MATCH MADE IN MONTANA
Rachelle Paige Campbell

Warning: Not intended for persons under the age of 18. May contain coarse language and mature content that may disturb some readers. Reader discretion advised.

Cover Art Design by: Kelly Moran/Rowan Prose Publishing
Photo Credit: Adobe Images
Editor: Katie O'Connor
First Printing
ISBN: 9781961967403
Rowan Prose Publishing, LLC
www.RowanProsePublishing.com
Published in the United States of America

FINDERS KEEPERS, Cowboy

MATCH MADE IN MONTANA

Rachelle Paige Campbell

Acknowledgments

First and foremost, I want to thank the late Dawn Dowdle of Blue Ridge Literary Agency. Dawn read an early version of this book (about twenty thousand words less than it is today) and signed me as a client. For a little over two years, she was my agent. Her kindness and patience came at the right moment of my career. She believed in me and my books, and I'll be forever grateful for the time we worked together.

A huge thank you to Kelly Moran at Rowan Prose Publishing for picking up the entire trilogy and to my fabulous editor, Katie O'Connor, for making this story shine. As always, I am grateful to my husband, my kids, and my parents for their unwavering encouragement.

Last, but not least, the Panera Supper Club supports every idea no matter how wacky. Thank you Kelly, Shannyn, Tammy, Kelly, Julie, and, of course, Miss Pamala for being the best writer friends in the whole world.

CHAPTER 1

Ryan Kincaid hated wasting time. Hank, his grandfather, called him impatient. His late grandmother, Susie, used to berate him for twitchy legs. If he had focused more on fixing the flaw at any point in his thirty-eight years, he wouldn't have been in such a rush today. Could he have saved himself from nearly cutting off his finger? *Probably.*

The day went downhill before he even got out of bed.

The phone rang ahead of the alarm.

BRING. BRING. BRING.

The loud ringtone blared.

He stifled the growl building in his throat. The peaceful tones he'd selected for his alarm should gently rouse him. The electronic chime blasted, drawing attention for the caller.

Instead of sitting and reaching for his cell phone, he kept his head on the pillow and fumbled for the device on the nightstand. He swatted the phone off the smooth surface, it landed with a thud on the wooden floor.

The phone stopped ringing. He turned his head to the cool side of the pillow. Good, maybe he could get another few minutes of sleep.

Under his four-post bed, the cell rang again, louder than before.

Grumbling, he rolled out of bed and knelt on the floor. With his cheek pressed against the boards, he groped, his fingers connecting with the device near the back corner. Reaching, he caught the cell and tweaked his shoulder. Grunting, he retrieved the device and frowned at the screen. Two missed calls from his ranch hand, Ted.

In a rush, he pulled on his jeans and work shirt, groaning as his aching shoulder stretched. Downstairs in the kitchen, he operated on autopilot, brewing coffee without too much thought. He tapped a quick text message to Ted, grabbed a travel mug, and reached for the glass pot. He grabbed the carafe off the coffee maker too early. Hot coffee scalded his hand and spilled onto the floor. With paper towels, he soaked up the mess but couldn't rid the room of the lingering stench of burnt coffee.

He rinsed his hands with cold water. The icy chill did the caffeine's job, jolting him to full alertness. He wasn't sure he'd survive his next slip-up.

He didn't wait to greet his grandfather to review the day's plans. Striding from the house, he was out the front door as the sun rose. With the opening day approaching and guests arriving soon, he didn't have time for pleasantries. His grandfather, a dyed in the wool cowboy, would understand.

Missing those moments with his grandfather, however, nagged Ryan for hours. Since losing Grandma, he never wanted to take a moment for granted. Their time together was too precious to let a single second slip past unremarked or a beautiful morning go unnoticed.

The Kincaids had been ranching outside Herd, Montana since the nineteenth century. As one of the three founding families, their legacy was awash with intrigue and back-stabbing. Eventually, they'd found stability and mutual respect with their only remaining neighbors, the Hawkes. Over the past decade, however, the Kincaids had been the last ranchers standing. And then Ryan had sold off the cattle and chased after an unexpected idea. High-end tourism.

Hopping into his truck, he drove out to the former Hawke property and the site of the newest lodging for the ranch's guests. Grass stretched toward the horizon, unbroken and abundant in every direction. The ground rose and fell in gentle undulations. His property had been claimed by his forebears for its pond and the creek that ran through the eastern boundary, believing a false claim of gold. But this stretch of landscape had been coveted by many a Kincaid for its seeming infinity.

He met up with Ted and the rest of the crew at the yurts. The traditional canvas tent home for nomadic tribes had been a unique choice for additional accommodation. Circular in shape, the structures both stuck out and blended into the rolling grass landscape. Set back from the new property line, he couldn't see his annoying neighbor Megan's house nor could she see his. He didn't want to encroach on anyone's privacy, legal right or no.

Sniggering, he shook his head. The woman would talk to his guests until they cried uncle and ran away, but he was steering clear. He wasn't some selfless neighbor, but a man looking out for his best interests. Since childhood, Megan had been an incessant chatterbox. Had she ever had a moment of quiet contemplation? Could she keep a thought or opinion to herself without blurting every idea to any passer-by? Didn't she have friends for girl-talk? He hated feeling cornered at every encounter.

Of course, Hank didn't care. She was thick as thieves with his grandfather. Always had been. In his youth, their bond stuck in Ryan's craw. Couldn't she spend her summer vacation with her family and leave his alone?

Grandma had understood. She was quiet like Ryan. To his chagrin, Grandma, his staunchest ally, had found Meg charming in the sort of head-scratching, bewildering way he reasoned everyone must like her. He wanted peace. Meg craved chaos. Even now, when she wasn't physically close, she was stirring up his mind.

He parked the truck, leaving the keys in the ignition and hopping out of the cab. He scanned the worksite. Cupping hands around his mouth, he whistled.

His lead ranch hand, Ted, and the two men hired for the summer turned their heads. Standing near the first of three yurts, they circled the erected frame.

"How's it going?" Ryan called, strolling toward the group.

Ted turned away from the men and strode toward the boss. "Glad to catch you. I haven't had luck finding a replacement yoga instructor with such short notice. Most of our back-ups have accepted other roles."

8

Ryan nodded. He wasn't surprised. Before he'd turned the ranch into a resort, he wouldn't have imagined many in town had ever heard of the exercise discipline. Their corner of the world wasn't awash with yogis. "I asked Joe to put the word out at school. One of the teachers might have a hidden talent."

Ted stroked his jaw.

Joe was a middle school teacher and, in the summers, tour guide. His knowledge of the history of the ranches and Herd was unparalleled. With a love for meeting new people, he was a natural for the part-time role.

"Or you could fill in?"

Ted grunted.

Ryan chuckled and clapped a hand on the cowboy's shoulder. "Never say never, right?"

"Sure, learned that since I started here."

Dropping his hand, Ryan scrubbed his face. While he employed a few additional cowboys in the summer season to mend fences, maintain the property, and separate wildlife from guests, he mostly employed spa staff. The old bunk house was now co-ed, and Ted managed people more than animals.

Life had definitely changed in ways unimaginable even a generation earlier when this land had been devoted to grazing cattle. "Never mind that problem. If someone doesn't turn up, I'll issue refunds for the classes already booked. I'll come up with something else to add to the schedule. You could teach meditation."

Ted chuckled.

"How's the progress out here?"

"Good. We're almost ready to stretch the canvas over the frames," Ted said.

Ryan grinned and rubbed his palms together. "I'm right on time."

"You sure about this?" Ted tipped his head to the side.

The question was fair. Ryan's latest venture wasn't a guaranteed success. When he'd first considered the idea of adding more campsites to the property, he'd hesitated.

For a while, he'd been in discussion with several wildlife groups about reintroducing a bison herd to the town named for the grouping. If the environmental impact and ecological study was approved by Herd's town council at their meeting in the fall, the first bison would be introduced in the spring.

The needs of the bison would take precedence on his land. He had no intention of swapping cattle for bison and raising the animals for profit. He wanted to restore the balance of nature to the ecosystem, and he'd be glad to let the animals take over the grass. Too much time and money had been spent on mowing and maintenance that the bison would handle for free.

The yurts might last one season. Ryan understood and accepted the risk. When he decided to make reparations, he was prepared for the potentially expensive and short-term chance. He profited off a complicated family legacy of arrogance that settled the land and placed man's will above nature. His family had been at least partially responsible for the devastation of bison herds.

The animals had been eradicated from the environment by force. Their treatment was only one in a long list of historic misdeeds. He was glad to do his small part to correct past wrongs. But he couldn't let fear of tomorrow's failure hold him back today. The ranch's lodging expansion was happening. "I'm ready. Show me what to do."

He listened, without comment, to Ted's instructions on completing the yurts. While the tents were Ryan's idea, he had tasked Ted with deployment. Construction could be tricky and dangerous. Withing a few minutes, Ryan proved his point.

In the process of stretching the canvas over the first frame, he reached for his knife to slice the material. In a second, he lost his grip and plunged the blade too far. He yelped and swore. Holding the finger tight, he staunched the bleeding with his shirt.

"You better clean up and find a bandage. I'll finish this," Ted said. "Can't have you bleeding over the yurts or dying of an infection on opening weekend."

With a grumbled, muttered oath, Ryan nodded and retreated to his truck. He drove the rutted road toward the house, cradling his injured hand to his chest and steering with his right. Hitting each bump and dip jarred him, and he winced.

At the fork to the house, he drove around back and slowed on the gravel drive leading to the barn. He kept a first aid kit on a shelf inside the doors for treating guests quickly. He couldn't remember where band-aids might be stashed inside the ranch house. He could ask Hank but would probably bleed out before Hank finished some non-relevant anecdote. His grandfather loved to spin a yarn.

He parked next to the barn and frowned. Motion in his peripheral vision caught his attention. He snapped his head and spotted her. Megan.

"What in the world," he muttered, pocketing his keys, and hopping from the vehicle.

In a few quick strides, he reached the outbuilding Hank had assumed control of years back. The uninsulated, man-cave was not to be entered without express permission of its rightful laird, Hank Kincaid. Not that a person could sneak in. A chain strung through the door handle and an iron ring was secured with a lock.

Ryan had never seen the key. He'd only been inside once with Grandma, and the visit lasted ten seconds. Hank had packed the structure from floor to ceiling. Grandma and Ryan hadn't managed more than three steps inside. The collection didn't allow for a person to take their time and survey the contents. They had retreated, walking backwards to do so, and neither mentioned the shed again. Their determination withered with the reality of the project.

Today, however, some clever person—or rascally Grandfather—found a way inside.

Stained, cardboard boxes surrounded the shed's perimeter.

With each step, he discovered more debris, and the throbbing in his temples increased.

A pile of old magazines was stacked on a broken chair against the side of the shed. The furniture leaned to one side. Another few ounces of weight, the precarious structure would tip and the yellowed pages would scatter.

Breathing in through his nose, he willed a calm he didn't feel. Patience was a virtue he couldn't find. He had enough work to do without adding another project. Cleaning up after Hank's mess wasn't ideal on a good day, let alone when he didn't have the use of both hands and was under a time crunch.

Surely the old man couldn't have gotten himself into this much trouble alone. He was no longer capable of this much physical labor in a relatively short amount of time. Shutting his eyes, Ryan shook his head and breathed deep.

A familiar floral scent tickled his nostrils. High-pitched chatter danced in the air. He swallowed the groan building in his throat. Frustration pounded in his forehead in time to his heartbeat. *Why is Meg the root of all problems?*

"Of course, I had to take the chance. Right? You understand," Meg said.

Who was she talking to? His hand throbbed. Was Hank inside, listening to the inane prattle?

Ryan stepped over the threshold and frowned. "What is going on here?"

A low woof woof responded.

He stood in the doorway, blocked the exit, and squinted into the dark interior. Without power, the outbuilding had no light source making it hard to confirm if she was alone or not. Blinking, his eyes adjusted.

At the back, Meg sat on the floor, a pink skirt floating around her like a gauzy cloud and her arm wrapped around a salt and pepper colored, mid-sized dog. She cooed to the dog, glaring at the entrance. "You scared her."

"What?" He poked his chest with a finger and strode forward. "Me?"

The dog howled.

"Yes, you. Who else? Is someone behind you? Are you hiding Hank?" She turned to the dog. "Shh, shh, Colby. It's okay." She returned her gaze to him. "Hold out your hand."

"Excuse me?" He drew back his chin. She trespassed on his property and had the nerve to dictate orders?

"You heard me." She got to her feet, straightening, and pulling back her shoulders. "Hold out your hand. Colby needs to sniff you. She needs to know you're a friend."

Am I? He frowned. Adding a dog bite to his list of injuries wasn't worth holding his ground against her. The black and white poodle mix was a stray Meg had rescued a few years ago. He'd worried she was getting herself in over her head by owning any dog, let alone one with unknown origins. Instead of telling her, however, he did the next best thing. He told Hank and let the old cowboy warn her off. Not that it had made any difference.

"It's okay, Colby. He's nice." She patted the dog on the top of the head. "To animals." She studied him.

He stared at her until she had the sense to glance away.

The dog trotted forward, sniffing the air, and wagging her tail.

He held out his hand.

She nosed his knuckles.

The cold sensation caught him off-guard, and he tightened his fist, wincing as he added pressure to his fresh wound.

"Oh, no. Are you hurt?"

He sucked in a breath and raised his hand, elevating the finger and holding it to his chest.

She neared, stopping inches away. "Hold out your hand. Can I see?"

"Why?"

"Because I can help." She rolled her eyes. "You don't have to be the macho, tough guy all the time."

Is that what you think? She wanted to fling insults and accuse him of casual misogyny? While destroying his land?

"Oh, stop shaking your head. Just hold out your hand and let me see," she insisted.

You're not dressed for it. She wore some sort of floaty, flimsy pink dress with a jean jacket over top. She always wore the clothes she wanted and not what was suitable to the task. He wouldn't get anywhere arguing against her outfit. He'd tried that too many times over the years.

She reached for him, grazing her fingers along the back of the hand resting near his collarbone.

He'd left the top of his work shirt unbuttoned and revealed an inch of tough, tanned skin on his neck. With the wide brim of his hat, he hadn't worried about overexposure. Until too late.

11

Her light touch sent shockwaves through him. He stared at her hand. What would happen if he looked at her and acknowledged the strange surge pulsating between them? He didn't have time to ask the question let alone learn the answer.

If he didn't have a second to stop his finger from bleeding, he definitely didn't have another minute for the odd sensation stirred up with her subpar nursing skills. "No, get out," he murmured.

"I'm sorry? Did you say something?" She tilted her head to the side.

Had she not heard him? He wasn't sure if he should laugh or cry. "Leave, Meg. Now," he delivered the words with as much stoicism as he could muster. "I don't know why you're here. Or what possessed you to trash my yard. In five days, the first guests arrive. You have single handedly added hours to my day. I know you don't like me. But why are you sabotaging my ranch? The tourists who stay here spend plenty of their dollars in towns at stores like yours." He kept his voice steady, never raising to any level that might be misconstrued as yelling. But he wanted no misunderstanding about his seriousness.

Red-cheeked, she straightened, flaring her nostrils. "Hank invited me. He asked for my help."

Well, he didn't tell me. If he wasn't annoyed, he'd admire her backbone. Instead of shrinking, she stood tall and held his gaze. He wasn't sure what was worse, the uninvited, stubborn woman on his property or his secretive, rule-breaking grandfather. While running a business together, they'd established one very important rule. Talk to each other. Hank, his grandfather, had not kept Ryan informed today.

"I'm asking you to go." He lifted his injured hand high on his chest, shielding the wound from view but redirecting the blood flow back into the limb.

She pulled back her shoulders and took in a breath.

Here comes the wind-up. He knew her cues and didn't want the fight she was readying for. He wanted so many other things. Top of his list, he sought every ounce of serenity he could muster in the dwindling days of solitude on the ranch.

Once the resort opened for the summer, his house would be a revolving door of guests and staff. No inch of his ten thousand acres would be spared from incessant chatter. For a loner, he chose a shocking new direction for family business. If he righted some past wrongs and saved the land for another generation, every sacrifice would be worth the effort.

"Okay, I'll go." She held up her hands, palms facing out. "You can tell Hank you ran me off. I'll leave the clean-up to you and Ted. Come on, Colby. Let's head to the store. We've got a business to run."

If rumors were to be believed, her words weren't mere segue to escape an uncomfortable situation. He'd never seen much of a crowd at her antique store. Was she struggling? He almost asked. Neighbors helped each other here. But he was too frustrated to form the words.

With the dog at her heels, she strode down the significantly widened center aisle. The shed's very own equator had been transformed from a thin line to several feet wide. For the first time, he spotted the plywood floor, a mismatch of different scraps unified by a dark stain.

If he didn't have junk littering the lawn he wanted to mow, he'd be impressed by her handiwork. She must have been the one to clear the path. Hank couldn't be decisive about his things. She'd moved quick on sorting the items. Hank picked the right person for the job. The man needed to learn how to choose a better moment.

She reached the door.

Her light, lavender perfume wafted on the cool, late spring breeze. He breathed in the scent and studied her.

Her chin trembled, and her hands shook.

She was too delicate for ranch life. Every year, he expected her to cut ties and run. She was slight and pretty. She wasn't a western woman. He'd known that since childhood. The day she finally realized she might find real purpose in her life, somewhere far away, he'd cheer if he didn't fear she'd take that as encouragement to stay. Now, he stepped to the side.

She exited.

The dog sniffed his hand and licked his palm.

The sandpaper tongue tickled his lifeline, and he jumped. He'd have to teach the pet what her owner already knew. He was tough and unyielding. He had to be. He had no room for sweetness or sentimentality. His life dealt in absolutes, and she was all murky grays.

He stared straight ahead, not daring to turn and glance her way. He stayed in place, counting to a thousand. At a thousand and one, he turned and spotted his grandfather strolling down the path.

Hank held up both hands. "You've scared her away?" His tone was incredulous.

Scared? Ryan would laugh if he wasn't so annoyed. Meg Hawke was intimidated by nothing and no one. "You know this is the worst time to start a project. Why send her here? She always gets in the way." He folded his arms over his chest.

"I have my reasons." Hank stopped a few yards away and pointed. "You want to bandage that cut before you start hauling everything back? Or maybe you should apologize to her first. Be mad at me. Not Meg. I called her."

"Why?" He muttered the word like he snuck in a swear. On the best days, Hank was entertaining. At his worst, he was exasperating.

"You've been mad at me about this mess for years. She has a business that could help me out. It's a win-win. You waste your energy searching for any reason to not like that girl. You're about the only person around who doesn't."

If that was true, why does she spend her time alone? Arguing with his stubborn grandfather wouldn't do any good. "Maybe the problem is I see her too clearly."

"Or maybe you're the fool who can't see himself for what and who he is."

Ryan held perfectly still, his injured finger throbbing in time to his pounding heart. If Hank wanted to illuminate who Ryan was, he'd listen. Most days, he kept his head down, racing from one task to the next. Focused on the business and the community, he'd admit he lost himself somewhere along the way.

A road map or instruction manual would be welcome, if Hank had either handy. Meeting his grandfather's steady stare, however, he nearly shuddered. In a single look, Ryan traveled back through time and was again the lost child, alone except for his grandparents. Disappointing his grandfather remained the worst sin.

Hank raised him better than to lash out at a longtime neighbor and accuse her of trespassing without cause. Ryan entered the shed burning from a hundred other frustrations that didn't involve Meg. She hadn't deserved his tirade. He shamed his family with the outburst.

Hank nodded slowly. "Come on, let's get you fixed. Then you can call Ted to help you clean the yard. I'll leave it to you to figure out how to apologize and get her back out here. We don't have all the time in the world for my project."

Don't I know it. "I'm not saying I'm sorry."

"Pardon?" Hank narrowed his gaze. "If you don't make time to do the right thing, you'll regret it."

Exhaling a sigh, Ryan sagged his shoulders. Why couldn't he have one exchange with Meg that didn't end in total frustration? He couldn't shake off Hank's words. For no reason, he'd been mean. Hank was right. Ryan owed her an apology. "I'm not running over there today. I'm too busy."

"Maybe you can't go tonight. Fine. You've got chores. But you need to make amends sooner than later." Hank strode away.

Ryan studied the ground. He wouldn't pretend he wanted a friendship with the girl who'd always gotten under his skin. For the honor of his family name, he'd admit he'd been wrong. First time for everything since he was always right.

CHAPTER 2

Kneeling behind the front window display of her antique store, half-hidden from passersbys on Main Street courtesy of the Frontier Days poster taped to the glass, Meg sprayed furniture polish directly on the water-stained floorboard and rubbed with a rag. With the fading daylight, she wasn't making any progress. Improving the decades old spot from a long since repaired window leak hadn't been a task she could cross of her to-do list. Which was exactly the point.

If she suffered frustration about something she couldn't change, she'd rather deal directly with an immovable object. The spot couldn't calmly berate her and, in a few seconds, send her back to her youthful misdeeds and every idea that ended in disaster. Under the steady, disappointed gaze of her childhood nemesis and neighbor, a rational defense had abandoned her. In the heat of the moment, she'd flinched at his words.

She sat back on her heels and dropped the rag, circling her aching wrists. Of course, her current location, wasn't exactly proof that she'd matured and changed.

Finders Keepers, her store for the past five years, struggled. When she had floated the idea of moving into her late grandmother's ranch house and using her savings from years of gallery work and living with her mom in their Chicago home, Meg had a champion in her mom. She'd been happy to know the ranch house would be lived in and cared for and even more thrilled that Meg would use her education and love of antiques to establish herself somewhere that had always felt like home.

Her savings funded her lifestyle. With the money dwindling, however, she needed the store to cover overhead costs and then some. If she couldn't turn a profit, she'd do what she should have done years ago and head back to Chicago. Mom wanted Meg to stay and succeed. But building a life in a small town in Montana wasn't easy.

For some, like unstoppable force Ryan Kincaid, sheer determination and willpower carried dreams from thoughts to reality. Meg admired him for what he'd done in transforming his ranch and revitalizing an entire community. Without him, the town would have disappeared from most maps. And his purchase of her family's land, leaving the ranch house untouched, set Mom up for the rest of her days.

Meg was grateful to him but wanted more. In her entire life, she had never revised Ryan Kincaid's opinion of her. Why grant him the power to upset her again? He had made his annoyance known more times than she could count. *The definition of insanity*....

Heaving a huge sigh, she sat back on her heels. Her issue was she sort of liked him. Sad as it was, he was her only age-appropriate, friendly acquaintance within a hundred miles. She wasn't oblivious enough to claim friendship. She'd like to though and had tried for years.

He was quiet and calm. While she'd never admit such a thing out loud, she appreciated his subdued personality. She was well aware others considered her a handful, overhearing the description a few times in town over the years. In his stoic company, she relaxed.

During every encounter, she vowed to do better. With advance warning, she gave herself a pep talk to listen and pause before speaking. At some point in each meeting, however, she slipped. She'd ask a question or make a comment. Instead of an immediate reply, he'd shoot her a look or tilt his head. She'd be so concerned about what he wasn't saying she'd blurt out anything to fill the silence with nervous chatter. If he couldn't remember why he shot her a stern expression, he'd stop judging her. Or so she had convinced herself.

The morning's encounter ruined everything. In her experience, she wasn't always met with his best manners, but he was unfailingly kind. In the grand scheme, she valued the latter more. Nice was about keeping up polite appearances. Kind was real depth and caring for other people. She had been so flustered by the whole encounter that she'd left with hurt feelings. Now she didn't know how to proceed without more awkwardness between them. She promised Hank, and she couldn't renege.

Their impromptu interaction in the shed kept replaying in her mind. With cool fierceness, he asked her to leave. His tone burned her skin like a sharp, biting, winter wind. She'd been shocked at his raised tone.

Red-cheeked and sputtering, she bolted and spent the rest of the day berating herself for both showing up without his permission and kowtowing to him, abandoning Hank and the project. She couldn't be righteously indignant when she accepted an equal share of the blame. In the past, she'd been guilty of machinations to involve him in her goals against his will.

A paw reached out, stroking the long-sleeve of her jean jacket.

"Sorry, Colby. You're right." She dropped the cloth and turned to the dog lying next to her, belly up. "I'm making no progress on my work. I might as well be useful to someone."

Petting the dog in long strokes, she fell into the rhythm of the motion, but the repetitive action wasn't enough to stop her whirring brain. She had thought she was being useful to Hank. Regardless of Ryan's opinion and whether or not she cared, she genuinely liked Hank.

With no memories of her grandfather, she gravitated toward Ryan's. Hank was quick-witted with a twinkle in his eye. After losing Susie, he dimmed. One bad joke at a time, he bounced back. She'd been happy to be part of the resurgence. She wasn't ready to lose him.

She had her suspicions the consignment idea wasn't pulled out of thin air. The only way she could be sure, however, was a call straight to the source. She leaned forward, pulling her cell from her back pocket and hit speed-dial.

"Hello? Meggie?" her mom greeted.

She smiled. Mom's voice was sing-song and bright, a perfect fit for her occupation as an elementary school art teacher. "Hi, Mom. Sorry I haven't called."

"It's okay, sweetie. I figured you were getting ready for your busy summer season. Besides, I've been following along on your blog."

Meg turned, resting her back against the wall. She pulled Colby into her lap. *Not much to follow at the moment.* "You and Hank are the only subscribers. I see the updates every time you *like* something."

Her blog was her first attempt at modernization, combining her love of history and storytelling. She couldn't stop herself from creating a backstory for every item that came into her shop. While the craze for blogging had faded in favor of other social media sites, she kept sharing entries on her website. If she spent less time on the not at all profitable venture and more time learning to code, she wouldn't be at her make-or-break moment now. "Speaking of Hank. Have you called him recently?"

"Old Mr. Kincaid? Your neighbor?"

Meg would like to witness Mom call him *old* to his mischievous, grinning face. "Yes, that's the one."

"Sweetie, why would I do that?"

Dragging in a shaky breath, Meg focused on the dog in her lap. At fifty pounds, Colby wasn't small enough to comfortably curl up on a human. At least not in the opinion of the human. Meg rested the dog's ribs and shoulders on her lap, stroking the dog's chest. With her legs losing feeling, she shifted the dog and stretched her limbs one at a time.

"Honey, are you there? Did I lose you?"

"Sorry, Mom. I was adjusting. The dog is on my lap."

Mom chuckled. "You mean the moose is on your lap."

"Colby is a show-quality doodle of murky pedigree and perfectly sized for a watchdog."

"No arguments about her size. She'd have to stay awake long enough to be qualified for a security role. What's going on with Hank? Why did you ask if I've talked to him? Any problems with the house?"

Meg exhaled a heavy sigh. "Did you call Hank and tell him the business is struggling and I might have to move back in with you in Chicago?"

"Umm ... I didn't call *him*."

"Oh, Mom." Meg groaned.

"Sweetie, I'm sorry. You know we care about you and want the best. Grandma loved Herd as much as you do. I want you to stay. If you need help, you can reach out to others. Dreams don't happen without help."

"I know." She wasn't the first to head west with a grand plan that never reached fruition. The pioneer spirit lived deep inside her. Grandma stoked her sense of purpose and adventure with tales of their ancestors.

Every summer of her childhood, she had relaxed here in a place she belonged. Spending her days roaming the land, she never had to adapt to please anyone else. Free to be herself for a few months, she recharged in time to return to life in Chicago with her single mom in a thousand-square-foot, two-bedroom condo. Mom grew up on the ranch in Montana and left the moment she could, preferring high rises and crowded streets.

Not Meg.

Growing up, she'd cherished the close-knit community and dreamed of moving here. After college, Meg had worked various gallery jobs, wishing for the chance to open her own store. Antiquing was a hobby born from visiting Grandma and loving history. Her family had owned their ranch since the nineteenth century. Meg loved the stories passed down from generations, often through objects, and absorbed everyone.

When the opportunity had arisen—a store for sale in town around the time Mom sold the land to the Kincaids—Meg jumped at the miraculous chance. At the start, she hadn't minded being an outsider. Five years later, she remained an out-of-towner to the locals. She wanted to belong.

Mom never made her feel ridiculous for wanting to head in the opposite direction. She encouraged the move. Had she anticipated the difficulties? She'd known the land and people with better insight. Meg hated to give up. Her choices dwindled. "I need a better plan."

"Did Hank help you find one?"

Not much of one. "No, but that's okay. It's not his problem, and it's not yours. I'm thirty-five, you can't keep rescuing me."

"I'll always help. You're my daughter."

Her mom encouraged every dream, promising a safe landing if she fell. She was both a safety net and a cheerleader. Meg found strength from her mom's love. "Within the first month of the summer, I should know if I can make a profit. It's not fair for you to miss out on the prime rental season." Her voice cracked. "I won't stay. I'll be out before the Fourth of July."

"Honey, please don't. I don't need to rent the house. I'm fine, and I'd hate for you to leave."

Meg knew the response she'd get. But she also was determined. "I have to face facts."

"I'll support whatever decision you make."

"Thanks, Mom." While Meg hated emotionally unloading over the phone, she appreciated the results. Without the weight of her potential failure, she held her head a little higher and pulled back her shoulders. She could admit the truth. "I'm hoping for a miracle."

"Which would be?"

"A consignment worth enough to garner attention and cover costs for the next year." The statement was hardly the sort of actionable goal she'd learned about during her years in business.

"You never know. Funny things happen in Herd. It's a special place full of possibilities."

The front door opened jingling bell over the entrance. A pair of boots clicked against the floor in a rhythm too familiar to ignore. Colby jumped to her feet and padded to greet the visitor.

Meg stood and spotted the last person she expected to see.

Ryan shut the door behind him and held his palms out.

With a wagging tail, Colby sniffed and licked his hands.

Meg hated the flutter low in her belly. Ryan didn't want her friendship. The awful truth was she'd always craved his. "Mom, I have to go."

"Of course. Bye, sweetie. Love you."

Hanging up the call, Meg stuffed the phone into her back pocket, dusted her hands on her jeans, and stared at him. For once, she had nothing to say.

Ryan pulled the ten-gallon hat off his head, holding it against his chest.

He wore dark jeans and a pressed black Western shirt. The outfit was one of the dressier options in his closet and something he typically only donned for his guests. Most often, he sported worn jeans and faded flannels. He'd gone to some trouble. For her? Her heart skipped a beat. She wouldn't read into his appearance. More likely than not, she wasn't the reason.

"Hi, Meg. Do you have a second to speak?"

Now he wanted her to talk? She traced the ridges on the roof of her mouth with her tongue, fighting the urge to reply.

Shifting his weight from foot to foot, his gaze darted around the room. He was uncomfortable. She nearly cheered. Only her desire to prolong the moment kept her quiet.

"Yep, okay, probably deserve the silent treatment." He sighed and ran a bandaged hand over his flattened hair.

"Oh no, you are really hurt?" She clapped a hand over her mouth, hiding her frown. In a second, she'd relinquished the upper ground. She couldn't be silent about an injury and didn't regret caring. As she accused him of putting on airs, he had suffered? Her stomach twisted.

He smiled. "Nothing that excuses my behavior yesterday but maybe helps make sense of it."

She nodded and frowned. How oblivious was she to the extent of his pain? While she was busy with a lifetime of frustration, what else had she missed?

Ryan held his hat over his heart, muffling the sound of his pounding chest. In the antique store, he was too much. If he lifted his arms, he was liable to knock something off a shelf. When he spoke, his voice was too loud and shook the baubles hanging off the chandelier. He didn't fit.

Wide open spaces suited him best. He preferred the outdoors with no obstructions. He didn't have to be mindful of anything more than his task.

Meg stood a few feet away, narrowing her gaze. Her focus rested solely on him.

He felt warm and sticky like he'd gone for a long ride at midday. Now he regretted changing into his best outfit. He'd have to wash it as soon as he got home. With any luck, she'd appreciate the effort.

"It's a clean cut. Ted poured antiseptic into the wound as he bandaged me." The memory of the burning in his finger during Ted's first aid session snapped Ryan back to the present. "I'll be fine."

She nodded. "Better safe than sorry. You don't want to contract an infection."

His throat squeezed shut. Now she was saying his tired, clichéd lines. He scanned the room, looking for hazards. If he slammed into something fragile, he'd add to his mounting debt.

She strode toward the register. Her hair swung with every step. She was as pretty as anything else in the room.

Her store was her domain. Every spare surface, from shelves to dresser tops to mantles, held a variety of objects from delicate vases to tiny figurines. Furniture scattered throughout the space in groups of twos and threes. She'd crammed thousands of items into her store. The room should feel crowded and cluttered. Somehow, her overdecorating worked. *Controlled chaos like her.*

He followed, grateful to reach an open space he could stand in. And then he dropped his gaze. Every time he noticed the tiny details that made her *her*, he berated himself a little more. She wasn't the enemy. She looked out for his grandfather, including setting vermin traps under the porch. She was kind.

And she wasn't a child anymore. Neither of them were.

"Let me see, please?" she asked.

Dropping his hat to the counter, he rested his hands in the center of the glass case. Inside, shiny, pretty things lined a velvet shelf.

She inched her fingers toward his injured digit.

With every tiny motion forward, he tensed. She wouldn't hurt him anymore than he'd already accomplished. He fisted his other hand.

She brushed her fingertips over his calloused palm.

The whisper soft touch of her silky, smooth skin over his work-hardened hands sent a jolt through him. "I'm fine."

With a mental growl, he drew back his hands. Every time she touched him, she activated some sort of response he couldn't define or explain. If he hadn't moved, he'd have cracked the display. He dropped his arms to his sides and breathed deep, inhaling lemon furniture polish and lavender.

Woof woof woof.

The dog trotted toward him, sniffing his boots and bandaged hand. Nails clicked against the hardwood as the dog circled him. Finally, she sat next to him, leaning against his leg.

He smiled and stroked behind the dog's ears. The mutt tilted her head, exuding a goofy exuberance. If he was out of place in the store of fragile things, he wasn't alone. The dog didn't let it impact her. Neither should he.

"Meg, I'm fine. Really. Don't waste your time worrying about me." *I don't deserve your goodwill.*

She crossed her arms over her chest.

He couldn't get out of speaking today. He'd come to eat crow, and he barely swallowed the first bite. "I am sorry about earlier. I was rude." The words were stiff and halting. He trudged ahead. "You've given me no cause for my poor behavior." *At least not recently.*

She nodded.

The dog woofed and trotted around the glass case to her owner. She plopped onto Meg's feet.

Loyalty was admirable no matter the species. He liked seeing the black and white dog so trusting. Meg had rescued the stray from a pound several years earlier. At the time, she had asked if they had any spare supplies. He had found an old kennel. Hank had vetoed the artifact and told Ryan to buy something. When he had dropped off the brand-new bed, he had been introduced to a terrified mass of fur.

The mutt's even temper was a credit to Meg's handling. She must have convinced the pup some humans were decent and worthy of love and respect. *When you know, you know.*

He wished he had such clarity. As the hours ticked past, he didn't have the luxury of getting lost in his thoughts. If he didn't keep the ranch in top-shape, meeting, and exceeding guests' expectations, he'd lose the business. In a few more years, he'd have the financial security he needed. Every morning, he focused on what was required to save the future. He had little to spare for the present and even less for the past.

Lifting his gaze, he met her steady stare. He shrugged. "If you're not talking, I'd better go."

"You want me to talk?"

"I'd like an acknowledgment of my apology. You can be mad. I don't want bad feelings between us." *We've weathered worse.*

She frowned.

A soft *tick tock tick* echoed in the silence.

In the glass case, he spotted a gold pocket watch resting on a pillow. He could mark every second as she absorbed his words. Fixing their perceptions of each other was a two-person job. Preferably, he'd wait until the summer was a success and the plans for the bison were officially underway before inviting her to tackle the shed. Waiting created another, bigger problem. Only a fool would give his neighbor and his grandfather three months for stewing and plotting. Reaching for his hat, he slid it over the glass.

She grabbed his wrist, curling her thin fingers over his joint. "No, wait, please?"

Her voice was muffled and subdued. He glanced at her. He never thought of her as anything less than a force of nature. He'd swear the weather changed on her arrival and departure every summer of their childhoods. The year she stopped coming, the air hung heavy and stagnant.

"I'm sorry, too." She swallowed. "I should have waited for your permission. I definitely shouldn't have accused you of toxic masculinity. You're always respectful."

"I appreciate your apology. As far as an invitation, don't worry about it. It's Hank's ranch. He has every right to do as he sees fit." *I wish I knew his motivation.* Hank never did anything without a purpose, hating to waste his two most valuable resources of energy and time. If his goal involved Ryan, Hank wouldn't rest until a conclusion was reached. Ryan shuddered.

She pursed her lips.

He raised a hand to smooth the hairs on the back of his neck. "You know what I mean."

"I do. Hank might own the ranch. Without you, he'd have sold years ago."

With one finger, Ryan traced the brim of his hat. Her words were high praise. His lips twitched as he attempted to hid a smile, schooling his features into an expressionless mask.

"I know your opinion of me. I knew what I risked."

He lifted his gaze. They'd circled this conversation for years. He avoided putting out his thoughts for her thorough inspection. Had she done her own analysis while he was pre-occupied with work?

"I shouldn't have stepped onto your property. You hadn't invited me." She held up both hands. "Believe me, it won't happen again."

Was she offering surrender? He wasn't prepared for her to capitulate. The stubborn girl he'd known would never have admitted defeat. And he didn't like her waving the white flag now. But he couldn't focus on that comment. Instead, he circled back to the most critical statement on her list. He shifted his weight from one foot to the other. "My opinion of you?"

"You think I'm a nuisance." She dropped her hands to her sides. "You barely hold yourself back from rolling your eyes every time I talk."

"I've never said that." He wouldn't correct the latter opinion. Every now and then, he struggled to keep his gaze straight ahead. On occasion, he'd press his fingers against the vein twitching in his temples.

She shrugged. "You don't have to say it out loud."

He gritted his molars. She was wrong. More often than not, he stilled his features best he could, unable to stop both his cheek and eye from trembling as he stifled laughter. She was the funniest, boldest person he'd ever met. She was candid and free. He appreciated silence and calm. He liked to consider his words. Typically, before he could reply, she'd said something wry or self-deprecating, and he had to stop himself from responding with a chuckle. "I'm sorry if I've given you that impression."

"Don't worry about it. I appreciate the apology." She grabbed a cloth and rubbed a nonexistent spot of dust on the metal edge of the counter. "Tell Hank I'll be back tomorrow. I know you have guests coming this weekend and want the lawn clear before then. And I know you hate things disorganized and messy."

Pot meet kettle. She claimed in-depth knowledge, but would she listen to the truth? Was she content to persist in projecting her opinions of him onto him? He stared hard at her half-averted profile willing her to face him. "It's not strictly about tidiness. If you leave the junk from the shed scattered over the lawn, you'll kill the grass."

"Can't you buy sod or something?"

He narrowed his gaze. "Sure, if I have enough lead time. A few days isn't adequate. The guests like to stroll the lawn in the evenings. If the grass is dead, and I can't get new turf fast enough, and it rains, I have a muddy mess."

She tipped her head to the side. "Again, not that big of a deal."

Everything is a big deal. "Time isn't infinite, and my minutes are stretched thin as it is. Once the tourists arrive, I won't have energy for unnecessary chores. It's wasteful to my resources."

"You mean expensive?"

"Well sure if we're talking finances. I've got a lot at stake this summer." He ran a hand through his hair. Didn't she understand cost was comprised of many factors? With a quick glance around her empty store, he dragged his gaze back and studied her.

Hunched and quiet, she looked defeated. Since she moved to town, she kept to her land and her store. He'd never caught her in his house but her light scent lingered in the air some days. On those occasions, he guessed from Hank's pleased expression she'd visited.

He didn't want to fight. They'd made some progress toward mutual respect and understanding. He hated to risk the tenuous truce but couldn't let her misconceptions persist unchecked. "We've moved ahead with the new yurts on your old property, but we haven't booked every weekend. I held off on corporate retreats until the end of the season. I need to at least break-even this year. To do that, I have to sell-out a minimum of four weeks in the next three months."

Or I can't take my next big gamble. If the town didn't believe in him, he'd be out of luck. He needed the full backing and support of the community to successfully reintroduce the bison to the area.

Unlike his ancestors, he wouldn't assume his was the only opinion that mattered. His neighbors relied on him and vice versa. He vowed to change the legacy from winning by force to shared success for all.

She dropped the cloth and huffed. "Is it always about money? Is that your stress?"

At his sides, he clenched and unclenched his fingers. The circular conversation trapped him in a loop. "No, of course not. Dollars aren't the only resource. Don't discount someone's time, too. I'm lucky if I can sleep five hours a night. I'm needed everywhere. I'm coming home, eating dinner, and heading back to work. I am grateful for your friendship with my grandfather. He'd be lonely if you didn't look in on him so often."

"Hank has always been good to me," she said. "So was Susie."

"Like when she was helping you trick me at Frontier Days?" He probably should have kept the thought to himself, like he usually did. Nothing good came from being open and easy for others to read. But sometimes he couldn't fight the urge to tease her. Provoking her was second nature.

She sucked all the air in the room into her open mouth, her cheeks flushing.

He wouldn't smile, but he was glad she suffered guilt from her involvement in the most embarrassing moment of his life. Growing up, he danced with Grandma in the kitchen. He couldn't remember a time before waltzing and two-stepping across the slate tile floor.

When a thirteen-year-old Meg had wanted to participate in the talent show, she had recruited their grandmas to lure him onto the stage. Once he had gazed at the crowd, he had wanted to run. He had never liked a trick or a prank. Her forehead had beaded with sweat and her eyes had grown round. She had looked petrified and had punished herself with the thoughtless plan. He couldn't leave her alone to her fate and had joined her act, spinning her around the stage. The moment he had finished his bow, however, he had vowed never to dance with her again. *Promise kept.*

He sighed. "Your grandma was good to me, too. All I'm asking is that you and Hank don't make more trouble for me right now. Stop and consider what impact your actions have on those around you. Specifically, on me."

She clasped her hands in front and released a heavy breath. Her entire body shook.

Should he prepare for impact? As a kid, he'd swear he heard the crack of thunder before she launched into one of her tirades. He'd endured plenty of them over the years. What if he used a different tactic?

He leaned close and reached out, grazing her elbow with his palm. "I don't want to fight or rehash the past. I came to say I'm sorry. I was injured and frustrated. I lashed out, and I was wrong."

Her hot breath tickled his neck. Near enough to breathe in her exhale, he watched her eyelashes flutter as she looked to the ground. The air sizzled. Instead of her bluster and thunder, lightning threatened to strike. His new plan might not be the better choice. He neither wanted nor needed another complication in his life and especially not a romance with the neighbor who drove him crazy. "I repeat. I'm sorry. You'll come back?"

"Yes."

"Good." He stepped back, breaking contact and dragging his burning palm over his jeans. "I'll get out of your way." He grabbed the hat off the counter and pulled the brim low over his forehead. "I'll see you around." In a few long strides, he reached the front of the store.

The bell jingled as he stepped over the threshold and shut the door behind him.

Outside, the temperature dropped ten degrees and chilled his skin. Whatever just happened wouldn't be repeated. Meg was all sorts of trouble both good and bad. He had no intention of engaging in either.

CHAPTER 3

Meg shivered, tugging the sleeves of her oversized sweatshirt, and covering her hands with the threadbare cuffs. She knew better than to bring only a worn sweatshirt as an additional layer. Never leaving home without at least three pieces of outerwear was fundamental for life on the ranch no matter the season. While sipping her coffee at the kitchen window, she had studied the dark sky and reasoned the temperate weather pattern would hold. Besides, she would be indoors. At the last minute, she had decided against a skirt. Thankfully.

Hours later, the morning had never quite dawned.

Spring was unpredictable. A day could start bright and clear but erupt with hail before lunch. Overcast skies were blown off-course with strong winds. Although, today, she'd welcome a change in the weather. Gloomy, gray skies that hung around all day weren't her favorite.

In her rush to the ranch, she had forgotten to factor in the uninsulated shed. The breeze whistled through the gaps in the wooden boards. With no windows, the chill couldn't be blasted with sunlight. The thin rays breaking through the clouds didn't promise much warmth.

Her priority had been getting to the ranch before Ryan changed his mind. She wasn't quite sure what to think about yesterday evening's encounter. While the morning run-in had been a heightened version of status quo, the second meeting was a marked change. For the first time ever, she had held her tongue in his presence, and he had spoken more than three words.

With every replay, she couldn't think of a better word to define his speech than an oratory. He had never shared his thoughts or his feelings or his concerns with her. It was easy to imagine the man robotic.

He proceeded through life with quiet efficiency, moving from one success to the next with no hiccup in any plan. When he had purchased the bulk of the Hawke ranch, enabling her mom to retain the house, he had done so with his typical few words and stepped aside as the lawyers handled the details. Over the past five years, she had often wondered why he took action. Was the transaction only to grow his business or to help her family? Or both?

She fisted her hands and raised both to her mouth, blowing hot air on her icy digits. Until yesterday, she had no idea he had feelings. Had she ever given him the chance to speak and explain? Or did she cut him off before he could say what she feared?

She based her assumptions about him on her experience and interpretation. Was she wrong? Another shudder racked her body, and she lifted her gaze studying the lone, uncluttered corner of the shed.

Hank sat on a nineteenth century side chair, the walnut frame creaking under his weight. In his lap, he held a box. Rifling through the contents, he focused on his task.

She navigated through the maze of boxes, picking her feet up and stepping over the variety of crates and cartons. The shed had taken years to fill. At various moments, some attempts at preservation had been made.

Analyzing the layers was like studying the strata in the earth's crust. Labeled cardboard levels separated rows of plastic bins on top of wooden crates. If she had to guess, she'd identify the organizational attempt as Susie's handiwork.

Her grandmother's friend had been a strong, stoic woman, much like her grandson. Unlike Ryan, her silence wasn't threatening but comforting. When she did speak, she made every syllable count. She had the best voice, kind and warm, and loved to read stories aloud to others.

Meg had spent many years in Susie's kitchen, seated at the oak table too mesmerized to speak. While her grandma gossiped, Susie baked, her fluid movements like a dance as she whipped up everything from biscuits to croissants. Grandma's voice droned in the background like a classical score for a ballet. The warm air hung heavy with yeast and sugar. *And love.* She couldn't pass a bakery without entering and breathing in the aroma, transporting herself back to a cherished memory for a precious second.

She missed both women with a fierce, sharp pain she doubted would ever ease. Did Hank miss the calm peace of the house from the women's combined presence? He often dropped in to kiss Susie on the cheek and share an enticing tidbit with Grandma. He'd chuckle and head out the back door. Spending time with the Kincaid men wasn't a substitute but at least something of a consolation. She wasn't alone. If Ryan wasn't her friend, he had her back anyway.

Had he grown even more stoic after losing his grandma? In the immediate aftermath, she hadn't noticed. She hadn't made more of an effort to act like a good neighbor. Instead, she restricted her visits to avoiding Ryan altogether. Was she oblivious or self-absorbed? *If you want a friend, be a friend.* She'd do better.

"Hank?" She called. "What did you find?" She stopped in the center. With the shed door propped open, light spilled into the room along the aisle. She crossed her arms, tucking her hands against her armpits and lowering her trembling chin into her collar.

"I'm not quite sure. I reckon I need to take this box and that one," he pointed to the large cardboard rectangle on the ground next to Colby, "inside for a better study. It's getting cold out here. We earned a break."

She nibbled her bottom lip. She doubted Ryan would agree. When she had arrived, she listened to the rules Hank established for the sake of harmony on the ranch. The items that had been removed already were handled. Ryan had loaded the donation pile into his truck and driven to the next town. With Ted's help, Hank had stored his keepers in the barn attic.

While the first efforts hadn't produced anything worthy of consignment at the antique store, she wouldn't be disappointed. The initial disruption created enough space to work inside the shed and a small pile of goods was stacked outside the shed to be loaded into her SUV at the end of the day.

Finishing the project before the ranch opened for the season was unlikely. If she could continue inside the shed and out of view, she hoped Ryan wouldn't mind her presence, and he'd let her keep working while guests roamed the property.

He was changing. Without a big discovery inside the shed, she wouldn't be around long enough to witness the full transformation. She didn't want to leave now. She loved her life in Herd.

Hank set the box on the ground. He stood, his joints cracking.

Colby howled.

"I'm fine. Don't you get started, too." Hank scowled at the dog.

Colby got to her feet and pressed her nose against the cowboy's knee.

Hank reached down and scratched the dog behind the ears. "Want to come inside and rest for a spell?"

Thump thump thump. The wagging tail slapped against the chair's legs.

"Calm down, or you'll hurt yourself. Sprained tail is no joke," Hank said.

Meg froze, pressing her lips together and swallowing her reaction. What happened to his claims her made when she adopted Colby that the animal should be treated like a dog and not a human? The pair was adapting to each other's cues. Hank spoke in the same tone and cadence as his usual voice, indicating he conversed with an equal and not an inferior.

Hank bent and groaned.

She rushed forward, extending both hands and lightly touching his shoulders. "Let me carry the boxes, please?"

He wrinkled his brow.

"It's for my sake, okay?" She bent and grabbed the boxes, stacking one on top of the other. She'd ask for forgiveness and not permission. Yesterday, she had regretted letting him do too much. The old cowboy's ways weren't likely to change, and he never let her do anything he thought he ought to handle. She had to try.

"If you insist," he muttered and shuffled forward.

Colby followed on his heels.

She tightened her grip on the boxes, her chin resting on top creating a wedge with her arms. The boxes were awkward and heavy, her cold hands slipped. She couldn't show the struggle. The bigger than life cowboy in front of her, leading the way to the house, would jump in and hurt himself.

Growing old was a gift and a curse. She understood his frustrations at not being able to bound in and keep pace. Her entire life, he'd been the quintessential western man, rugged, tough, and strong. She wouldn't let him feel his age if she could help it. As long as she remained in Herd...

She stumbled, catching herself in time. Frowning, she glanced at the rock in the otherwise clear path. She'd focus on the present and leave worrying about the future to the side. For one day.

"Hey, can I help?"

She turned in a slow circle.

Coming around the side of the house, Ryan waved and jogged toward her.

Dressed in his usual flannel and jeans, he wasn't as formal as the last time she'd seen him. She wasn't sure she had a preference. Today's light gray buffalo check shirt looked soft and warm. She'd love to cuddle up in it. *Not appropriate.*

Colby raced to him, jumping up and catching him mid-chest with both paws.

He chuckled, petting the dog. "Okay, Colby, down. You're a good girl."

Colby obediently dropped to the ground. Her whole body shook from the excited pump of her tail.

"Good to see you. We were about to take a break," Hank said.

Ryan strode forward and grabbed the boxes from Meg.

He stood close, his hot breath tickling her cheeks. Through her thin sweatshirt, she absorbed warmth from his palms. Would his rough, calloused hands scrape her skin if she pushed up her sweatshirt sleeves to her elbows brushed? Her cheeks heated. Better not to think about it.

He arched a brow and smiled. "You okay?"

She nodded, pursing her lips.

"Speechless, again?" He tipped his head to the side. "Did you lose a bet?"

She rolled her eyes. His tease snapping her out of the moment. "I'm fine. Hank and Colby are taking a break. I thought I'd keep going."

"No, you should take a break, too." Ryan frowned. "I've got something I want to show you. Wait here, I'll get Hank and Colby settled."

She widened her eyes but didn't reply.

He passed Hank and the dog, striding up the path and into the house. The back door swung shut, the slap of the screen into the frame echoing in the otherwise quiet air. When the trio disappeared, she pressed cold fingers to blazing cheeks.

Why was he suddenly so different? Had Hank read him the riot act and demanded politeness? Had *he* lost a bet? Or maybe his total personality shift was an indication that anything was possible, including her chance at staying in Herd and mattering to the community—and people—she loved.

Turning on his heel, Ryan pounded the path under his boots, his heavy steps echoing as he climbed the steps behind Hank and the dog. He slipped inside the screen door before it shut and slid across the slate tile. Behind him, the screen slammed against the frame, bouncing twice.

Usually, the sound made him jump. Living in a hundred plus year home, he learned early to never test the limits of a hinge. He eased every door and drawer closed with care. Today, he didn't flinch. Slowly, he scanned the room, his gaze unseeing.

He was too aware of what had happened moments earlier. When he had reached to grab the burden, he brushed her arms, and the air charged with electricity. Again.

He gritted his molars and crossed the room, setting the boxes on the table. She was his longtime neighbor. If he judged her by her dedication to her grandma and her attentive friendship with Hank, he supposed she was nice enough. She didn't need more of his time or his admiration.

Clearly, he needed to right the balance of the world. His axis was leaning wildly to the left, and he'd be knocked to the ground. The answer was simple and elementary. He'd keep his hands to himself. He groaned.

"You all right, boy?" Hank asked.

Ryan glanced at the old man settled at the head of the table.

Colby circled, her nails clicking against the floor, and laid down at the old cowboy's feet. With a sigh, she rested her head on her paws.

Hank leaned forward, scratching the dog behind the ears. "Well? Are you?"

Ryan narrowed his gaze, crossing his arms over his chest. "Are you?"

Hank shrugged. "She's a good dog. Not many out there this calm. I like her company." He met Ryan's gaze, wrinkling his brow. "Don't tell, Meg."

Ryan smiled and shook his head. He had his own share of secrets to keep from the neighbor. "I'm taking her over to the yurt to show her the progress."

"Riding?"

Ryan caught his breath. Meg could only handle one horse, Grandma's Cupcake. Ryan hadn't saddled the horse in a long time, letting Ted take care of the dear animal. He stopped by with sugar cubes but couldn't bring himself to spend any time in the horse's company. Missing Grandma knocked him sideways some days. "No, not today, but maybe another time."

Hank sighed. "Whatever you think is best." He pulled a box to his lap and focused on his work.

Why are you doing this? What's your motivation? The questions tickled the end of Ryan's tongue. Hank hadn't been so devoted to a task in years. He approached the shed clean-out with focus and resolute determination. The timing of the project wasn't the biggest issue. Ryan had the nagging doubt some deeper purpose propelled the effort.

Besides the annoyance of having one more person poking around the house on the last few days of peace, he couldn't have his ranch hand, Ted, tied up in helping Meg either. The bulk of summer employees wouldn't arrive until the second week in June. The first few weekends operated with a reduced crew, each person shouldering a huge amount of work. Ryan opened his mouth, but nothing came out. Maybe he was better off not knowing the answer. "I'll be back in a bit."

Hank waved but didn't raise his head.

Stuffing his hands in his pockets, Ryan strode to the door. He spent all morning trying to show he regretted his bad behavior. He believed in doing and not talking. Rising early, he drove the three hours round-trip to drop off the donations from Hank's shed to the nearest city. Sitting behind the wheel, he waited as the staff insisted on unloading the pickup and returned with a receipt. All told, he was at the facility for fifteen minutes. The flat, monotonous landscape of his drive gave his mind too much time to wander.

On the drive home yesterday, he had replayed that weird charge in the air at Finders-Keepers. It was only because he caught her by surprise, and she was silent. The change between them wasn't his concern. He couldn't afford to expend any energy or time on a distraction.

After making up his mind to ignore her, he had parked his truck and hopped out of the cab. Her voice floated past. Following, he decided his best path forward was to help. With actions, he'd prove he wasn't mean and cruel. When he stood close enough to breathe in the hint of lavender clinging to her clothes, his heart skipped a beat.

Pulling back his shoulders, he strode through the open doorway and headed back outside and down the path. He understood his next course of action. With a little more time together, she'd start yammering again, falling into their old patterns. He'd remember he didn't like her because he couldn't think when she was around as she filled every moment with a random stream of consciousness. He needed her constant chatter to annoy him so he could stop wondering if she drove him crazy or if he was crazy about her.

He jogged down the steps toward her. His palms itched, but he kept his hands in place in his pockets. No fast motions or he'd do something stupid. Like reach for her. "Hey." He called.

She turned her head.

A shaft of light broke through a cloud, beaming on her brown hair. Streaks of gold shimmered. No, not gold as much as red, like copper. *What? Huh?* Why waste his time comparing her to precious metals? She had brown hair, like dirt. "Do you want to go for a drive? Give Hank a moment to sort through his boxes? You've earned a break."

"I'm not sure." She nibbled her lip. "We haven't made much progress."

"I bet you have. You're a hard worker." Why couldn't he stop talking? He crossed his arms over his chest and gripped his biceps until he twisted and burned the skin through his jacket. He sounded like a fool.

"You really don't mind if I take a break?"

"Of course not." He frowned. Was he that much of an ogre? Had he made her feel unwelcome? He'd raised his voice before, and she'd never been scared away. What changed? *I don't want to know.* "Come on. I want to show you something. We'll take my truck."

Strolling at his side, her head reached the top of his shoulder. She swung her arm wildly at her side like the thin limb could propel her. *But she isn't talking.* He had to stop picking at every little thing. He wanted silence. He got it. At thirty-eight, if he didn't know his own mind by now, he never would. Rounding the side of the house, he strode toward his vehicle and opened the passenger door on his truck.

She climbed inside.

He caught himself reaching forward, his fingers almost to her elbow. He pulled his hand back and shut the door. Crunching the gravel under his boots, he strode around the bumper, wrenched open the door too hard, and hopped in behind the wheel. He turned over the engine and reversed out of his spot, depending on the mirrors. He would not reach behind the passenger seat and turn. He'd be too close.

Pulling out of the drive, he steered onto the dirt road toward her property. From the corner of his gaze, he studied her.

She looked straight ahead through the windshield.

Her expression was blank. Was she mad? He searched for flaring nostrils, a sweaty brow, or her pinched lips. He found nothing.

Her silence was unnerving. Was she waiting for him to yell? Processing the surge of pulsating energy between them? Nope, he was not going there and couldn't let her confuse the quiet either. "I wanted to give you a look at what's happened on your family's land."

"It's your land now."

His chest squeezed tight. He'd always think of it as hers. His earliest memory was riding in the saddle with the grandfathers and learning the boundaries between the properties.

The men had a cordial relationship based on respect for the other's domain and authority. Of course, shortly after, her grandfather suddenly passed from a massive heart attack. Her grandmother relied on his family for help whenever necessary and offered the same in reverse. She hadn't been a burden. Miss Betty was a sweet chatterbox with a compliment for every person she met. Helping her was a gift.

When he had the chance to preserve her land, he claimed it. For years, he had not developed the acreage. He hadn't done so for her sake. He'd indulged his own nostalgia for keeping the area as pristine as he could. With increased demand and more overhead costs from the purchase, however, he had to find a way to cover the costs. He hoped his plan was a decent compromise.

The additional acreage also secured the ability to partner with the bison foundation. The situation was one win after another. He never asked if she regretted selling. *I would.* "The yurts are set back from view. I had to run infrastructure out here. Otherwise, the land is undisturbed. If it doesn't work, I can pull the tents down and break up the slabs. I'll restore the prairie. I don't think you can see the new lodgings from your house?"

She shrugged. "I haven't noticed any changes."

"Good. I didn't want to disrupt your life." *Or maybe I do.* A lump stuck on his Adam's apple. He coughed. "I mean I don't want my guests to wander over and bug you. I know you appreciate your privacy."

"You can do what you need." She turned in her seat and faced him. "I trust you."

Why? Was her faith in him based on being a good neighbor or something more? Did she feel the sudden shift in their world?

Why now? He'd never been swamped with doubts or questions. His life suited him. He worked to maintain his legacy for at least another generation. While he understood the world in black and white, he accepted she believed in the murky grays somewhere in the middle of his perception. She was decent and a perfect neighbor. Why must everything change and why the bad timing?

People aren't preserves. They don't keep.

Grandma's words weren't a comfort. He understood he couldn't wait forever. If he could get through the summer first, focusing on his business and paying off the mortgage on the Hawke land, then he'd reevaluate his personal life in the autumn. He promised.

CHAPTER 4

Adjusting the seat belt across her chest, Meg leaned forward. Hot air blasted from the vents onto her icy hands. The moment of sunshine was too brief to stave the chill in the air. Although, his smile had warmed her.

Through the windshield, she surveyed the passing landscape. To some, the grassy land might be boring. A seemingly endless expanse stretching to the horizon. But to her? She'd never seen a more beautiful sight than the sea of green rippling in the wind like waves in the ocean.

She hadn't ridden inside Ryan's truck in years and never alone. On her last trip, during her first Christmas living in Herd full-time, he had fussed over helping cart the trees she and Hank got from the sale on Main Street. While he wasn't berating her this time for tracking needles and sap into the carpeted interior, he hadn't made his vehicle any more comfortable for passengers during the past five years.

The cab was clean and empty. No paper receipt, food wrapper, forgotten tool or other item littered the interior. She sniffed, breathing in only the faint hint of musky aftershave. How was it possible to use a vehicle as much as he did and leave behind no clue about the owner?

Did he clean up after himself constantly? He never carried anything extra like a toolbox or a fanny pack. By comparison, her SUV was a neatly organized garage on wheels. She was prepared for any situation. *Except sitting close to him.* Her senses heightened to a painful degree with the close proximity.

"Hey, are you, okay?" Ryan asked.

"Why wouldn't I be?" She focused on the dashboard.

"I don't know. Why would you sniff my truck?"

Heat crept from her hands straight up her neck and across her cheeks. Had she been loud? *Better out than in.* Hank loved that expression. His meaning was slightly different, but she'd follow the spirit of the directive. "Why doesn't your truck smell?"

He chuckled.

"It's...unusual. There isn't any sort of scent. Not even a hint of your aftershave lingering in the upholstery."

33

"I guess I don't spend enough time to notice. Is the lack of scent a good thing or a bad thing?"

His tone was soft, thoughtful. From the corner of her eye, she glanced at him. "I'm not sure."

"What does your SUV smell like?"

"If I don't use air freshener, it smells like dog."

"Hmm."

She turned her head. A loud crack snapped the crick above her spine.

"Yikes." He winced. "Seriously, are you okay? What's wrong?"

She straightened, tucking her hands under her legs. "I'm fine. I'm a little sore from the physical labor."

"I can understand." He rolled his shoulders. "I don't know how Hank dragged you in to this. I never thought he'd go through that shed." He smiled. "It's why Grandma put the lock on it in the first place. To stop him from adding more."

She liked how the corners of his eyes crinkled when he grinned. She liked being included in his jokes. She liked belonging. "But she gave him a key?"

He shook his head. "No. He found it."

She chuckled, shaking with the belly laugh. She covered her mouth with both hands. "Sorry, I shouldn't laugh."

Grinning even broader, he kept his face forward, looking out the windshield. "No apologies necessary." He tapped the steering wheel. "The cold snap is supposed to let up soon. By the time the tourists arrive, it'll be mid-sixties and perfect during the day."

"Twenty degrees warmer in a few days?"

"I'm only repeating the forecast."

"I believe you," she said. "If for no other reason than your business needs good weather, and your family has always had good luck."

"Not always, but we're an optimistic sort. We've never wasted an opportunity. When it comes to nature, however, we're all at the mercy of the elements. Here we are."

She turned away, reluctantly. When was the last time she'd seen him smile? When had she ever been the cause in a good way?

He parked the truck at the top of a hill.

From the shotgun seat, she couldn't see much. Unbuckling her seat belt, she opened the door and hopped to the ground.

Set in a small valley, she spotted three large yurts. The short, white cylinders should have stuck out against the landscape. Instead, the dwellings suited the setting. Tall prairie grass rippled in the wind surrounding the buildings. Like they'd always belonged.

Sunlight broke through the clouds, and a shaft of light brightened the property. She held her breath. The setting was magical and peaceful. She exhaled a deep breath and relaxed her shoulders. She sort of liked not talking and listening. Being quiet was peaceful. Maybe she didn't have to fill in every moment. She could let someone else take the lead. *If it's Ryan.*

With a shake of her head, she faced him.

He dragged a hand through his hair, frowning. "What? You don't like it?"

She shook her head. "I haven't been here in years."

"It's nice land." He covered his mouth with a fist and coughed. "The yurts aren't permanent. We take them down and store them before the winter. We'll give the land time to rest and heal."

I wouldn't think you would. First and foremost, he was a caretaker. "I'm glad you bought the land. Selfishly, of course." She faced the yurts again. "Thank you."

"You don't owe me any gratitude."

His sharp tone grated on her nerves, scraping her cheek with the bit out sentence. Did it strain him to be nice and accept her thanks?

She opened her mouth to reply and stopped. Knee-jerk reactions were their default mode of communication. The past few days showed her a chance at something different. She wanted better for both of them. Instead of assuming his mood, she should stop projecting and ask. She could be wrong and her initial assessment correct, but how would she know for certain? She faced him.

He stepped forward and reached a hand out, hovering near her shoulder.

She frowned at his fingers. Why didn't he touch her? Was he afraid she'd bite him? She met his gaze. "What about weddings?"

He drew back his hand and frowned. "Not sure I follow your train of thought."

She didn't either. The words burst out of her without any planning. She could think on her feet and hid her wariness of any change in their relationship status. "I guess not only weddings. Big events, too. Why not expand the resort offerings? You've already made Herd a destination. Isn't this the next step?"

"It's a major industry within the hospitality world." He turned toward the valley. "I guess I never really had marriage on the mind."

She nibbled the inside of her cheek, unsure whether she should be heartened or discouraged by the statement.

"Do you think anyone would want to get married on this lonely stretch of grass?" His tone was teasing and a gentle curve lifted the corner of his mouth.

I would. Her grandparents had married in the exact spot. With wildflowers blooming, Grandma had carried a freshly picked bouquet.

Growing up, Meg spent so much time studying the photos she created fake memories including herself in the event. Her mind supplied the warm feel of the sun, the smell of sweet grass in summer, and the sound of happy laughter as her grandfather dipped her grandmother before the pastor following the vows.

With a hand, she shielded her gaze and considered the spot for a modern audience with no tie to the land. She scrunched her nose. "Sure, the spot might not be ideal especially if you're dealing with high-maintenance bridezillas." She sighed. "You'd need parking and bathrooms. Building permanent structures would change the landscape here forever. This patch of prairie is perfect as is. What about an expansion at the barn?"

He scoffed. "Oh sure. Leave your house alone but give up my backyard?"

She heard the tease in his tone. "Not necessarily. The barn is plenty big enough as is. You could build a deck with an open pergola overhead. String up lights across the beams. You'd have plenty of space for ceremonies on the back deck and cocktail hour inside."

"You've given this some thought."

Not really. She spoke as the ideas formed but could picture the entire setup. Getting married on the ranch would be magical. Could she convince him to both expand and let her be involved?

"You sure you don't have a secret admirer, stoking bridal visions?" He narrowed his gaze.

His question was delivered like an accusation. Under his direct stare, she flushed and glanced away. Of course, she didn't. The small town of barely two thousand residents didn't provide a range of romantic options, and secrets were nonexistent.

"I'm kidding." He sighed. "I like the idea, but you're talking about a major expansion. Catered events and weddings have a lot of pressure and high expectations. The enterprise is very stressful."

"You could focus on smaller events in the beginning."

"True, but I'd need to do a test to be sure everything ran smoothly for my customers. To rent the whole ranch in my busiest season, I'd charge a lot."

"I'm sure you'll find interested guests. Even at an exorbitant rate in the shoulder seasons."

"Do we have those?" He arched a brow. "Seems like the snow falls earlier every year."

She widened her gaze, clapping a hand over her mouth. A sudden, inspired thought sprouted. Would Ryan go for it?

"What?" He uttered the word with his weary, put-upon tone. The same one he'd used since childhood.

"I know the perfect test run. Hank's ninetieth birthday. What could be better? He would love a huge, town-wide affair."

Ryan shook his head. "Please, don't give him the idea. I'm begging."

"Will you... consider it?" She scrunched her nose. *Please, please, please.* When the shed project with Hank wrapped up she wasn't sure she'd be content to being respectful but distant neighbors again. She wanted a legitimate reason to be here. To be near Ryan. Working together could be that opportunity.

"Yes, it's a good thought. I'm always interested in diversification. I'm looking for every opportunity I can. The old-time photography studio could become an official vendor."

"I'm sure they'd appreciate the business. Everyone does. You've done a lot for the community."

"I can't sit around and wait for my chance at success. In this life, we have no guarantees."

The breeze whipped past. The environment shook her as her thoughts threatened to do the same on the inside. Her tie to town wasn't a strong rope but a thin ribbon. Without her last name, she wouldn't belong. If she didn't fit here, could she find home anywhere?

"I better get back to work."

She nodded and lifted her gaze, but she didn't move away.

Neither did he.

They stood closer to each other than ever. Nearer than the weird moment at her store yesterday afternoon when her skin electrified. She'd been convinced if she touched anything she'd be jolted by a static shock.

Today, she was sure the spark in their touch would cause a wildfire on the dry prairie. If she inched closer, would he step back? Better not to risk the land she loved. She sighed and turned to gaze over the grass again. "I probably should return, too. We're making progress on the shed."

"It won't be done by the weekend though."

She pressed together her lips, stifling her smile. She didn't hear the usual admonishment today. "No, it's a long project. I promise I won't be in the way."

"You aren't," he murmured. "Thank you for coming."

She caught her bottom lip. In a moment, she trespassed on unknown territory. She struggled to process the words of someone she'd known—and never understood—almost her entire life. Warmth spread through her from head to toe.

"Let's get back." He stepped away, turning toward the truck.

He saved her from a response she wasn't sure she was ready to think let alone verbalize. Following, she grabbed the door handle and pulled herself into the truck, buckling her seat belt.

He turned the keys in the ignition and circled the vehicle onto the road.

"How's the store faring?"

Her stomach twisted. She sucked in a sharp breath, breathing through the stitch in her sides. He'd rescued her once already. If he knew how bad things were, would he try to swoop in again? Why?

"Oh. Do you need he—"

"Stop, please." She held up a hand. "I'm working on a plan. You don't need to get involved. You owe me nothing." *I don't want to be an obligation.*

"I don't mean to offend you." He scowled, gripping the steering wheel tight.

"You didn't." She sighed and focused on the dashboard. Now she was being flippant and unkind. Pride was no excuse to cut him off. "I need to improve business for the rest of the year after the tourists leave." She kept the true depths of her problem to herself. If he knew, would he help her? Would he feel forced to ride to her rescue? He'd purchased her family's ranch and thus enabled her to move here. He didn't owe her more.

"Do you have any ideas?"

"Some," she murmured.

"If you're modernizing, I can help," he said. "I had to establish our website and e-commerce system. I didn't want to pay someone to set us up initially or charge us every time I need to change a tiny detail. I can teach you."

"Thanks." She turned toward him and smiled. Sharing her burden was both harder and easier than she'd imagined. She was glad to have someone to take her job seriously enough to ask. How strange to consider him a confidant. "If I get to that point, I'll take you up on the offer."

He turned his head and arched a brow. "Promise?"

She nibbled her bottom lip. He studied her so earnestly. What was happening? She nodded.

Sliding his gaze back to the road, he pulled the truck in front of the house and braked. The engine idled.

She unbuckled her seat belt. "Are you coming inside?"

He shook his head, wrinkling his brow with deep lines. "No. I've got some work to do. I'll see you later."

She shivered. Reaching for the door, she opened her side and hopped to the ground. Without glancing back, she rounded the house to the shed. She'd thought they were thawing. Had she been wrong? Again?

One hundred forty-eight, one hundred forty-nine, one hundred fifty.

Ryan halted. He'd reached the corner of the barn. Swiveling on his heel, he strode back to the approximate center of the building.

He hadn't intended to spend his evening pacing his property. After dinner, however, he couldn't stop thinking about his conversation with Meg. The sun didn't set until nearly nine in late May. While chill lingered in the air, he wouldn't waste the extra daylight. He had time, and he preferred action to sitting around.

He also couldn't ignore a good idea, no matter how unlikely the source. A cool breeze stirred. He raised the collar on his jacket and stared across the rolling prairie of swaying tall grass.

She'd looked so wistful as she discussed the idea. When she had mentioned her grandparents, she almost glowed. She'd lost her beloved grandmother, too. They had an unspoken understanding of each other's grief because of the gift of knowing each other's family.

Her grandmother, Betty, had talked nonstop, making Meg seem restrained by comparison. He couldn't remember a time in his youth Betty's deep voice didn't echo from the kitchen.

She had loved jokes. She wasn't always skilled in the delivery, but her contagious good humor was impossible to ignore. Everyone laughed with her. She had an instinct about people and never pushed. Several times, she came to his defense with a smile and an off-topic story, distracting Susie and Hank from reprimanding him.

Since his apology to Meg, he recognized the fundamental shift in his opinion of her and vice versa. After years brushing her aside as an annoyance, he couldn't label her so simply anymore. She had thoughtful ideas and depth he never suspected. Whatever came next, he couldn't return to their previous status. He didn't want to.

"Hey, boss. You need help or something?"

Only two people called him boss. It was a nice change from answering to *boy*. He didn't need to face his companion to know Ted stood behind him.

California born and bred, the ska-music loving cowboy listened to his tunes almost constantly while working on the open range. The low sound of a horn line from a late nineties hit filtered out from the headphones dangling from Ted's neck in the seconds before he hit pause.

Hank had hired him years ago. At the time, Ryan had been annoyed his grandfather made a major decision without asking for any input. In the years since, Ryan was forever grateful for his grandfather's gut instinct about the quiet. Ted's positive pragmatism and hard work encouraged Ryan through the tough times.

"Good evening," Ryan said. "I'm finishing up. Sorry if I disturbed your rounds."

Ted approached with his heavy-footed strides.

Ryan glanced again at the red painted boards. The barn was painted every three years. The southern-facing side faded quick.

"It's no bother, boss. Everything is in order. The first wave of staff is settled in at the bunk house. We'll have our orientation in the morning."

"Good, good. I'll be sure to drop in," Ryan said over his shoulder. He pointed at the wall. "Since you're here, you can give me your opinion. Do you think we could build a deck here? Add French doors off the backside of the barn?"

"For a cost, anything is possible." Ted stroked his chin. "You'd have a short window to build during the fall and spring so guests aren't disturbed. Why? What are you thinking?"

"I'd like the deck in a semi-circle shape extending out from the barn. I don't want it covered but a retractable roof might be a nice addition if it's too sunny or a little drizzly. No one could be out here in a full-blown storm. I'd want a clear view of the stars overhead." Ryan glanced up, shielding his gaze with a hand.

In big sky country, the night was a display not to be missed. Overhead, the constellations burned brighter than a planetarium. He'd hate for guests to lose an opportunity for stargazing. Joe, middle school history teacher and ranch tour guide, might be keen to give talks. He'd probably have to do some research first. Luckily, Joe loved learning more than anything else.

Years ago, Hank had taken Ryan and Meg cowboy camping. The plan was to sleep under the stars without a tent. Once Meg started talking about how bright the stars shone, she never stopped. The next morning, she remained chipper and chatty. He and Hank dragged with exhaustion. The experience was never repeated.

"Sounds expensive." Ted folded his arms over his chest.

"I know." Ryan sighed. "Everything is."

"I can't see the upside. Why invest so much without a way to add revenue?"

Ryan shrugged. "Maybe we expand into weddings and events."

Ted whistled. "Welp. Now I've heard everything. I wouldn't have thought you'd turn your focus to romance."

"I haven't. I'm not." Ryan frowned. "It wasn't my idea."

"Meg's?"

Ryan nodded.

Ted looked across the landscape. "It's a good plan. We're busy enough but always smart to have another revenue stream."

"Yep. If we host events, we can extend the season on either side. The guests' focus would be the wedding. We wouldn't have to worry if Joe can't take off time from school for excursions. The guests would be otherwise engaged."

"Gives Abby a chance to extend her season, too. Running a food truck in the winter is a non-starter."

Ryan nodded. Abby Whit operated a barbeque food truck on par with the best restaurants he'd ever visited. In two years, she established herself in town as the best chef and accomplished the remarkable feat of keeping her personal life and history secret. She'd arrived in Herd with a fully-fledged business and never offered much in the way of relatable anecdotes or childhood story.

He didn't mind. She approached him about catering, and he'd been happy to sign the contract. Questions were Hank's forte and not his. The more he considered Meg's plan, the more he liked it. He only observed potential and no pitfalls. His blind spot made him apprehensive. What was he missing? Where was the hiccup? "Any change needs Hank's approval. Retrofitting the building, again, wasn't my plan." Ryan turned and considered the paint-chipped boards on the side of the barn. "We've already patched and pieced so much together. Wouldn't mind the chance to build from scratch."

"Losing the building and a big piece of history would be a shame. The roaming bison might change how we operate," Ted said. "Perhaps we need time to co-exist with the new herd before pouring footings."

Ryan studied the prairie. After selling the cattle, he adjusted to the absolute silence at night. He hadn't understood how much noise the animals made until they were gone. He'd also grown lax about watching his step for cow patties.

The new herd would disrupt the environment for a time until everyone acclimated. *Sort of like living with Meg's chaos.* He agreed with his cowboy's assessment.

How often had Ryan reconsidered a plan lately? Reintroducing the bison would heal old wounds from generations past. He couldn't overlook someone in the present either. Ted hadn't watched Meg's face light up as she discussed the idea. As much as Ryan found her presence complicating, he couldn't imagine living here without her. "I doubt the bison would get this close to the house. But you're right. A lot to consider."

"Sure, have seen a lot of her lately."

Ryan wouldn't insult either of them by pretending he didn't know which *her* Ted mentioned. "If Hank's happy, who am I to complain?" Ryan shrugged. "Did you need me? Were you looking for me?"

"Yes, I have a couple things. Number one is do you have any leads on a new yoga instructor?"

Ryan shook his head. "No word yet from Joe but I'll reach out and touch base with him. See where he's at with it."

"He hasn't mentioned any names?"

At the quizzical look, Ryan paused. Did Ted know Joe's colleagues? Was he worried about someone in particular? Ted and Joe were Ryan's closest friends. He couldn't easily transition from his role and responsibilities to the town into a carefree guy having fun on a night out. The same couldn't—and shouldn't—be said of the cowboy. Ted and Joe probably socialized with a wider group. Ted had a whole other life including a sister and niece. Ryan didn't know everything about his employee's personal life.

"Never mind."

"Sorry for my distraction lately." Ryan scrubbed a hand over his face. "I wouldn't make a hire without your involvement. You're a great manager of people and livestock."

"I enjoy the people more than I imagined. I've met a lot of different folks from all sorts of places since the spa opened. I've learned a lot from listening to their stories."

Ryan envied him. He couldn't admit as much because too many depended on him for their livelihoods. He was always the boss. No one ever opened up to him and vice versa. *Except for Meg.* "You mentioned two items to discuss?"

"Heads up, the vet is coming tomorrow to check on the horses and to re-shoe Cupcake."

Cupcake was Grandma's mare. The sweet old horse only got ornery when she spotted the vet. It took a lot of sugar cubes and Hank's soothing voice to calm her down for any procedure. "Thanks, I'll be sure to tell Hank so he can be there."

Ted turned toward him. "For the record, I like the event idea. You don't pay me enough to be your yes-man. I have to find the flaws."

Ryan chuckled. Ted was a good friend. He'd started as a cowboy during the final year of cattle ranching. Ryan changed the rules by transforming the property into a travel destination. Luckily, Ted continued in a new role. They kept each other on their toes and helped the other through grief for Ted's late wife and Ryan's grandma.

"Do you need me to keep an eye on the shed project? Make sure those two stay on task?"

Ryan studied the cowboy. History meant reading between the lies from a hundred paces off. Ted sensed something was different between Ryan and Meg. Ryan read it on his friend's face. Unless Ryan screwed up, he was assured of Ted's silence on the matter. For his discretion, Ted was more valuable than gold. "I'll manage them. Have a good night."

Ted reached for the brim of his hat, tipping his head.

Ryan strode around the barn and toward his house, passing the shed. Progress happened everywhere at different paces. The middle of nowhere wasn't immune to life surging forward in leaps or tiny tiptoe steps.

He'd focus on the positives and leave the worries about the changing nature of long-held acquaintances. But that wouldn't stop him from replaying what they'd said. Or spend the rest of the night debating the best excuse for another meeting.

CHAPTER 5

A t the desk in Grandma's front parlor, Meg rubbed her weary eyes and leaned forward. Squinting at the screen, she clicked on the toolbar and enhanced the resolution of the nineteenth century, black and white cards again. She should go to bed. In the lower corner, she spotted the time. Almost midnight. She hadn't stayed awake so late in a decade. Her vision blurred.

Until she accomplished one task, she wouldn't be able to sleep. Working on the best chance at hidden treasure was a better prospect than dragging herself for what she did and did not say to Ryan. Did he like her event space idea, or was he humoring her? She hated not knowing if he laughed at or with her.

Grandma never had that problem. *As long as the person's smiling, I'll take it as a win.* Not for the first time, Meg wished she possessed more of the woman's moxie.

She leaned back in the chair and tapped her fingers against the edge of the walnut secretary desk. Her initial excitement at the potentially valuable discovery was quickly tempered by the process. Much like the rest of her day, she wasn't certain if she was better off than when she started. One step forward and two miles back.

She hadn't seen Ryan again after he dropped her off at the house. He had plenty of work to do with guests arriving soon. She understood but couldn't ignore the odd twinge in her gut. She didn't miss him. The idea was preposterous, but she had the weird sense she had never spent time with him before today. Would she get another chance at a relaxed, friendly conversation?

What about expanding into events? She had no experience, and nothing to offer besides her willingness to help. Would he take her seriously enough to consider?

This newly talkative, attentive man was the opposite of the neighbor she'd known. His company was enjoyable, and he tempted her with his offer to help with her store. Proficiency in social media wasn't quite the same as extensive html knowledge. She couldn't claim knowledge in either sphere. Shortly after moving to the ranch, she'd given up sharing updates and photos of her personal life in favor of blog posts highlighting her business. She didn't want to open her home to public scrutiny and speculation and finally understood Mom's constant railing against over-exposure. She gave her head a shake and focused on the screen, moving the cursor to adjust settings and click start.

The scanner whirred, and a bright light flashed under the lid.

She jumped, startled by the sudden burst of blue. She blinked and rubbed her tired eyes. Swiveling the chair, she looked for her supposed companion.

On her back on the velvet couch against the wall, Colby was unaffected. Her paws moved, her tail thumped the cushions, and she snarled. In her dreams, the sweet shadow must have imagined herself a fierce huntress.

The dog might not be alone in personal misconceptions. How wrong was Meg about herself? Was she the friendly neighbor? Or a nuisance? Or both?

The scanned image flashed on the screen.

With higher pixel count, she had a clearer view of the faces than with the naked eye. She leaned close and squinted. Her gut instinct, based on memories from school textbooks, told her she knew the bearded man in the cowboy hat and the Native American man seated beside him. Seeing wasn't always believing. The card wasn't an original photograph and could be one of thousands of reproductions.

She zoomed in again on the signature, studying the bleeding ink. The likelihood of Hank planting a signed fake in the shed, stoking her hopes, were slim. She couldn't shake her skepticism of the sudden good fortune if the card was authentic.

She uploaded the image to the facial recognition database she found after a quick internet search, tapping her foot against the desk chair leg. If today held one miracle, friendship with Ryan, why couldn't she hope for more?

After the expedition to the yurts, she had spent the rest of her day in the shed. Sorting through crumbling boxes and broken furniture, she'd created three piles for Hank's assessment. Once again, the consignment stash was the smallest with only a handful of salable items. Why bother Ryan and ask for help creating on online store for nothing?

Working alone, she had made better progress, but the process was lonely. She had especially missed Colby. While the dog only made noise in her sleep, she had a presence that relaxed Meg. Keeping her head down, Meg had focused on one task at a time and had only stopped at the knock on the shed door.

"I reckon it's quitting time," Hank had said.

She turned toward the door and stared past him into the twilight sky. "Already?"

"We made good progress today." He reached to his side.

Seated, Colby pressed against the man's legs and lifted her furry face to gaze at him.

The dog adored the cowboy. Meg bit the inside of her cheek. Over the past few days, she'd appreciated the renewed companionship, too. She wasn't as independent as she wanted to believe.

"How come you haven't updated your blog this week?" he asked.

She wasn't sure her best response. Because she was using her free time on his property or because she had nothing to say. Should she tease or answer truthfully?

"Guess I set you up to fail with that question." He chuckled. "I like the stories you tell. Sometimes I worry you spend too much time observing and not enough living."

She stared, slack-jawed. He'd picked that up from a few paragraphs here and there? "I'm not sure I always..." *belong.* If she admitted as much, she knew her concerns would be brushed aside. Hank had always been the heart of the community. How could he relate to her troubles? "Not every item has a story worth sharing. Besides, if I posted about the shed, all your business would be shared with the whole world. Do you want that?"

"Hmm. Maybe not." He smiled. "I've got something for you inside the house. Might be worthy of a tall tale."

She frowned. "You do?" Her chest squeezed tight. If he was about to offer her something of Miss Susie's, he'd be disappointed by her response. She would not stoop to selling his memories, no matter how desperate her business was for income. The shed was turning into a bust. With her head held high, she'd help a neighbor who always did the same in return. She didn't need payment.

"Remember those boxes from this morning?"

She remembered too much from this morning. When he grabbed the boxes, he'd flashed her a lopsided grin and electrified her every nerve ending from her fingers to her toes. Her heartbeat pounded, and her throat closed. She nodded.

"I found a bunch of old photographs and signed cards," Hank said. "I think some are from the Wild West Show."

That snapped her back. "You mean Buffalo Bill Cody and Annie Oakley?"

"One and the same. I don't know if they are old souvenirs or originals. They don't mean anything to me. I think they could be valuable."

He was probably right. Western art remained a hot niche of the fine arts market. On the rare occasions she got a print or statue, she couldn't keep them in stock. Would photographs be the same? She could be out of her depth. If she was honest, she'd admit to handling smaller items worth, at most, several hundred dollars. She'd never sold something worth five figures or more. She couldn't let him down with her lack of connections. "Should I call an expert? Like a museum or an auction house or something?"

He shook his head side to side. "A deal is a deal. I want you to sell these for me."

"I don't know if I can." She exhaled a heavy breath and hung her head. "The first step is authentication. Whether real or not, I want to get you top dollar. As collectibles, the set is desirable. I'm not sure how to price the collection."

"You're clever. You'll figure something out. Come on, let me show you."

She'd followed him inside. Spread across the kitchen table were black-and-white images of bearded men in over-the-top western wear. Fringe along every seam of velvet buckskins, the too much persona was Buffalo Bill's signature. The collection of images included one with an older Native American man in feathered headdress seated next to the buckskin clad, bearded figure. Could it be Sitting Bull and Buffalo Bill? She'd seen a few pictures of each man individually but didn't recognize this shot.

Hank had helped her pack up the photos and load her SUV. With reluctance, Colby had jumped into the vehicle. Driving away, Meg had banished her thoughts of Ryan for a time. She considered the various paths she could take to sell Hank's goods for top dollar. Central to any plan, however, was identification.

Ryan provided the answer. Their talk about modernization sparked an idea and an internet search. Couldn't facial identification software spot a well-known historical figure? Buffalo Bill and Sitting Bull were famous since their time. With hundreds of images available, A.I. would be able to tell her definitively right away. She'd have one problem solved.

Seated behind the computer at midnight, she curled her toes and grinned as the results popped up on the screen. She had a reason, and now she had a path to stay.

Ryan woke early the next morning. Or, more accurately, he had left his bed an hour ahead of schedule. He couldn't wake up when he'd never quite fallen asleep. After their visit to the yurts, he had dropped Meg at the house, he had vowed to focus. Almost immediately, he had broken the oath. The rest of his day—and night—was plagued with thoughts about her.

He took up every chore he could, staying away from the house as long as possible. Because he didn't know what would happen when he ran into her again. He wasn't scared. He wouldn't deign to empower the change with an emotion.

The situation was absolute madness. For the time being, he couldn't start thinking about her as anything other than someone to manage. In the future, when he finished paying off the mortgage on her ranch and saved enough of a nest egg to feel in control of his future, he could maybe indulge these new thoughts.

She implied concerns about her future. How could anyone live for the moment when they were terrified about tomorrow? He knew Hank didn't understand. Every issue in his grandfather's life resolved itself almost by magic.

Ryan didn't begrudge anyone their good fortune. His path wasn't one of faith but focus. Approaching any new situation, he learned the variables and navigated to safety. He wasn't spontaneous. He was steady.

When she spoke of her worries, she couldn't have guessed how she spoke to what weighed so heavily on his heart. Somehow, she was different. Since the apology, she wasn't the girl she'd always been. Or maybe he'd changed and was no longer so set in his opinion of her that she surprised him. The moment at the store hadn't been a fluke. Unfortunately.

Something shifted, and he understood her in an entirely new way. Instead of the electricity in her company, threatening him with a bolt of lightning, yesterday he found peace. She knew him. He didn't have to explain every thought. He wanted to correct her misunderstanding but didn't want to upset the calm of the momentary ceasefire.

Standing on the hill, looking across the building site, she had looked serene like an angel on a Christmas Tree. She was contemplative and content with pretty features and lustrous hair.

He swallowed a groan. The hair thing bugged him. Couldn't he reset their relationship and avoid the painful, hyperawareness? Shouldn't people have a factory setting mode so he could meet her again for the first time without any of the past mistakes?

Tightening the belt on his robe, he jogged down the stairs and through the hall, pushing the swinging door to the kitchen. He only had a few more days of leisurely wandering through his own house in his pajamas. The one downside to the business was utilizing the main house as the lobby. He did his best to separate his personal and professional lives. He'd installed the door at the end of the hall to block the kitchen from view. Growing up in the house, he often forgot the changes. More often than not, he smacked his forehead into the panel door, remembering what had been and forgetting the present.

In a couple years, with enough capital, he'd build a special lobby away from the house. If he raised a family, he wanted to give his wife and children the privacy and freedom he had loved as a kid. He frowned. Again, with the family talk. He had to get himself under control.

At the sink, he filled the coffeepot reservoir, added grounds to the filter, and started the much-needed brewing cycle. Spending time together should have summoned a return to old habits. Familiarity should breed contempt. He'd been counting on her talking too much.

She hadn't fallen into her old patterns. During the last few encounters, every word she uttered was a devastating blow to walls he hadn't realized he had erected. Each touch stirred up more feelings than he ever remembered. Lately, she forced him to operate in the moment with heightened awareness of how fleeting time was. He longed for peace but worried their former status quo equaled a resumption of mixed signals. Couldn't the revelations wait a few weeks, or months, for a more convenient time?

Loud knocking echoed in the quiet room.

Spinning on his heel, he frowned at the panel door. Had he imagined the sound? The sun hadn't risen. Who would be on his property so early?

If Ted had a problem, he'd call. Or let himself in. Ryan must have imagined the noise and turned away.

The pounding resumed.

"Coming." He strode across the slate tiles, his slippers gliding over the floor. Reaching for the doorknob, he twisted and pulled open the unlocked door.

Meg stood on the other side, bouncing from foot to foot. Colby sat at her feet. "Hi, Ryan. Sorry about the early call."

She's here? He shut his gaping mouth. "No, no, it's umm... Fine." He opened the door wider. "Please come in. It's cold in the dark."

"Thanks." She passed inside, her steps muffled.

Colby's nails clicked with each step.

He shut the door and stuffed his hands in his robe pockets. Maybe he should have started dressing for the day to get ready for the visitors. Or prepared for the possibility she had almost total access to the ranch. He couldn't kick her out without ending in the same sort of trouble that demanded his hat-in-hand apology and free-access to the ranch. "Can I get you a coffee?"

She lifted on tiptoe, glancing around him toward the stairs. She dropped to her heels. "Hmm? What did you say?"

He frowned. He hadn't mumbled. Was she distracted? He wanted her focus. "Can I get you a coffee? I'm brewing a pot."

"Oh, sure." She smoothed a strand of hair behind her ear. "I probably need it." She chuckled. "Sorry to drop by so early and unannounced. I have something big to share. I barely slept last night."

Her cheek-to-cheek smile warmed him. It was like standing outside at midday on a cloudless summer day. Except better. Her cheer worked from the inside out, without threat of sun burn. He didn't need his hat for protection or shielding. He had a clear view. "What is the good news?"

"Well, I..." She rubbed together her palms. "I really ought to share my discovery with Hank first." She scanned him from head to toe, and her cheeks pinked. "Don't let me get in your way. I'm sure you're ready to start your day."

He liked her embarrassed. It was almost like old days. Dropping his hands to his sides, he leaned back against the stairwell. "I've got plenty of time. Like I said. I woke up early."

"We got company?" Hank's voice bellowed from the second floor.

Ryan frowned, turning toward the stairs. Had they been loud enough to wake the notoriously heavy sleeping Hank?

Trudging steps sounded from the second floor.

A low "woof woof" echoed.

Meg spun in a circle. "Oh, not again," she murmured. "That dog is stealth."

Ryan faced her. "Not again?"

"She's passionate about mattresses. She sneaks upstairs every chance she gets. Even at a stranger's house."

And we're strangers? The thought stung.

Meg stepped around him to the foot of the stairs and cupped her hands around her mouth. "Colby Woofington Hawke, get down here this instant."

"Your dog has both a middle and last name?" He tipped his head to the side.

"Of course." She narrowed her gaze.

Her incredulous stare knocked him off-balance. "Of course?"

She shrugged. "How else does she know when she's in trouble?"

With his tongue pressed to the roof of his mouth, he held back his retort. He could think of any number of other methods for a dog to know it misbehaved. Every scenario he conjured required a firm differentiation in the pack roles. He suspected neither woman nor animal would understand.

Arguing wasn't earning him points. He didn't want to get shooed away before the big reveal. He was curious. Why was she visiting early in the morning? "If that dog is on my bed, you're washing the sheets."

She turned and glared, pulling back her shoulders.

Nails clicked on the hardwood steps. Colby trotted down the stairs, tail wagging.

Not far behind, Hank descended. He'd thrown on jeans and a shirt. He had advance warning about their guests.

The thick white stubble highlighted the deep grooves of his wrinkled skin. Ryan dropped his gaze. In the mornings, his grandfather looked like an eighty-eight-year-old man. Ryan hated the reminder.

"Morning, Meg. Ryan, you want to put on something decent?" Hank asked.

Crossing his arms over his chest, Ryan locked his knees. He was acceptable for surprise company. He wasn't moving.

"Hank, great news. I got a hit on the photos. You're right. It is Buffalo Bill," Meg said. "Velvet clad and all."

"Like Cody?" Ryan asked.

"Is the man next to him Chief Sitting Bull?" Hank asked.

Ryan dropped his hands to his sides, twisting his neck to study one and the other. What on earth were the pair talking about? Why were they ignoring him?

"I emailed an expert on Native American art and photographs from an auction house in San Francisco. With luck, we'll find out the next steps for evaluating and pricing the collection," Meg said.

"You'll handle the sale, right? I don't want anyone else involved." Hank frowned.

She held up her hands. "I promise I'll be involved in helping you get the right experts on board. I will ensure the property is handled correctly."

Hank grunted.

Ryan darted his gaze between the pair. He was definitely the odd man out of the conversation. His interjection wouldn't be appreciated.

"It's a long shot," she said. "If the expert gets back to me quickly and wants a meeting, that has to mean something, right?"

Too many maybes. Ryan wanted to interject and interrupt. The pair of dreamers needed caution. One of them had to stay on the ground, or they'd both float away into the heavens.

If he was honest, he'd admit he hated being left out. Of course, he didn't have time to involve himself in their business. His exclusion was for the best. He wasn't part of their project, and the sooner he removed himself from their business the better. He had real work.

"What about other options?" Hank asked.

"I'm searching for museums and private collectors. While I sort out what we have uncovered and run my store, I won't be able to help in the shed. I hope you understand. I can resume the project again after the photos are resolved." She glanced at Ryan. "I know you wanted the project finished before the guests arrive on Friday. We should have enough space to pick up our work inside the building. I won't disturb the yard again."

"Sounds like you have your hands full. We understand. We do, too. I'll get out of your way." With a nod, he spun on his heel and continued to the kitchen. Everything was working out. He wouldn't have to worry about bumping into her anymore. He could focus on his business.

Back to normal was exactly his goal. He wasn't a child. The sooner he got the future settled, the faster he could lean into what was happening. He was unhappy about being pushed out of the project. For everyone's best interests, he'd hit pause here and revisit their discussion later.

As long as she did the same.

CHAPTER 6

As Meg stood in line at the grocery store, holding a basket full of microwave meals for one, she mentally drafted a post on the blog about the shed discovery. She wanted to share the thrill of finding documentation tying the present to the past. Did the sentiment sound a little sad?

She'd never worried about the perception of her words but she'd clearly underestimated her audience. She swallowed the sigh building in her throat and unloaded her groceries on the moving belt. She hadn't received a response from the auction house yet. The big company was probably busier than she could imagine. Shouldn't she have, at least, received a confirmation email?

"Dear?"

Meg glanced over her shoulder.

A petite, white-haired lady in pearls and a sweater set stood behind her in line. "Do you mind grabbing the plastic divider? If I'm not quick, my grandson will wander into the ice cream aisle."

Meg smiled at the hushed, conspiratorial tone. "Of course." She unloaded her groceries on the belt, set the divider behind her order, and slid the plastic basket into the holder.

"Nana?" a deep voice called.

"Over here." The lady waved a hand above her head.

Will Buck, owner of the General Store, approached.

Meg did a double-take. She'd pictured a teenager loading up the lady's cart with pints of rocky road, not a man.

"Hi, Meg," Will said.

"Do you know this young lady?" Will's nana unloaded her groceries onto the belt.

"I do. Meg owns the antique store," Will said. "Meg Hawke, this is my grandmother, Lana Buck."

"Pleasure to meet you, Miss Hawke" Lana extended a hand. "I'm surprised I haven't seen you around before."

Meg shook Lana's hand. "I guess my store fills a niche role. Not like the General Store. Anyone in search of a good cup of coffee has to stop by and order a cup of coffee from your grandson."

"I'll have to look for you at Frontier Days," Lana said.

"It's not really her scene, Nana," Will said.

It's not? Meg thought.

At the same time, Lana replied. "Isn't it?"

"Do you like line dancing, Meg? Carnival games? I've never seen you in town after working hours," Will said.

He had a point. Meg liked to get home. She hadn't realized she'd been such a loner in the town's eyes. Making friends as an adult was more involved than during childhood.

"Paper or plastic?" the cashier asked.

Meg faced the woman behind the register, grateful for the excuse to get out of the conversation. "Paper, please." She inserted her credit card into the checkout terminal and glanced at Lana once more. "It was nice to meet you."

"You as well."

The cashier quickly scanned the stack of frozen food. "Here's your receipt."

Meg accepted the paper slip and pulled her credit card out of the terminal, tucked both into her purse, and grabbed her groceries. With a paper bag in her arms, she pushed out the revolving front door of the grocery store and turned left on Main.

Herd embraced their Wild West heritage, and nowhere was that more visible than downtown. False front architecture dotted the one- and two-story buildings on either side of the road. Painted vivid shades like red, blue, and green, the stores stood out against the otherwise flat landscape. Most of the buildings were wooden. A few stone structures had been erected at great cost not long after the town's founding.

The bag she carried did nothing to ease the weighed-down feel in her limbs. No one had entered her store. She'd spent the day entirely alone. All she needed was a plan to get people inside. With a shake, she shrugged off her doldrums. She'd head home, make dinner, and distract herself with a good book.

She shivered when a cloud blocked the sun, and a chilly breeze blew past.

A hot meal and a cozy cuddle with a warm dog would soothe her. As she stepped off the sidewalk at the next block, another shudder racked her body. She turned her face to the dark sky and gulped. Overdue for rain, she hated to wish away the clouds.

When the weather changed on the plains, it was with dramatic rapidity. A sunny morning could transform into thunderstorms in less than a few minutes. Three blocks away from her vehicle, she didn't like her chances for staying dry.

She glanced across the street at the wooden false-fronts and pitched roofs extending over the plank walkway opposite. She was, of course, in front of the post office at the middle of the block of stone and brick buildings without awnings.

She could go inside and wait out the storm. Standing in the elements was dangerous.

Hail was always a possibility during the tail end of spring.

A late in the day rain could last anywhere from ten minutes to ten hours. Colby waited at home. The dog hadn't been out in hours and would demand dinner soon. If Meg didn't hurry, she worried what she would find. Meg had to reach her vehicle and get to her dog before Colby took matters into her own paws.

In Meg's thirty seconds of indecision, the sky darkened to pitch black. Rain poured down like an upended bucket. She tightened her grip on the bag, climbed the steps onto the next section of walkway, and tucked her chin against her chest.

She couldn't raise her face to follow her progress, or she'd be pelted in the eyes by the fat drops. She trusted her memory of town to guide her. With each passing moment, her clothes became wetter and clung to her body. She focused on warm thoughts like the hot cocoa packets in her pantry. She could manage. She'd dealt with worse.

A truck rolled past, hit the pothole in front of The Golden Crown Saloon, and splashed water like a wave, thoroughly drenching her.

She lifted her gaze at the idling vehicle, her mouth forming a circle and freezing on the gasp.

The truck's passenger side window rolled down.

"Meg?" Ryan asked. "Hop in, warm up," he commanded.

The door unlocked with a loud click.

In normal circumstances, she wasn't one to be bossed around and especially not by him. He always thought he knew best. Arguing was pointless as she shivered in the rain. This one time, he was right.

She hopped into the cab, sliding her groceries onto the floor mat. "Thanks." Her teeth chattered.

With a frown, he turned up the heater. "I'm sorry I added to your misery."

"I should have known better." Keeping her hands on the vents, she turned toward him. "If I'd been thinking, I would have driven to the grocery store instead of leaving my car in the municipal lot. I wanted some fresh air and a little exercise."

"The temperature will improve by the weekend. You've lived here long enough to know one truth." He lifted the corner of his mouth. "Nice weather never lasts."

Nothing good does. She stared into his amber eyes. The amusement in his gaze invited her into a private joke. She didn't want to lose the new connection. Once she finished at the shed, she wouldn't have any reason to seek his company. Worse, she could end up back in Chicago if she didn't make progress on her online store or those cards failed to pan out.

She had to find contentment one day at a time in the present, ignoring her inclination to race ahead. Her tomorrows might not include him so she couldn't squander her todays.

She pointed at a clip on one of the vents. "You bought air freshener?"

"Hank had some in a drawer." Ryan shrugged. "I can't tell a difference."

Shutting her eyes, she breathed deep. "It smells like cedar." She turned her head and met his gaze with a smile.

A car honked.

He broke away from her gaze, raised a hand to the driver passing him, and pulled into traffic. "Can I get you dinner by way of apology?"

She shook her head. "I've got to get home to Colby. A ride to my car would be more than enough."

He nodded and turned at the next intersection, driving onto the side streets and backtracking to the lot on the edge of downtown, a few blocks past her store. "You left the dog at home? Doesn't she accompany you everywhere?"

He keeps tabs on me? The thought was cheering and a little jarring. She wasn't sure she wanted to be so predictable and boring. Or maybe he knew her that well. "Typically, she does." Meg pushed her limp, wet hair behind her ears. "She's in time out for behavior unbecoming of a lady this morning at the ranch."

Ryan chuckled.

Her heart lifted at the deep, rumbling sound. "Why are you in town? Aren't you too swamped to leave your property? Only a few more days until the first guests arrive."

He exhaled a heavy breath. "Believe me, I know. Cupcake was reshoed today, and I spent the rest of the day with the spa staff. My brain is counting down the seconds. Occasionally, a meeting pops up that can't be rescheduled and is easier handled in person." He paused.

Oh. She swallowed hard. Was she a fool for wanting him to seek her company? Their fledging friendship might be endangered if he did. She shouldn't expect more than either of them could give.

He lifted his shoulders. "I was serious about my offer. I'm heading over to Church Street. Joe and I have business to discuss, and I'd like to review the catering orders for the first few cowboy dinners with Abby Whit. She'll have everything handled, of course. But two big events in less than a week is a lot. I figured we might as well grab dinner from her food truck while we're there. Really, it's a good excuse to do just that."

Meg licked her lips. She loved Abby's pulled pork sandwich with mustard coleslaw on a pretzel roll. Eating out was a luxury she couldn't afford at the moment. His offer was tempting. With Joe there, no one could accuse Meg and Ryan of a date. Her cheeks burned. She wasn't sure she'd mind the assumption.

"You want to reconsider now that you know my plan?" He arched a brow and shot her a quick glance before refocusing on the road.

"Don't tempt me."

He pulled into the public parking lot behind Main Street and turned down the first row. All alone, her white SUV waited for her. He parked next to her vehicle and turned toward her.

"Hey, before you go. I want to tell you how much I appreciate your work with Hank. It's a lot to deal with and sort. You helping means a lot."

His sincerity scrambled her brain. How could she form an appropriate response when he was so earnest? She nodded.

"I also wanted to tell you the event space idea is a good one. I am looking into it. Not sure how feasible it will be with some other projects in the mix, but I am considering it."

"Wow. That's great. I'm... glad." He took her seriously. She would have expected him to brush off her idea and never mention it again. He surprised her in the best way.

"I do want to urge caution about the stuff you found in the shed. Might turn out to be nothing, and I'd hate to get Hank's hopes raised only to dash them."

Irritated by his lack of faith, she found her footing. Sitting up straight, she faced him. "You are good at your job. I'm good at mine. Trust me. I would never deceive or hurt Hank." *Or you.*

Ryan scrubbed a hand over his face. "I never accused you of treachery. I'm saying be careful."

She didn't want to fight. How quickly any comment could be filtered through their history and misconstrued. She was overreacting, but she couldn't shake off the foul mood with continued company. "Okay." She reached for the handle and opened the door. Hopping to the ground, she grabbed her sodden bag of groceries. "Thanks for the lift."

With a foot, she kicked the door closed and walked around her bumper to the other side of her SUV, away from his piercing gaze. She had dropped her guard only to have him grab her by the shoulders and shake. Metaphorically speaking.

He probably didn't intend his words as a challenge. Regardless, she'd fight and prove him wrong. She wasn't toying with Hank's emotions or hers.

As Ryan rolled through town, he imagined the community's collective sigh. In addition to much-needed rain during an unusually dry year, the sudden storm encouraged tourists to seek shelter.

The General Store would be hopping with folks looking for souvenirs or hungry for a piece of fudge. Olden Time Portraits would be packed with customers in costumes, snapping sepia-tinted photos. The Golden Crown would be stuffed to the rafters with the supper crowd.

Too bad Meg closed up for the evening. She might have had her best sales yet this year. He couldn't worry about her. She made it clear that she didn't welcome his concern.

On the opposite side of town, he reached his original destination. The rain stopped as soon as he pulled out of the parking lot. *So much for a grand, gallant gesture.* Meg could have waited inside the saloon and avoided him altogether. She would have been better off than after their impromptu encounter. As he said the words about Hank, her hackles visibly rose.

He hadn't intended a professional attack. After she had left the ranch as suddenly as she had appeared, she stirred up all sorts of talk inside the Kincaid house. Hank was jollier than Christmas morning. Ryan wanted to join in the glee but couldn't. What if it all went wrong? Meg could be mistaken about the value.

Their unexpected encounter in town was the perfect opportunity to speak frankly. She cared about his grandfather and would appreciate the concerns for the older man's heart. Ryan made a huge miscalculation. He forgot who he was dealing with. She was equally as determined and stubborn as him.

He wouldn't have responded well to a perceived critique of his work skills and business competency. He hated ruining the otherwise pleasant encounter. Under no circumstances, however, would he retract the sentiment behind the statement.

Hank was larger than life but not immortal. Any big upset in either direction could overwhelm him. Ryan couldn't see the future without his grandfather's presence. He didn't want to be left on his own. If he continued to antagonize, however, he'd scare Meg away. His future looked very lonely without her in it.

He parked and turned the key in the ignition, cutting the engine. The large, open parking lot behind the historic, Presbyterian church faced the town's cemetery. Many people swore the hallowed grounds were haunted. He brushed off the comments. Any old graveyard looked spooky as the iron fences surrounding family plots rusted, the stones discolored from age and acid rain, and the ground uneven due to erosion.

Wrenching open the truck door, hinges squealing, he pocketed his keys and strode toward the food truck parked on the other end. Abby chose the location due to its size and access downtown, successfully petitioning the town for permission. As a member of the council, he supported the enterprise. The spookiness of the location didn't detract from customers. Diners flocked to the spot for the best barbeque for a hundred miles in any direction.

He joined the back of the queue and breathed deep, savoring the mingled smells of damp earth and smoked meat. He'd overstepped with Meg by being too harsh. What he meant as a tease wasn't properly conveyed. One step at a time, he'd fix it. Not tonight. He had to focus on the business at hand and worry about Meg later.

"Hey, boss."

Ryan turned and waved.

Joe jogged across the wet pavement.

"Hey, Joe. Thanks for meeting me. I know you're swamped with end of school stuff."

"It's fine." Joe stuffed his hands into his coat pockets. "To be honest, I'm surprised you had time to leave the ranch."

A popular opinion. If he had phoned, he wouldn't have had the unfortunate run-in with Meg. He couldn't regret riding into her rescue. She would never be a damsel in distress, making an opportunity to help rare.

But his dwindling hours were stretched thin. He'd spent most of the day onboarding the new spa employees and greeting those who'd become summertime fixtures.

"I like to review the order for the first cowboy dinners of the season in person. Two in one week is a big ask. Figured I might as well grab supper, too. Thanks for stopping by on such short notice."

"Of course." Joe sniffed, twisting his neck side to side. "Is it just me or does it smell like a sauna around here?"

Ryan pressed together his lips, resisting the urge to sniff his collar and draw attention to himself. If Meg's face hadn't lit up when she noticed he took her advice, he'd toss the clip-on air freshener.

"Never mind." Joe shook his head. "You mentioned you wanted to follow-up about potential yoga teachers?"

Ryan nodded, holding his breath. He needed every staff position filled as soon as possible.

"I put the word out at the school teacher's lounge. No luck upstairs with the middle school wing. But I struck gold in the kindergarten through fifth grade portion of the building. Stephanie Patricks expressed interest. She isn't just a kindergarten teacher. Turns out she is a certified yoga instructor, too."

The line moved forward.

If only every problem was so easily solved. Ryan shuffled a few paces ahead, staring at the ground. "Great news."

"You okay?" Joe asked. "You're sort of radiating nervous energy."

Ryan let out a bark of laughter. "I am? Sorry."

"It's okay. Opening week stress, I get it." Joe darted his eyes side to side and shifted his weight. "This is a weird place for a food truck. Don't you think?"

Ryan met Joe's gaze and frowned. Was he trying to deflect Ryan's attention? "It's the biggest parking lot in town with good proximity to Main Street. Makes sense to me. Besides, the benches are on the unclaimed land. Good to see it put to use."

Joe rocked back on his heels. "I hate waiting around for the hundred years to pass. Can't we get a lawyer involved and speed up the process?"

Ryan had no response to the bitter tone. In less than eighteen months, the land the parking lot sat on—formerly owned by the Whittier family—would be absorbed back into Herd. No one ever stepped forward to state they possessed the deed. Why pursue unnecessary litigation? "I don't want to put the money and time into it. Have you uncovered anything in your research that makes you think it should be pursued?"

Joe shook his head. "No, the genealogy records stop with Hoss. I can't find any mention of him owning property or getting married. I haven't located his death certificate. He can't be alive, or he'd be well over a hundred."

"He probably didn't last long after leaving town," Ryan said. "He struggled with his demons."

"I've run into Abby at the library several times."

The words were almost a hiss. Ryan couldn't understand his friend. Something was off in Joe's mood. With the end of the school year and the start of tourist season, he was busy, too. In addition, he toiled on his history of Herd, a project he'd dedicated all of his free time to for the past decade. Ryan gave him a pass on his attitude today.

"We don't have to get dinner."

Ryan would readily admit his own inner turmoil and distraction. He guessed he wasn't alone in the sensation. "No, I promised, and I'm starving. Join me. We won't linger. I know you're busy wrapping up your school year."

Joe nodded. "I have a lot on my mind."

"Next," Abby called.

With a wave, Ryan stepped up to the window. "Good evening, Abby. We'd like a couple three meat samplers, pork, brisket, and sausage with the works. I'm wondering if you got the order I emailed?"

"Hey, Ryan. Good to see you. Hi, Joe."

Joe raised a hand to his shoulder and dropped it to his side.

Weird greeting for an effusive person. Ryan couldn't get distracted by other people's problems. He had enough of his own, and he wasn't Hank. Ryan didn't try to insert himself—by force, if necessary—into other people's personal lives.

"I got the email," Abby said. "I've already reached out to my suppliers. We should be set for both events. If there is an issue, I have plenty of time to find a solution for Friday. Monday will be taken care of, no matter what."

"Good, thank you." Ryan nodded. "Catering twice in one week is a lot to ask."

"Nothing I can't handle. Have you had a chance to think about my proposal to park on-site once a week?"

Joe snorted.

Ryan snapped his head toward the sound in time to catch a corresponding eyeroll. He glared at Joe.

"Sorry. Allergies," Joe said. "I'll get a seat." He strode around the truck toward the grass on the other side and the row of wooden picnic tables.

He moved too quick for a reprimand of his out of character behavior. He wasn't exactly rude, but neither was he nice. "Sorry about him. Allergies." Ryan rolled his eyes.

Abby chuckled and waved a hand.

At least she was good natured enough to brush off Joe. Ryan wouldn't take advantage of her kindness. "I have to run the idea by Hank and Ted. I'll be honest, something popped up recently and has me totally sidetracked. I'll get you an answer soon."

Abby nodded. "No worries. Steve has your order ready at the other window."

Ryan smiled and followed Joe's path. As Ryan cleared the front of the truck, he spotted Joe claiming their meals.

Ryan continued to an empty table and sat down. Pulling his cell out of his back pocket, he shot a quick text to Ted and Hank before he forgot again. Hitting send, he placed the phone face-down on the weathered plank top.

Joe slid a metal platter in front of him and handed a cup of water.

"You feeling okay?" Ryan asked, studying his friend.

Joe stepped over the bench seat opposite and sat in front of his tray. "Ever get the sense you're not being lied to but you don't know the full scope of a person or situation?"

As far as cryptic statements went, Joe was an unrivaled master. Ryan ran a hand along his jaw. "Am I supposed to understand your meaning?"

"I'm glad if you don't." Joe shook his head and speared a slice of brisket. "Should I have Stephanie call and set up an interview?"

"I can call her if you'll send me her phone number." Ryan raised his plastic cup. "Let's toast to a good season." *Including resolving issues with as little disruption as possible.*

Joe set his fork down and grabbed his water, touching his plastic cup to Ryan's before taking a sip.

Ryan drank a large gulp. After a dry, dusty day on the ranch, nothing was as satisfying as water. Maybe Meg wouldn't agree today after he drenched her. If she was warm and toasty at home, perhaps she'd reconsider the encounter and realize his words weren't meant as a taunt or a test.

If she was upset, then she had misread the charge in the air between them. A sense of anticipation collided with fate. He wasn't sure if he loved or hated the new and different feelings. He hoped she welcomed the change.

CHAPTER 7

With her laptop open on the antique store's front counter, Meg refreshed her inbox. Since sending the email late on Tuesday night, she'd spent too much of her time on Wednesday and Thursday staring at her computer screen. Finally, Friday dawned and with it the promise of tourists. She hadn't seen one in the hour since she'd opened.

Propping her chin in her elbow, she sighed at the empty email account. She didn't even have an update from a mailing list about a limited time sale. Had she been wrong to raise Hank's hopes about potential interest?

Ryan was right. Her indignation had been in vain. She should head to the ranch and apologize. Spending more time with him—even to say she was sorry—threatened their status quo. She didn't mind the provocation. Did he?

Instead, she'd focus on the photographs and cards. She pulled up her blog, hit compose, and stared at the flashing cursor on the blank page. The discovery was exciting but unknown. Could she share anything without jinxing herself? Or worse, revealing too much? Hank had guessed at her feeling like an outsider through her entries. She was guilty of waiting on the sidelines as life happened.

What if she put herself out there? If she joined the knitting club that met at The Golden Crown or directly asked Stephanie about helping with Frontier Days, what was the worst possible outcome? Being told no?

Her neighbors weren't rude or unwelcoming. She hadn't attempted to befriend anyone besides Hank and Ryan. She had to do better or she'd never belong.

In her back pocket, her cell phone vibrated. She pulled out the phone and smiled at the screen. She answered the call, pressing the cell to her ear. "Hi, Mom."

"Well? How's it going on your treasure hunt at the ranch? Anything to report? The blog hasn't been updated all week."

Meg chuckled. Her loyal—and top—follower would know. "I doubt I'll have much that I'll be allowed to share." She nibbled the inside of her cheek.

"Oh? Really? Why?" Mom's voice pitched high.

Had Hank called Mom? She'd grown up with Hank's son, Ryan's dad. Mom talked to Hank every so often. Were they in cahoots about saving the store? *Probably.* "We found a box of old photographs and souvenir cards from the nineteenth century. I can't say much more at the moment. The discovery could be valuable." *Although, now I have my doubts.*

The bell over the door jingled.

She straightened and smiled, meeting the gaze of a teenager.

The ponytailed girl blushed and backed out, shutting the door.

The glass rattled in the frame.

"Is someone there?" Mom asked.

"No, just the wind." Meg sighed. "I'll keep you posted about any new developments. In the meantime, don't expect much on the blog. I am focusing on the website."

"You should. Couldn't Ryan help you? Didn't he have to build one for the ranch?"

Meg nibbled her lip. Hank and Mom played the same tune. They were wrong. Two people of the same generation—like Meg and Ryan—weren't automatically friends. With their occasionally acrimonious history, Meg and Ryan should be well past any sort of clunky *setup*. Too bad their respective families didn't understand the definition of futility, and informing Mom of Ryan's offer of help wouldn't win Meg's argument. "I'm not sure what he does on his ranch. I'll ask Hank. I better go, Mom. Don't want to discourage customers with a phone plastered to my ear." She forced a chuckle.

"Bye, sweetie. Good luck! I'm rooting for you." Mom ended the call.

Rolling her shoulders, Meg shut the laptop and tucked the computer and phone into her purse on the floor. She needed to dust off her customer skills, or she'd scare everyone away on the first day of the busy season.

Herd was in a celebratory mood. Every store was open. Flowers filled planters. Flags hung on lampposts, and banners strung over the street. A few wandering cowboys strutted down the sidewalk, playing up the Wild West for tourists.

She loved the small town in every season but especially during the contagious cheer of summer courtesy of outsiders. Her sleep deprivation shouldn't dampen her spirit. A heart heavy with questions and concerns slowed her. Grabbing the feather duster from under the counter, she stood and started cleaning.

The mindless motion gave the appearance of activity while her brain drifted to a ranch not so very far away. When she'd been splashed by Ryan's truck last night, she hadn't shared the details she and Hank had worked out in the morning. Over coffee in the kitchen, she had devised a plan, and Hank agreed with a condition. She didn't want Hank to miss out on a big payday.

He'd use the money to help the ranch. No doubt, he'd pay off the mortgage on the land Ryan bought from her. She'd feel a lot less guilty about the Kincaids riding to her rescue. Without the stress, Ryan could slow down and enjoy himself.

Had he ever?

She snorted and dusted the first row of shelves at the back of the store. Hank had insisted she take a cut of the final sale price of the photographs. She had no intention of doing so but would save the disagreement for another day. First, she needed contact from the auction house.

Jingle jingle jingle.

With a smile on her face, she turned slowly toward the door. "Hello, welcome to Finders-Keepers." She used the brightest, cheeriest tone she could muster.

A man strode over the threshold and shut the door. He turned.

Each quarter inch of action happened in slow motion. Dressed in a slim cut, light blue dress shirt and tailored, charcoal slacks, he stood out from the usual jeans and T-shirts crowd of locals and tourists alike. He was instantly the most interestingly out of place stranger she'd ever seen. When he connected his gaze with her, he smiled.

He looked like an old movie star. With dark hair and dark eyes, she couldn't quite tell the color of either. A cleft in his strong jaw deepened with his grin.

Ryan's more handsome because he's real. The thought slipped into her mind and she couldn't shake it. This stranger's beauty was undeniable. But she was drawn to the inside of a person.

The man tipped his head and approached.

With each step, he came into focus. He wasn't quite five ten, but his trim figure gave a lanky impression. *He's going to change my life.* The complete thought was like a bolt of lightning surging through her veins. She wished she understood the how and why of her certainty as much as she instinctively knew the what.

If such a thing were possible, she'd throw the idea to the ground and crush it under her heel. She wasn't ready. She wanted everything to stay the same for as long as she could hold on. Or, if she could have a hand in manipulating fate, she longed for Ryan to be the one to spark change.

"Hello, are you Megan Hawke?"

His voice was smooth and deep, lower than she expected. She coughed, raising a fist to her mouth. The feather duster tickled her nostrils. She dropped her hands behind her back. "Yes, hello. Thank you for stopping in." Her voice cracked. "Are you looking for anything in particular?"

He stopped a few feet away. "I'm Eric York, from Campbell and Company Auctioneers in San Francisco." He arched a brow.

"Oh, wow. You came?" She clapped a hand over her mouth, her cheeks burning.

He grinned again. "I did. Your photographs are worth an examination in person." He extended a hand.

She reached forward, batting him with the duster. "Oh, sorry." She tucked the duster into her back pocket and tried again. "Thank you for coming so quickly."

"My pleasure."

A loud yawn echoed in the room.

"Is someone here?" he asked.

Colby trotted out from behind the front counter, tail wagging and nose sniffing the air.

"This is my coworker, Colby."

The dog stopped at her side and sat.

Eric kneeled on the floor. "Pleased to meet you, Colby."

When's the last time I mopped? He'd ruin his pristine slacks to greet her mutt. She couldn't offer to pay for dry cleaning. The town didn't have such a service. She remained motionless, fighting to keep her cringe internal.

The dog lifted a paw.

Eric shook and reached forward, scratching behind Colby's ears before straightening to his full height. "Very polite."

"We try." Meg shrugged.

He reached into his pocket and retrieved a business card. "A first-hand examination is paramount before we go any further."

She grabbed the extended card and held it in between both thumbs and index fingers. The heavy weight of the smooth card hinted at a company with means. Her business cards felt shabby and rough by comparison.

She drew in a shaky breath. Had she overcorrected? Maybe the find wasn't worth his time. What did she know? Running a small-town antique store was hardly equivalent to his experience, she squinted at the card, as lead expert in Western and Native American artifacts.

"I wanted to stop by and see if we could set a time to review the collection in person."

"Oh, yeah, of course." She scrunched her nose.

"Is there a problem?"

She lifted her gaze. "I think I explained in the email that I'm helping a friend? I'm not the owner. I would like to coordinate with that person before moving ahead."

He nodded. "Absolutely. I'm sorry I stopped by unannounced." He rested a hand on his heart. "I found an opening at a nearby resort and wanted to jump at the chance. I'd like the opportunity to do some research in town, and lodging was booked until mid-July after this weekend."

She smiled. "Herd is a popular destination."

"I can see. I wanted to introduce myself before I check-in at the resort."

"I'm glad you did." Dropping her shoulders, she relaxed. He was direct and not pushy. She could handle straight-forward, business interactions. She had no doubt he'd put Hank at ease. Hank's feelings mattered, not hers. "I'll speak with the owner today."

"Great. I'll be staying at the Kincaid ranch. Do you know it?"

"I do." She smiled. He made her job much easier. "In fact, the photographs are at the ranch."

He rubbed together his palms. "Better and better. Perhaps I can do some on-site research as well."

As long as you don't get in Ryan's way. The thought was unkind. Her experience shouldn't color a stranger's. Especially since she wasn't sure how to categorize the state of her interactions with her neighbor. He wasn't a close friend, but neither was he an enemy.

She shook her head. "If you want, you can follow me to the ranch. I'll speak to the owner while you check-in."

"Are you sure you want to close?"

She shrugged. "I'll only be gone for a little bit. I'll leave you to settle in. With any luck, I can introduce you to the owner, and he might have more information to share to get you started."

"That sounds wonderful. Please, lead the way, Miss Hawke." He waved a hand in front of him, turning toward the door.

"Please call me, Meg." She smoothed her hair behind her ears, brushing her hot cheeks with her fingers. "Everyone does."

"As long as you call me, Eric."

Her stomach dropped at his smooth delivery. Was he flirting? She wasn't looking for love and especially not with someone who wasn't from Herd. She dried her clammy palms against her sides.

I might not be a resident much longer, either. Not sure anyone will notice. She couldn't think like that. If she wanted a friend, she had to be one first. With the stranger's arrival, she might soon have enough capital to buy time and try.

"Let me grab my bag." She returned to the front counter and grabbed her purse off the floor. Greater concerns than romance waited her. She wouldn't read anything into the stranger's physical tics. She had a hard enough time deciphering the actions of someone she'd known her whole life. One more man was too much trouble.

"You're all set," Ryan said. With a smile, he pushed back his chair from the folding, banquet table and stood. Reaching over the table, he handed a set of keys to the guests, a couple celebrating their twentieth anniversary in cabin five near the fishing pond.

"Thank you." The wife turned to her husband.

With silver streaks running through her dark hair, she didn't look young, the cheeky smile she shot her companion was youthful. The couple exited through the ranch house's propped open front door.

Stretching his arms over head, Ryan twisted one way and then the other. A morning spent seated wasn't his usual modus operandi. His muscles ached, and his stiff back needed a heating pad. He'd settle for a little movement instead. Dropping his arms to his side, he glanced at the wall clock. Barely ten a.m., he'd checked in almost all the cabins and two of the three yurts.

"Hey, Ted," he called to the table set up kitty-corner. "I'm putting on another pot of coffee. You want some?"

"Yes, please." Ted widened his eyes and nodded.

With a chuckle, Ryan turned toward the kitchen. He'd set the check-in table to block access to the heart of the home, giving Hank some peace when possible. In the front room, he'd constructed the adventures sign-up table. Helmed by Joe, the middle-school social studies teacher during the school year and ranch guide by summer, a steady stream of guests stopped by to approve their itineraries, change activities, and add more experiences.

At some point, Ryan needed to discuss the bison plans in-depth with the teacher. His summer employee and full-time friend earned a stellar reputation within the community. Joe was well-respected and well-known. Between his work at the school and his years of interviewing older citizens for his book, he'd become a person many in town knew and like. His public approval of the plan could do a lot to ease potential concerns that might arise regarding the introduction of a free-roaming herd.

Ryan pushed through the door to the kitchen, the panel swinging shut behind him, and headed straight to the coffee maker on the counter. If the pace continued all summer, he'd meet his goal quicker than planned. He might need to invest in another coffee maker to properly fuel his staff.

Filling the water reservoir, he found the filters and scooped the grounds into the machine. He hit brew and leaned his hands against the edge of the counter, rolling his neck from one side to the other. Almost every inch of him ached from manual labor. He could stretch for hours and still feel sore. Was town as busy as the ranch? How was business at the antique store?

None of my concern.

He sighed. He was glad for the busy morning. Between final preparations and checking in guests, he didn't have a second to think. Which was good. Because any moment of quiet turned into contemplation. Meg was becoming a nuisance. Again. For an entirely different set of reasons.

As shocking as her appearance yesterday, while he was in pajamas, she somehow belonged. Of course, she should treat the home like she could arrive, unannounced, at any moment. She'd practically grown up inside the four walls.

Less pleasing was the time he spent wondering about her and wanting to see her. After their second encounter, he wanted to apologize again. Would she show up at the ranch today and give him the opportunity?

The house hadn't had any female energy to ease the machismo since Grandma passed. He hadn't understood the loss until the constant presence of Meg. She fit. What did that mean? He liked her?

She drove him crazy. *Or am I crazy about her?* He shook his head. *Get back to work and focus on your job.* Once he secured the future with a successful summer season, paying off the mortgage on her land and ensuring the arrival of the bison, then he could let his mind drift to other thoughts. He needed time.

"Woolgathering, boy?" Hank asked.

Jumping, Ryan pressed the heel of his palm against his beating heart. He squinted and turned, spotting Hank at the head of the table. His grandfather had been so quiet, Ryan assumed he'd gone to the shed. "Didn't realize I had company."

The coffee maker beeped.

He pulled three mugs off the hooks on the wall. "Can I get you a cup?"

"No, I'm fine." Hank sighed.

Ryan frowned, leaving one mug on the counter in case Hank changed his mind. Grunts, growls, and groans were Hank's non-verbal forms of communication. Not silence or heavy exhales. He filled his mug to the brim. "You okay?"

"Feels wrong not to see her."

I know what you mean. Ryan woke up, came downstairs, and started calculating how many hours it had been since seeing her. He couldn't let Hank see this mental quandary, or he'd force Ryan to act. "She can't stop by every day."

"Well, I don't see why she can't. How different is it for her to be there or here?"

Ryan returned the coffeepot to the machine and turned. Leaning back, he blew across the top of her steaming mug. "She has a whole life without us. I'm pretty sure she'd be offended if you implied her day to day was incomplete without a man."

Hank shook his head. "I'd have to disagree. She's missing the ranch as much as the ranch misses her."

Ryan had no response. Why on earth was Hank digging in his heels about Meg? He'd never concerned himself with seeing her before. She'd always been around. If a few days went by without a visit, why not call?

The kitchen door swung inward.

Ryan spun, but he didn't spot an intruder. Did he need to add trapping a ghost to his ever-growing to-do list?

"COLBY!" Hank called with glee.

A flash of black and white raced past.

Shaking his head, Ryan grabbed his mug and turned to watch the pair.

Wagging her tail like a fan blade, the dog approached the old cowboy at top speed. She rested her paws on his legs and stretched, lavishing his face with licks.

Hank chuckled. "Oh, I missed you, too. I was talking to Ryan about you." He pet the dog and grinned broadly.

Oh. Why had Ryan assumed Hank meant Meg? Because Ryan couldn't stop thinking about her?

A knock shook the door.

Without waiting for a response, the door cracked open.

Meg poked her head in. Her gaze met his and then she twisted her neck toward Hank and the dog and back again. "Hi, is it okay that she's here?" She murmured. "Sorry, she didn't wait for permission."

"She doesn't need permission. Neither do you," Hank said. "Come in."

"Umm, well, actually. I can't. I have someone with me," she said.

Who? Ryan frowned. He didn't like the way her voice dropped when she said someone. Holding the mug, he couldn't curl his hands into fists. He lifted the coffee and sipped, grateful for something to do besides question her.

"Whoever you brought is welcome, too," Hank said.

She stepped back, and the door swung shut.

Ryan turned to his grandfather and arched an eyebrow. What was the old cowboy playing at?

Focused on the dog, Hank was too busy for Ryan's pointed look. Or smart enough to avoid the steady stare.

The door swung open.

Meg entered, followed by a man.

Setting his mug on the counter behind him, Ryan pulled his shoulders back and strode forward.

The guy had styled hair and loafers. He looked slim but not strong. Dressed nicer than most Herd grooms on their wedding days, the stranger didn't belong. He couldn't imagine anyone more out of place on the ranch, including the wide variety of guests the Kincaids had welcomed over the years.

Ryan wrinkled his brow. *This pretty guy can't be her type.* Why did that matter? In a few steps, Ryan closed the gap and extended his hand. "Ryan Kincaid."

The man returned the grip with surprising force. "I'm Eric York, from Campbell and Company in San Francisco." He twisted his head back and forth between Hank and Ryan. "I've come to look into the photographs, and I've booked a yurt for the weekend."

A chair scraped the slate floor.

Ryan dropped his hand and turned away. He hated to break first and show any hint of weakness to the new arrival. Letting Hank overexert himself because of Ryan's pride, however, was a non-starter.

Hank got to his feet with Colby at his side. "I'm the man to see about the photographs once you're settled. It's no rush." He chuckled. "I'm not going anywhere." He bent and scratched Colby behind the ears.

"I can get you checked in if you go back out into the hall." Ryan waved to the exit.

Eric turned to Meg and lifted a brow.

She nodded.

Two strangers had an unspoken language? Ryan pressed his lips together. Growling at a guest wasn't top tier customer service.

She walked to the table, brushing past, and sat at Ryan's usual seat.

Hank sank back to his chair.

No hello? No how is the morning going? He turned toward the counter and grabbed his mug. Spinning back around, he met the expert's gaze. "If you'll join me in the front room?"

Eric nodded and strode across the kitchen.

Ryan glanced at the table. Hank, Colby, and Meg made a picture-perfect trio. He wished he could pull up a seat and join them. With a shake, he exited through the door the stranger held open with a hand.

He had guests waiting and a business to run. This pretty boy was probably exactly the right person for Meg. He understood old things and could drop everything to turn up someplace else for a week. She'd like that spontaneity.

The only time Ryan's plans changed were for emergencies. This scenario was the best possible outcome. The surest way to get her out of his thoughts was for her to overtake someone else's.

CHAPTER 8

U nder a bright, still blue sky, Meg turned off the dirt road and steered her SUV onto the gravel drive. With a glance at the clock, she read seven p.m. on the dash. If her cheeks didn't ache from smiling at customers all day, she'd be fooled into thinking she had nothing but time. She snorted. When she wasn't worried about tomorrow, she'd enjoy today. Maybe in a few months. Hopefully not from her mother's condo in Chicago's Logan Square.

The tires crunched over the tiny rocks. In the shotgun seat, Colby sat up. Tail whacking the upholstered seat, she turned toward the windshield. She emitted a low woof.

Meg smiled. At the store, she'd had her biggest sales day in eight months renewing her hope for a future in town. Receiving a call from Eric, asking her to drop by the shed for news, lifted her to new heights. She'd pinpoint her joy on her business and not on the prospect of bumping into Ryan.

She shook her head and narrowed her gaze on the circle drive in front of the house. She hated the tense visit to check-in Eric that morning. If she stopped by to address the subject, she wasn't sure what she would say.

Hi, Ryan, we've been such good friends lately, and I'd hate for you to think I have feelings for some random guy that I showed up with at your ranch when I was trying to help check him in so we could work on the project for Hank. She blew out a sigh. Rambling went nowhere with Ryan, and she hated the defensive twinge in her prepared remarks. She wanted to be friends and had done nothing to owe him an apology.

Tightening her grip on the steering wheel, she navigated as close to the edge of the lawn as she dared. With guests visiting, she knew he liked to keep the front drive clear. Using the house as the check-in meant the gravel path filled up quickly at peak times though she wasn't likely to block any new arrivals arriving this late in the day.

Parking the car, she leaned over to open Colby's door.

In a flash of black and white, the dog bolted to the front of the house.

Meg hopped to the ground and locked the car. "Come on, Colby. Hank is in the shed."

The dog jogged down the steps and raced around the side.

At a subdued pace, Meg followed, looking eager wouldn't earn her any points. *Maybe Ryan's around here somewhere.* She stiffened. She absolutely refused to dwell on him. Instead, she filled her lungs with a deep breath and inhaled the sweet perfume of summer grass.

The clean scent should be bottled. Montana summer promised a few thunderstorms, the occasional hail, and endless, glorious blue-sky days. She'd lived other places but she'd never enjoyed the hottest months of the year so much. The annual childhood escape from her big city hometown recharged her spirit for the rest of the calendar. She'd spent enough Junes, Julys, and Augusts in Chicago as an adult to appreciate fresh air.

The shed door was propped open. Colby pushed it wide and trotted inside, tail swishing.

As she neared the building, she strained to decipher the low voices of the men in conversation drifting through the doorway. If she was a subject of conversation, she wanted a heads up. Inside, she spotted two figures seated at a small table in the back corner. In the center, a battery-powered lantern barely illuminated the surface.

Had Ryan done this? How sweet to make Hank more comfortable. She should have thought about it.

Squinting, she spotted Hank and Eric. Neither turned toward her. She couldn't shake the unsettling feeling the stranger hadn't come with the sole purpose of helping with Hank's project. The unease of déjà vu hyper-charged her senses. Whatever Eric's purpose in her life, she didn't want romance.

Eric was perfectly fine, but she'd never let him be more. Because if she did, she'd move, leaving her heart behind. "He's only visiting. He'll go home," she murmured. "I'll stay."

With a shake, she narrowed her gaze again. Where had her dog gone?

Lying under the table, Colby rested on top of Hank's feet. Her snores echoed in the small space. The dog was the master of sleep.

Meg smiled and knocked on the doorframe. "Hello?"

Chairs scraped the floor.

"Meg, come in, come in." Hank rose and waved a hand. "We've set up shop back here."

She entered; her steps silent on the plywood floor in her soft loafers. "This is very cozy." She pulled out the chair opposite, careful to avoid her sleeping dog's paws.

"Eric's idea." Hank smiled and sat.

Oh. She didn't know why, but she was disappointed. She smiled at Eric.

He was nice, and thoughtful. Wasn't that a positive? Especially if Hank was about to enter into a lucrative business agreement with him? She wasn't upset with Eric as much as letdown that typically thoughtful Ryan hadn't noticed and anticipated the need.

"Thank you for coming so quickly. I hope we didn't cut your workday short." Eric frowned, wrinkling his smooth brow.

"Not at all. I was already closing up for the day," she said. "You have news?"

Eric nodded. "Hank has been gracious enough in assisting with the process today."

"My pleasure." Hank puffed out his chest.

"I can confirm the collection of photographs and signed souvenir cards are authentic including the images of Buffalo Bill Cody and Chief Sitting Bull," Eric said.

Meg sucked in a sharp breath. "Wow. Really?" She twisted her neck, gazing from one to the other and back again. "I mean. I knew they were. The computer software already told us. The confirmation is ... thrilling."

"To be honest," Eric interlaced his hands and leaned forward. "We've had an influx of false identification because of the artificial intelligence software that you utilized."

Heat crept up her cheeks. Her victory was very short-lived. She was little more than an armchair historian? She didn't share his illustrious credentials. Her undergraduate degree was in comparative literature. During her years of handling antiques, first as a hobby and then as a career, she thought she'd gleaned some knowledge.

"You were one hundred percent correct." Eric smiled. "You have a good eye."

She pressed cold hands to her cheeks. Now her skin burned for a completely different reason. "I'm confused about the origins. Why would the Wild West Show perform here? The town wasn't on the railroad, and the population was under a thousand at its peak during the era."

"I don't believe they did stage the show here," Eric said. "With the proximity to the reservation, Buffalo Bill probably came to recruit more native people into the show. Some Lakota were pushed over the South Dakota border and onto Fort Peck along with other tribal nations. Of course, Chief Sitting Bull only participated in the show for a short period. I believe he'd already left the production when these cards were originally acquired."

She drew back her chin. "Would the tribe want to join? Wasn't it sort of pretending to lose their battles all over again?"

Eric nodded. "It was. The pay was good. He offered a chance to send money home to family struggling under difficult conditions on the reservations. The show toured the world, performing for monarchs across Europe."

She crossed her arms over her chest, rubbing her shoulders. She supposed his explanation made sense, but her heart ached for the poor choices Indigenous people faced. She lifted her gaze. "What do you think, Hank?"

"I'm glad something in this shed has value. I've proved Ryan wrong. I'll be crowing over him for the rest of time." Hank grinned and winked.

She chuckled. What would she give for the same chance? Nothing. She'd rather have his friendship. "Are you prepared to sell the collection? You don't want to keep them in the family?"

"I had no idea of their existence." Hank shrugged. "I'd rather see a little good come from your hard work cleaning out this shed to get my grandson off my case. I'll be happy to see you take a nice chunk of money."

She shook her head. "You owe me nothing. This is your property. Besides, finders keepers. Right, cowboy?"

Hank shook his head and waggled a finger. "A deal is a deal, miss, and I'm a man of my word."

She knew better than to imply anything else. In good conscience, she couldn't take a cut of his payday. Arguing in front of a stranger, however, was inappropriate.

"Besides," Hank continued. "Mr. York explained the finder's fee is a percentage of the auction company's cut and not mine."

Could that be true? She wasn't sure how to accept payment for doing nothing. She offered him a discreet nod. Turning, she faced Eric. "What are the next steps? What do you need from us? Are you heading back to the auction house right away?"

"I'd like to stay for a few more days. The auction wouldn't be until the fall. I'm in no rush to catalog and photograph. I would like the opportunity to do research." Eric coughed. "I was hoping you might be able to help."

Why me? She poked her index finger into the center of her collarbone. The physical tap wasn't strong enough to convince her she wasn't dreaming. He'd raised and dashed her hopes several times. She wasn't sure of her footing anymore.

Eric nodded.

"I'm not a historian. I'm not sure how much help I could provide," she murmured.

"You know this place, this land." Hank held her gaze with a steady stare.

His confidence was like a fuzzy blanket, wrapping her in warmth. How soon until he snatched it away again? With Ryan, she always understood he respected her. He didn't always like being around her, but he never made her question her worth or shake her self-confidence.

"Can you help?" Eric asked, leaning forward.

Neither Eric nor Ryan asked for her heart. She was the fool reading too much into the sudden interest of two men. She'd be a fool to miss a professional opportunity. But she didn't have a ton of time. She shrugged. "If you think I can be of assistance, you can find me at the store. You can stop in whenever. I'll be there."

"Good." Hank pushed back his chair and stood. "Don't let me keep you. It's past supper."

Eric got to his feet and slid the chairs into position.

Her stomach growled. *Always classy, Meg.* She bit the inside of her cheek.

Hank laughed and waggled a finger. "See? I know what I'm talking about."

She giggled and pushed back her chair.

Colby followed Hank, tail wagging.

Hank hung an arm at his side, brushing the dog's head every time she neared.

The pair brought a smile to Meg's face with every encounter. The rough cowboy and the lazy mutt were a perfect, opposites attract, couple. She didn't know too many pairings that didn't end in spontaneous combustion. *Like me and Ryan.*

She slung her purse onto her shoulder, exiting the shed. Until Hank's project, she had avoided the younger Kincaid like she was paid for each snubbing. Now she couldn't go more than a few hours without finding herself on his land, hoping for a run-in. He drove her crazy, and she came back for more.

Eric followed her out, shutting the door and walking beside her.

"Thank you," she murmured.

He clasped his hands behind his back and lifted a brow. "For..."

"For taking my call seriously and showing up."

"I'm glad you reached out. It's quite a find." He smiled. "I love solving a good mystery."

She did, too. As long as ghosts were left undisturbed. She stifled a shiver.

"I'm heading in." Hank yelled. "Call your dog, Meg."

She spotted the cowboy at the backdoor. With a wave at Hank, she whistled.

Colby turned, with great reluctance, and trotted toward Meg.

"Would you believe he doesn't like dogs?"

"Not one bit," Eric said.

"It's true." Meg bent, turning a palm toward the dog trotting her way.

Colby kissed the hand and leaned against Meg's legs.

"Some cowboys change their ways," Meg murmured.

"Not most, in your experience?"

Her throat tightened, cutting off a response. The cowboy she cared about wouldn't change.

"Why is Meg's SUV blocking my drive?" Ryan's deep voice boomed in the stagnant air.

Her cheeks burned, and she bit her lip. Did he have to bellow in front of his guests? "I'd better move my vehicle."

Eric nodded. "See you in town tomorrow? Your store?"

"Stop by around one. That's my lunch break. I can close up and get you started at the library."

Heavy steps pounded the ground.

She turned.

Colby, heedless of the glowering expression, ran to greet Ryan.

Meg met his gaze and gulped. She lost track of Eric, her focus solely on the cowboy. With the fading light at his back, Ryan stood with his chiseled face in shadow. He was the definition of tall and dark. *And handsome?* Her memory filled in his hidden expression. How his brow knit and his full lips pursed at every encounter, like he wasn't sure if he should be amused or annoyed. Her heart skipped a beat.

If he didn't care, he wouldn't expend his energy. He was a master of efficiency. Was he missing their friendship, too? Something changed over the past week. He transformed from a man of few words into a poignant conversationalist.

When he showed her the development of her family land, he proved with actions what his words never had. He valued her. She wasn't sure if she was thrilled or terrified.

Ryan shook his head as he glowered at the guest standing too close to Meg on his lawn.

The yard was off-limits to guests. *That's not what I told Meg.* He gritted his molars and narrowed his gaze. The man hovering around Meg lurked somewhere between customer and vendor. The gray area demanded respect. As long as he stepped away from Meg.

With a nod to her, the man strode down the path toward the barn. Was he walking all the way back to the yurt he rented? Ryan squinted, watching the guest's progress.

Ted intercepted him at the door and lead him to a gator. He'd drive the man where he belonged. *Can the vehicle get good mileage on the highway?* Ted could take the guest all the way back to San Francisco as far as Ryan was concerned.

"Ryan? Hello?" Meg called.

He turned his head to meet her gaze and winced. His whole body ached. He agreed to give Miss Stephanie, the teacher and a colleague of Joe's, a job interview for teaching yoga classes. While he wasn't one for meditation and stretching, he valued the appeal of the exercise to his clientele.

What he hadn't anticipated was participating himself.

In the barn a little over an hour earlier, thankfully with the doors closed, Stephanie, who was only a few years out of college, had insisted on leading Ted and Ryan through a beginner's class. He didn't think she understood how far he was out of his depth. He didn't bend. He wasn't a noodle.

Ted was a natural. The ranch hand twisted and turned like he was a secret gymnast. Or a human pretzel. Stephanie had praised him, and Ted had turned red, offering some random movie reference Ryan hadn't understood.

Judging by Stephanie's sudden silence, she hadn't either.

Witnessing his unflappable employee's embarrassment, Ryan had lost focus. Balancing on one foot, he'd lost control. He had circled his arms but couldn't stop his crash to the ground. A pulled pectoral was almost worth the price to see the rough cowboy blush. Ryan had hired Stephanie on the spot, if only to torture Ted about becoming the assistant teacher.

Colby padded back to him.

Ryan scratched the dog on the head once and then raised the hand to massage his aching chest. "You heading home? Or you plan on blocking my drive for the rest of the evening?" He frowned at Meg.

She rolled her eyes. "I've been here all of ten minutes. Don't blame me for your poor timing."

Or good. "You know, for someone who once accused me of rolling my eyes at her, I can't help but point out you are almost always staring heavenward in my company."

She blushed.

He smiled and scrubbed his hands over his face. When had he pulled behind her little SUV, he whistled an upbeat tune. He wanted a chance to apologize for his poor behavior this morning and fate provided him the opportunity. He dropped his hands to his sides and lifted the corner of his mouth. "You're probably right."

"Excuse me?" She widened her gaze. "Can you please repeat your statement?"

He gritted his molars. This was exactly the reason he never admitted to being wrong on the few occasions the rare occurrence happened. Other people tended to gloat when he needed grace. "I'm sorry."

"Hmm. Not quite what you said, but I'll take it. She smiled and sashayed past him, elbowing him in the sore ribs as she passed. "Walk me to my car, cowboy. I've had a long day."

Up close, he caught a hint of lavender wafting in the air again. He could identify the scent anywhere. He remembered watching Grandma and her best friend work on the little sachets. In the first few months after her passing, Hank had declared himself allergic to the herb. He wanted all trace of the potpourri eliminated from the house.

Ryan hid one heart-shaped packet in the bottom drawer. Try as it might, the little sachet stood no chance against the lingering stench in his socks even after a thorough laundering. If he focused on thinking about his smelly feet, he'd ignore the other sensations racking his body at her hot breath so close to his collar. She made the same lavender scent her own, different from the sachet with a hint of soap he couldn't identify. He tipped his hat and turned. "Ma'am, let me escort you and your dog off my land."

She batted his arm and laughed. "Stop teasing me, and don't be mad. I only came by at Hank's request."

"Oh?" He studied her from the corner of his gaze.

"Eric authenticated the photos. I'm sure Hank wants to tell you the details. I'd hate to spoil his fun." She sighed.

He narrowed his gaze.

"Oh, okay, I'll tell you a little more. Eric wants to do research, so he'll stay a little longer on the ranch. I promised to help, when I can of course. I had a great day at the store. It's a nice first wave of tourists you've brought here. Very deep pockets." She smiled.

Warmth spread through him. He couldn't take any credit for the shoppers but was glad for her good day. He didn't want her to leave. His silence encouraged her old pattern of rambling. Instead of the flare of annoyance as she spoke, he almost smiled. He liked how she couldn't hold herself back from blurting every thought in her head. He only had one issue. "Eric?" He arched a brow.

She turned pink and fumbled with the purse on her arm. She studied the contents with far more interest than him or her path.

Rounding the house, they'd reach her vehicle in another few strides. First, they had to cross the bigger rocks he'd hauled up from the pond to create a boundary so Hank didn't drive the truck into the porch. She wasn't looking. She stepped on a rock, lodging her shoe and flailing her arms.

He reached out and grabbed her, hauling her against his chest as he lifted her over the rock. In his arms, he wrapped an arm around her waist, gripping her slight frame. If he wasn't careful, she'd slip through his grasp. He was so used to her being a force of nature he never considered how small her actual stature was. He set her down on the ground but didn't drop his grip or move back.

Her chest rose and fell with rapid, shallow breaths.

In the light from the porch, her hair glimmered and sparkled again. Her eyes shone bright, more rich mahogany than mud brown. She couldn't hide her surprise or her reaction in his arms.

Eric couldn't do that. Ryan wouldn't give himself the satisfaction of saying out loud what they both knew was true. The expert was a slim, city man. Not rugged and rough, with muscles honed from manual labor instead of trendy gyms. She couldn't leave him for Eric and a new city.

"Ryan?" She croaked.

"Hmm?" He studied her face.

"I'm safe. Can you put me down?"

I can't lose you. With a nod, he dropped his hold and stepped back.

She raised her key fob and unlocked her vehicle. Colby raced to the passenger side.

He followed the dog, opening the door. At least he could be useful while giving them both a chance to catch their breaths.

Her SUV door opened, and she hopped behind the wheel as he shut the passenger door and rounded the car to her side.

She lowered the window.

He rested his hand on the roof of the car, leaning forward. *I could kiss her.* Standing close, he noticed everything about her. The light hint of shampoo and laundry was the best perfume he'd ever inhaled. At the base of her throat, the delicate skin meeting her collarbone fluttered. Once again, her hair glimmered in the fading light, the copper streaks luring him to reach out and smooth the strands to see if he could touch a bit of the magic.

"You're sure it's okay if I visit the shed? I know you have guests all week. I promise I won't be in the way. I want to do my part for the research. To help Hank."

He nodded. Helping Hank. Right. Ryan pushed off the door and stuffed his fists into his jeans' pockets. He winced again, the twinge of pulled muscles in his torso aching. Yoga was rougher than the old days doing cattle drives and sleeping under the stars. "Of course. You're always free to do as you please."

She smiled. "Thanks. I'll be around." She twisted the key in the ignition. The engine turned over.

Lifting a hand, he waved until her vehicle pulled onto the road and disappeared from view. Never let Meg out of his sight was another lesson he'd learned years ago. On her own, she stirred up all sorts of trouble. *Maybe being with her wasn't much better.*

He turned toward the ranch house. Movement around the side of the building caught his attention.

Ted and the guests celebrating their twentieth anniversary, Marcia and Ford Clayton, studied a row of chest-high waders and the lost and found collection of old, mismatched rain boots. As he got closer, the stench of dead fish and rubber permeated the air.

Ryan pinched his nose, unprepared for the sensory assault. "Good evening. What's going on here? Can I help?"

Ted lifted his chin, meeting Ryan's gaze and subtly shook his head side to side.

"Yes, please, Mr. Kincaid," Marcia said.

The tilt of her head and hands on hips posture assured him she'd suffered fools already and would endure no more. He kept his mouth shut and clasped his hands behind his back, leaning forward. "Ryan, please."

"Okay, Ryan. Please call me Marcia and this is Ford." Marcia pointed to her husband. "Tomorrow, we are panning for gold in the creek near our cabin. I'd like to be properly outfitted. Ted thinks we only need boots. I like to be fully prepared."

Ryan nodded. Now he understood. "Marcia, I'm sorry to tell you the gold was only a legend. No one has ever found a fleck." He glanced from wife to husband.

Ford grinned. "Told you."

She rolled her eyes. "I did some reading before we came. One of your ancestors found something and claimed the land for his ranch."

Acquiring the worst plot in the process. Gold in the western portion of the state fueled settlement of the Montana territory in the 1860s. South of the Missouri River along the eastern boundary, however, no one struck it rich near Herd. "I know the book, ma'am. The family wasn't consulted. If my grandfather had been approached, he'd have informed the author of the man's undiagnosed vision problems. The saloon in town is named after his find."

"Golden Crown like a tooth?" Ford asked.

Ryan nodded.

Ford chuckled.

"Still. It's an adventure, and I want to go." Marcia shrugged.

"The creek is less than a foot deep, but the current is strong in some sections, especially near the mouth of the fishing pond," Ryan said. "I don't recommend wading into the water no matter the precautions. I'm sorry to say we haven't used these waders in quite a while. They smell like they should be thrown out and not lent to guests. I can't, in good conscience, give you these old things."

She lifted her chin higher. "I'm not squeamish. I'll be fine."

She remained undeterred? Ryan turned to her husband. The man hadn't turned green from the smell. That was a promising sign.

"I'd rather avoid whatever calamity we'll find the in creek," Ford said. "I'm against the plan but pro defensive measures."

Ted stepped forward. "I think they'll be much more comfortable in boots. No need to be restricted."

"I agree with Ted's assessment." Ryan nodded. "The waders can be pungent. Only guests determined to go on one of Joe's all-day, offsite, fly-fishing expeditions wear them. Because they have no choice."

"Fine, I'll stick with boots. I concede." Marcia held up her hands. "I will pan for gold in the creek along the shore."

"Somehow, I know I'll end up in the bottom." Ford winced. "I don't want to be right and muddy."

"Oh, darling. Don't worry. You won't be." Marcia wrapped an arm around her husband's waist and stretched up on tiptoe, kissing his cheek. "You'll have fun."

Ford smiled. "Or else."

Marcia giggled. "You're so smart."

"Please wait until tomorrow. The sun sets soon." Ted extended a pair of boots. "Drop the boots off at the checkout when you leave. If you need anything else, let me know."

"Or me." Ryan reached for the other set. "Have fun."

"If I find anything good..." Marcia accepted the boots from Ryan. "You'll never know."

Ryan chuckled.

The couple waved and turned away, each carrying a pair of boots.

They were a curious pair. The husband and wife had to be in their mid- to late-sixties, judging by the streaks of gray in their hair and firmly established laugh and smile lines. At that stage, a person knew their own mind. Why partner with someone who pushed all your buttons? Was it comfort?

"You good, boss?" Ted asked.

"Tired. You'll keep an eye on their adventure?"

Ted bent and grabbed the waders by the straps. "Of course. I'll put these away before we attract hawks."

"Thanks, Ted." Ryan strode around the house to the front door without another look. Maybe the smell would lure a certain mutt next-door to return. He wasn't sure what to think of the prospect.

After months of quiet, the first day of hosting guests took a lot out of him. He wouldn't let his strain lead him to any rash decisions about his life. I looked like Meg would stay. He didn't need to make a big deal about it.

When life settled down, he could reevaluate how he would like their friendship to proceed. He wasn't in a rush and didn't need to be. He had to focus on the bigger picture before he could worry about minor details. *Like romance.*

CHAPTER 9

Meg tied a bright pink ribbon on the handles of the shopping bag and slid the purchase across the front counter. Smiling, she met the customer's gaze. "Thank you for stopping by today."

The older woman returned the grin, grabbed the package, and strode toward the door. The bell jingled.

Meg followed the paying customer's progress, ignoring the latest round of selfie-takers near the hats and boots. Should she lock up the valuable goods? For the most part, the accessories were treated with care. If she removed the tempting items to a locked case, she'd eliminate the lure. Today wasn't the day. She appreciated having any company at all.

From the corner of her gaze, she glimpsed the empty dog bed on the ground. Her chest squeezed. While Colby rarely made noise, she had a presence that soothed Meg's soul.

After she had dressed for the day, she had turned toward her companion lying on the bed. "Want to go to the store?"

No response.

"Want to go to town?" She infused her question with as much cheer as she could muster.

The dog sighed and turned the other direction, facing the wall.

Meg didn't need to be a pet psychic to understand. Crawling across the four-poster bed, creasing the quilt, she stroked the dog's belly. "We can't visit today. I promise you'll see him soon."

The dog shifted and licked Meg's palm with one flick of the tongue. Then she laid her head on her paws, shut her eyes, and snored.

Meg could take a hint. On her own, she had opened the store for the day. Within twenty minutes, she greeted her first guest in what became a near constant stream of customers. Busier than she'd been all year, she had no second to spare. Still, she missed her dog.

Was this the future if she had to leave town and return to working for someone else? She hadn't yearned her desk job at someone else's gallery. Would she return to days under florescent lights without Colby's calming presence? She'd worked the same long hours in her previous roles but hadn't been fulfilled. And she'd crave interaction that didn't revolve around her career.

In her pocket, her cell phone chirped.

She jumped and reached for the device, silencing the alarm.

On cue, the front door opened again, and Eric walked in.

Dressed in a V-neck sweater and jeans, Eric was more casually attired today, yet he remained too sophisticated for his setting. Was the navy-blue sweater cashmere? Were the jeans tailored?

He nodded at the two girls posing in the cowboy hats. With bright red cheeks, the girls deposited the hats on the nearby rack and raced out the door. The overhead bell nearly shook off its hook.

Meg chuckled. "That's one way to close up for the afternoon I suppose."

"I get you for the whole afternoon?" Eric approached, each step creating another beat in an even melody against the pine floor.

Now it was her turn to flush. Grabbing the phone, she tucked the cell in the back of her worn out jeans. "You know what I mean. Just my lunch hour."

"I'll savor every second. How's business today?"

She lifted her gaze and met his smiling face.

A couple good days weren't enough to make the store suddenly profitable. The stranger didn't need to know that. Neither did Hank, or he'd insist on her accepting the auction house's proposed finder's fee cut when the signed images sold. "Things have been great all morning. Most people will be eating lunch. We should have the library all to ourselves."

He swept a hand toward the door. "After you, please."

She grabbed her purse, pulling out her keys and lacing her fingers between each one. It was a reflex. Growing up in a big city, she hadn't relinquished her street smarts training in tiny Herd. She doubted she needed to defend herself against Eric. Appearances could be deceiving. *Like Ryan and his constant scowl.*

Last night, for a second, she had sensed a charge in the air. Ryan had leaned in her vehicle window. The tiny hairs on her arm had stood on end. She'd studied the quirk of his lips and wondered what kissing him would be like. The urge had been unsettling and overwhelming. Shaking off the thought, she flipped the sign in the window and opened the door.

Eric stepped out first.

She followed, pulling the old wooden door shut and jimmying the frame as she spun the lock in the dead bolt. She pocketed her keys and tipped her head. "This way."

Eric fell into step beside her, his gait matching hers as they passed the edge of her store.

Herd's downtown consisted of an approximately five block strip of stores and businesses on either side of Main. Wind gusts rolled the occasional tumbleweed through town in late summer, delighting tourists with the visual cliché. The nineteenth century style false fronts played up and romanticized the town's early days.

"Have you ever seen bison roaming in Herd? Or out here on the ranches?" Eric asked.

She nibbled her lip, scrunching her nose. Had she? "I don't think I have."

"With the name, I'd rather assumed you'd be outnumbered." He smiled and scanned the street. "It is charming."

"We aren't much, but we do pack a punch." She grinned.

"It's almost a theme park style Wild West town."

The metallic clang of metal on metal from the blacksmith shop filtered down the street, punctuating his sentence.

He smiled, and his look was genuine bemusement. She wasn't sure if his enjoyment was directed against the town or in its favor. From the saloon to the old-time photo studio, Herd embraced the sanitized version of its past.

"Hard to believe this is original," he said.

She nodded. With wooden sidewalks extending along either side, she studied the timber structures on her side of the road and the stone opposite. "Herd is historic. On this side of the street, the buildings date to the eighteen-eighties when the three families founded the town."

"What about the other side?" He tilted his head across the road to the post office, saloon, and grocery. "Rather interesting to see stone all the way out here. Unusual, isn't it?"

"Rather a sad story." She nibbled her lip. "A little ruthless, I'm afraid." She dropped her chin to her chest, studying her steps. Airing dirty laundry wasn't her style. The town might not consider her one of their own. In her heart, she remained a loyal citizen.

He nudged her with a shoulder. "Now, I'm dying of curiosity."

She reached the alley between the buildings. Stepping off the main sidewalk, she stopped against a wall near a dumpster. "A fire spread from the original saloon in 1894. In 1904, the rest of the block burned from another blaze. The Golden Crown was a fiery pile of ash for the second time in ten years. The townsfolk came together for justice. They demanded that side of the street be rebuilt in stone."

He chuckled. "Can't make this stuff up, can you?"

She gritted her teeth at his ringing laughter. Something about the teasing tone riled her. A local could joke about the foibles of the community but not an outsider, no matter how otherwise polite and charming. Her hackles raised.

"My apologies. I didn't mean to offend you." He turned and pressed a hand to his heart.

His expression was sincere. She shook her head. "It's fine. The townsfolk blamed one man for both incidents, Hoss Whittier. His father was a successful Boston businessman who was one of Herd's founding families."

"Along with the Kincaids and Hawkes?"

"Hoss wasn't the same as his father. He struggled with alcohol and fighting. After the second fire, it was decided by a council that the Whittiers would pay to rebuild the street in stone. To do so, the ranch was sold and split down the middle."

"What happened to Hoss?"

"Run out of town. It's sad to think all the hard work his father did amounted to nothing in the end. The family retained one plot of land in town but left soon after Hoss." She shrugged and strode back to the sidewalk. "I'm sure the families whose livelihoods he impacted twice couldn't handle another disruption."

Passing the next few storefronts, she slipped into silence. How would Ryan have taken the out-of-towner's chuckle? Perhaps with better humor than her. The stoic cowboy had grown accustomed to tourists.

The blasé response irritated her. Of course, the town's founding involved backstabbing and machinations, her ancestors teaming up with the Whittiers to give the Kincaids the worst plot. In a little over a decade, the Hawkes changed allegiance again to run the Whittiers out of town. Until, finally, the Kincaids owned it all.

"We've reached the end of the block. Did I miss the library?"

His question cut through her inner monologue. "Nope. Here we are." She opened the door in the corner entrance of the building at the end of the street. "After you, please."

With a nod, he entered.

The library had been one of the first attempts at historic preservation in the 1970s. While Herd sidestepped much of the destruction of old properties by nature of being so far out of the way, it wasn't until her and Ryan's grandmothers had banded together for a concerted effort to save the town that laws and codes were changed.

Visiting the building brought Meg comfort. She had spent so much of her youth checking out as many books as she could carry under her arms. She'd read until her vision blurred. In the years she hadn't traveled to Montana, she relied on the library for that instant connection. Summer was symbolized by plastic-protected hardbacks.

The main room of the former store housed the checkout counter and shelves devoted to children's books and popular fiction. She nodded at Miriam, head librarian.

"Good afternoon," Meg said.

"Hi, Meg and mister?" Miriam removed her reading glasses, letting the frame dangle on a chain around her neck.

"Eric York." He extended a hand and a warm smile.

Miriam brightened.

"Mr. York wants to look into some history about the ranches. I'll help him settle in upstairs and then head back to my shop," Meg said.

"Certainly. If you need anything, Mr. York, please let me know." Miriam turned toward Meg. "It so nice to see you with a friend."

Miriam meant the words kindly. But the off-hand comment stung like a slap. Meg nodded and strolled past the desk and through the stacks to the spiral staircase. She glanced over her shoulder, readjusting her slipping purse.

Eric nodded.

Her steps clanged on the metal risers. At the top, she stepped to the side and breathed deep. A curious mix of wood and vanilla scented the air from the aging books. In the winter, a small potbelly stove in the corner heated the room and added the smoke to the aroma. She found the scent intoxicating, often losing track of time in the warm room during the long, dark months. "Sorry, I always forget how loud it is on the stairs. But once you're up here, the sounds from downstairs and outside are muffled."

"Is the bulk of the collection up here?" he asked.

She was glad he focused on the task at hand and not her unnecessary apologies. "It's sort of a hodgepodge of nonfiction, public records, and microfiche."

He widened his gaze. "I'm captivated. I love research."

Thank you for not commenting on being declared my only friend. In this moment, he might be. She never found an eager partner for pouring through nonfiction texts. "I can help get you started, and then I want to head back. It's been a busy weekend."

"Say no more." He held up a hand. "I appreciate your time."

She nodded and strode through the windowless room. Along one wall, an empty research desk faced four oak tables with lamps. Pushed together, the tables formed a large rectangle. She crossed to one and flipped on the light, dropping her bag to the table.

He mimicked her actions at the table opposite.

The soft glow of the pair of lamps softened the harsh glare of the overhead lights.

She scanned the room, hoping to spot Joe engaged in his research. He could prove invaluable. His knowledge of the town was unrivaled. *He's leading a tour.* The realization landed in her gut like a heavy stone. She didn't mind being alone with Eric but wasn't entirely comfortable in his company.

Eric shot her an expectant look.

Dusting her hands on her jeans, she pointed behind him. "Those shelves are the nonfiction books. It's a wide range of topics, but the first row is local and state history. I think I know of something that might be interesting to get started."

"Please, you're an excellent guide. I put my faith in you."

At the shelves, she reached for a red, leatherbound book. The cover was stained, the pages dog eared, and the spine cracked. Cradling the book in her arms, she gingerly brought it to the table and opened the front cover. "This book was donated by Susie Kincaid, Hank's wife. She was part of the committee that fought for the library in this location."

"Fought?"

"It was the seventies." She shrugged. "The locals were used to the bookmobile and preferred the convenience." She flipped through the first few pages, running her index finger down each margin as she read the dates handwritten in pencil annotating the text. She stopped. "Oh, my goodness."

He leaned close and squinted at the page and then turned to her with a broad grin. "I didn't think it would be that easy." He chuckled.

This time his mirth lifted her soul. The first book she pulled off the shelf, an old Kincaid ranch ledger, mentioned the auditions at the Kincaid ranch. The calendar marked off the day from typical operation for the special occasion. "I'm sure you'll want to do more research to verify."

"Of course, I will, and I have a date to help pinpoint my study. Maybe this is a good opportunity, since you've shown your exceptional skill, for another piece of business." He paused and studied her. "I'd like to offer you a job."

Her jaw dropped.

"It's not always this fun." He held up his palms. "I deal with a lot more dead ends than hidden treasure. Often, my research time is measured in hours and not weeks." He dropped his arms to his sides. "You have what it takes. You have a good eye."

She shook her head. "I don't know about such praise. Didn't you pretty much say it was a fluke that my software made an accurate hit?"

"I did. What were the odds you would make another instantaneous hit? You have a good memory and an eye for details. I'm always looking for someone to train with those qualities."

She nibbled her bottom lip. Approaching the auction house had not been meant as a job interview, but maybe it was supposed to. Maybe this was her next step.

Her initial impression of him carried an immediate understanding he'd change her life. She'd—wrongly—assumed with a romance and entered every conversation apprehensively anticipating some sort of move on his part.

This job could be fate. She told Mom she would let her know with plenty of time to rent out the old house before the Fourth of July. She had a back-up plan now.

Maybe her success depended on taking herself seriously and not relying on her family name alone. If she applied a little determination and self-belief to running her store, could she stay in Herd? Or would she fail the moment she tried?

She blinked against the sudden sting in her watery eyes and rubbed a hand over her nose. Leaving was her worst-case scenario and most likely option. Could Ryan be her back-up plan? If he moved forward with events, he'd need a coordinator. He told her he liked the idea but would he really do it or had his agreement been lip service?

"Don't give me an answer now," Eric said. "You don't even need to tell me before I leave. Just consider the option."

She nodded and dropped her shoulders. For the first time since meeting Eric, she relaxed. The path he offered—and his importance to her next step—suddenly made sense of what she had felt in the moment they met. She wouldn't choose to totally upend her life, but she was glad for a choice. "I will. I'll leave you to your research."

"I have one more request. If it's not too much trouble?"

"Of course not. How can I help?"

"Come on the ride tomorrow. It's late afternoon. Hank suggested I go. I would feel a bit awkward by myself. I would appreciate some help in asking questions of the adventure guide."

"You mean Joe? He's about the easiest person to talk to."

"I'd appreciate an insider approach." He lifted a shoulder. "Mr. Kincaid suggested you might want to come."

She considered Eric. He dropped his gaze to the ground and shifted his weight from foot to foot. He wasn't being entirely forthcoming.

She wasn't sure what his motivation was. Getting her to agree to the job? She wouldn't mind an excuse to see Ryan. Perhaps she could prod him a little about events and find out if he would hire her. The slow thaw in their relationship heartened her. After a vague sense of childhood animosity, their years of acquaintance mattered. Shared memories were special.

She owed Colby a visit with Hank. What did it mean that Hank put Eric up to asking her? What angle was the old cowboy playing? Matchmaking? She figured it was only a matter of time before the opinionated older man got involved in the personal lives of his friends and family. But she wouldn't have pegged Hank for wanting to pair her off with an outsider. Did he want her to move on? "Yes, thank you. I would love to join you tomorrow."

Eric grinned. "I won't take up anymore of your time today."

She spun on her heel and strode toward the stairs. With each step descending the metal staircase, her steps rang out. While she didn't mind giving him time, she owed her business more attention. Leaving town was her last resort. For her best chance at staying, she had to get to work.

Slowing the pickup in front of the house, Ryan parked and cut the engine. He moved without any hitch and his end of the day lower back tightness was gone. Maybe yoga wasn't so bad. After a full night's rest, his usual aches and pains had disappeared.

When he had stepped out of bed and stretched his arms overhead, he reached a little higher than yesterday morning. Had one class been the magic tonic to boost his flexibility? *If only I'd let her get to the meditation part, I might have peace during my day.*

With a fully booked resort, however, controlled chaos was his best hope. From sunrise to sunset, he'd been on the move. He was grateful he hadn't wasted much time with his thoughts. He was promised nothing but anxiety if his mind strayed to Meg and where she might be. And who might be keeping her company.

Shaking his head, he hopped to the ground from his truck and strode to the front door. The sky finally darkened. A hint of woodsmoke curled in the air. He sniffed again. A vaguely fishy, muddy scent wafted past.

Deep, rumbling laughter floated around the corner of the house.

He turned from the door and jogged down the steps, rounding the side in several long strides.

Drenched and mud-splattered, Marcia and Ford Clayton trudged from the barn and across the lawn in socks.

Ryan winced. Wet socks were the worst thing on earth. He could—and had—assist in a live birth and stitched a gushing wound without flinching. Ask him to do anything that ended in soaking socks squeezing his soles, and he bowed out before his stomach churned.

"Good evening. Can I help you two?"

"Good evening, Ryan," Ford said. "We dropped off the boots we borrowed at the barn. Marcia has something to say." He stepped back and motioned for his wife to walk forward.

Marcia grinned broadly and pushed her stringy, soaked hair behind her ears. "You were right. We didn't find gold. My husband was right. We fell into the creek."

"Ah, I never get tired of hearing her say that." Ford chuckled. "Makes every bad idea worthwhile."

"Hey." She swatted her husband's arm. "Don't you have something to say?"

Ford grabbed her hand, raised her fingers to his mouth, and kissed her knuckles. "You were right. I had a lot of fun." He faced Ryan and shrugged. "I always do. I'd never do anything outside my comfort zone if not for my wife. I wouldn't have so many memorable tales."

Ryan smiled and nodded, hiding his confusion. Why had she pushed? If two people hadn't sanded off each other's rough edges with twenty years' together, how was this bliss?

"I learned the hard way," Ford said. "I prefer having her push all my buttons to sitting around in silence."

Marcia kissed her husband's cheek.

Because—in spite of differing points of view—they like the end result.

Meg definitely pushed Ryan into uncomfortable encounters. The talent show was the most prominent in a childhood of awkward, on-the-spot moments. He could write a thousand-word essay for every day spent together. The years she stopped coming were all one giant, boring mass of memories. He couldn't fill even a single sheet with his recollections from the decade without her.

"Will we be seeing you at the campfire tonight?" Ryan asked.

"Absolutely," Marcia said.

Ford rolled his eyes.

Marica giggled. "See you soon."

Ryan nodded and waved, watching the pair stroll away hand in hand. He dropped his hand to rub against the ache in his chest. If Meg had a decision about what came next, what would she choose?

He couldn't ruminate on Meg. Dropping his hand, he glanced at his watch. The campfire started in thirty minutes. He'd come home to pick up the guest of honor, Hank, and for a break from his public persona.

Saturdays in summer meant smiling nonstop. Opening the front door, he scrubbed a hand over his face and aching cheeks. Faking cheer wasn't his style. If he'd bumped into Meg, he might have a reason to grin.

Or more of a headache. The moment he almost kissed her burned him. He should have leaned forward and pressed his mouth to hers. It would have gotten the whole will-they-or-won't-they dilemma over with. Or created a bigger problem.

Pushing for something to happen was asking for trouble. At the moment, he had enough on his plate without getting involved in *them*. She hadn't stopped by, and he should be glad for the space. He pushed through the swinging door into the kitchen, heading straight to the sink to wash up. With the faucet running, he turned his head and frowned.

At the head of the table, Hank hunched forward over a pile of papers.

His wrinkled, tanned skin highlighted his white hair. The opposites enhanced the other to an unflattering extreme. He looked old.

Ryan shuddered. Shutting the faucet with the back of a hand, he tore off a paper towel and dried his hands. "Hey, Hank. You almost ready for the campfire?"

Hank lifted his head and scowled. His eyes were unfocused and glassy.

Is he confused? Ryan caught his next breath. He'd been grateful his grandparents hadn't suffered from any of the diseases that stole a person away in their later years. Nearing ninety, however, Hank entered unknown territory. He was the longest living member of the family. If he started to lose himself... Ryan shook off the thought. He'd do whatever he could for the man who'd loved him unconditionally.

"Is that tonight?" Hank rubbed the crust from his eyes. "Guess I forgot the time. I've been going through my papers, looking for anything of interest to the expert."

Ryan slid onto the bench at the large oak dining table. The kitchen could serve a crowd, but the pair were often alone. He hadn't missed company. Until she stopped dropping by. *It's one day, and I'm busy.* "What are you looking at there?" Ryan pointed to the pile.

"Susie's papers." Hank waved to the sheets fanned across the table. "She was quite the historian. I reckon you know she gave several boxes of old records and books to the library when it opened." He propped an elbow on the table, resting his chin in his palm. "I'll have to remind Meg, so she can show the expert."

"She probably already did," Ryan muttered.

Hank widened his gaze and leaned forward, peering closely.

"It's nothing. I talked to her while she was leaving yesterday."

"And?" Hank drummed his fingers on the table.

Ryan fought off a flinch, meeting his grandfather's gaze without blinking. "And...what?"

"Did you tell her how you feel?"

Ryan propped his elbows on the table.

"Oh, come on, boy. You are the most frustrating person on this earth."

Ryan rolled his eyes. *Takes one to know one.*

Hank held up both hands. "At least I know I'm trouble. The problem with you is you're always so wrapped up in the future and the big picture you're missing right now."

"If I don't, I won't have a future. Neither would anyone in the town. Living in the moment is a luxury. I have to plan ahead. For all our sakes."

Hank scoffed and leaned back in the chair at the head of the table. Crossing his arms over his chest, he glanced at the ground.

"Fine. You know you're trouble." Ryan sighed. His grandfather's self-awareness had a blaring blind spot. "You accuse me of worrying about tomorrow. What about you? You're trapped in yesterday."

Hank shrugged. "At least I'm trying. Cleaning out the shed isn't easy. I don't want to go through the memories. I've been too focused on what I'm missing. I'm taking my days for granted. I'm here. I don't want to waste another second."

"What's inspired the introspection?"

"I miss Meg and Colby." Hank sighed. "I want them to stay. You know she chose to make her home in Herd even though it's hard. We have some opportunities but not a lot. She's special, and she'd different for most folks."

"I know." Ryan nodded.

"I worry she's lonely. She needs more than work for a good life." Hank shook his head. "She doesn't even have much of that. Now the big city fella is here, and she'll see what she's missing. He'll tell her stories about his life and work. He'll present her with tantalizing tidbits."

And she'll leave? Ryan couldn't imagine Meg running off. She wasn't a grass is greener person. She had a good—if quiet—life here. He'd been glad he could present a solution to the initial problem of her leaving by purchasing the land. In the years since, had she been too scared to fully commit to life in town? Did she have friends besides his grandfather and her dog? He never asked the questions.

Hank held his gaze.

What wasn't the cowboy saying? Did he know more information he wasn't sharing about Meg? Had the auction house expert said something in front of Hank? No, Ryan wouldn't read into everything. He didn't have time. "We all make sacrifices."

Hank snorted and pushed back his chair. "Like my beauty rest. Come on, let's go tell some stories so I can get to bed."

Ryan followed his grandfather to the back door. If he didn't tell Meg how he felt, would she go? Or would his honesty propel her escape? Maybe she didn't share his feelings. Maybe he made her feel uncomfortable in his company and that was why she stayed away today.

He'd focus on what he could control and worry about the rest after the guests left. Could Stephanie walk him through a meditation over the phone? Otherwise, he faced a sleepless night.

CHAPTER 10

Riding horseback on the open range wasn't the place to let a mind wander. Meg knew better. As she followed the tour group across the Kincaid ranch, however, she couldn't seem to focus.

After another successful weekend at the store, Meg had hated to close early on Monday afternoon. Would she jinx her recent string of good luck? If she kept pace with the tourists, she'd cover her overhead costs for the summer by the end of the month. With her immediate costs covered, she could build her internet store and get her business ahead. She could—conceivably—stay without involving Ryan, Eric, or anyone else in her decision.

Her plan depended on too many external factors she couldn't control. She'd hate for Mom to miss out on a lucrative time to rent the ranch house. Mom didn't need the extra income. On several occasions, she assured Meg of that fact. Meg couldn't get it out of her mind, however, that she was taking something away from Mom and providing no benefit.

Meg would like to stick around at least until the Frontier Days at the end of June. Mom had again reiterated that she didn't want Meg to rush into her next move against an arbitrary deadline. If she could somehow earn enough to cover costs through the rest of the year, she'd feel better about staying. Resetting the window display, she'd straightened the sign advertising the event.

In between helping customers, she'd created a tableau featuring the hats and boots, effectively stopping the selfie-takers and luring in new buyers with the merchandise. During the first hour, she had several compliments on the display and sold one of the hats. She was conflicted about leaving but promised both Colby and Eric.

The group of riders ahead of her stopped.

"Whoa." Meg pulled back on the mare's reins. Astride the oldest horse in the Kincaid stables. She didn't have to use much force to convince the horse to stop. Getting Cupcake started, however, was another matter.

She leaned forward, patting the mare's neck with long strokes. "Good girl, Cupcake."

"You are a natural," Eric called and walked his horse over.

Meg snorted. Only city folk thought what she did looked *natural*. She grew up around horses but never caught the bug. At her elementary school, she was the only pre-pubescent girl not obsessed with the creature. She preferred her own feet as mode of transportation.

Whenever she got the chance, she loved to watch Hank and Ryan ride. Both men moved with their animals in perfect harmony. She understood why the Greeks dreamed up a centaur. Some people were born to gallop.

Not Meg. Astride the back of a horse, she was too high off the ground. She didn't move in tandem with the creature but struggled against her. In the old saddle, she hit every bump and jostle, every twig and uneven patch of ground. With her two feet on the dirt, she controlled her motion and center of gravity. If she rode, she wanted the easy-going mare. "Hardly. Cupcake here is pure sugar."

"She looks quite..." He frowned.

"Ancient?"

He nodded.

"She used to be Hank's wife's horse. He's sweet enough to let me ride her. I'll probably have to turn her around and leave the rest of the group soon." She nodded her head to the rest of Joe's morning tour.

A family of four, including two elementary school-aged kids, a retired couple, and a trio of twenty-somethings celebrating a bachelorette made up the motley band of wannabe cowpoke.

Joe stopped the group near the two-foot wide, rocky stream, cutting through the valley.

A couple of the horses bent their heads to drink the clear water.

Pulling up the rear, Meg was content to take things easy. She wasn't in a rush. Scanning the terrain she knew by heart for the possible location of the Wild West Show auditions was like discovering the land for the first time. She could hardly believe the empty prairie had ever seen much excitement. "Do you suppose this is the place?"

He nodded. "It must be. From what I read the show needed lots of land for the fake stampede. This space would have been perfect."

In the beautiful valley, tall grass waved in the slight breeze under a bright blue sky. Sunlight warmed her from the top down. Inside her boots, she curled her toes.

She could almost feel the earth shake as hundreds of hooves pounded the ground. If she shut her eyes, she heard the call of the Lakota feigning a battle as onlookers cheered.

"It was quite unusual. Buffalo Bill didn't often set up large scale tryouts like this. He had scouts do the work for him. After the show got going, people came to him. This situation was different."

She wondered who enjoyed the show more. The city folk glimpsing what they must have assumed was an authentic encapsulation of life past the Mississippi? Or the performers eager to pretend the old days persisted? "How so?"

"My research also uncovered the reason you've never seen any bison," Eric said.

"Really?"

He nodded and shifted on the saddle. "Apparently, the show needed more stock for the stampede. When the auditions came to town, Buffalo Bill put out a call with a price for every bison caught in good condition. In one swoop, the cowboys rounded up every last one. The other ranchers had relocated most of the animals onto Kincaid land years earlier. When the herds from all surrounding areas were gathered, John Kincaid made a fortune."

"The bison were forcibly removed from their environment? Taken from their homes?"

He nodded.

"The babies, too?"

He held her stare.

She turned and gazed at the grass again, blinking back the tears. On the wind, she heard the pained grunts of the animals. Were the Kincaids solely involved in the round-up? Her family must have participated in some fashion, too. They were neighbors and, when the moment suited, allies. She'd never looked too far into her own past because she worried what she'd find.

Her privilege allowed her to ignore what happened in the nineteenth century and form her own sentiment. Her west wasn't the Old West. She'd grown up with modern amenities in the big city during the school year and absorbed the slower pace of life every summer.

Montana meant spending every second possible outside, picking wildflowers in the morning and catching fireflies at night. Her past held the feel of the warm sun on her skin and the rich earthy smell before the first strike of lightning streaked the sky and the boom of thunder shook the ground. She never questioned her right to the land.

Her heart ached for the bison. Did Ryan know? He benefited from the sale both historically and in the present. The money exchanged over a hundred years ago kept his family around long enough for him to operate his enterprise without the hiccups of wildlife. In the original rancher's position, would he have done the same?

The more worrisome question remained. If her presence in town was only a given because of her family's legacy, what did that mean when the history was bloody and tarnished? Did she belong here?

Eric offered her a way out. His job opportunity was the ultimate chance to prove she could be successful on her own merit. *I'll have no excuse for failure.* Was that unfortunate truth? Was her fear of not being enough her real motivation to stay?

Her unhelpful thoughts weren't fair. The silence stretched on too long. Any uncomfortable history shouldn't be shared with an outsider. She shifted on the saddle. "Do you have everything you need?"

He nodded. "I do. Tonight is the cowboy dinner. I'm sort of looking forward to it."

She lifted the corner of her mouth, forcing a smile. "You're in for a treat. It is a real cowboy hootenanny."

"A rootin', tootin' good time?"

She didn't respond. Another laughing at the town comment? Or teasing her with an exaggerated twist of her words? He delivered the question with a charming smile. She couldn't quite judge the situation.

"I definitely can't miss it. Have you been? Will you join me?" he asked.

What would Ryan think? She froze. Why did her brain immediately go *there*? Perhaps, because, as much as she wanted a minute alone with Ryan to chat, she understood showing up with another guy might send the wrong message.

Or did it? Ryan hadn't made any move that she'd considered romantic. Eric was only a friend and colleague. She hadn't been to one of Ryan's cowboy dinners in years. She had nothing going on. Why not? If she got a minute with Ryan to talk about the collection and her plan to turn down the finder's fee, she'd prove herself more than another of his burdens.

They could meet as equals. Then, the spark between them might have a chance at a real flame.

She met Eric's gaze. "Thank you. I will join you tonight."

He smiled.

"Meg!" A deep voice roared.

She turned her head toward the sound. Racing like a thunder cloud, Ryan strode from his truck parked several yards away.

Good. She unclenched her jaw and relaxed her defensive posture. He was here and could provide answers. She'd gratefully lean into their well-established roles. Ryan was the stoic reasoner, anchoring her mental flights of fancy. He'd reassure her of their legacies' importance.

Stomping down the hill, he moved like a force of nature. He wasn't smooth or refined like Eric. Ryan was rough. From the stubble on his chin that never seemed to be completely shaved in the morning to the simple responses, he didn't put on airs or a façade. He was always real.

Her heart stuck in her throat. Looking at him now, she reconsidered her eagerness to meet him. He glowered. Where was the thoughtful, longtime acquaintance? This Ryan was a version she hadn't encountered before. Red-faced, he practically blew steam from his ears.

"What do you think you're doing?" He glowered, stopping at her side.

Without a hat, his frown was on full display as he stared up at her on Cupcake's back. *Nothing much.* Heat crept up her cheeks. What did he imagine she was up to? His scowl could tan a hide without the lye. She gulped.

Raising a hand to shield his gaze against the bright glare of sunshine, Ryan scanned the horizon behind the house. Squinting and frowning simultaneously might be a skill. To him, it was the start of a pounding headache that threatened to rage all day. Spotting no one, he pounded the path to the house and strode in the backdoor.

His hat was gone. Ted or Joe might be playing a trick on him. Ryan wasn't in the mood to be teased. Sunglasses bothered him. He liked being able to see clearly what was in front of him. He scrubbed a hand over his face, tightening the reins in his other. He'd heard enough of Hank's lectures lately to be aware he was almost legally blind in regard to one person in his life.

After several hours under the cloudless sky, he returned to the house. He needed a ball cap or something. When he spotted Colby on the floor of the kitchen, he released the heavy breath he'd been holding. Where there was a dog, the owner wouldn't be too far away. He shut the door and turned. "You got a visitor?"

Hank grinned. "I do. We're heading to the shed in a little bit."

"Are you dog sitting, or is Meg joining you today?"

"I'm sure she'll be around in a little bit. We didn't get into specifics. She dropped off Colby for a visit and headed out. She can't stay here all day. She said she's been doing a lot of sales in town."

"That's good to hear." Ryan sagged his shoulders, relaxing his tense body for a second. If she was busy, she couldn't spend time with that well-dressed guy. Ryan had a shot. *Do I want one?* He wasn't sure.

Before the stranger's arrival, Ryan had sensed the shift between them. After years of avoiding each other, he found every excuse to interact. He wasn't ready to address *them* or face any upset to his status quo. The stranger almost forced his hand. With the pair separated, Ryan had no concerns to plague him. *Except, that's not what Hank said.*

"Wait. Back-up. What do you mean *stay here all day*? Is she here?" *With him?* At his sides, he flattened his hands against his jeans. He would not curl his fingers into fists.

"At the moment, she is on a ride with Joe and the tour group. She earned a break. Sounded like a good opportunity to combine business and pleasure. When I ran into Eric, I suggested he tell her about it."

Ryan's heart pounded in his chest. Hank said the words with nonchalance. The old cowboy was never careless in his speech. Was he warning Ryan? "Oh?" His voice cracked. He winced.

Focused on the dog, Hank scratched Colby behind the ears and smiled.

The grin could have been meant for either of them. Ryan didn't relax, poising for the latest round of the verbal tug of war.

"Eric went, too," Hank said.

"Oh." The word was more grunt than comment. Of course, *Eric* did. Ryan pressed a finger against his throbbing temple. "Why?"

Hank shrugged and dropped his hands from the dog. Leaning back, he folded his arms over his chest. "He's a guest."

"No, why did she go with him?"

"Reckon it's about the photographs and cards." Hank tapped a finger against his bicep. "I'm not sure. I didn't ask specifics. She dropped off Colby a little while ago, and I told her to take Cupcake."

"What?" Ryan gasped; the air sucked from his lungs. The conversation jumped from bad to worse to terrible with every new sentence.

"The horse needs exercise."

"Not that much." Ryan fisted his hands at his sides and dragged in as deep a breath as he could manage.

The mare was twenty-six years old. Losing Cupcake was inevitable. He didn't want to speed up the process. It wasn't like ripping off a bandage. Once gone, he didn't get over the pain after the initial sharp sting. He accepted the ache of missing a loved one and sometimes forgot his loss. The pain never lessened.

Without Cupcake, Hank was the last living link to Susie and childhood. *I'd have Meg.* Would he? He turned and frowned at Hank. "Where did they go?"

"Joe was leading everyone to the creek and then the big valley," Hank said. "I'm sure Cupcake is fine. Meg cares about that horse. She won't push her."

I can't take the chance. Ryan headed outside, pounding the grass to his truck. He turned over the engine and sped off, ditching the road in favor of a short-cut only accessible due to the drier than normal weather. Otherwise, he would have driven into mud too deep for the truck's tires to traverse.

As it was, he ripped up enough prairie grass to be noticeable. Ted wouldn't appreciate his rash actions. *Well, I don't like hers.* She knew what the horse meant to him and Hank. How dare she use Hank's good nature, sweetened up with the re-appearance of his new best friend Colby, to get her way. In another few miles, he reached the crest of the hill and slowed the truck, rolling down the hill. He spotted the group a few yards away. Cutting the engine, he hopped from the truck and strode toward the group.

The horses stood too close. Dangerously close. Apart from the rest of the group, the light brown mare stood almost shoulder to shoulder with Heathcliffe, a young colt with attitude.

Ryan gritted his molars. This was what happened when amateurs played cowboy. Good animals got hurt. "Meg!" he yelled.

She turned her head and frowned.

In three long strides, he reached Cupcake. "What are you doing? Get those horses apart." *And their riders.* He shook his head and grabbed the reins on Cupcake, leading the sweet mare to safety a few feet away. If Meg was a real ranch girl, she'd have had more awareness of the animal. She never quite shook off her city lifestyle.

"Sorry, Ryan. You're right. I didn't realize how close we were." Her cheeks pinked.

He bit the inside of his cheek. She couldn't hide her guilt. Why? Did she have feelings for the stranger?

"I was turning back anyway. I don't want to push Cupcake."

"Or leave Hank to do all the work?" He hated rhetorical questions but couldn't seem to stop himself.

She blanched. "Is he? Oh no. I'm sorry, Ryan. I only came for a quick tour on my lunch. I have to get back to the store. I can stop by tomorrow afternoon."

She didn't deserve his lecture. Hank wasn't in the shed but resting in the kitchen. The only person who earned condemnation was himself. But he couldn't stop his tirade. "Don't apologize to me." He kicked an ant hill. "You sort yourself out with Hank."

"I will." She sighed. "Did you know your family contributed significantly to endangering the world's population of bison? They rounded up and sold every animal they could. They didn't care what happened to the creatures as long as they got paid."

Huh? Why was she talking about this? He turned to her companion.

Eric winced.

"I'm aware," Ryan said. *What game was she playing?* He didn't appreciate her shrill tone or accusatory words. With months of work devoted to the bison conservation project, he didn't deserve a lecture. He was trying. The past couldn't be wiped clean. The Kincaids were part of a larger effort in the nineteenth century to force Indigenous people onto government lands by exterminating a critical part of their culture. Her family wasn't innocent either.

He focused his energy on the future, building a better tomorrow for everyone. Had she wanted to be involved? He dropped the threads of the conversation. She could cling to the past like Hank all she wanted. Without Ryan, however, she would be flung into an unforgiving present alongside Hank.

"Do you have anything to say?" she asked.

I don't like that you're dismissing my hard work based on assumptions. He set his jaw, grinding his molars. Couldn't she pick a better, private moment to argue?

She widened her eyes and flared her nostrils. Preparing for a verbal attack? Ryan scrubbed a hand over his face. He hated explaining himself but especially in front of a stranger. "Save it. Please."

She turned toward her companion but not before Ryan glimpsed her quivering chin. Oh no. Had his words been too sharp? He wanted peace, not to reprimand her in front of her colleague. She hadn't cried in years. At least, not in front of him.

A wave a nausea threatened to knock him off-balance. He hated her tears and especially detested being the source. But he wasn't in the wrong at this moment. He wouldn't cave.

"I'll get going. I've stayed too long," she said. "Bye, Eric."

"Later?" Eric asked.

Ryan didn't want to listen but couldn't walk away. Making plans? While his grandfather pet sat? The pair were supposed to be helping Hank, not cavorting around his property.

She nodded and wrinkled her brow.

Ryan caught her gaze. His throat squeezed shut, cutting off his airway. An apology caught on his Adam's apple. He coughed.

She nudged Cupcake with her heels. The good-natured mare turned toward the stables and trotted, swishing her tail from side to side.

Turning, he caught the outsider's stare. Dressed in fancy jeans and white sneakers, the man was out of place. Yet, he had the nerve to look perfectly comfortable. Ryan grunted. He didn't like the knowing look in the man's gaze.

With a wave, Eric whistled and turned his horse, rejoining Joe's tour group.

Ryan headed back to the truck. He had the cowboy dinner tonight. He couldn't be in a bad mood in front of his guests. Many checked out in the morning. He didn't want his scowl seared into their last memory of the ranch. Could he find a reason to smile? Or at least to stop frowning?

He'd have to track her down and apologize. Keeping her informed was a full-time job. Since he'd taken her input on his business, however, he faced a new reality of sharing his ideas with someone who'd voice an opinion. Hank approved plans without getting into the particulars and his employees never offered a thought. Meg was his equal. His poor treatment of her shamed him. He reverted to pushing her to the side instead of involving her in discussion.

If he kept shoving, he'd push her out of his life completely. *She'd leave for a job with someone who clearly respects her.* With a growl, he hopped into his truck and turned over the ignition.

CHAPTER II

O nce Meg pointed the horse in the right direction, she didn't need to do anything else. Cupcake knew the way home. The mare picked up her pace and trotted. In the saddle, Meg bounced around, but the shaking couldn't snap her out of her reverie.

Ryan was mad at her. Why? His anger rolled off him in waves, and he spoke with such short, curt words. She'd seen him annoyed, frustrated, and indifferent. She could handle those reactions. Him thinking poorly of her? She shuddered and tightened her grip on the reins.

She knew how important Cupcake was to the Kincaid men, on par with Colby to Meg. She trusted Hank with the dog, and Hank returned the favor with the horse.

Ryan was the hitch.

Always.

To drive over, hunt her down, and berate her in front of an audience was clear proof of his low opinion. To do so in front of a professional colleague was even worse. Her ears burned, and her cheeks scalded. She sniffed, scrunching her nose. She would not cry. If asked, she'd blame her red face on wind and sun.

How could she take herself seriously when he didn't? How could she drop the invisible shackles she imposed on herself if she didn't have his support? Would he ever value her as an equal?

She'd never been so embarrassed in her whole life. It was exactly the sort of behavior she might have expected out of the old Ryan, the one she'd grown up with. The one constantly trying to avoid her or blame her for some tiny infraction. Not the Ryan she'd gotten to know since starting the shed clean-out project.

He was right about one thing. She'd left Hank on his own with Colby. She knew the pair would head to the shed to continue the process of clearing through a lifetime's worth of boxes. The old cowboy would overexert himself. If anything happened due to her negligence, Ryan would never forgive her. Nor would she.

Meg lifted her gaze, scanning her surroundings. "Whoa, slow down, Cupcake." Meg pulled on the reins.

The mare stopped and whinnied, shaking her head.

Ted waved and jogged toward the pair. He opened his palm, displaying sugar cubes. "You're back early. Did the old girl give you any trouble?" Ted rubbed the horse's neck, wrinkling his brow. Cupcake gummed his palm.

"No, she's perfect. Like always." She extended the reins to Ted.

He grabbed hold of Cupcake.

Meg swung her leg over the saddle and dropped, her boots hitting the ground. She'd have to sneak into one of Stephanie's yoga classes to loosen up. Straightening, she sighed. "Thanks, Ted."

"Sure thing. I...ugh...don't suppose you've seen Ryan around?"

With his down-turned mouth and shifting gaze, Ted transformed into the physical embodiment of guilty conscience. "Why?" She frowned at the ranch hand.

"I might have grabbed his hat by mistake this morning."

"How? Isn't his head huge?"

Ted shrugged. "I didn't notice until I was on my rounds and the wind blew the thing off my head. I had to chase it down. Took half the morning." He chuckled. "I cleaned it up and put it back on his hook. No harm, no foul."

Speak for yourself. She pressed together her lips. Was she simply collateral damage in a bad day? Ryan's words cut her deep. She needed an apology. *I was accusatory.* Inwardly, she cringed. She didn't want to owe him anything after his treatment, but she owed him an apology.

"Heard about your events and weddings idea," Ted said.

She held perfectly still. *Heard about it* as in Ryan shot down the plan and laughed at the notion? Or *heard about it* as in the concept earned serious consideration from Ryan's most trusted employee?

"Could be a good thing for the future." Ted smiled.

Don't blush. The slow warming crept up her neck. After one confusing interaction, she didn't need another. If Ryan liked the idea, he would have only business reasons at the heart of his acceptance. "Do you mind taking care of Cupcake? I need to check on Hank and Colby."

"Sure thing. He's in the shed. Come on, Cupcake. You've earned a bucket of oats."

Cupcake whinnied and lifted her head and tail.

With a tip of his hat, Ted led the horse into her stall in the stables.

Meg had a half mile walk toward the shed.

With the beautiful weather, guests were scattered throughout the property on different adventures and tours. The lawn behind the house was empty.

She filled her lungs and slowly exhaled, making her way to the shed. Hank had witnessed her grow up. He'd spot any display of emotion, no matter how small, and want an explanation. Until she processed how Ryan hurt her so deeply, she didn't want to talk about her feelings with anyone else.

Strolling to the shed, she rubbed her lashes and dried her clammy palms on her jeans. With her fingertips, she pushed open the door, slipping inside the darkened interior. "Hank? Colby? Hello? Is anyone in here?"

Squinting, her gaze adjusted to the dim light. She walked to the back of the shed. The air was stagnant and heavy, holding the smell of aging paper and old tobacco. The building must have been where he'd stashed his pipe after Susie demanded he stop. There was no smoke in the air, so he hadn't taken it up again. But she was surprised by the changes.

In a few days, the shed had transformed from hazard to cluttered retreat. A roughly ten-by-ten area free of boxes and clutter opened at the back of the shed. On her last visit, she had sat at a small bistro-sized table with three chairs. Now, two card tables were set up along with a battery-powered table lamp. She didn't see either her dog or her friend. "Hank?"

"Over here, Meg."

She turned toward the sound.

A tail and a pair of shoes stuck out from behind a box-shaped igloo.

She'd passed the pair in a cardboard fort and had no clue. "Colby?"

The tail wagged, thumping against the ground.

"Come on out of there, silly dog." She knelt near the opening. Inside, she spotted the cowboy. "Hank, this isn't safe. The boxes could topple on you."

"Hold on. I've just about got it." He grunted, dragging a box.

"Let's give him space, Colby." Meg patted the ground. The dog crawled out.

In another few seconds, Hank followed on his hands and knees, pushing a box. He spotted her and sighed. "What are you doing here? Is Joe cutting his tours short?"

She narrowed her gaze. Something was off. Doubt tickled the back of her neck. What if Eric's invitation hadn't been so spur of the moment? What if a masterful puppeteer lingered in the background, pulling a few strings? "Did you encourage Eric to ask me on the ride to get out of your hair?"

"Why would I do that?" His tone was steady. He stared at the ground.

She pursed her lips. The cowboy was up to something, but she didn't know his motives. She pushed off the ground and reached for the box. "Should we examine this at the table? I'm not much for sitting on the ground."

Hank nodded and slowly got to his feet, his knees cracking as he stood. "I probably shouldn't either. I wanted to grab one more box before that fella leaves tomorrow."

She nodded and walked to the card tables, carefully setting the box on top. "I understand. I wish you had waited for me. Or even let me know you needed to get something specific out of the bottom of the stack. Do you have more to sort through today?"

Wincing, he walked toward her.

Her breath caught in her chest. "Are you okay?"

He held up a hand. "Just stiff. I'm fine. Don't start makin' a fuss. That's what I like about you. You don't fuss. You treat me like an adult and not an invalid."

She bit her bottom lip. What she liked about him was he didn't put her in tricky situations between her conscience and her ego. Present circumstances excluded.

He reached the table, pulled out a chair, and sat down. He sighed. Colby trotted to him and rested her head on his lap. He smiled at the dog and scratched behind her ears. "I wasn't alone, if that's what concerns you."

Only partly. She grabbed a chair, scraping the feet against the rough plywood floor and plopped into the seat.

"I have to admit." Hank pulled the box across the top. "I didn't think I would. But I like that city fella. He's nice and knows his business. I appreciate dealing with someone so upfront."

She nodded her commiseration. Once she understood Eric's motives, she'd relaxed. Moving past the odd initial greeting at her store, she had stopped trying to control the situation and focused on her responses. Was seeking domination in their interactions her hiccup with Ryan? She wasn't sure what either of them wanted anymore. *Besides respect.*

"Colby must agree because she didn't bite him," Hank said, his voice scratchy and rough.

Meg frowned and rested her arms on the table. "You sound disappointed."

Hank shrugged. "I guess I'm not used to you having someone with so much in common."

Neither was she. As an adult, she chose Herd. She wanted to belong here. Desperately. Most days, however, she didn't fit. No matter how she smoothed her rough edges, she stuck out. With Eric, she hadn't needed to explain her passion for history. She enjoyed his company. *But with Ryan, I can be one hundred percent myself.*

"I almost think..." Hank wiggled his bushy brows.

Heat crept up her cheeks. Please let her de facto grandfather never inch closer to discussing romantic attraction. "He's helping us with the project. That's it."

Hank held her gaze.

The cowboy's knowing look rankled. She pressed a cold hand to her hot cheek. "It's nice to talk shop with someone. But that's it."

"Really? I thought he might want to steal you away. You're too smart to stay hidden here."

You guessed? How had he so accurately understood while she'd been so oblivious? She was tempted to ask more of his opinions. With irrefutable proof, however, she couldn't lie to herself. "Leaving isn't my choice, you know that."

He smiled. "Nice way to avoid the conversation."

She shook her head but wouldn't deny his spot-on assessment. "I've got to head back to the store with Colby. Will you promise not to go digging through that pile over there?"

He crossed a finger over his heart.

"Can I grab a particular box for your and bring it inside? You'd be more comfortable at the kitchen table, and I'd feel a lot better."

"Okay. I suppose that's fair. Just pick the one on top."

She pushed back her chair and crossed the room, grabbing the box he indicated. "Come on, Colby. You need to make an appearance at the store. You've been missed."

Tail wagging, the dog licked Hank's palm and trotted to the door.

"Hank? Are you coming?"

"I'll be along in an instant. I promise."

With a nod to Hank, Meg followed the pup outside. Try as she might, she couldn't erase the censure in Ryan's condemnation. He'd been right. Left unsupervised, Hank immediately chose to endanger himself. She hated being at odds with Ryan. Without another confrontation, she couldn't make amends, and the fight wasn't in her.

From his window overlooking the yard, Ryan stood sentry. The second he had opened his mouth; he had understood he was dead-wrong. Back there, standing on the hill, he'd spotted her with that guy and spewed hurtful words. He couldn't stop himself.

As he paused for a breath, however, she took her shot. She gave as good as she got. He was fully aware of the misdeeds that established his family and continued to support him. He just didn't know she knew. He was making amends.

Not fast enough.

He hated arguing in front of a visitor. At least the other guests hadn't noticed or reacted to his poor behavior. Bad customer service and airing dirty laundry in public ratcheted up his frustration until his blood boiled. She had the sense to flee. It wasn't until he returned to his bedroom, spotted his hat suspiciously returned to its hook, he hadn't fully processed his behavior or calmed down.

When he did both, he was smacked in the face with the truth. The other man was her colleague and his guest. In one momentary lapse, Ryan ruined both of their prospects. After giving her a head start, he drove his truck the long way and reached his house in time to spot her talking to Ted.

He'd headed upstairs and straight to his window, overlooking the yard and the shed.

While he couldn't see inside the building, he knew in his heart she was inside. Of course, she'd go straight to his grandfather. She had a heart for him. Ryan had demanded it and heaped on the guilt. The old cowboy wasn't her responsibility. Ryan knew how much each valued the other. Pitting one against the other was a low blow. Adding in Cupcake was petty.

The shed door swung open.

Head down, Meg emerged with a box in her arms and Colby at her side. She moved quickly. No second glance to see if he was around?

His chest tightened. He couldn't blame her for making a quick escape, but he had to intercept her. He strode from the room, raced down the front steps, and flung open the kitchen door, the panel crashing against the siding.

He winced and turned toward her. "Hey, can I help?"

She strode straight towards him and pushed the box against his chest without any comment.

He secured the cardboard in his arms.

And she disappeared from view.

Where had she gone? How had she moved so fast? He set the box on the table and jogged through the house to the main entrance.

She strode toward her SUV, crunching gravel with each determined stride.

He cupped his hands around his mouth. "Meg. Wait, please."

She froze.

He jogged down the path, leaving the door wide open.

With a wagging tail, Colby raced toward him and jumped, nearly knocking him to the ground with her front paws.

I'd deserve it. He widened his stance and petted the dog. "Down, Colby."

The dog dropped and sat.

He raised his gaze to her owner. Meg's cheeks were bright pink. Her lips puckered, like she fought from frowning. Her gaze held steady on the ground.

"Meg, hey, please look at me?" His voice cracked. Raising a fist to his mouth, he coughed. He strode toward her, narrowing the distance from feet to inches.

She ground a rock under her heel. "Why? You want to yell louder? You don't have an audience around to hold back. You ready to really unload your grievances against me?"

"No, listen please?" He reached out a hand, brushing her elbow.

She caught her breath.

Dropping his hand, he tucked both into the pockets of his jeans. He had barely touched her, his fingertips grazing her soft skin. He would never use physical force or presence against another person. "I'm really sorry."

She met his gaze. "For?"

Everything. By virtue of wearing her heart on her sleeve, she was an open book. When she had smiled at the other guy, she looked so happy and free. Tiny creases had formed at the corners of her chocolate brown eyes. Her mouth had lifted. Her skin had almost glowed. She had been prettier than ever.

And he had seen red.

"Bye, Ryan," she bit the words out.

"No, wait." He lunged forward, stepping in front of her path. "I was out of line."

She stiffened. "Because of a hat?" She stared into his eyes.

Who told her? He reached up a hand to the back of his neck, rubbing the sunburned skin. Her blunt statement only added to his feeling of failure. He couldn't hide from the truth.

"Yes, and a lot of other things."

She broke from his gaze.

"I'm sorry. You don't know what I have going on behind-the-scenes, and you didn't deserve poor treatment. What happened back there in front of one of your peer?" He shook his head. "I was wrong. I behaved poorly. I know your work is important to you. I should have treated you with more respect, especially in front of a colleague."

She folded her arms over her chest and popped a leg out, tapping the foot. "And?"

"I am deeply sorry for what I implied about Hank and Cupcake. I know both mean a great deal to you."

"I wouldn't endanger anyone."

"I know. I just..." The words stuck on his tongue. Why was apologizing so hard? "I have to address your accusations."

She lifted her chin.

"When you brought up the bison..." His thoughts jumbled together. He wasn't quick with snappy replies. He needed to think his words through.

The longer the silence stretched, the deeper she frowned. Had his inability to form a speedy retort caused some of the misunderstandings between them? "I fully understand the privilege I have. I stand to inherit a lot of property. Not everything was acquired in ways we'd view as moral with our modern lens. All of this land..." He extended his arms and dropped both to his sides. "The founding families settled the valley. The land was unoccupied because military force cleared it. Doesn't mean it was unclaimed. I can't change history, but I am trying to right a wrong. You hit me with a sensitive subject." He swallowed. "I haven't shared the information with many people off the ranch. Please keep what I'm about to tell you between us."

She arched an eyebrow.

Probably the best encouragement he could expect. "I'm in talks to reintroduce bison to the prairie. If all goes according to plan, we'll have a herd next summer. Properly reestablishing the animals to the environment takes time. It's not a lot. But it's something." He finished before his voice shook with frustration and fear.

With the weight of his small corner of the world on his shoulders, he struggled. He couldn't show his worries to anyone else. He accepted his role as a town leader with all the positives and negatives inherent in the position. But he desperately needed her support and understanding.

Her chin quivered. She scrubbed her face with both hands. "I'm sorry, too. I had no clue about your plans. Of course, you don't owe me an explanation. You have done more for this town and community than anyone else. You shouldn't be accused and interrogated. Least of all by me."

He widened his gaze.

She dug the toe of her boot into the loose gravel. "I shouldn't leave Hank on his own. I caught him and Colby not being as cautious as they should be."

"He's not yours to worry about. I'm supposed to be minding him. I promised..." His throat swelled shut. "I shouldn't have put you on the spot. You have your own business to run. I appreciate how much time you've devoted to us."

"Speaking of my work." She studied him. "I won't be able to help at the shed again until after work on Saturday and Sunday. Think late. Like past nine. It's been quite a busy week. I'm heading to the store now."

We won't see you for four days? Why? His stomach dropped to his boots. The thought was too charged for consideration. He wanted to question her reasoning. Was there a difference between a weekend and a weekday in retail? Was she expecting something—or someone—needing her time after work during the week? "Guess I'd better find some more extension cords and lights."

"Will you do your best to keep Hank out of the shed until the weekend? He's in there now. Eric has everything he needs and is leaving tomorrow."

Is that the real reason? Was she avoiding him or had no more motivation after the other guy left? Ryan coughed. "I can try. I might see if Joe needs his help on any tours this week. I'll put Ted on rotation to check the shed every hour."

"Thanks. Hank means a lot to me."

Do I? Ryan hated this superficial conversation. Everything he wanted to ask and say lurked deep in his mind, beneath the surface of non-controversial pleasantries. *Why was talking to her suddenly so hard? What happened to her nonstop chatter that always left an opening for a reply?* "Can you come to the dinner tonight? It's our first cowboy event of the season. I'd appreciate all the support I can get."

She tilted her head to the side and narrowed her gaze.

Under her study, he didn't shift his weight. He hated the subtext between them. Should he extend a different invitation? Dinner and a movie wasn't an option. If he offered her anything close to a real date, he'd anticipate hearing *no.* "I have something to show you."

He regretted the words as soon as he blurted them. If all he could offer her were professional obligations, he'd do what he needed to keep her here. Without compromising his feelings, he'd offer her a piece of the future. Though he'd been pacing and thinking, he hadn't marked the potential deck event space in any meaningful, physical way. Now, he'd have to.

"Okay, I'll see you tonight." She spun on her heel and stalked to the SUV.

Why had she hesitated? He followed with Colby, helping the dog with the passenger side door. Having thumbs meant he was occasionally useful to the pair of independent women. He owed Meg so much more than an apology, and wouldn't read into what she hadn't said. With any luck, he could formally start his groveling tonight in front of the biggest audience around. He shut the door and backed away from the car, waving as she drove off.

CHAPTER 12

A t the open barn doors, Meg stood very still. The sun wouldn't set for another couple hours, and the daylight made the well-lit interior extra enticing. She couldn't go inside yet.

She wasn't sure where, or if, she belonged.

Scanning the crowd, she swayed with the bluegrass music and suppressed the very persistent urge to twirl. In her bedroom, she hadn't been able to resist. She didn't often don her favorite dress, the floral, sleeveless, cotton garment with the full skirt Grandma had made decades ago.

Meg had saved a few of her late grandma's dresses. The quality of the home sewn vintage garments couldn't be matched in modern factories. Every time she wore one, she linked the past in the present. Antiques weren't merely a commercial enterprise but a way of honoring those she loved and lost.

Digging her cowgirl boots out of the back of her closet and applying eyeshadow and dark lipstick, she'd completed the look. She was probably overdressed. When she asked Colby, she barely got a glance. After a few hours at the store, customers cooing over the good girl, the dog was exhausted and happy. Meg hoped Hank was too. Grabbing her jean jacket off the hook, she'd hopped in her SUV and headed back to the Kincaid ranch.

In the entry, she didn't twirl. She didn't watch to catch anyone's eye. She wasn't sure if she'd accepted Ryan or Eric's invitation. Pressing together her lips, she refreshed her lipstick. She had the unnerving sense that it mattered which man she greeted first. Not that she was sure why.

Eric had offered her a job. Ryan had extended a hand for friendship. She wasn't in the middle of a tug of war. She should have told Ryan she had already been invited when he asked her. But he'd flashed such a soft smile. She hadn't wanted to ruin the moment or push him away.

Inside the barn, the cowboy festivities were well underway. Under the hay loft, the seven-piece band performed on the stage. The fiddle dueled with a banjo, whistling through the night air, inviting all to tap their feet to the upbeat rhythm. The entire red painted structure hummed with the buzz of excited conversations and tittering laughter.

Footsteps sounded behind her.

A couple passed, the wife brushing Meg with a shoulder. "Oh, I'm so sorry, dear."

Meg waved off the concern and crossed her arms over her belly, grabbing her elbows. She was at fault, standing awkwardly in the way. She stepped over the threshold, rolling her step from heel to toe in careful consideration. The worn, leather boots had a higher heel than her typical sneakers.

Darting her gaze, she spotted him.

Standing near the buffet, overseeing service, Ryan grinned. The expression brightened his whole face. The rare, genuine look of pleasure warmed her.

I wish he'd smile at me. Following his line of sight, she drew in a shaky breath. If he beamed at another woman, she'd be crushed.

On the other side of the line, guests—a family of four—returned his grin. He chuckled, throwing back his head.

He was natural with kids. Better than when he was a child. He'd always been destined to be a grown up running the ranch. With circumspection, she understood how being young must have been a struggle for someone who needed control.

"You made it."

Eric's voice snapped her to attention. She turned, tugging her jean jacket closed. "Hi, Eric. Yes, I'm here. Ta-da." Why did she say that? She might as well have flashed jazz hands.

He stepped back. "I grabbed us a spot in the corner. Follow me."

She nodded, glad when he turned. She nibbled the bottom of her lip. Where was Hank? Too tired after the long day? She strode behind Eric across the dance floor to the table in the opposite corner from the band.

Passing the buffet line, she met Ted's and Joe's gazes and smiled. Ryan never looked her way. She turned back and focused on Eric.

He reached the table and pulled out a chair.

This isn't a date. She tensed. She appreciated chivalry and compliments but didn't want any confusion. He'd offered her a job. She wasn't planning to accept, but neither was she interested in more. She didn't want to project the wrong idea to him or the community at large. On occasion, small-town living could be claustrophobic.

He walked around the table and sat opposite.

She dropped her shoulders a half inch. At least he wouldn't insist on pushing her chair into the table for her. Or draping her lap with a napkin. She sat and scooted the chair forward.

"I realize this might be..." He raised a fist to his mouth and coughed.

Inappropriate? She wouldn't supply him with his lines. She didn't have a copy of the script.

"Have you had a minute to think about the job offer?"

She nodded, pressing her lips into a straight line. The career change remained top of mind. One good week at her store wasn't enough to salvage the business but could give her time to diversify. She had to get the online store running.

"I'm guessing from your serious face, your answer is no?"

She pursed her lips. Taking him up on his job offer was the sensible choice. Lately, she'd had the urge to leap and try for the big, scary unknown. Ryan had a lot to do with her change of heart. Looking at Eric, *I'm sorry* tickled her tongue. She wouldn't apologize.

"I won't bug you about it. I am disappointed. If you ever reconsider." He reached into his jeans pocket and pulled out a business card, sliding it across the table.

She smiled and pocketed the card. Her tight stomach eased. After Hank's implication, she worried she'd given Eric the wrong impression. "Thank you. I appreciate your time and consideration."

He snorted. "You sound like a formal rejection letter. I understand." He scanned the room, staring past her. "Herd is a special place. Carving out your own path here is almost a throwback to another time. It's a rare chance."

I wish I knew it was the right one. If she was being honest, which she tended to save for self-reflective nights with Colby, she'd admit she was afraid of failure without any excuse to make herself feel better. She turned in her chair and scanned the room, waving at acquaintances.

Stephanie helped the bluegrass band, moving the mic stands.

Entering through a side door, Abby from the barbeque food truck carried three stacked, covered trays. Ted and Joe grabbed the trays and settled each in respective chafing dishes. Brisket and corn bread scented the air. Meg's stomach rumbled. She lost track of Ryan. Twisting all the way around, she spotted him in the doorway, assisting Hank. *I should help.*

From the corner of her gaze, she spotted Stephanie backing away from the band. Meg couldn't give up on participating in the Frontier Days. At the very least, she could donate a few baskets for the raffle. Everything converged into this moment.

She started to rise from her seat and froze. Where would she go? She would get in the way. She had no role. Wasn't Ryan always frustrated she was underfoot?

Stephanie disappeared from view.

Meg scooted her chair closer to the table. She'd stay put. Five years and a childhood of summers wasn't enough to make her a true resident. The stranger showed her in a handful of days she didn't truly blend in with her surroundings. She might never belong, but she had to try even if she'd always stand out.

Lifting her chin, she faced Eric again. She nodded. "I have to give the store everything I've got. I owe my grandmother and my mother." *And myself.*

With luck, she didn't have to spell out for him what had only—in recent days—become clear to her. She chose Herd. But she hadn't made a real effort to get to know anyone else. It wasn't too late to try. "Should we get some food while we can? The line is almost empty."

"After you, please." Eric smiled.

She pushed back her chair and strode with her head held high. She might be a temporary member of town, more guest than resident. But she wouldn't give up and walk away. She'd stay and fight. Sometimes, the best course of action was a life well-lived. She'd start by enjoying herself tonight.

Ryan couldn't catch a break. For the past hour, no matter which direction he turned, he glimpsed Meg's smile, inhaled her scent, or bristled at her laugh. He yearned to be included in the joke. Behind the buffet table, he rubbed a palm over his heart. Yearned? He hated even thinking that word, but it was spot-on.

He grabbed the last of the silver frames, holding the chafing dishes, off the table. He looped the empty rectangles over his wrist like a ridiculous oversized bracelet and strode the length of the buffet.

"Hey, Ryan."

Stopping at the end of the table, he turned and met Abby's gaze. In a few steps, he reached her. "Thanks for increasing the order so quickly. I didn't realize we'd have so many plus ones tonight."

She shrugged. "I'm always glad for the work. Thanks for letting me park my truck for lunch during the week. Let me know if you want to do anything for you-know-who." She widened her gaze.

He frowned. For Meg? Was he that obvious? Turning, he spotted her again with Eric.

She was lucky vampires weren't real. She kept throwing back her head and flashing her long, white neck as she chuckled along with what Ryan could only assume were dry, history-related jokes nobody else would understand. Ryan frowned. He'd invited Meg and yet she made no effort to say hi.

Abby snapped her fingers. "Yoo-hoo, earth to Ryan. Ryan, do you copy?"

He shook. "Sorry, you were saying?"

"Hank's birthday?" She lifted a shoulder. "It's not the big nine-oh, but every year is worthy of a celebration."

"You're right." He nodded. He'd totally forgotten. Was getting older the impetus for Hank's clean-out? Was he worried about leaving the project unfinished? Or did he want an excuse to focus on the past and the people long gone? "I'll keep you posted."

She smiled. "Please do. I'll get out of your hair now. Have fun."

He opened his mouth to protest he was working not playing and stopped. Not every comment needed a reply. He used to know that. He smiled, pressing together his lips.

She turned and strode past him toward the exit.

Joe approached, extending both hands. "Need any help?"

"I'm good here. Go check on Abby."

A funny look passed over Joe's face. He puckered his mouth like he bit a lemon and tried to cover it with a smile. Ryan would have to invite the guy around for poker if he made such bizarre facial expressions. He could only imagine the tells. *Another night, when I have time.* "Please?"

"Of course," Joe said.

Ryan reached the end of the table and nodded at the bluegrass band, comprised of more of Joe's colleagues from the kindergarten through eighth grade school. The towns-folk stepped up to the task of putting on a good show for the tourists. He was grateful for everyone's help and willingness to jump in and lend a hand. *Why hadn't Meg joined in?*

He passed the bathrooms, heading into the walk-in closet lined with shelves. When he had converted the barn into the event space, he'd carved a storage space in a slim hall opposite the newly added bathrooms behind the stage. Scanning the contents, he found the correct spot and deposited the frames in position one at a time. The first cowboy dinner of the season always had a few kinks. He couldn't complain about her. He invited her but hadn't specified what the request meant.

The band started another tune. The fiddler taking the lead in kicking off the dancing with a lively number. A cheer erupted.

"Why are you hiding out here?"

Ryan turned toward the open doorway and frowned at Hank.

The old man shuffled through the tight space.

"I'm not hiding. I'm doing my job. What are you doing back here?"

Hank shrugged. "Went to the bathroom and heard a commotion. Figured I'd better make sure you weren't making trouble."

That's your job. Ryan set the last frame on the shelf and strode toward his grandfather. "I'm heading out right now."

Hank held up a hand. "Let me stop you for a second, boy. You have anything to tell me?"

Ryan stared at the older man, unseeing. Had Hank witnessed the almost kiss a few days ago? Ryan slipped a finger under the starched collar of his checkered western shirt. He dressed up for the guests, but the start of the season involved reassessing what shirts no longer worked. This one almost choked him.

"About whatever's happening behind my barn? I spotted the string lights on my way inside. What're you playing at?" Hank narrowed his gaze.

I wanted to take Meg outside and show her I value her input. And her. Ryan unbuttoned the collar and resisted the urge to fan himself. The storage closet was stuffy. He'd add improve building ventilation to the project checklist. "Meg had an idea about expansion. Nothing's been decided. There is no conspiracy or attempted coup here. I'm developing the plan and determining feasibility. I would never move ahead without involving you."

"Oh. Meg?" Hank softened his hard stare. "Puts a different spin on it. Are you taking her outside? Showing her the view? Lots of stars tonight. Nice atmosphere."

I was... Ryan frowned. If, when, and how he acted, he wouldn't follow a dictate from his grandsire. On the flipside, however, following orders took off some of the weight of free will. He clenched his jaw. Back and forth uncertainty wasn't good for his stress levels. "I'd better get back out there."

"Good. You need to start dancing."

"Excuse me?" Ryan frowned.

"You heard me. Why did you invite a pretty girl to a dance if you're not going to twirl her around the floor?"

Ryan gaped. Did Hank have spies everywhere?

"Close your mouth, you look like a fish."

Ryan pinched the bridge of his nose. Getting into a fight with Hank served no purpose. "I don't know. She seems happy with him. Why should I interrupt?"

"You're not going to do anything? You're going to stand by and smile?"

Ryan squeezed his nose tighter, his vision clouding with spots.

"Boy, you need to act. Why have I gone to so much trouble? I never would have encouraged those two to spend time together if I had thought you'd continue to be so obtuse. I was hoping a little jealousy might force your hand. I was wrong. You're too stubborn for that." Hank snorted. "Why don't you admit what everyone else in town already knows?"

Ryan dropped his hands to his sides and stared. After their earlier fight, he'd spent the rest of his day setting up to impress her. Worried he'd lose her; he'd devoted hours to a showy task made the more frustrating because half the string lights were dead. He'd been played by his grandfather the whole time?

Hank exhaled a heavy sigh. "No more games. No more tricks. Just honesty. You two belong together."

"That's not true," Ryan murmured. "No one thinks of us as a couple. Eric has more in common with her. She's always smiling around him."

"Boy, you're a fool. Opposites attract." Hank reached out, dropping a hand on Ryan's shoulder, and squeezing. "Me and your grandma were all the proof you'd ever need for that. Go ask Meg for one dance, and I'll leave it. I've got my sights set on helping out the rest of your sad friends."

"Who? Ted?"

Hank shook his head. "Ted is a tough case. Widower. No, I'll get to him eventually. I'm taking care of all the easy-to-match folks first. Joe is next on my list. I've got someone in mind."

A laugh bubbled up Ryan's throat. With verbal confirmation of his troubling suspicions, he felt lighter than he had in a long time. Should he tell Hank to stay out of his business? Berate the old man for his meddlesome ways?

Ryan stepped forward and embraced his grandfather. If Ryan stopped fighting and took Hank's advice, what would he find? *Happiness*. He hugged the man tight. "Thanks."

Hank kissed his cheek. "Always." He stepped back, reversing to the entrance and tipped his head to the side.

With a nod, Ryan followed. He strode around the corner, pausing at the edge of the dance floor. On the platform, the band performed with vigor. Guests clapped and hollered, but the crowd remained seated. The empty pine planks looked lonely.

Hank was right, again. Ryan rubbed a hand along his slack-jaw. He shouldn't have been surprised, but he was. He continued on to his destination, weaving through the tables until he reached one in the corner. "Excuse me."

Two heads turned in his direction.

She looked at him with a steady, questioning stare.

He swallowed his discomfort. This was his chance. He extended his hand. "Meg, will you help me jumpstart the dancing?"

She stared at his hand.

The second stretched to eternity. Hank was wrong. Ryan shouldn't have done this. He shouldn't have invited her. He could back away and pretend no one saw. The table's prime position, however, ensured the opposite. He was on display for consumption and dissection of the entire town and all the guests.

She put her fingers in his and nodded.

He smiled and helped her to her feet. Once clear of the tables, he lifted his arm and spun her in a circle. Her dress fanned out.

When she returned to her starting position, her gaze widened, and she laughed. "Aren't you the guy who absolutely swore you'd never dance with me *in public again*?"

He lifted a shoulder. She was right. When he wanted to make a grand gesture, he found her steel-trap memory an inconvenience. For the gift of a long relationship, however, he'd pay the small price of having no secrets. "As long as you don't start to shuffle off to Buffalo in the middle of the two-step..."

Knitting her brow, she wrinkled her nose.

He grinned. "Seems a shame to waste such a pretty dress seated behind a table all night." He grabbed her other hand and lifted both, twirling her in the opposite direction.

"It's one of my grandma's. I was happy to have a reason to wear it. I'm not wearing my tap shoes tonight. You're safe from my spontaneous choreography." She bit her lip. "Thank you for inviting me. I didn't get a chance to say hi."

"Are you having a good time?" He reached for her waist and spun around with her, whirling across the floor. With a glance over her head, he nearly sighed.

The couple celebrating their anniversary joined in. As did a young family. Several other tables were getting to their feet and participating in the contagious good spirit.

"I am." She spun back into his arms. "I want to disclose, Eric invited me, too."

"Oh?" He arched a brow. Any other reaction wasn't appropriate. He'd taken too long to realize what she meant to him. He'd had nearly four decades. He couldn't be mad a smarter man wouldn't make the same mistake.

"He offered me a job. I think he wanted another chance to present his case before he leaves in the morning."

"And?"

She held his gaze. "I'm right where I belong." Her smile was soft and sweet. "Herd is my hometown. I'm not leaving."

My place is here with you. Under his palms, he felt her shudder. Was this the moment for truth? Was she staying only for the town? Or was he included in her list of reasons? "Not sure if you caught a glimpse on your way in, but I marked out the proposed deck with spray paint in the corners. I strung up some lights in case you wanted to see."

"You're going forward with it?"

He adjusted his hand on her waist, liking the delight in her response and the feel of her in his arms. If he could keep his grip, he had the illusion of control. "I'm considering it. If I did, I'd need your advice to optimize appeal."

She blushed. "I'm sure I'm not the person to ask."

"You had the initial idea. You see the world differently. You make me ask questions." *You challenge me in the best way possible.* He couldn't tell her how much she scared him. Every encounter left him a little shaken, but he wanted more. If he invited her outside, what would happen?

First and foremost, he had to focus on keeping her in Herd. With enough time, he'd sort through the emotions and fears blocking his way. "I can help with your online platform."

She frowned, scrunching her nose.

Had he overstepped? "We talked about it?"

The day she had smiled and his heart had started beating for the first time in recent memory. She didn't remember? He'd never forget. They'd been standing on her old property talking about weddings. She had looked so beautiful and fragile. A fully formed picture of her in a veil with a sweet grin popped into his mind.

She continued to stare, tilting her head to the side, gliding across the floor with him.

No pressure. "I wasn't sure if you needed any assistance. You've been so generous with your time, clearing out the shed. We owe you." *I owe you.* Why was speaking honestly so hard? He'd known her forever. She must see his struggle. But he didn't want her to give him a way out or to ease away from the difficult part. Until recently, he'd never seen her.

"I was kind of hoping you'd ask me for my than advice," she murmured.

She did? What question did she want him to ask?

She cleared her throat. "Should we discuss plans for Hank's birthday?"

He nodded. "I'm not sure about this year. I don't want to do too much and overtime him. The shed has been taxing." He adjusted his grip on her waist. Under his palm, she was slight and small. He never thought of her as less than a tornado, but she was a woman underneath it all. "If I make any plans, I'll let you know." He lifted his arm and spun her again.

Her dress fluttered around her.

When she returned to his embrace, she frowned for a second. Then she wiped the look off her face like she'd never had a second of hesitation.

Back to business as usual? He hoped so. Why did he feel like he'd dodged a bullet and missed his shot? How many other bad clichés would attack him?

He darted a glance at the doors leading outside. Stringing the lights had been a lot of work. He'd cursed under his breath more than once in the process. What would she think of his handiwork? Would she have ideas for improvement?

He had a niggling sensation he should ask her to join him at the ranch as the lead of the new events department. No one would do the job better or bring more creativity to the role. But then she'd be his employee. A romance would definitely be off the table if she was his subordinate.

Maybe that was for the best. Same with avoiding the proposed deck. Before their dance, he hadn't thought through all the repercussions of leading her to such a cozy, almost intimate spot. It would look like he wanted more than friendship.

If she wasn't going anywhere, she didn't challenge him to change his stance and tell her the truth of his feelings for her. Maybe she didn't want him to. Maybe it wasn't just his foolishness separating them but her clarity that they'd be a disaster. He'd have to follow her lead. He could always count on her to be upfront and honest. Come what may.

CHAPTER 13

On her front porch the next morning, Meg blew across the top of her coffee and snuggled under the afghan Grandma and Susie Kincaid had crocheted decades earlier. The chill lingered from last night's after midnight rainstorm. She'd been home and tucked in bed long before the first drops fell. She should have been asleep.

Instead, she'd tossed and turned. At four am, she gave up on sleep and came outside. The damp morning air refreshed her tired eyes, and, once she'd gone back inside and brewed it, the coffee added a jolt to her system. After two hours of woolgathering, she needed to get ready to head to her store. She couldn't seem to give up the comfort of sitting on a wicker armchair, drinking a hot beverage (her fourth), and tracing the spirals in the hand-made blanket.

She still didn't know what to make of Ryan.

Last night, he had shocked her speechless.

He had approached the table as Eric had relayed a funny story about a recent sale at the auction house. With his eyes shining, Ryan had extended a hand and asked her to dance. Sure, he'd invited her to the dinner, and dancing was part of the evening's festivities, but his request surprised and confused her all the same. When she couldn't catch his gaze for a wave hello, she had contented herself that she misunderstood the intention of his invitation.

On the dance floor, Ryan had twirled her with a deft hand. He'd moved quick and light. The cowboy had a prowess for dance. She liked spinning with him. As he held her tight, her stomach fluttered and her limbs felt fizzy, like her blood was pure champagne. But she hadn't wanted to be anywhere else. In his arms, she was content and safe.

At the first chance, she explained her behavior. If she'd been thinking correctly when he asked, she would have told him on the spot she had already been asked to attend by Eric. She'd been so blown away by Ryan's request that she imagined he had asked her on a proper date. Of course, she'd been wrong to assume. When she had discussed her plans to stay, she'd been hit with disappointment.

He had no response? He wasn't glad? His face turned to unflinching stone and his gaze darkened. She had tensed in his arms but shook it off. She couldn't be mad at him.

Only herself. He had offered his help like always. While she appreciated the gesture, she couldn't help but wonder if she was simply another burden. His delivery was automatic, and his tone was emotionless.

And then she'd almost asked him if she could work for the ranch with the events department.

She took a final sip of her coffee, the rich roast clearing out the sour taste in her mouth at her mishandling of everything. Setting the mug on the ground, she reached into her pocket for her cell phone. She had no messages or missed calls. While she hadn't expected any, she'd hoped for a valid distraction. She dialed home.

The phone rang and rang.

"Please pick up," she murmured. She wanted a break from her thoughts with a third party unaware of current events.

She couldn't fight the worry that she'd screwed up. Not just about not telling Ryan she had another invitation last night or not seeking him out and greeting him when she arrived. She couldn't shake the gut-clenching certainty that she'd officially brushed off any chance for more to develop between them.

With his hand on her waist, he'd looked into her eyes, and her legs had turned to jelly. She didn't know what came next. And she'd been terrified. What if her feelings weren't reciprocated? Backed into a position of vulnerability, she had given them both an out. She volunteered information instead of making him ask directly. Would they slip back into their old ways? She couldn't go back.

Adjusting on the chair, she tucked the blanket under her legs and held the phone against her ear. It was a Tuesday. Mom had a few more weeks of teaching before her school year ended. But she should be free for a quick phone call before the bell rang in thirty minutes.

The call connected.

"Hello? Meggie?" Mom said.

"Hi, Mom." She exhaled a heavy sigh.

"Sweetie, are you okay? You sound a little off."

Meg scrunched her nose against the tickle in her nostrils. "I'm a little tired. I've been selling a lot at the store. Tons of customers. I'm heading in soon and will be there until late."

"Really? Oh, that's such great news. What happened with the photos? Did the expert leave?"

"He leaves today. He thinks the signatures are real and plans to include the entire collection in the September auction."

"Wow. How wonderful for Hank. Are you blogging about it?"

Meg frowned. She wasn't sure if she should. "I don't think so, Mom." How could she extricate herself from the photographs and souvenirs? The project spurred her toward change, and she couldn't untangle her journey from the discovery. "The expert offered me a job in San Francisco."

"Oh, are you considering it?"

"No. I want to stick around Herd. I'm more determined than ever to get the website going. We still have half the shed to clear out. We might find items for consignment."

"I'm glad you're staying. Did Hank try to get you to sell the photographs yourself?"

Meg smiled. "You know I'd never let him. I can't watch him miss such an important opportunity."

"Your honest, caring heart might be what I love the most about you."

Does Ryan love something about me? Meg hated that she cared.

A red sedan drove down the country lane and turned into the driveway.

"Mom, I think I have a visitor. I'd better let you go."

"Of course, bye, sweetie. I love you."

"Love you too." Frowning, she ended the call and shook off the blanket. She slid the phone into her back pocket. Just in case. She'd never had an unexpected guest. Nor had she ever struggled with the uneasy concern she was too far away from help if she needed it. She got to her feet, shading her gaze with a hand.

The driver's side door opened. Eric exited the car, waving.

She sagged her shoulders.

He shut the door and strode across the gravel. "Hope you don't mind that I dropped by. I remembered you said you lived next-door. It took a little bit of driving, but I figured out what that meant."

She stifled a laugh. Next-door was fifteen miles from the ranch house. "Of course, I don't mind." She strode down the steps. "Can I get you a cup of coffee?"

"No, thank you. I'm headed to the airport. Thought I'd say goodbye and try that job offer once more in person."

She stopped a few feet away. Eric was nice. More than once, she had caught herself sharing in his contagious grins. He shared a love of history and asked questions, eager to listen to the answers. She hated to disappoint him, but she owed herself a chance at her dream. She drew in a deep breath.

He held up a hand. "I get it. You don't owe me another explanation. I've pushed too much. If anything changes, you have my card."

Was he speaking purely in a professional capacity? Or something more? Her answer remained the same. She couldn't force herself to change her feelings into something more convenient. If she had any power of persuasion, she'd utilize her skills to get Ryan to call.

"Goodbye, Meg. I'll be in touch. Maybe you can bring Hank to the sale."

She smiled. "Have a safe trip home."

He nodded and retreated to his car.

She crossed the lawn to Colby, sunning her belly on the damp grass and unconcerned about their visitor. Meg sat on the ground, extending her feet in front of her and holding onto the dog. The red sedan backed out of the drive and turned onto the road, heading toward town.

In her pocket, her phone vibrated. Dropping her hold on Colby, she swiped her finger over the screen and raised the device to her ear. In the bright sunshine, she couldn't read the name on the screen. "Hello? This is Meg."

"Meg? It's Hank. Listen, can you stop by the shed today?"

She scrunched her face. She hated to tell him *no*. While Memorial Day—yesterday—was the unofficial start of summer, tourists didn't descend for another week, after many schools finished for the year. If the past week was any indication, she would be a few very busy months. *With any luck.* But she'd closed the store early too many days lately to take another one off.

"You still there, Meg? Meg?"

"Hi, Hank. Sorry." She heaved a sigh. "I'm not sure if I can make it until later in the week."

"This doesn't have anything to do with the fella leaving?"

"No, of course not," she said without a breath.

"Maybe you don't want to stop by because you're afraid about running into someone else?"

She nibbled her lip. Lying to Hank was impossible. "I had a long day followed by a late night. I'm tired."

"When can you stop by?"

The weekend? She couldn't do that to a friend. "Later? I might have a spare moment after the lunch rush and before the dinner crowd. Downtown has a lull around four. No promises. But if I have time, can I swing by for a quick visit then?"

"Alright. I'll wait 'til then. Last night was a lot of fun. It was good to see you dance."

It had felt good. When she had entered the barn, she'd vowed to enjoy herself. For a short while, she'd shrugged off her worries and had fun. Then, she'd screwed everything up with Ryan. Maybe she saved herself a lot of heartache. She couldn't be mad at him for setting boundaries. Doing so was healthy and an exercise in protection.

She'd do better to learn from his example than rail against him. Starting now, she'd respect the distance between her house and the ranch. "I'll see you later. Bye, Hank."

CHAPTER 14

Ryan ripped the sheets off the mattress, balling up the bedding and tossing it on the floor. He wasn't usually so quick to housekeeping. Changing linen and cleaning toilets wasn't his favorite task. Today, he made an exception.

Once the guest checked out of the yurt, he wasted no time turning over the room. A last-minute booking scheduled for tomorrow meant Eric couldn't extend his stay. If Ryan stayed busy with the cleaning, he avoided confronting Meg with the inevitable frank conversation.

He shook the pillows out of the cases. He had been tricked by the feel of her in his arms. She was strong and small at the same time. Her skin had been softer than the worn quilt at the foot of his bed. He had liked holding her. Hank was spot-on to push them together. His heart had jumped into his throat, and he had opened his mouth to speak.

Then she had told him nothing would change.

She wanted to remain status quo? He had spun her through the rest of the song. He did his best to move and operate like a normal person. By the end, the dance floor had been packed.

Ted had approached him with a problem.

Eric had strode onto the floor, heading straight to her.

Ryan had left, and she didn't stop him. He had spent the rest of the night on his normal tasks of cleaning up and helping guests. In the chaos, he had lost track of her.

He had stayed at the barn until late into the night, sweeping, mopping, and thinking. After everyone had left, he strode around the back and unplugged the lights. A light rain had started, preventing him from lingering at the site.

He loved Hank. The meddling cowboy wasn't infallible. He was an opinionated rascal with too much time on his hands.

Ryan twisted the sheets around his hands, wringing the cotton. More than anyone, he blamed himself. He listened to Hank when he should focus on work. How could he take on one more problem? As much as Hank might argue otherwise, he couldn't deny what Ryan witnessed with his own eyes.

While it lasted, love was great. Once it was gone, the loss was devastating. Grandma's passing nearly killed Hank. If the worst had happened, and his grandfather succumbed to his broken heart, where would Ryan have been? Struggling with a business he couldn't handle on his own. How long could he have lasted?

Luckily, Meg figured out she needed to draw a line between them and stated her decision. Before he let his guard down and put himself out there for her rejection, he knew the truth. He had walked away unscathed, unlike the torn apart yurt.

"What happened in here?"

He turned toward the door.

Ted strolled in, frowning. "Did that city guy leave it like this? Should we run up a charge for extra housekeeping?"

"I'm cleaning." Ryan bent and grabbed the bedding off the ground.

"Oh, that's what you're doing?" Ted scrubbed a hand over his face. "I wanted to ask about the bison. Any more word?"

"Oh, right." Tightening his grip on the bundle in his arms, Ryan rocked back to his heels. "I have to follow up with the town council. I forgot."

"Not like you. Any particular reason why?"

None that I care to discuss. Ryan never backed down from a confrontation, but he had no good reason for his distraction lately. Hank might argue the point. "Nothing out of the ordinary. First week is always an adjustment. I owe the mayor another call."

"You've been busy." Ted grabbed the bundle from his arms. "Let's leave the rest for the professional crew."

Ryan rolled his eyes but didn't correct his ranch hand. The cleaning crew was scheduled to stop by in an hour. He'd barely finish dusting at that point. He knew his skill set. While he could manage the house at his own pace, he didn't have enough time for the guest rooms. "Fine. Go out, and I can lock up."

Ted left.

Ryan scanned the room once more. The circular space felt expansive and welcoming. With a slim bathroom and closet set in the outer band, the inner sanctum focused on a comfy bed. What more could a guest need? *A companion.*

He shook his head, flipped off the lights, and locked the room. He jogged to the gator. Ted had dropped the linens into a basket on the back of the vehicle.

Ryan secured the basket with bungee cords, looping over the handles to create an x and prevent the sheets and towels from escaping. Chasing after bedding as it blew across his land wasn't how he wanted to spend his day.

With his luck, the sheets would blow into her yard, and he'd have to head there. Was she home? Would she want to chat? She made a concerted effort to explain she wouldn't be stopping by all week. What if she turned him away?

Ted secured the last cord. "Are you heading back to the house?"

Ryan shook his head. "Opposite direction. I figured I'd follow Joe."

"Why? You don't trust him?" Ted crossed his arms over his chest.

"Of course, I trust him." Ryan scrubbed a hand over his face. "Don't start now."

"Guess I'm not sure who I'm dealing with some days."

Ryan frowned. "And that means?"

Ted shrugged. "Nothing. I've got to head back to the barn. Repairs on the outdoor lights. I'm on the radio if you need me."

Ryan nodded.

The ranch hand headed toward a pickup parked on the dirt road past the three yurts.

Had Hank put Ted up to the controversial remark? Ryan didn't have time for nonsense today. He'd focus on work, redoubling his efforts where he was wanted and needed. He'd avoid drama.

Climbing into the gator, he drove toward the cabins. Joe scheduled a group of first-timers fishing at the pond. Ted was right to question why Ryan would micromanage the seasoned adventure guide on a basic outing.

Because he'd take any excuse for space. The wind whistled past as he sped along on the gravel road. He knew the blind spots of every dip in the narrow one-lane road. He'd rather not deal with a head-on collision with one of his guests. An accident would be too much distraction from his everyday duties.

He reached the top of the last hill and cruised down the slope toward the cabins. In front of number five, third from the right corner, he spotted the Claytons at the trunk of their beige, mid-sized sedan. Ryan slowed his vehicle and stopped off the road. "Good morning." He called and hopped out of the vehicle.

"Hello, Ryan," Marcia said. "I've got to run inside." She pointed at the cabin and bolted.

Ryan smiled and approached the trunk. "Are you checking out today? Need any help?"

Ford lifted a suitcase off the ground and dropped it in the trunk. He exhaled. "We are heading home. I've got the packing under control." He shifted the suitcase into position next to several others and slammed the trunk. Dusting his hands on his jeans, he extended a palm. "Wanted to thank you for a memorable trip. Marcia doesn't want to leave."

Ryan shook the man's hand. "Glad to hear it. You'll definitely want to return next year. The property will have some major changes on your next visit."

Ford dropped his hand. "Really? Anything to do with your dance partner?"

Was Ryan that obvious? He nearly gaped as his throat swelled shut.

"Sorry, I shouldn't have overstepped. I wasn't the one who made the observation. After Marcia pointed it out, though, I couldn't shake it."

Ryan coughed. This was the most uncomfortable encounter he'd ever had with a guest. Meeting up on the trail ride, he'd nearly growled at Eric. Somehow this exchange topped that moment. "Pointed out what?"

"Well, you and the young lady had a very opposites-attract vibe. You couldn't keep your eyes off each other. Reminded Marcia of us."

"Meg is my neighbor. I've known her forever." Ryan said the words by rote. His brain processed the action of his speech, but he no longer connected with the sentiment. She meant a lot to him. He had to accept the feelings might not be mutual. Why else would she push him away at the exact moment he wanted to bare his heart?

"In that case." Ford wiggled his brows. "Maybe you're even more like us than we realized. Marcia and I were next-door neighbors. She was my best friend's kid sister. She followed us everywhere and drove us crazy with her incessant talking. She ratted us out to her parents more often than not." He sniggered.

Ryan nodded. As kids, when Meg wasn't involving him in trouble, she was setting him up to take the fall. The corner of his mouth lifted. Her heavy-handed attempts were pretty funny now. At the time, he didn't appreciate the little girl with the chocolate covered face blaming him for eating all the cookies. Or how Hank's scowl slipped at the obvious lie. "What changed?"

"I went off to college and got a good job. I came home for the holidays but never stayed. I didn't realize she was avoiding me, too. While she was the annoying kid, she had a crush on me and tried to spend time together whenever she could. When my best friend got sick, I came home. I finally saw what was there the whole time. How funny and smart and amazing she is, and how much she lights up my life. I wasn't smart enough to hold onto her then. I almost lost her. We broke up for a few months. She found someone else." Ford lifted a hand and snapped his fingers in mid-air. "Like that. She'd be fine without me. I can't live without her. Don't be like me. Don't wait for a life-or-death scenario to spur you. I saw you two dancing. Don't miss your chance."

What if I already have? How could he trust his heart when his brain so clearly told him to slam on the brakes? He wasn't the type to ignore someone else's feelings. Last night, he'd decided against honesty by not showing her the deck. Had he let them both down?

"I have to thank you. Our trip has been our most memorable vacation."

"I'm glad. You'll have to try a yurt next year."

Ford grinned. "Marcia is ready to book now."

Rusty hinges squealed, and a screen door slammed shut, snapping into the metal frame.

Ryan glanced up.

Marcia strode toward the car, stopping a few feet away. "Ah. Much better. Thank you for a lovely trip, Ryan. I'll have to try my luck gold panning again next year."

Ford rolled his eyes. "Not me. Thanks again." He strode around the car and hopped in behind the wheel.

Marcia leaned forward. "Did he speak to you?"

Ryan nodded.

"Good." She flashed a self-satisfied smile, striding to the passenger side.

Ryan stepped back and waved as the Claytons drove off. They were right. He didn't want to wait for the worst to happen to spur him to change. If Meg didn't feel the same as he did, what happened next? She'd always been there. What if she was gone? Or what if she remained? Would his heart break a little more with each hello?

He needed time. A couple days to get his work in order. He'd dropped the ball on his bison project and needed to follow up with the mayor and town council about setting up some meetings.

He had another new round of tourists to settle in. He could wait until later to discuss his feelings. It wasn't life or death.

CHAPTER 15

L ounging around the house got old, fast. Meg finished the laundry, cleaned the bathrooms, and started supper in the slow cooker before noon. If she stayed home much longer, she'd launch a full-scale renovation. Adding to her physical exhaustion did nothing to alleviate her emotional strain. She couldn't avoid Ryan forever.

By one o'clock, she stalled long enough. She loaded Colby in the little white SUV and headed to the ranch. The front of the house was quiet. Ryan's pickup was gone. She exhaled a heavy sigh. She wasn't a coward. She wouldn't be afraid to face someone because a situation hadn't worked in her favor.

Hopping to the ground, she followed the dog around the house to the shed.

The door was open. The interior was dimly lit.

With a woof, the dog brushed past and raced inside.

Stepping over the threshold, Meg scanned the nearly emptied interior. Without boxes stacked to the ceiling, the building didn't have the claustrophobic atmosphere she'd first encountered.

Hank continued to make progress without her. Her heart squeezed. Had she disappointed him? Had he overexerted himself?

"Hi, Meg. Thanks for coming," Hank said, his voice carrying from the back.

She strode forward.

Hank sat with his back against a wall.

Colby laid on the floor at his feet.

Twisting her neck, Meg surveyed the room. Without stacks of cardboard, she glimpsed the uninsulated plank walls. A few knots had dried and fallen out of the wood. Crumpled up newspaper filled the holes, duct tape securing the make-do patches in silver crosses. With the unconventional patches, the exposed-to-the-elements building would be unbearably icy in the winter. Could the building be repaired and insulated?

She shivered. "You're almost finished. I can't believe it."

"I'm motivated." He pointed to one side of the room. "Only that stack left to go through." He sighed and met her gaze. "I'm sorry to tell you I haven't found anything else of interest. It was boxes of broken knick-knacks and old paperwork."

She nibbled her lip. She wished he'd waited. One man's trash could most definitely be another's treasure.

"You're disappointed. I promise we aren't talking anything older than the nineteen eighties." He crossed a finger over his heart. "On my honor. I wanted to finish, and Ted helped load the truck since he needs to run an errand in Miles City. It was all donation. We might hit pay dirt in that stack."

She nodded and pulled up a chair at the table. "I'm happy to help finish."

"Good." He smiled. "I remember boxes of old, hardcover books. Some are leather-bound." He wrinkled his brow. "I'm not sure how those will fare at an antique store."

She straightened. Maybe she hadn't missed a chance after all. "Actually, I'm starting an online store front, too. Books can definitely spark interest from the right crowd."

"I'm not talking first editions here."

She shook her head. "You don't need to. A lot of books are purchased for their looks. Designers use them to decorate shelves in high-end homes."

He chuckled. "We were happy to have something to read. Never cared what the spines looked like. I probably have some of Susie's paperbacks, too. Early in my marriage, I boxed up most of my books in our library to accommodate hers. She needed space for all her romance books. Some boxes of paperbacks are here somewhere."

"Romance books will definitely fly off the shelves inside my store." Meg grinned.

"Some summers, we had our power knocked out by storms once a week. She used to read to me."

Meg propped her elbows on the table, resting her chin in her palms. She couldn't dream of a better way to spend a rainy afternoon. During her childhood, she remembered a handful of such nights. Her summer days were filled with reading as much as she could. "I remember. On a few rainy days, she read to me, too. Susie had a great voice. I loved her accents."

"She was happy to have such a captive audience. What did she read?"

"*Anne of Green Gables* and all the books that followed. She gave Marilla a raspy voice." Meg smiled. "What did she read to you?"

"Her romance books. Everything from Jane Austen to Danielle Steele."

Reminiscing, Meg didn't feel the ache of missing one of the most important people in her life. More than a neighbor, Susie Kincaid poured love into everyone she cared about. Meg warmed at the shared memories. She and Hank hadn't spoken of his wife since her funeral. Why the change? Meg straightened. "Is missing Susie the reason for cleaning the shed?"

He shook his head. "Trying to get you to sort out your feelings for my grandson is the impetus."

She dropped her jaw. Over the years, she'd had her suspicions. Convincing herself she was mistaken; she'd shoved aside her concerns every time Ryan appeared instead of Hank. She never imagined confronting Hank or that he'd so readily admit to his matchmaking.

"I've seen how you look at him." Hank leaned back in his chair. "Just like me and Susie. You're so confused at his silence and overwhelmed by his speech."

Her skin burned.

Hank chuckled and bent, scratching Colby behind the ears. "Getting to spend time with this little lady and helping your business is the icing on the cake."

Meg coughed. "Am I so obvious?"

"Only to a trained eye." Hank winked. "You've got to make him see sense, or he will never be honest."

She frowned. "With me?"

"No, worse. With himself. You've always been his conscience."

She wasn't sure she agreed with the assessment. For as long as she could, she had happily lurked in status quo as Ryan's frenemy. Progress couldn't be held back indefinitely. Herd and the community were changing. Did she have a role in town? Or worse, could she only stay if she was connected to the Kincaids?

She had plenty of reasons not to ask hard questions. She couldn't put off what she knew was true, but she needed a plan. "Let's finish things up. You have the makings of a nice man-cave here."

"You can change the subject, because I know you'll take my words to heart." He sat back. "I'll admit to you, because it's going no further, I'm a little stiff today. Do you mind bringing the boxes to me?"

She smiled. Admitting weakness wasn't standard protocol for the cowboy. She appreciated his confidence in her and owed him the same in reverse. "Of course, I don't mind."

One at a time, she carried the boxes over for Hank's inspection. At his direction, she divided the piles into donate, sell, and throw away. By the end of the hour, she acquired a tidy stack of boxes full of vintage romance novels and old hardcover books. She started trekking the pile around the house from shed to SUV and back again.

She should have parked closer. The parking lot at the barn was empty and half the distance to the shed. But she didn't want to potentially sneak up on Ryan. Her parking spot on the circle drive in front of the house would alert him to her presence.

On her fifth trip, she paused to help Hank into the house.

The shed felt like a never-ending project, like excavating London with centuries of history layered on top of each other. Hank promised to leave the haul-away to Ted and to wait on the final boxes until she had time later in the week. She hated noticing how he slowed down but couldn't ignore worrisome signs that the stubborn man had overtaxed him in recent weeks. While she believed his confession of matchmaking was truthful, she didn't think that summed up his entire purpose in the endeavor.

On her final trip, she whistled to Colby and set the box down outside the shed, shutting the door. She rolled her shoulders and her neck, her upper back aching from a day of manual labor. Bending, she groaned as she grabbed the box. Why had she saved the heaviest for last?

Colby woofed.

Frowning, Meg followed the dog's gaze, pointing toward the barn.

Ryan stood in the doorway of the big, red building. His hat shaded his face. She couldn't be sure he was looking at her. Tiny hairs stood on end on her skin. She felt his gaze. She couldn't move or speak, her throat closing. She wanted to shout. Her heart skipped a beat as she willed her heavy limbs into locomotion.

What would she say? *I think we're a match. Hank agrees. I might not stay. Maybe I should leave?* She hated the ultimatum implication. Staying was about more than him, but she was honest enough for the admission leaving wouldn't be. She could fight her feelings for only so long.

He lifted his head, changing the angle.

Meeting his gaze, she smiled.

He turned away, striding back inside the barn.

Hank was wrong. She was a fool who talked herself into a fantasy. She was Ryan's neighbor and sometime burden. Every exchange had been heightened by her overactive imagination.

121

"Come on, Colby. Let's get to the store," she murmured.

The dog spun around and raced to the SUV.

Meg followed at her own pace weighed by the heavy burden of disappointment. She'd let down herself more than anyone. Any effort on his part must have been fueled by pity. She didn't need to come back and subject herself to that again. She'd stay in town, or on her property, for as long as she could.

CHAPTER 16

"Welcome to Finders-Keepers," Meg greeted an older couple entering her store less than thirty minutes later.

The woman lifted her gaze and smiled. "Good afternoon." She turned to her companion and handed him her purse.

With a sigh, the man kissed her on the cheek and walked to the wall kitty-corner the front window, and leaned against it.

The woman hustled toward the front counter. "I promised I wouldn't take too long." She tilted her head to her companion. "He's been a good sport for a long lunch at the saloon and a costumed photo session. I've delayed our departure long enough. I'll come out and ask."

The no-nonsense manner raised her hackles. Was Meg being put on the spot or her merchandise?

"Do you have any ice cream molds?"

Releasing the pent-up breath, Meg dropped her shoulders and rounded the counter. "Yes, ma'am. Right this way." She strode toward an Eastlake vitrine and opened the center doors, stepping back, to reveal two glass shelves of pewter ice cream molds. From flowers to animals to holiday emblems, she loved the whimsical shapes. Popularized in the U.S. around the turn of the twentieth century, the molds hinted at the luxury of the upper classes. To have the ingredients, refrigeration, and time to produce and shape ice cream suggested above average means. Her family never had any. The Kincaids owned several.

"What is that?" The woman pointed at one on the top shelf.

Carefully reaching inside, Meg grinned and grabbed the most talked about item she'd ever listed for sale. She wasn't sure she could post it for sale online without having the listing flagged for indecency. Opening her palm, she rested the five-inch object in the center. "What do you think it is?"

"A topless, pregnant woman's torso," the woman replied.

Meg shook her head and opened the mold. "I did too, until I tested it. This makes a Thanksgiving turkey."

The woman chuckled. "Oh, I have to get that. I have every other holiday in my collection."

Meg extended the mold. "How many George Washington busts?"

"Too many."

Meg smiled. In her excursions for inventory, she came across many commemorative molds of the first president.

The woman closed her fist around the turkey breast. "I haven't been surprised in a long time. Before the internet, I had a lot more fun discovering different pieces."

Meg nodded. "My mom says the same. She used to visit flea markets and estate sales for Depression glass. Once stores started posting their goods on websites and online auctions, it changed the dynamics. But..." She pressed together her lips.

"What?" The woman tipped her head to the side. "Is something wrong?"

"I suppose you'll think I'm a hypocrite. I am in the process of opening an online store myself."

The woman grinned. "Then I'll look forward to checking in on your site every so often." She held up her hand. "This piece is perfect. A unique souvenir from a special vacation. We stayed on the outskirts of town."

"Oh, you were guests at the ranch?" She inflected a hint of surprise, like the Kincaid ranch wasn't the only lodging within forty miles for out of towners.

"Yes. We had a marvelous time. I can only imagine what you might find on that property."

The stranger had no idea. In the last few weeks, Meg discovered valuable objects and painful truths. She wouldn't trouble the customer with either.

"Where did you find this? I haven't seen one like it."

"I picked it out of a box at a garage sale in Chicago. I was visiting my mom and dragged her along one Saturday."

"Chicago?" The woman whistled. "That's a long way from Montana. What made you leave a big city? Did you grow up here?"

Meg shook her head. "No, ma'am. My mother did. I spent summers here as a child. My family owned the Hawke ranch, next door to the Kincaid's place."

"I'm sure you must have had a lot of family heirlooms, too." The woman turned toward her companion, raising on tiptoe. "Ford, I need my wallet. See? Record time."

Ford pushed off the wall.

Meg hustled behind the counter and rang up the mold, accepting and swiping the extended credit card before handing it back with the receipt. She grabbed a stack of tissue paper, setting it on the glass.

The woman placed the mold in the center.

"What is *that*?" Ford asked.

Meg suppressed a smirk at the incredulous tone and wrapped the mold. She grabbed a paper bag emblazoned with the Finders-Keepers logo and placed the mold inside.

"Get your head out of the gutter, dear. It's a turkey." The woman grabbed the bag by the handles and pressed it into his chest. "I'll meet you outside."

Ford shrugged and tipped his head toward Meg.

"Can I help you with anything else?" Meg asked.

"Do you have a mailing list? Any way I can follow your store before your website is up? I'll be back to visit Ryan next summer of course."

The guest was on a first-name basis at the ranch? Meg grabbed a card from the holder next to the register.

"I think I saw you dancing at the barn last night."

Meg couldn't escape from public view at her store? Was her house the only remaining refuge? She wasn't sure where the bossy stranger would direct the conversation. She wanted it to stop here. She flipped over the business card and jotted down the website address she'd secured in pencil on the smooth back, extending it with a tight smile.

"You make a nice pair." The woman grabbed the card. "Good bye, and thank you again." Without a backward glance, the customers left.

The overhead bell jingled as the door opened and shut.

A loud yawn echoed in the silent room.

Meg stared at her dog.

Stretching, Colby got to her feet and pressed against Meg's thigh.

Absentmindedly, Meg stroked the dog's head. If she couldn't escape her feelings at her store, how would she find peace in Herd? She had an inkling but wasn't ready. Because once she laid her heart at his feet, he'd either trample it or embrace her.

She wasn't sure which scared her more.

Instead, she reached into her purse and pulled out her laptop. Powering on the device, she clicked on her blog and hit compose on a new post. She stared at the blinking cursor against the bright, white digital background.

If she penned her letter to the town, poured her hopes and fears into a searchable document, she wouldn't be able to shy away from the problem. "I can't hide from myself."

Colby woofed.

With a smile at her dog, Meg rolled her heavy head and focused on the screen. Lifting her fingers to the keyboard, she dashed her hands across the keys, the rapid clicking not quite keeping pace with her thoughts.

"History is messy, and small-town living is complicated.

"Herd isn't uniquely immune to real-world problems. Perhaps, to visitors, we are a picture-perfect Old West town trapped in time. Locals and transplants, however, know we chose this place and reaffirm our commitment to it every day.

"Not every mistake can be fixed. I'm starting to think that's the point. We can't unsay hurtful things yelled in ignorance, but we can strive to do better. I'm not sure how many people actually read this blog besides my mother and my favorite cowboy. If you are a regular visitor here, you're used to getting stories of some of the unique objects I sell in my store. This post is different.

"Recently, I've learned some history about our town that is hard to process. Full details are not my story to tell, but I can share the following. Under the tourist friendly image is a legacy of loss and betrayal. During the early years, neighbors treated each other with a cutthroat ruthlessness and did the same to the greater landscape.

"Today, our Herd is a kinder place, and we are blessed to live during easier times. The town wouldn't exist without the founders, but reconciling their actions for our positive outcome is difficult. As the last Hawke in town, my presence has never been questioned. I have struggled to fit into the community.

"I have doubts about how I connect. Am I here because of name alone? I've loved this place from my earliest memories and am grateful for the ability to try to build a life for myself here. I strive to do my best to honor the people who came before and the promise of those to follow.

"Herd was founded for a new chance. Under the greed and pain, the initial premise was good. I want to carry that spirit into the future. One person is presenting the community as a whole with an opportunity to pay retribution. It's not my place to tell. When the news comes out, I hope you'll listen. I want us all to lean into everything that makes us great as we repair past hurts."

Colby snored and swatted the ground with her paws, scratching the pine floor.

Meg hit publish, closed the laptop, and returned the computer to her purse. If she determined to be brave, she couldn't back down from her words now. Of course, she had no guarantee the person she wanted to read the words would. "I have hope," she murmured.

Ryan spent the remainder of his day in a rush. From one request to another emergency, he stumbled into the busy pattern of his normal life. He usually liked it.

Guests had questions, comments, and concerns. He was the ultimate authority on the land. Some might find the process too cyclical with the constant turnover of the rooms. Not him. He'd rather have work than endless time on his hands. This was one of the reasons why he started the enterprise.

He locked up the barn and headed toward the shed. After ripping apart the yurt, he almost banished thoughts of the historical expert from his mind. He couldn't shake Meg.

She said she wouldn't leave but that didn't mean her life wouldn't change. She was alone. If he didn't have Hank, he would be, too. He couldn't bear it any more than he could watching her with someone else. He was jealous and foolish.

He cut through the yard, close to where she had been earlier. When she had turned, the sunlight had dappled on her profile and shimmered on her copper strands. She had waited. For a declaration? He had had no idea what came next. Like a coward, he had escaped.

Sniggering, he shook his head. The truth was always a sound starting point. He needed more time. If he could secure the ranch's future, he'd focus on personal matters. He sniffed and caught a phantom hint of her lavender scent on the breeze. He was right to put distance between them.

He had his life, and she had hers. Besides Hank, they had no reason to interact. He opened the shed door and squinted in the dark interior. The building was nearly empty. He sighed and kicked a box left on the ground. She'd written donate on the cardboard in loopy letters.

He rolled his eyes. She always had to be noticed. *Not fair. I can't help but stop everything and watch her.*

"Hey," a voice called.

With a jerk, he twisted around and pinched a nerve in his lower back.

Ted frowned. "Sorry, should have knocked. You okay?"

Ryan winced, rubbing a hand on his back. "How can I help?"

"I'm finishing for the day. Wanted to give you a heads up. I'll take those boxes into town tomorrow. Then the project is done. Just in time for Hank's birthday. Who would have thought?" Ted shook his head.

Definitely not me. Ryan couldn't shake the ominous feeling. He was missing something important.

Hank wouldn't have cleaned up without a purpose. What was it? Really just match-making, like he implied?

Or a fear of his mortality? At almost eighty-nine, Hank was the longest living member of the Kincaid family tree. If Ryan had any say, he'd keep his grandfather around forever. One day, he'd have to let go.

"I'm heading home for supper. Thanks, Ted. See you tomorrow."

Ted strode out of the shed.

Ryan followed, shutting the door.

With a wave, Ted set off for his cabin. For nine months for the year, he ruled over the opposite side of the pond by himself. His two-bedroom abode was a recent build next to the renovated bunk house, now a co-ed dorm for summer spa staff, facing the guest quarters. Change was inevitable.

Ryan dragged his gaze to the darkened house and frowned. For years, Hank teased Ryan about Meg driving him crazy. But Hank never conducted such sloppy setups. Was he worried about running out of time?

Jogging up the back steps, Ryan opened the door to the kitchen. The house was silent, dark, and still. No hint of cut herbs and simmering spices curled in the air. No snoring greeted him. Twisting his neck from one side to the next, he squinted but saw nothing. He stepped forward, letting the door slam shut and cupping his hands around his mouth. "Hank!? Hank!?"

The kitchen was empty.

He strode across the slate floor, pushed open the swinging door, and blinked rapidly. The lights in the front of the house were on. He darted his gaze through the family room turned lobby, and his heart dropped to his knees.

"Hank?!" The name ripped from his throat was more guttural than enunciated.

Sitting in a spindle back armchair near the stone fireplace, Hank slumped. He was ghostly pale.

"Hank! Hank!" Ryan leaped across the room, narrowing the gap in seconds with one big jump.

Hank's head lolled against his chest, spittle dripping from the corner of his mouth. His chest barely moved with shallow inhalations.

"Don't worry, Hank. I'm getting you help. You'll be fine." Ryan pulled the phone out of his pocket and texted Ted *9-1-1*. Then he called the paramedics.

Within seconds, the front door opened and crashed against the wall.

Ted raced into the room. "Let's get him into the truck. Maybe we can meet the ambulance at the end of the road."

Ryan nodded. He lifted his grandfather under the armpits, hoisting him to his feet. In his hold, the once strong bull of a cowboy was slight and shrunken. *You can't go anywhere now. I won't let you.*

Ted grabbed Hank's legs. Together, they carried Hank out the front door. By the time they reached the gravel drive, flashing lights and blaring sirens stopped them in their tracks.

Ryan tightened his grip. He couldn't let go. Readjusting his hold until his knuckles whitened, he clutched the one person who had been his constant in life. *I need more time.* How much did he need to learn about life from Hank? His work wasn't done. If Ryan had to fight or bargain with a higher power, he'd do exactly that.

In slow motion, the ambulance parked. An EMT jumped from the driver's side, leaving the door ajar and racing to the back. After an interminable few seconds' pause, the EMT reappeared wheeling a gurney opposite another uniformed person.

Holding up Hank offered Ryan the only tangible, physical support. He locked his knees and stood as straight and motionless as possible.

The EMTs stopped inches away and motioned for Hank.

For a second, Ryan pulled back. This was all wrong. None of this was supposed to be happening. Hank shouldn't die alone in a hospital, forgotten and scared. Tears stung the back of Ryan's throat.

With a reassuring word from the paramedics, Ryan, Ted, and the two professionals lowered Hank onto a gurney. One EMT fastened an oxygen mask, covering Hank's nose and mouth. The other explained instructions.

A low buzzing filled Ryan's ears. What started low increased in volume like someone playing with a dial on a car radio. What were the EMTs saying? He couldn't make sense of the words as he stared at their moving lips.

Thankfully, Ted remained. He listened and nodded.

Ryan stood in place, having difficulty in processing information and senses.

Ted was mobile. Taking the front steps two at a time, he raced up and locked the house. His heavy footfall, as he jogged back down, registered somewhere in Ryan's mind.

Ted loaded Ryan into the truck and drove to the hospital, following the flashing lights.

Was the siren blaring? Ryan took a deep breath, straining for any sound outside of his body. He heard nothing.

The paramedics didn't need to blare the emergency alert. In the middle of nowhere, they didn't need to stop traffic. Neither would they need to draw attention to the sad news. Without a doubt, everyone in Herd would know within twelve hours.

But would she?

He turned toward the window, biting his nail. Why hadn't she been there? Where was Colby? Weren't dogs supposed to alert others to danger and get help? Blaming her didn't ease his guilt about avoiding the house after letting down his grandfather the night before. Forcing her to be the scapegoat was his only option.

If Hank succumbed, he'd abandon Ryan. On his own, he'd be alone all over again. The prospect shouldn't be as terrifying as an adult as it had been in his childhood. His primal fear gripped him tight. He hated the fate he couldn't seem to escape. At least, this time, he had a villain. This was Meg's fault.

CHAPTER 17

After Meg sold the ice cream mold, she helped another customer. She smiled and chatted, selling a pair of boots and a hat. She rang up the purchase and followed the woman from the store. She was ready to lock up for the evening and start inventorying the books. Standing in the open doorway, she waved goodbye.

"Meg!" a feminine voice called from down the block.

She turned toward the sound, cheeks burning. The voice was crisp and commanding, like a teacher correcting a naughty student. When she spotted the blonde in the colorful dress barreling down the sidewalk, she widened her gaze. "Stephanie?"

"Hi," Stephanie said, slightly breathless, and stopped a few feet away. "Glad I caught you. How are you?"

Meg pressed a hand to her collarbone. "I'm fine." She scanned the other woman. In a dress, she was a little too put together for a regular day. Had she been at a meeting for the school? "Do you need something?"

Stephanie held up a finger and slowed her breathing, taking several big gulps of air. "Yes, I do." She drew in another deep breath. "By any chance, could you be the master of ceremonies for the auction and dinner at Frontier Days?"

Meg twisted her neck but spotted no one else on the stretch of wooden sidewalk. "Are you sure you mean me?"

"Yes, you would be doing me a huge favor."

"I don't know if I'm qualified. It's a big role."

Stephanie nodded. "We need a good storyteller. That's you."

Me? Meg shook her head. She wasn't a writer and couldn't spin a yarn, not like Hank Kincaid. Neither was she the town historian like Joe. Where had Stephanie gotten the impression Meg had any qualifications? She hated to miss the opportunity to participate, but she couldn't lead Stephanie on. "Are you certain you mean me?"

"Of course. I love reading the Finders-Keepers blog. My colleagues first told me about the site. You tell some great stories about the town. Not lately, though."

Meg stiffened. "I've been busy."

Stephanie shook her blonde hair behind her back. "I was touched by what you just posted. I get alerts on my phone."

Meg cringed.

"No, don't be embarrassed. You were real and vulnerable. I don't think I could be so staggeringly self-aware in such a public way." Stephanie smiled.

The friendly expression softened the sting. If she thought she had an audience, she would never have shared such a vulnerable entry. She wasn't sure why she turned to the internet instead of a notebook. Next time, she'd do better.

"I relate a lot to the sentiment. It's tough to take pleasure in what our town has to offer when we know more of the pain in the past," Stephanie said.

We all have the opportunity to make some amends. Yet another gift Ryan bestowed on the town.

"In fact, I'd love to have you come in to speak to my class next year," Stephanie continued. "History is complicated, but untangling memories piece by piece is illuminating."

What could Meg say to a bunch of kindergartners? Why not ask Joe? He was the go-to resource for the town's past. Wasn't he writing a book and interviewing everyone he could?

If you want a friend, be a friend. A chance to participate in the community, to be someone others leaned on, might never come again if she turned Stephanie down. "I'd love to help with Frontier Days. I'm not sure about presenting to five-year-olds."

Stephanie chuckled. "You'd be great at both. I'm ecstatic to have you involved in this year's event. Thank you so much."

"I don't know what to do. How should I begin? What are your expectations?"

"We can meet and go over the whole thing. I'll help. It'll be fun." The beaming smile brightened Stephanie's whole face.

Would it? Meg had wished for an opening to participate. The last time she had graced the town stage, she hadn't been alone. Ryan couldn't be lured to her aid again. If she wasted her chance, she squandered an opportunity at a friendship, too. She couldn't remember her last interaction with a peer in a social setting. "Okay, I'm in. I'll look forward to it."

"Great. Can we meet tomorrow at The Golden Crown? Let's meet for supper at six. I'm running late for an appointment. I've got to run now." Stephanie waved, spun on her heel, and jogged down the wooden sidewalk.

Turning, Meg stepped inside her store. She felt lighter than she had in years, since first deciding to move. Her dreams stood a chance.

Ryan included? She strode to the back and gathered her things and her dog. She'd rather do the work of inventorying from the comfort of her home. She couldn't handle another person acknowledging what happened last night or what she'd just posted on her blog. Locking for the night, she and Colby hopped into the SUV and drove home.

She opened the trunk and grabbed one box of books, leaving the rest for the morning. If only she could push aside her thoughts for a few hours, too, she might have peace. Shutting the trunk, she followed Colby, jostling the heavy box in her arms and leaning against the siding as she fiddled with the keys.

She couldn't shake the worry she'd let down Hank. He'd been one of the constants in her life. From her early childhood, she knew she could count on Hank Kincaid. He had never asked her for anything before showing up at the store and inquiring about the project. She shut the front door and dropped the box on the kitchen table, next to stacks of library books and a legal pad filled with more questions than answers.

Why had Hank asked for her help now? What was she missing?

While she'd turned to him for assistance with everything from a skinned knee riding her bike between the ranches to repairing the leaky faucet in the kitchen, she couldn't remember him every doing the same in return. He showed up with a smile and a friendly word. He was the closest she'd ever had to a grandfather.

As she served Colby dinner and ate leftovers over the kitchen sink, she mentally drafted another blog post about the discovery. She wouldn't divulge the particulars of the value but rather how the experience changed her. Without the unexpected shake-up in her routine, she would have been locked into one perspective her whole life.

No, she couldn't do the fun part. She had to put in the real work for her business. Pulling up a chair, she sat at the kitchen table. Covered with books about website building and the basics of coding, she'd ignored the work for too long. She grabbed the legal pad and found her laptop in the purse on top of the box. She grabbed the slim device and powered on the computer. Her to-do list grew every day. She uncapped a pen and added another: list books online ASAP.

With a sigh, she pulled up her website. She could only learn so much from reading and worrying. She needed practical experience. For several hours, she focused on the work, her vision blurring as she typed code and attempted to fix flaws in the long strings of letters, numbers, and characters. Her handiwork might have improved or ruined her website but at least she made progress. She stretched her arms over head and arched her back, adjusting on the chair behind her kitchen table.

In the corner of the room, Colby snored. She earned her snooze.

Meg dropped her arms and rolled her neck. She wished she could say the same. Had Hank wanted her to take charge of her destiny? She owed him a call and a thanks for the push. She scanned the room, where was her cell phone? Had she left it in her purse? Shortly after moving in, she gave up on the house line. The cost was excessive for one person who was usually in town.

Rifling through her bag, she came up empty. She swallowed the groan at the mental slip. Leaving her phone in her vehicle was dangerous and irresponsible.

She grabbed the keys and raced outside. In the cupholder, the phone screen flashed bright. She frowned. A call? She must have turned the device onto silent at some point. She opened the door and grabbed the phone, frowning at the screen. She'd missed calls and texts for the last three hours.

In her clammy hands, her grip loosened, and the phone clattered to the ground under the car. She shut the door and laid on the ground, reaching for the phone. With her fingertips, she brushed the device's edge. Scooting under the car, she grabbed the cell, pinching the nerves in her neck. Wincing, she uncoiled her body and straightened.

She unlocked the phone and stared at the list of calls. All from Ryan? Her heart skipped a beat. As much as she wished he sought her out to apologize for the day's snubbing, she feared the worst. He wasn't the type to call nonstop. On a good day, he was an uneasy conversationalist.

She called back, and the other line rang and rang.

She bit her bottom lip. Did he think she'd been purposefully avoiding him? Was he trying to give her in-kind treatment?

"Hello?" Ryan said.

She scrunched her nose at the gruff tone. "Ryan, hi. I'm so sorry. I got busy and left my phone in the car."

"Meg, stop. You need to come to the hospital. Hank passed out. I don't know what happened."

She sucked in a sharp breath, tears stinging her eyes. "I'm on my way."

She hung up the phone and raced inside, grabbing her purse, kissing Colby on the head, and locking up the house. She hopped behind the wheel, turned over the engine, and prayed hard. She had to make it to Hank. She had to do what he asked her and be honest with Ryan. Or, harder, be truthful with herself.

CHAPTER 18

Ryan hated hospitals ever since, as a young child, he had woken up in a bed with Grandma stroking his hair and Grandpa explaining what had happened. A car accident. No one's fault. A tragedy.

Ryan had lost his memory of that night, and he'd never regained it. He accepted it as a small mercy. While he couldn't remember his parents' final moments, he could hold on to every other piece of his life before and be grateful for everything that came after.

Loss never defined his life. He'd grown up surrounded by love. He'd put all his faith in his grandparents and was never steered wrong. Now he sat on a hard chair in the lobby, waiting for word and fearing what came next.

Shortly after arrival, he'd flagged down the paramedics and was given the news. Hank had been rushed straight into emergency. They couldn't share more and told Ryan to wait. In the lobby, he paced back and forth. Meg should be here.

He'd put distance between them. She waved, and he turned away. Because he couldn't do more without being absolutely vulnerable. He'd never wanted to be so scared and out of control as he'd been at five, the only survivor in a car accident. Controlling every variable kept him safe.

Today, his need for sameness endangered everything that mattered. He'd pushed her away. She'd left, and Hank had been unattended.

Because he refused to be honest and accepted her announcement as pushback against any change to his comfort level, he was alone. It was his fault.

A call from the ranch sent Ted back after twenty minutes. Alone, Ryan started calling her. With each hit to her voice mail, his blood pressure rose. After a few terse words, he'd hang up and start the process again. He couldn't stop. Because doing so meant giving up or accepting she didn't care or worse was in danger. He couldn't lose her, too. For hours, he tortured himself with unanswered calls. Until finally, she had called him.

She's never been mine. The phone call was brief. He couldn't say more without breaking down. Resting his face in his hands, he stared at the tile floor and breathed in the smell of industrial cleaner. He wanted to leave this place as soon as he could.

"Mr. Kincaid?"

He snapped up his head and frowned at a young doctor, scrubs peeking out from under the white coat. Ryan stood, dusting his palms on his jeans. "Yes, hello. I'm Ryan. Hank's grandson. How is he?"

The doctor, a man probably a few years younger than Ryan, nodded. "I'd like to keep him overnight. Possibly for two nights. I want to monitor him, but he didn't have a heart attack."

"What happened?"

The doctor frowned. "We are still running tests. The best guess is a panic attack."

"Panic?" Ryan drew back his chin. Hank the big strong cowboy was overwhelmed and incapacitated by panic? How?

"It can mimic a heart attack. Given his age, I'd like to observe him for a couple nights to be sure we aren't missing something else."

Ryan couldn't argue with that but had trouble connecting the pieces. Had he been the source of anxiety for Hank? "He'll be here for his birthday on Thursday?"

"Not necessarily. He's awake. Would you like to come back and see him?"

"Sure." Ryan rubbed together his clammy palms, turning toward the door. She wasn't here yet. He faced the doctor again. "A family fr..." He coughed. "I have more family coming. Can I leave her name with someone so she's allowed to visit?"

"Is her last name Kincaid?"

Ryan shook his head.

The doctor pulled a piece of paper and pen from his pocket. "Write it down, and I'll let the front desk know."

Ryan scribbled the name and handed both back to the doctor.

"Mr. Kincaid, your grandfather is a healthy man. We are being cautious. I want to assuage your fears about why we are keeping him."

"Thank you. I appreciate that."

The doctor turned and pushed through a swinging door, leading the way down the corridor.

The bright, white space was blinding. Florescent lights bounced off every surface.

Ryan's vision blurred. He blinked back the tears, overcoming the emotion he'd buried so deep in his efforts to be every bit the cowboy Hank was. Had he missed the biggest hurdle? Love? Hank had Susie. His strength was wound so tightly with his faith and respect for his wife. She remained his guiding force years after her death. What did Ryan have besides work? *A woman I've loved and kept on the sidelines.*

The doctor stopped and twisted a doorknob, opening the door. "I'll leave you two alone."

Ryan entered the room. Stuffing his hands in his pockets, he dragged in a shaky breath and inhaled the cleaner smell again. Past the bathroom, a bed faced a TV and window.

Dressed in a gown with a blanket over his lap, Hank pushed the buttons on the remote. He looked too human for Ryan's lifelong image of the man as a superhero.

"Oh good. You're here. Can you fix this thing?" Hank dropped the remote on the bed and folded his arms over his chest. "Stuck in a hospital for my eighty-ninth birthday, and I can't even find the game."

Ryan frowned and approached the bed, grabbing the remote and powering off the TV. "What game?"

"Any game. I'd settle for golf at this point."

Ryan rolled his eyes. "It's late, and you need to rest so you can celebrate your eighty-ninth birthday. Do you remember what happened?"

Hank shook his head, pursing his lips.

"Were you alone and overexerting yourself in the shed?"

"No, after Meg left, I went into the kitchen. I felt a little dizzy, and my gut burned." Hank rubbed a hand along his breastbone. "I sat down. I woke up here."

Exhaling a pent-up breath, Ryan relaxed. He didn't want to blame her but struggled with his default setting. Trouble and Meg were synonymous. "Any tightness in your chest? Pain in your arm?"

"It wasn't a heart attack." Hank rolled his eyes. "I don't know how else to describe what happened, but I know it wasn't my chest."

"What did you feel?"

"I was starting supper. Suddenly, I felt weak like all my energy drained. My head started spinning so I sat down."

"I'm so mad at Meg." Ryan gritted his molars, rubbing his jaw. "She should have been there."

"Boy, what are you talking about?" Hank pushed himself up on the hospital bed. In the thin, blue-patterned gown, with a blanket draped over his lap, he couldn't assure his usual, stern expression. "Did you hire me a babysitter while I wasn't looking?"

"No, of course not."

"Pardon?" Hank folded his arms over his chest. "Am I mistaken then? Did you give her another reason to hang around?"

Ryan strode to the window and gazed at the parking lot. Meg was her own person and had reasons for her actions. Answering Hank's question would only push the man's buttons.

Had Ryan somehow caused Hank's episode? With his stresses mounting, Ryan hadn't paid attention to his grandfather. He'd disappointed his grandmother's memory. He was supposed to take care of the older man, and instead he neglected him. While Ryan was distracted, had he missed obvious signs of poor health?

Turning around, he leaned against the windowsill. "Can I ask..." He pinched the bridge of his nose. Pressure built behind his eyes, his temples throbbing. "What was the real reason you started cleaning out the shed?" He dropped his hand to the side and met his grandfather's gaze. "Were you trying to set me up with Meg? Or settling your affairs in case you..."

"In case I died?"

Ryan pushed off the window, folded his arms over his chest, and broadened his stance. He hated saying that word. As the silence stretched, he nodded.

"I'm not afraid of dying, boy. When it's my time, it's my time. I wouldn't mind seeing my Susie again." A wistful smile lifted the corners of Hank's mouth. "I worry about you."

I know. Ryan frowned and gripped his upper arms. "The reason?"

"If I say both, will you be mad?"

Ryan shook his head. Years ago, he and Hank reached an agreement that neither would hold a grudge if the other was being honest.

"Then that's my answer. I'm tired of waiting on you and Meg to figure out what is right in front of you. I thought maybe I could get you two together and clean out my shed in one go. Now I'm done, and I can't enjoy the new space. I'm not going anywhere anytime soon. At least not according to the doctor." He sighed. "I can't have cake."

The words were so bitter, Ryan lifted the corner of his mouth. He couldn't stop the smile.

"They told me I'm here for at least two nights, and I'm on a salt free, sugar free, fun free diet." Hank held up his hands. "And I didn't have a heart attack! This place is the worst."

"Hank, it's one birthday. You'll be okay."

"When you get to eighty-nine you don't skimp on any celebration."

"We'll have cake when you get home. If you do as the nurses say, maybe you can go home on your special day. Two nights counts tonight."

"I better get to leave. The wish only works if you blow out a candle on the actual day and eat the cake."

"Why are you so feisty? Did you have a wish lined up?"

Hank lifted his chin. "I always do."

A knock sounded on the door, saving Ryan from formulating whatever response he could muster. He hated for Hank to waste any wishes on him.

The knock sounded again.

Ryan stepped around the end of the bed. "Come in."

The door opened.

Meg poked her head around the side of the panel. "Hi," she murmured.

"Come in, come in, he's decent." Ryan turned to his grandfather and arched a brow. "Or as decent as he's going to get."

Hank narrowed his gaze. "Don't listen to him."

Meg passed Ryan, approaching the bed and hugging Hank.

Her light, lavender scent saved Ryan from the overpowering aroma of hopelessness the walls of the building contained. She grounded him. Why hadn't he understood until his grandfather's life was endangered? *Don't wait for life or death.* Marcia and Ford had warned him.

"Hank, are you feeling alright?" She stepped back, out of the hug, but remained at the bedside.

Hank held her hands. "I am, darling. I'm disappointed about my birthday. I wanted to celebrate at the ranch."

She turned to Ryan, tilting her head. "He won't?"

"We don't know yet. Maybe. I promise, with a witness, your ninetieth will be a celebration Herd has never seen."

Hank's grin lit up his entire face, his color brightening. "You swear, boy?"

With one finger, Ryan crossed his heart. He'd do anything to keep his grandfather hale and hearty, including the probable disruption of his ranch for the better part of next summer. He lifted his gaze to Meg.

She nodded.

Their unspoken communication remained operational. What would happen if he was frank with his feelings? *Now or never.* "Can I talk to you? In the hall?"

She widened her gaze, her cheeks pinking.

Hank patted her hands. "Go with him. I'll be fine. Just a little scare, but they want to keep me for a few days."

"Better safe than sorry. Have a good rest, Hank." She kissed his forehead and strode to the door, biting her lip as she passed. The door shut behind her.

"Don't mess this up, boy," Hank said.

Ryan hoped he wouldn't. He exited the room and spotted Meg leaning against the opposite wall.

She met his gaze and stepped forward. "Please understand I wasn't avoiding your phone calls and texts. I legitimately forgot my phone in the car. I was working on the website and lost track of time."

"I didn't think you were."

"You didn't?" Her voice cracked. "There were so many messages and voice mails. I haven't checked them all. I didn't want you to think I was trying to play a game with you because you didn't acknowledge me today."

He swallowed pushing down the horseshoe sized lump stuck on his Adam's apple. He had snubbed her. "I know you aren't petty. I didn't think you were playing tit for tat."

"So...why?"

Her words were so soft. *Because you're the only person who would understand what I was feeling.* She slipped between his defenses like a knife slicing between his ribs and lodging straight in his heart. He spent his time wrapped up in worrying about tomorrow. In doing so, he ignored today.

When he got home from the hospital, he realized what he pushed away—happily ever after. Was he ready now? He hated his vulnerability. "I needed you to know."

"About Hank?" She tiptoed toward him, cutting the distance between them from feet to inches. "Is there anything else I need to know?"

"I...can't talk about..." He scrubbed both hands over his face. Why was this so hard? He didn't need another pep talk about honesty. He'd had his fill. He felt raw and exposed.

Was it the location? The subject matter? The brush with death? Hank never let him live in fear. Any time Ryan hesitated ever, his grandfather jumped in to encourage him to try. What if Hank's words at the dinner last night had been the last piece of advice?

The doctors only wanted to keep him for a short period but what if something else happened? Ryan learned to focus on the future so he could manage his daily expectations. No living soul was guaranteed a tomorrow. He stopped worrying about the next day and looked a year or three into the future, constantly moving the target. The advice was to live in the moment. He'd never figured out how.

"I wanted to talk earlier today," she said, her chin trembling. "After a discussion I had with Hank. I've disappointed him."

"No more than I have, I'm sure." Ryan shook his head.

She sniffed and swiped at her glistening eyes.

His gut clenched, and he set his jaw. He could handle anything but tears.

"When I thought he was gone?" Her voice cracked.

"Shh." He closed the distance between them and reached out, brushing hair behind her ears. He only touched her with the very tip of his fingers. Any more and he'd crumble.

Under the fluorescent lights, against the stark white of the sterile space, she was beautiful. Her hair shimmered with red catching in the artificial light. She stood before him with no artifice.

Holding his gaze, she dragged in a breath and looked straight through him. "I promised Hank."

Ryan removed his hand and stepped back. "Please, not..." He wasn't even sure how he intended to finish. Not now? Not here? Not ever?

"Okay." She nodded and dusted her hands on her jeans. "I'm heading home. Please make sure Hank knows if he needs anything, I'm around." She spun on her heel, her shoes clacking against the tile.

The door at the end of the hall opened and shut, the swinging creating a breeze that blew away her lavender smell and left him with pain. He had himself to thank.

CHAPTER 19

The next evening, Meg pushed through the swinging front door of The Golden Crown. Her senses were assaulted from every direction. Animal mounts loomed overhead, staring at the occupants with beady eyes brightened by the rows of electrified kerosene-style hanging fixtures. Underfoot, sawdust covered the floor in a thin layer, muffling heavy steps. Though no longer required to soak up the tobacco spit, the sweet sawdust smell covered the scent of spilled beer.

The saloon was the only official restaurant in town and welcomed families as well as regulars. Along one wall, the impressive walnut bar spanned the length of the building. In the back corner, the poker club held court. The low rumble of masculine laughter from the card players mixed with the buzz of conversations and occasional high-pitched squeal of laughter.

Twisting her neck, she scanned the crowded space. She should have called and canceled the meeting with Stephanie. In light of last evening's events, the kind-hearted teacher would understand. Hank's hospitalization was a convenient excuse for her inner turmoil.

Ryan asked her to talk later. But did he really want to have the conversation? Or had he pushed her away and, for once and for all, rejected her? Meg spent the day feeling useless. She wasn't sure she could handle company but at least the meeting promised her a distraction from her pain.

At a table near the center of the room, Stephanie sat with sheets of paper strewn across the circular, oak top.

Meg navigated through the maze of tables and stopped at the seat opposite. "Hi, Stephanie." She pulled out a chair, the feet scraping the ground.

Stephanie glanced up.

For a second, her stare was as blank as Big Barry, the massive, stuffed bison head mount centered on the back wall.

"Oh, hi, Meg." Stephanie gathered the papers into a messy stack, clearing the table. "Sorry, just going over some details for Frontier Days. Please sit. Thanks for meeting me. I wasn't sure..."

Word traveled fast, as Meg expected. She scooted her chair closer to the table, moving her purse into her lap and retrieving a small notepad and pen. "Yeah, I wasn't sure either."

She still wasn't. Her closest confidantes were Mom and Hank. With one in the hospital and the other over a thousand miles away, she had no one to commiserate with about the Ryan situation. Instead, she spent her night replaying the whole scene. "I need to feel useful today."

"Will he be alright?" Stephanie asked.

"He's getting great care." Meg forced a smile. He was. The scare shook her to her core. She knew the fragility of life. No one could live forever. Hank almost convinced her otherwise. "Persuading him to take things easy when he gets home will be the real challenge."

"How are you?"

Meg rubbed a hand over her itchy nose. Did Stephanie mean about Hank or Ryan? In small towns, everyone knew everyone else's business. The hospital hallway discussion was probably overheard. Meg anticipated the question. The genuine caring in the teacher's delivery pierced Meg in the heart. "I'm a little shaken."

"Of course you are. He's pretty much your grandfather, too. You must have some amazing stories about growing up here."

Meg shook her head. "Not as many as Ryan. I only spent my summers here. We did manage a certain amount of good-hearted mischief."

"I don't think I've ever heard Ryan in anything less than a professional capacity, and I've definitely never heard any personal anecdotes."

"He takes his responsibilities to town very seriously. He's always been stoic. Even as a kid." Meg lifted the corner of her mouth as a memory tickled the back of her brain. "Once, he did prank Hank. I helped. Hank had been giving Ryan a hard time about being too responsible. Ryan did his chores and then some. If he wasn't working at the ranch, he was reading and studying. He always wanted to make Hank and Susie proud."

"I'm confused. Where's the trouble?"

"Hank wanted Ryan to be a kid and not act like a small adult. Hank used to say all the time, we'd have years of being grown-ups." *He was so right.* Hank was as stubborn as he was talkative and charming. Shaking him off an idea was nigh impossible for anyone but Susie.

The problem with always having a lot to say was others had trouble knowing when to listen. Everything Hank said had value. How could anyone absorb each piece of advice?

Stephanie leaned forward.

"Ryan decided to give Hank what Hank claimed he wanted. I lured him to the stables, and he tripped a wire. A bucket of corn syrup upended onto his head. Ryan popped out with a fan and blew a bag of feathers on his grandpa. I've never seen Hank so angry or Ryan run so fast. After getting punished, Ryan went back to being his industrious self, and Hank never said a word to discourage him again."

Stephanie chuckled. "I can't even imagine those two acting like that. Ryan goofing and Hank yelling is so out of character for both." She propped her other elbow on the table, interlacing her hands. "What was town like?"

"Quiet. For me, it was such a welcome, restful change from living in the city. All the space and fresh air rejuvenated me. As an adult, I can think back and understand how strained the economy was and the toll on folks. The turnaround has been wonderful."

"I'm glad for it. I can't imagine living anywhere else," Stephanie said. "I'd love if you could include tidbits about your experiences into your master of ceremonies role."

I'm not sure how much I can include when it mostly involves Ryan. If he pushed back against Meg last night, he wouldn't want her implying they had a connection on stage. Was he interested in someone else in town? The thought burned like the old Kincaid ranch branding iron. "How much do I need to prepare? Is this like a monologue?"

Stephanie shook her head. "Don't worry, you need an oratory. You'll welcome the guests and give a run-down of the evening's events. You'll run the auction and introduce the band. Any point where you can add a personal point of reference or anecdote is what we're looking for."

Like the time I tricked Ryan into partnering me on stage? Heat crept up her face.

Stephanie riffled through her stack of papers. "I should have something to guide you in here. Let me look."

With her head down, she was hopefully oblivious to Meg's burning cheeks. Pressing a cool hand to her hot skin, she darted her gaze through the room. In the corner, she met Ted's steady stare.

He nodded and pushed back his chair, striding toward her.

Her heart stuck in her throat. Was he about to deliver bad news? Why else cut short a round of cards with his friends?

"Here is a timetable and a list of auction prizes so far." Stephanie slid a paperclipped bundle across the table. "If you want to get started, you can keep this and make your notes. We can meet up again whenever you're free. I'm not teaching summer school this year, and my classes at the ranch finish before noon. I have a lot of availability an—"

Booted steps cut off the rest of her speech.

Ted stopped at the side of the table, between Stephanie and Meg. "Evening, ladies." He reached for the brim of his hat and tugged it off.

Meg's chest tightened. "Hello, Ted. Are you here for poker?"

For a second, he frowned then scrubbed a hand over his face. "Yes, ma'am. Every week if I get the chance."

Good, he'd taken her lead on public niceties and nothing serious. "Will you participate in the tournament in September?" Meg persisted with questions she knew the answers to. *How is Ryan?* She couldn't think the words without a lump clogging her throat.

Ted opened his mouth.

"Oh, I'm sorry. I'm being so rude. You know Stephanie, of course." Meg cut him off. If she gave him the opportunity to speak, would she like what she heard? She wasn't sure she could take the chance. "She's in charge of the poker tournament among so many other things."

"Good evening." He tipped his head to the other woman. "I've had positive comments from the first round of guests about your yoga classes."

In response, Stephanie stared, slack jawed.

"I'm participating in Frontier Days." Meg barreled through the half second of awkward silence. Any lapse could provide an opening for bad news. "Stephanie has asked me to be the master of ceremonies. Seeing as I love to talk, feels like a natural fit."

"You'll be great." He turned to smile at Stephanie. "You've made an excellent choice."

Stephanie might have said "uh huh" or pushed back her chair. A squeak sounded but her face didn't move. The reaction was strange given Ted's bland grin.

"We're reviewing the responsibilities of the role." Meg shuffled the papers. "Good to see you, Ted. Please don't let us keep you from your game."

Ted shook his head. "Sorry to interrupt your work. Could I have a word, Meg?"

Meg sucked in a breath. He wasn't letting her escape the conversation. She glanced at Stephanie. The frozen woman turned beet red. Who knew embarrassment was so contagious. "I'll be a second, Stephanie. Should we get dinner? Maybe you can flag down a server and get a couple menus?"

"Okay," Stephanie croaked and covered her mouth.

Meg pushed back her chair and stood. "Can we speak outside?" she asked Ted.

He nodded and waved her ahead.

Retracing her earlier route, Meg wound through the other diners and pushed the door outside. She strode toward the replica hitching posts in front and leaned back against the wooden rail. If she needed solid support for the conversation, and the churn in her stomach told her so, she couldn't do much better.

Ted stood opposite. "I'm not good with small talk so I'm coming straight out with it." He crossed his arms over his chest. "You need to come to the ranch."

Her chest tightened. Ted was a good man and a solid friend. He never made demands or requests. His tone was unequivocal. She wanted to do what he asked. She couldn't. "Ryan doesn't want me there."

"He's upset. Whatever was said ... whatever happened ... doesn't matter. You're his family. Come to the ranch."

I'm not. She could have been but Ryan pushed against change. Was there more to Ted's speech? If Ryan felt like this, and shared his concerns, why didn't he come out and address her directly? Why was Ted a mouthpiece? She narrowed her gaze. "How much did he tell you? Did he put you up to this conversation?"

"To answer your questions in order, nothing, and no. He doesn't know what he wants. I have eyes and a brain. I can make sense of other people's relationships. He's hurting."

"How would I know what's best? My appearance might set him off."

Ted held her stare.

She understood Ted's sentiment with startling clarity. She'd known Ryan the longest, second only to Hank. If anyone knew him, it was her. No matter how he felt about her, they'd always have their shared memories. They were connected. He'd flounder when the time eventually came for Hank and Susie's heavenly reunion.

Meg owed Hank and Ryan her undying loyalty even if Ryan would never want her heart. After he pushed her away, however, she couldn't show up unannounced. "I'm sorry, Ted. I can't help. If he invited me, sure. I can't show up. He'll consider it an ambush."

With a slow nod, Ted released a heavy breath and put his hat on his head. "Have a good night."

Unlikely. "Good night." She pushed off the post and strode back inside the saloon. She'd have to swallow her pride for the sake of friendship. But not yet. Her heart throbbed. Eventually, the pain would lessen, and she'd accept the return to their previous roles. Not tonight.

Rinsing the bowl under the kitchen sink faucet, Ryan stared through the window and across the lawn toward the shed. He had so much left to tackle before Hank came home.

He didn't wish for more time. He hated the house without his grandpa's booming voice bouncing off the walls.

He couldn't trust himself around the few remaining guests from last weekend and wasn't ready to check-in the new arrivals. Instead, he sequestered inside the shed. Alone with his thoughts and his pain, he started the final push to complete the shed.

He had patched and repaired worn plywood. He'd insulated and added drywall. Electricity would have to wait for a few weeks until the scheduled appointment with the electrician to power the shed with lights and a mini-split to keep the climate comfortable. He needed to paint and lay a proper floor.

With so many tasks remaining, he might stay awake all night to last another painfully silent morning on the ranch. He was so bone-tired from a sleepless night, a full workday, and an evening on the project, his knees almost buckled under his weight. If he went to bed now, however, he'd end up staring at the ceiling on a second night of replaying all the ways he screwed up with Meg. Should he call? Show up? Let her say words he wasn't ready to hear?

The backdoor slammed.

Ryan frowned, meeting Joe's gaze. Why was he here? It was almost nine.

"Are you going to get that?" Joe called, cupping his hands around his mouth.

"Huh?" Ryan moved the bowl to the dish rack and turned off the faucet. He stared at his prune textured fingers.

"The oven," Joe yelled. He jogged across the tile floor, grabbed a pot holder, and opened the door.

Smoke poured out, curling in the air.

Oh no, the cake. With a jolt, Ryan snapped to the present and shut off the timer and oven. Grabbing a thick dish towel, he reached for the rectangular cake pan in Joe's hands. He raced back across the room, throwing the blackened cake in the sink and opening the window.

Blinking through the haze, Ryan batted at the smoke-filled air.

With a fist covering his mouth, Joe coughed and shut the oven door.

He hadn't noticed he ruined the birthday cake. Oblivious to the blaring timer, the pungent burning stench, or how long he'd been rinsing the same bowl, he was trapped in place as he argued with himself. If Joe hadn't alerted him, what would have happened?

Opening the back door, he tilted his head to the exit.

Joe raised his arm, covering his mouth and nose with his inner elbow, and jogged outside.

Ryan followed, leaving the door ajar.

"I hope that wasn't your dinner." Joe coughed into his elbow.

"It was Hank's birthday cake." Ryan leaned against the siding. "I did a pretty good job, too."

"Scratch or mix?"

Ryan shot him a look. His grandfather cooked his meals. On his own, Ryan survived on canned foods and cold sandwiches.

Joe sighed. "I can pick up another box for you tomorrow. Or, better yet, let me call in an order to the General Store."

"I'll get the cake. I'll order it."

"You promise no more unsupervised cooking?"

Ryan rolled his eyes. Under normal circumstances, he could handle light teasing. Joe picked the wrong moment. Nothing was typical today. "Why are you here late? I don't need babysitting."

"I lost track of time." Joe raised a hand to the back of his neck.

Ryan didn't believe him for a second. Ted would be playing poker in town tonight. Had he and Joe come up with a plan to make sure Ryan wasn't unsupervised? He wanted to be righteously indignant. Since he almost charred his home, however, he couldn't argue in his defense.

"I stopped by because I wanted to see if you needed anything. I wasn't checking up on you. I was worried. I'm trying to be a friend."

Ryan snorted. Joe was a good friend. Ryan didn't have a good track with other people in the last twenty-four hours.

"Are you pushing me away, too?"

"What does that mean?" Ryan drew together his brows, his upper lip curling. Anger bubbled under the surface like a hot spring. What did Joe know? Had Ryan's hospital conversation been overheard and recounted? He hadn't said much but managed enough to hurt someone he cared about deeply.

"It means why isn't Meg here? Why are you alone? You had a huge scare. You shouldn't be by yourself. It's not typical for her to mind her own business as far as you and Hank are concerned. I'm pretty good at putting two and two together." Joe shrugged. "I was a kid detective."

The comment was almost enough to lighten Ryan's mood. He could picture a kid version of Joe holding an oversized magnifying glass and snooping around. Ryan didn't want to be so transparent. It hurt too much. He scrubbed a hand along his jaw, unshaven whiskers scraping against his skin. At least Joe wasn't well-informed enough to know specifics and start refuting Ryan's arguments. "I'm better like this."

"No, you're not." Joe shook his head. "I'm worried you believe your lies."

The soft sincerity threatened Ryan. He couldn't be weak. Everyone—an entire economy—depended on his strength. "Isn't that what we all do?" He croaked and coughed, clearing his scratchy throat. "Don't we tell ourselves what we need to make every day bearable?"

Joe stepped closer, wrinkling his brow. "Hey, are you okay? Should I stay? I'm very worried right now."

I am too. Under the close inspection, Ryan almost caved. He slid down the wall and sat on the porch, legs extending in front of him. Without Hank and Meg, he was trapped in a house and a life haunted by memories and regrets, exactly what his grandpa worried about. In the moment, yesterday, he'd been too terrified for truth. Letting them continue status quo was meant to save them from pain. Neither happened. He still lost, and he got hurt.

If he let her speak or—better—told her the truth about his changed feelings, how suddenly he realized he'd taken for granted the person he needed more than anyone else, would he be out on a covered porch utterly dejected and nearly burning down the legacy he fought so hard to modernize for the chance of a future?

Maybe, maybe not. Fear stole his options. He ended up with no one, like he always feared. Once upon a time, his problems were solved easily. Either a conversation and bear hug from his grandfather, or an apology and ice cream cone with Meg fixed everything. He was desperately unprepared to navigate life alone.

"Do you want me to call her?" Joe sat. "Ask her to stop by?"

Ryan lifted his gaze and stared, unseeing. His next move had to be the opposite of his last. The call to action couldn't be spurred by someone else. He needed a plan, courage, and strength. At the moment, he was an empty shell. He'd finish the shed, seeing a project to completion, clean himself up, and head over to her place after Hank came home. "I know what I need to do. And I promise no more cooking."

Joe chuckled. "I'm glad I stopped you from setting the whole place ablaze. It's been a solid start to the summer. A lot of great tours so far. Guests are very interested in history. I'd hate for everything to go up in smoke."

Ryan smiled. "Thanks for the heads up about Stephanie. She's a nice fit for the job."

Joe nodded. "She's a sweetheart."

Ryan widened his gaze.

Joe held up both hands. "Not for me. She's too young. I talk pop culture in the teacher's lounge, and I can see her eyes glaze over from the door."

"I wouldn't hold that against her."

Joe scowled.

Ryan chuckled. "I did want to mention. I promised Hank a huge celebration for his birthday next year. I'm anticipating an all-hands-on deck scenario. Be ready."

"I look forward to it. You sure you're alright?"

Ryan nodded and got to his feet. At the door, he sniffed. While smoke lingered, the haze cleared from the kitchen. "I will be. Thanks for being a good friend and stopping by."

Joe stood and tipped his head, jogging down the stairs. "I'll see you tomorrow."

Ryan nodded and walked inside, shutting the door. He had a lot to squeeze into a short time. He could do it. When life shoved him against a wall, he pushed back harder.

CHAPTER 20

M eg tightened her grip on the steering wheel and shifted forward in the driver's seat. She'd only been to the hospital once and wasn't sure where to go. Until a couple nights ago, she hadn't appreciated her luck with good health.

In the shotgun seat, Colby whined.

"Shh." She reached out a hand and petted the dog, never taking her gaze off the road and the signs. "We're picking up your cowboy. I promise."

Slowing, she turned into the circle drive in front of the medical building. She parked and turned on her hazards, swiveling in her seat to face the automatic doors. For two nights, she'd done nothing but stew. If Ryan hadn't cut her off, she would have put everything out there for him. She'd have done as Hank asked.

Ryan's scared face haunted her. While the small mercy of stopping the conversation ripped her heart in half, she had no other choice. Instead of honesty, she vowed distance. Time healed all things. She'd keep to her land and her house, inviting Hank over to her turf. Maybe one day she could stand to look at Ryan again.

While she waited for any word, she spent her time creating her online store from behind the register of her physical branch. Once she stopped asking questions, she started learning the answers. Why had she been so scared and intimidated to start? Was it her fear of failure? She'd had enough falling flat on her face in recent weeks to forever abolish any such hang-ups.

Slowly but surely, she began to list the books from Hank's consignment. She hit publish on the site only an hour ago and already her phone pinged with sold notifications.

She could do this. She could stay. Grandma thrived on the ranch for years on her own. Meg would be as strong and independent.

A knock sounded at the window.

She turned and lowered the window a crack.

"Are you picking up Hank Kincaid?" A fresh-faced, ponytailed, twenty-something woman in nurse's scrubs asked.

"I am. Should he sit in the front or the back?"

"Back."

RACHELLE PAIGE CAMPBELL

Meg nodded. "I'll hold the dog so you can help him."

"Is this Colby?" The nurse smiled.

Colby woofed and wagged her tail, thumping the upholstered seat.

"Mr. Kincaid has been talking about you all morning, little girl. We'll be right out." The nurse walked away.

Meg rolled up the window and reached for the dog's collar, holding her around the shoulders with both arms. "Shh, shh."

Excitement radiated off the dog's body. Her pants came fast and furious.

The back door opened.

Hank grunted, reached for the door handle, and pulled himself inside.

The nurse helped him with his seat belt and shut the door. She waved at Hank and flashed Meg a thumbs-up.

Colby howled.

Hank chuckled. "Well don't stand on ceremony for me, pup. I won't break. Get back here."

"You sure?" Meg frowned.

Hank nodded and grinned.

Meg let go of Colby.

The dog vaulted over the center console and into the back seat. She landed with a thud and launched into licking Hank's face. The loud slurping sounds were greeted with warm laughter.

Meg turned in her seat, put the SUV into gear, and drove through the parking lot. She navigated onto the highway. For most of the ride, only the sounds of Hank's laughter and Colby's tongue filled the SUV. Meg was glad for the silence. She feared telling Hank the truth. She'd ultimately disappointed him. She couldn't feel worse if she was confessing to her own family.

When the sounds of joy quieted, she studied him in the rearview mirror and smiled, meeting his gaze. "Happy Birthday."

"Not much of one." He sighed.

"I double checked. You'll have a cake." Although sending a quick text to Ted was the coward's way out of dealing with the ranch. He'd replied and asked her to pick up Hank.

"Ryan promises a big celebration next year, and I'm holding him to it. I already have a few ideas."

I'm sure you do. Hank's plans and schemes kept him active. If meddling in her life helped him, she was glad to have been a pawn as long as not sticking to his script wouldn't pain him. She wanted to be part of the birthday. A beautiful summer evening under the stars would be the perfect backdrop for Hank.

She needed distance. For Ryan's sake and hers, she had to stay away. How did she explain? She lifted her gaze to the rearview mirror.

Hank scratched the underside of Colby's neck.

Colby licked the side of his face.

At least Meg wouldn't have to break up this pair. "I started the online store. I silenced my phone before I came to pick you up. Your collection of hardcover books are the first items up for sale, and they are flying. Within seconds of publishing the first few listings, the books were sold."

"Oh, that's good. Not that I'm surprised. I don't work with amateurs." He winked. "You planning on staying in town then?"

She nodded. "As long as I can."

"Good, you're a little piece of sunshine."

She peeked at him again and smiled.

With both hands petting Colby, he focused on the dog with adoration. He could have been speaking to the dog.

"I don't drive you crazy with my chatter. Or my dog?" she asked.

He chuckled. "This dog is special. Not a lot like her."

There are plenty more that need a chance. Colby was a rescue, but, following the unspoken code of dogs, she saved everyone around her. Given a chance, every dog astounded the humans in their orbit with their limitless capacity for love and forgiveness.

Meg turned onto the dirt road leading to the ranches. She passed her house and eventually pulled in front of the Kincaid ranch house.

The drive was full. Three pickup trucks occupied most of the gravel.

The full cavalry? She steered her SUV to the end of the drive and parked, twisting the key in the ignition. At least she wouldn't need to go too far for assistance. "Stay here, Hank. I'm sure I can get you help."

Opening her door, she hopped to the ground and raised a hand to shield her gaze against the bright sunshine. Crunching the gravel under her heels, she had never felt more conspicuous or unsure. She'd approached this house countless times. Did she have a right to walk onto the property without an invitation?

On the porch, Ted and Joe stood shoulder to shoulder.

The full-time cowboy and part-time adventurer were lanky. Neither man was as broad-shouldered as Ryan. Between them, they had enough muscle to accomplish the task.

Her stomach clenched. She wasn't sure what she would say if she did see Ryan. Blurt her feelings before he could cut her off? At least then she wouldn't walk around with the nagging tickle of unsettled business. A smarter person would accept that he'd already turned her down. She whistled and waved.

Ted and Joe descended the steps.

"Thanks for getting, Hank," Ted said. "We were on decoration duty."

She widened her gaze and twisted her neck from one to the other.

Joe held up both his hands. "Not our idea. Luckily, I had some input from the other teachers on what to buy."

Where's Ryan? She didn't ask. He made his stance pretty clear two days ago. She hadn't thought that he'd avoid her. He could, conceivably, be preparing for a new round of guests. It was Thursday. He probably had a full booking. *He should be here.* "I have the birthday boy in the SUV. He's in the back seat with Colby. Can you help him?"

"Of course," Joe said.

Ted nodded.

The pair approached the SUV. She followed a few paces behind.

Ted reached the vehicle first and opened the back door. The men helped Hank to the ground.

"Don't coddle me. I'm not an invalid." Hank shook off the men.

Meg nibbled her lip. The doctor and nurses might have a better response to his declaration. Letting him get worked up would only set Hank back.

Colby jumped down to the ground.

Meg closed the door behind her pet.

"Just help me inside to the kitchen. Then you two can go," Hank said and turned toward her. "Do you mind if Colby sticks around for a little bit?"

Meg shrugged. "Of course not, if that's what you want."

"It is. I left something in the shed. Do you mind getting it for me?" Hank asked.

Now? She wanted to sing the birthday song, stay for a slice of cake, and then go home. With enough of a crowd, she wouldn't feel awkward. She could handle the new normal as long as she knew what to expect.

Heading to the shed wasn't in her plan. How could she say no to Hank? She'd pop over, find whatever he needed, grab it, and head out. Maybe she didn't need any cake. Her stomach growled. She cleared her throat, covering the treacherous sound. "Sure. What am I looking for?"

"You'll know it when you see it." Hank winked.

Joe and Ted led Hank toward the house, Colby excitedly barking at their heels.

She scrunched her nose against the tickle and burn of coming tears. She had an idea what she would find behind the house. She wasn't sure she was up for a formal rejection. Was he about to finish his "I can't?"

Well, fine. He'd have to tell her to her face. She sniffed and rubbed her eyes dry. Crunching the gravel under her shoes, she strode around the side of the house. At least she would know where she stood. For better or worse.

Ryan had never been more grateful for the community than during the two nights Hank remained in the hospital. He required assistance with the resort operations. Driving back and forth from the hospital, he counted on others.

Stephanie sat behind the front desk, answering questions from guests after her yoga classes. The members of the bluegrass band, all teachers at Joe's school, similarly stepped up to interact with guests, filling the void left by Hank, arguably the biggest draw to the property. Joe and Ted helped shuttle Ryan back and forth.

He found the drive impossible alone. He wasn't scared of much, but every fear resided within the hospital's four walls. If he hadn't been such a coward, would he have found the courage for honesty with Meg? He knew what she was getting at. Maybe if he'd have let her kill his hopes for a future at the place that terrified him, he wouldn't be prepared to ruin his ranch with her rejection.

Scanning the interior of the shed, he studied the two-nights' handiwork. Late into the night, he painted and laid laminate flooring over the subfloor. In the attic, he found a rug to warm up the space and added an armchair and ottoman. The room wasn't perfect. Luckily, his grandfather valued effort.

He told his grandfather to come down the minute he got out of the SUV. He couldn't wait to show the space to its owner. He wanted to reward Hank for finally fixing up the mess. *If only I could do the same.*

Ted had informed him of Meg's text. Ryan had dictated the reply. He needed a moment. If he raced from his grandfather's return into the big romantic gesture he had planned, he'd crash.

On his trip into town, he'd purchased a cake and ordered something special for her. Will at the General Store had shot him a curious look. Ryan had ignored his peer, thanking him for the two-tier chocolate frosted cake and leaving before he had bumped into anyone else.

A knock sounded on the shed door.

He turned toward the entrance, watching the panel slowly open.

Meg stood on the other side, twisting her neck as she took in the transformed space. "Wow." She stepped inside, leaving the door ajar. "When did you do all this?"

He shut his eyes, her lavender scent wafted in the air and tickled his nose.

A rain storm was predicted before sundown. If he stayed in the shed with her, he knew the electrical surge between them would cause a lightning strike. He opened his eyes and met her gaze.

Lifting a shoulder, he shrugged. "I didn't sleep much the past couple nights."

She rubbed her palms. "Me, too."

Because of Hank or me?

A cold breeze snaked through the entry.

She scanned the shed. "It looks nice." She rubbed her hands together. "Very cozy."

"It will be. I'll add heating and a/c and lights."

"Maybe a dog bed? I'm sure Colby will love to be here with him." She lifted the corner of her mouth.

The smile was hesitant and shy.

"Where's Hank?" He frowned. This wasn't the plan. He wanted to ride over to her house later with the roses he ordered. After he was certain Hank liked the room, Ryan wanted to apologize and explain.

"He told me to get him something down here." She nibbled her lip and crossed her arms low over her belly. "I think he meant you." Her cheeks flushed, and she stared at the ground.

Tell her. Now or never. This moment wasn't what he planned or—more accurately—rehearsed. He'd meant to catch her off-guard and leave her in no doubt of his intentions. Instead, every word caught on his Adam's apple, choking him.

With a sigh, she turned. "I can go."

"No, please stay." He cleared his throat. "I'm sorry about..."

"Giving me the wrong impression?" She shook her head. "Don't be. Hank had all sorts of ideas. You were right to stop me the other night." She met his gaze and sniffed. "Let's not make this any harder or more awkward than it already is."

"Too late."

She stiffened. "I want to help with your events. Let's be careful to keep our relationship civil."

In a handful of steps, he reached her.

She shuddered. "Don't push me away for good."

His heart slammed into his ribcage. "Is that what you think I want?" he murmured. "For you to leave?"

She lifted a shoulder. "To leave you alone, yes. That's what I think."

Joe was right. Hank was right. Everyone in town was probably of the same mind. Ryan should have listened. He'd let his misconceptions and fears take her for granted and then push her away. "Meg, you drive me crazy." His words tumbled out, more growl than speech. "Your constant need for chatter bugs me. Every time you walk into a room, you demand my attention. You've been this way your whole life. You're never growing out of the behavior."

Wrinkling her brow, she pressed together her lips but kept her attention on the floor.

This is all wrong. How had he gotten so off-script? He meant to flatter her with pretty words and entice her to take a chance. Who would waste a second on a jerk like him?

She didn't move.

Had he struck the right balance? If he was lucky, his impromptu honesty would mean more than any practiced compliment. She'd see through smooth lines anyway.

"No comment?" He arched a brow. "Good, I need to finish. Because I realized I don't like it any better when you are quiet. When you don't speak, I have to. I end up saying way more to you than I've ever said to any other person living or dead."

She shrugged. "I'm sorry I'm such a bother."

"No, you're not, and you never have been." He stood a few feet away now. If he extended his arm, he could graze her cheek with his fingertips. "I was foolish. You challenge me. No one else ever has. And the most surprising thing is? I like it."

She rolled her eyes.

"Fine. Don't listen to my words. Look at my actions. At sixteen, I vowed to never dance with you again in public." He reached for her hand. "I was foolis—"

Squeezing his hand, she lifted her quivering chin, her eyes glittering with unshed tears. "I love you."

"You stole my line!" He gaped. What was the point in preparing a speech and ordering a bouquet if she was going to do all the work? Was this his lurking in the bottom of a muddy creek future like his guests, the Claytons? He could only be so lucky.

She stuck out her lower lip.

In another second, she would turn pink and launch into some speech. He chuckled. The laugh shook loose the last bits of tension stiffening his spine. He knew every expression and could anticipate every rebuttal. Still, she surprised him in the most unlikely ways.

She could find someone else in a second. He'd be miserable for the rest of his life. Ford's advice was also a warning. Thank goodness Ryan heeded both in time.

Wrinkling her brow, she pursed her lips. "What's so funny?"

The corner of her mouth twitched. She was barely suppressing a smile.

Gently, holding her fingers with a light touch, he tugged her close. He reached for her waist and pulled her against his chest, wrapping her in both his arms. He would never let go as long as he breathed. Without her in his embrace, his world made no sense.

"I guess, since I love you, what's mine is yours."

She widened her eyes. "You really love me? Or you sort of love me? Or you l—"

He lowered his mouth to hers and kissed her like she was the tall glass of water after the dusty ride through the ranch in August. She was more than the past or the future. She was his present.

If he could focus on one day at a time, he'd have all he needed in the world. The trouble would be keeping her occupied so she didn't start her chaos without him.

CHAPTER 21

A week later, Meg raced up the front steps of the ranch house at six thirty. Without knocking, she twisted the doorknob and strode through the front entrance, shutting the door behind her. She inhaled the scent of roasting meat and buttery bread. Her stomach growled. Strolling to the door at the end of the hall, she pushed inside.

At the stove, Hank stirred a pot.

Colby sat at his feet, tail wagging.

Joe, Ted, and Ryan sat around the big table, laughing and smiling.

She lifted the corner of her mouth, feeling the contagious, happy spirit in the room. "Did I miss dinner?"

Hank turned and glanced over his shoulder. "You're right on time. Go and wash up."

At the sink, she scrubbed her hands under the faucet. Turning off the water, she grabbed a paper towel, dried her hands, and turned. "Oooff!" She spun straight into Ryan's arms, hitting her forehead on his chin.

He dropped his arms and stepped back, rubbing his jaw. "Might need a bit of work on my timing."

She smiled and stepped forward, reaching on tiptoe and draping her arms around his neck. "Let's try again."

He lowered his head and kissed her.

Warmth spread from her heart to her toes. The gentle press of his soft lips on hers and his strong hands on her waist reassured her. They might have taken the scenic route, but they ended up where they belonged.

He dropped his hands and stepped back.

"Hank? Can I help?" she asked.

"No, I made those three set the table. Just get a good seat." He turned and winked. "Come grab the pot, Ted."

Ted nodded and pushed back from the table.

She slid onto the bench, next to Ryan.

Hank sat at the head.

Ted set the pot in the center of the table and motioned for the bowls, filling each to the rim.

When she grabbed hers, she breathed deep. Beef stew was Hank's specialty and the ultimate comfort food for the ranch.

Ryan passed the bread basket.

She bit her lip, grabbing two.

He arched a brow and turned, extending the basket across the table to Ted.

She liked having inside jokes. For so long, she felt like he laughed at her. Sharing humor together brightened her day. "Did you get the email from Eric?" she asked Hank, leaning around Ryan. "He cc'd me."

Hank nodded. "I did. Do you think those prices are real?"

"For a signed souvenir photograph card, apparently yes." She shrugged.

"I wish you sold the collection for me," Hank murmured.

"I don't regret anything." She shook her head. "You'll get five figures from the auction house, and the consignment is already sold out both online and in my store."

"Really?" Ryan turned. "Wonderful news. You're on a roll."

"Speaking of. How's your Frontier Days speech coming?" Joe asked. "Stephanie is pleased you agreed at the last minute."

Ted grunted and raised the bowl to his mouth.

Meg wasn't sure what to make of that sound. She was thrilled to be involved. "I think I have a good start. I'll be meeting her at the end of the week to go over what I have so far."

"You've got plenty of town stories to share," Hank said.

"I'm not sure how many I'll be allowed to divulge." She bumped Ryan with her shoulder.

"As long as I'm not the bad guy or the punchline of every joke, I'll be fine," Ryan said.

"Okay, cowboy." He might play rough and tough for others, but she'd only just begun to understand how marshmallow soft he was on the inside. Their strengths and weaknesses complimented each other. They were far better together than they'd ever been apart.

Under the table, Ryan reached for her knee and squeezed.

"I wish you'd taken a cut from the sale," Hank repeated.

"I'm doing fine." She smiled. "I set aside enough profit from selling the entire collection of Susie's books for a special order for the corner of my store."

"What's that?" Joe asked, stuffing the last bite of a roll in his mouth.

"A photo booth," she said. "I got tired of shooing away customers. I'll keep a selection of cheap props. The good stuff is on display in a locked cabinet. Hank, do you think you'd be up for a trip to San Francisco in the autumn? Might be fun to go to the sale."

Hank rubbed his jaw. "I could be interested. I have plans for the proceeds."

"You do?" Joe asked. "I never think of you as a spending money before you have it type."

"I'm not, and we don't know how much we'll get. Ryan's yurts just about covered the loan on the Hawke land. I'd like to invest in the future, too. I'd like to buy into the events side of the business." Hank smiled at Meg. "If you two will have me?"

She nodded, tears stinging her eyes. She could think of nothing better.

"I'll join you in the city," Ryan said.

"We're going for business, boy," Hank replied.

Meg's cheeks heated. Was it wrong she'd merge her professional and personal lives at the first chance? With any luck, her future became part of the Kincaid legacy.

"I have professional reasons," Ryan said. "The zoo has one of the oldest American Buffalo herds in the nation. The zoologists and caretakers have a wealth of knowledge. When my forebears were rounding them up, a park superintendent bought a couple bison and started conservation efforts in the nineteenth century. Thought they might have a few tips to share. I'm always interested to learn what I can." Under the table, he squeezed her knee.

"A good idea." Ted nodded. "The herd will be a big adjustment to operation next summer." He turned to Joe. "How are your town education efforts?"

Joe covered his mouth with a hand and held up a finger. Swallowing, he dabbed his face with a napkin. "I have an informal, educational night planned at the end of the month. The school gave us permission to use the building. I should have a booth up and running at Frontier Days, too. I'll be happy to answer questions and dispel any rumors."

Ted raised his bowl to his mouth and slurped.

Meg widened her eyes but didn't comment. Her exposure to life on the ranch had always been restricted. Now she had the full experience. *If this is the worst I see today, it's a good day.*

"Sorry, ma'am," Ted said. "I'll dust off my manners soon enough. Don't forget, Ryan, I should have a quote for the deck build next week."

She bit her lip to keep from crowing.

Under the table, Ryan squeezed her knee. "You'll get your big celebration for ninety, Hank. Meg had an idea for expansion, and you're our test run."

Hank leaned back. "As long as I am thoroughly feted with catering, balloons, and fireworks, I'll be your guinea pig."

Ryan shuddered. "I knew agreeing to your demands was risky."

"Demands?" Hank asked. "You mean strongly worded suggestions, and I have my first one. Joe, I want you and Abby in charge of the entire event."

"Entire event?" Ryan murmured. "What does that mean?"

Meg elbowed him in the ribs. It wasn't a time to tease.

"Are you sure you need both of us?" Joe asked. "Don't you think it's better to have one person in charge?"

Hank shook his head. "Teamwork makes the dream work."

Ryan leaned close to Meg. "He's not even trying for subtlety."

"Boy, hush." Hank waved a hand. "I know what I want and it's a two-person job."

Joe nodded.

"Might have to be in town if we get an early snow or a late thaw. I can't start construction until the summer tourist season is over," Ryan said. "Other projects and repairs come first."

Meg bumped her shoulder into his. "Don't worry. I'll be here the whole time to oversee the building project."

"I'm counting on it," Hank and Ryan said in unison.

Meg chuckled and the others joined in. "Full steam ahead," she said. She liked being part of life on the ranch. The changes were significant and exciting. She was thrilled to be included in the conversations, even if she agreed to helm the biggest celebration in the town's hundred plus year history.

"Hank, thank you for dinner," Ted said. "I better go do my rounds."

"I have to get going, too," Joe said. "Last staff meeting in the morning and then summer vacation officially starts. You'll get me and Stephanie full-time." He pushed back from the table, grabbing his empty bowl and plate.

She widened her gaze and glanced at her full bowl of stew. From the corner of her gaze, she spotted Ryan's almost finished dinner. She'd have to eat faster to keep up with the others in the future.

"Have a good night," she said.

"You too," Joe said.

Ted grunted.

Hank crossed his arms over his chest and slowly nodded, acknowledging the goodbye.

With boots clicking against the tile floor, Ted and Joe left through the back door.

Ryan pushed back from the table, carrying his bowl to the stove, and ladling in another hearty serving.

Meg turned to Hank. "What was that look about?"

Hank shrugged and leaned back, scratching the dog behind the ears. "Just thinking."

She shook her head. She knew better than to attempt to discourage him. Once he set his mind on a path, stubborn Hank wouldn't quit. His focus wasn't a bad thing. She could personally attest to the success.

Ryan set his steaming bowl of stew on the table, stepped over the bench, and settled next to her.

She leaned against his shoulder, and he scooted closer. Draping an arm over her leg, he squeezed her knee. Warmth spread from his palm to her heart. She belonged here with these Kincaid men. She didn't have much more figured out about them but had the rest of her life to learn.

Their bond was deeper than blood, strengthened by choice and time. Every day, she was more grateful for the catalyst that finally launched her into her role in this house. Family had each other's back. In Herd, everyone was Hank's family.

CATCH A
Cowboy

BOOK TWO

MATCH MADE IN MONTANA

Rachelle Paige Campbell

Acknowledgments:

Thank you to my friends and family for their support of my career. Having an author in your life presents its own challenges. From staring off into space to holding one-sided conversations, I appreciate that everyone accepts and expects me to jot down notes (and sometimes borrow their names for characters).

The Panera Supper Club, Kelly, Shannyn, Tammy, Kelly, Julie, and, of course, Miss Pamala, remain the best writer friends in the whole world. We encourage each other and sometimes write the demise of someone's enemy into our books. There is no better group for bouncing ideas, commiserating, and celebrating the wins. New writers, the best advice I can give you is to find your people!

Thank you to the wonderful team at Rowan Prose Publishing. Working with you, especially Kelly and Katie, has been the most validating and uplifting experience.

Readers, I am so grateful you have found this book, and I can't wait to take you back to the town of Herd soon. Thank you for the gift of your time.

CHAPTER 1

Stephanie Patricks readjusted her crisscrossed legs on the thick yoga mat, tucking her feet under her thighs, and rested her hands lightly on her knees. In late morning, sunshine brightened the studio. Early September brought golden days with a hint of chill in the air, promising the cold on its way. Her noisy inhalation filled her lungs to capacity as she counted to ten in her head before her loud exhale.

The air in the room whooshed as her class of ten followed along.

She smiled as she met each participant's gaze. She loved yoga, both practicing and teaching. She had no choice but to focus on the current moment. During each session, she forced herself to be present, and not worry about the thousand other tasks on her ever-growing to do list. As a person who took action, she had difficulty with not resolving every situation decisively ASAP. Sometimes, she needed to sit and stew on a problem.

While focused on breath and movement, she found a few moments of peace.

Pressing her palms together, she raised her hands to the center of her chest. "The light within me honors the light within you. Namaste." She bowed, lowering her torso until her forehead touched the floor. She stayed folded in half for another cycle of breath. When she returned to upright, she smiled at the class.

The mixed group of men and women from their early twenties to mid-seventies clapped.

"Thank you. I hope you've enjoyed your vacations and that we'll see you again next summer." She swallowed the small lump in her throat. Three months had passed in an instant. She'd miss her tranquil days here.

With murmured thanks and goodbyes, the class gathered their mats, blocks, and straps and exited the class.

The yoga studio was the corner room of the spa barn at the Kincaid ranch. Ten years earlier, the last remaining legacy ranchers, Hank and his grandson Ryan Kincaid, transformed their business from a traditional cattle operation into a high-end resort. It was a big risk in a small town with no tourism. But Ryan had a vision and revitalized his land and Herd's economy. Within the first year, visitors flocked to the Old West town and the business flourished each following summer.

She was grateful for the opportunity to practice yoga in a brand-new facility with eager students on a gorgeous piece of land. Facing South, the wall of windows flooded the room with natural light, enabling her to turn off the overhead fluorescent bulbs for shavasana. In a building dedicated to massage and facials, quiet and stillness permeated the entire structure.

She liked it here. Teaching was her passion. While instructing adults in the techniques of a Hatha practice was different from her regular job, she enjoyed sparking joy in others. One of the selling points of her vocation was summers off. But she wasn't the sort to sit around. In less than two days, she'd start her fifth year as a kindergarten teacher. She had one full day off.

And was already dreading how bored she'd be. She exhaled a heavy sigh, got to her knees, and rolled the pink and purple mat into a tight cylinder, securing it with her strap.

The door shut slowly.

Typically, the slam that followed the last person's exit echoed in the silent room. Today, the closing was muffled and restrained. She wasn't alone, but she didn't tense. She knew the mystery person's identity. He wasn't betrayed by a sound.

It was a smell that confirmed her suspicions.

Mint and leather. She was reminded simultaneously of a sun warmed car interior on a lazy Sunday afternoon drive and iced tea with the fresh cut herb from a kitchen garden. Unlike the man, both gave her a feeling of contentment.

She lifted her chin, raising her gaze to the newcomer. Her chest squeezed and her throat seized. She frowned. Did that rhyme? Could she work that into a lesson for her kindergarten class? At least then she could turn what would inevitably become another awkward encounter into a positive experience.

Ted Stirling, staff supervisor, pressed a palm flat against the door. With one leg raised and the ankle crossed over the opposite knee, he slipped off a boot. Then he repeated the motion. For a big man, his movements were surprisingly poetic and soft. His balance was impeccable. And his actions? Seeking to respect her space by padding across the floor in socks only solidified what she admired most about him.

He's kind and caring. And he's my boss.

She swallowed a lovelorn sigh. Her body would do at least the minimal motion. Really, she struggled against a full-fledged swoon. He was so dreamy. She knew better. He'd never direct his energy toward her so why let her unrequited crush restrain her? She wasn't exactly tongue-tied in his company. She couldn't remember how to think and speak at the same time.

In bright white socks, he tiptoed across the floor. "Mornin, Stephanie. Figured I'd help you gather your things and get your keys back from you."

The smell of fresh laundry mixed with the other scents, saturating the room. She leaned back on her heels, pressing her knees even harder into the floor. Somehow, he carried every aroma she found most intoxicating in a heady cologne. It was like he embodied a list of her wants. Of course, he didn't know her preferences. How could he when she didn't have the courage to say more than a few words?

Under her knees, the solid surface was unrelenting. Not that it could shake the words out of her throat or stop her palms sweating. She opened her mouth—wanting to deliver a cheeky, flirty comment—and grunted.

He smiled. "Just point to what you need help with, and I'll start loading your car."

Dragging in a shaky breath, she brushed her hair out of her face, her clammy hands extra cold against her burning cheeks. At least her momentary muteness only happened with arguably the nicest person in town. If she couldn't hold her own, she never would have lasted against some of the extra concerned, very involved parents at her school.

She lifted her knees and—balancing on the balls of her feet—slowly stood. The deliberate motions regulated her breathing and her pulse. Grabbing her purse from next to the mirror at her back, she threw the tote-style bag over her shoulder and slung the yoga mat over the other arm, straps creating a crisscross pattern on her back.

As long as she didn't look at him, she was fine. She could pretend she was in charge as the teacher and ignore how his thick lashes highlighted his gray eyes or the deep cleft in his chiseled chin that made him look like a cowboy from an old movie. She crossed the room, averting her gaze, and pointed to a stack of plastic milk crates holding foam blocks and another with woven blankets. "Thank you. I'll get the rest."

She didn't wait to see if he did as she asked. She knew he would. That was the sort of person he was. Within her first few years living in tiny Herd, Montana, she became familiar with every townsperson. Ted always stood out in her mind. Beyond his broad shoulders and good looks, he had a calm, controlled energy she admired.

But she was unable to verbalize at every encounter. Unless she was unquestionably in charge.

The door cracked open, flooding the room with light.

She bent and grabbed the crate holding straps, throwing her purse on top. Turning toward the door, she froze mid-step.

With his back holding the door open, he waited.

She glanced down, he'd slipped back into boots silently. Inelegantly, she jammed her feet into her flip flops, stubbing her big toe. She winced.

He stepped forward.

She shook her head and strolled past him. If he offered her help, he'd wreck her. He couldn't be kind to her. She didn't need to encourage her heart any more to pursue this ridiculous, one-sided, crush.

Down the flagstone path, she continued to the small, employee parking lot behind the building. Hidden from view of the windows behind a row of buffaloberry shrubs, the recently paved rectangle wasn't in keeping with the overall cowboy aesthetic. She was glad for a slight break from the dusty ground. And, although it hadn't been a problem this year, she was glad to avoid her tires getting stuck in the mud during the typically heavy summer storms. A cool breeze shook the dry leaves of the plants. Snow wasn't too far off.

She shivered and walked to her car.

The little red coupe needed a wash from the dusty, gravel roads leading from town to the ranch. Dirt was the least of the vehicle's woes. The backseat was loaded with plastic containers holding school supplies. In the shotgun spot, she set a banker's box full of files and paperwork from the last civic event—Frontier Days—to the next in a week—the annual charity poker tournament. She'd get around to cleaning and organizing the car over the next week.

She would unload the supplies in her classroom tomorrow. In a few more days, she'd co-host the poker fundraiser. Then she'd put her events files in her bedroom closet to wait until she was called to volunteer again. In a small town, she could be conscripted into service sooner than later. She didn't mind. She set the milk crate on the ground, rifled through her tote for her keys, and popped the trunk. Lifting her gaze, she spotted his gaping mouth.

He coughed.

For a second, reversing the speechless roles was nice. Until she remembered why he gawked. She was the sort of person who constantly made piles. As soon as she cleared away her things, she started a new stack.

Stephanie grabbed her milk crate and strode past, brushing his shoulder as she rounded the bumper. Her arm scalded from the accidental touch. She set the crate in the trunk and removed her mat from her shoulder, slipping the strap over her head. Her cool confidence lasted less than ten seconds.

Ted set the other two crates in the trunk and shut the trunk.

Gripping the tote bag style purse with both hands, she faced him. He looked oddly expectant. If she was supposed to say something, she'd love a script and some lines right now.

"Keys?" he asked.

Duh. She reached into her bag for her studio keys and slipped the yoga studio's door off the clip. She extended the key.

He held a hand out, palm flipped up.

She dropped the key, grateful to avoid any other accidental touches.

"Thanks, Stephanie. Will we see you tomorrow night? It's our last Cowboy Dinner and we like to invite all the employees to enjoy the festivities. Our way of celebrating the season together. I promise, no work."

She nodded. She'd helped at several of the events over the summer but never been invited as a guest. *Not his guest.* He said we. Of course, he meant in his role as the spa staff manager for his bosses Hank and Ryan Kincaid. It was practically a royal we around these parts. The Kincaid Ranch saved the town's economy by transforming from ranching to relaxation.

"Great. I'll see you tomorrow." He reached up like he'd tip the brim of his hat. Instead, he swiped his forehead. "Forgot I left it at home this morning." He chuckled. "Have a good day."

He spun on his heel and strode away.

"You too," she whispered, her words evaporating on the breeze. She walked around her car and hopped behind the wheel. If she ever kept her nerve around him, what would she say?

With each booted step, Ted kicked up more dirt. Striding from the staff parking lot to the barn to lock up and back again to his truck, he walked through a cloud of dust of his own making. He couldn't remember a drier summer. The grass had lost its luster by mid-June. He ripped up roots on the dead lawn with each step.

In a few days, he expected the environmental impact study about the bison's return to the land in his inbox. He and Ryan needed to review the details before sharing information with Joe Staunch. Social studies teacher and part-time tour guide, Joe would ultimately lead all discussions about the herd with the town. With a reputation for respecting others' opinions and understanding the history of the area better than anyone,

Joe was the perfect intermediary between the ranch and the town. He was the face of the program.

The reintroduction of the animals was the right decision for countless reasons. But the community would push back. Change was hard. Ted knew he shouldn't try to guess what the study would reveal. He couldn't stop himself. He was brimming with questions and playing out what-if scenarios.

What would happen with the bison next summer? If the prairie grass dried up, what would they eat? Would he have to feed the way he used to for the cattle in the winter, throwing hay off the back of his truck?

Or he could focus on one day at a time and be glad for checking one item off his to do list, getting the studio keys from Stephanie.

He had hoped for more acknowledgment than a nod. He was confident in his managerial skills but worried he put her on edge. Could she give him feedback to improve?

When he had started at the ranch, he accepted a career handling animals. It fit his degree and his personality. He never anticipated he'd be in charge of humans. But he couldn't have predicted any of the twists and turns his life had taken over the last decade plus. If he had? He might have been too scared to take even a step.

Still, he didn't like that Stephanie was so quiet around him. She was known for her capable, take-charge-attitude around town, running a variety of civic events with admirable efficiency. But she never opened her mouth and uttered more than a visceral sound in response to him.

The age gap between them was the prime suspect for her discomfort. He was nearly over a decade and a half older. Their different generations spoke their own languages, he assumed. Beyond that, he carried his emotional burdens in a heavy steamer trunk like he was setting off for a new land and would never return home. He suspected she traveled light. But he couldn't know.

She'd have to speak first.

Shaking his head, he climbed behind the wheel of his pick-up and drove down the gravel road toward the red barn. With one Bluetooth earpiece in, he tapped the steering wheel in time to his favorite music. He learned early on in his time on the ranch, over eleven years ago, that no one in Montana appreciated the Southern California ska punk scene quite the way he did. If he didn't want to listen to the ranchers' complaints about his taste, he couldn't blast the songs he knew by heart on the stereo.

As a transplant from the farming belt in the heart of the Golden state, however, he kept what ties he could to the hometown he had once imagined he'd never leave. He hadn't been back for a year. The longest stretch he'd ever managed without a California sunset or a slice of his favorite pizza. He owed one spot in particular a visit. After he wrapped up the paperwork for the summer employees, he'd make a visit. It'd have to be quick before the chance of snow hung heavy in the air in about a month.

His sister and niece were the only relatives left in their home town. Earlier in the summer, he'd floated the idea about relocating to Herd. She hadn't said anything in response. Oh well. His reasons for visiting wouldn't change if she moved and neither would his hurt lessen. He wanted her nearby. As far as little sisters went, she wasn't too terribly annoying. And her daughter was his favorite person on earth which almost made his sister's bratty years worthwhile.

He pulled the truck to the side of the barn and parked. Jumping to the ground, he pocketed his earpiece and shielded his gaze with one hand. The wooden structure was overdue for a coat of paint but would have to wait a little while longer. He saw no point in doing a job twice. If the owners moved forward with the deck addition, the barn would be plenty beat up during construction. Cutting a giant hole in the back wall and adding French doors guaranteed a touch-up job.

Strolling toward the back of the building, he headed toward the deep low rumble of a heated conversation. Maybe he spoke too soon. Progress couldn't be reached at an impasse.

At the corner, he dropped his arm to his side and approached his bosses. Both equal owners. The eighty-nine-year-old legacy rancher and his thirty-nine-year-old grandson. Scowling at each other in symmetry, like they were mirror twins.

"Ah, good. Sense has arrived. Come over here, Ted. Help explain my side," Hank, the octogenarian, called.

Ryan rolled his eyes heavenward and dug the toe of his boot into the dirt.

Ted wasn't sure he counted as good advice, but he always urged caution. Taking risks was Ryan's forte and how the ranch prospered. Ted needed time to warm to one of the new ideas but ended up in full support. "What's the problem? Didn't we work out the deck's size and position? I have the crew coming to pour footers. I have permits. We are scheduled and ready to start."

"I think we're wasting an opportunity here," Hank said. "This old barn has been fixed up more times than I can count. Why don't we raze the whole thing and build something modern? We keep adapting the structure to fit our needs. Let's take the opportunity to really build what we need."

Ted widened his eyes. Shaking his head, he stared at the ground. If he'd had a guess about today's Kincaid intergenerational debate, he wouldn't have used it on this topic. Demolishing a piece of ranch history? And Hank being the one to lead the destruction?

When Ryan had first broached the idea of selling the cattle and appealing to tourists, he had waged a war with his grandsire, battling to change a single speck of dirt on the land. Ted knew. He'd been part of many of those arguments. Now, Hank wanted to rip out the original barn? Anyone who thought a person couldn't change past a certain age was a fool. "Mr. Kincaid, sir, are you serious?"

"Ha!" Ryan pointed to the cowboy. "See? Told you he'd be on my side."

"I don't want to come between you two," Ted said slowly, drawing the words out to give his brain a chance to catch up. *I know better.*

Grandfather and grandson were equally matched when it came to stubbornness. Only the girl next-door, Ryan's girlfriend Meg Hawke, could cure either of their pig-headed ways. The Kincaid men shared a blind spot for her. She could almost do no wrong. What would she think about the new idea?

"Mr. Kincaid, you're right," Ted said, stroking his jaw. "It would be great to have a clean slate. We'll be scrambling to retrofit the interior to meet the needs of the event guests and staff."

Hank lifted his chin and grinned broadly at Ryan.

"But I agree with Ryan."

Ryan clapped Ted's shoulder. "Good man."

Hank glowered.

"I'm not in favor of keeping the old barn forever." Ted held up his hands in surrender or defense, whichever proved the more effective stance against either or both of the Kincaids. "You have a good point about the needs for an event. We squeeze into a tiny storage closet when we need something. We'll no doubt be storing at least double or more. Abby Whit has spoiled us about catering because she's on wheels. Her kitchen is parked outside, and she hauls everything in as needed," Ted said.

"Hey, you're supposed to be talking up my plan." Ryan frowned.

He didn't want to choose a side and sometimes the stubborn pair insisted on all or nothing. "The biggest argument to keep the barn is simple. We can't risk losing time during the start of the summer season if the build goes long. And builds always go long."

"My thoughts exactly," Ryan said. "We'll get a new barn. Eventually. We have to know the events are going to pull in a profit first."

"Oh, they will. With Meg in charge, I don't doubt it." Hank extended a hand to his grandson.

Ryan shook it with a smile.

Hank was a gracious enough loser to admit defeat. Of course, he was also wily enough to include praise for Ryan's girlfriend. Sharp and nimble, Hank was a formidable ally or foe. Ted always kept his caution around Hank. "I was heading inside to double check provisions for tomorrow night. I invited Stephanie, after she handed in her key," Ted said.

"Good, good. Did Stephanie get out ok? Was she pleased with working for us this season?" Ryan asked.

Ted stroked his jaw. "I think so, not like she'd tell me."

Ryan chuckled. "Yeah, why do you have to be so scary all the time? You don't have to inspire fear to earn your employee's respect."

Ted scowled. He couldn't take the joke for fear of the truth hidden in the jest. Was he intimidating? The ranch was his first experience as a boss. He didn't want anyone frightened of him.

"Oh, give the man a break." Hank interjected. "Not his fault the woman clams up around him. It is peculiar though."

Ted agreed. She was a puzzle. He admired her spunk and bubbly personality. He'd glimpsed her beaming smiles directed at others. Whenever he neared, however, he heard nothing. He supposed it shouldn't matter. But it did.

He could fight his own battles but was always grateful for a reprieve. Especially about Stephanie. All he wanted out of life was to keep the status quo until he reached the end. He was most definitely not looking for romance and kept his guard up around his matchmaking, elder boss. With so many years between himself and Stephanie, they'd have nothing in common and no reason to interact besides work. If he was going to pursue a friendship with someone, however, he might choose her.

As the silence stretched, Ted became aware of the collective stares of his bosses. He cleared his throat. "She did a nice job. Hopefully, she'll be back."

Ryan nodded. "Wait a second." Scrunching his face, he turned to his grandfather. "Why is he a man, and I'm a boy?"

Hank shrugged. "I never had to wipe his butt."

Ted smiled at Ryan's red cheeks. Not a lot could embarrass him, but Hank knew every touch point. While the pair weren't Ted's family by blood, he was glad they'd embraced him anyway. Tragedy spurred him to uproot his life and change everything he'd ever known. Where he landed was just about perfect. With the opportunity to work with animals again next spring, he couldn't ask for more.

He wanted everything to stay perfectly the same forever.

At the main road, Stephanie signaled and turned toward town. She had agreed to an end-of-summer lunch to savor every last second, even though she'd end up talking about work. Her destination was The Golden Crown saloon. She was meeting with her fellow kindergarten teachers—and arguably her best friends. In another town, the location might be a scandalous destination for three teachers before noon. Only about a third of their school population resided in Herd. The rest of the kids came from neighboring towns in the greater surrounding region. The likelihood of running into students and their families was small.

Named for the failed prospecting discovery that established the town, when a would-be miner fished someone's golden tooth out of the creek on the current Kincaid ranch, the saloon was less rowdy bar and more family-friendly bistro. It was also the only full-service restaurant in town. During the summer and on warm weekends, Abby Whit operated a food truck from the disputed land near the church at the end of the street. Her food was exceptional but her location was al fresco. Stephanie had doubted her fellow teachers wanted to spend their last few hours of summer exposed to any passer-by.

She drove down Main Street, past the blacksmith shop and the antique store, past the costumed Old West portrait studio and General Store, parking in front of The Golden Crown. Turning off the car, she glanced at the banker's box full of her plans for next week's event.

James, the saloon owner, was kind enough to host the annual, historical dress encouraged, fundraiser. After three years, he understood what was needed and expected. Still, she liked to be fully prepared and work through the entire checklist several times over.

A knock on the window had her snapping up her head.

"You coming inside?" A very pregnant brunette asked, leaning an arm on the roof of the car.

Stephanie scrambled out of the vehicle, grabbing her purse off the center console. "Lauren, you should be inside and off of your feet."

The other woman waved off her concern, resting both hands under her swollen belly and leaning her back against the old hitching post in front of the building. "I'll have plenty of time to lay around later."

Stephanie eyed her dubiously. She'd never heard of any parent of multiples finding time for rest after their sweet, twin bundles of joy arrived. But she also knew better than to disagree with Lauren and especially not now. Calling her bluff only provoked a challenge. "Let's get a table. I'm hungry." She rubbed together her palms and continued to the door, holding it open for her friend.

Stepping inside, her eyes adjusted to the dimly lit interior. The Golden Crown saloon was a large space and had hosted an occasional hundred person plus reception when needed. Most days, however, the place felt cozy with smaller vignettes created by huge posts throughout the room.

A polished, walnut bar took up the length of the building, hugging one wall. Behind it an antique mirror reflected the patrons' faces as they savored their drinks. The sweet smell of sawdust hung in the air, a throwback to the early days when The Golden Crown used it to mop up spilled beer and spit tobacco.

At a table near the back, under a kerosene style hanging light, an older woman stood and waved.

Stephanie and Lauren strode toward their comrade.

Kelly Strong was nothing like her namesake. From her soft and flowy garments to her hushed voice, she was the matronly type Hollywood would cast to portray an early childhood teacher on screen.

To her good friends, Kelly was known for her deep laugh, strong drinks, and love of family. Her kids were in college, only a little younger than Stephanie and a decade younger than Lauren. Kelly never treated the women as a mother hen but rather worked hard to guide them as a trusted and respected mentor.

Kelly pulled out a chair for Lauren.

Lauren sank into the wooden seat like a bag of horseshoes.

Kelly grabbed another chair, tugging it out from the table. "For your feet."

"I'm fine," Lauren protested weakly.

Kelly shot her a teacher face and returned to her spot.

With a sigh, Lauren rested her feet in the chair and propped one arm on the table, sitting in profile. "This is probably better anyways. I can't scoot my belly under the table."

Stephanie sat in the free seat. "Are you sure you want to start the school year? You can still change your mind. Bill understands."

Their principal was well regarded. Raising twins of his own, he appreciated Lauren's situation better than most. Definitely better than Stephanie. She only vaguely grasped the impending changes to her friend's life. With a husband, Lauren's world was already a step removed from Stephanie's. Kids would only heighten the differences between them.

"I'm fine. I can't take any more babying. Steve is monitoring my every move. Wouldn't surprise me if he pops in." Lauren rolled her eyes.

"He's excited. Good for you and him." Kelly pushed a water glass forward.

Lauren grabbed it and drank.

Stephanie was glad for the break from Lauren's gripes about her sweet, nurturing husband. If opposites attracted, the pair were a perfect match. Not to discount Lauren's good qualities. She and her husband shared kindness. But their difference was in the delivery. "Soon enough, your kids are grown and gone. Your job is done like that." Kelly snapped her fingers. "If you need anything, you call me. Any time. No questions asked."

Lauren nodded.

"I'm looking forward to a good year," Kelly continued and turned to include Stephanie in the conversation.

With so much happening in their personal lives, Stephanie didn't like to admit she felt like an outsider at times. She had too much to do for wallowing or self-pity. *You get one life, what are you going to do with it?* Her mom's mantra pushed her forward every day.

"Me, too," Stephanie chimed in. "I might stop by and drop off another round of supplies at my classroom." She smiled, feeling it down to her toes. Creating a safe space for every kid in her class was just as important as providing them with the tools to excel and love learning. She had a new plan for the school year to further erase any differences. She wanted everyone on an equal standing within her four classroom walls.

Focusing on her kids was better than thinking about her one-sided, unrequited crush.

"I need a good, smooth, quiet year," Lauren said, her gaze sliding to Kelly's.

Kelly shook her head.

The motion was so slight, Stephanie might have thought she imagined it. But with five years of working together as a duo before Stephanie was hired, the pair sometimes exchanged looks and non-verbal communication with significant implications. "What is it? What's wrong?"

Kelly frowned.

Lauren leaned forward. "Nothing's wrong, per se. But be careful. The PTO president's youngest kid is in your class this year."

"Oh, okay." Stephanie tipped her head to the side. She'd only had positive interactions with the woman, Candace Vane. When Stephanie first had her idea to do a fundraiser to cover the costs of food service for the entire building, thus eliminating any difference between kids receiving free and reduced lunches and those paying full price, the woman had supported her and had called on a corporate connection that met the donation, thus doubling the gift and adding breakfast to the offerings. "Do you suppose she requested me?"

"Maybe?" Lauren grimaced and shook her head. "I taught the eldest Vane child my first year."

"What was the problem?" Stephanie asked. "My interactions with Candace have all been good. She has a real heart for the school and doing her part."

Kelly darted her gaze side to side and leaned forward. "She likes to play saints and martyrs. Either she portrays herself as utterly magnanimous and you adore her because she's so selfless. Or you are her persecutor and how dare you when she's only trying for the greater good. She never does anything without seeking public support."

Stephanie puzzled over that, folding her arms over her chest, and nibbling her bottom lip. Was that her angle? Trying to be esteemed by the public at large? Did people really spend so much time caring what others thought about them?

"Just be careful is all we're saying," Lauren said.

"I will. But don't worry about me. You'll be on leave soon," Stephanie said. "Focus on staying healthy for your babies."

"I want you there when I get back," Lauren murmured.

Stephanie lifted her menu, cutting off the unhelpful conversation. Talking wasn't her style. She much preferred taking action over pretty words. When her plan was in full effect and the kids were excelling, then she'd be vindicated.

She didn't want to be on edge at school. After a summer tiptoeing around Ted Stirling, she wanted to fall back into her role as self-confident, career woman. She appreciated her friends' words but knew she'd have to live the experience to understand for herself the caution they urged.

Thankfully, a server approached the table and took their orders, clearing the way for a total conversational shift. She would do what she did best. She only had to survive one more awkward encounter with Ted, and then she vowed to put her feelings for him away for good. What was the point in liking someone if she was too scared to say hello?

CHAPTER 2

Stephanie was nothing if not maddeningly self-aware. As predicted, her day off was torturously long. When the clock finally struck five, she grabbed her tote style purse and headed out her apartment door. An early riser her entire life, she forced herself to stay in bed in her one-bedroom apartment in the complex between the regional school she taught at and Herd's historic downtown, roughly ten miles of empty prairie separating her from each. She'd had to drive another fifteen past town to reach the ranch, putting more miles on her car over the past three months than in the past three years.

Meal prep and laundry kept her busy most of the day. She liked the days she didn't need to drive at all. The newer apartment building sat in a redeveloped strip mall complex. If she'd wanted, she could walk to the little coffee shop on the corner, past a convenience store, gift shop, dry cleaners, and two-screen movie theater. But she didn't need anything else keeping her awake today.

She could have stopped by school to drop off the supplies taking up her backseat. But she hated to drive even a single mile extra. Besides, she'd wake up early enough tomorrow morning with plenty of time to unpack her car long before another teacher arrived and asked if she wanted help.

As a do-er, she resisted any hesitation in a plan. Working with another person—even for something as simple as unloading a vehicle—meant she'd have to slow down and explain herself. She preferred to be in charge without any hint of micromanaging. When her younger brother had married, she'd officially handed over making his appointments to his wife. Her sister-in-law had been shocked an adult didn't know the number for the dentist or when the next physical was due. With two, full-time working parents, Stephanie had taken care of Tyler, earning praise in the process.

Late in the day, leaving for the cowboy dinner, she exhaled a heavy sigh. She was eager to get on with her life and excited to see Ted, despite the churn of her tummy. The scenery passed in a blur. If she had spared a glance, however, she wouldn't have enjoyed the view.

The prairie grasses and wildflowers died early in the season. A lack of summer rain dried the ground until deep cracks broke the earth. For the first time ever, she'd welcome the snow and—with it—the hope of quenching the parched earth.

At long last, she pulled her car in front of the ranch house. Parking at the end of the circle drive, she grabbed her purse off the shotgun seat and exited the car. She swung the tote over her shoulder, tucking her hands into her jean jacket. The late summer evening held a chill in the air. She probably should have worn something more substantial than her favorite cotton sundress and ankle boots.

She wanted to look nice. Just in case. Crunching the gravel under her heel, she crossed in front of her car and continued around the side of the main house. She had only talked to Ted—successfully—once. During her audition to teach, she led him and Ryan through a class. When she leaned into her skills, she was confident. As long as she held still in tree pose, she conducted a conversation with ease.

This evening presented a challenge. Her prospects for success were very slim. Balancing poses were hard enough without adding a plate full of baked beans.

A screen door slammed shut.

She jumped.

"Stephanie?" A feminine voice called.

Stephanie stopped and raised her gaze to the covered, wraparound porch. Squinting, she spotted the face of her newest friend and waved. "Hi, Meg. How are you?"

"I'm doing very well, thank you. But I think you're the person who should be answering the question." Meg walked down the front steps and stopped at her side.

Why? Stephanie sucked in a breath. Had Ted said something? About what? She hardly replied with one-word responses to his questions. Her skin burned. Of course, he could be joking around behind her back.

"Ready for school in the morning?" Meg asked, crinkling the corners of her brown eyes as she smiled. The pretty brunette wore a floral dress that floated around her. She moved with an ease Stephanie envied. *Because she was the girl next door and knew this ranch by heart? Because she was lucky in love?*

Releasing a shaky breath, Stephanie smoothed her hair behind her ears and nodded. "I'm all set."

Meg looped her arm through Stephanie's.

With almost five inches height difference, Stephanie focused on the ground as the pair started walking. After a few steps, she found the rhythm. Meg was considered average height. To Stephanie, however, she was tall.

"I'm glad to see you. This has to be your busiest week of the year, huh?"

"Well . . ." Stephanie considered that. The start of the school year was quickly followed by the holiday season. Between work and civic life, she operated in a loop of busyness. Once winter came, her town commitments diminished as her career ramped up with parent-teacher conferences, curriculum meetings, further education, and after-school activities. Then came the spring and summer and the return of tourists. Did she ever have a slow time of year?

Meg chuckled. "Never mind. I think you're always busy."

"I like to be productive."

At the back of the house, they crunched brittle, brown grass under their feet, careful of the deep cracks in the dry earth. Stephanie missed the sweet smell of fresh-cut grass but watering the lawn would cost an exorbitant amount. She lifted her gaze toward their destination.

The doors were fully opened. Light spilled out and the buzz of conversation floated past, welcoming company for a fun evening.

Cars parked on the grass next to the barn. During the summer, resort guests were the primary customers at the cowboy dinners, thus not needing a large parking lot. Had Stephanie been presumptuous to park in front of the house? She nibbled the inside of her cheek.

"Do you need an extra hand at the poker tournament?" Meg asked. "The auction was pushed back so we aren't leaving for another week."

"Oh, that would be great." Meg sighed. "Can I stop by the store on Thursday?"

"I'll be there. I might be working on my packing list. I haven't visited San Francisco in years."

"I've never been." Stephanie couldn't hide her wistful tone. Images of cable cars and brightly colored Victorian homes flashed in her mind.

"Really?" Meg pulled back, studying her. "I had family nearby years ago. I'm not excited to see how much has changed. But I am looking forward to visiting my favorite spots in the city."

At the entrance, Meg unhooked her arm and leaned close. "I confess my volunteer involvement at the fundraiser won't be entirely selfless."

Stephanie tipped her head to the side. "It won't?"

Meg shook her head. "I would love to pick your brain about event planning. The ranch's next venture was my idea. But the more reading and research I undertake, the more I'm overwhelmed."

Stephanie nodded. "I understand. Believe me. When I first took over Frontier Days, the task seemed Herculean. You have to start small and be willing to learn. I have a few checklists I can copy for you as a starting off point. Weddings are a different beast."

"Maybe I can convince you to help me part-time?" Meg asked. "We both have full-time careers demanding the bulk of our attention. If the business takes off, an on-staff coordinator will be hired. It'll be a bare bones operation at the start."

Stephanie nibbled the inside of her cheek. She preferred to work on one event at a time rather than a vague promise to help out indefinitely. She liked having clear deadlines and set budgets. If Meg asked for wedding help for her nuptials, Stephanie would agree straight away. "I'm sure I can give you an answer without more specifics. I'll help where I can. I'll bring copies of my calendars, too. Everything I have, I'll share."

"I'd appreciate it, thanks," Meg said. "I better see what trouble Hank is getting into," she murmured.

"Don't let me keep you. Thanks for the escort." Stephanie smiled.

Meg strolled forward without a backward glance like she owned the place. She almost did. Her family had owned the next-door ranch, and were one of the town's founders. She grew up spending summers on her land and this property. Dating Ryan Kincaid, the owner's grandson, she'd no doubt be a part of the legacy of this land very soon.

Stephanie was happy for her and knew the now very serious and seemingly inevitable pairing had been a lifetime in the making. Would it take her that long to work up the courage to talk to Ted?

A shove from behind pushed her forward.

She gasped and turned, eyes wide.

"Sorry, Stephanie," Joe said, peering around the large box in his outstretched arms. "I didn't see you."

"Totally my fault for lurking. Can I help?"

"Actually, yeah. Grab one end, please."

Stephanie nodded, not that he could see, and did as directed. While she'd heard whispers of a job opening on the ranch at the start of the summer, she owed her position to her friend, Joe. She'd help him however he needed.

In the K-8 school, she had the opportunity to get to know her fellow teachers as they shepherded their kids from one grade to the next. Joe taught middle school social studies. In a year, he'd be working with her first class of students. She marveled at how fast time sped past for the kids while she barely changed.

"Just behind the catering table," Joe said. "I'll walk backward." He sidestepped until he stood in the position.

"What's in the box?" she asked.

"Huh?" he called.

"What are we carrying?"

"The box?"

She blew out a sigh. Curiosity wasn't enough of a conversation starter tonight. She didn't really care. But she'd made an effort twice, might as well go for the third time. "What is in the box that we are carrying?" she raised her voice, hovering just under a yell.

He stopped walking and started to lower the box to a table.

With her attention focused on the cardboard, she set it down, straightened, and her skin flushed.

Ted stood next to Joe, quirking an eyebrow at her.

In amusement? Oh, please let her be anything but a source of ridicule.

"Thanks," Ted said. "The box has favors for everyone, to celebrate another great year. We have a photographer set up near the band, and we'll pass out commemorative frames. The photos will be mailed."

"Oh," she murmured. Again, the words caught in her throat. She might have only thought the response.

Ted focused on the box, slipping a hand under the flaps at the end.

"Are you trying to open it? Use a knife," Joe said.

"No, I got this." Ted waved him away.

She scrunched her nose. What was it with men not accepting help when offered? If Joe said nothing, would Ted have pulled out his own pocket knife?

"First, you have to grip it. Then you rip it," Joe said.

Ted chuckled. "Okay, Bogey Lowenstein." He rolled his eyes and ripped the box open.

"Wait? What?" she asked.

His comment snapped her out of her stasis real fast. Was that all it took? Adding in a hearty dash of utter bewilderment to loosen her tongue? Too often, in Ted's company, the useless muscle lolled in her mouth.

Two male faces stared at her with mixed expressions of amusement and outrage.

She wasn't in the wrong here. If they wanted to make bizarre comments, they'd have to explain themselves. And for once she found her voice.

She spoke? In front of a witness? To him? At a public event?

Ted widened his gaze. Her confusion was enough to make him ignore the very painful paper-cut he'd given himself from the surprisingly well sealed box. He should have used a pocket knife. Once Joe opened his mouth, however, it went against Ted's code to give his friend the satisfaction. That was their friendship in a nutshell. Fine and dandy until one opened their mouth gave the other advice. No matter how prescient.

"Who's Bogey Lowenstein?" she asked.

"Ah! She speaks." Ted grinned and widened his stance on the old pine boards, folding his arms over his chest. He couldn't believe his luck any more than he understood her lack of knowledge of one of the seminal movies of his generation. "And I'm offended. It's not who, the question is, what's a Bogey Lowenstein?"

She darted her gaze from one to the other. "I'm supposed to know what that means?"

"It's a classic line from a great movie," Joe said, exasperated.

Her eyes widened.

This was the first time she'd engaged in a conversation with him. Ted hated to waste it by being offended. But he was equally as flabbergasted as Joe. "It's from 1999?"

"I was five." She shrugged.

Joe groaned.

I was in college with Liv. And just like that, the moment shattered. Not that it mattered. Ted was never moving on from losing the love of his life and definitely wasn't looking for a connection with someone so young and unhurt by the world.

Stephanie was sweetness and light. She didn't know pain the way he did. He hoped she never would. They'd never have anything in common besides their zip code.

Ted scrubbed a hand over his face. "Regardless, the film has one of the best soundtracks of all time."

"Truth." Joe raised his hand and fist-bumped Ted.

"I thought the music from that time was all horn lines and . . ." She frowned. "What was it called? Ska?"

Joe threw up his hands. "This is too much."

Ted agreed. Maybe he liked her better not speaking if she was going to challenge the pop culture pillars of his life. But he was equally amused at finally having a conversation with her. He couldn't let it go. "What's better than ska? It has a point of view and a message."

"And that is?" She asked, staring at him with a quizzical gleam in her sapphire eyes.

Ted enjoyed seeing any expression other than confusion and bewilderment on her pretty face. He'd probably regret giving her an answer. Her tone hovered between teasing and serious consideration.

"Because every song I've heard had the same, vague, parents don't understand vibe," she continued.

"Ah. Okay. I get it." Ted regained his footing. "You prefer country slash pop?"

She nodded.

"Aren't some of the most popular songs too hyper focused on the artist's personal life? Why dunk on someone else's ex?" Ted asked.

Her cheeks turned pink. "Heartbreak is universal. The specificity makes it more relatable."

Did she have a bad break-up in her past? Opening his mouth, Ted wasn't sure he wanted to know. The idea of Stephanie dating someone made him feel as hot and weary as he did after a long day of mending fences under the summer sun. But he liked talking with her. What he would have said remained a mystery.

Joe paled, whiter than the clouds, and stepped forward, hunching his back.

"Stephanie, please cover for me," Joe hissed. "Hank's coming towards us with Abby, and I really don't want to be bamboozled tonight."

"No, you're an adult. Just tell him to back off," Stephanie said, rolling her eyes. "You're starting to be rude. Be honest with Mr. Kincaid. Although, I don't understand why you don't like her. She's the only person even remotely interested in your town history project."

Joe glared. "Once I finish the interviews and publish the book, I can promise you everyone will be interested."

Ted studied the pair. He had the sense they'd had this conversation several times before. He hated feeling like the third wheel, especially with them. But he couldn't insert himself into a chat he only guessed at.

Hank Kincaid had spent the summer heavy-handedly manufacturing meet-ups between Abby Whit, food truck owner, and Joe. Ted should be grateful he wasn't on the old man's radar. Love wasn't part of his future. He clung to the memories of romance like a comfortable pair of faded jeans. Someone new wouldn't know his moods or understand his love of silence.

He'd come to Montana seeking peace on his own terms. While he'd become part of a community, slowly over time, that hadn't been his goal. Friends he cared for like family was an unexpected gift. He wouldn't ever seek more. He wouldn't challenge fate again.

"She's hiding some kind of secret," Joe said.

Stephanie rolled her eyes.

"Or she's laughing at me," Joe rushed to add. "Either way it's awkward. Please, come on. I'll owe you big time."

"I flat out refuse." Stephanie shook her head. "The last thing either of us needs is a rumor that we're together spreading through town."

"Fine," Joe bit out the word.

"Besides. I like Abby. I don't understand your issue. If she's catering," Stephanie licked her lips, "I'm eating every plate I can. The food truck is only operating for a few more weeks. I won't get a chance to stop by again once school is in session."

Heavy, bootsteps clicked against the wooden plank floor.

Joe scrubbed a hand over his face, wiping away the grimace.

Smart. Hank deserved no less than everyone's respect. He'd been a town mainstay, supporting any neighbor who needed help and never asking questions. While he might have a bit of a reputation as a gossip, he didn't push. People shared.

About six months into Ted's tenure, he confided in Hank. The pain could never fully be eased but sharing helped shift the boulder off his heart. Hank didn't demand an explanation or play by play. When he had lost his beloved Susie, he had sought Ted for a chat. The pair had reached an even deeper bond.

Hank clapped a hand on Joe's shoulder. "Good evening, everyone. Nice to see you, Stephanie."

"Hi, Mr. Kincaid. I'd better get a seat while I can." Stephanie smiled and waved, backing away.

Joe might have uttered *coward*. Or maybe Ted's imagination filled in the dots. But he had enjoyed the evening's unexpected encounter, learning more about both his friend and his former employee.

He'd been corrected. She was only fourteen years his junior. In the grand scheme, the difference from twenty to fourteen was marginal. But at least it explained why perhaps she never really attempted to talk to him. She probably had no idea what to say.

If she didn't, she wouldn't be the only one.

The problem with falling in love at fifteen and getting married at twenty-two was he'd only really interacted with one girl outside of his family circle. And when he vowed forever, he meant it. He'd shake off his concerns about his run-ins with a random acquaintance. *Except she wasn't random, and she was than an acquaintance.*

"Ted?" Hank snapped his fingers.

With a shake, Ted focused on the new group. "Sorry, thinking about what to do next."

"Good man," Hank said, nodding. "I'm going to steal Joe, if you don't mind. Since Abby's here, figured it's a good time to talk logistics."

Joe frowned. "We don't really want to interrupt her in the middle of service."

Hank waved off the comment. "Oh, it'll only take a second."

"I'm all set here. Thanks for your help, Joe," Ted said, sort of enjoying his friend's frustration.

"Right this way." Hank gestured down the table.

Joe smiled and turned, flashing a finger behind his back.

Ted chuckled. After Hank successfully paired off his grandson and their beautiful next-door neighbor earlier in the summer, he focused his newly found matchmaking energy on Joe. In this case, Ted didn't mind being forgotten.

In Ted's back pocket, his phone vibrated. He pulled out the device, staring at the screen.

Jen Cade: We're here.

His palms went clammy. Why now? Was something wrong?

He'd called his little sister a few days ago, and she'd given him no clue about a visit. His heart slammed into the front of his chest. The text was plural. He could rest easy that had to include at least two. If it was three?

Swallowing the lump in his throat, he dried his hands on his jeans. He could be cordial—if distant—to his niece's father. Jen would expect no less. Probably why she'd given him no warning about her impending arrival. If he snuck out now, he could be back in fifteen minutes.

The crowd settled at tables. The photographer roamed the room, snapping candid pictures. The staff helped Abby carry covered trays from her food truck outside, through the side door, and set them onto chafing dishes. Meal service would start soon.

Everything was set-up and running smoothly. But he couldn't disappear, abandoning his post without a word. Crossing the room, he pulled Ryan from a conversation with Meg near the bandstand.

"I need to go to my cabin. I should be back in half an hour. Forty-five minutes, tops," Ted said.

"Why?"

The question wasn't unexpected. Ted shifted his weight uneasily. He wasn't sure he knew the reason and didn't want to lie.

"Should I be worried?" Ryan tipped his head to the side. "Do you need someone to go with you?"

"No need. Nothing I can't handle." *Liar liar.* Ted cleared his throat. "I'll be back soon."

"Okay." Ryan nodded.

Without further explanation, Ted spun on his booted heel and stalked out of the building. In a few long strides, he crossed the lawn and made his way through the maze of vehicles. He wrenched open the door of his truck, turned over the engine, and peeled out of the parking spot. He reached his snug, wooden, two-bedroom cabin on the other side of the pond, opposite the tourist cabins. Parking his car next to an SUV pulling a trailer, he hopped to the ground.

"Unc!" A little voice called and barreled into his legs, nearly knocking him over.

Chuckling, he reached down and grabbed his niece, embracing her in his arms for a big bear hug. The little girl always looked askew. Her curly mop of thick hair fought against any attempts at taming it. So did the child. He kissed the side of her cheek and, for the first time in twenty minutes, he felt calm, his pulse slowing and his breath evening. "Maddy. So good to see you. I didn't know you were coming." He set her back on the ground and raised his gaze.

His sister sat on the front stoop.

Alone. Thankfully. He refrained from releasing a heavy sigh. With limited time and a complicated custody arrangement, his sister's ex-husband had joined them on visits to Montana in the past. Ted preferred advance notice in such situations. Relief that his former brother-in-law hadn't joined the pair wasn't a particularly charming response to the impromptu family reunion.

"Hi, Teddy." Jen pushed off the top step, dusting her hands on her sherpa jacket and jeans.

Only a few inches shorter, she shared the same gray eyes and brown hair. He often thought she looked like him in a wig. Not that he'd ever say so. She had a wicked right hook.

He pulled her in for a hug.

She returned the embrace and released a shaky exhale. "I got a job at the local hospital. Like you recommended."

She could have called and told him. She knew he hated surprises. Little sisters never stopped being frustrating. He dropped his arms and studied her face. "And everyone is okay with that?"

She nodded. "He's taking a job overseas. We both decided I should be near family. He'll visit us here."

Ted pressed together his lips, holding himself back from what he wanted to say. He wouldn't speak ill of a man in front of his innocent child. When he'd floated the idea about the job opportunity, he'd received no response from his sister.

He figured she wasn't able to pursue the option or wasn't interested in a move. He couldn't blame her. With a child and an ex, her life was complicated without uprooting everything for her brother. Besides, he'd been the one to leave their childhood hometown. If he wanted family close, he should have stayed.

"Are you 'cited, Unc?" Madison asked.

He smiled down at the little girl. "More than you can know. Come on, let's get you settled inside."

When he lifted his gaze to Jen, he noted the dark smudges under her eyes. Exhaustion clung to her like chains. She was here. He'd keep them both safe. If he had to watch his tongue around Maddy, so be it. But he'd never let down the people who loved him. Not after failing one person so completely that he'd never be fully healed.

CHAPTER 3

Stephanie chose her career because she loved children. Summers off was one of the selling points, too. Until she started working and realized the break wasn't relaxing for a person who thrived on external validation.

In that aspect, she supposed she'd never shake her childhood lessons. Her parents instilled in her that a person could have it all as long as they weren't afraid of hard work. The phrase was motivation and cover. Happy to shine the spotlight on others, she shrank in the overhead glare of a direct beam and kept to the background as part of her head down approach to any job.

Since she'd started working, she focused on any chance to make someone else's day a little brighter. She could worry about her own happiness at some distant point in the future. Or if she ever worked up the courage to speak to Ted again.

Behind her desk, she yawned and glanced at the clock on the opposite wall. She had ten minutes to show time. Last night, after the dinner, she had stayed up too late watching the movie he mentioned. She still didn't quite get the appeal. Was that his high school experience?

The amount of in-person interaction was what shocked her the most. Of course, without social media or even widespread cell phone usage, she supposed that was what they had to do. Speak to each other. She cringed. She'd rather send a text than have to look at her crush in the face and worry what her expression said.

A knock sounded on the door.

"Come in," she called and stood, brushing her hands on her skirt. For work, she dressed in bright colors with often cartoonish, cutesy themes. Today, her shirt dress was covered with crayon appliques.

"Good morning, just checking you're all set?" Bill, the principal, asked, entering the room. Dressed in his usual suit, he also used his wardrobe to set him apart in his role. Without the collared shirt and dress shoes clicking against the twelve-by-twelve tile floor, the kind, soft-spoken man wouldn't be nearly intimidating enough for the older kids.

With a smile, she strode toward the neat stack of school supplies she'd unloaded from her car. She pointed to the boxes of crayons and pencils. "I'm ready. Although, first day of kindergarten usually involves more tissues than markers."

The middle-aged man nodded enthusiastically. "I'm sure you're right. The incoming class is our largest ever. I'm stopping in to double check if you, Kelly, and Lauren have any last-minute requests."

"No, I'm good." She grabbed the stack of fliers off the top of her desk, holding the text to her chest. Was he truly here to offer bland first day greetings? Or had Kelly and Lauren met with him?

"You're aware you have Candace Vane's daughter, Amelia, in class this year?" he asked.

"I am." Stephanie dragged out the response.

"Candace asked for you specifically."

"Oh, that's nice." Stephanie released a shaky breath.

He tugged at his necktie, loosening the Windsor knot.

"Or . . . it isn't?" she asked.

"If you need any support, please come to the office. If you anticipate any problems, you don't even have to knock on the door. Just enter and tell me. Keep me in the loop."

Two warnings in less than twenty-four hours had to count for something. She wasn't the type to follow other people's advice without question. But she always listened when someone shared a personal anecdote. Still at the start of her career, she remained mostly untested. "I appreciate it. I have worked with Mrs. Vane for the past several years."

"You have, and the free meals for all program has been wonderful. She can be formidable as either an ally or an enemy. Be careful."

The bell rang over the door, metallic clanging reverberating through her.

She jumped, the papers in her arms fluttering. "First day. That always gets me."

He chuckled. "Have a wonderful day, if you need anything, you know where to find me." He turned and strode out the open door.

When her boss was out of sight, she released a heavy breath. She wasn't a brand-new educator. She could handle her class and was eager to lean into her strengths.

High-pitched chatter mixed with the squeak of sneakers against the freshly washed floor. The doors whooshed and crashed from constant opening and shutting. The organized chaos of the school year began.

In a few minutes, she'd have to go pick up her kids from the multi-purpose room, shepherding her students down the hall after the older kids were settled upstairs. She held her papers out, scanning through the text again. She never second-guessed a decision and especially not when her motives were so clear and logical. But all the talk lately left her slightly off-balance.

On the fliers going home today, she spelled out her expectations of the year. She wanted her kids to learn in a safe, fair environment. To that end, she was limiting volunteer opportunities in class. She hated seeing the tears of children whose parents both worked and could not be the mystery reader while other children's moms and dads stopped by on multiple occasions per week.

She'd been that kid without any parental involvement. She'd taken it upon herself to be her brother's mystery reader to save him the pain of everyone else feeling special and him feeling singled out. Neither had she wanted her wonderful parents—with two equally high-powered careers—to feel guilty they couldn't take off time.

At the wall of cubbies, she slid a brightly colored sheet in each slot. While parents might initially balk at the change, they would come around. Earlier in the summer, she'd informed the families of her incoming class about the shared school supply format. The crayons, markers, and glue sticks would not be kept at each child's desk. Instead, she would have supplies available for everyone from a communal table. A few had raised complaints insisting their student should have their own supplies, but after discussion about teaching the importance of sharing, parents had agreed. She wouldn't have to worry about this.

The bell rang again.

With the last paper in the final cubby, she pulled back her shoulders, plastered on her teacher smile, and strode into the now quiet hallway. Everyone was safe and equal at school. She wouldn't flinch from her purpose.

She breathed deep, inhaling the smell of freshly sharpened pencils and industrial cleaner as she walked from her classroom to the multi-purpose room at the end of the corridor. With each step, the buzz of furtively whispered conversations filled the air. She would miss this.

While nothing had been officially announced, the large incoming class signaled a change in the town and the school's future. The economic rebound—spurred in large part by the success of the Kincaid ranch—meant more families moving into the district and others staying put. She was glad everyone could earn a solid livelihood.

The expansive school boundaries weren't being redrawn with the population boom. But the building couldn't house too many more grades of seventy plus kids. She'd been pleased to teach roughly fifteen to eighteen children each year. At twenty-four, this would be the most students she'd taught on her own ever. She'd student taught a large class and found the situation overwhelming.

An idea had been floated to separate the kindergarteners into their own building. She'd miss the other teachers. The elementary grades were a family within the larger community. They worked together, sharing ideas and practices for the benefit of the entire school society.

The multi-purpose room's door stood ajar.

She entered and stayed close to the wall. She waved at the first and second grade teachers, and stood next to Lauren and Kelly.

"You're late?" Kelly whispered, leaning close.

Stephanie gripped her elbows behind her back. "First day pep talk from Bill. Nothing to worry about."

Lauren stepped forward out of the line of teachers. "Good morning boys and girls."

"Good morning, Mrs. Simmons." The chorus of voices of the first and second graders filled the room.

Lauren smiled at the room, meeting the gazes of the confused kindergarteners on the ground in front. "When I call your class, I'd like you to please stand up and form a single file line. Your teacher will lead you down the hall to your new classroom. If you aren't sure who your teacher is, please wait until I ask for the remaining students to step forward. Miss Patricks' class."

Stephanie stepped forward and grinned.

A gaggle of children stood, gathering their backpacks and lunchboxes. They formed a somewhat single file line. A few pairs clung to each other.

With her finger as a guide, Stephanie counted to twenty-four and flashed Lauren a thumbs-up. "Please follow me."

A little girl dressed in head-to-toe pink, with a huge, satin bow expertly tied around her ponytail and velvet ballet flats, stepped forward as the line leader.

Stephanie fought her frown. The child assumed the first-place spot and the others let her. Not a good omen. Stephanie kept smiling. If she had to guess, she'd wager the child was Amelia. She carried herself with the same confidence as her mother. Stephanie had good interactions with the parent and wouldn't read too much into the child. But she also counted herself a good judge of character, and worried about the mean girl vibe she got from the too-sweet-to-be-genuine expression.

"Please follow me," Stephanie repeated, this time with a little more confidence, and turned. As she exited the room, the little girl put her hand in Stephanie's.

She glanced down and smiled, again fighting the urge to recoil. She wasn't a fan of the teacher's pet. Favoritism wasn't her style but could be a struggle against a person's natural inclination to gravitate towards one over another. Under the guise of turning to glance over her shoulder, she dropped the little girl's hand and counted again to twenty-four. She checked the numbers two more times as they walked the twenty yards to her classroom. At the door to the room, she stopped. "Good morning class. I would like to shake everyone's hand as you walk inside. Please find your name on a cubby and place your backpack inside. Then, if you'll take a seat on the brightly-colored carpet in the story corner, we'll start today with a book."

Kneeling, she held out her hand to the little girl. "Good morning, I'm Miss Patricks."

"Amelia Vane," she said and bounced into the room.

Stephanie turned to the next child, a little boy with tear-filled eyes. Pulling a tissue from her pocket, she extended it.

The boy blew his nose, loudly, and held it out to her.

She had a long day ahead, but she'd focus on one step at a time. This would be the best year ever, she'd except no less. And avoiding the snotty sides of the tissues whenever possible was key.

Ted paced outside the closed door, clicking his boots with each step. He hadn't stepped foot inside a school in over two decades and never this particular building. But some things a mind and body couldn't forget. The whiff of pencils tickled his nostrils and brought back the long-forgotten anxiety of coloring in bubbles on a standardized test. He did well in school, but tests overwhelmed him every time.

As his ribs tightened, his vision blurred. He stilled, leaning against the painted, concrete wall.

"Unc, you okay?" Maddy asked, shaking their clasped hands.

He glanced down at his niece, swallowing the bile rising in his throat. He wasn't the one who should be nervous. He wouldn't be starting a new school a day late. He cleared his throat. "Yep. Sorry, squirrel."

The bell rang.

The loud clang preceded the classroom door opening and cacophony of high-pitched voices filtered into the hall.

Maddy ducked behind him.

"Alright, single file behind me please," Stephanie said. Her voice was kind but firm.

Until yesterday, he hadn't really heard it. Was that only yesterday? Might as well have been a year ago. After he had settled his sister and niece into the extra bedroom at his cabin, he had returned to the Cowboy Dinner. Jen and Maddy were invited but skipped it, following the long drive they were wiped. By the time he had finished and returned home, he knocked on their bedroom door and opened it to see the pair curled up together and snoring in sync. They'd been so peaceful. He hadn't had the heart to wake his sister and get more specifics about her move or her next steps. He'd regretted that choice all day.

Stephanie walked backwards into the hall and turned, glancing over her shoulder. Frowning, she froze for a moment.

Wearing a crayon-patterned dress, she embodied her role as a kindergarten teacher. He'd grown used to seeing her in yoga pants and ponytails. He'd never noticed that her hair only grazed her shoulder or how the light made the blonde shimmer. She wore minimal makeup, but she looked more pulled together than he was used to.

A child pushed another forward.

"Please, let's be careful of everyone's space," she said, facing her students again. She walked backwards, facing a line of boys and girls.

When she glanced his way again, she dropped her gaze to the child. Nodding, she flashed him a thumbs up. "We'll go to the multi-purpose room again for dismissal and then I'll come back to the classroom. You'll be called by your bus or your last name if you are being driven home."

Was that directed at him? Should he duck inside the room?

She tilted her head toward a classroom door and shot him a look.

Yep, he definitely stood out. In dirty jeans and an old flannel peeking under the hem of his brown coat, he came straight from the ranch without changing. He had washed his hands but that was the full extent of his cleaning up before his arrival. As the last child in the line filed past, he tugged gently on Maddy's hand and strolled into the classroom.

Bright colors greeted him from every corner. Posters with cheerful greetings, inspirational messages, and class rules were interspersed on the two long walls. Opposite the door, a wall of windows overlooked the playground and in front a play kitchen sat behind a large alphabet motif rug. To the left of the door, cubbies hugged the corner. Circular tables with little chairs filled the center of the room.

He breathed easier. The space was warm and inviting. "Let's sit. Miss Patricks will be here in a minute." *Hopefully.*

He didn't like the way Maddy's lower lip quivered or her sheepish posture, her chin practically glued to her chest as she stared at her feet. She'd been fine until she saw the other kids. Had he missed something? In the car on the drive over, she hadn't stopped chattering about going to school. He'd been glad for her enthusiasm.

At the table closest to the adult-sized desk, he pulled out two chairs. He sat, his bones creaking.

Maddy giggled.

With his bent knees almost at his shoulder height, he felt like a bear riding a tricycle at a circus. The image was ridiculous, and the position was painful. He didn't care. Earning her smile was worth the physical cost.

Like usual, he had arisen before the sun to take care of the horses. Animal husbandry was his favorite part of the job, and he left his cell in his truck's cupholder for a spot of peace as he started his day. But when he had returned to the vehicle, he'd missed about a hundred calls from Jen and frantic texts.

He had no choice but to head home. At his front door, his sister had explained what she had failed to mention the night before. She needed to return to California, to finish her final shifts and finalize both the sale of her house and her custody arrangement. The new job hired her sooner than she intended but she couldn't pass up the chance. She'd be gone for the next ten days, coming back for a weekend visit before finishing her last week at her current job.

She would have stayed in California and moved with Maddy in a few weeks. But Maddy needed to start school. Jen had filled out some forms online but didn't get a chance to stop by and drop the paperwork. If he showed up, he could probably manage the rest of registration.

Overwhelmed, he hadn't done more than listen as the information was tossed at him. No sooner than he found his voice, he had watched his sister maneuver the SUV and trailer and head down the road the way she came. He'd turned to a still sleepy Maddy.

He had never stepped in as a parental figure. His role had always been the fun uncle. Right now, she needed security. He had no idea what to do with a child. But he couldn't show fear. There had to be some similarities between skittish animals and small kids.

So, he had fed her and loaded her into the truck. They had spent the rest of the morning doing his usual work. She wasn't as much of a hindrance as he feared. But neither could he modify his schedule every day to be child friendly. While he had toyed with the idea of keeping her with him until her mother returned, he understood he'd be doing them both a disservice. After lunch, he couldn't delay the inevitable any longer. He needed to get her into school. Luckily, he knew just who to ask for help.

The door shut with a gentle thud.

He turned toward the sound.

"Hello," Stephanie said softly, approaching with eyes only on Maddy. "I'm Miss Patricks. I'm a teacher."

For a split second, he was jealous. She addressed the little girl with such care and attention. He wanted some of that, too.

Stephanie walked to their table, pulling out a seat opposite and sinking down. "What's your name?"

"Madison Cade," the little girl whispered.

Stephanie beamed. "It's a pleasure to make your acquaintance, Madison. Do you have a nickname you like?"

The little girl nodded.

"Can you tell me what it is?" Stephanie asked.

Maddy froze, turning toward him with a deer in the headlights expression of terror.

Jen did a good job raising her daughter to be afraid of giving any information to a stranger. But—with any luck—Stephanie wouldn't be unknown for long. Mentally, he shook himself. She wouldn't become closer via him. Stephanie would be Maddy's teacher. He put a hand on his niece's shoulder. "This is my niece, Maddy. She arrived in town last night, and I guess I messed up her first day of school. Her very first day."

"Oh, that's where you went?" Stephanie said the words in a rush.

She knew I was gone? He widened his eyes.

She coughed. "Sorry, at one point Hank needed you and . . ." She waved a hand. "Doesn't matter. Did you go to the office? Fill out registration? I didn't have an extra name on my attendance list this morning." She wrinkled her brow.

He liked her cute look of confusion. But his screw-up wasn't her fault. "My sister had forms I was supposed to bring but then I lost track of time today." He glanced down at his niece. Her hand felt tiny and vulnerable in his grip.

"Did you just walk in?" Stephanie shifted her weight from one foot to the other.

"No, I stopped at the office. I gave them my I.D., but I told them I was here to see you." He hated the off-balance feeling of not knowing exactly how to right a wrong and worse, letting down his niece in the process. "I really need some guidance here. Can you help?"

A curious look passed over her face. An almost triumphant gleam to her eyes. She smoothed her hair behind her ears and focused her attention on Maddy. "So, Madison, are you starting kindergarten?"

Maddy nodded.

"Well, that's perfect. I teach kindergarten," Stephanie said. "Would you like to be in my class?"

Yes, please. Relief washed over him. If Maddy ended up in Stephanie's class, she'd be safe and looked after. He wouldn't worry.

Maddy faced him, her mouth gaping.

"It's okay, squirrel." He rubbed a hand over her back and glanced at Stephanie.

Stephanie mouthed the word *squirrel?*

He shrugged. When his sister showed him the ultrasound, he couldn't make sense of it. The blob in the center had looked more like a tree rat than a baby. "You can talk to her. She's nice."

Stephanie smiled. The expression came from deeper than the lift of her lips. Her eyes sparkled and her whole body seemed to radiate with happiness. From a single, obvious, statement? Was his opinion important to her?

He couldn't let it be. For both their sakes. He was glad she relaxed enough to talk to him. If she returned for another summer on the ranch, she wouldn't be so on edge again. She was a sweet person and so light and full of life. Her bubbly persona was a genuine gift.

Maybe being on her turf, she felt confident enough to take the lead. While he wanted a change in their interactions, from silence to friendship, he complicated that by needing her help. This time, the power balance shifted toward her.

"Yes, please call me, Maddy. I would like to be in your class." Maddy exhaled a heavy sigh. "Did I miss a lot today? Will I be behind? Did everyone make best friends? Is anyone else new?"

Stephanie grinned. "You did not miss anything, and I don't think you'll find it difficult to make a best friend. We have a nice class. It's big. With you, we'll have twenty-five kids."

"Is that too many?" He shifted forward on the hard, molded plastic seat. "Can you teach that many kids?" He hated to impose on her. He couldn't imagine watching two five-year-olds let alone twenty-five. Would Maddy be shifted into another class? She warmed up quickly and had a knack for making friends. If something went wrong, though, he wanted to know. Stephanie would keep him informed.

"I'll be fine. Why don't you head to the office and start the paperwork?" she asked.

He reached inside his coat pocket, pulling a folded stack of papers. "My sister, Maddy's mom, already started filling out the forms. I need to drop them off. But I think I have more to do? Something about proving residency? Do you know if everything is online or if I'll have more to fill out or . . ." He was rambling.

Stephanie smiled. "Wendy, in the front office, can help with every question."

Stephanie was such a calm presence. He found her comforting. Maybe he hadn't messed up too much. Letting down Maddy was far worse than the lecture he'd get from Jen when she learned what happened. "Thank you. I'll do that."

Stephanie nodded. "Maddy, do you have any questions I can answer?"

"Yes." Maddy slipped her hand out of his and crossed her arms over her chest. "Trick or treating. How does it work here? In California, we have sidewalks and live close to each other and go door to door. Unc lives in the middle of nowhere here. I didn't see any sidewalks when we drove to school from the ranch. It's all country." She sighed.

He covered his mouth with a fist. Her put-upon-tone always tickled his funny bone. Maddy was serious from birth, an old soul trapped in a child's body.

Stephanie nodded. "At school, we hold a costume parade for parents and uncles to attend. Then we have a party in the afternoon. Instead of trick or treating from one house to another, the town holds a big trunk or treat. It's a lot of fun. Cars and trucks get decorated and park up and down Main Street. You go from car to car. Don't worry, you'll get plenty of candy." Stephanie winked.

He hadn't ever attended the Halloween event. By October, the weather was cold and night fell early. He usually completed his evening routine with the horses and, with the exception of poker night, was back in his home reading over his supper by six.

Now he was looking forward to attending the special holiday celebration. He'd loved Halloween as a kid. Children were a gift, forcing the grown-ups in their lives to snap out of their doldrums and look at the world with wonder. Did Stephanie experience that on a daily basis thanks to her job? Or was she just sort of magic on her own?

With hands pressed flat against his thighs, he forced himself out of the too small chair with a groan. His knees cracked. He was relieved he hadn't been trapped in the seat. Although, he wouldn't mind a few more minutes in Stephanie's classroom. The space was comforting and cozy, as warm as the teacher.

She shot him an expectant look.

He cleared his throat.

Stephanie flashed him a thumbs up. "Can I show you around my classroom, Maddy?"

"Yes, please. Does everyone get a cubby?" Maddy asked, her voice chipper.

He strolled to the door and glanced over his shoulder.

Stephanie and Maddy spoke with animation, totally focused on their conversation and not him.

He preferred the status quo. If any change was going to happen, though, this one was welcome. Having his family near would be worth the momentary upheaval. But that was it. Pretty young teachers who'd never known heartache—and good for them, he'd begrudge no one a lovely life without hindrance—were best left to their own devices.

CHAPTER 4

Stephanie held open the door to the multi-purpose room with her back. The second day of school passed in a blur. She liked to leave her students with a sunny smile and a positive affirmation. She wanted everyone to feel good about their school day.

Teaching kindergarten, she learned staying calm was paramount to success. Getting overly worked up about anything aggravated both good and bad situations. With a gentle reminder tomorrow held no mistakes, she could encourage those students who had a difficult time in class.

As usual, Amelia and her oversized, satin bow led the line.

Stephanie bit the inside of her cheek. The child was well-behaved. She spoke and acted with a sugar sweetness that set Stephanie's teeth on edge. No one could be so cute all the time. How did the little girl act when Stephanie wasn't watching?

Tomorrow, she'd institute classroom jobs and give everyone a fair turn at leading the group. She waved and winked at each student as they passed her into the room for end of day pick-up. At the back of the line, Madison strolled forward with confident swagger.

Stephanie was glad. The other students welcomed her instantly. The room was tear free for most of the day. The school year was off to a banner start.

"Bye, Miss Patricks. I can't wait to see you tomorrow." Maddy squeaked.

"Same, Maddy. Have a good night." Stephanie stayed in place until her classroom reached their marked spaces on the wooden floor and sat. Then she stepped away from the door and strode back down the hall. Inside her classroom, she shut the door and exhaled a heavy sigh.

The first week was always an adjustment. She forgot how much energy she had to summon and utilize for each day. Being present required a lot of focus.

Rolling her neck and shoulders, she started her work of preparing for the next day. She cleared the dry erase board, wrote out the next day's in-class announcements, and picked up stray items for their lost and found. Back at her desk, she organized the thick stack of photocopied worksheets she'd requested which would carry her class through the end of the month, and checked her to-do list.

She opened her laptop and pulled up her inbox to check on any messages she had missed. During quiet time after lunch, she usually caught up on her emails from parents. A few trickled in later in the day. Sure enough, she had a message from Candace Vane.

Curious, she clicked on it and scanned the text, sucking in a sharp breath. Candace had issue with the reduced volunteer opportunity, and her daughter didn't like sharing classroom supplies. Stephanie reread the missive but wasn't exactly sure the point of the email. A warning? A threat? General observations?

No request was made. Stephanie wasn't sure a response would be the best course of action. Both complaints were part of Stephanie's strategy to create a safe space for all. Candace was financially blessed, or so she gave that impression to everyone in town. Stephanie balked at the idea of flaunting status in general but especially in front of five-year-olds.

With her fingers hovering over the keyboard, she tried to think of the best way to handle the situation.

A knock shook the door.

"Come in," she called.

The school secretary, Wendy, opened the door and entered. "Good afternoon, Miss Patricks. Sorry to disturb you. I'm here with one of your students."

A hiccupping cry bounced off the walls.

Stephanie stood, rushing out from behind the desk and pulling the pack of tissues out of her skirt pocket. "Of course, of course."

The child was hidden behind Wendy's legs. The pair stopped near the first table.

Stephanie knelt on the ground and glanced at Wendy.

New girl. Wendy mouthed.

Stephanie widened her eyes. "Maddy? Sweetie? Can you tell me what's wrong?"

The little girl peeked around Wendy's knees. Her face was swollen and red. "Unc isn't here."

Stephanie shot her gaze to the clock on the wall. Almost an hour had passed since the end of school. In a silent room, she often lost track of time. She hadn't realized how late the day had gotten.

"I can't get ahold of him," Wendy said.

"No problem." Stephanie stood, dusting her hands on her skirt. "Maddy, I can call him, and we can read and color while we wait for him, okay?"

Maddy let go of Wendy and lunged for Stephanie's outstretched hand, the backpack dangling off her back and threatening her balance.

Stephanie hadn't asked any questions yesterday. She should have. Where were the little girl's parents? Why was she suddenly living with Ted? Stephanie stroked the child's back. Maddy had such a great first day. Bile rose in Stephanie's throat, and she struggled to swallow it. She hated this ending.

Wendy offered a grateful, sad smile and strode out the door.

Stephanie led Maddy to the carpet and pulled a bin from the shelf under the window, full of coloring pages and crayons. "Let me call him," she said softly and handed a tissue.

The child blew her nose and extended the used tissue.

With years of training, Stephanie didn't flinch as the snotty square was dropped into her open palm. The little girl stopped crying. That was the most important thing at the moment.

Maddy raised her gaze, nodded, and sat on the carpet, rifling through the bin with determination.

Stephanie crossed the room, dropping the tissue into the waste basket, washing her hands in the room's sink, and returned to her desk. In the bottom drawer, she retrieved her purse and found her cell phone. She dialed Ted's number. He'd given it to her over the summer in case she needed anything while working on the ranch.

The phone rang and rang, never clicking over to a voicemail box. Then the line died. She dialed it again.

She'd never called. What was the point if she couldn't speak? When the situation involved one of her kids, she trusted she'd find her voice. She would always have her students' best interests at heart.

The line rang and rang. Then nothing.

Dialing again, she couldn't imagine where he was or why he didn't set up a way to receive voice messages. *Pick up pick up pick up.* From the corner of her gaze, she studied the little girl coloring with gusto. Stephanie was glad Maddy didn't react.

As she held the phone to her ear for the fourth redial, she flushed with frustration. Wherever he was, and whatever held him up, he had a responsibility to his niece that took precedence. She had a clear—if atypical—solution. He'd asked if he could list her as an emergency contact. She'd agreed, not imagining she'd ever be required to step up and drive her student anywhere.

"Maddy, I have a booster in my car. I can drive you to Unc's house and talk to him about pick-up. Is that okay?"

Maddy got to her feet with a huge smile. "Yes, please."

Stephanie smiled. Was this a gray area? Would Bill frown at her for taking charge in this way? She'd take care of the child first. Grabbing her purse, she waited as the child put the bin away a bit haphazardly.

Stepping out into the hallway, she darted her gaze from one end to the other. Most of the other teachers had left for the night. The off-pitch tones of fourth grade band filled the space. She held her hand out to Maddy and led the child out the doors to the teacher parking lot.

She settled the child into the backseat of the car, hopped behind the wheel, and turned over the engine. Her pop music playlist launched as she steered out of the lot and onto the main road. When the song approached a questionable lyric, Stephanie turned off the stereo and glanced in the rearview mirror.

Maddy faced the window, her swollen cheeks still puffy but her eyes less red.

Stephanie focused on the road. She had a lot of driving to do tonight, and if it was all in silence, she'd never last. Exhaustion overtook her in the quiet moments. "Do you have favorite songs to listen to in the car?"

"Mommy and I like musicals."

"Really?" Stephanie glanced in the mirror again, catching the child's emphatic nod. She would have figured Maddy would say the soundtrack to an animated movie or the kid-friendly versions of current songs. She kept both on her school-approved playlist. "Any musical in particular?"

"My favorite is the Christmas one because . . ."

Stephanie smiled. "Because it's Christmas? No explanation needed. I don't think I know which one you're talking about."

"The one with the sisters. Mommy and Unc sing that song."

"They do?"

"Unc always has to tell Mommy which way to turn."

In the rearview mirror, Stephanie met the little girl's gaze. "What do you mean *turn*?"

"Mommy and Unc have a routine. Just like the movie. He's a great dancer."

He dances?! Oh, she had to see that. Stephanie's icy ire thawed as her imagination took control. But something else came into clearer focus.

Maybe her ability to speak to him was the clearest indication she was over her ill-fated crush. She felt a connection with him but maybe her lonely heart planted a false idea. When she did meet the right guy, she wanted to be a priority. For the first time in her life, she would be someone's number one.

Shaking the can of white spray paint, Ted bent and marked an x on the ground. With a hand to his aching lower back, he groaned. His day had skidded downhill like a truck left in neutral. The last guests had checked out yesterday. The seasonal staff had departed by midday. And he was caught somewhere in the middle.

Today, he had started the work of figuring out how much he had to do while the weather cooperated. Surveying every building for needed repairs, he'd been called to the barn to oversee the start of the deck. But the crew had never arrived. And at some point, the markings of the deck had been washed away, so he had rolled up his sleeves and taken care of business.

Most days, he didn't feel like he was forty-three and middle aged. After a day spent on repetitive physical tasks, ending his chores by bending over and marking the ground for the proposed deck behind the red barn with several cans of spray paint, he reconsidered. His muscles ached and tweaked. When he talked to Stephanie, he didn't feel any younger.

She'd been so delightfully deadpan when she had called his favorite movie out of touch. He smiled despite himself. Rolling back his shoulders, he straightened, shrugging off annoyance. At least he finished this task.

He was never afraid of getting his hands dirty. Physical labor had kept him sane when he lost his wife. No one expected to be a widower. Let alone at the age of thirty. Their organic farm had only started turning a profit when Liv was killed in a car accident.

Grounded with a job that demanded the use of his muscles more than his brain, he worked each day methodically as he checked items off his to-do list one at a time. Life on the ranch was easy—if not especially meaningful. That was okay. He wasn't the boss worrying about employees. He did his tasks and didn't get caught up in anything that could add deep commentary on his life choices. For that, he had his family.

The start of the morning was surprisingly smooth. Maddy was an old soul. She made thoughtful—often hilarious—observations and connections on the world around her. Dressing herself with care, she had helped him pack up her bag for her first day of school. When he had dropped her off, he had lingered in case she needed another hug. But she had never turned around. She had strolled into the school like she owned it. He couldn't wait to hear how her day went.

Icy dread gripped him tight. His palms went clammy, his forehead beaded with a cold sweat, and he frowned at the low tilt of the sun. *What time was it? Oh no, I forgot Maddy.*

Spinning on his heel, he ran to his truck, parked in front of the barn.

Tires crunched gravel.

He lifted his gaze.

Stephanie's little red coupe neared.

What was she doing here? He had to go get his niece. He opened the door to his truck and found his cell in the cupholder. The screen was full of missed calls from her.

"Hey, I've got her," Stephanie shouted, her voice carrying out an open window.

Ted slammed the truck door shut and approached the slowing car. With a hand shielding his gaze, he spotted Maddy on a booster seat in the back. *How could I have forgotten to pick her up? How could I have let her down?*

The red car stopped.

He reached for the rear door handle, waited for the click of the lock, and then opened it.

"Hi, Unc," Maddy said, her face looking a little red and her cheeks chapped, but otherwise okay.

He could have cried. His knees buckled, and he locked them to hold his position. "Hi, squirrel. I'm so sor—"

"BZZT," Stephanie said.

Huh? He met her gaze in the rearview mirror.

She shook her head and mouthed *no*.

He wasn't supposed to apologize? He'd let down his niece. What was expected of him if he wasn't allowed to grovel? He turned back and unbuckled the seatbelt.

Moving out of the way, he stood next to the car and waited for either female to direct him on what came next.

"Can you hold my backpack?" Maddy flung it at him. "I'm gonna run up and tell Mr. Hank about my day. He asked me to." She yelled over her shoulder, racing across the lawn toward the back of the ranch house.

She didn't want to yell or cry? She didn't want a hug? He held the pink and purple bag and watched her climbed the porch and let herself in the back door.

He exhaled a huge shuddering breath, rolling his shoulders forward and hunching. "Thank you for bringing her home. I can't believe I forgot."

He wanted to shrink to the size of an ant so someone could squish him under their boot. Abandoning Maddy on her very first day of school ever? Jen expected more. Maddy deserved better. What if he didn't have a friend who cared enough to bring the little girl home? He met Stephanie's gaze. "I owe you."

"It happens."

Her voice was oddly flat.

He slipped the backpack onto a shoulder and turned, facing her. Had he disappointed her, too? Was he less than in her eyes now? He didn't want that. "I am truly, truly sorry."

"I know you are." She softened her face, just a little, glancing at the ground. "Sorry I cut you off mid-apology. I didn't want you to get her worked up again. She was in tears at school. I calmed her down on the car ride."

He appreciated she was the expert here, and he'd have to follow her lead. But he didn't like her darting gaze or crossed arms. She was standoffish. While she'd only recently begun to speak to him, she was a sunny, open-book. Not today.

"I promised my sister. I really hope I didn't scar Maddy."

"We've all been left by a parent or caregiver." Stephanie lifted a shoulder. "It's almost a rite of passage."

Was it a painful experience for you? Her hesitation hinted at something he couldn't decipher. He was intrigued.

"Where are her parents?" Stephanie asked, frowning. "I'm sorry to put you on the spot. But what is going on?"

"My sister and her husband divorced when Maddy was a baby. They've been good co-parents since the beginning. She doesn't know any different." *Thankfully.* Jen and her ex fought from day one. A mismatch from the start, Ted wanted to warn her that if the easy time was complicated the relationship was doomed.

But he hadn't offered an opinion. Knowing his stubborn sister, she would have ignored him. Or, worse, she pushed him away. She needed him and vice versa. So, he kept his mouth shut. "Maddy's dad is moving overseas for a job. My sister is starting at the hospital soon but needed to finish up her job and sell her house. She came on Labor Day so Maddy could start school."

"A little abrupt. She didn't give Maddy a chance to settle in."

He held up his hands. "Maddy is so good at being flexible with plans. My sister takes that for granted. I know I do."

Stephanie nodded.

He waited for her to ask more. She had every right. He'd put her in a tough spot.

"How long is your sister gone?"

"She'll be back for a visit in ten days. She'll be up here for good the week after." He held his breath.

Stephanie wrinkled her brow in the cute way he understood meant she was working through an issue. He hoped it didn't involve calling the authorities about his negligence.

She tipped her head to the side. "Do you want help with the afternoon pick up? I can drop her off after-school if that makes life easier."

Oh, it does. He dropped his shoulders and exhaled a heavy sigh. "That would be wonderful. I'm great at getting up early. Once I'm on the ranch, I lose track of time."

She nodded. "I did, too."

"I truly am so sorry this happened today. You can't choose the memories children make." He scrubbed the corners of his eyes, wishing he was stuck in a bad dream. "I love that little girl so much, and I don't want her holding onto the time Unc let her down. I never want her sad."

"I appreciate that sentiment, but you can't beat yourself up over every mistake. Isn't it better she sees you accept responsibility, apologize, and move on? Give tomorrow your best shot. You can't and shouldn't give a child some perfect, no problems worldview. That's just not real life."

"What is?"

She lifted the corner of her mouth in a half smile. "Trying."

Could it be that easy? With parents in another state, Maddy depended on him. Intellectually, he'd grasped the concept. Until he was left in charge as the sole adult, he hadn't tested the weight of the role. Now he carried every ounce.

"You should take her home, explain what happened, and let her move on. Read a book. Make a good memory. She had a great first day at school."

"Thanks, I'll do that."

With a nod, Stephanie strode back to her car. As she moved, a hint of citrus wafted past his nose. The smell was sweet like candied orange slices.

"Wait," he called.

She paused, glancing over her shoulder.

"Can you stay for dinner?" He shouted, his voice cracking. He hadn't intended to ask. But now he wanted her to stay and prove that he was a capable guardian. "You've driven over here. It's getting late. I owe you."

"I don't know." She tapped a finger against her chin.

"Did you already eat?" he asked.

She frowned.

His foolish question hung in the air. "It's just... I thought I smelled candy. Like oranges?"

"Oh, that's my shampoo." Her stomach growled. "Now that you mention food, I am hungry." She covered her stomach with her arms, muffling further sounds. "Should I trust you with cooking? It involves some time management skills that might be out of your wheelhouse?"

He chuckled. He liked her teasing. "I'm great at dinner because I start in the morning. It's my go-to slow cooker alfredo. Maddy's favorite, and she has quite the discerning palate."

"Okay, sounds good." She tucked a loose strand of blonde hair into her ponytail. Her cheeks pinked.

Great, with a few exceptions, they were back to normal. She spoke now, which simplified and challenged their interactions. But he could handle the change. He was interested in friendship and Maddy's well-being. If the twin goals could be combined, he'd come out on top.

CHAPTER 5

Sitting on the opposite bank of the pond, the snug log cabin stood apart from the guest cabins. With a stone chimney on one side and a low-pitched roof over the porch, mirroring the entrance of the larger ranch house, the charming, one-story building blended perfectly with its surroundings. The setting couldn't be more picturesque if it had been created by an artist.

Stephanie slowed her car as she neared the front of the house. Maddy rode with her uncle, giving Stephanie a break from Maddie's chatter. Her mind took full advantage of the quiet to daydream.

She pictured sitting outside in a rocking chair at night in the summer, catching fireflies. On a crisp autumn morning, she'd cuddle under a blanket, sipping a hot cup of coffee. In winter, she'd bet the smoke curled from the chimney in wisps while the home nestled in a snowbank, demanding its occupants slow down and enjoy the indoors for a spell.

Every scenario included Ted. It was too easy to imagine. She'd always been glad for her boundless depths of creativity, but now she hated it. Her one-sided crush was doomed to remain unrequited. First, he'd been her boss. Now, she was his niece's teacher. Each association raised ethical concerns.

But if they were a couple? Her skin flushed thinking about the warmth of his smile. Her toes curled, remembering the tenderness and vulnerability when he realized he forgot his niece.

Parking next to his truck, she pocketed her keys and grabbed her purse off the shotgun seat. Out of the car, she strode up a flagstone path toward the front door. Could she regain her righteous indignation and find her confidence—and voice—again?

He'd been so earnest and so genuinely upset when confronted about his mistake. She'd lost her balance. But she hadn't wanted to slip into the old patterns. She wanted to move forward. The night of the cowboy dinner sparked a change. Teasing him about his pop culture taste had been natural.

If Maddy hadn't shown up, would the encounter have been a one-off? Stephanie would have returned to teaching full-time with no excuse to stop by the ranch. Would she have

193

spoken again if they bumped into each other in town? Or would the moment simply have been a shared memory that floated past with no significance?

Lifting her fist, she knocked on the door.

The knob spun.

She took a step back.

Pulling the door open with a smile, Ted waved her to cross the threshold. "Please, come inside."

Cautiously, like a sudden movement would snap her out of the moment and back to reality, she entered the home, stepping into a small entryway onto a handwoven rug. The rectangle was—at first glance—red. With closer inspection, however, she noticed the variety of shades of rust, burnt orange, and salmon, coming together. It was the sort of piece someone might pick up at an artist's fair. Did he buy it? Was it a gift?

She lifted her gaze, studying his profile as he shut the door. She really didn't know him. For as much as she knew that his gray green eyes never crinkled when he smiled, she had no clue about his personal life. He kept himself removed.

Maddy, at least, wouldn't let him remain aloof. When she returned, his sister would humanize him, too. Nothing like family to suddenly force a person to stop faking and start being real. Would Stephanie be close enough as a friend to witness the change?

"I hope you don't mind waiting for a few minutes." He gestured to a room on the left. "Maddy wants to set the table."

"Of course, not." She turned toward the open doorway leading to a sitting room.

A large window overlooked the front yard. The stone fireplace took up most of one wall, the mantle extending over low, built-in bookcases on either side. A pair of leather armchairs with ottomans sat before the fire. A worn quilt was thrown over the back of one. Again, a surprising touch of softness and care. Was that why he smelled like leather? Did he fall asleep in the chair?

Heat crept up her neck, and her ears burned.

Opposite the window wall, a smaller doorway opened to the eat-in kitchen. No TV? How did he watch his beloved teen movies? She faced him, readying her question.

"I'll go and check on her. She loves to decorate and could take the whole night if not otherwise managed." He wiggled his eyebrows. "What would you like to drink with dinner?"

"Water, please."

He nodded and walked into the kitchen, through the other doorway.

Interlacing her fingers, she strolled toward the bookshelves, curiosity lifting her onto her toes. Above the bookshelf nearest the window, she spotted a certificate mixed in with candid photos. A college degree? She was both surprised and unshocked. Any time her role as a teacher came up, he spoke with a deference about education. What did a cowboy study in undergrad?

She narrowed her gaze and studied the words Animal Sciences.

Sparing the degree only another momentary glance, she turned toward the other frames. She recognized Maddy and assumed the pretty woman, who looked like Ted in a wig, was his sister. Leaning closer, she didn't spot any other mystery woman in any of the pictures. Childhood photos were mixed with a few recent shots, most including Maddy. If she had to guess, she'd wager the sister provided all the images.

She exhaled a heavy sigh. She was glad she hadn't spotted any romantic shots of him and another woman. Just because Stephanie's love life was non-existent didn't mean anyone else's was. He had fourteen years on her. He had ample time for a meaningful romantic entanglement. She couldn't get jealous about his past, and she should know better than to snoop.

She studied the top shelf. Near the window, she bent and read the spines of the books in the dim ambient light from a wall sconce. With each title, she widened her eyes a little more. *Young Adult fantasy novels?*

"She's almost ready."

Stephanie straightened, stiffening, and tweaking her lower back. She sucked in a sharp breath.

"Sorry, didn't mean to startle you."

"I'm fine." She forced a smile and gestured toward the shelf. "I'm a little surprised by your book collection. Did you get these for Maddy? They are advanced for her reading level."

He folded his arms over his chest. "No, those books are for me. I love them."

"You do?"

"Is that wrong?" He lifted a brow.

His expression was quizzical. She hoped her tone wasn't judgmental. She loved to read and hated when she was condemned for enjoying romance novels. Still, she was surprised by his choice. She cleared her throat. "I've never met a cowboy who loves dragons."

"Maybe I'm not really a cowboy."

She widened her gaze. He wasn't? Who was he? She nibbled her bottom lip. Or was he flirting with his cheeky comments? Her cheeks heated.

"I wanted to let you know. I apologized to her and told her the new plan." He took a few steps closer and stopped a foot away. He dropped his hands to his sides. "Thank you. You're really helping me out here. How much do I owe you for gas?"

"Oh, that's not necessary." She waved a hand. Standing near, she had the perfect opportunity for an up-close perusal. She didn't need to look to know concern would be etched in a deep furrow across his brow. She shook her head. Once she made it through the first month of school, after the poker tournament, she'd start a profile on an online dating app and get over her crush.

"Will you get in trouble for driving a student home?"

"It's a temporary solution. It'll be fine." She hoped it would be, but she wasn't exactly sure. She wasn't breaking any hard and fast rule. She'd have to remember to tell Bill to stay ahead of any gossip. "I'm glad you two talked. She's a great kid."

"That's all her mom."

"Not her dad, too?"

A shadow passed over his face. Earlier, he had spoken so highly of how his sister and her ex co-parented. What wasn't he saying? Something lingered there, but it wasn't her place to push her way into family dynamics.

"Dinner is served," Maddy's high-pitched voice called. With an apron wrapped around her waist and a paper towel draped over her arm, she appeared in the doorway.

He leaned close. "She's playing restaurant. She's the maître d', and server, and chef."

Did that mean they were on a pretend date? *Might be the closest I ever get to the real thing.* Her cheeks burned, and, with her luck, he'd spot her heightened color.

Taking in a deep breath to calm her nerves, she breathed in his mint and leather smell. Instead of peace, her pulse jumped. She'd always thought the smell was from handling saddles and reins. Now that she knew how he lived, she'd picture him here, in his chair near the fire, reading aloud with his deep voice.

Why not torture herself a little bit more with a pretend date now? She swallowed. "We'd better go. I've heard this place doesn't take reservations."

"Yes, it's exclusive." He winked.

Standing behind Stephanie, Ted pressed together his lips, holding in his chuckle. He was glad to use the woman as a shield.

Maddy expected to be taken seriously, always. Even when she was being exceptionally cute like right now, pretending to run a restaurant. He knew better than to laugh, however sorely tempted he was to start chortling.

"Table for two?" Maddy asked, stopping by the only table in the whole house.

He loved booth seating. When the opportunity presented itself, and he only had himself to please, he purchased a pair of high-backed, oak banquettes and slid a table in the center. He always felt cozy and warm, imagining he could smell garlic and oregano like he was at a pizzeria.

Stephanie turned him, widening her eyes as she glanced over her shoulder.

"Three," he said. He wasn't quite sure how to interpret the teacher's look. Surprise? In a good or bad way? The whole week had been one unexpected moment after another. He wouldn't take offense at something else going off script.

"Of course." Maddy nodded and pointed to one side of the table. "Please be seated."

Stephanie slid into the appointed spot.

Maddy turned toward him. "Excuse you."

Again, he swallowed the laugh. Eight times out of ten, she mastered the cliched sayings she heard from adults and TV. Those two instances she got it wrong, however, tickled his funny bone every time.

Maddy slid into the booth, pressing against the wall.

He joined her, taking the outside seat. His knee brushed Stephanie's.

She blushed and tucked a strand of hair behind her ear.

He sat straighter. "Please, dig in."

Maddy wasted no time. She spun her fork in the pasta and slurped.

He smiled at Stephanie, but she focused on her meal, neatly twirling the noodles onto her fork. The sauce covered pasta fell off the tines.

She glanced up. "Do you have a spoon?"

He nodded, slid out from the booth, and crossed the kitchen. He pulled open the utensil drawer, and at the loud sound of Maddy's chewing, grabbed the extra napkins off the top of the counter. He handed the spoon to Stephanie and a napkin to Maddy.

The little girl blotted her face. "Thanks, Unc." Her words were muffled with a full mouth.

He frowned and sat, scooting next to his niece. He'd have to work on her manners if they had more company. Did he want that? From under his lashes, he studied Stephanie across the table. Using the bowl of the spoon, she created a perfect pasta swirl on her fork and raised the bite to her mouth.

He held his breath. He hoped she'd like it. When he threw together dinner in the slow cooker that morning, he hadn't thought he'd have to please anyone besides himself and his niece. But it was nice to share a meal with someone else. He'd grown used to keeping his own company and ate mostly by himself. The Kincaids invited him to supper at the ranch house about once a week. He enjoyed the often-teasing chatter but didn't mind returning home to eat in silence the next day.

Would she get in trouble for staying? She assured him she wouldn't, and he had to take her at her word. It was nice to have support. With his niece, he was so out of his depth for full-time care. He'd babysat but never longer than a few hours. He didn't anticipate Maddy's needs. He had a lot to learn and was glad for the teacher across the table. Serving her a meal was a simple way to show his thanks for her help today and what he was beginning to realize would be almost every day while his sister was gone.

Stephanie reached for her napkin, dabbing her mouth. "This is really good. Can you send me the recipe?"

"Sure, of course. It's really easy. I'm not much of a cook. But I have a couple recipes I like."

"Isn't that better? My grandmother always said *jack of all trades, master of none*." She took another bite.

He considered her words as he started eating. She had a shyness to her but the more they talked, the more he felt he knew her. And the more he knew he couldn't overstep. Stephanie was so positive, resilient, and caring. He couldn't remember ever being bright and shiny with no predestination.

Marrying his high school sweetheart after college graduation meant he'd been checking off one to-do after another. He loved Liv. She'd been his past, present, and future. For fifteen years, he didn't have to explain himself. He lucked into meeting the person who knew him best before he could even drive a car. And then, all he had to do, was go along with her plans.

Losing her was devastating. Thirteen years later and he still wasn't sure he'd ever find who he was again. His interactions with Stephanie were nice and a pleasant diversion. But their situation was temporary. He could be appreciative and fully aware of the limits of the arrangement.

"I can't wait to bring Shakes home," Maddy said.

With a start, he frowned. He'd been in his own zone, mindlessly eating and unaware the other two were conducting a conversation. He looked down at his empty plate. If something named Shakes was coming into his sanctuary, he needed to get involved. He reached for his water and cleared his last bite. "What is Shakes?"

"Not what. Who," Stephanie said behind a napkin.

"Our class pet," Maddy said. "Everyone gets a turn to take care of him for a weekend. And then you add to his scrapbook. And I can't wait to show him the ranch."

Class pet? He shuddered. Oh, those poor creatures. Shouldn't one of the animal rescue organizations have put a bill forward banning class pets from schools across the country? He remembered a series of terrified, anxious hamsters sitting in glass aquariums near the teacher's desk and a window. A few had been lost during their weekend stays with his classmates.

"Shakes is a stuffed animal," Stephanie said. "He's a Golden Retriever, to be more precise."

He dropped his shoulders.

She arched an eyebrow. "You don't like animals?"

He shook his head. "I love animals. That's the problem. Didn't you see my degree?"

She nodded. "I did. What is Animal Sciences?" She propped her elbows on the table, resting her chin in one palm. "Is it Veterinary Medicine?"

"It can be a pre-vet course. It can also focus on the science and technology of enhancing animal products with well-being. My focus was on more general agriculture."

"Why did you pursue it?"

My wife. "I grew up in farming country. As a kid, everyone focused on adapting to the newest technology and efficiency. I was more interested in old techniques. Organic was starting to become a buzz word when I was in high school. In college, I started to pursue the idea of everything in relation to one another. I studied animals to understand the interconnectivity of life and the land."

"Wow." She leaned forward. "You were a farmer?"

"For a time."

"How did you end up ranching in Montana?"

My wife died. Again, he left the biggest reason unsaid. He missed Liv every day. He didn't hurt when he thought about her or talked about her. But having to drudge up all the emotion again to explain himself was draining. Although, he had the oddest sensation that if he ever wanted to talk to anyone and be understood not pitied, Stephanie would be the person. "Farming was tough on my own. I sold the farm and started wandering. I wanted to focus on animals and my little portion of the job instead of constantly being responsible for a big picture. I was in Montana, passing through and met Hank. He offered me a job."

She crossed her arms over her chest, her mouth gaping.

"Is that not what you expected?" He didn't want to care, but he did. Her opinion mattered.

"I suppose it's as good a job interview story as any other. Weren't you scared to start a career with no experience?"

He shrugged. At that moment, when he had met Hank, he hadn't been scared of anything. In the aftermath of the worst days of his life, he had operated without fear. "I'm an avid reader and hard worker. Learning to cowboy was good for me and gave me direction." And, being so focused on studying for his job in the early days, he hadn't had time to think about anything else.

"Are you excited about the bison?"

He nodded. "I am. It's a chance to learn. I'm always grateful to take on something new." And he was. He'd been wandering around the country, considering an RV, when he'd decided to visit Montana for a while. He liked to be grounded and hadn't needed much convincing to transplant his uprooted self on the ranch.

Ryan and Hank were content with his resume and references, and Ted had proved himself adept in the role. Stephanie was the first person to prod. But her questions didn't feel intrusive, and he found himself answering.

She set her napkin on her plate. "Thank you for a delicious dinner."

Do you want seconds? He wanted to stall her. He wasn't eager for her to leave. But he didn't want to apply any sort of pressure to convince her to stay longer. "Of course, my pleasure."

Stephanie slid out of the booth seat and turned toward her plate.

He reached a hand to still hers.

She jumped at the touch.

He drew back his hand. "It's quite alright. We'll clean up. Let me walk you to the door." He stood and motioned for her to walk ahead. Following behind, he kept several feet distance between them. At the door, he strode in front of her, to hold it open. "Thank you again for your help."

She nodded. "It's no problem. Have a good night."

With her gaze downcast, she didn't look up at him. He watched her get into her car and waved as she turned over the engine and reversed out of the spot onto the gravel road. Shutting the door, he crossed back into the kitchen. "Okay, squirrel. You go take a shower while I clean up the kitchen. Maybe we can read after you talk to Mommy."

"Three chapters?" Maddy looked expectant.

"Hmm." He stroked his chin. "Maybe two. If you hurry."

The little girl raced out of the booth and down the hall.

He chuckled. He wasn't quite sure what to make of the day, but he knew he had hours left before he settled into bed. And for once, he was excited.

CHAPTER 6

On Thursday night, Stephanie was still puzzling over Wednesday's unexpected dinner date. Not date. Her cheeks flushed. Lifting her gaze, she scanned the saloon. She'd arrived too early for the dinner rush and was—blessedly—alone. With one day until the poker tournament, she'd stopped by to review plans.

She reached for her glass of ice water, her hands slipping against the condensing sides. Sipping the cool drink, she relaxed. Last night hadn't meant anything. And, in case anyone got the wrong idea, she had knocked on the principal's door first thing that morning and explained exactly what happened and what would be continuing. He'd raised no concerns. As she expected. Her crush on Ted remained unrequited and inconvenient. But she would push through.

Following another successful school day, she had dropped off Maddy at the cabin but remained in her car. When he had spoken to her over a pasta dinner, he had held himself in check. He answered more personal questions than she had ever thought to ask before the quiet moments in his home. A niggling doubt, that she wasn't hearing the full story of his past, bothered her. Instead of confronting him, she backed off. She didn't want to push too far and make him shut down.

James Rabbitt, saloon proprietor, approached her table. He'd grown a full beard, and was almost unrecognizable. Only the historical garters he insisted on wearing over his shirt sleeves, like the original owner of The Golden Crown, gave away his identity. "Thanks for the updated timetable for tomorrow night."

"My pleasure, truly."

He chuckled.

After several years working together, he knew to take her at her word. She loved a schedule and an organized event. Until Candace Vane stepped up, Stephanie had run the evening with James for support in the food and beverage logistics. Even with the other woman's involvement, much of the planning still fell to Stephanie. She wasn't upset about being left to tackle most of the work alone. She was never one for group projects.

"Can I get you anything besides water?"

"I'm meeting Meg. She'll be here soon. I'm sure she'll be hungry." Stephanie leaned forward studying James' red blond beard. He looked more like a Viking. Typically, he took great care at accuracy for the grooming habits of a nineteenth century man for the special, costumed evening. "Interesting choice."

"Oh, this isn't the final look." He stroked his beard, smoothing the whiskers. "I'm shaving tomorrow right before opening the doors to the ticketed event. I'll be sporting an Imperial."

She appreciated that he thought she was educated enough to know the term. But she wasn't Joe the social studies teacher and town-historian. She participated in one historic event a year.

"Mutton chops connected with a mustache." He gestured with his hands.

"Oh." She couldn't visualize the description. She liked a clean-shaven man. Like Ted. She ignored the heat in her cheeks. When she had the chance, she'd have to search for the facial hair style on the internet. "I'm sure Joe will approve."

"It's hard to beat the waxed mustache from last year. A crowd favorite. But I like to try something new." James smiled. "I'll grab a couple menus." He walked away from the table.

The door swung open, light filling the entrance. A cool breeze snaked into the room.

Stephanie dragged her attention toward the front. Meg strode in, swinging her brown hair over her shoulder and waving at James and the other occupants she recognized.

As the last of her founding family in town, Meg Hawke was the closest Herd came to royalty. Her relationship with Ryan Kincaid, member of the other prominent family, solidified her status as town darling. Until recently, however, she'd felt like she didn't belong. Meg had confided to Stephanie her struggles with her place in the community. Stephanie remained aghast that the confident, beautiful woman ever questioned herself.

"Sorry I'm late." Meg stopped at the table, her floral skirt catching on the breeze. "Hey, did I see you at the ranch today?" She sat opposite and scooted the chair closer to the table.

Stephanie fought a groan. So much for avoiding the topic of Ted. Better to address the situation head-on with the only person who guessed about the crush—or the only one to say so to Stephanie's face. "You did." She nodded. "I'm helping Ted and his niece."

"Oh, I heard about his niece. I haven't met her yet although Colby has." Meg smiled every time she mentioned her rescue dog, Colby. The one-time stray was a pampered pup now and could most often be found asleep on a well-padded surface. "Hank says she loves the little girl."

"I think it's hard not to like her," Stephanie said. "She's in my kindergarten class. I haven't met her mom though. Have you?"

Meg shrugged. "No. Ted is close to his family, but usually he goes to visit them. Although, according to Ted, his sister looks like him in a wig."

Stephanie chuckled. "I concur."

Meg arched an eyebrow. "I thought you hadn't met her?"

"No, I've seen her photo in Ted's cabin."

Meg lifted both brows clear into her hairline.

Stephanie covered her mouth with a hand. If she'd done that earlier, she wouldn't have blurted such a suggestive statement. She hadn't behaved inappropriately and wouldn't incriminate herself. Straightening, she dropped her hands flat to the table. "Nothing happened. I'm dropping Maddy off for Ted at his cabin. He is having trouble navigating the afternoon pick-up. Yesterday was sort of a surprise that it happened, and Ted was nice enough to invite me in for dinner as a thank you. It's strictly business." She turned and reached into her tote, grabbing her clipboard, and ignoring Meg.

Meg couldn't possibly read Stephanie's mind. Stephanie wouldn't allow it despite her friend's reputation for being a shrewd judge of character. Their friendship was in its early days. What began as a mutually beneficial exchange of skills and time at Frontier Days in June continued naturally over the summer.

By the time the poker tournament approached, Stephanie couldn't fathom asking for help from anyone else. Stephanie pulled the sheets off the clipboard, handing a stapled stack to Meg.

Meg accepted the stack of sheets without comment.

No matter what may or may not be happening in her personal life, Stephanie wouldn't lose sight of her focus. The poker tournament raised funds and eliminated the stigma for the families that relied on the help. She'd heard stories of some kids not eating lunch so they wouldn't be spotted getting their meal at a free or reduced price. If she didn't fight for the kids, advocating everyone should be treated equally, she worried no one would. She couldn't let anyone down.

"Corporate sponsorship?" Meg asked after checking the sheets.

Stephanie nodded. "Yes, Candace got the backing. Last year, her corporation supported the event with a very generous in-kind donation. She didn't want to ruffle anyone's feathers so she approached a friend."

"Must be nice to have high-powered friends."

"Better than enemies." Stephanie hoped her under the breath comment hadn't been intelligible. She hadn't received any further communication with Candace since the annoyed missive earlier in the week. If she was upset, she'd let Stephanie know. Still, something nagged.

"What's wrong?" Meg asked. "If it's about you know who, you don't have to worry. I won't tease you. Just consider me a sounding board."

"Thanks. No, this is about my class." Stephanie sighed. "I think I've annoyed a parent. But I know everything will be fine."

"Dare I ask what happened?"

"The long and short of it is the parent does not agree with my management style. The parent thinks they deserve more of a say in how I run my classroom."

"And does the parent have a valid argument?"

The question was asked without any inflection. Stephanie flinched all the same. She wouldn't write off one parent's frustrations as invalid or unimportant. Everyone had a say when it came to their child. She respected that each parent was trying their very best for their kids. She'd been blessed to only have loving, involved moms and dads in her classes so far. What would happen with the reverse? She shuddered. "Yes, but my side is valid, too." She had another note already sitting in the cubbies for the kids to put in their backpacks tomorrow afternoon. "I'm probably making something out of nothing and being defensive. The parent sent an email with a comment. If they want to discuss the situation, I know I'll get a phone call or a meeting request."

"You know you'll always have my support. And not just because I need your help, too."

"Thanks." Stephanie bent and grabbed an accordion file off the ground. The heavy file landed with a thud on the table. "Speaking of my help."

Meg widened her eyes and gulped. "Your event checklists?"

Stephanie nodded. "And a little bit more. I included some contracts, budgets, planning calendars, etc. I wanted you to get an overview of what goes into an event. Although

I'm not sure all the information is transferrable to the ranch. Most of this came from my brother's event a few years ago. Weddings will have their own set of issues. I gather you'd have a list of preferred vendors for your guests to choose. You might be able to glean a bit of how far in advance you'd ideally need to book." She paused.

Meg reached for her water and sipped, drinking steadily until she emptied the glass. "This is a lot of information. I knew asking you was the best first step. You're an expert. I can only imagine what a good teacher you are for the kids. They're lucky to have you. If the parents can't appreciate your work, you should come to the ranch. We'd value you. Handsomely."

"Thanks." Stephanie smiled through her gritted teeth. Chasing a big payday wasn't her style. She hadn't needed it to be. With her college education fully funded by her family, she started her career debt-free and continued to live that way, saving whatever she could. "I just wish I could be a little bit more like your boyfriend. Ryan has strong beliefs and a unique vision. He's celebrated."

Meg frowned. "Well, I'm not sure your situations can be compared. I don't fully understand what you're dealing with but the scenarios are different."

"Because I'm not rich?"

"No, because you don't have the ultimate authority for your decisions. You answer to the parents. Whether everyone agrees on the methods or not, you and the parents are bound by a duty to the children. Ultimately, the parents carry the final choice. They are responsible."

Stephanie couldn't argue with that. Maybe she'd been focused on the wrong aspect of her battle. She'd remember every side of the argument going forward.

"I'm sure Ted won't raise any complaints." Meg shot her a knowing look. "If you're worried about getting on your crush's bad side..."

Stephanie's cheeks flushed again. "Am I that obvious?"

"Not anymore. Now that you sort of talk around him, you don't make it so clear how you feel."

Stephanie pressed cool fingers to her hot skin. In a small town, every action was observed and studied. Doing so wasn't necessarily a conscious choice on the part of the observer. Patterns became expectations. Any behavior out of the ordinary would be observed as a curiosity, not necessarily to stoke gossip. Her little conversation at the dinner continued to draw notice and get comments.

"I'm proud you've found your voice," Meg said.

"Well, maybe it's because I know nothing will happen." Because if Ted was going to make a move, he would have done so by now. Stephanie partially took her summer job to spend more time around him. But the plan backfired. Instead of forced proximity, she'd ended up complicating their roles by becoming his subordinate. And now she was his niece's teacher. Could the situation ever be simplified?

"Don't say that around Hank, he might take is as a challenge and set you two up."

Stephanie snorted. "If I thought that would work, I would have told Hank how I felt years ago. Matchmaking might be old fashioned, but it is effective."

"I don't think a set-up is a guarantee."

It worked with you. At the start of the summer, Hank pulled out all the stops to throw Meg and Ryan together. Within a month, the long-time frenemies were officially the town's favorite couple. Stephanie wouldn't mind a little of Hank's meddling magic.

"Are you sure you're not interested in Joe?" Meg asked.

"And mess with the set-up between him and Abby?" Stephanie lifted an eyebrow.

Meg chuckled. "Hank won't push with Ted. He might be the only person to get a pass."

Stephanie frowned and leaned forward. "Why?"

Meg lifted a shoulder. "He's a widower."

Stephanie hadn't known. The explanation answered so many questions. She understood why he was alone when he had such kind soul and warm heart. Losing someone must be the hardest tragedy to overcome. Pressing a hand to her chest, she rubbed her aching heart. The biggest question remained. Would he ever be ready to try again?

Inside the old red barn, Ted held a measuring tape to a wooden board and pulled it taut to the end. He lifted the end, letting the tape recoil slowly back into its case and grabbed the clipboard he'd left on the ground. With a pencil, he checked off the last of the boards.

It had been a good, too busy to think, sort of day, exactly the kind he'd come to the ranch for. Running from one task to the next didn't leave a person with any time to themselves. For good reason.

At the same time the lumber had been delivered for the deck build, another crew had poured the footings outside. The concrete mixer had needed extra care, navigating around the old building. Ted couldn't stand in one place and direct the guys where to stack the boards. Too bad the back wall hadn't been pushed out yet, or Ted could have directed everyone from one spot. Instead, he was in and out the entire day.

With men and machinery everywhere, he'd been in the center of the storm, directing the chaos. The mechanical whir of the saw, appropriately slicing each board and post to order on site, had mingled with the hum of the mixer to create a white noise symphony. Ted had signed the lumber receipt with the caveat he'd be checking each board. After setting the posts in the concrete, the crew had called it quits and left.

In silence, Ted filled his lungs and immediately his mind drifted, wondering what Stephanie was up to. He could barely take care of himself let alone watch out for his niece. He couldn't take on more people. He was better off alone.

But he hadn't been lonely until he realized what he'd been missing. That was the sting. A person could know something with the certainty of absolute zero and still find themselves struggling to reconcile the head and the heart.

Maddy had arrived on the ranch an hour earlier, in the midst of the day's work, and been happily ensconced in the ranch house with Hank and Colby. He probably needed to head up to fetch her and start thinking about dinner. Before Maddy came, he survived plenty of days on a piece of fruit and a cup of coffee until he headed into town for dinner. That wouldn't fly with taking care of a child, and he didn't need his sister thinking she couldn't count on him when it mattered.

He wanted Maddy and Jen nearby, just not as the sole responsible adult overseeing everything. At least he'd managed to look pulled together once, for Stephanie, when it mattered. Maybe she wouldn't totally think him an old fool.

The big barn doors slid open, the wheels squealing on the track. He'd add *oil hinges* to his list.

"Hello," a deep, gravelly voice called. "You still back there?"

Ted smiled, striding to the entrance. "Yes, sir, Mr. Kincaid."

Hank Kincaid, sunlight glinting off his white hair from the open doorway, surveyed the interior. "Huh. With all the tables stacked up and the chairs in storage, I'm having a hard time picturing what it'll look like. Do we need more tables? Less?"

"I think we'll be fine." Ted scanned the space, trying and failing to gaze with fresh eyes. He had no problem imagining the space.

During the tourist season, the barn came alive with evenings of dinner and dancing. Some of the local teachers formed a bluegrass band and were happy with the opportunity to perform regular gigs. Stephanie had sung with them a few times. Her voice was as sunny and bright as her personality. She had lit up on stage.

"Hey, you were supposed to get me," a deeper voice, slightly out of breath, added. Ryan Kincaid entered, his chest heaving as he pressed a hand to his side.

"Boy, I can't wait around all day," Hank said.

Ryan lifted his gaze to the ceiling.

Ted pressed his lips together. The eyes to the sky was all the eye rolling Ryan allowed himself in the presence of his grandfather. The eighty-nine-year-old man was spry, both mentally and physically. He did what he wanted, when he wanted, and what he didn't want was answering to the child he'd raised. Even if said child now stood over six feet, was closer to forty than four, and had single-handedly saved the family legacy with the idea to sell off the cattle and transform the ranch into a resort.

No, Hank still had his opinions. Ted cleared his throat and tucked the clipboard under his arm. "I was checking the boards again. Everything is correct. I'll be ready to start with the flashing and ledger board tomorrow, if Ryan has time to help."

"I'll see you tomorrow morning after the school drop-off, come get me," Ryan said.

"Great. Should we head outside and see the footings?" Ted asked.

"Lead the way," Ryan said.

Ted strode through the open door and around the building. He'd spent most of the summer planning the deck build. The project demanded precision in its execution both for the scope and timing, to not disturb the guests. As he rounded the last corner and the site came into view, he gasped.

No amount of x's on the ground or hastily drawn sketches could prepare him for the scale of the actual construction marked with concrete footers. The deck was to be built in such a way that, if needed, they could eventually extend the boards to wrap around the sides of the building. He'd fought against starting with that vision. It would ruin a visitor's first look at the historic barn. He wasn't a history buff like his buddy, Joe, but he did have an opinion on the ranch. He'd soaked the ground with his sweat and hoped he'd memorialize himself on this land. Somehow.

Hard to live forever if you don't have kids to remember you after you're gone.

He turned around to gauge his bosses' reactions.

Ryan stroked his jaw.

Hank nodded. "It's good. I trusted Meg. She has vision. But I'll admit I was worried. Seeing this now?" He rubbed together his palms. "Gives me ideas."

"Ideas?" Ted frowned.

"He's circling back to his matchmaking. He'll twist any comment into an infinity loop for his favorite topic," Ryan said.

Ted's heart hit the front of his chest. Hank couldn't be thinking about him, right? Ted wasn't looking. *And if I was, I found my own match.*

"Boy, now you've scared him." Hank shook his head. "Don't worry, Ted. I have big plans for my birthday celebration. I'm not plotting anything for you."

Ryan sniggered. "Your birthday celebration is the whole ruse. You've got to back off. Joe and Abby don't need this much time to plan. And, even if they did, they could tackle a lot on their own."

"That's not the point." Hank spit onto the ground.

Ted could find his voice for his friend. Joe didn't dislike Abby as much as he had expressed his frustrations and concerns about her. *She's hiding something, and I think it's big.* Joe had told Ted at the last poker game. "Mr. Kincaid, sir. I have to caution you. Joe doesn't care for Abby. I don't think they could even be considered friends."

"There's a very shaky boundary between love and hate. Those two have something," Hank said.

Ryan shook his head.

"Maybe you should set him up with someone else?" Ted asked.

"I thought about Stephanie." Hank stroked his chin.

Ted caught his breath, the air burning his lungs. If Hank set up Joe and Stephanie, the pair would be happy. As a couple, they'd make a lot of sense with so much in common. Hank was one for one on his matchmaking skills. He'd probably score another win with those two.

"No spark there," Hank said. "And she's too young."

Slowly exhaling, Ted didn't find much relief. If Stephanie was deemed too young for Joe, what about Ted? He was two years older than his buddy. He shook his head. The conjecture didn't matter. While he never intended to be alone forever, that was his lot in life, and he wasn't going to change course now. How could anyone else claim his heart? Even a good person with a sweet, soft smile could break him.

Focusing on status quo was his path to a contented life. He loved and cared about his family and was happy to have them unexpectedly close. Despite his love of a friendly game of poker, he wasn't a gambler. When he had married his high school sweetheart, he had lucked into a once in a lifetime love. No guarantee he could find that again. Marriage didn't come with a warranty. If he had a kid, he still didn't have any assurances. He could end up divorced like his sister. Was that fair to a kid?

"Ted?" Ryan asked.

Ted lifted his gaze. He hadn't realized the conversation continued without him. But he was glad for it. "Sorry, thinking about the next steps on this project. Did you need to discuss your birthday?"

Hank grinned. "That's why you're the best cowboy we've ever had. You're always looking ahead and spotting problems. I don't think we'd be able to reintroduce animals to the land without you here."

"It's quitting time," Ryan said. "Your little lady is getting hungry. We came down to fetch you for supper. Will you join us tonight?"

Ted nodded. These men stepped up for him at a time he'd been so lost. And again, their kindness and caring extended to him like he was their kin, too. They invited Maddy into their lives without a second thought. "That sounds wonderful." He meant it. Status quo might not be overly ambitious but it was peace. He wouldn't lose that for anything.

After dinner at the ranch house, he drove home and started the new nighttime routine at the cabin. While Maddy showered and brushed her teeth, Ted swept up the kitchen floor and ran the dishwasher. Having a house guest forced him onto a schedule.

If not for the little girl, he'd probably have missed dinner and started the deck. Working around the clock was his norm. He could push himself past pain and through hunger, if he engaged his muscles and his mind in manual labor.

"Unc? Can we read?"

He lifted his gaze to the pink pajama clad child. "Of course. First, I promised Mommy we'd video chat."

"Yes, please." Maddy grabbed the cell phone off the table and handed it over.

Sliding onto the bench after her, he unlocked the screen and dialed his sister. He handed the phone to his niece and sat next to her, angling close.

"Mommy!" Maddy squealed.

"Oh, sweet girl. Hi! I've missed you!" Jen sounded exhausted and wistful. Like she could start crying in a second.

He wouldn't be surprised if she did. She was doing her best in a tense situation. His sister shouldered a lot of worry and guilt. Maddy was the proof of his sister's wonderful parenting skills. Remembering Stephanie's advice, Ted had to insert himself in the call and aim for levity. "Don't worry about me."

Maddy giggled. "Unc is here, too. Mommy, I can't wait to show you everything. Mr. Hank and Miss Meg and Colby and the barn and school and Miss Patricks."

Jen chuckled. "Sure sounds like you've settled in. Good job, sweetie. I'm glad I'll have a local to take me around town."

Maddy beamed at the praise.

Ted almost sighed. Jen regulated her voice to normal. Crisis—and bad night's sleep—averted. "How is everything? No hiccups?"

"None whatsoever," Jen said without hesitation.

Ted swallowed the sigh of relief, glad to know they'd be nearby for good. Ted wasn't sure he could go back to living totally on his own. The girls wouldn't always share his house. Taking care of Maddy grounded him, and he couldn't give it up. In a few years, he could look forward to off-tune school concerts and maybe attending a few sports events. He couldn't wait.

"I'm heading to work soon," Jen said. "I'm off tomorrow, and then I'll work six days straight. I'm driving up with some of our things next weekend."

"Not everything?" Ted asked.

"I'll have one more week of work before I close on the house. Slight hiccup. The movers will follow me in two weekends."

He didn't mind, but he couldn't quite comprehend what his sister was going through. The separation from her child had to be excruciating. He couldn't let the call linger or everyone would be sad, realizing what they were missing. "We'll be happy to see you."

"Mommy, do you want to see my backpack and my papers?" Maddy stood on the bench and jumped over him. Holding the phone, she raced to her bedroom.

Ted chuckled. His motion sickness prone sister was in for a doozy. But he wasn't going to micromanage the call. He'd give the pair space.

Maddy could dazzle her mom with tales of school, and he could be grateful for the twist of fate that brought his family to his chosen hometown even if he avoided adding to his list of nearest and dearest. He refused to read into the motivations for Stephanie's help. She'd be kind to any child. Maddy was special to her family.

He was grateful. Because he couldn't be anything else.

CHAPTER 7

In her high-necked prairie gown, Stephanie stood perfectly straight. She had no choice. Sitting was uncomfortable. Running was impossible. Talking too loudly was most definitely not an option. The worst part about her ensemble? She didn't even have pockets. Her historically accurate dress seemed to shrink the longer she wore it. She took in the deepest breath she could and calmed down. Not long to go now.

While the poker tournament was nearing its end after several loud, raucous hours in The Golden Crown saloon on Friday night, she remained in constant motion with no opportunity to slow down or sit. Helping wherever she could, she had run to the back to grab her cell phone, almost forgetting to snap a few pictures of the event to share on the school website, loan to the town's tourism page, and keep as a personal memento of another successful night.

The outfit restricted her ability to perform even the most basic of her tasks. At least her wardrobe was temporary, and she'd been born over a century later, long past the fashion for up-to-the-chin collars and floor length hemlines. She was glad she didn't have to teach her students in the school-teacher garb she wore. Although, she wondered if some might enjoy not having a teacher focused on them but too attuned to her own aches and pains.

Pushing through the swinging door from the employees only area to the main room, she plastered on a smile and pulled up her camera app. Angling her device this way and that, she snapped hundreds of photos in a handful of minutes as she circled the perimeter. At the start of the evening, the circular tables were occupied with card sharks. As the play dwindled down, only one table remained with an active game. Couples, families, neighbors, and friends now gathered around the buffet tables, enjoying the meal their entrance fee purchased. With her device, she captured smiling faces and heads thrown back in laughter. It was a fun evening for a good cause. Everyone got the memo.

For the most part, the crowd was attired in nineteenth century costumes. The annual event had become a town spectacle. Locals stashed period clothing for the tournament. Kim at the Old West photography studio began an enterprising side-hustle, renting out her costumes to interested tourists. The room was filled to capacity with bowler hats, vests, corsets, and ruffles.

She would be jealous of the women dressed in saloon girl outfits, if the corsets didn't look more restrictive than the tight collar on her gown. She had a role to play at the end of the evening to officially close the night and needed to look the part. Still, she was sweating through the dress and couldn't wait for a cool shower and soft pajamas at home.

Striding past the bar, she snapped a couple shots of James in action. His beard was definitely the stand-out facial hair of the year. Most of the other men stuck to either a mustache or beard. A handful sported a few days of scruff, also in keeping with the time period. No one had taken the same level of care as the saloon owner. She angled her phone and snapped a picture, flashing him a thumbs up before crossing toward the last table still in play.

Hank Kincaid operated as the house. The local blacksmith and a man she recognized but didn't know sat in front of him. Joe and Ted were there as well.

She held her breath, transfixed watching Ted. With his cards face down on the table, he stared straight ahead. He could have been carved from a glacier. Nothing showed in his expression. He barely breathed, holding still and steady. Even playing a game, he exuded safety and certainty. She'd been drawn to those qualities. *I'll always be able to count on Ted.*

The longer she studied him, the chillier she grew. She crossed her arms, tucking her phone into the crook of her elbow. She couldn't snap pictures and risk the flash disturbing the men.

Hank dealt two cards to each player.

Ted focused on the game, providing a rare opportunity to study him. Gray hair threaded through his temples. Not a ton, but enough—along with the fine lines around his mouth and eyes—to highlight their age difference. She didn't find the years between them insurmountable. She liked his cautious approach to the world. She found herself barreling ahead and flailing around, but she liked that he was more thoughtful.

The players placed their bets.

His gray eyes flashed like melted silver. For a split second, he warmed up like he'd been plunged in a crucible.

The change was slight, but she noticed. And his moment of victory was contagious. She smiled for him, feeling the heat from her head to her toes.

Hank gestured for the players to show their cards.

"Pair of Kings," Ted said. The others sniggered and took sips of their drinks. Hank pushed the pot to Ted.

She took a step forward, eager to congratulate him. A cold hand seized her elbow and squeezed. Wincing, she turned and frowned at the back of a saloon girl.

She let the woman drag her from the crowd, across the room to the corner near the kitchen. She wouldn't cause a scene and interrupt the last table at play. Her mind reasoned the kidnapper must be an acquaintance, and she was in a very public place. She wasn't about to be snatched, no matter how many of her true-life crime shows told her otherwise.

Free of the crowd, the woman turned.

Stephanie sucked in a sharp breath. Her eyes almost bugged out of her head.

In arguably the skimpiest saloon girl costume of the evening, Candace Vane glowered.

"Oh, hi." Stephanie pressed a hand to her collarbone and forced a laugh. "Good evening, Candace. I didn't recognize you. No wonder I hadn't seen you yet. I'm glad you found me."

"I thought you were deliberately snubbing me."

The haughty tone befit royalty. The corresponding sniff and lift of her chin complimented the expression. Only the costume ruined the effect. "I apologize if I gave you that impression. I think this might be the best event yet." Stephanie smiled, the corners of her mouth lifting in a shaky grin.

"I know it is. The corporate donations alone have secured the program for the next year."

"We couldn't do any of this without you."

"Hmm. Interesting. I appreciate your praise. I thought I must have offended you somehow." Candace studied her bracelets.

Stephanie darted her gaze, looking for escape, a witness, or solid ground. Anything to hold onto. The subtle cut of each word sliced deep with repetition. "Of course you haven't offended me." Stephanie forced a laugh.

"We aren't quite the partners I had imagined." Candace lifted her gaze and held Stephanie's with an unblinking stare. "You didn't respond to my email on Wednesday."

I completely forgot. The stifling costume threatened Stephanie with heat stroke, trapping her flushed skin under a high collar and long sleeves. She hated being scolded and did her best to avoid reprimands. "My sincerest apologies. I didn't realize you required a response. Your email didn't pose any questions or ask for any action."

Candace lifted her hands to her tiny, corseted waist. "At least this went well. Let's return to more formal terms, Miss Patricks. From what I gather from Amelia, you have been showing a lot of particular attention to specific children at the expense of the others."

Stephanie's throat went dry. "I don't follow."

"Oh, I'm sure you do. Your closeness to one child and her guardian hasn't gone unnoticed. Since I seem to be on the outside looking in, maybe this is the natural end of my help with your fundraiser."

Stephanie was speechless. Threatening the kids and calling her out, Candace cut her down to size. Hot emotion bubbled up inside Stephanie. She wasn't sure if she should laugh or cry.

Candace strode past Stephanie, brushing against her shoulder.

The shove was too powerful to be an accident. Lauren and Kelly had warned Stephanie about Candace, but she wanted to believe she'd taken the measure of the woman during their years working on this event together.

With a glance over her shoulder to make sure no one noticed, and she wouldn't be missed, Stephanie strolled toward the antique half door. At least she had the valid excuse of putting away her phone to steal a moment to calm down. She pushed her way inside and continued to the line of hooks near the back door. She shoved her phone deep into the bottom of her purse.

Filling her lungs, she caught a hint of mint and leather. And she almost collapsed and started to cry. She pulled back her shoulders. Ted must have noticed her disappearance. She wanted him to care about her so much more than he ever could. But it wouldn't be fair to him if she leaned into his solid chest and hugged him, though she desperately longed for his strong arms to wrap around her and reassure her everything was okay.

Her world was changing. Whether she wanted it to or not. She wouldn't compound her sins by dragging him down with her. No matter how tempting.

She turned, brushed her hair out of her face, and smiled as she strolled towards the one person she feared really saw her. She wished he'd be her friend and nothing else right now. "Hi, Ted. Good round out there. We should get back."

"Wait," he murmured.

She felt the softly spoken words down to her bones and the light tone frightened her worse than Candace Vane's bluster and fury. Stephanie twisted her fingers to stop from doing something over the top, like reaching for him. She was a fool to imagine anything more than the momentary friendship based on her helping him out. She couldn't seem to make her heart understand.

We could be happy if you let us.

For the past several hours, Ted was unnervingly aware of Stephanie's every move. Without turning his head, he knew exactly where she was in the room. It was torturously hard to keep his focus on his game-playing. But he managed. Somehow.

He had debated skipping the event. After a long day of work on the deck, he ached. Every muscle in his body was strained from unusual twisting and stretching. As had become their habit, Stephanie had pulled her car in front of the ranch house and walked around the wraparound porch to flash him a thumbs up. Then, Maddy had let herself into Hank and Ryan's house and Stephanie had left.

He'd wanted to talk to her and thank her. The rest of Maddy's week had been much smoother since the grown-ups in her life had started working together. As a result, his world had been restored to its axis. Was this what prompted his sister to put aside her differences with her ex? For Maddy's sake? He hadn't understood the importance until he'd lived it.

He had been holding a piece of metal flashing when he had spotted Stephanie on the porch, and couldn't do more than nod his head in acknowledgement without ruining his work. She deserved better. Exhausted from his labors, he wanted to kick back at the cabin with Maddy. He'd never been so grateful for a weekend. What would next week, the first five days of school, bring?

He looked forward to quiet and a weekend spent recharging. But Ryan volunteered to babysit since he was dog sitting for Meg. The pair, Colby and Maddy, were evenly matched in energy levels, making the job easier as the child and dog entertained each other. Ted thanked Ryan, grateful. Ted had to show up and support Stephanie's event. Friendship required kindness from both parties. He couldn't offer her more of a relationship, but she deserved every ounce of his respect.

He was good at playing poker. Participating in a tournament was hardly a stretch for him. Careful to never play with the seasonal ranch hands, he had a standing weekly group and, as he expected, those five were the last men standing in the tournament.

When Meg had approached the table during the last hand, she brought with her a strange sense of calm. He relaxed at her nearness, maybe because he didn't have to subconsciously track her around the room. She stood close enough for him to catch a whiff of her citrus-y smell. And then he'd been dealt a winning hand.

He accepted his winnings, turned his head toward her, and frowned. She disappeared. Reaching a hand to his chest, he rubbed the dull ache in his ribs. One person in a crowd shouldn't hold the power to make or break an event. For him, she did.

"Hey, Hank, will you watch my chips?" Ted asked the dealer.

Hank arched a brow. "Okay, but we're only taking a quick break before the last hand."

Ted nodded, pushing back from the table. He accepted the congratulations and positive comments from friends and neighbors as he wove through the crowd. Everyone knew the evening's winner didn't take home the pot. The money was donated back to the school as part of the fundraiser. But the winner earned a positive reputation in town. In a small community like Herd, a person's integrity was prized above all else.

He spotted the door to the kitchen still swinging. With a frown, he noted the angry saloon-girl nearby, nostrils flaring like a bull.

His pulse raced. Was Stephanie in the back? Was she okay? Slipping through the door while it swung open, he carefully strode into the kitchen.

His boot slid on the tile. He froze but slid forward a half an inch. He stared at the floor. He hadn't realized how slippery tile could be with his all-purpose boots. With his gaze on the floor, he didn't see her approach he felt the change in the air as she tiptoed toward him.

"Hi, Ted," she said. "Good round out there. We should get back."

He heard the hitch in her words. Had she been crying? Her face was a little red and puffy. What happened?

He was terrible at dealing with tears and his flight control took over command of his body at the first sign. Right now, however, he wanted to stay here and comfort her. *We are friends. Friends don't abandon each other.*

She brushed past his shoulder.

"Wait," he murmured. When he turned his head to speak, he stood only a few inches away.

She froze.

Up close, he couldn't even see her breathing.

Dressed in a high-neck gown with long sleeves and a busy print, she was one of the women portraying the Ladies' Society for the Health and Moral Well-Being of the Youth of Montana. The group had worked to abolish gambling in Herd during the early days of the town. They'd been unsuccessful.

She shouldn't be the most beautiful woman in the room, but she was. Her unusually tight posture was all wrong. She was lightness and positivity. She should never have a second of sadness. He had enough for the both of them. He'd take on even more pain if he could spare her a second of sadness. She should always be bright and happy.

Dragging in a shuddering breath, she stepped back and met his gaze. She offered a tight smile. "I'm okay. Don't worry about me."

It's hard not to.

"I'm just preparing for my big entrance." She reached up and pinched her cheeks. "You had a great round out there." She repeated her earlier praise.

"I got lucky." Could his winning streak continue? It hadn't. For much of his life, he had one perfect thing, one good moment, or one glorious victory. And then everything crashed down around him. *What if my luck changes?* "What happened? Why are you upset?"

She sighed and shook her head.

"You can tell me. We're friends . . . right?" He desperately wished that were true. Because that was all he could ever have with this special, wonderful human. And he needed her goodness and spirit in his life. He'd lose that when Jen returned. She would assume control of the pick-up and drop off. She would meet with Stephanie for parent teacher conferences. Jen would step up in all the ways involving Maddy. And he'd have no reason to speak to Stephanie again. Until the summer? June was an impossibly far off date in the vast and distant future.

"You're right, we are." She took in a deep breath. "To be honest, it was a little bit of a power play. Someone trying to put me in my place. Under their heel."

He'd dealt with that before and—if he ever left the ranch—he would probably have to face it again. "Do you need me to do anything? Can I help and speak to someone?"

"No, but you're sweet for trying." With a shaky breath, she stepped forward.

He opened his arms wide and wrapped her tight in a warm hug. Until he made the gesture, he hadn't known what he'd intended. Holding her felt right. He needed the embrace, too. She'd been slumped and defeated. He wanted to lift her up figuratively and literally.

After a few seconds, her breathing evened, returning to normal. She kissed his cheek. "I'm needed for my grand entrance." She strolled toward the swinging door, pulling back her shoulders and lifting her head high.

He liked this version of her almost as much as the soft peck she'd planted on his cheek. He let the light touch soak into his skin.

She turned. "Come on, you better go win it all so we can finish this night properly."

He had to take her word that she was fine. He had hoped hugging her would reassure him that she was okay, he wasn't sure it had. He knew she was the same sort of prideful as he was. Like recognized like. And more than anything, he was certain sometimes a person had to tell others what they wanted to believe about themselves. But the reflection of himself didn't change what he wanted. Her dampened spirit had only a tiny flicker of its usual spark. He cleared his throat. "Okay. See you soon."

Striding past her, he headed straight toward the table. At his sides, his hands shook. Not from nerves but the sudden desire to reach out and touch her again. He sat at the table as Ryan announced the last hand.

The final round was quick and—shockingly—Ted won. He didn't lose it all at the last minute. He was applauded and clapped on the back.

The front door of The Golden Crown crashed against the wall.

The room fell unnaturally quiet. The crowd parted.

Standing into the center of the saloon, holding a sign reading *For the Children*, Stephanie strode in with her band of other modestly-garbed women. She played her role to perfection. Joe had researched the event but allowed Stephanie to take liberties with the script. She demanded the cowboys cease and desist at once.

At the table, she lifted her chin and held his gaze. He adored the flicker of amusement and cheek as she continued to rail against him. Finally, she finished. He pushed the winnings forward. The crowd erupted into cheers. After a few minutes, James announced the record-setting donation amount, everyone clapped, and the evening concluded.

Ted tried—unsuccessfully—to catch her eye but Stephanie had stepped away to finish up her duties for the evening.

Playacting for one night was okay. But he preferred the real person under the costume. From the corner of his eye, he caught what looked like a heated argument in the opposite direction. He turned his head and observed Joe and Abby at war again.

Ted shook his head. Hank was usually a shrewd judge of character. There was no way he would find success matching up Joe and Abby. Ted had a surefire way to take the heat of Hank's matchmaking off his friend. If Ted made a move on Stephanie, he'd be sure to grab the old cowboy's attention.

Ted glanced at Stephanie, smiling so pretty near the bar. Holding her hadn't been about anything more than providing comfort. What he found, however, had shocked him. She belonged in his arms, as natural as pulling on a hat on a sunny day. The longer he'd held her, the more he realized he needed the warmth of another person's embrace too.

He didn't want to need her but couldn't deny the way she enhanced his life. Was that emotion tougher than fighting against lust? While it might be more tempting, he'd hold strong against her allure.

He had his family in town now, and she had her own life. She deserved so much more than a broken-down old cowboy like him. But a tiny part of him, deep down, wanted her in his life. As more than friends.

CHAPTER 8

Stephanie parked in the driveway of the cheery yellow house, and turned off the car. Reaching for her travel mug, she took one last long sip of the cooled coffee. She hated room temperature coffee. Today, however, she savored every last ounce of caffeine and peace. Saturdays should be for sleeping in. The day after the poker tournament, however, was anything but restful.

Last night, she'd gone home exhausted and spent the night tossing and replaying the past few hours. She'd been shocked by the confrontation with Candace. The PTA president's threat to stop her participation—and thus the majority of the fundraising—left Stephanie speechless. Could the other woman be so vindictive she'd impact children's welfare over a personal frustration?

Before Candace's involvement, the event raised only modest sums to help pay the lunch balance owed by a few students at the end of the school year. Since the woman took over the project, however, the increased corporate sponsorships had helped raise their goal to almost unimaginable heights, covering the fees for every child.

Stephanie was upset, frustrated, and disappointed. Inwardly, she raged against Candace for threatening a program that did so much good out of spite. Mrs. Vane, she corrected herself. Formal terms only with an eyeroll. In the moment, Stephanie hadn't stood up for the kids. She'd acted like a coward.

If she was honest, she was more annoyed with herself both that she'd let the event depend so heavily on one person's involvement and that she hadn't practiced her due diligence in reaching out to a parent. She had put herself in a questionable spot.

Compounding the issue was driving Maddy every day after school. If she didn't know Ted, would she have helped him? She couldn't argue that it was on her way home. She had to drive miles out of her way and circle back. She'd informed Bill, keeping administration abreast of the unusual situation. But deep down, she knew she used it as an excuse to see Ted. Otherwise, she wouldn't have any reason to fan the flickering flames of their new friendship.

A knock on her window snapped Stephanie to attention.

Lauren stood next to the car. "Are you planning on coming inside? Or are you busy plotting an escape?"

Stephanie pocketed her keys and swallowed the cheeky response. She was here because after three early morning texts, she'd agreed to help Lauren today. Otherwise, she'd still be in bed resting.

Slowly, Stephanie opened the car door, grabbing her purse off the center console as she slipped from the driver's seat. "Sorry." She shut the car door. "Lost in thought."

"Remember, you said any time I needed help?" Lauren's voice shook, heavy with emotion.

Stephanie reached for her friend's hand and squeezed. "I did, and I meant it." She forced a smile.

Lauren sniffed and pulled her hand free, swiping her eyes.

Stephanie knew better than to ask what was wrong. Lauren never responded to that question. She bristled like a cactus growing spikes on time-lapse when pestered about private matters. As her fluctuating hormone levels impacted her emotional state, she would not appreciate any prodding.

"Did you get home late?" Lauren asked. "Are you tired?"

Stephanie shook her head. "I'm ready to get started. What's today's project?"

"Nursery furniture. Packages have been accumulating in the room. I didn't want to open anything until I could organize. I finally got the furniture yesterday. But it's all in flat pack boxes and needs to be put together. And I have to get the room straightened and sorted. Steve doesn't understand the urgency."

"I'm sure that's not true." Stephanie struggled to keep her voice even. Lauren was sensitive to tone without the added upheaval of her changing body.

"It is. The packages arrived late last night. After seven. I wanted to get started. But Steve had to go into the office this morning for monthly inventory. He made me promise I wouldn't start on my own. The room is packed, and I can't do anything."

Stephanie nodded solemnly. Obviously, Steve hadn't read enough of the baby books to grasp the importance of nesting. And he assumed he could reason with his agitated wife. Stephanie would have to talk to him. "I'm here. I'll get to work, and you can tell me where everything goes. Okay?"

Lauren inhaled and exhaled, loudly. Her nostrils flared. Her eyes went a little wild.

Stephanie remembered the same breathing techniques from her sister-in-law's pregnancy. She copied the pattern for two rounds. "Better?"

Lauren smiled. "Yes, much. Come on in, and I'll get you another cup of coffee before we gets started. You probably need it after last night."

Stephanie pressed her lips together. Her honest reply would only worry her very distressed pregnant friend. Stephanie followed her friend into the house, slipping off her shoes inside the front door and climbing the stairs to the second level. "I'm okay. A little hard work is all I need."

The Cape Cod style home boasted three bedrooms and two bathrooms on the upper floor. Stephanie tried not to notice her friend's labored breathing as she climbed the steps. She remained silent as she approached the open doorway.

"I'm relieved to hear you say that. Because here we are." Lauren's voice caught.

Frowning, Stephanie peered inside and dropped her jaw. Boxes filled every inch of the room like some complicated stacking game gone awry. Steve was right not to let Lauren start assembling on her own. Or at all. She was liable to hurt herself even stepping foot inside.

Telling Lauren her husband's judgement was sounder than hers wasn't a good start. None of Stephanie's thoughts were helpful or encouraging.

So, instead, she faced her friend with a smile. "Why don't you rest on your bed? I will start moving the boxes out so I have room to work on the furniture. That might take me a while. Once I start building, I'll let you know so you can tell me where to put the pieces."

"I know it's lot. I can't remember what is inside every package anymore. I really need to set up the room."

"It's no trouble. I'll help today, and then you can take your time with the little things, and you'll feel so much better." Stephanie utilized her most placating tone. "Are you going on a babymoon soon?"

"Maybe." Lauren sniffed. "I don't really want to go anywhere. I feel miserable. What's going to change if I go to a hotel? Will my heartburn suddenly stop? Will the babies stop kicking my bladder at three am?"

"A night away might be a nice mental break," Stephanie said, interjecting her voice with as much whimsical optimism as she could muster. "You could let someone else cook and clean. Take a few days off."

"I'm not sure. I have so much to do."

"Don't worry about this." Stephanie waved a hand at the room, not able to assess the space again without pulling a face. "I'll get everything straightened and sorted."

"Thanks, Stephanie. Truly." Lauren wiped at her eyes. "You're such a good friend. It's why I don't want anything to happen while I'm gone."

"Gone?" Stephanie cocked her head to the side. "Where would I go? I don't take vacation during the school year." She hadn't taken a real trip in years. She'd love to but always used her time off to help her friends or visit her brother.

"No, I don't mean a trip to the beach. I'm talking *gone*." Lauren widened her eyes.

Stephanie frowned at her friend. "Gone like fired?"

Lauren nodded.

A chill swept down Stephanie's spine. Lauren wasn't the sort to gossip or invent a story. Had Lauren heard about the argument last night? Had someone been listening? Or was Candace spreading the story?

Stephanie gritted her teeth. Candace Vane's threats rattled, but Ted buoyed Stephanie's flagging spirits. Lauren hadn't been at the event. How would she know? "What do you mean?"

"I had a dream a couple nights ago. It was so real, but I didn't want to call you and tell you over the phone. I've been waiting to talk to you in person."

"Ohhhkkkaaay," Stephanie dragged the word.

"You were called into Bill's office and cleaned out your room." Lauren reached for Stephanie's hands and squeezed. "Please be careful."

Stephanie swallowed her sigh. Dreams weren't reality. Her heartbeat returned to normal. "I will." She pulled her hands free. "You were missed last night. No one rings the school bell to publicly shame the gamblers with quite as much gusto as you."

"Did Kelly take over for me as the dowdy school marm?"

Stephanie nodded. Her relief at not being gossiped about was fleeting now that she realized a frustrating truth. No one had taken notice of her distress and disappearance last night. Neither had anyone spotted that she had returned disheveled and overwrought.

While she was glad to avoid more gossip, she couldn't help but wonder why she flew under the radar. Was everyone too wrapped up in their own problems? She still wanted to matter to someone. Her childhood insecurities resurfaced in an instant. She drew in a deep breath.

Ted saw.

He might never look at her the way she wanted. He might never offer her more than a polite friendship at arms' length. But he still cared. She'd accept the crumbs of his affection like a starving woman.

"I think I will lie down." Lauren yawned. "Only for a little bit."

Stephanie waited until her friend disappeared down the hall before entering the nursery and shutting the door. She sank to the free spot on the carpet, resting her back against the door. Hot emotion tickled her throat and eyes. Frustration? Anger? Both?

As far as the town was concerned, the fundraiser had been another success. Ted's comfort had felt real. Unfortunately, both highlights were tainted by her mistakes that led to the argument with Candace, and the potential loss of fundraising going forward.

Sharing her concerns with Lauren would only reveal her sense of guilt. She hadn't done anything worthy of condemnation. Focusing on someone else, she remained out of the spotlight and in control. But she couldn't shake the unease that had taken hold. Her only way out of her problem was to get through it. She'd find a solution both to the funding and to fighting Candace's veiled threats. She stood, dusting her palms on her jeans, and got to work.

Despite being exhausted from a nearly sleepless night, Ted sat at the kitchen table in the ranch house, eager to get on with his day. The night before had left him with a sense of unresolved issues and nagging worries. He'd hated witnessing Stephanie's breakdown.

A kind, caring person should be treated with respect. She shouldn't be crying in the back at a successful event she had spearheaded. Anyone would feel angry and defensive on her behalf. But he didn't want the surge of protectiveness.

He hadn't experienced the rush of anger for another person in years. Until only a few months ago, he had avoided any sort of emotional sway in either direction. He chalked his feelings up to friendship. He'd be as protective if something happened to Meg as Stephanie. The only difference was Meg had Ryan to defend her.

He didn't want more. Scratch that. He couldn't handle more. Under the bench, he crossed his ankles and leaned forward, resting his forearms on the table.

Last night, he had picked up Maddy from the ranch house and tucked her into bed, he spent the rest of the night staring at the ceiling. He had no clue how to best move forward with his feelings. The word elicited a shudder. Hadn't he left behind inner turmoil years ago? He didn't want to go back. Unable to sleep, he had arisen and escaped with what he did best, work.

With his niece in tow, he'd come to the ranch to discuss the results of the study that popped into his inbox late yesterday. He had dashed off a text to Joe for good measure. Maddy had scampered off with Hank, Meg, and Colby, on a walk around the property.

Ted had let himself in, following the sounds of grumbles as his friend, Ryan, slapped buttons on the coffee maker. Ryan paid him no attention as the coffee brewed.

Fine by Ted. He let his mind wander to another problem. How to entertain Maddy for the next two days. He'd already used every trick he had and then some, looking up Internet articles about how to keep kids happy and engaged. He was glad he only had one weekend solo. His sister returned next weekend for a quick visit.

He wouldn't let either his sister or niece down. Now that he had Maddy here, he wasn't sure he'd be able to return to the way things were before. He'd be happy to relinquish his role as the sole decision maker for the little girl's health and well-being. But he loved hearing her funny thoughts, and reading out loud together after years of silence in his cabin.

He suspected he wouldn't find contentment by himself anymore. To his surprise, he needed people. His comfortable hermit lifestyle had been destroyed. He'd knew he'd be lonely once his niece left and moved into an apartment with her mom.

And Stephanie wouldn't have any other reason to drop by and interact with him. He'd miss that, too. The admission made him shift and squirm. He wouldn't run from the discomfort. Friendship was the full extent he would offer either of them. She had to understand.

The coffee maker beeped.

Ryan poured himself a cup and turned, facing Ted as he sipped.

Eye contact and a nod were Ryan's typical greeting before the first cup of coffee. Despite being a legacy rancher, Ryan wasn't a morning person. The morning after a late night, the minimal responses were hardly surprising.

Ted needed action not circumspection. He did not want a discussion about the event or what happened. He'd steer the conversation. "Did you get a chance to look over the report?"

"Sort of." Ryan covered his mouth with a hand, ineffectually shielding a yawn.

Ted turned away. Nothing good came from pointing out his friend's exhaustion. He was tempted to ask why Ryan was so tired. Ted had stayed late to help clean-up The Golden Crown following the poker tournament and woke up early with Maddy. The little girl rose with the dawn every day no matter how late she'd been awake the previous night. She had requested chocolate chip pancakes for breakfast. Ted had been up for hours already.

Ted looked at his friend and boss again, studying the other man. Ryan had accepted babysitting duties alone. Had Maddy run him ragged? Had the dog? Before Ted had adjusted to the energy and noise levels from his niece, he must have been in a similar state of exhaustion to those around him. Why had Ryan volunteered to stay with Maddy and Colby? And then it clicked. Ryan was ready for fatherhood, or at least wanted to prove his caregiving capabilities to Meg.

"Did I miss anything interesting?" Joe asked from the doorway.

Ted watched Joe stroll in with a notebook and pen. His smiling countenance and loose gait giving him a jaunty air.

Ryan might have groaned or growled or both. Sipping from a mug, it was hard to decipher if he'd made any noise at all.

"A rehashing of last night?" Joe asked, arching a brow, and shooting pointed stares at both men.

Ted wasn't about to bite. He might be curious about Ryan's sudden caretaking side but not enough to put his own behavior under the glare of his friend's shared stares. Ted didn't want Joe asking where he'd gone before the last hand. "Thanks for stopping by so early on a Saturday," Ted said. "I'm sure you'd rather be sleeping in on your first weekend of the school year."

Joe slid onto the bench across the table. Opening his notebook, he uncapped a pen. "Of course. I'm anxious to get my part of the project underway. Bison education."

Ryan dragged his feet, his slippers scuffing against the slate tiles as he approached the table. He glanced at the armchair at the head.

Ted caught his breath. Did Ryan dare assume Hank's throne?

Ryan slid next to Joe on the bench. "Me, too. I scheduled a meeting with the zookeepers to get a little more insight into the care and handling. Ted, I'm sure I'll have to make another trip and I'd like you to join me next time."

"Thank you. I'd be glad to," Ted replied.

Reintroducing a herd of free-roaming bison to the surrounding ranch land had been Ryan's passion project. Ted had thought his days of animal husbandry were long gone following the sale of the cattle. At the Kincaid ranch, however, he'd learned to never say never. He would appreciate a chance to speak with the people who dealt with the animals on a daily basis. But he'd also prefer to do so with his boss and no one extra.

The San Francisco Zoo wasn't providing the animals but had cared for a herd since the nineteenth century. With generations of hands-on experience, Ted appreciated the insights from personal anecdotes the keepers would provide. The upcoming trip was scheduled for Meg and Hank to attend an auction that included an antique photograph from the Kincaid collection. Ryan was their plus-one.

"The data in the email is remarkably straight forward and optimistic." Ted interlaced his hands on the table. He liked feeling the worn top of the solid piece of furniture. With time, the rough edges had been smoothed and softened.

Joe nodded. "The more positives the better. I've been informally polling the town. I'd like to get ahead of any problems. The biggest concerns revolve around property. Most folks are worried about destruction. One lady used the word *stampede*."

Ryan snorted. "We're not suddenly descending into the chaos of the eighteen nineties. We won't be welcoming bandits next."

"Change is hard." Ted stroked his chin. While Ryan always did his best for the town, he wasn't a selfless philanthropist. He prioritized his business and—for the most part—the town benefitted.

Ted did not want any part of the bison project to be misconstrued. "We should look into the fence on the boundary closest to town. I need to be sure it's in good shape. The blockade will discourage the wanderers from heading toward town. Hard to anticipate the herd's patterns but I'd like to be prepared."

"From the old records I've seen," Ryan said, "the herd mostly kept to the original Kincaid land."

"Yep," Joe added. "In fact, part of the reason for the success of the cattle on the ranch was the presence of the bison. They established a critical ecological balance the settlers didn't appreciate."

Ted shook his head. Man forcing his will on nature was an old tale. Eradicating the bison threatened the entire prairie. Not that the proud settlers understood their folly.

"After the summer drought, anything to help the landscape will be welcome. But a boundary would serve to show our endeavor is real and valuable and not just a bandage to an old wound," Ryan said. "The expansion onto the neighboring ranches will help create a buffer zone. But I'll ask the zookeepers if there is anything we need to be aware of. If they get easily spooked by loud noises, that sort of thing."

"I'm sure the conservation group bringing the animals will have more information about the particulars of the herd," Joe added.

"Are we still on track with the feed truck?" Ryan asked. "Extra hay?"

"Yes. We can make do in the horse stable for the time being," Ted replied. "We might need another barn. Is the Hawke property available?" The last of the original ranches, the Hawkes sold their land minus a couple acres around their ranch house, to Ryan years ago.

"No. I don't want to develop that side of the ranch," Ryan said. "But the Whittier land is available. I had an idea we might repurpose an old building over there into a restaurant for Abby. Offering her a more permanent spot could benefit everyone. She could operate year-round and help with the events in the off-season."

"Are you serious?" Joe asked, aghast. "You would give her a building?"

Ryan shrugged. "It's an idea. I'm never opposed to trying new ventures."

"Yeah but...a restaurant? Food service is a notoriously hard industry. Turning a profit isn't guaranteed. The hours are long. Most new places close in the first year." Joe shook his head. "Not to mention who you'd be getting into business with. Can you trust her to do her share?"

Ryan frowned, deep furrows marring his brow.

"Let's table expansion talk," Ted interjected. He didn't want anyone to speak without more thought.

Joe's temper was short on any topic peripherally related to Abby. Ted hoped—for everyone's sake—the pair found common ground. But glaciers made faster progress. Joe and Abby weren't his top concern. "We won't want another barn for the animals too close to guests."

"Even if we do give Abby one of the old buildings out there, we still have plenty of space for bison on the Whittier land. No one will mind," Ryan said sharply.

Ted shared a look with Joe. The other man only shrugged. "I think I'll go take a look at the fence closest to town. Get a sense of what we need to do. Can Maddy stay with Hank for a little while longer?"

Ryan nodded. "He'd insist on it. Let me know what you find."

Ted slipped out of the room and hopped into his truck, steering toward the boundary with town. He was glad for an escape from founding families talk.

The Whittiers had founded the town along with the Hawkes and Kincaids. Ultimately, however, the Whittier family fell from grace and left town under a cloud of scandal. While the current Kincaids didn't often speak to the publicly held sentiment that the good for nothing Whittiers got what was coming to them, they were as susceptible to town prejudice as everyone else. Joe—an amateur historian working on his first book about the region—often fought for a more open-minded view. But even he wasn't one to speak up in their favor.

On the horizon line, the split rail fence came into view. The barrier had never been much of a deterrent for trespassers and wasn't used as such for the past hundred years. After the Hawkes and Kincaids booted the Whittiers from town, their vengeful reputations kept too many from crossing into this part of the land. *Don't cross a Kincaid man* was some of the first advice spouted to Ted, not that he'd ever seen any cause for the phrase.

Ted parked close and hopped out of the cab. The fence ran along the perimeter of the property where the ranch met asphalt roadway. From a distance, he spotted flaking white paint but nothing major to concern him. He'd replaced several sections six months ago but hadn't touched this part.

He'd come to the corner by two intersecting roadways. To get to the other side, he'd have to drive the long way around, or he could hop the fence. He chose the second option.

He tested the post's structural integrity before climbing onto the bottom rail. Swinging one leg and then the other up and over the top rail, he intended to jump to the ground. He'd done the motion countless times over the years. Muscle memory should have been enough to give him a little boost. But today, conditions conspired against him.

In the second after he'd lifted his second leg, as he supported the bulk of his weight with his two hands on the post, he heard a noise. A car. He was far enough from the roadway, the fence set onto the ranch property and not at the line, to allow for egress should a car need to pull off the two-lane roads.

But then he'd glanced up at the car. A little sedan driving along with music blaring from the stereo and out the partially rolled down windows. He knew the song because Maddy had educated him on the music of Taylor Swift thanks to Stephanie's influence.

Instead of paying attention to what he was doing, he focused on the car, hoping Stephanie might be the driver. And she was. He swung down his leg, glad for a chance to chat again and make sure she was okay.

Except, he didn't land on the ground with his usual grace. His jeans snagged on the top rail and his back foot caught. His palms scrapped against the rail. He fell in a heap on the ground, denim ripping as the weight of his leg pulled his foot free.

Tires squealed as the car stopped on the shoulder.

"Ted? Are you okay?" Stephanie shouted.

He winced and sat up, easing his legs out in front of him. Testing his muscles, he'd ache in the morning but hadn't twisted any major leg joints. He waved a hand. "Yeah, I'm fine."

"No, you're bleeding. Hold on," she called.

He sucked in a breath and flipped over his palms. She was right. He'd torn through the top layer of skin and bled in several sections. The wounds didn't look deep enough for stitches, but he'd have to keep bandages on and use his work gloves for a few days. He should have worn the gloves before he'd hopped the fence, but he'd been so sure of his abilities that his ego led to his fall.

"May I see?" Stephanie asked in a soft voice.

He met her concerned gaze and swallowed the lump in his throat. With her knees pressing into the ground, she was close. Almost as near as last night when she'd kissed him.

His cheek burned from the memory of the tender press of her lips. Kiss was a rather hopeful word to define the peck. But he couldn't stop from hoping she might kiss him palms. He didn't think that would make him all better but he wasn't about to stop her from trying.

"May I?" she asked again.

"Of course." His voice sounded scratchy, and he coughed, clearing his dry throat. "I mean. Please."

She furrowed her brow as she studied the angry dashes on his palms. Then she reached into her purse for a small red case with a cross on it. "First aid kit. Occupational hazard." She smiled.

He returned the grin, liking the conspiratorial gleam in her eyes.

When she wiped his palms clean with a wet towelette, however, his smile faltered. The shock of cold and the sting of the alcohol was fleeting. She produced antibiotic ointment next, careful to dab but not rub the cream into each wound before covering each palm with a large square bandage. "All done." She sat back on her heels, putting space between them.

"Thanks. I'm a little surprised you had normal bandages and not something covered in cartoons."

She chuckled. "Oh, I have those too." She rifled through the kit and produced a fluorescent purple bandage with unicorns. "But your injuries required something a little larger."

"I'm not sure if that's a good or a bad thing." He shook his head. "It's strange to see you dressed down."

"What do you mean?" She held out her arms and stared at her olive-green corduroy jacket and dark rinse jeans.

"I like the bright colors you wear to work. You know the smiling crayons and stuff." Was he rambling? He felt like he was.

She shrugged. "I do have a full adult wardrobe in my closet. It's not all yoga pants and over the top sweaters. But . . ." she tapped a finger to her chin. "Now that you mention it, I've never seen you in anything but flannel and old jeans."

"I can clean up when I need to," he said. "I just don't need to."

She giggled.

"I'm grateful you stopped by and helped." Although, he'd admit to himself, he might have had a chance at staying whole if she hadn't.

"I am, too. I don't know what you are doing out here. But I suppose we're even now. You saw me cry. I saw you cry."

He rolled his eyes at her smirk. "Friends don't need to keep score but sure, we're even." He made his next mistake by meeting her gaze again only to study her lips. She hadn't kissed his boo-boos. Had he imagined the charge between them at the saloon?

"What are you doing out here?"

"Inspecting the fence. Looking to see what sections need to be replaced before the bison arrive. Once winter hits, I won't be able to fix anything and the snow drifts can last long into *spring*." He made air quotes with his fingers and winced, as he reaggravated his palms. "I'll need to paint the fence again but I was starting to walk the perimeter when I . . . fell."

She pressed her lips together and her eyes sparkled.

Suppressing a giggle at his expense? He appreciated the effort.

"Bison can jump fences. They are powerful creatures," she said.

"But at least we can try to establish boundaries for them. Hopefully they'll get the idea."

She leaned back on her palms and scanned the fence behind him. "When I was a kid, I helped paint a fence. My friend had the brilliant idea to toss the paint from the can, and I would very quickly use my brush to spread it around."

"And how did that work out?" He grinned, already knowing the answer.

"We were taken off the job by my friend's dad." She smirked back. "I can help if you need an extra pair of hands."

"No, I'll be fine. It's my job, not yours." He shook his head. "What were you doing out here?"

"Helping a friend."

This time he threw back his head and laughed, a deep belly chortle that rose up from deep inside him. She joined in, her giggle light and melodious and a perfect harmony for his. Spending time with her was nice, almost intoxicating. If he wasn't careful, he'd get addicted to the joy she exuded. And then he'd want to give up all of his good intentions and get closer to her.

He slowly got to his feet. Besides a twinge on one side, he was fine enough to keep going about his work. And he needed to before he did something crazy, like kiss her on the cheek.

"Are you really okay?" she asked, getting to her feet and dusting her palms on her jeans.

"I am. Thank you for stopping. See you afterschool tomorrow?"

She nodded and flashed a thumbs up before turning her back to him and striding towards her car.

Ted wasn't sure but he thought in the moment before she nodded, she might have been about to argue. Instead, she walked away. Once he heard her car door open and shut, he did the same, heading in the opposite direction to inspect the fence. He was glad. In large part because a little distance between him and Stephanie might be the cure for his odd sense of longing. Or he'd be in even deeper.

CHAPTER 9

On Monday morning, Stephanie sat behind her desk, scanning her email, and eating a sandwich. She could go to the teacher's lounge for her break. But the forty-minutes passed so quickly, while the kids ate in the cafeteria and played on the playground for recess, she often lost track of the time. With the earliest lunch slot of the school at ten thirty, she and the other kindergarten teachers were usually still nursing a coffee and finishing breakfast.

She could have gone to Lauren's class next door, sneaking through their shared bathroom, or wandered across the hall to Kelly's. She'd had a lot of dealing with people at the event, however, and was glad for a break. She needed downtime to recharge.

Besides, her muscles still ached from manual labor at Lauren's house and her heart ached after her encounters with Ted. She couldn't accept another round of kudos for her help. Focusing on others instead of herself brought her clarity and control. She didn't seek praise and found it uncomfortable.

She chewed her last bite of sandwich and crossed the room to the sink by the door. She wouldn't have to worry too much longer about any wrong impressions. Maddy's mom was expected to return soon. This would be the last week of the atypical carpool. And then she'd have no reason to see Ted.

She'd just found her voice around him. She hadn't wanted to stop talking. And maybe, just maybe, he felt the same. Friday night, he'd followed her to the kitchen to check on her. He'd noticed she was gone. He'd noticed she was upset. What was she to make of that?

He was concerned because he's kind and a good friend. She pumped foaming soap into her hands and rubbed, covering completely every inch of skin. Scrubbing for thirty seconds was too long for her to be alone with her thoughts. The weekend was too long.

She replayed the quiet moment in the kitchen. *We're friends . . .right?* He asked so softly, and she wasn't sure how to answer. She wanted to be more, but she'd have to settle for friendship. When she spotted him on the side of the road, she'd been glad for a chance to help him. Up close and personal, holding his hands, she hadn't wanted to let go. But she had. She hadn't wanted to push her luck.

She rinsed her hands under the running water, grabbed a paper towel, and was drying her hands when she turned toward the door and jumped back.

A woman with brown, shoulder length hair neatly styled, a full face of make-up, a cream-colored shirt, and pressed jeans stood with her fist to the door. "Oh, hello." She smiled. "I'm Grayden's mom. I'm here to volunteer."

"Oh." Stephanie gasped. She took a step back, glancing at the clock over the door. She only had five minutes until the kids returned to the classroom. "I didn't get a call from the office."

Grayden's mom crossed the threshold and strode toward the cubbies, swinging her purse off her shoulder and into her son's marked spot. "I checked in and scanned my I.D. They must have thought I'd be going to my older daughter's class. Oh, well. Here I am."

She was tall and strode with purpose, like she belonged. Her confidence caught Stephanie off-guard. Tossing the balled-up paper towel in the waste basket, Stephanie shook her head. "I'm sorry for the confusion. We don't have volunteers in our class yet. Sign-ups will be posted after Back-to-School night. I'm going to need to ask you to leave."

"What?" The woman turned and frowned. "Kindergarten is always asking for help with the reading and math centers. I was in my older daughter's class at least once a week."

Until we hired more educators and aides this past summer. "Typically, sign-up sheets aren't posted until Back-to-School Night." Stephanie reiterated slowly. "But our classroom won't need too many volunteers this year. We are lucky the district hired plenty of help." Stephanie aimed to keep her tone light and the conversation vague. She hated confrontation and shied away from it at every turn. Her palms felt clammy. She shouldn't have thrown away the paper towel.

"Oh, it's no trouble." The woman smiled and waved a hand in the air. "I'm happy to help."

"I . . . ugh . . . I'm . . ." Stephanie stood in between the door leading to her shared bathroom and the door leading to the hall. She darted her gaze across, willing Kelly to save her from this situation.

No, she'd have to step up for herself. She'd let Candace Vane walk all over her on Friday night and still felt terrible. While this mom wasn't waging a war with the same venomous tone, she wasn't backing down and taking a hint either. Stephanie never let parents call the shots over the good of the kids, and she couldn't start now.

"Did you receive the newsletter on Friday?" Stephanie knew the answer before asking the question. Earlier, she'd checked the clicks on the links embedded into the email. Every parent had received and opened the message.

"Well . . . I did." She stretched the word to three syllables. "An oversight, I'm sure."

Stephanie stood her ground, pulling back her shoulders as she faced the stranger. "I'm sorry for any confusion. I need to ask you to leave. I'll be stepping out to get the kids soon, and I don't want anyone upset."

The woman flushed. "Well." She turned toward the cubbies, grabbing her purse. Swinging the bag onto her shoulder, she momentarily lifted her gaze to Stephanie. She pursed her lips, giving herself a pinched, just bit into a lemon, look. She continued past and out the door, without a backward glance.

Stephanie waited until the woman left, then she hunched forward, drooping as she let out a heavy breath. She felt horrible. Was this what she could expect her whole year? Saving the kids from having their feelings hurt by constantly battling one entitled parent after another? Why had the woman come? If she had an older child, she knew it was too early for volunteers.

"Was that Grayden Foxx's mom?" Kelly asked.

Stephanie spun around.

In the shared bathroom between her class and Lauren's next door, Lauren and Kelly stood shoulder to shoulder.

They must have been working on a project together in Lauren's class. They had been nearby the whole time. They had her back. But she wasn't at ease. She waited for another parental ambush. She'd never had such an encounter before. Until last week, she'd thought she had a very good, open, understanding style in communicating with parents.

Stephanie nodded.

"She's best friends with Candace Vane," Lauren said, gripping her belly underneath with both hands.

Stephanie glanced from one to the other. Her friends had tight expressions, mirroring each other. At her sides, Stephanie's hands shook. She took a deep breath, willing a calm. In a couple minutes, she'd have to get the kids. She couldn't be upset or they would feed off that energy and her day would be ruined. Young kids were finely attuned to emotions. She strove for peace and contentment for everyone's best interest.

Still, she was rattled. "Do you think Candace put her up to it?"

Lauren frowned. "Why would she?"

Because I didn't email her. Because she threatened me the other night. Stephanie couldn't say the words. She hated feeling like a naughty child when she hadn't been wrong. The email hadn't required a response. Just because everyone else in Candace's life kowtowed to her didn't mean she could expect that treatment across the board. "I figured I was in the clear until Back-to-School Night with the other parents. The sign-up sheets for volunteers don't go up until then anyways. I want to explain why visitors are limited in person. I've never had someone just walk in without advance notice."

The office should have called. Unless the parent gave another reason for striding into the building. Stephanie shivered. She didn't want to see a conspiracy everywhere she looked. But the oversight was chilling.

Kelly shrugged. "Maybe Candace said something. Or she could have taken the initiative on her own. You know we support you, but . . ."

"It's a big change," Lauren said. "Sure, letting parents help in the classroom comes with its own set of challenges. But you can't block every helicopter mom out there. Pick your battles."

Stephanie bit the inside of her cheek, fighting the burn in her nostrils. Her colleagues had become her dearest friends. Their advice was always for the best.

She had to do what was in the kids' best interests, even—perhaps especially—if she had to live through the discomfort of establishing something new. "I'm sure this is the right plan for these kids. Yes, a handful of them are blessed with very involved parents. But for the most part, the parents are already pulled in too many directions. I can't tug them in one more, and I won't let the kids feel left out because Mom or Dad can't miss work. I'm not blocking access. But I don't think it's helpful to the classroom to have the same parents underfoot every day of the week. I'll explain everything at Back-To-School night."

Lauren nodded. "We support you."

Should Stephanie be more forthcoming? Should she open up about her reticence and her nerves? She glanced at the strain in Kelly's smile and Lauren's white knuckles gripping her belly. Only a few more weeks until she left for maternity leave.

The bell rang.

"Let's go get those kids," Kelly said. She plastered on a bright smile and led the way out through Stephanie's door and down the hall toward the playground. Stephanie followed behind.

Should she have explained her situation with Ted and Maddy to her friends? They must know. She hadn't kept the arrangement a secret. But she also hadn't felt she owed anyone a lengthy diatribe about the scenario. She wasn't doing anything wrong.

In a small town, talk spread faster than a brush fire. But no one would talk about her and Ted. What would they say? No one would misconstrue the arrangement. Ted wasn't interested in her in a romantic way. She might be seen as desperate. And—since her sudden recklessness was the truth—she had no reason to lie.

Ted had had big plans for the rest of his weekend. He'd intended to barrel ahead with the deck project and get the joists in position. He'd need help. While Ryan frowned at working on the weekends, Ted counted on Ryan being unwilling to leave Ted to do a two-person job alone, especially once it became clear he was going to continue by himself until the task was accomplished.

With Maddy occupied at the ranch house, Ted had no excuses for distraction or delay. But he hadn't counted on torturing himself about Stephanie after two encounters that left his heart aching. She had slipped into his thoughts at the strangest moments. The breeze had carried a phantom hint of citrus like her shampoo. He almost swore he heard her laughter, and nearly hammered his thumb in the process of looking for her.

The relief of her imagined joy was particularly jarring. Friends didn't find such pleasure in each other's happiness. Neighbors definitely didn't.

The weekend work had been slow and frustrating. He couldn't go on plodding through work with only half his attention. Accidents happened with a lack of focus. He'd proved that when he fell off the fence. When he returned to the ranch after his inspection, he'd found his work gloves and his concentration.

By Monday, he was resolved. He knew the cure. Once he saw her again, he'd act totally normal and friendly. She would do the same out of politeness. Soon, they'd fall back into their usual ways of a cordial—if distant—acquaintance. No feelings necessary.

Reaching into his back pocket, he pulled out a bandana and mopped at the sweat beading on his brow. He had finished the joists earlier, thanks to Ryan for his help. Now he was double checking every screw and nail. The next stage of the build should move faster.

By himself, time passed in strange ways. Hours could go by without him noticing. Or the seconds stood still. With his hands busy, he struggled to focus and not let his mind slip to Stephanie and how much everything would change when Jen returned. He didn't want to miss Stephanie but couldn't seem to stop his thoughts from creeping back to the kitchen at The Golden Crown.

She'd been so broken, and he'd hated it. He didn't want to see her diminished in any way. He would have stormed out and yelled at the offending party if she'd given him the a-okay. He would have done so even without her permission, except then maybe he'd have to start acknowledging she could be someone special. Feelings remained dangerous.

He was off balance with his family life suddenly in upheaval. He'd mellow after his sister returned, and he got back into his normal routine. He stuffed the bandana into his back jeans pocket behind his phone. He owed his sister a call.

Dialing her number, he held the cell against his ear and fought the sigh building in his throat as the line rang. Jen worked nights. Part of the appeal of her new job nearby was the switch to days. Getting ahold of her could be a task but on the fourth ring the call connected. "Hey, Jen. It's me, your brother."

"Hi," she said, her voice slightly husky. She cleared her throat. "Sorry, just got up. How's it going? Thanks for the emails and texts. I miss Maddy. I'll be glad once I'm finally moved to Montana."

"Things are good. Maddy is settling in. She loves the ranch. You might have trouble convincing her to move into town." He chuckled. He'd have trouble watching her go.

"Good, I'm glad to hear. She's not too much trouble for you?"

"Never, and you know it. That girl is an old soul. She's fitting in well with her classmates, too."

"Oh, good." Jen sighed. "I've had a few emails from the teacher and—to be honest—I'm not quite sure what to think."

He frowned and dropped his gaze to the ground. He didn't want to care. But his heartbeat picked up its pace and his throat started to go dry. "Really? How so?"

Kicking at a rock, he dug the toe of his boot into the dry, dusty ground. Did Jen disapprove of Stephanie? He wanted them to get along. At the very least, Stephanie offered him a massive amount of help he could never repay. He didn't want to put either woman in a difficult spot of being forced to get along with someone they didn't like. Beyond that, he thought they could be friends. Unless he'd read them both wrong.

"Nothing bad. She sent the emails to the entire class. Just her expectations of the year and I guess she wants to limit parent involvement. I got one like a few minutes ago about needing to schedule ahead if you wanted an in-person meeting."

"I'm sure she had a reason. She always has others best interests at heart." *Even when they don't deserve it.* A flash of Stephanie's sad smile popped into his mind. Until he'd hugged her, he hadn't realized how he'd longed to hold and be held by another person. She stirred up all sorts of long buried emotions. *And soon it'll be over.* He had to get through the next week. Then they'd fall back into a more comfortable, easy friendship. He could avoid her and not have to worry about pesky personal problems. "She's been a big help to me with Maddy."

"I'll be glad to meet her and get a feel for her myself. Maddy loves her. I'm sure she's great."

She is. Stephanie would be someone worth risking pain and heartbreak for. Ted never intended to be alone and childless. But he couldn't have a family of his own. He had to be content to be close to his sister's. Because love was no guarantee of forever. While his wife had been tragically taken in an accident, his sister had been broken by simply pulling apart.

Jen and her ex moved further away from each other one inch at a time during a difficult pregnancy and the subsequent infant year. Cracks that had been patched and smoothed over, her husband's lack of empathy a major factor, could no longer remain hairline. The fissures stretched until the foundation rotted. And they split.

"You don't think she's great?" Jen asked.

"What?" He shook his head. "Sorry, I'm distracted. In the middle of a big project, you know how it is."

Jen snorted. "Yep. I'll be glad to finish packing and meet the movers."

"When does Dane leave?"

"In about a month. He'll come up to say goodbye and make sure she's settled in."

How nice of him to care about his child. Ted's upper lip curled but he didn't say the cheeky remark. Dane wasn't the guy his sister deserved, but he wasn't a villain. In fact, he'd been remarkably reasonable throughout their marriage and divorce. Co-parenting was complicated.

Ted could take a chance on love and start a family only for the whole scenario to blow up in his face. And what if his future ex wasn't as level-headed? Why bring a child into a doomed world AND a miserable marriage?

Life didn't hold guarantees. He might gamble the occasional hand with other players he could read like a book. But he never played for high stakes. Falling in love demanded a vulnerability that he couldn't accept again.

Not even for someone as sweet as Stephanie. He was jumping ahead, and he knew it. But he couldn't stop himself from analyzing a situation from all sides. "What is your plan? Have you found an apartment that'll work?"

"Not yet. Is it okay if we bunk with you for a little while? I'm having the movers take everything to storage close to the hospital. Then, when I'm ready, they'll haul it all to the final destination. Although, part of me wants to just sell everything and start over completely."

"Don't do that. You'll regret it."

"You did," she murmured.

And he had second thoughts for the first year. As a widower living in his hometown, he'd been given advice from everyone at all times. He'd been told not to make any big decisions by lifelong family friends, the bank teller, his dentist, and—more significantly—his lawyer. They'd all advised to stay put for a year and then make choices.

But the morning of day three hundred and sixty six, he couldn't stay put. He'd never had a wandering heart and always been content in their town. Once Liv was gone, she took the light out of the golden state. He sold the farm and almost all his belongings. He gave hers to her family. Now, years later, he wished he'd held on to some things. But he feared creating totems and holding himself back. He didn't need to worry about objects; his mind took over the task all on its own even from several states—and a whole lifestyle—away.

"ETA is Sunday?"

"I'll try for Saturday, but yes, realistically, Sunday. Tonight is my last shift. Then I'll just be packing."

"Okay, sounds good. Bye, Jen."

"Love you, Teddy."

He hung up and stuffed his phone back into his pocket. He had to get off the line before he stirred up more thoughts. He preferred action to premeditation. Especially when he couldn't take any deed.

Stephanie glanced at the bag in her hands and back up to the cabin's door. Nibbling her lip, she couldn't decide if self-confidence or self-sabotage had spurred her to drive to Ted's house after dark. Whatever motivated her, she was here, readying herself to knock with the lamest excuse possible.

She fisted her hand and raised it to the door, knocking quickly before dropping the heavy appendage to her side to grip the tote bag again. Like a flimsy canvas sack containing an assortment of Maddy's things—mostly socks and sweatshirts she'd slipped off during the school day—from her car would provide her with protection from embarrassment. She couldn't stop thinking about the stolen moments she'd spent together with Ted. Each had been spontaneous and natural. Tonight, she was forcing an encounter.

The door opened.

"Stephanie? Hi," he murmured, slipping outside. "I thought I heard a knock at the door but wasn't sure. What's up?"

She thrust the bag forward, hitting him square in the chest. "I've been collecting Maddy's lost clothing. I realized just how much I had and figured you'd probably need it. You know. To do her laundry?" Stephanie's voice was squeaky and awkward. Her skin flushed.

"Oh, right." He held the bag to his chest. "Thanks. I appreciate it."

She took a deep breath. She was glad he hadn't asked why she didn't just give the items to him tomorrow or let Maddy bring them inside. She'd wanted to see him. But now, once again, her small talk skills vanished. So much for the progress she'd imagined them making. "Well . . ."

"Maddy is asleep inside, and Hank is here, watching her for me. I wanted to stop by the barn and give Cupcake a little extra attention. She had a minor cut that I've been applying salve to every night."

"Did she jump a fence, too?"

He stared at her for a long second. Stephanie held her breath. She'd thought she was charming him. Was she wrong? Tonight was a mistake. She was only proving that she couldn't pursue anything because of her awkwardness.

And then he chuckled, the sound warm and welcoming. He rocked back on his heels, turning his face up toward the sky and the moon shining on his broad grin. "That's a good one. Do you want to join me?"

"Can I? I've never spent much time around horses. Would I be a liability?"

He shook his head. "You'll be fine. Hold on a sec." He opened the door a crack and dropped the tote bag inside. He shut the door and motioned for her to follow him down the path that led around the pond. He didn't speak again for several minutes.

She didn't mind. Sure, her inner voice might be telling her he didn't want to draw attention to their presence. He didn't want people to know she was here. But she squashed that unhelpful voice.

"I don't like to talk too much on my rounds," he murmured, leaning close as she fell into step beside him. "I hate to spoil the quiet out here. It's so peaceful."

She nodded, gratitude welling up inside her and cutting off a verbal response. He'd somehow guessed what she'd been thinking. She enjoyed the companionable silence the rest of the loop to the horse barn.

Set at a distance from the spa barn and lodging, the steel structure was the last new structure Susie Kincaid championed. Royal blue from the roof to the walls and the trim, the horse barn was a bright pop of color against the brown structures nearby. On a sunny day, the building shone as sparkling as the sky. During the snow-filled winter months, the sight was inspiring, reminding Stephanie of brighter, warmer days ahead.

Ted continued to the man door, unlocked it, and held it open for her.

She stepped inside, passing him by mere inches. She couldn't focus on that when the smell of hay, manure, feed, and wood overwhelmed her. With a hand, she covered her nose and mouth and stepped to the side.

"You get used to it," Ted said. He tipped his head to the right. "Come on, she's down here."

Stephanie followed his lead, passing the horses in their stalls. Neighs and whinnies greeted them as they passed. Ted offered the friendlier horses pats on their noses but didn't stop for long.

"Is this your favorite part of the job? Taking care of the animals?" she asked, remembering his degree.

"It's the most cut and dried part of my job," he said over his shoulder as he continued walking. "It's why I was hired."

She nodded. At the height of the ranching days over a century earlier, more than fifty horses lived and worked on the land. By the end of the cattle operation, however, the Kincaids only had thirty-five horses. Since then, the numbers had hovered around twenty.

At the last stall, Ted stopped. He pulled a pair of work gloves out of his pocket.

She noticed he hadn't changed his bandages and frowned. "You need to change the dressing and check for infection."

He slipped the gloves on. "I did. These look the same because they kind of are. I liked what you used so I bought some like them at the store. Thanks again for stopping to help."

"Any time."

He lifted the latch on the door and let himself inside, shutting himself in with Cupcake. He focused on the horse, pulling out several sugar cubes from his back pocket for her as he approached. But he kept talking to Stephanie. "And, while I appreciate the offer, after careful consideration, I won't be taking you up on your offer for painting the fence."

She grinned. "Your loss."

"Probably," he murmured.

Cupcake gummed his palm, happily munching and shaking her tail.

"May I see your leg, ma'am?" he asked the horse in the same tone of voice he'd speak to a human.

Cupcake shook her mane and neighed.

"Please?" he asked, holding firm with his tone, and only lifting an eyebrow.

Cupcake lifted her front leg onto a hay bale in her stall.

"Good girl, Cupcake," he said, pulling the salve from his other pocket and making quick work of applying the protectant to a raised bumpy section. "Don't tell the others, but this is why you're my favorite." He finished rubbing the product into the horse's skin and pet her nose.

"Wow. You're great." Stephanie flushed at her breathless exclamation. "With her."

"She's the easiest horse. She's probably a person reincarnated. She gets all the credit."
He slipped out of the stall, careful to latch the door closed.

"I've never ridden a horse."

"Really? How is that possible?"

She shrugged. "I didn't grow up around here."

"Neither did I. But we still had horses." He bumped her with his shoulder. "Would you like to try?" he asked, his voice a breath above a whisper. "I can take you out."

"Can it be . . . not in front of other people? I don't want to flail for a crowd."

"But you don't mind falling in front of me?" he asked.

His question sounded almost wistful. "Of course not. Because we're friends. I trust you." Her voice almost shook on the last part. The more she got to know him, the man she'd had an unrequited crush on for years from afar, the more she liked him. She was probably a fool to keep putting herself in his path. She'd probably end up with a broken heart. But she couldn't seem to help herself.

"Thank you," he said. "Then I'll have to find time to schedule something soon. This is a good time of year to ride without too many people around. Cupcake is the horse to ride. She's a sweetheart."

"I'll hold you to it."

"You'd better." He grinned. "We'd better get back. It's a school night, after all."

She wouldn't forget it. Every moment together was printed onto her brain for posterity. Unfortunately, her heart carried the same burden.

CHAPTER 10

Stephanie spent Tuesday looking over her shoulder. She hadn't received any more emails from parents or surprise drop-ins. But she obsessively checked the inbox after she got home last night, when she first woke up, and throughout the school day. During quiet time and morning snack, at recess, after lunch, she hit refresh on her email account almost minute by minute. And she crept towards the classroom door, scanning the hallway, more often than she could count. By the end of school, she was exhausted.

She didn't need to glance in a mirror to see the dark smudges under her eyes. She felt the scratch every time her eyelids closed over her dry eyes. Her students were unnaturally quiet, too. Kids fed off energy, and when the teacher was completely wiped, they either acted up or were silent. Luckily, they chose calm. She wasn't sure she'd have the stamina to last the whole day with naughty behavior.

As it was, she didn't use different character voices during story time. She leaned heavily into independent work time today, passing out more coloring sheets than ever. She usually viewed her students' antics from a good-natured lens. Today, optimism wasn't so easy.

No one woke up and decided to be terrible and mean. Sometimes, a person acted up without any real justification. Honest mistakes could hurt feelings just as much as a premeditated moment. She encouraged grace among the kids and treated them with such herself. With not-so-subtle threats from two of their parents, however, she was on edge.

As the last bell rang, she dropped her shoulders and rolled her neck. Thank goodness. She stood at the front of the room, writing sight words on the dry erase board in giant letters. She recapped the marker and turned, plastering on a bright smile.

At the tables, the students stared at her with rapt attention. No jumping up to race out of the room. Kindergartners still loved to learn.

She wanted to inspire them to keep the positive momentum going through all the years of their education ahead. "Who knows this word?"

Four hands shot up. The usual suspects.

She scanned the whole room, giving each child another opportunity.

At a table in the center, Maddy held her hand at her shoulder. Her fingers trembled, and she slowly lifted and lowered her arm.

"Maddy? Can you give it a try?" Stephanie asked, eager to give the little girl a chance. She was smart but uncertain when speaking in front of the entire class. In her small reading group, she shone. With practice and encouragement, she could build her self-confidence among her peers.

"Nn . . . oo . . ." She scrunched her brow.

A few murmurs filled the room.

Stephanie shot a stern look at each table.

"Now?" Maddy said.

Stephanie grinned, beaming for the first time all day. "Great job. That was a tricky one. Okay class, please line up, and we'll head to the multi-purpose room."

Chairs scrapped against the floor, and the room filled with excited chatter.

She strode toward the door. In forty minutes, she could be on her couch with a good book. If she could give herself a night off from overthinking . . . She shook her head and dropped her gaze to the class.

In the back, Grayden and Amelia stood close, whispering, and darting glances her way.

At least the little girl wasn't jockeying to be line leader. Stephanie wouldn't be intimidated by the child or her mean girl mother. "Ready?"

The children quieted.

She opened the door and led her class down the hall to the multi-purpose room. The students filed into the room one at a time. The second and first graders had already been seated. Her class took space on the floor at the front.

Maddy hung back, near the door.

Stephanie lifted her gaze to Kelly, the teacher in charge of this week's dismissal.

Kelly flashed a thumbs up and a soft smile.

With a nod, Stephanie stepped into the hall, Maddy at her side, and let the door shut behind them. Next week, Stephanie would be the adult in the multi-purpose room. She'd have to remember to pack extra ibuprofen.

The multi-purpose room sat at the end of the early elementary hall connecting to the front offices. From the corner of her gaze, she spotted movement. She turned and spied the back of a woman's head.

Slicked back hair in a smooth bun, the severe style didn't fit any of the teachers. Stephanie frowned, who could it be? Someone from the board of education? Then the woman's profile came into view.

Candace stood in the waiting area for the principal's office.

Stephanie sucked in a breath. She would know the other woman's determined chin and haughty tilt of her head anywhere. No one else dressed to kill. Being a female in a high-powered career meant she navigated a world where her femininity was used for and against her. Stephanie respected the difficult balance. But she did her best to avoid the woman's spiky, slim stilettos.

Stephanie took a step down the hall, out of the line of sight of the office. She extended her hand.

Maddy reached for her fingers and squeezed.

Stephanie smiled. For the thousandth time, she reminded herself helping a child wasn't a capital offense. The guilt didn't shift. They strolled down the hallway and back into the classroom.

Stephanie shut the door, scanning the hallway. She was acting paranoid. Candace Vane had other children at the school and plenty of reasons to be in the building. Stephanie crossed to her desk. "Maddy, let me just get some things pulled together, and then we'll go."

The little girl nodded, sat on the alphabet rug, and pulled a book out of her backpack.

A knock sounded at the door

Stephanie's breath caught in her throat and her chest squeezed tight.

The knock sounded again.

"Come in," she croaked and dried her palms on her slacks. She hadn't even pulled out her chair and already she was set for an ambush? She'd waited all day and still she wasn't prepared. Her arms hung heavy and limp.

The door opened and a head peeked around the frame.

"Joe?" Stephanie sighed.

He entered and shut the door behind him. With a smile for Maddy, he crossed the room. "Sorry if I'm a disappointment."

She waved a hand in the hair. "Not at all." *You're a relief.* She didn't want to lose her job or be put on the spot in her classroom where she'd always felt safe. "How can I help you?"

"I wanted to congratulate you on the poker tournament." He smiled and stopped in front of her desk.

He made no move to sit or get comfortable. Whatever he had to say wouldn't be a long chat. Good. She wanted to leave. "Thank you. It's become a real community effort. I'm glad to do my part."

He nodded. "We all chip in and help each other. Can I help you with anything else?" He tilted his head to the side and raised both eyebrows.

On the rug, Maddy dragged her finger through the lines of her book.

She probably wasn't reading as much as giving a good performance for the grown-ups. It tugged at Stephanie's heart a little bit. The little girl was living through a lot of emotional turmoil at the moment. Moving to a new state, her father leaving, staying with her uncle, her mother gone, and she'd started school. It would be too much for most grown-ups.

Maddy was sensitive and tough. She was a surprising combo of both and reminded Stephanie so much of Ted. The little girl had provided both a reason to interact with him and a rare chance to get to know him better. She'd always be grateful for both. And with only a few more days left in her carpool, she wouldn't squander even one opportunity to see him.

Clearing her throat, she met Joe's quizzical gaze. She understood his warning but she couldn't back down now. *In for a penny, in for a pound.* "We're great. Heading out now."

"Okay." He stepped back. "Bye, Maddy. Tell your Unc I said hi."

Maddy nodded.

Joe strolled out the room, leaving the door ajar.

Stephanie opened the bottom drawer of her desk, grabbed her purse, stuffed her laptop into the bag, and pulled out her keys. "Ready?"

Maddy scrambled to her feet. She hadn't taken off the backpack so she nearly toppled from her adjusted center of gravity. But she caught her balance and rose, clutching the book to her chest. "We're having dinner at the big house tonight. Mr. Hank said I could come over right after school and help. Miss Meg is there baking." Maddy licked her lips.

"Okay, the big house it is."

With one reply, Maddy began to chatter.

Stephanie smiled and tuned out the excited rush of words. She had too much floating through her mind to focus on Colby's new tricks. She turned off the lights, shut the door, and led Maddy down the hall and out the doors to the teacher's parking lot at the back of the school. She helped Maddy into the car seat and got behind the wheel. She turned the keys in the ignition and reversed out of her space. She started to relax, and then she turned forward, put the car in drive, and met the gaze of Candace Vane.

Crossing the lot to her own vehicle, Candace turned her head from one side to the other.

Maybe she hadn't spotted Stephanie and Maddy. More likely than not, she had.

Stephanie gulped. Paranoia and frustration could control her if she let them. She wouldn't. Because she refused to regret a single second of the past few weeks.

Ted strode along the covered porch of the ranch house. Under the guise of a break, he'd timed his arrival to coincide with Maddy's drop-off. Hopefully she had remembered to tell Stephanie to bring her to the main house.

Leaning against the post near the stairs, he stared across the dusty, dead grass toward the road. His conversation with Jen still nagged at him a day later. Through the day, as he made steady progress on the deck working from one side to the next, nailing in each board, he replayed his sister's words about her downsizing and relocating plans.

You did. She couldn't know the taunt from the obvious reply. He had sold his belongings in hopes that he wouldn't look at a random object and be thrown to the ground, overwhelmed with a wave of longing and nausea. But distancing himself from the things he'd owned during his marriage hadn't worked.

For the longest time, even the sun had mocked him and revived memories long-buried. At the time of her death, he'd spent half his life in love with Liv. Now he'd lived over a decade without her. And he had started to forget the details of day-to-day life. He wanted those random scraps to prove their time together hadn't been a dream.

Because he felt a pull towards someone new. And he knew he couldn't trust himself and she especially shouldn't. He'd let down Liv. If he hadn't asked her to go to the store, he would still have her. It was a random, tragic car accident. No one blamed him. Except his conscience.

In the distance, a red car appeared, driving toward the ranch. After Jen returned, she'd take over Maddy's schedule. If he bumped into Stephanie, then maybe he'd see these past few days in a different light. With distance in time and space, he hoped to stop thinking about the meaningless, chaste kiss and feeling the phantom press of her lips on his cheek. When they were on an even field, neither holding power over the other, then perhaps reality would strip some of the magic from his memories.

As the car neared, music blared.

He came down the steps, straining for the melody.

The car entered the half circle drive in front of the house and stopped.

"Sisters" from *White Christmas* filtered out of the car. The engine kept running, even after the vehicle stopped and parked.

With a wave, he jogged toward the driver's side, leaning against the side mirror. "I didn't know you liked musicals."

Stephanie turned and smiled. "I don't. But Maddy suggested this soundtrack for our drives, and I finally remembered to download the music to my phone."

"Yep," a little voice said in the backseat. Maddy grinned. "And now Miss Patricks knows all the words for her part. She's Betty, and I'm Judy."

Stephanie shot him a frown, the corner of her eyes pinched and her mouth down-turned.

He swallowed a chuckle. She looked put on the spot, like she worried he'd test her.

"Your family has provided quite the education in movies," Stephanie said.

He studied her face. She looked unwell. Her eyes were almost sunken and her skin too pale. He should let her go. But he didn't want her to leave. "Thanks for dropping her off. Would you like to come inside? Hank cooks for a hundred."

She shook her head. "Not tonight."

Her words were soft and sad. He wanted to ask her a follow-up and wipe that down-trodden expression off her face. He'd seen her upset two times too many. He was power-less. He stepped back from the driver's side and opened the backseat door for Maddy.

The little girl hopped down and raced around the car. Her heavy steps thudded against the front stairs.

With a chuckle, he shut the back door. "Thanks again."

She nodded.

He stepped away from the car and waved an arm, watching her pull out of the spot and drive away. She wasn't her usual friendly self. Last night, she hadn't needed much encouragement to join him at the horse barn. Was she regretting their time together? That didn't seem to fit the companionable chat they'd had.

Joe might know what was troubling her if it involved the school. Stephanie worked so hard and tirelessly, it seemed doubtful anyone would have an issue with her. Except for jealousy. She came into town and started to impact the community in real, positive ways almost from the start.

He'd lived in Herd for years before she arrived and hardly knew another person in the community. She wasn't exactly walking around and introducing neighbors to one another, but she helped facilitate more events for the whole town to come together. If he called Joe, what would he say? How would he open the conversation without sounding suspicious?

Shaking his head, he crunched the gravel under his boots and strode up the front steps. Maddy had left the door ajar. He entered, toed off his boots, and shut the solid wood panel behind him.

From the front entry, Ted could turn his head to look into the front room or up to the top of the stairs and the gallery overhead leading to the second-floor bedrooms. In both directions, he spotted a wide collection of chew toys, blankets, and no less than three dog beds. A certain cowboy, who once declared pets were frivolous and that animals served only work purposes, had changed his tune. Careful not to step on one of the squeaky stuffed animals, he picked his way toward the kitchen, following his ears and nose.

Melted butter, braised beef, and a rich broth floated on the air. Water rushed out of a faucet. Low timber laughter mixed with a high-pitched giggle.

Ted strode through the open doorway and into the kitchen. In tourist season, when the ranch house doubled as the check-in, a swinging panel blocked the heart of the home from visitors. With the summer over, the door was propped open and invited everyone to come in.

The large kitchen overlooked the backyard and backside of the wraparound porch. At the sink, Meg tied an apron around Maddy's waist as Maddy washed her hands. An eight-burner stove took up the short wall to the right. Hank stood with a spoon, stirring a stew.

In the corner at a farmhouse table battered and bruised from generations, Ryan sat behind a laptop screen, his face brightened by the glow of the computer, in his seat to the right of the head of the table. Nearby, a fifty pound, black and white mutt slept on yet another dog bed. Snoring louder than Ted's college roommate, the dog's tail thumped a nearby cabinet as she beat an out of rhythm syncopation.

Although he was glad to be welcomed into the warmth, the kitchen scene was domestic chaos. Only a few months ago, the equal numbers of females to males, dog included, would have been strange. Since the passing of Hank's wife, Susie, the ranch had been a testosterone zone. Hank was a good cook, but the conversation was lacking. After a few words of gratitude and compliments on the meal, talk usually turned into a companionable run down of the day's work, and maybe conversation of whatever sport was currently televised.

Now, with the addition of Meg and Colby, he never knew what to expect. Meg ran the antique store in town and had a penchant for learning interesting facts. She loved to read, talk to newcomers, and always picked up tidbits here and there. She wasn't a gossip and never spoke ill of anyone. Rather, she discovered anecdotes and articles that made a person stop and consider a different perspective. Over the summer, she had changed the tenor of the mealtimes for the better.

While Maddy was a new arrival, she clearly fell into step with the crowd. It did him good to see his found family and his blood come together. He knocked on the doorframe.

Four heads turned in his direction.

"Thanks for having us over," Ted said.

"Of course." Hank turned back to the stove.

"Maddy and I are going to make the biscuits," Meg said.

The little girl hopped off the stool at the sink. "All yours, Unc."

He chuckled and walked to the sink. After thoroughly scrubbing his hands, he approached the table, sitting opposite his boss.

Ryan lifted his gaze off the screen. "I sent you the itinerary for our trip. It's going to be a busy few days. But you can always call if you need anything."

Ted knew, but he wasn't planning on reaching out. The trio would be busy, squeezing in several big meetings into a few days. Before Memorial Day, Hank's last-ditch attempt at setting up Meg and Ryan involved cleaning out the old shed and—by luck—the uncovering of a treasure trove of antique souvenir cards and photographs from Buffalo Bill Cody's Wild West Show. With the items now up for sale at an auction house in San Francisco, Hank and Meg had been planning to attend for months.

Ryan was an add-on to the original trip, citing the bison as his reason for joining. Ted wondered if Ryan didn't have an ulterior motive for the trip as well. The city by the bay was romantic for a proposal. While Meg and Ryan had only dated for a few months, their fate seemed written in the stars. A quick engagement and marriage wouldn't surprise anyone.

"I'm sure we'll be fine," Ted said. Over his shoulder, he glanced at the still sleeping dog. The hardest part of his weekend would be keeping Maddy from trying to play with the mutt around the clock. Colby liked rest.

"When is your sister coming?" Meg asked.

Lifting his leg, Ted sat sideways on the bench to keep an eye on everyone.

Standing at the counter with Maddy, Meg oversaw the cutting of the biscuits.

"Probably Sunday," Ted said.

"Are you okay to bunk here at the big house with Colby?" Hank asked.

"Absolutely. We'll take good care of her," Ted said.

"I've got a sleeping bag, Mr. Hank," Maddy chimed in.

"Oh, I'm not worried about you, darling." Hank winked at the little girl.

"What else is happening?" Ryan asked. "Do you need more room at the cabin? Are you cramped? You can use one of the guest cabins while your sister and Maddy get settled."

"Thanks." Ted nodded. "We're good. I like having the company."

He glanced at his niece. Her broad smile brightened him from the inside out.

What would it be like when she moved away? Would the quiet become oppressive? He couldn't think about losing her. Her arrival had been an unexpected blessing, as the good things usually were.

Life on the ranch offered more than he could ever have imagined. Change was good, bad, and inevitable. As long as he limited his variables, he'd be fine. If he expanded his social circle too quickly, he'd pop like an overinflated balloon.

CHAPTER 11

Nothing could snap Stephanie out of the doldrums faster than being helpful. When she had arrived home on Tuesday night, she answered an urgent call from Kelly. Lauren's doctor put her on bedrest effective Friday. The surprise school baby shower had to be moved up a few weeks to Thursday.

Tuesday night, she called Will at the general store and ordered the cake and balloons. The science teachers would no doubt frown at the use of helium as the world's supply of the resource dwindled but needs must. She'd pass out if she had to inflate the balloons herself. She reached out to Abby Whit, owner of the barbeque food truck, and scheduled a lunchtime treat for the staff. While not every grade took lunch at the same time, Abby would be parked outside for several hours to give everyone the chance for a complimentary meal. It was the biggest expenditure for the party but well worth it.

On Wednesday, she sent emails to the entire staff about the change. Those who were able coordinated with aides to watch their classes so, at the very least, they could be present when Lauren walked into the lounge. With a firm deadline, Stephanie focused.

The old adage *if you want something done, give it to a busy person* was almost her guiding life principle. She didn't like downtime and had never done well with time on her hands. She found her purpose and happiness in working and helping others.

As a result, her kids perked up. Wednesday was the smoothest day of school so far. No tantrums or tears. Everyone shared nicely and actively engaged in learning. She left the building feeling light as a feather with a broad smile.

Until she dropped off Maddy and saw Ted and reality slammed into her. She'd only have two more—rational, non-stalker—days to see him. Nothing had changed. Since she found her voice, she hadn't gone back to silence. But they sort of stagnated at pushing any further ahead.

She had no other conversation starters. Once again, they had nothing in common and no shared interests. How could she bring up his love of ska music or the movies of his youth without coming across as a total creep?

244

The age gap didn't matter to her, and she didn't think anyone in town would particularly care. But he must see it as a non-starter. Technically, they were from different generations. He grew up in the last era without social media. That was a huge blessing. Navigating puberty through the lens of influencers had been a nightmare. If anything, that pushed her to work with children too young for the various platforms. She couldn't imagine having to explain the ins and outs of the apps or warning signs to be on the lookout for when everything changed so rapidly.

She would be glad for Maddy's life to return to her new normal with her mom's move. Stephanie would be glad too that any hint of impropriety would be gone in her interactions. But she would miss Ted. Deep in her bones she knew for certain they could be happy if he let her in. She swallowed the sigh building in her throat and sat still in her chair.

Jumping out and yelling at a very pregnant woman was probably exactly the sort of thing Lauren's doctor wanted her to avoid. Stephanie scanned the room. In the teacher's lounge, with all the lights on, everyone gathered and sat, waiting for the guest of honor. It was decided slowly walking into a room full of people was enough of a surprise without causing a shock.

Kelly's voice filtered down the hall.

Stephanie sat straighter.

Lauren entered the room, stepping through the curtain of blue and pink streamers. With wide eyes, she twisted her neck from one side to the other. She covered her mouth with her hands.

Stephanie held her breath. Oh no. Had she miscalculated? Should she have let Lauren start her leave without a celebration? Stephanie pushed back her chair and reached her friend.

Kelly stood on Lauren's other side.

Lauren sniffed and met Stephanie's gaze with watery eyes. "Did you do all of this? For me?"

"Is that okay?" Stephanie asked.

Lauren nodded, tears streaming down her face. "Uh huh."

Kelly pulled out a tissue and handed it over not a moment too soon.

Lauren blew her nose, loudly. "Thank you all. So much." Her shoulders shook as a sob wracked her body. "You are too kind to me."

Stephanie wrapped an arm around her friend's shoulders and squeezed.

Lauren tilted her head, resting on Stephanie's shoulder.

Kelly stepped forward. "Okay, let's eat cake. I know a lot of you have to get back to your classes. Don't forget, Abby Whit is in the parking lot serving lunch today. It's our treat."

A cheer sounded and the room erupted into applause.

"Is this okay? Do you want to leave?" Stephanie whispered into Lauren's ear, rubbing her back.

Lauren nodded her head and stepped away.

Kelly handed her another tissue.

Dabbing at her face, Lauren balled up the tissue and lifted her red, splotchy face. "This is wonderful." She extended her hands.

Stephanie grabbed one and Kelly the other.

Lauren squeezed their hands. "Thank you both. For everything. I was really hoping to make it to Back-to-School night."

"We'll cover for you," Stephanie said.

"We always have each other's backs," Kelly added. "Come on, let's get you and the babies some cake. You need to put those feet up."

Stephanie dropped her hold and winked as Lauren rolled her eyes.

Kelly rarely played her leader card but, when she did, the other two knew better than to fight her. With a tug, she led Lauren toward the table in the center. The older grade teachers formed a line to grab a pre-plated slice of cake and then file past Lauren and offer their congratulations.

Joe approached Stephanie with a wave.

"Hi," she said. "You're getting quite cozy in the elementary wing lately."

He chuckled. "Mere coincidence, I assure you. I have to ask. When did you have time to throw this together?"

She lifted a shoulder in a shrug. "If it's important, you make time. Friends are always worth it."

He nodded. "Maybe you'd be better at party planning for Hank's big ninetieth celebration next summer."

She turned toward him, studying his face. His tone was forced. Was he pretending he'd just had this brainstorm idea? Or waiting for the perfect opportunity to unload? "Well, I probably would."

He frowned.

She stifled a laugh. *If you don't want the answer, don't ask the question.* "I'm already swamped with Frontier Days at the same time. And if I'm working on the ranch again next summer while finishing up the school year here, I'd really be too busy. But . . . to be honest?"

He faced her.

He looked hopeful. She hated to be the one to dash his plans but owed him the truth. "I already asked Mr. Kincaid if he wanted me to take over, and he refused."

Joe sighed, rolling his shoulders forward.

His animosity with Abby Whit was well-documented and unavoidable. Although it didn't make a lick of sense to her. The food truck owner was kind, friendly, and helpful. A recent transplant, she'd become a pretty indispensable vendor for both civic and private events. What could Joe possibly have against the woman? She smiled too much?

"Thanks for trying. I'd better give Lauren my regards before I head upstairs," Joe said.

She nodded and stepped back, her legs hit something. Startled, she turned and spotted the principal seated at the table she'd walked into. "Oh, sorry." She frowned.

On the tabletop, a splash of coffee formed a ring around the mug nearest her boss.

He waved off her concern, pulling a paper towel out of his pocket. "I don't go anywhere in this building without paper towels."

Smiling, she pulled out a chair and sat. "Thanks for your help with this last-minute switch."

"Of course. I'm honestly surprised she lasted this long. When my wife had our twins, she went on leave at seven months."

"Wow."

He nodded. "She was on bedrest for a month. A very, very long four weeks. Hopefully Lauren's time will be easier."

Stephanie smiled. She had nothing to add but made no move to leave. She sat, giving her principal plenty of opportunity to request a meeting or speak frankly. Following the run-in Monday and spotting Candace on Tuesday, she hadn't heard a peep from administration. Neither had she received any more emails from the parents.

"Good to see you and Kelly coming together. Kindergarten is a real team," Bill said.

Stephanie smiled. "We are. Lauren will be missed, but Kelly and I will help her sub."

"Good to hear. If you'll excuse me, I have to get back to a few meetings." He pushed back from the table.

"Of course. Don't let me keep you."

With a nod, he turned and made his way over to Lauren.

With a deep breath in, she held the air in her lungs for a count of five and slowly exhaled. She could and would continue to advocate for her students and the entire student population. Luckily, with only herself impacted by her choices, she wasn't risking much.

Ted loaded the last of the luggage into the back of the SUV and frowned. The back of the vehicle was packed floor to ceiling with suitcases. The small SUV was the tiniest of the vehicles they could have chosen. Meg had argued against one of the trucks, pointing out the complexities of parking in a city.

Perhaps she had a false impression of how much was needed for their trip. For a long weekend away, the trio had probably overpacked. The worst offender was Hank, dropping off two large rolling upright suitcases at the last moment.

Luckily, Ted didn't mind a challenge or re-doing all his hard work. He emptied the trunk and reconfigured the bags in record time. He didn't want to be the reason the group was held up. Not that any of them would blame him.

Ryan decided to leave Thursday afternoon instead of Friday morning, squeezing in more time at their destination. For someone who planned everything, the sudden spontaneous switch was suspicious. And had more likely than not been his schedule all along. As to the reasons, he didn't share the details with his traveling companions or cowboy. Ted had his guess.

Taking a step back, Ted shut the trunk door and wiped his hands on his jeans. He strode to the driver's side. "You're all set. Have a safe drive."

With the window rolled down, Ryan leaned against the door, behind the wheel. "We will. Meg's practically opened up a coffee shop in the front seat." He pointed at four travel mugs, occupying every cupholder.

"I don't love starting a long drive late in the day. Caffeine it is." Meg leaned over Ryan. "If you have any problems with Colby, please call."

Like, trouble getting the dog to walk? Colby hadn't left the couch to bid adieu to her humans. The dog expended no extra energy. Ted had no non-cheeky response. He nodded.

The backseat window rolled down. "Hey, do me a favor," Hank called.

Ted approached the back seat. Hank sat in the center with pillows on either side of him. Either he'd be asleep in no time, or he'd comment on Ryan's driving from the safety of his comfortable perch. Maybe a little of both.

"Yes, sir. What do you need?" Ted asked.

"Keep an eye on Abby and Joe. If you can nudge those two together, I'd appreciate your assistance," Hank said.

In the driver's seat, Ryan rolled his eyes. "We're off. Bye, Ted."

Raising his hand to his shoulder, Ted stepped back and waved.

The SUV pulled through the end of the drive and turned down the road. Once the vehicle disappeared, Ted grabbed his phone out of his back pocket. School had ended, but it would be a bit before Stephanie and Maddy arrived. If he started a chore now, he'd be stuck at it too long. Night would fall, and he'd have to turn on the lights to finish. Maddy would be left alone in an unfamiliar in the dark house.

He didn't need to do more than heat the oven to make dinner. The kitchen was fully stocked for the weekend. Hank had prepared one of Maddy's favorite dinners, stuffed peppers. Ted could wander the property, alone with his thoughts for a while. But then he'd circle back to Stephanie and the dwindling time together. And then he might do something stupid like come up with an excuse to see her over the weekend. Asking her to stay tomorrow night after drop-off for a movie as a thank you hovered on his tongue.

He had only one alternative for how to occupy his time. With official confirmation of Hank's meddling from the man himself, Ted owed his friend a heads up. Dialing Joe's number, he pressed the phone against his ear. "You're right," he said without preamble as soon as the line connected.

"I usually am. What is it this time?" Joe asked.

"Hank is setting you up with Abby. Any luck getting yourself off the birthday bonanza project?"

Joe's whoosh exhale answered first. "Stephanie can't help. Bad timing."

Why? Does she have plans? Ted didn't like the boulder that had settled in his gut. Nor could he shake the surge of jealousy. He pinched the bridge of his nose. Hank's birthday wasn't until May. She could hardly plan that far ahead for a date. And if she did? He'd have to be happy for her. She deserved everything she wanted as long as he wasn't included in her plans.

"Ted? You there?"

"Sorry." Ted coughed. "Why can't she help?"

"Frontier Days and working at the ranch, if you'll have her."

Of course I will. He dropped his hand to his side and rolled his shoulders up and back. He needed to focus on the present conversation and not on himself. He'd have his hands full enough over the weekend and didn't need to add on with his own issues. "Hank probably already took that into consideration when the idea first came to him," Ted said. "If you tried, you couldn't get out of it. Why don't you just stick up for yourself with Mr. Kincaid and tell him you don't like Abby."

"As if I haven't made my distrust clear enough already?" Joe snorted. "Do you think my opinion would stop him from his goal? Have you ever tried to stand up against his matchmaking?"

No, he hadn't. After Hank settled Joe, however, would the old cowboy turn his attention in Ted's direction? Or was Ted a lost cause? Maybe Hank would help Stephanie find love. *I don't want to watch that.*

"Can I speak frankly?" Ted asked. While he prided himself on truthfulness, he also understood not everyone could handle bald facts and strong opinions at all times.

"Of course," Joe replied.

"I don't like the way you speak about Abby. Hank isn't even around half the time you speak poorly of her. You don't need to have such a personal vendetta against her."

"I'm only being honest."

"No, you're almost mean when her name comes up."

248

"When?" Joe's question held barbs and prickles, deflecting the accusation.

"During the conversation the other day with Ryan about helping get her a proper building for her restaurant. She's a good partner for the ranch and a kind neighbor. She needs a little help. So what? Why do you care? Leave your feelings aside and realize she's an important part of the community. Like you. Like all of us."

"Fine." Joe sighed. "You're right. But if I ease up now, I'll only convince Hank I'm softening on her. My best bet is to fall in love over the weekend. The sooner I'm taken, the better for me. If I can find someone in the next seventy-two hours, I'll propose on the spot. I'd love for him to get back and focus on Abby and some other poor schmuck."

Ted rolled his eyes. "Do you have anyone in mind?"

"Of course not. I don't spend my time thinking about her."

The reply had a sharp edge to it that was a little too venomous for the situation. Or did Joe do the opposite? How much of his day was spent circling back to his issues with Abby Whit? "Isn't she friendly with Ian?"

"The blacksmith? No. That wouldn't work. Not at all."

The delivery was crisp, clear, and concise. *And confusing.*

"Why not?" Ted asked. Before the turn in the conversation, he never really noticed or cared. But Joe sure had opinions. "Isn't he helping her with her new smoker? Shared interests is a solid start for a couple. Seems like that pairing would be a good set-up for Hank to pursue next. Take some heat off you."

"Just because I want to save myself doesn't mean I'm going to throw someone else in her path."

Ted shook his head. "What do you have against her? She seems nice enough to me. Every time we've needed help, she doesn't hesitate."

"She's hiding something, and I hate it."

Ted couldn't figure that out. As far as he was concerned Abby was an open book. What could she hide? But he wouldn't say anything to Joe. There was no point. "Okay, I relent. I didn't call to fight. You know I'm out for poker again this weekend?"

"Yep, already told the guys. After your sister gets back, you'll be expected at the saloon every week. No excuses."

After his sister came back, he'd have none. Neither would he have a reason to see Stephanie until the late spring. At least she was planning on working at the ranch next summer. Perhaps by then she would be in a relationship, and he could return his focus to his work and family. His status quo was in the midst of a shake-up. He hadn't planned on change but was finding he didn't hate it. He would hate missing her. "Sounds good. Bye."

"Catch you later."

Ted hung up the call and strolled back towards the house. With the fading daylight, the sky was awash with pinks and blues. He loved the autumn sunset, the soft colors easing the end of his day, but he hated the long nights. In summer, the days stretched into eternity, matching his working hours. Montana hadn't been meant to become his home. He settled down while he was busy ignoring the future.

Was he again at a crossroads? He'd stumbled into a good life and, despite the career changes, managed to keep his world controlled. Something different pulled at him, tugging where his heart used to be. Could he love someone else, even knowing he'd be doomed to fail her? Stephanie would be so easy to fall for and so hard to get over. She was the town's darling, and he wasn't ready to be exiled for hurting her.

He kicked at a large chunk of gravel in his way and strode toward the house. Colby would be expecting her evening meal and then her bed. For one woman, he could meet expectations without tangling his heart in the mix.

CHAPTER 12

Stephanie smoothed her hair behind her ears and dried her clammy hands on her long, flowy pants. Striding down the hall, her heeled steps echoed off the tile floor. Without the buffering of childish giggles or a teacher instructing her class, she only listened to her self-created noises.

The corridor looked like an optical illusion sketch. Could she actually reach the end or would she hit a solid wall painted as an illusion? Could she pick her preferred option?

She had never felt so alone, and her senses confirmed her solitary status. With twenty minutes until the end of the day, she'd thought she was in the clear. Yesterday, at Lauren's baby shower, she had expected a comment from the principal. When he didn't take the opportunity to ask her for a meeting, he gave her hope she had been mistaken.

Perhaps Candace's appearance in the front office earlier in the week after Mrs. Foxx's sudden visit was mere coincidence. Or—more likely—with older children also in the building, Candace simply had other targets for her attack. Last night, Stephanie had slept easier, knowing she only had to make it through one more day and then she'd have fulfilled her obligation and take the weekend to rest and recharge.

Of course, she wasn't totally free of her feelings. Her heart still twisted when she considered next week and the long months ahead until she had a reason to be at the ranch. Couldn't Ryan hurry up and propose to Meg already so the town could celebrate together?

Then, she'd have an excuse to help out around the ranch again. Only, this time, she would have no power imbalance with Ted to get in the way. Although, she didn't think that was the issue. He held himself in check. He wasn't the sort to express any big emotion, swinging from one extreme to the other. Was it because he lost his wife? Did he still grieve her? Stephanie only wished she could have an ounce of that sort of affection directed at her.

She had been happily going through her day. Until a few minutes ago when a knock had sounded on the door. She'd set down the book she'd been reading to the class and opened it to an unknown face holding a note. Could she please come down to meet with the principal as Mrs. Lamb watched her class? Stephanie had smiled to the kids, reassured them she'd be back soon, and strode out the door.

Now, she reached the glass door leading to the front offices. With a hand on the cool, metal pull, she filled her lungs to capacity, tamped down the hot emotions flooding her face. She could do this. Sure, she'd never been asked to come to the principal's office during the day nor had she ever been surprised with a substitute at the door. That didn't mean anything. First time for everything.

She opened the door wide and entered, smiling at the school secretary. "Hello, Wendy. I'm here to see B—"

"He's expecting you," the older woman interrupted.

Stephanie widened her eyes and froze at the curt greeting. Well-past retirement age, Wendy was an excessively kind, grandmotherly type woman. Dressed in matching pastel sweater sets with her silver hair permed, she greeted everyone with a smile and soft word of welcome.

Not me. Not today. With a nod, Stephanie continued past the desk to the open doorway. She stopped outside and knocked on the panel.

Behind the desk, Bill focused on a desktop angled away from the door, toward the windows overlooking the parking lot. He turned toward her, pushing back his chair. "Come in, come in." He smiled and waved to the chair in front of his desk.

She stepped over the threshold and crossed the short distance to the chair. The carpet muffled her steps, but nothing could slow the rapid beat of her heart.

He shut the door.

The click of the lock settling was like a shot. She jerked and lifted her gaze.

Unbuttoning his blazer, he settled behind his desk. He rested his forearms on the top, leaning forward. "Thanks for coming down. I'm sorry for the short notice."

She lifted a shoulder. That was the best response she could give. Inside her chest, she felt fluttery and dizzy. Like she could float off or fall down.

"I'll come straight to the point." He cleared his throat and tugged at his Windsor-knotted neck tie. "Allegations of favoritism and exclusion have arisen from your classroom."

She dropped her jaw. She'd never been accused of either. She knew Candace plotted something unseemly. These words were particularly cruel and carefully chosen, mirroring what she had endured as a child.

"I've been made aware that you have turned away help from a parent in your classroom."

She shut her dry mouth and swallowed. "Yes."

He sighed. "I was hoping that was an exaggeration."

She frowned. "Typically, we don't even put out the call for volunteers in the class until after Back-to-School night next week. The other classrooms haven't sent out any sign-up sheets. I was stunned the parent showed up."

He propped his elbows on the desk, steepling his fingers. "But the parent has older children and would have a reasonable expectation of being welcomed as a volunteer."

How did the parent get inside the building? She couldn't fling that accusation at the principal. But the lapse would need to be addressed at some point for the safety of all. "I was ambushed."

He widened his eyes.

She lifted her chin. "I believe the parent was set up to fail by someone else. I feel bad for the entire situation. I could have handled the impromptu appearance better. But I think Mrs. Foxx was used."

"That's quite a lot to claim."

"It's what happened."

He scrubbed a hand over his face. "Stephanie, you're a great teacher and an asset to this entire school."

But but but her mind rang with the word. She didn't want to supply his lines. She wanted to escape this room and this conversation.

"Are you still driving one of your students home?"

She nodded. He knew she was. Was she on a collision course with losing her job? Over one infraction? About something she'd cleared with the administration? Should she laugh or cry? She wasn't sure one wouldn't inevitably lead to the other. "Today is my last day."

"I wish you would have told me what happened with Mrs. Foxx. When it happened. I could have helped before. . ."

"I didn't want to give it more energy." Her voice cracked from the weight of her honesty. She'd had thought coming to the principal with a *she said-she said* argument was counterproductive. Clearly, someone else disagreed. With everything that had happened since the poker night, she'd pushed the incident from her mind.

"But now you have put yourself, and the school, in a difficult position. You are directly assisting one family but turning away others. I know you are trying to help, but the appearance is misleading and has created a tense situation."

Driving Maddy was a short-term situation. She had asked Mrs. Foxx to leave because, once she allowed one volunteer into the classroom, she would have a rotation of the same few helpers involved every week for the long-term. The kids with working parents would be left out. She never lost sight of her end goal. But she couldn't deny the optics were off.

"I am sorry to say that there is a hint of impropriety, too," Bill said. "Whispers have reached me about your connection with your student's temporary guardian. You have been seen spending time together beyond dropping off your student."

It's nothing. Her ears burned. Any response dried on her shriveled tongue. Ted definitely didn't have any sort of feelings for her, but she couldn't deny her regard.

"The look of the whole thing is the problem. Until I can straighten out the drama, I need to ask you to take a paid leave of absence starting after school today."

What? She gasped. Her mind whirred, and she darted her eyes from side to side, searching for any way out of this situation. "Because I'm driving a child home? I'm in trouble with disciplinary consequences for that."

"It's a little more complicated. Your choice to limit classroom access has created a tense situation for some of our more outspoken parents. Apparently, a petition has been floating around to start a disciplinary hearing into your behavior."

Her jaw dropped. She couldn't believe what she was hearing. But she did. Everyone warned her. Candace Vane was determined and difficult. On a good day. Stephanie shook her head, reaching up to press her cool fingers against her throbbing temples. "I was helping a family. I would do the same for any of my kids. You know that."

He held up a hand. "I believe you. When you first told me about the situation, you were upfront and honest. Today is the last day you'll be driving her home?"

Stephanie nodded, sniffing.

He extended a box of tissues over the top of the desk.

She grabbed one and blew her nose.

"It's a temporary review. You aren't being fired. But we have to go through the motions." He left the tissues on the desk and interlaced his hands.

"I haven't done anything wrong."

"No, you haven't. But perception is reality. Mrs. Vane is convinced there is impropriety. Until we straighten out the mess, we can't have you teach. We have to be seen as taking the correct steps. We support you. I'm doing everything I can to get you back in your classroom as soon as possible."

Perception is reality. If only that were true. Did some people in town think there was more going on with her and Ted? Or was she the desperate woman willing to do everything—including risking her reputation—for a man who wasn't interested?

Or was a cunning person crafting a narrative to manipulate the system and get her way? Stephanie had never heard anyone whisper anything about her and Ted. Would she now? Had Candace spread gossip in town?

"I am sorry to have you gone for any amount of time but especially with Lauren's maternity leave. Hang in there. We will get this figured out. Come to my office on Monday at 10:45 in the morning. We'll talk more then."

She stared at the tissue box. Tears burned her nostrils and clouded her vision. It would be all too easy to curl into a ball and sob. She could crumple.

Tucking her fingers against her palms, she dug her nails into the meaty flesh of her palms. She refused defeat. Instead, she could leave with her head held high and cling to her dignity. She hated when tears were weaponized and wouldn't be caught in that trap herself. No matter what happened next, she wouldn't be accused of manipulation.

She pushed back her chair, stood straight as an arrow, and met his gaze. "Thank you. I'll wait to hear more."

Tipping her head in a tiny nod, she swiveled on her heel and retraced her steps. She wasn't going to cry because of a mean girl's power play. Nor would she glance left or right and catch sight of a frown or commiserating head nod by a member of staff.

With her chin lifted in the air, she strode in determined steps down the hall and back into her classroom. She'd say goodbye for now to the kids but not for good. She'd drive Maddy to the ranch, and then she'd head home and plot. One setback wasn't enough to stop her. She'd found her strength, and she wasn't going to lose.

Ted had never resorted to begging a dog to move. But he'd never taken care of Colby by himself before. Standing at the ranch house's front door, he jingled the leash in the air.

From her perch on the couch in the front room, the dog lifted her head and set it back down on her front paws.

He was sure he'd heard a sigh. Could have been his. Since he returned to the ranch from the school drop-off, he'd tried to encourage the dog to leave the couch with the same poor results. What was he doing wrong?

Didn't dogs love to walk? Wasn't that their thing? A chance to sniff and go to the bathroom and chase squirrels? He frowned. Not many squirrels on the ranch but plenty of other rodents of interest to a canine.

Last night, with Maddy's help, he progressed through the dog's routine with ease. They'd fed her, walked her around the perimeter, and made sure she was comfortable in her bed next to Hank's. He'd been feeling proud of himself and brushed off the notion he'd need to call Hank or Meg. His success had all been an illusion.

As soon as Maddy left, the dog nestled on the couch. He'd come back to check on her as the hours passed, but the dog had only moved from laying on her side to her back. The black and white mutt was unimpressed by him from the start of the day. He just hadn't been smart enough to realize.

The dog gave him the cold shoulder. He wouldn't have thought a dog could snub a human. This one did.

For most of the day, however, leaving the dog in the house to sleep had been the easiest option. He'd checked on her water and petted her as he passed. But if he wasn't offering food, he was of no interest.

He glanced at his watch. Maddy and Stephanie would be home soon. He needed his niece to convince the dog to leave the couch. This was too pathetic. A grown man hired to care for animals shouldn't be overwhelmed by one spoiled, finicky pet. She was probably upset he wasn't Hank or Meg.

What if the dog was ill? Should he drive her into town to see the vet? Doc Hampton would probably make a house-call if necessary. But what if the dog was fine, and he'd charged an astronomical fee to the account for his own stupidity? He was tempted to call Meg but didn't want to worry her over nothing. He had to make another try. "Please come on? A quick walk and then we can eat?"

The dog tilted her head.

"Eat? Do you want food? After our walk?"

The dog hopped off the couch and padded over, her nails clicking with each step. Stopping a foot away, she yawned and stretched her legs one at a time. She sat very still.

"Okay, good. Let's go quick, and you can have dinner." He bent to attach the leash to the collar.

The dog's crooked tail swished over the slate.

If he hadn't spent all day internalizing, he could have made better progress. Who knew the dog understood English? He looped the leash in his right hand, opened the door, and strode outside. The more he thought about it, however, the more obvious it became.

Colby spent her days with Hank and Meg, arguably the two most talkative people in the whole state.

Ted, on the other hand, was so used to keeping his own company that he often forgot to speak. Sometimes, he felt awkward when he remembered the social niceties and found his voice following what was inevitably a too long conversational pause. *Never with Stephanie.* He liked the not needing to explain himself. No wonder he misunderstood her general friendliness as affection.

Shutting the door behind him, he jogged down the front steps and led Colby on the path around the house and toward the barn. Exercise could help clear his head where his day's labors had failed. Stephanie wasn't interested in him more than anyone else. She was outgoing. Soon, she'd find someone else.

Too bad Joe had already declared her off-limits, or he'd solve his own problems with Hank. She'd be so easy to fall in love with. Who wouldn't want to hear her light, lilting laugh? Or stare deep into her blue eyes as she considered a trademark thoughtful response?

She was perfect.

For someone else.

And Ted would have to try really hard not to hate that guy when he showed up. At least it wouldn't be Joe. He couldn't stand to be the third or fifth wheel on nights out with Meg, Ryan, Joe, and Stephanie.

Shaking his head, he dropped his gaze from the sky to the dusty ground, matching the pace of the dog at his side. For a couch potato, she was remarkably fluid and walked like she'd been trained to follow a human. Would she go to the bathroom? Or was this another moment he needed to give her permission?

Dogs and women. Why were they so confusing, discerning, and adoring? Did he need to be upfront with Stephanie? Did he owe her a full accounting of why he couldn't be the guy for her? He'd focus on one problem at a time. "Colby, please find the toilet."

The dog tilted her head in his direction and walked a little further out, pulling the leash another foot. And then she took care of business.

Was that the secret to both? Talking? Then he was doomed. While he might adapt as necessary for family, he wasn't a chatty person. A big part of the appeal of the ranch lifestyle was the solitude.

In his back pocket, his phone rang. He frowned, pulling out the screen and swiping his thumb over the image of his friend. "Two calls in two days? What's wrong?" He chuckled at his joke.

"It's Stephanie," Joe said.

"What?" Ted gasped and tightened his grip on the phone, pressing the hand against his head and readjusting his clammy hold on the leash. "What's happened? What's wrong?"

"I don't know specifics. No one is really talking here. Hopefully nothing."

"What do you know? Is she hurt?" Ted shut his eyes. If something happened to her and Maddy, how would he go on?

"Ted?" Joe asked. "Can you hear me? Are you there?"

"What was it? An accident? Where is she? The hospital?"

"Oh, no. I'm . . . I'm an idiot. Sorry. She is physically fine."

Ted let out a shuddering breath. He rocked back on his heels like he'd dropped a heavy saddle off his shoulders. "What are you talking about then?"

"School. Something has come up here," Joe said. "I should have led with that."

Ted dropped his tense shoulders. *Yeah, you think?* He pinched the bridge of his nose. Colby yelped.

"Sorry, girl," Ted murmured. He'd forgotten they were attached. He'd lost track of everything as the adrenaline rushed his body, electrifying every cell and nerve. If she was hurt. . .

"Girl?" Joe asked, his tone dripping with disgust.

"I'm walking the dog. She responds to verbal contact."

"Oh, huh. Makes sense I guess," Joe said. "Meg acts like the dog understands English. Maybe Colby learned a few words. About the other thing. I wanted to give you a heads up. I know this is the last day she's dropping off Maddy. Stephanie might be upset. Be easy."

"How do you know she's in trouble? What sort? What happened?"

"I stopped by the office to grab a package and watched her storm out of the principal's office. I've heard rumblings about the PTO president being upset with Stephanie. My guess is she's made trouble and filed a complaint."

"What could she do? Can the PTO fire a member of staff?" Ted was incredulous. How could one self-absorbed parent impact someone doing so much good for a classroom full of little kids? Why should one too loud voice ruin others' lives?

Without Stephanie, Ted knew Maddy wouldn't have adapted half so well to her new living situation. To move away from the only home she'd known, and say goodbye to her parents, not knowing when she'd see one of them again, and stay with her uncle was traumatic for someone three times her age. But Maddy had soared, hardly noticing the little hiccups as she settled in, and he learned caretaking on the job.

He owed it all to Stephanie. Had her helping him but her in a bad spot? She swore it hadn't. But had she been trying to protect him?

"Candace Vane is a powerful enemy," Joe said. "I'm in my car, heading home. I'm guessing Stephanie will probably stop by in the next ten minutes or so. I wanted you to be aware of the situation. I'll give her a call over the weekend to see if she needs my help."

Would she need mine? Ted hated to be powerless on the sidelines, watching. "Thanks."

The crunch of tires on gravel echoed through the otherwise still air.

"They're here," Ted said. "Better go."

"Yep. Bye."

Ted hung up the call, slipping the phone into his back pocket. With long strides, he retraced his steps. Colby matched his gait perfectly. If the dog was treated less like a human, she'd probably be the ideal animal. *Except she's prized for her companionship skills.*

He shook off the thought as he rounded the edge of the house.

Maddy skipped out of the car and up the front walk, chattering a mile a minute.

Stephanie walked with her, smiling sweetly.

With each inch forward, her expression came into clearer view. She looked soft and thoughtful. How dare a brazen, brash, bossy broad ruin this woman's happiness? No one should have their joy stolen. Especially not Stephanie.

She turned her head and met his gaze.

Her face froze in a look he couldn't quite read. He cleared his throat. "Good evening. Just walking Colby. Thanks for dropping off Maddy." He'd reached the bottom of the steps and glanced up at her and his niece at the front door.

"And Shakes," Maddy said, holding the little yellow stuffed animal in a tight squeeze.

"Very nice to meet you, Shakes," he said.

"It's been no problem. My pleasure," Stephanie said with a wink at Maddy before turning back to him.

Something glistened in her eyes. Unshed tears? What happened? What was wrong? He could assure himself later he'd only said it to be a kind, caring friend. It wasn't because he didn't want her to leave. It was because he had a heart. He would have helped anyone who looked so sad and broken. Because Stephanie needed his help was beside the point.

"Come inside. We're making our own pizzas for dinner and watching a movie. Please join us," he said, resting his free hand on the railing and looking up at her.

She held his gaze and slowly nodded.

"Yes," Maddy murmured, opening the front door, and barreling inside. "Colby let's get your dinner."

The dog lunged forward, nearly taking off his arm.

At least he had back-up. He climbed the steps and stood inside the door. "Please, come in."

She passed by him, biting her lip.

He was glad. If she was truly upset, she shouldn't run off home. She shouldn't be alone. She could do or say something she'd regret.

Was he about to sow a relationship with a fateful consequence? A sigh built in his chest. He forced it down, turning to shut the front door. For a little while, he could content himself with a little taste of how easy it could be to spend time in her company. And then she'd go home, and he'd feel better. Two lonely souls making each other a little lighter for a while. He couldn't—and wouldn't—ask for more.

CHAPTER 13

Stephanie had never been more grateful for her carpool than driving home from school on Friday following her official rebuke. Which, all things considered, did a better job arguing she'd expressed favoritism than the hearsay evidence Bill presented. If she hadn't had Maddy in her car every day, Stephanie would have avoided her career doom.

But the little girl made Stephanie smile and lightened up her afternoons with conversation varying from wisdom to whimsy in seconds. Adding in the opportunity to talk to Ted each day, and she had no regrets. In truth, she hadn't known what she'd been missing.

With her friends and her projects, she was busy but not necessarily engaged. She'd participated without fully immersing her mind, her heart, and her soul. And now she would lose the companionship when she needed it the most. She probably shouldn't have accepted the invitation to stay for dinner. But she had.

As she stepped over the threshold of the old ranch house, she passed him, breathing in his mint and leather smell. Had she swayed into him, sniffing his collar? She hadn't received her official punishment yet. Was she now in a sort of double jeopardy state? If she was accused of favoritism due to a personal relationship, could she pursue said romance? Should she?

She stepped to the side, tamping down the streak of wild, recklessness surging through her veins. "Shakes shouldn't give you too much trouble. Take lots of pictures as he tags along with Maddy. She'll present a slideshow on Monday and talk about their weekend together. You can send an email with the photos on Sunday night." Stephanie sucked in a sharp, stinging breath.

No, he couldn't.

She wouldn't be there.

Swallowing, she forced her scratchy, dry throat to open and close. "Actually, I'd better give you Kelly Strong's email. She's another kindergarten teacher. She'll know what to do."

He nodded. "Follow me into the kitchen. I'll grab a piece of paper from the junk drawer, and you can jot it down?"

259

She lifted her gaze to his. With her admission and acceptance of her altered schedule, she lost some of the spark of indignation and daring that fueled her. She should excuse herself and send him an email from home with the pertinent details. She couldn't stand being alone right now, as fragile and transparent as a sheet of glass. He was strong and stoic. She longed to lean into his arms and break down, knowing he'd hold her.

Instead of leaving or launching herself at him, however, she cleared her throat. "Kitchen?"

Nodding, he pointed toward the back and an open doorway. "We can't make our own pizzas out here."

She'd only been invited into the Kincaid house a few times and on those occasions the home had been overflowing with guests and laughter. She'd been awed by the craftsmanship and scale of the home. The building had stood strong for over a century and would keep shielding and protecting its occupants, come what may. Tonight, with only three humans and one dog, the four walls felt cozy and warm. Intimate.

Her cheeks flushed, and she strode down the hall and into a large eat-in kitchen.

At a sink overlooking the back of the wraparound porch, Maddy stood on a little stool and washed her hands. She tucked Shakes under an arm, clutching him tight around the neck, and struggled with the plastic bag holding a pre-cooked pizza crust.

Loud crunching echoed in the room. In the corner, Colby happily munched, her crooked tail swinging side to side. Ted entered behind Stephanie and crossed the room quickly, helping Maddy open her bag and the other one on the counter as well. Together, Maddy and Ted positioned the crusts on cookie sheets spread across the stove.

Stephanie should excuse herself. But her tongue stuck to the roof of her mouth, and she wasn't sure she could loosen her jaw to speak if her life depended on it.

Ted turned around and flashed her a quick smile. "Just one second." He carefully removed Shakes from Maddy's embrace and set the stuffed animal a safe distance away on the counter to observe. He strode along the counter, pulling open a drawer and approaching Stephanie with a notepad and pen.

Stephanie smiled and jotted down the details, aware he'd moved away.

"After pizza, we're watching a movie," he said, drawing her gaze again.

He grabbed an apron off the counter and slipped into it, standing near the stove.

His movements were smooth like a dance. She stared trying to figure out the steps. He grabbed another apron off the counter. Stopping a few feet away, he extended it. "You're going to need this. Trust me."

She stuck out her hand, thrusting the notepad and pen forward with too much power and hitting him in the process. Her cheeks burned.

"Specifically, we are watching *White Christmas*," he said. He swapped her pen and notepad for the apron, his touch light and fleeting.

She was grateful he hadn't commented on her jerky motions. But she refused to fall back into silence around him. Teasing suited her. "Isn't it a little early to watch Christmas movies?" She arched a brow.

The corner of his mouth lifted.

Her stomach flipped.

A loud gasp sucked all the air out of the room.

Turning toward the sound, she spotted Maddy pushing up her sleeves with a wide-eyed gaze. On a stool at her side, Shakes sat at attention, equally unimpressed by the lack of seasonal cheer.

Ted chuckled, shaking his head. "It's okay, squirrel. She doesn't know what she's missing." He stepped away from Stephanie but not before shooting her a wink.

She felt the flutter down to her toes. She slipped the apron on and tied it around her waist.

Ted helped Maddy with her and snapped a picture on his cell phone of his niece and the class pet. He opened a jar of sauce and set it on the counter with a spoon for Maddy. Then, he arranged containers of cheese and toppings nearby.

Maddy focused on creating her dinner.

He shot Stephanie a look.

She took the hint, washed her hands, and strode to the workstation. She took the space on the end with Maddy in between her and Ted. "What am I missing about watching Christmas movies in September? Don't most people stick with the holiday season?"

"It's a family tradition," Maddy said.

"When I was a kid, my mom taped all my favorite Christmas specials onto a VHS for me to watch whenever I was home sick. It always cheered me up," Ted said with a smile, staring at the pizza crust as he evenly spread sauce like a professional. "I find the movies comforting when I'm not feeling good."

Stephanie could definitely use cheering up. She'd imagined herself safe only to have that security snatched at the last second. The timing of the afternoon meeting felt particularly cruel. Bill had assured her he had her back. What happened?

"Although . . ." He lifted his chin and met her gaze. "I'm guessing that's one of those things you didn't deal with as a kid."

Sadness? She frowned.

"VHS. Video tape? I wore out the tapes. I loved everything that recorded, including the commercials. Maybe especially the commercials."

"Hmm." She tapped her chin with a finger. "I think I've heard of commercials. From the dark ages. Before fast forwarding live TV."

He rolled his eyes and chuckled.

She curled her toes. Anticipation swept through her at the low rumble of his laughter. She liked teasing him. She'd never been much for banter but with him, she had the impulse to say the coquettish retort.

I'm not that young. The words tickled the end of her tongue. She didn't say it. With his niece between them, she had to be careful not to cross over any boundary. Although, of course, she wasn't sure dividing lines existed anymore.

"Regardless, it is a family tradition to watch holiday movies whenever we feel like it. And I feel like it today. How about you, Maddy?"

The little girl nodded. "And now you can watch the dance routines and learn your part."

Stephanie nibbled the inside of her cheek. She definitely needed cheering up. Choreography might be the cure. "Will you and Unc perform along with the actors?"

Maddy grinned.

"Oh man, what has she told you?" he asked.

Maddy's giggle was the only answer anyone needed.

Stephanie met his gaze over the top of the little girl's head. For the first time all day, she felt light. As of this moment neither owed the other anything. Her staying at his invitation started something new. And she was glad for it. If she was already in trouble, her career at risk, why not actually be held responsible for following her heart?

For the first forty minutes of the movie, Ted was an active participant.

Maddy loved to sing and dance through the opening numbers with a partner. Tonight, she chose one human and one stuffed animal. By the time the cast of the movie reached the inn, however, she settled down on the couch and stayed in place. He snapped a picture of the pair, careful not to include Stephanie in the frame.

When she had explained where to send the email about the class pet, she had looked shell-shocked. Her situation had become real in that moment. Instead of crumbling, however, she had stood straight, her eyes had gleamed with valiant determination. How could anyone not admire her strength? He clung to reason, ignoring any deeper meaning.

Maddy snored. With a full belly, a warm blanket, a stuffed animal turned pillow, and a sleeping dog next to her, she curled into a little ball. Colby joined her in a symphony of nasal congestion that threatened to overshadow the movie.

Stephanie turned her head, widening her eyes.

He flashed a thumbs up. He knew what he was doing. A full belly and favorite movie were the secret ingredient to babysitting success on a weekend night.

But he didn't turn off the movie. He loved the scenes of struggle at the inn. As he got older, he respected the nuance of the film; showing how people could be forced out while still in their prime, how second chances weren't a given, but how magic could change everything.

Sitting in silence, he observed Stephanie as she stared at the screen, her eyes bright. Transfixed? He hoped so. Watching a beloved classic with an outsider was an act of vulnerablity, like showing someone his bedroom as a child. But she didn't make a sound.

Fighting the urge to sing and deliver the lines, he forced himself to watch the movie as much as he was able. Her presence proved more distracting with each second as the onscreen characters lost and found each other.

As the credits rolled, he studied her again from the corner of his eye. Curled on the couch with a blanket, she didn't show her reaction. No swooning. No laughing. No tears.

He rubbed a hand to his side, easing a sharp pain in his ribs. Did she hate the film? Did she think less of him for loving the movie?

He wanted her to connect with the story and the characters. That was probably a tall order. Life in a small Western town was not quite the same as the fictional Vermont of the fifties. Some things, however, were timeless. Reaching for a dream, continuing against the odds, and finding love remained primary motivations for so many.

"What did you think?" he asked, cutting through the silence and turning toward her. Whatever her opinion, he'd take it face to face.

"I loved it." She turned, widening her eyes. "I can't believe I've never seen it before."

"Me either."

She rolled her eyes. "Not another comment on the age gap. The real difference between our generations comes down to good luck and opportunity. You graduated college with plenty of both. When I graduated, I had neither."

A retort stilled on his tongue. He'd never thought of their differences so starkly before, but she was right. The dot com burst and 9/11 came during her formative years. Before she'd have much luck in the workplace, she'd hit the housing market crisis.

"You have a tendency to make yourself sound like Hank's peer. I'm pretty sure he wouldn't understand your references either."

Ted chuckled. "Fair point but face it. My favorite movies are your classics. Something like this, that came out when my parents were children, is practically part of the silent era to you."

She turned toward him, resting a hand on the back of the couch. "My lack of pop culture knowledge would be the same if we shared the same birthday. I didn't really watch much TV or movies growing up. I was too busy."

That he could believe. She didn't just randomly start being the overly involved town doer in her twenties. She must have been the kid with a packed schedule from birth. He could picture her in every afterschool club available. "I shouldn't have absorbed as much as I did. I spent plenty of time reading and playing outside. I've always been drawn to stories. I couldn't help but pay attention to the TV if it was on."

"Too bad you didn't read to Shakes tonight. I'm sure he would have appreciated one of your dragon books."

"There's always tomorrow." He held her gaze. His palms itched to trace the curve of her cheek. "Thanks for all of your help. I'm sorry about what happened."

"Joe called." She lifted her mouth in a sad, half-smile. "I wondered if that was why you didn't question me about the email. I'm sorry if pity was the reason you asked me to stay."

"No, I wanted you to," he murmured. He was approaching a delicate topic. Raising a fist to his mouth, he cleared his throat. "I wanted to thank you for your help. Are you okay? Do you want to talk? I'm sorry you are in a bad position because of us." He pointed at the sleeping child.

Maddy's blanket covered torso rose and fell with her deep even breaths. She was truly asleep. The little girl slept harder than anyone he'd ever known. He could speak freely without worry of upsetting his niece.

"Maddy's mom is coming up this weekend?" Stephanie asked. "For good?"

He nodded. Living with his sister again would be challenging. Jen was a messy, multitasker. She operated best at a hundred miles per hour, tackling more in sixty minutes than most did in sixty days. She exhausted him.

He liked the cozy little cabin with him and Maddy. He enjoyed the daily meet-up with Stephanie. Everything was about to change. He'd finally accepted his new normal. He felt a pang of nostalgia for the past couple weeks.

Maddy missed her mom, and he didn't begrudge the little girl for wishing the time away. The pair would stay with him for another few months before settling in a new home or an apartment. For someone who sought solace in the status quo, the constant upheaval should be upsetting. He was more worried about the shifting dynamics. He'd only found his footing. He wasn't ready to let go.

Stephanie lifted a shoulder in a shrug. "I think I know what I like most about the movie."

If she wanted to jump to another conversational topic, she'd come to the right guy. He was a master of deflection. "My singing and dancing?" he asked.

"Both are excellent." She smiled.

The expression was the same soft, sad twist of her lips she'd had when he said hello and invited her in. He would never push. He knew too well that people built up their walls to protect themselves. If he wanted his personal safety respected, he owed others the same. But still, he almost did push her. Maybe he was the only one who could.

"No what I liked most is it made showbusiness seem like such a natural job opportunity," she said, her tone wistful.

"Isn't it?"

"If only. No career is easy."

"We can get lucky. Find ourselves in the right place at the right time." He had. If he hadn't stopped in Herd, he didn't know where he would have ended. Coming to the town felt like kismet when it happened. Everything that happened in the years since only reinforced his feelings.

"I don't know how many details you've heard. But I'm on leave pending a review. I don't know what to expect."

His chest tightened. Because of Maddy and him? He reached a hand to stroke his jaw, swallowing the metallic aftertaste filling his mouth. He should ask her why she did it. Why she helped him.

She could claim it was helping a child. She'd have done the same for any of the students in her class. But she hadn't. She'd done this for him. She risked her position and reputation. Her job needed her. The town needed her.

Did he? "I'm really sorry," he said.

"Don't be sorry. I knew what I was doing." She stretched her arms over the back of the couch again. "I thought I had administration support. I didn't. But don't be sorry because I'm not. I don't live with regrets."

He wished he could say the same. He would have claimed it even a few hours ago. But that was in the time before when their interactions were an equal exchange at every turn. And now they'd reached a different moment. Words couldn't go unsaid any longer. They'd reached either the end or the beginning. He wasn't sure what he was hoping for.

"Be honest. Do you really think the age difference between is us fourteen years?" she asked. "Not what the passage of time says. But does it *feel* like we have a double-digit gap separating us?"

He opened his mouth.

"Because I don't feel it. You've had more experiences than me. Everyone has. Age and time are fluid concepts. Hank could be in his thirties for how cheeky and wry he is. Some days, I feel ancient."

"You're right," he said, quickly and reached a hand to hold hers. If he didn't stop her, he'd never get a chance to speak. "The years between us is more of an outward concern than inward."

Her hand twitched.

"I don't care what society thinks about me," he said. "I'm lucky to be here in this place. We value our neighbors."

"But?" she murmured.

"You are so sweet and so unaffected. I'm dark and moody. You need someone better. Don't get lumped in with me."

She snorted and rolled her eyes, tugging back her hand to fold her arms over her chest.

"It's true." He glanced at his sweet niece. He'd spared her the worst of his sad and angry days by moving out of their hometown long before she was born.

As long as he'd stayed on his farm, he couldn't shake the tragedy. He'd been long gone when his sister announced her pregnancy. While he'd had a momentary pang for moving away and missing out on Maddy's day to day growing up, he'd been glad that she hadn't known the version of him he'd been in California. With Maddy and Jen's move, Ted came out ahead, finding home and family in the same space again. "I told you I'm a widower."

She nodded and arched a brow.

And? Her expression spurred him on, challenging him. "I had a whole, full life with someone else in another place."

And? She didn't move.

"I was different before."

"I didn't know you then."

"I can't be that man anymore."

"I'm not trying to change you, and especially not into a stranger," she murmured.

Her words were soft and honest and heartbreakingly poignant. He'd always love his wife. But Liv was gone. And if the roles had been reversed, he would have wanted her to move on and have the family and home they'd dreamed about. Even if it was with someone else.

He drew in a breath but instead of hitching along every rib, he was lighter. He could no longer remember why he'd built a wall around his heart. Why was he acting like there was no future but also refusing to live in the present?

If they had no tomorrow, why not be honest and a little reckless tonight? If it's all going to end, why not take the risk? He leaned forward. With his fingertips, he reached out and grazed her cheek and chin.

She licked her bottom lip. Her tongue darted quickly across her mouth.

The air changed. The space between them suddenly charged. He leaned forward. He couldn't go back once he did this. He wouldn't. No matter what came next.

She sighed, and her eyelids fluttered close. She tilted her face towards him.

From the corner of his eye, he saw a spark. He dropped his hand and turned. Maybe he'd imagined the streak of lightning. Then came the ground rattling boom. He'd be glad for a thunderstorm if it meant rain.

She sucked in a breath.

He faced her, tipping his head to the side and considering her pale face.

Lifting an arm, she pointed out the window. Her hand shook. "Fire," she murmured.

CHAPTER 14

Stephanie had imagined herself in a dream. All too soon, she found herself in a nightmare. Swiveling off the couch in one smooth movement, Ted could have been a dancer. As her mind formed the thought, she knew how unhelpful her brain was. But she couldn't focus on what or where she was needed. She stood on wobbly limbs, locking her knees to stay upright. She was moving through gelatin or quick sand or anything else better suited to a sitcom than a life or death problem. A real emergency unfolded, and she couldn't quite send the signals from her brain to her body and back again.

Thankfully, he didn't have the same problem. He raced out of the room and flung open the front door. It crashed against the wall and snapped her back to the present.

She padded toward the entryway. The tiles were icy under her sock covered feet. A horrible, acrid smell filtered into the room. Why did the outside smell like plastic? She'd always been comforted by the smell of woodsmoke. But this overwhelming stench was different.

Wrapping her arms around her torso, she crept onto the covered porch. In the dark, she squinted. Beside the orange light of the flame, she couldn't see anything. It was a cloudy, moonless night.

She pulled the front door closed and walked down the front steps. With each step, she adjusted to the dark. When she spotted him, she sighed.

Holding a hose, he followed a thin line of fire, soaking the ground. He was fighting with success. And he moved fast. The grass fire was nearly put out. Thank goodness. The ground was so dry, they could be encapsulated in a ring of flames within seconds.

How had it started? She hadn't heard thunder. Was she too distracted to notice? She cupped her hands around her mouth. "Hey."

He lifted his head, briefly acknowledging her presence. Then lowered his chin again.

The ground shook. A streak of lightning brightened the sky with a terrible glow.

He dropped the hose on the ground, turned toward the house, and took off at a jog disappearing from view.

Where was he going? Had he heard her? He'd sort of acknowledged her but not in any significant way. He hadn't asked for help or offered instruction. She hated not knowing what to do.

Facing the house, she saw the next bolt of lightning and felt the heave of the earth with the boom of thunder. If the streak wasn't so close to those she loved, she would have marveled at the ferocity. Instead, she ran.

She chased after him, rounding the side of the house. She raced ahead and collided with his back.

He was frozen in place. Why? Then she saw it, the most awesome and frightening sight she'd ever beheld. Flames licked the left side of the barn. An old structure that had seemed immortal now succumbed to Mother Nature.

"Oh no," she murmured. Her heavy limbs trembled. What could they do?

Crackling echoed in the otherwise silent night. It was horrible. Shouldn't something so devastating and destructive sound an alarm? Wasn't the outbuilding retrofitted with sprinklers?

He grabbed her shoulders. "Call Joe and James and Ian. Call the brigade. Call anyone."

She nodded, wide-eyed and took a step forward. She'd help. She could throw a bucket of water onto the flames.

"No, don't. Go back inside. Take care of Maddy and Colby. Get the fire extinguisher by the front door."

She opened her mouth to object.

"Please." He squeezed her shoulder and dropped his hold.

The single word was a shaky plea. With a nod, she spun and raced back around the house to the front. She let herself inside and shut the heavy door. If only she could shut out the bad things happening on the other side as easily.

She was helpless.

A whimper came from her left.

"Maddy? Colby?" she murmured, tiptoeing away from the door toward the front room. She retraced her steps. She should turn on a light. She didn't know this house well enough to navigate in the dark. Why didn't she have any issues finding the door when she'd left?

The TV had been on.

She bumped into a table, the sharp edge hitting her thighs. She sucked in a sharp breath, wincing at the pain. She'd found her way out thanks to the ambient light of the television, and the front door left ajar by Ted. Now the space was plunged into darkness. The power was out.

A transformer had blown somewhere. She went to the wall, flipping the switch in an act of futility. But she had to try. *Fire extinguisher by the door.* She felt her way there, finding the cold hard cylinder on the ground and then slowly made her way back to the couch.

"Shh, shh, shh," she murmured. To herself or the dog or the child? Didn't matter. All three needed comforting.

With her hands outstretched, she hit the back of the couch.

Colby woofed under her breath.

"It's okay, it's me," she said, cooing to herself, the dog, and any ghosts that might haunt the old home. "Maddy? Are you here?"

"Uh, huh," came the shaky, voice cracking reply.

Feeling her way along the back of the couch, Stephanie returned to her spot on the right side. Close to the girl and the dog just in case. Colby was fond of humans but in a tense situation, anything could go wrong. "Sweetie, it's okay." Stephanie sank onto the cushion and reached for the little girl, smoothing her hair.

Maddy remained curled into a tight ball with Colby resting her furry muzzle on the little girl's legs. Her body wracked with shudders, shaking the furniture with the same force as the thunder. "I've got sh . . . sh . . . Shakes." Her teeth chattered. "He was scared."

Stephanie drew in a deep breath. Outside she had been out of her depth. Whatever may or may not be happening with Ted threw her for a loop. But she could be strong for a child.

Grabbing a throw blanket off the back of the couch, she wrapped the thick knit around the little girl's shoulders. "The power is out, but we are okay," she said softly, stroking the child's hair. "I need your help. Do you know where the house phone is?" *Or my purse?* She could barely see a few inches in front of her face.

"In the kitchen." Maddy sniffed. "Colby knows the way."

The mutt hopped onto the ground, her nails clicking against the slate floor.

Carefully, Stephanie stood.

Maddy got to her feet. "Do you think I can leave Shakes here? I don't want him to be scared."

Her kindness in the face of her own vulnerability touched Stephanie's heart. "He'll be okay. He knows you need him to be brave."

"Okay." Maddy draped the blanket around the stuffed dog. Bending, she held onto Colby's back. "Follow us."

Stephanie rested a hand lightly on the little girl's back. The unlikely conga line made their way through the front room and hall and into the kitchen.

Red-tinted light poured in through the windows. The awful fire lit brightness reflected the painted barn as it became engulfed in lashing, licking flames. But she could see. In a few steps, she crossed to the wall and grabbed the cordless phone off its cradle, dialing the emergency number.

"Oh, no. Unc!" Maddy stopped near the sink.

"Shh, Shh." Stephanie pressed the phone to her ear. "It's okay, sweetie. He's fine. Let's call for help. Everything will be fine. We need to do our part. Unc has everything under control."

She hoped. Because she'd never been less certain of a situation in her whole life. And this wasn't the moment for anything less than her best.

Ted hadn't believed in signs. He had never put much stock in fate or karma either. Losing Liv couldn't have been destiny. No higher power could be so cruel and expect worship. But maybe he should reconsider. He stared at the flames on the side of the barn, frozen in place for several seconds as his brain processed what was happening.

He had to stop it, as much as he was able, before the fire spread. The hose attached to the back side of the house wouldn't stretch far enough to save the barn. He hoped the hose still running on the front continued to pour water onto the cracked ground. He'd build a moat around the house to protect Maddy and Stephanie if he could.

Instead of water, he'd run inside the barn to grab the extinguisher. With his elbow, he slammed the glass case near the entrance, shattering the door and pulling out the fire extinguisher. The old beams and boards released a pleasant smell of woodsmoke. After the grass fire, the scent was a relief. His eyes watered from the plastic, chemical like emission.

He pulled the pin and scanned his surroundings, shocked by the turn of events. The barn had stood for generations. *If it burns, we can rebuild.* Hank had expressed the sentiment with a shrug of indifference, frustrated by the efforts to retrofit the building instead of new construction due to sentimentality.

Ted would never have guessed he'd be alone, fighting to save it. If he had, he would have pushed to add a sprinkler system when he'd learned of the updated codes while overseeing construction of the spa barn. Grandfathered in with building codes, Hank and Ryan had waved off the safety concerns over a decade ago.

Ted heard a crackle and then a creak. He glanced up in time to see one of the beams overhead catch fire. He raced out of the door. He wasn't a hero and wasn't sticking around to die like one. He had to make sure Maddy and Stephanie were safe.

By the time, he felt cool night air on his cheeks a wave of heat pushed him forward. He turned, fire extinguisher at the ready.

The roof collapsed inward. The crash of heavy beams and splintering wood echoed.

For a second, he didn't move. The horror of watching something that had stood sentry for generations rattled him. A family's history gone in an instant. It was horrible to witness.

He couldn't save the building, but he could make sure the flames didn't spread. He started to run. Lapping the barn, he sprayed the perimeter with retardant until he reached the deck. Then he had to lengthen his strides, jogging past his hard work. The fire had already begun to catch on the lumber he'd toiled over.

By the time he returned to his starting point, the smoke thickened. Panting from exertion, he breathed in the billowing air and coughed. His throat and lungs burned. He stopped, bending over to drag in deep shaky breaths.

The fire extinguisher ran out of the contents. He threw it to the ground, his mind racing as he triaged the situation. He couldn't do more for the barn. As much as he hated to walk away from the deck after months of work, he had to focus on containment.

He raced to the side of the ranch house, turning on the spigot and grabbing the garden hose. Stretching the hose as far towards the barn as possible, he sprayed the ground. The water rolled off the cracked earth and brown grass. It might take as long as half an hour for the drought-stricken land to absorb the moisture. He wouldn't worry about time. He'd stay and do his best.

This was why he'd been right to be alone. No matter how much Maddy's childish jokes brightened his whole day. No matter Stephanie's shy smile made him feel like he was living a good life. Caring about people meant he was vulnerable. He couldn't handle losing someone he loved again. He was a coward, but he wasn't a fool.

Please let the rain come. He snorted and shook his head. If willing was manifesting, he would never have arrived on the ranch. He'd be at home in California with a couple of kids by now.

Flashing lights and a siren drew his attention to the side of the house.

He exhaled, nearly collapsing forward, and dropped the garden hose. Help had finally arrived. He strode around the covered porch.

Joe and the rest of the volunteer firefighters reached the ranch.

Ted cupped his hands around his mouth. "It's the barn." His hoarse voice croaked, and he started coughing.

The fire engine drove around the house without slowing or stopping.

The flames must be visible from the road. He'd strained his voice for no reason. *Powerless.* He hated the feeling. He raced back around the house.

The fire engine parked. The crew descended and got to work on the barn. Two of the team worked in tandem to unfurl the hose and douse the flames. Another produced an ax and walked around the back.

With their training on full display, Ted realized he was out of his element. The adrenaline drained out of him, leaving him numb. How much time had passed since he sent Stephanie inside? The minutes stretched to an eternity as history turned to ash. But where was Maddy? Stephanie? Why weren't the lights on?

He backtracked to the side of the house, turning off the water and letting himself in through the back door. "Maddy? Stephanie? Colby?" He coughed again, shutting the door, and slipping out of his boots. He couldn't see. Crossing to the wall, he flipped the switch but nothing happened. The brief electrical storm had cut the power.

"Unc?" A little voice asked.

His heart cracked as a small body collided with his legs. Bending, he squinted and reached for Maddy. Embracing her, holding her tight against his chest. A rough tongue licked his cheek. "Oh, hi Colby," he croaked and coughed.

Maddy giggled.

The dog continued lapping his face with her sandpaper tongue.

"Okay, okay, enough." He petted the dog and stood, holding onto Maddy's hand. He couldn't lose track of her again. When his sister came back, he'd be able to resume his rightful place in the sidelines of his niece's world. His ultimate fear almost came true again. He can't protect those he loves. He desperately wanted the love of his family, but he couldn't be in the midst of it. He'd endanger those he held most dear. Because when the worst happened, he was useless.

"The fire is almost out," Stephanie said.

Silhouetted by the kitchen window, he couldn't see her face. Her hunched posture looked defeated and fragile. "Thank you for taking care of them," he murmured, forcing the words out of his scratchy throat. "Squirrel, let's go in the family room. I can't find the way upstairs without the lights."

"Okay," Maddy whispered.

Clutching his niece's clammy hand, he led the way back down the hall, humming one of the songs from the movie musical. He felt Maddy relax, her tense grip lightening. He settled her on the couch, tucking the blanket around her.

Colby jumped up and laid down next to the little girl, resting her head on the girl's legs.

"Good dog," he murmured. "I have to go outside for the firefighters. Stay here with Miss Patricks. Please?"

Instead of a reply, a snore escaped the little girl.

Stephanie sat on the other end of the couch. "Go. I'll take care of her."

Ted wanted a few more moments with Stephanie. But in the dark, after the fire, he didn't know what to say. Maybe another person would be compelled to seize the day after surviving a life or death scenario, but not him. He couldn't take a chance on love again. He couldn't be the man she needed or deserved, so he left.

CHAPTER 15

Stephanie stretched her arms over head, her fingers hitting something soft and solid. Her bed had no headboard. This morning, she touched fabric and not drywall. She opened her eyes and stared up at a ceiling. She pressed her hands to her sides and raised herself against a smooth, cool cushion. Where was she? She surveyed the room including the massive stone fireplace and hardwood floors.

Realization slammed into her. She was angled on the leather couch in the front room of the Kincaid ranch. Next to her, Maddy and Colby slept, curled up in twin tight balls. On the ground, Shakes, the stuffed retriever, laid on his side. His glass bead eyes somehow bore into Stephanie, peering deep into her soul. Ted was gone.

Slowly rolling off the couch, she stood. She stretched her neck from one side to the next and twisted her torso. After the fire, she hadn't left. She told herself, the power was out, and she wasn't sure she couldn't leave if Ted needed help again.

In the morning light, she saw how slim her excuses were. She remained because she wanted to be here. She was touched by his tenderness. He knew exactly what to do in every situation from fighting the fire to calming his niece. She'd been awed. She felt safe and secure with his steady, stoic presence. After her rollercoaster day, she really needed him, and he came through.

She had been relieved when he hadn't asked her to leave. Exhaustion slammed into her within seconds. Curled up on the couch, she had fallen asleep, unconcerned with what anyone might think or the crick she'd get in her neck from the awkward positioning on the cushion.

Last night was long gone. Thin streaks of sun poured through the front window. She grabbed the stuffed toy off the floor, tucking him next to Maddy. She crossed the room and gazed at the front yard and circular drive. A patch of burnt grass was visible from the front window. The sky remained full of clouds but these didn't seem heavy with rain any more than the ones from last night. How bad was the barn? She shuddered. She was grateful the fire had been contained.

On her drive over after school, she had mentally talked herself into acting like the consequences wouldn't matter. She thought she could live like there was no tomorrow. She hadn't been prepared for the terror of thinking her days might end. On tiptoes, she turned and crept toward the kitchen. Last night's fire had proven her new mindset was the right one.

As she entered the kitchen, a blinking light caught in the corner of her eye. She turned her head. The microwave and oven flashed twelve o'clock. The power was restored.

Turning toward the table, she spotted her purse on the bench. Inside, her phone was on silent. More likely than not, she would have missed a couple calls and texts from Kelly. She hoped not from Lauren. If Stephanie stressed her friend and risked Lauren's well-being, Stephanie would never forgive herself. But neither of her friends would expect an immediate reply. She wasn't quite sure how early it was and didn't have to race out of here.

Doing so would be irresponsible. She couldn't leave while Maddy was inside unaccompanied. At the very least, she'd have to find Ted and say goodbye. She might as well make coffee before doing so.

A yawn hit her hard. She spotted the coffee maker next to the sink. She filled the reservoir, located filters and grounds in containers next to the machine, and hit brew. As the percolating started, she stared out across the backyard toward the remains of the barn.

A pile of red and black wood occupied the space.

She recoiled. She hadn't grown up in Herd. Like many, she was a transplant. The small-town was either the starting point or the final destination, but not many people stayed their whole lives. The Kincaids were the exception. Ryan and his grandfather Hank were both born and raised. Seeing their historic barn reduced to ashes shocked her down to her core. What stood for generations was gone in one night. Everything could be erased in an instant.

The night taught her one important lesson. Stop wasting time by not being honest. She owed herself that much.

The coffee maker beeped.

She jumped.

"Miss Patricks?" A little voice asked. Stephanie turned and spotted Maddy and Colby standing inside the doorway.

Maddy flicked on the light switch.

Stephanie blinked. Now she was definitely awake. She plastered on a smile for the child. "Good morning, Maddy."

"Do you know where my unc is?"

Good question. "I'm not sure. I just woke up, too."

A stomach growled. Colby woofed.

"Me and Colby are starving," Maddy said. "Shakes, too."

"Sure." Stephanie wiped her clammy palms on her pants and crossed to the fridge. She rooted around someone the fridge like she belonged there. Already pushed out of her polite comfort zone. After she fed Maddy, she would march out of the house, find Ted, and kiss him. She vowed to stop wasting time waiting for permission.

She scanned the fridge's well-stocked contents. Every ingredient needed more preparation to craft a meal then she felt comfortable tackling. She didn't want to turn on the stove and make eggs or whip up French toast in the oven. "Toast with cinnamon and sugar?"

Maddy licked her lips. "Yes, please." She strolled to the dog's bowls set in the corner.

Stephanie made her way to the corner of the counter, housing the toaster, bread basket, butter, and spices. She made quick work of the easy breakfast, as the sounds of kibble hitting the metal bottom of the dish and running water at the sink for the water bowl filled the room.

Stephanie opened the upper cabinets, finding the glasses, mugs, and plates. She pulled down a few of everything and opened various drawers, utensils clattering with the tug of each handle. The morning soundtrack was reassuring.

She buttered the toast, sprinkled the cinnamon and sugar over it, and carried the plate over to the table. Shakes was propped on the top, waiting for his temporary owner. Maddy approached with a carton of milk, Stephanie poured the glass and returned the half gallon to the fridge. Movement outside the window caught her attention.

Ted walked toward the destroyed barn, his chin down and shoulders slumped.

Now or never. "Maddy, I'm going to go talk to Unc. Can you and Colby stay inside?" Maddy shook her head.

"You can't?" Stephanie's stomach dropped. She'd just talked herself into what she had to do and hadn't factored in resistance.

"I need to take Colby out. I'll put her on the leash."

"Can you stick very close to the house? I don't think it's good for either of you to get too close to the burned sections."

"Okay," Maddy said through a mouthful of toast.

Stephanie chuckled and strode toward the mugs she'd set next to the coffee maker. Filling both to the brim, she held both mug handles in one hand, opened the back door a crack and slid outside, shutting the door behind her.

A chilly breeze snaked past her, blowing the smell of smoke. She shivered and curled her bare toes against the ground. She should go back inside and get shoes. Hadn't she warned about the dangers out here? If she turned back now, however, she'd lose her courage.

Under her feet, the ground was cold and hard, rising in misshapen lumps with footprints scattered across. She'd heard water running but hadn't realized he'd turned on the back hose. Heat from the mugs warmed her chilly hands. She put one foot in front of the other, heading toward the barn. With each step, the smell became stronger, and acrid. Stopping as close as she dared without shoes, she breathed in charred wood mixed with melted metal and plastic. The flames had been indiscriminate, burning the whole structure.

"Stephanie?"

She turned her head, gaping. He stood near what had been the deck. From her position, she shouldn't have been able to see him. A building should have blocked her view.

Her heart sank. All his hard work reduced to nothing. His time wasted. But not hers. If he hadn't worked on the project, he wouldn't have needed help with pick up. She wouldn't have chatted with him so much. She held up a mug. "I brought coffee."

Walking in a loop around the ash, he accepted the coffee. "Thanks." He took a long sip and glanced down. Meeting her gaze, he frowned. "Where are your shoes?"

"I didn't . . . I wasn't . . ." She cleared her throat. "I hadn't planned on coming outside until I spotted you." *And I couldn't waste a second once I did.* She sipped her coffee. She preferred creamer to cut through the bitter taste but was glad for the extra jolt of caffeine. "How can I help?"

"Is Maddy awake?"

"Yep, and Colby. I fed her, and she took care of the dog. She might walk Colby on a leash close to the house." Stephanie drank again. With the mug raised, she glanced at him over the brim. He was quiet.

She was used to his stoic, reserved personality. But this morning was different. He stood in front of her but was hiding somehow. His jaw was set, and his eyes clouded. Only a few feet away, he was distant. The friendly man of last night had vanished.

Not surprising. He was probably trying to figure out how and what he'd tell his bosses. The fire was hardly his fault, but it was a major catastrophe and would impact the business. Not just in the immediate clearing of debris and rebuilding but long term.

Their community had never been so dry as this year but that was only after last year's record-setting drought. Wildfires burned faster and longer. If every year became the worst in a century, the community couldn't count on problems only every couple generations.

"What can I do?" She pulled back her shoulders.

He looked at the ground again.

She rested one foot on top of the other. "After I get shoes on, of course. I can help. What do you need?"

He shook his head and took a long drink of coffee.

"Come on, it was a good thing I was here last night. Let me keep helping." She hadn't intended turning the conversation in this direction. But now that she was here, it felt right. She had to be helpful. If she wasn't, if she didn't advocate, who else would? She wasn't backing off the conversation about where they headed next. Instead, she was providing a more natural opportunity for the talk to spark organically. "I can help."

"You can't. One person can't change a thing," he snapped. His words were sharp in a foreign tone. He turned away.

She wouldn't be put off so easily.

He faced her. "You don't have to always be the one leading the fight. Sometimes you just need to sit and listen. There are other people who can step up. Doesn't always have to be you."

She wasn't sure she understood. "Maybe you're right." She said the words softly. She didn't believe them. If he did, however, he wouldn't respond well to badgering. "I can't stop everything bad from happening."

He snorted, his shoulders shrugging.

She inched forward. "But what if one person could make real change? They just had to be brave?" She reached a hand toward his shoulder.

He stepped away. "Then I'd wonder if it was courage or foolishness. We have differences too big to overcome."

She drew back her hand and clutched the mug. His words had been a verbal slap. He'd shifted from a broad discussion to a narrow argument so quickly that he'd almost pushed her away. She wouldn't be so easily put off.

She drank the last of her coffee. Was he going to break up with her before anything had started? All she was going to get was one almost kiss? She refused to accept that. The bitter coffee couldn't compete with the foul taste filling her mouth. She could pretend she didn't understand him. But she did, all too well. She was tired of games. "Are you talking about our age gap? If I was older?"

"No, that's not it."

"If I had some big tragedy?"

He sucked in a breath.

She'd put her foot in her mouth in spectacular fashion. Good thing she forgot her shoes, or she'd start choking. She was a jerk for even thinking it.

"I would never want that for you," he said. His words were almost a growl. Was the huskiness from smoke inhalation or emotion? "You deserve happiness. Always."

Just not with you? "Tell me why?" she asked, her voice cracking.

"Because I lo—" He shook his head and faced the ashes. "Just go, please."

For a painfully long second, she couldn't function. Her brain couldn't process how to make her limbs bend and move. She couldn't save herself from this pain. A laugh built low in her belly. The shudders wracked her torso and restarted her locomotion. She had just enough dignity not to linger.

She stalked back to the house, grabbed her purse, hugged Maddy goodbye, and was out the door and in her car. At least she wouldn't have to face anybody. Since she was on leave. What a joke. She was being blamed for favoritism and following her heart. In truth, she'd skidded in a brick wall and been too oblivious to avoid the head-on collision.

Ted drummed his fingers against his thighs and stared—unblinking and unseeing—at the horizon. He didn't look down at the mess on the ground. Since waking a few hours ago, he'd toured every inch of what had been the barn and deck. With only the foundation intact, the whole thing needed to be rebuilt.

Now he focused on keeping still. On not turning around and apologizing and agreeing he wanted to give them a chance. He needed to let Stephanie walk away. It was the kindest thing he could do. For either of them.

He curled his hands into fists, counting to a hundred. When he left her sleeping on the couch, curled up next to Maddy and the dog, he almost reconsidered. She looked so peaceful despite the awkward twist of her body to fit onto the sofa. He knew she wouldn't complain. She was so accommodating and yet firm, a perfect mix of strength and spontaneity.

But he couldn't. Overextending himself emotionally, he'd stood on the brink of ruin last night as the terror of the fire highlighted everything he stood to lose. He couldn't endure another tragedy.

Stephanie wouldn't give him a chance at peace or rest. Her angelic, sleeping face hid the truth of her constant need for advocacy. She wasn't a person who spent much time relaxing. His quiet evenings spent reading alone would be gone. He appreciated her fierce spirit. But he couldn't imagine joining her in every battle she waged. If his ultimate goal was calm, he wouldn't find it in a relationship with her. He was right to push her away. He forced a momentary hurt for her good, not that she could see it yet. She'd probably leave if her job was gone. Why stay?

His jaw tightened. He opened his mouth and shut it, forcing the muscles to clench and unclench. Taking in a deep breath, he filled his lungs with the still smoky air. A relationship with Stephanie was doomed to fail.

"Unc, what are you doing?"

He turned and squinted, rubbing the crust from his eyes to clear his vision.

Colby tugged the leash, panting as she led Maddy down the yard toward him.

"Stop there, squirrel." He jogged the few yards toward her. "I'm not sure how safe it is. There are sharp things like nails mixed with ashes in the ground. I don't want you getting hurt."

"You're dirty."

He scrubbed his face with the hem of his shirt. Soot and sweat collected on the cotton. "I need a bath."

"Miss Patricks left."

He swallowed the sigh building in his chest. He knew.

"But Mr. Joe is here." She pointed toward the house. Joe raised a hand and waved from the porch.

Thank goodness. This time he didn't hold in his heavy exhale. He needed another able body. Stephanie could have been the help, but he couldn't separate out his feelings from his needs. "Squirrel, can you go inside? Are you hungry? Do you need food?"

"Miss Patricks made me cinnamon toast." Maddy licked her lips and widened her eyes. "We need to show Shakes the ranch, remember?"

He chuckled. He'd probably regret the little girl eating sugar first thing in the morning, but he wouldn't second-guess what had already happened. If he started down that path, he'd wallow in self-recrimination for the rest of the day. Stephanie did the best she could in the circumstances. He had to do the same. "Okay. I'll be in soon. I need to talk to Mr. Joe."

She shrugged and tugged the leash. "Come on, Colby." The dog happily sniffed the ground, wagging her tail and leading the way.

Probably eager to lay on a bed. He waved a hand to Joe. who crossed the yard, greeting the ladies as he passed. He wore heavy work boots.

Ted wasn't sure what compelled Stephanie to traipse outside in her bare feet. Had it been him? Hoping for a resolution to the almost kiss? He shook his head and stared at the ground, kicking a rock with his boot.

"Hey, good morning," Joe said.

"Hey." Ted lifted his chin and nodded.

Joe whistled and approached the remnants of the barn.

Ted followed and stopped at his friend's side. "Yep."

"I was afraid of how bad it would look in the morning. Somehow this is worse than what I imagined."

Ted had no response. He agreed. He could only be grateful the fire had been successfully contained and put out by the crew. The rain never came. The ground remained dry as kindling.

"Any luck reaching the Kincaids?" Joe asked.

"Nope." Ted dragged the toe of his boot into the thin layer of ash. With a rake, he might be able to scrape off the soot. He wasn't sure any efforts would ease the shock of the changed landscape. His feeble words wouldn't offer much consolation either. He raised his gaze to his friend and shrugged. "I left messages for Hank and Ryan this morning. I'm not likely to get a call back. I think it might be a big day."

Joe widened his gaze. "Are you talking about a proposal?"

Ted nodded. While Hank was known for losing his cell phone, Ryan was fused to the device. Last night, Ted had decided against waking the men. By the time the fire was out, the hour had grown too late.

This morning, Ted tried again. Ryan's must be powered off. Every call immediately received the voicemail message. Only a big reason, like a proposal, would justify Ryan turning off his phone. Ted was happy for his boss and friend but his ribs tightened and his eyes burned. He'd admitted to himself—and almost to her—that he loved her. He couldn't offer her the happiness she deserved. He wouldn't begrudge anyone their joy. "I haven't seen a ring but I have my suspicions. I wasn't a kid detective though."

Joe chuckled at the jibe. "Hank will be truly incorrigible if Meg says yes. He'll take all the credit."

Ted shot his friend a pointed look. Meg and Ryan were destined for each other. Everyone knew it.

"Alright." Joe pulled a pair of work gloves from his back pocket and slipped them over his hands. "Where can we start? And don't push me away. You can't do this alone."

It's not hard when there is nothing to salvage. Ted nodded and strode to the gravel parking lot on the side of the building. Earlier, he had driven to the spa barn and collected every trash can he could find and parked close to the ruins.

In silence, Joe followed.

Together, they grabbed the empty cans from the bed of the truck and filled each one with sharp items they found amid the debris. After they had the loaded each garbage to the top and neatly arranged all in the bed like a puzzle game, they closed the hatch.

With a sigh, Ted turned to survey. Their hard work had barely made a dent in the clean-up. Now he'd have to drive the load to the dump and see about arranging several dumpsters for the rest. All of that would wait. He didn't want to permanently remove any piece of history from the ranch without Hank's say so.

"Thanks for stopping by. And for last night."

Joe shrugged. "I'm sorry for all your hard work on the deck."

"It's not worth anything anyway."

Joe drew back his chin and stared.

Flinching, Ted turned away. He couldn't help his cold attitude. Despite an hour's work, he remained cold from the inside out. "I'm glad you came quick last night. I'm grateful to you and the crew."

"I got the call from Stephanie." Joe crossed his arms over his chest and leaned forward. "Was she here last night?"

"Yes, but it wasn't like that." Ted hated the suggestion of any untoward behavior. Stephanie didn't deserve to be the subject of gossip.

"How was it?"

Joe asked with such tenderness and care that he threatened Ted's hard exterior. "She dropped off Maddy. You told me she was upset. I didn't want her to think no one cared or appreciated her. She stayed for dinner." He scrubbed his face with both hands. He wasn't going to rationalize or justify yesterday's actions. "Doesn't matter because it's over."

"Is it?"

Whirling around, Ted crossed his arms over his chest. "Zip it, Joe. Why did you come here?"

"To help." Joe held up his hands. "But you want to be alone."

No, not now and not ever. That's the problem. He sagged his shoulders. "I'm sorry, and thank you. I think there's nothing left to do here at the moment. Hopefully Ryan checks his messages so he won't be shocked when he gets home."

"I don't think that's possible."

Ted agreed. From a long-standing structure to charred remains, the landscape's sudden change was shocking. The point of a surprise was being totally unprepared for it. It's why he'd always hated the unexpected. He had no time to steel his response and lessen the impact. Love the first time had been a long slow build giving him ample opportunity to jump ship before reaching the next level of seriousness.

In life, he could only control his actions and responses. Never another person. Growing up with Liv had meant knowing her well enough to anticipate her needs and yet still enjoy the thrill of her questions and answers. She'd surprised him in the best ways with her contagious joy.

Stephanie was both a stranger and a friend. But he had the same awareness of her, understanding her wants, during a much shorter amount of time. He shouldn't know her as well as he had known his wife.

This time, he'd been smacked on the side of the head with love. And he'd never be the same. Because he couldn't give her what she needed. She deserved much better.

CHAPTER 16

Angry pop anthems and rage cleaning could only do so much for Stephanie. *We could be happy if you let us.* The words thrummed through her veins, pulsing in time with her heart. As she stripped her sheets, washed every linen, beat her rugs, and scrubbed her grout, she couldn't shake the mantra. She should have said it to his face.

He was frustrating. He was such a puzzle at a time when she didn't have time to fit pieces together. He opened up and invited her in only to push her out and slam the door.

He provided a good distraction from her work frustrations, but she wasn't content to categorize their exchange so superficially. He couldn't get hurt if he wasn't actively engaged so he hovered on the fringe of life. And once he finally started to interact with her, he couldn't let it continue.

She understood him better than he wanted. She was terrified of tragedy. But instead of hiding, she took action. She guided her path. After the fire, she wasn't going to sit around. He might have been short with her, but it wasn't anything new. She'd heard the whispers for years. *What's the deal with your savior complex? Do you live for the praise?*

She'd argue she needed no accolades and hadn't received any. If she didn't make something happen, it didn't happen. She preferred action. Clarity slammed into her.

He wanted to wait around. He wasn't ever going to let himself love or live. Stephanie left, and he didn't stop her. They had been getting close. She felt it in her heart and soul, but she couldn't make him love her back.

She redirected her feelings into cleaning, losing herself, until a text message interrupted her playlist. Lauren was admitted to the hospital for observation. Stephanie pushed aside every concern, racing to her friend's beside.

As she signed in at the front desk, applied her name tag, and waited for the door to open, she focused on her breathing to still her dread. She would not get emotional. She would not upset her friend. And—under no circumstances—could she discuss her leave of absence.

Her steps echoed in the hall as she plodded toward the room.

The door was ajar, propped with a doorstop. Kelly and Lauren's muted voices filtered out. Raising her fist, she knocked.

"Come in," Lauren called.

Stephanie pulled the small gift bag out of her giant tote and entered.

Lauren pushed herself up from a pile of pillows on the bed. Kelly stood next to her.

"I brought you contraband." Stephanie wiggled her eyebrows and set the bag on the tray table next to the bed, and squirted some of the giant bottle of hand sanitizer into her palm.

Lauren reached for the bag, looked inside, crinkling the tissue, and grinned. "I'm hiding this from the nurses and Steve." She tucked the bag under her blanket.

Stephanie laughed. "I'm sure you're allowed a little treat." Gummy bears and corn chips weren't a combination Stephanie cared for, but Lauren had a weakness for both. Stephanie had purchased the junk food to bring to the hospital after Lauren's delivery. But with doctor mandated bedrest, she needed the distraction now.

"Not according to anyone here." Lauren exhaled a heavy sigh. "I'm being monitored and evaluated. Everything is being recorded including my food. It's so boring. I thought it was bad at home. It's so much worse here. I have none of my stuff. I can't do any work. The TV has limited channels."

"Really?" Stephanie looked to Kelly for guidance. "Having someone else cook and clean sounds pretty good right now."

"I agree." Kelly nodded. "And she should enjoy the chance to rest before the babies get here."

"What do the doctors think? How much longer?" Stephanie asked.

"Maybe by the end of the week. They've given me some steroids to help with the babies' lung development. Which sounds really scary, but Bill told me his wife had the same. Their twins didn't have to stay in the hospital too long after they were born," Lauren said.

Stephanie offered a tight smile. "Oh, well. He would know."

Lauren folded her arms over her belly, interlacing her fingers. "Yep, he knows quite a bit."

Stephanie glanced from Kelly's frown to Lauren's pursed lips.

"You've heard what happened." Stephanie felt spotlighted by the overhead fluorescent bulbs. Her nostrils stung with the alcohol stench of the sanitizer and cleaners. She wasn't escaping this conversation. She nibbled her lip, her teeth sinking into the flesh. She didn't want to aggravate her friend. The dark smudges under her eyes and heavy breaths told Stephanie how worn-out Lauren was.

"You aren't going to stress me out by talking about your leave of absence. Kelly told me everything. What can we do? How can we help?" Lauren asked.

Stephanie lifted her chin and met the determined set of Lauren's chin and the soft smile in Kelly's gaze. Her friends always had her back. They had warned her. But she hadn't listened. Instead of telling her *I told you so* or shaking their heads in contempt, they consoled her. The unease of the last twenty-four hours drained the last of her anger, leaving only exhaustion and sadness. The tickle in her throat became a gasp as her eyes overflowed with tears and her nose started to run.

Kelly handed over a tissue box. Lauren squeezed her arm.

It was going to be okay. With the support of people Stephanie cared about, she would manage her way through. The truth stung. She couldn't hide from it and expect to feel resolution enough to move on. She grabbed the tissue and blew her nose. With another, she dabbed at her cheeks. "I was taken aback by how far the situation escalated. I didn't tell either of you, but Mrs. Vane confronted me at poker night. She threatened the future of the fundraising event."

"Why didn't you tell us?" Kelly asked.

"At first, I was shocked. I couldn't believe she was willing to be so flippant about a program that has become so vital to the community." Stephanie shrugged. "I didn't want to believe it was true. But I should have understood the warning. She was determined to bring me down. Guess she has."

"But you told Bill you were driving Maddy. It was only for a short time. He knew." Lauren wrinkled her brow.

Stephanie nodded. "He knew. I couldn't really fight back though against the claims of favoritism. If I'm honest, I'd admit helping Maddy wasn't an entirely selfless act." She paused.

They didn't exchange knowing looks. They just listened without judgement or condemnation. How had she gotten so lucky to find these friends? And why had she almost ruined her relationship with them after their warning? "I would help any child in my class. By assisting this student in particular, I had the chance to spend time with Ted."

"And how has that been?" Lauren asked.

Stephanie snorted and grabbed another tissue, blowing her nose again for good measure. "Foolish. He's not interested in me."

"Someone else?" Kelly asked.

Luckily, no. Stephanie wasn't sure she could stand by and watch that. Was that what happened next? Was she just the wrong person? Would he find love with someone else? Her heart ached. She shook her head. "Kelly, he'll email you the pictures from the class pet's adventure-filled stay at the ranch. I don't know who my sub will be. Maddy was so excited about taking the stuffed animal for the weekend. I didn't have the heart to cancel."

Kelly nodded. "I'll take care of that. Don't worry."

"What comes next?" Lauren asked.

"Bill asked me to come to a meeting with him Monday morning, before the closed-door board meeting," Stephanie said.

"What are you going to do?" Lauren asked.

Stephanie frowned. "About Ted or my job?"

"Both," Lauren replied.

"I don't know," Stephanie murmured.

Kelly reached for Lauren and Stephanie's hands.

Lauren extended her other hand.

Stephanie accepted both and squeezed.

"I hope you fight to stay," Kelly said. "You're a wonderful teacher. We'd miss you. So would the kids."

Stephanie smiled but didn't reply. She wasn't sure. After facing down a fire and a formal reprimand, she wasn't sure who she was or what she'd be.

But she couldn't pick up from where she had been before. She had a day to process before her meeting with Bill. She wasn't sure what the future held for her career. She proudly stood by her moral code and wouldn't back down on taking action. Not to placate the people who couldn't support her. She wanted someone to be at her side and not hiding in the wings. If that wasn't Ted, then good riddance. If only her heart could catch up to her brain.

Ted had spent the rest of his Saturday taking care of the horses and his niece. Cupcake the mare was particularly upset. While the stables were moved far enough from the barn not to be under threat from the fire, the smoky haze carried on the wind, irritating the sweet old girl. He'd given her extra oats and a thorough brushing. The horse had responded well to both.

With Shakes tucked under her arm, Maddy had offered her words of encouragement. So did Colby. Or, rather, low barks of commiseration.

He'd finally heard from Ryan around eight pm. Ted's suspicions proved correct. Ryan proposed to Meg and spent the day with his phone off to enjoy the celebration. He didn't want bad news to ruin his plans. He'd been smart.

Ted hadn't slept easy. With their arrival scheduled for Sunday afternoon sometime around when he expected his sister, he had plenty of chores before the Kincaids returned. But that wasn't the reason.

Long after Maddy fell asleep, Colby curled up on her legs, on one of the two twin mattresses in the guest bedroom, Ted had headed downstairs with his book. Reading always transported him far away from his cares. It was hard to remain rooted in the real world when on the back of a dragon, soaring over a fantastic kingdom and engaging in the various plots and intrigues of a royal court.

But he couldn't stop thinking about Stephanie. His beloved mythical beasts were tinged with the memory of her astonishment the first time she dropped off Maddy and scanned the spines on his bookshelves. He smiled, thinking back on her cute, surprised face. He liked catching her off-guard. He enjoyed letting another person see the playful side of him he didn't freely share. With her, he embraced it.

And now that he pushed her away, he had to return to the man he'd been. The steadfast and safe person who others could depend on. He wanted to cry. Despite the words blurring in his vision, he must have fallen asleep. Because he started Sunday on the couch, aching and cold.

After waking, he fed Colby and Maddy, cleaned the kitchen, and led the pair on a long walk around the property. Exercise had always been his balm and antidote. Angry? Sad? Confused? Working his muscles and body gave his brain the freedom to either solve the problem or give up and move on. Topping out at forty minutes, however, he wasn't any lighter mentally, but his companions were exhausted.

He glanced down at the panting dog and his winded niece, their shallow breaths evenly matched. He fought the chuckle building in his throat. The pair were adorable. Always. He might not be ready to take on more dependents, but he was glad for them. "We're almost back. I promise we walked in a loop."

"Unc, are you sure? I don't recognize any of this." She frowned, twisting her neck from one side to the other.

The landscape was very monotone in the autumn. Dormant, golden grass stretched into the horizon. In a few weeks, snow would blanket the ground. On cloudy days, the line between heaven and earth would be indistinguishable. In the bright sunshine, the glare from the frost-covered landscape would be blinding. He didn't love all seasons but respected the process. The weather's constant change was a reminder to him that nothing was permanent.

"If you squint, you can see the bar—where the barn used to be." He reached up and rubbed his tight chest. Would he always ache at the events of Friday night? If he hadn't had the ultimate sign from the universe, he would have kissed Stephanie.

Tires crunched over gravel, the sound broadcast in stereo on the other wise silent air.

"Mommy!" Maddy shouted and dropped the leash, racing ahead.

He stepped forward too late.

Colby ran off after the little girl, happily barking and shaking her tail. Like she was always ready to run and not the dog who loved to snooze.

He shook his head and jogged behind them. The pair certainly found their second wind when properly motivated. He continued forward, rounding the ranching house, reaching them on the drive and catching the leash. Jen held Maddy in a tight squeeze, lifting the little girl in her arms until Maddy's feet dangled.

He chuckled. His sister wasn't a very big person, and Maddy wasn't a baby anymore. For motherhood, however, she tapped into a strength she otherwise hid.

Colby woofed under her breath, wagging her tail.

"Hey, sit," he commanded. With one more low bark, the dog complied, her tail dusting the ground.

"Thanks for taking care of her, Ted." Jen set her daughter on the ground, keeping her arms wrapped around the little girl's shoulders.

"Of course. Squirrel is easy," he said.

"The fire was hard," Maddy added.

Jen widened her gaze. "Fire?"

He nodded. "The old barn burned down. Luckily it was contained. No one was hurt."

"Yikes. Are you okay?" Jen asked, narrowing her gaze. "How long were you exposed to the smoke? I have to head over to the hospital soon to pick up my badge. I was going to take Maddy. Should you come and get checked out?"

"I'm a little bruised, but I'll live." At least he'd stopped coughing or his sister wouldn't give him a choice. He didn't want to elaborate about the location and severity of his injuries. Breaking his own heart wasn't something a nurse could fix. "I was outside for much of it, and the wind blew in the opposite direction. Glad you're here. Our cabin is fine. Are you still planning on staying with me for a bit?"

"As long as you'll have us. My start date was pushed back a week. I thought I might tour a few places, just so I know what is out there when the time comes to move. I'm guessing I won't be able to sign a lease until January," Jen said. "I'm sure you want your space and some quiet."

"No rush." He meant it. He wasn't sure how he felt about being alone or left in silence for too long. "The new year is fine."

"Mommy, this is Shakes. He's pleased to meet you." Maddy held out the stuffed animal like a talisman. "He's our class pet, and Miss Patricks let me take care of him this weekend."

Jen shook the stuffed dog's front paw. "Shakes, it's a pleasure. Sounds like you have had an exciting visit."

"And we took pictures," Maddy chirped. "Unc can show you. I get to talk all about his visit at school tomorrow. Can he take a picture with you?"

"Sure, honey. Even better. Maybe he can get an I.D. at the hospital, too." Jen smiled.

A car horn honked.

"Come on, let's stand on the porch," he said, grabbing the leash and leading the dog out of the way.

The white SUV appeared, driving fast, and stopping with no care for the shocks. The vehicle doors opened and slammed shut in a syncopated rhythm.

Colby howled and lunged forward.

"Alright, go and say hi." He dropped the leash.

The dog leaped from the porch to the ground, clearing the stairs, and launched herself at Hank Kincaid, knocking him backwards into the SUV's door.

"Oh, I missed you, too," the old cowboy cooed, stroking the dog as he was lavished with kisses.

Meg and Ryan strolled forward, passing the pair.

"She used to be my dog," Meg said.

"What's yours is mine and vice versa, right?" Ryan asked, lifting their intertwined hands, and kissing her knuckles.

A flash of light from Meg's left hand caught Ted's attention. Being right usually felt more triumphant. After the tumultuous weekend, however, he could only manage a pleased smile.

"When is the wedding?" Ted asked, glad to jump on this topic.

"I was thinking we could combine it with Hank's birthday extravaganza," Meg said.

Hank grinned from ear to ear. "I can't wait to update Joe and Abby." He rubbed his hands.

"I'm thinking all the events might be on hold," Ryan said. "Ted, you burned down my barn?" He arched a brow in an exaggerated, joking manner.

Meg glared at her fiancé.

Ted shook his head. He wasn't sure he was ready to find humor in the terrifying situation.

"How bad is it?" Hank asked, holding Colby's leash, and striding forward with a slight hitch.

"Come see for yourselves," Ted said. He led the group around the side of the house. Once they reached the yard, their murmurs stopped.

Joe had helped clear away what he could. Ted needed machine power, a dumpster, and a crew for the rest. Piles of charred wood and asphalt shingles were neatly contained within the general outline of the foundation. No part of the structure remained intact or in position.

"You didn't say it was as bad as that!" Jen hit him in the ribs. "Teddy!"

Ted rubbed his side, taking in a sharp breath and glaring at his sister's pointy elbows.

"It's okay, Mommy. Unc had it under control, and the fire men came. The scary part was being inside without power. But Miss Patricks kept me company."

"Miss Patricks?" Meg, Ryan, Jen, and Hank said the words in unison.

Could he quadruple jinx them and keep them from talking or asking questions for the rest of the day? As he scanned each face, ranging from inquisitive to skeptical, he was sorely tempted.

"Sure. Miss Patricks drove me home and stayed. We made pizzas and watched a movie. It was really fun." Maddy shrugged. "I thought she liked Unc, and Unc liked her. But she left yesterday morning, and I haven't seen her."

"Miss Patricks spent the night?" Hank asked.

Maddy nodded.

"Hey, squirrel." Ted bent to address his niece. "We had a really long walk. Why don't you and Colby go inside and get some water, okay? I need to talk to the grown-ups for a little bit."

"Okay. Come on, Colby." Maddy turned and waved to the dog. The duo went inside through the back door.

Meg shook her head. "I don't think Colby even noticed I was here."

Ryan wrapped an arm around her shoulder and squeezed. "I did."

"Do you want to survey the damage to the barn?" Ted asked.

Hank rolled his eyes. "No, I want to get back to you having a lady over and her spending the night under my roof."

Heat crept up Ted's cheeks. Blushing? In his forties? He hadn't done anything wrong, but the events sounded scandalous when laid out by his niece in her matter-o-fact way. "Not like that. We were watching a movie, it ended, she was going to leave and then lightning struck."

Hank stroked his chin. "According to Maddy, in more ways than one."

Ryan rolled his eyes. "The fire was an act of God? I worried bad wiring started the blaze."

Ted shook his head. The entire evening had seemed to be the work of the almighty. He'd made his displeasure at Ted's romantic feelings known.

"You must have been terrified," Meg said. "Especially with Maddy. I'm sorry you had to live through that, Ted. I'm glad you had another adult to help."

Ted was grateful too. But not just any grown-up could have stepped in quite the way Stephanie had. "I owe her a great deal. She kept Maddy and Colby safe and called the firefighters while I did what I could. The power cut, and she stayed. She could have left, but she didn't."

"Are you interested in her?" Hank asked.

Ted scrubbed his hands over his face. He didn't want to lie to himself or his friends.

"Are we open to outside opinions now?" Meg asked. "Can we finally be honest and tell you you're making a mistake and throwing away happiness by not pursuing her?"

"You knew?" Hank spun and stared at her, incredulous.

"I know Stephanie's interested." Meg shrugged and turned to Hank. "But you said you weren't going to put pressure on Ted so I thought it was okay to let the pair figure out their own path. I didn't realize they needed a helping hand."

"Of course they need help." Hank shook his head. "You two would never have taken the initiative if I hadn't pushed."

"Wait, I'm confused," Jen said. "Maddy's teacher that she loves and raves about? She's interested in you. You seem to like her. What's the problem? Why aren't you together?"

"You know," Ted murmured.

"Because you're a widower? I loved Liv, but she's been gone for a long time. She would not have expected you to remain alone for the rest of your days," Jen said. "You aren't honoring her memory by living like a monk."

He did not want to have this conversation ever and especially not in front of his employers. He glared at his sister. "No."

"What's wrong?" Jen asked. "If someone makes you smile, you need to run after that person and hold them tight for as long as you can. Life is too short and unpredictable to waste any time."

"Here, here," Hank said. "I blame myself. I've missed out on matchmaking this whole summer. I've been too distracted by other pairings. I'll fix that."

"Please, don't." Ted drew in a deep breath. "I'm not ready. It's not just about loving and honoring Liv. I miss her every day. It's . . . more complicated."

"How?" Ryan asked.

Had all his friends deserted him? "I'm not judging anyone."

"But . . ." Jen fixed him with a stern look.

"What if I end up married and divorced? You said yourself, life has no guarantees. I got lucky once. Why would I take the chance again when I can get hurt?" Ted asked.

Jen sighed. "Why are you affected by my failure?"

"Don't say that. You got Maddy. You won."

"You're right. But . . ." Jen shook her pointer finger, emphasizing the word. "We are talking about you and how you internalize others actions instead of taking action yourself. Divorce wasn't easy, but once I determined to do the best for daughter it wasn't the hardest choice to make. Navigating each other's adult feelings is hard. Leaving emotions out is difficult but not impossible. Why do you think you'll end up divorced? Don't use me as an excuse to stop from living your life." Jen folded her arms over her chest.

Ted glanced at the ground. She'd nailed a direct hit. No one could call him out like his sister. Except maybe Hank. With the people closest to him holding him accountable, he couldn't hide anymore.

But he could run. "I'm glad you're all back. I need a night off." He turned and strode away, seeking refuge away from those closest to him, and hoping for a break from himself.

CHAPTER 17

After a final round of hugs in Lauren's room and promises from Kelly to keep an eye out for Maddy's email, Stephanie lingered in the antiseptic scented hallway. Slowly ambling toward the exit, she tried to process the whirlwind weekend. She'd endured more highs and lows than a night at the carnival. Now she wanted off the ride so she could regain her balance somewhere sturdy. She wished Ted could have been what she needed. Her eyes watered, and tears sting her nostrils.

She hadn't expected to feel so emotional and raw after visiting Lauren in the hospital. While she was worried for her friend, her deep vulnerability exposed Stephanie's own insecurities.

She was so used to putting on a brave face, to tamping down her own feelings, to reframing her struggles as lesser than in the grand scheme of the whole world. And while she still believed all of those to be necessary functions as an adult, had she grown so used to discounting her own sense of self that she had no identity any more besides her work?

Fighting for her feelings hadn't done her any good. She had wanted Ted to see who she was and to be brave enough to take a chance. But maybe she had to do the same. She couldn't be afraid to be herself.

"Miss Patricks," a tiny voice called.

Lifting her chin, Stephanie plastered on a smile and spotted Maddy. With Shakes firmly clutched under her arm, the little girl beamed and held hands with her mom. Tall and lanky, Ted's sister shared his smile.

Happiness exuded off the pair as expansive and unending as the Montana sky. Despite her pain, Stephanie was glad. She didn't have to worry about her new pupil. She felt a little lighter and hopeful at witnessing the family reunion.

Stephanie stopped a few feet away. "Hi, Maddy. It's nice to see you and Shakes. This must be your mother?"

"Hello, yes, I'm Jen Cade." Jen extended a hand. "It's a pleasure to meet you."

"The pleasure is all mine," Stephanie said. "You have a wonderful daughter. She is a joy in class. Maddy, what is Shakes doing here? I hope he isn't having health issues."

"Oh no. Don't worry I'd take him to a vet if he was sick," Maddy said solemnly.

Jen chuckled. "I'll be joining the nursing staff here. We wanted to take a quick tour."

"Shakes is going to get a badge like mommy," Maddy added.

Stephanie was bursting with curiosity about Maddy's mom. Only the thought the other woman was probably brimming with wonder about the woman who had grown close to her child and brother reminded Stephanie to keep her tongue in check.

"I hope you are alright?" Jen asked. She scanned Stephanie like she had x ray vision. "Are you here for an appointment?"

Hopefully a broken heart wouldn't show up under such scrutiny. *The fire.* Stephanie shook her head. "I'm perfectly fine, thank you. One of my colleagues is pregnant with twins, and she's been put on bed rest and observation. I was visiting."

"Not Mrs. Strong?" Jen asked.

Stephanie frowned. No one would make that mistake. And then realization hit. Jen must be taking over all duties including Shakes' photo project and had the email address for Kelly. As Jen should. She was the mom. Still, it felt like giving up one last link to the unexpected connection with Ted. Stephanie shook her head. "No, not Mrs. Strong. I'd better get going before one of your new colleagues has to escort me out."

"Thank you for all of your help," Jen said. "Truly. I appreciate it more than I can say."

At least someone did. Stephanie forced a smile. "No thanks needed."

"We'll see you soon?" Jen asked

Stephanie pressed her tongue to the roof of her mouth. She never lied in front of a child. Starting now wouldn't do her any good. "Have a good afternoon." With a nod and wave to the mother-daughter pair, Stephanie continued down the hall toward the exit. She couldn't mourn what she'd never had. The best she could do was to keep moving forward.

She didn't stop until she reached the parking lot. Then she took in deep gulps of the air, breathing in the faint hint of smoke. Or so she imagined.

For the rest of her life, she would never forget the terror of the fire. As the flames licked the side of the red barn, she had been frantic looking for him. And then she saw him. And she knew. He was her home.

But he didn't feel the same way. And he rejected her enough times that she really needed to start listening to the message he'd so clearly delivered. She had to be enough on her own. She couldn't keep doing for others and ignore herself deep down. Inside her pocket, she grabbed her phone and tapped the speed dial.

"Hello?" A deep voice answered on the first ring.

"Hey, Ty, it's me."

"Steffy. Hey, Melissa has been asking about you. Are you coming to visit soon?"

Her little brother's low baritone was like a soothing balm. He should have gone into radio or voiceover work. But he found his passion in engineering, and she'd been proud of how he managed a demanding career with starting a family. His question should have been obvious before she made the call. She had the time. She should put it to good use. "Maybe."

"What's wrong?" Her brother asked.

Emotions bubbled up in her chest, and she felt like she was drowning and couldn't get air into her lungs. "I'm on leave. From my job."

"Oh no, what happened? Are you okay?"

She pinched the bridge of her nose stemming the tide of tears that threatened. "I don't know. I'll be ok about my job. Something will work out."

"Why do you sound so demoralized? Is there a guy?"

"Yes." Her voice cracked, and she blubbered. "I'm sorry. I didn't mean to call and get all emotional."

"It's okay. I wish I was there. What happened? Do you need me to beat somebody up?"

She snorted. "Do you want to take on a big lug of cowboy probably 200 pounds?"

"Hey, I'm not your kid brother anymore. I'm two twenty on a good day."

"Do you mean when Melissa is making healthy meals?"

He chuckled. "Something like that. If you need to get away, you should come visit us. You know we'd love to have you. And you don't have to worry about a thing anymore. I'm a grown-up now. I'm fine. It's ok to take care of yourself a little bit."

She knew he was right. And she knew she had people who would show up for her. She wasn't scared little girl anymore, worrying about being left at dance rehearsals long after pick up or not having mom or dad show up for parent day at school. But she didn't know how to let go of it all. "Do you ever get mad?"

"That's a very vague statement. Of course I do. Want to provide a little context?"

"Didn't you want Mom and Dad around more?" Her tummy tightened, her insides twisting like the binding on a battered spiral notebook. She breathed through the sharp pain. "Don't you ever wish things were different when we were growing up?"

"Not anymore."

"Really?" She spent too much time thinking up what if scenarios. Had he been so unaffected?

"I don't want to throw the whole it's different when you're the parent thing at you because that's not fair. Plus, I've been a dad for about two minutes. Everyone is entitled to their feelings about their experiences and to frame their life however they need," he murmured. "Please don't think I'm discounting you. All parents are learning on the job. We assume a huge responsibility with no training. Our parents were busy and dealt with any issue they were aware of. You had trouble advocating for yourself."

She still did. He had a point. But it was frustrating that her little brother could be so rational and insightful. Although, as an engineer, he dealt in logic.

"I know how much you did for me," he said. "You saw what I needed and took care of me. I couldn't do the same. I was too young to understand you had needs too."

She wasn't sure how much she really did in the grand scheme of things. Her brother was a good kid. Silly at times but determined to always do the right thing. And precocious. He'd skipped two grades and graduated college a semester before she did. On a fast path to success, he seemed to soar without any hurdles.

"I want to encourage you now. Don't be held back by fear. Learn from your insecurity about attention and make it your strength."

How? With Ted, she had taken charge and asked for what she needed. And she was still turned down flat. Maybe her problem was tying up her sense of security in one person. She had to be enough for herself. She had to speak up. She sighed. "When did you get so smart?"

"I made one good choice. Falling in love with Melissa. She taught me everything including the gift of forgiveness. That's why I want you to find someone who cherishes you. So, if you need me to come up and beat up this cowboy I will. Or maybe you can move by us."

If she didn't love the community as much as she did, relocating would be tempting. She knew better than to think she could simply run away from her problems. And she definitely couldn't leave behind her heart. She might be able to keep breathing, but she wouldn't keep really truly be living if she left. "I love you, Tyler. I think I just needed to talk it all out."

"If I can help, I will. Will you keep me posted on a visit? I know we owe you one but with the baby."

"Absolutely I will."

"Great I love you, sis. Bye."

"Bye." She ended the call on her cell phone and slipped the device back into her pocket. This time when she filled her lungs, she didn't breathe the smoke it truly had been in her imagination after all. Maybe Tyler was right, and she wouldn't understand the sacrifices her parents had made until she became a parent herself. Maybe she hung onto childish feelings as a way to deflect growing up.

But she was an adult. And she couldn't run away from her problems. She'd stride into the principal's office tomorrow morning, accept her punishment, and figure out the next phase in her life. Because she was going nowhere.

Ted swiped the broom against the hardwood floor, scraping the bristles along and against the grain. If he kept at it with such vigor, he'd probably scratch the boards. At present, he hadn't done much good. For his efforts, he was rewarded with a plume of dust, as he worked his way through the bunk room.

With summer in the rearview, maintaining the residential space for the seasonal employees was a monthly job. And a quiet one. And the most annoying. Which almost guaranteed he wouldn't be followed by any of those overly involved friends that had become family. Or—potentially worse—his actual family.

He hated the way everyone had invested so much of themselves in him. Because he was bound to disappoint. He'd done Stephanie the kindness he couldn't bring himself to do for anyone else that he loved. Leave them alone.

Loved? He grabbed a bandana out of his back pocket and blew his scratchy nose. He'd kicked up too much in his fevered attempts at cleaning. He wasn't scared of the word or the emotion.

He didn't think letting someone else into his heart was a betrayal of what he had felt for Liv. Not anymore. On the contrary, the last few weeks of getting to know Stephanie, reminded him of the capacity for living he only experienced when he was completely open and vulnerable with another person. He only reached that point of enlightenment once before when he'd fallen head first for his wife.

He'd nearly succumbed again. But then nature intervened. The fire had burned through him as fast as it did the old barn. Maybe quicker. He was drier than the timbers of the historic building, ready fuel for the blaze.

And the absolute rush of adrenaline, he had clarity of his purpose. He couldn't lose someone else. Even if that meant forcing himself back into a black and white world after living in Technicolor for the past several weeks, he'd do it.

"Whoa, whoa," a deep voice called followed by a sharp whistle.

Ted met Hank's gaze as the older man stood in the doorway leading from the TV room.

"You weren't kidding," Hank said, his breathing shallow. "Reckon, you really wanted to be alone to come all the way out here and do chores." He coughed, leaning against the door frame for support.

"Hank, you shouldn't have followed me." Ted crossed the room to the older man. Without asking, he draped Hank's arm over his shoulder and steered Hank back into the main communal gathering space, lowering him onto the couch.

Ted crossed the room to the sink, filling a glass of water and returning to his boss.

Hank stopped coughing and accepted the cup, drinking deep, and nodding. "Ahh. Thanks. Needed that. Tickle in my throat."

Ted wasn't so easily convinced.

At eighty-nine, Hank was definitely not spry and nimble. He tired easily and was now on even more prescription medication following a hospital stay earlier in the summer. He was so mentally fit and focused, it was easy to pretend he was a young man who would live forever. No one could.

"Take a seat and stop hovering," Hank said, curling his upper lip. "Makes me feel old when you're staring like that."

Ted understood. He didn't like fussing either. He sat on the sofa's armrest, propping one leg on the furniture and keeping the other foot flat on the floor. In case he needed to run again.

"I am here. To apologize to you," Hank said, cradling the empty cup in both hands. "I overlooked you, and I underestimated you. I'm sorry."

"I'm the one who was here when your barn burned down. I should be the person apologizing."

Hank stared at him. Hard. "We both know I'm not talking about the barn. But I am sorry to see it go. Losing a piece of your history, especially something you've taken for granted your whole life?" Hank shook his head. "I was cavalier about the old timbers. I floated the idea of tearing it down. I was wrong to be flippant. Probably caused the fire with my careless words."

"No one would ever accuse you of taking your legacy lightly," Ted said.

"Maybe. But I did. Those old boards have always been there. Like a beacon. To lose it?" Hank pressed a hand to his heart. "It's like getting knocked off your favorite horse. Hard not to reevaluate everything. In your case, though, I think it brought up some old trauma."

Ted couldn't disagree. He still didn't quite understand what Hank was sorry for. In his experience, however, Ted would only get the answer if he let Hank speak.

"A lot of change happening around here lately. Now even more with the wedding." Hank smiled.

Ted grinned, too. He couldn't help it. Hank's excitement was contagious for good reason. When two people found each other, and in this case after years of mutual uncertainty, it was hopeful for the rest.

"I'm sorry, because I skipped you. After my success with Meg and Ryan, I jumped straight ahead to Joe. I was focused on him and Abby and couldn't see what was happening on the ranch between you and Stephanie this summer."

Ted's throat constricted. He coughed. "Nothing happened this summer, sir."

"Maybe nothing big, but changes were underway. A friendship was developing and swiftly becoming something sweeter." Hank stroked his chin. "I couldn't find a better pairing for you if I'd been looking. I'm glad. I am sorry. I was treating you with extra care and space, and I forgot something important."

"I'm a lost cause?"

"You?" Hank widened his eyes and waggled a finger. "Oh no, you're no victim. I know your pain." He pressed the hand to the center of his chest. "I don't push you, because I don't want anyone to shove me."

Ted understood. In many ways, Hank had been an example and a mentor. At Ted's lowest, most fragile, Hank had been the one to offer a job and a purpose. They'd been united in their grief and status as widowers. "You were right. I'm not ready."

Hank snorted. "I was coming around to you as soon as I had everything else settled."

"Joe and Abby are not a match, sir."

Hank rolled his eyes. "Leave them to me. Right now, we're talking about you. You never mention your wife. My Suzie practically haunts this place, as much as I talk about her."

"Liv was. . . everything. My past, my present. And I thought my future."

"I wish you'd have had it all. Growing old with someone is a gift. Are you honoring her memory? Is that what you've been doing on your own? I can't understand why you are a hermit."

"I'm not anymore. I have you and my sister and niece now. Ryan will have kids. I'm not alone."

"But you aren't together. Not really. I've seen the way you always keep yourself apart and away from us. I'd guess you're trying to protect yourself from getting hurt?"

"I can't. . ." A sob rose in Ted's throat, choking him. "I can't lose Stephanie."

"And the fire put that fear through you again?"

Ted pinched the bridge of his nose, shutting his eyes tight and squeezing hard.

"You are already loving her from a distance. You don't get to enjoy what you could have. You are only suffering pain. Why are you pushing her away? Do you need permission to love again? Because that's what I'll do. I'll give you the freedom to follow your heart. Your wife would not have wanted you to be scared. What would have happened if you'd been the one that died? What would you have wanted?"

Ted dragged in a shaky breath and dropped his hand to his leg, numb on the armrest. "For her to have a family."

"And you don't think she'd want the same for you?" Hank murmured.

You're going to be the best Dad. Liv's voice filtered through his mind. He wasn't sure he agreed. And kids were a long way off. But he had a chance at a real, lasting love. If Stephanie wasn't too mad to look at him. . . He had to take his shot.

"Okay. You're right." Ted lifted his chin.

"I usually am. What are you going to do?" Hank asked.

Ted wasn't sure. Grovel? Apologize? She was woman who kept to the sidelines and gave others a moment to shine. "I'll come up with an idea."

At the determined glint in Hank's eyes and the cheek-to-cheek grin, Ted was glad he didn't ask for assistance. He didn't want help. He was ready for his life to begin on his terms. He'd managed to escape Hank's notice for his courtship, and he'd continue under the radar for as long as possible. "Actually, I have another question. How did you know I was here?"

"I didn't." Hank pressed his hands on his thighs and pushed up to standing, his bones creaking and cracking. "I went everywhere else first. When someone is important to you, that's what you do. You don't give up. You keep fighting."

Ted got to his feet. "Did you ever think maybe you had permission to enjoy your time here without Suzie? You should take your advice. If you met someone, you wouldn't betray your wife but might enhance your life. Never say never, right?"

Hank scoffed. "I'm the oldest person in town. I'm not finding love. Thanks for thinking of me. And I promise, if someone comes along interested in my stories, I'll give her an earful over a nice dinner. Let's go. You've got work to do. Good thing my old pictures sold well at the auction. If I know my grandson, I can expect a big bill from the new construction. More than just the insurance will cover."

Ted chuckled, the laughter lifting him up and making him feel lighter than air. Hank was right, per usual. Ted had work to do, and he'd get straight to it. He'd pull out all the stops to win back Stephanie.

CHAPTER 18

Stephanie stood outside the school's main entrance at ten thirty-eight, smoothing the jacket of her charcoal gray suit over her pants. She only owned the one suit and felt like she was on her way to a funeral every time she wore it. Or to trial. Which was worse?

The door buzzed, and the lock clicked.

She grabbed the handle and strode inside, making sure the entrance relocked behind her. She hoped she wasn't on her way to being sentenced. She missed her bright, colorful outfits with cartoonish details. Dressing in shades of black and white wasn't for her.

The glass paneled foyer gave visitors a peek into the school en route to the front office.

Movement caught in the corner of her eye, and she spotted the last few kids from Lauren's class in a single file line, heading to art. Stephanie was tempted to smile and wave. But she hadn't been recognized in her austere, professional garb, almost a disguise. The long-term sub would have her hands full on the first full week on the job. She wouldn't appreciate a disruption to whatever order she'd created.

At the door to the office, she reached for the intercom button.

The door buzzed.

She grabbed the handle and looked up.

Wendy smiled. "Good morning, Miss Patricks."

Stephanie stepped inside and shut the door behind her.

Wendy gave away nothing with her even tone. She offered a warm welcome to everyone who entered the school, but she knew all. She held out a hand.

Stephanie stared at her blankly.

"I.D.?"

Right. Stephanie reached inside her purse for her government identification, ignoring the flash of hurt, and handed it to Wendy. It was standard security practice, and she went through the motions like anyone else. Had Wendy always addressed her with her last name? Stephanie wasn't sure. She was desperate for clues to make sense of the situation and the state of her career, but now she saw conspiracy. She breathed in through her nose and slowly exhaled.

Wendy handed her the sticker visitor's pass and driver's license, motioning to a chair. "He'll be right with you."

Stephanie nodded her thanks and took the seat, perching on the edge and crossing her ankles. She slipped her license into the slot into her wallet.

Her phone rang.

Kelly's face flashed on the screen. It was the kindergarten planning period. Kelly had enough on her plate today with two substitute teachers filling in for the rest of her team. Kindergarten thrived on consistency and many of the kids would cling to Kelly with the new faces. But she took the time to reach out.

Stephanie breathed a little easier and silenced the call. She switched her phone to vibrate as a series of incoming texts from Kelly and Lauren began in earnest. Her phone remained loud with the wave of encouragement.

"Stephanie?" Bill asked.

She glanced up and almost sighed. At least she remained on first name basis with her boss. "Good morning." She turned off her phone, slipped it into her purse, and stood.

"Please, follow me." He smiled.

She did her best to focus forward, not daring to dart a glance anywhere else. A worried look or polite nod from her colleagues would pierce through the faux confidence she wore like armor. With her heartbeat thundering in her ears, she followed Bill into his office and sat at one of the two visitors' chairs in front of his desk.

Since opening up about her failures to her friends, her end of the road conversation with Ted, and being placed on leave on Friday, she wasn't sure she had any emotions left. She'd been squeezed and tossed like an old sponge.

Bill shut the door and took his chair.

She watched his mouth move but didn't register the words, instead listening to a low buzz. Her boss was speaking. She needed to listen.

Anxiety crushed her. If she lost her job as well as her chance for love, what did she have? Until it had been snatched, she hadn't realized how desperately she'd been searching for her place in the world. She wanted to matter to her workplace, to her community, to Ted, and to herself.

"What do you think?" Bill asked.

She shook her head. "I'm sorry. Can you repeat that last bit?"

"I'm sorry, if you felt blindsided. You were upfront with me the entire time about the situation. I needed to straighten out the information being flung at me. I've spoken to the board. Off the record, several members feel that the PTO president is unfairly exerting pressure and power of her position. They have worried about other situations she's been involved with. Her treatment of you has only solidified their concerns. A meeting will be called, and she will be removed. A special election will be held to fill her vacancy. The vice-president is taking over until then."

It was everything she could have asked for and then some. The words held no meaning.

She loved working with the kids and being part of her community. She didn't like not having her boss and colleagues on her side. She could pursue any number of jobs to provide a paycheck, starting with the much-needed role of wedding coordinator at the Kincaid ranch. If she returned, she needed more.

The silence stretched.

She studied her boss.

He held himself perfectly still.

"Does that mean I can come back to work?" She could have cheered for how even she kept her tone despite the chill running through her body.

"Yes, please." He sighed. "I shouldn't be saying this, I'm sure a lawyer would advise me to hold my tongue, but I have to tell you the truth. You are sorely missed today. We need good teachers. And I hope you look into becoming an administrator. We need fighters."

She lifted her chin and stared at her boss. Today was the first day in a long time, she felt seen and supported in her job. Could she believe it? Or was his comment a throwaway attempt at placating her? "Are you serious? Do you think I should move into the front office? Would you want me to join you in administration? I'm sort of a lightning rod now."

"I am, and I do. You have a deep compassion for the students. It's not a universal quality. Admin would be a good move." He steepled his fingers, pressing his hands to his mouth.

Being a principal hadn't been a goal, but maybe it should be. Why not expand her work and help more kids? "I'd have to take night classes. Maybe some summer classes, too." She wouldn't be able to teach at the ranch. *Probably make my life easier if I didn't.*

"The courses can take time, but you'd have our full support."

She took in a deep breath, letting the air expand her lungs and letting go of the pent-up frustration. "You say you want fighters, but I can't always fight. If I've learned one thing, it's the value of listening."

He grinned from ear to ear and stood, extending his hand. "Then I think you'll be very successful in the role."

She pushed back her chair and rose, shaking his hand. When she thought she'd lost her career, she wasn't sure what came next. But now—with a little humility—she understood she'd always rise to the challenge and find a new way. Even when it hurt. Maybe especially then. "Thank you, sir."

"We'll see you tomorrow?" He dropped her hand.

"Tomorrow? Really?"

"Yes, please."

She nodded, grabbed her purse, and exited the room. She might have to reevaluate, but she wasn't running away. She loved her town. For better or worse. And she'd take advantage of a rare free day to do something for herself.

Ted held the cell phone against his ear. No sooner than the line connected and it went to a pre-recorded message almost instantly. Straight to voicemail. Was that on purpose? Was she avoiding him? Did she bristle and send him on his way every time his name flashed on the screen?

He couldn't blame her if she was avoiding him. He told her to go away. At a vulnerable moment in her life, he pushed her out of his. Maybe it was all too presumptuous on his part, that feeling he couldn't shake that she could change his life if he let her. Why give so much power to another person? Why let an outsider control his destiny? For all he knew, she wasn't looking for forever. One date would give him an idea of what lay ahead. That's all he wanted.

"Stop pacing." His sister shouted.

Startled, he turned around and spotted Jen walking into the living room with a laundry basket on her hip.

"If you're going to walk in place, take off the boots for goodness sakes. It's like being at an out of sync tap dance recital."

"You know you are staying in my space."

"And I'm grateful." Jen set the basket on the floor and sat in an armchair. She pulled out a purple, child-sized shirt and folded. "But having roommates means making allowances even in the short term. Shouldn't you be doing something somewhere anyways? It's Monday at ten minutes to eleven in the morning. Why are you here?"

"I can't really do much today. Ryan is meeting with the insurance company. I'm not supposed to touch anything near the site."

"A day off?"

"Not really." He sighed. "I have to get things straightened with Stephanie. I can't get ahold of her, and I'm not sure what I do next."

Jen folded pants and socks.

"You don't approve?"

She shrugged, grabbing a sweatshirt, and shaking it out before folding it in half. "Do you want an opinion? You seemed to shut down the other day."

"I was." He sat in the opposite armchair. Without activity, he felt gangly and awkward. He was a man of the never-ending chore list. Quiet time was best avoided.

"Miss Patricks is lovely, kind, and sweet from Maddy's point of view." His sister leaned back and met his gaze. "I never thought I'd see you get back into the dating pool again."

"I had thought it was all behind me. But then a series of events made me realize maybe I shouldn't be alone."

"Like me barging in on your personal space?"

"That and becoming part of a community again. I didn't try to, but I found family here."

"For what it's worth, Liv would like her."

He didn't need anyone's blessing or approval. He didn't live his life by committee. Warmth spread through him regardless.

"They wouldn't be friends." Jen chuckled. "They'd have nothing in common. They wouldn't get coffee together."

He nodded. Liv was sarcastic and sophisticated. Stubborn and savvy. She had been a take charge personality that guided him for years, leaving him bereft on his own. He'd been happy in her wake. "How do you know?"

"I met Stephanie at the hospital when I got my badge. I'm known as a pretty shrewd judge of character."

He rolled his eyes.

"For other people," Jen said. "Liv wouldn't have stayed single forever. No one would have wanted her to be alone. Same goes for you."

"I'm rusty at flirting and all that stuff."

Jen snorted. "Aren't we all? At least you were friends first. It's a solid start. And you don't have to get on the apps." She pointed at the phone. "Are you trying to call her right now?"

"It seems like the sensible idea," he said, fighting the eyeroll. Little sisters might grow up, but they never stopped being annoying.

"Well, it's a Monday, and she's a teacher. She's probably at school. She's not exactly the type to stare at her phone all day."

Or she was at her review meeting with the principal. His stomach sank to his boots. Maybe her phone was turned off. Was she getting bad news? Had she been fired? Was she already packing up her apartment preparing to leave? Was she about to say goodbye before he had a chance to tell her he felt like she brought him back into the living world? That she could be someone very special? "I'm heading into town. Do you want anything?"

"Like what? Where are you going?"

"I'm not sure. I'll find out when I get there."

Jen grinned and slowly nodded. "I understand. You're about to make a big gesture. Convince her to give you a real chance?"

"Not that I deserve one."

"No, you don't." Jen shrugged.

He rolled his eyes.

"You know I won't flatter your ego. I'm not Mom. But I am glad. What's your plan?"

"I don't know what I'll do. Talk?"

Jen shook her head. "Too late. You need more." She snapped her fingers. "I have an idea. But we need to go up to the ranch house, and we need reinforcements."

"What are you thinking?"

"We have to go classic romantic comedy."

In his mind, only one movie had captured the ideal grand gesture moment. And it didn't involve a stereo or signs. It required a marching band and an outdoor stadium. He remembered the adorable wrinkle of Stephanie's brow when she completely misunderstood a pop culture reference between him and Joe. He'd be tempted to find a brass line if he didn't worry she'd think he was poking fun at her.

"She doesn't really watch movies," he said. "She won't get it."

"Maybe that's even better, she'll think you're being original."

He wasn't so sure. Wouldn't she appreciate something more from the heart? From him? His sister was determined to use every cliché she knew. If he asked for her help, he'd have to take what she gave. How would Stephanie react to knowing his sister was involved?

In a small town, dating relationships were hard to hide from public scrutiny. Everyone would have an opinion. They probably already did. Would she be embarrassed? Would it be too much too soon?

No, he should get others involved. Showing her that she mattered to him, in a public way, in front of those nearest him nearest and dearest to him, would matter more than anything. Because she mattered to him. And if he got a chance, he would show her. "She won't be at the school today." *Or for much longer.* "But I think I know where she will be." He glanced at the time on his cell phone screen. "I don't have a lot of time."

"Let's go to the ranch house. I'm sure they'll have what we need."

He wasn't sure he liked the flash of mischief in his sister's eyes. But he was glad she was here. He'd take a little inconvenience and over-involvement if it meant having everyone that mattered close. He had one piece of the puzzle left to finish the whole picture.

CHAPTER 19

Stephanie drove to town, only passing a handful of cars on her way. Her apartment was outside city limits, on the way to a bigger town and more job opportunities. Downtown Herd was tourist central. The Old West false fronts catered to those in search of a sanitized version of the cowboy past.

With the ranch closed for the summer season, most of the businesses shuttered until the late spring. She expected a tumbleweed to blow down the street. She was heartened to see a few locals out and about, walking into the post office, stopping at the general store, and frequenting the local businesses. The off-season focused on community spirit, a very worthy endeavor.

At the end of Main Street, she steered towards the church and cemetery. She turned into the gravel lot, crunching the stones under her tires like a heraldic welcome announcing her visit.

She hopped out of her vehicle and grabbed her purse, stalking towards the food truck.

"Stephanie?" Her friend, food truck owner and go to cowboy dinner caterer Abby Whit, exclaimed. "Wowza, you clean up nice."

Stephanie unbuttoned her blazer and tugged the hem. "Thank you. I feel a little too strict in the suit. It's like a strait jacket."

"You could be a lawyer. Who knew you were a shark hiding underneath all of those oversized dresses."

"I suppose we all have a few secrets."

Abby nodded, stiffly. "Did you have to defend yourself today?"

Stephanie wasn't surprised word had gotten around town about her situation. Neither could she stop her embarrassed reaction. As she tucked a strand of hair behind her ear, her fingertips brushed her burning cheeks. "I think I'll be okay." She darted her gaze side to side. No one was around. "Between you and me, I'm returning to school tomorrow. I'll be glad to shove this suit into the very back of my closet."

"That's great news are you here to celebrate? I can offer you a wide selection of anything on the menu." Abby chuckled.

Stephanie sniffed. Instead of melting butter, smoking meat, or baking bread, however, she breathed in industrial cleaner. "Are you sure you don't mind?"

"Of course, not." Abby tossed a dish towel over her shoulder, twisted a knob on the griddle, and squirted oil liberally over the heating surface. "Deep cleaning can wait. Trust me."

"Thanks. I'm glad you're still open. Not a lot of traffic in town today."

Abby nodded.

"When will you close up for the season?"

"Soon. Business always dwindles after the poker night. But this year it seems to be an even steeper drop. And the wind is cold when I don't have the griddle on."

Stephanie nodded her head in commiseration. Her apartment complex had seen a lot of recent development nearby. She knew of at least two new restaurants going up. While not many could compare with Abby's culinary skills, location was a big factor. As well as indoor seating. Too bad Abby couldn't set up shop in a building. She'd lure customers to downtown year-round, a boon for every business. "Could you make me a wrap?"

"Absolutely. I have some barbecue chicken in the fridge that I think will be perfect. I made a batch while testing a new rub in the oven earlier. And I'll whip up a smoky chipotle ranch dressing."

Stephanie licked her lips. "That's great."

Inside the food truck, a cell phone rang. "I better get that you can go sit down if you'd like."

"Actually, I think I need to grab something out of my car." Stephanie walked back towards her unlocked vehicle. She reached inside and grabbed her lip gloss from her purse.

She wouldn't admit it to Abby, but Stephanie didn't really want to be alone right now. She'd come out victorious. And the only person she wanted to celebrate with, Ted, had shoved her aside. She wasn't quite sure what to do or where to go. But sitting on a picnic bench overlooking a cemetery wouldn't make her feel any better. Angling her body, Stephanie observed her friend from the corner of her gaze. As soon as Abby hung up the call, Stephanie made her way back over to the food truck.

"Hey, do you mind testing out a few new recipes for me?" Abby asked.

"Sure. What did you have in mind?"

"I want to try a new hushpuppy batter. And I have a new macaroni salad I'd like to try. It may take a little bit of time. Are you in a rush today?"

"I've got nowhere to be. For maybe the first time ever."

Abby chuckled and glanced away. Her movements were sharp and rigid. Determined. Practiced.

Stephanie nibbled the inside of her cheek. Asking who had called was rude. But whatever was said during the short phone conversation must have set Abby on edge. She acted sort of bristly. Stephanie wasn't sure how to proceed without making things strained. She'd try anyways. "It sure is quiet here without the tourists around."

Abby nodded and started pulling ingredients out of the fridge, whipping hushpuppy batter, her utensils clanging against the metal bowls.

"Does it ever unnerve you?"

"The tourists?" Abby focused on her work, not glancing up. "That's the whole job."

"No. Working in a haunted parking lot." Stephanie kept her voice low so as not to disturb the ghosts. She wasn't superstitious, per se. But she didn't court trouble. Avoiding cats, cracks, and ladders, she also tossed salt over her shoulder and followed every other old wives cure to ward off evil.

"It's not haunted," Abby said, deadpan.

On the otherwise bright day, a cloud passed over the sun. A cool breeze kicked up, whistling through the cemetery. Stephanie shuddered.

"Isn't it?" she asked, pushing ahead with her theory. "Unclaimed land belonging to the most hated family in town next to the cemetery?" Stephanie shuddered. "At least you won't have to worry about someone swooping in and stealing your spot soon. The land reverts to the town within the next year. I'm sure you'll manage a hundred-year lease for like a dollar a year or something."

Abby nodded but didn't lift her head.

Did Stephanie imagine her friends' tight posture? "Gives me an idea about Christmas."

Abby raised her gaze. "Ghosts?"

"Of course. What is more festive than reflecting on the past? But you are already closed for the winter by then. Too bad. It could be almost like a historical reenactment of the shunning of the Whittiers. People in Herd still hold a grudge. The crowd would be huge. I bet you'd sell out of everything."

"Before you run away on a wild tangent with your ideas, you need to know. I can honestly say I have never been approached by a phantom, a poltergeist, or spirit of any kind."

"I suppose Joe would tell everyone if it was haunted."

"And I'm surprised you are put off by quiet. Considering who you like."

Stephanie cheeks flamed again. "Don't tease me about that. It's too raw. There's nothing there. Not like you and Joe."

Abby rolled her eyes. "Now you need to stop teasing. He knows a lot about history, and I'm interested in learning. That's it."

Stephanie knew the pair were like oil and water. They separated and couldn't be forced together unless vigorously shaken. Maybe that's what the town needed next. To really enter the next phase of their community's progress, to accept moving forward, they'd all have to get a little uncomfortable for positive change.

"Okay, it's going to be a little bit. I've got to get the water boiling for the macaroni. You don't mind waiting?"

Stephanie's stomach growled loudly.

Abby laughed. "Fair enough. Let me make your wrap really quick, but you cannot leave. At all."

If you see something say something flashed in Stephanie's mind. Abby wasn't the type to make demands. But she was acting a little peculiar.

"I have my guinea pig, and I'm not letting her go." Abby chuckled again, the sound a little forced.

"I'm not going anywhere."

Stephanie meant every word.

Holding a stack of posters in one arm and a boombox in the other, Ted waited in position at the end of the street. If he was right, and he really was hoping he was in at least this one instance, he'd be hard for Stephanie to miss as she left the food truck and drove back to her apartment.

He angled the posters against his chest, trying to avoid a finger cut as he readjusted. He wasn't sure how long lunch would take. He'd called Abby to stall, and she promised to do her best. He'd been standing in place for ten minutes already. Did he have another thirty to wait?

Under his boots, he had no give on the solid asphalt. His knees ached. He wasn't much for being in one place for too long, his body wasn't used to the way his legs locked. This must be as bad as sitting for the way gravity could stress a skeleton. In another ten, he might reconsider holding the props.

No, it's a big moment, I have to. Stephanie deserved to know and see and feel how wrong he'd been about her. About them. Since opening up to the extended ranch family, he'd felt both lighter and weaker. He was a worn piece of leather, dangerously thin but buttery soft. With any luck, he'd have enough of a head start on opening up about his feelings before he had too much of a crowd. Although, he wouldn't shy away from that either. Being vulnerable and honest was a lot less to carry around than hiding.

Tires squealed as a car pulled out of the gravel lot a few hundred yards away.

Ted widened his stance. He was an immovable object. As long as he didn't get hit.

The little red coupe appeared and stopped, suddenly.

Through the windshield, Stephanie's eyes went wide, and her mouth dropped open. She looked like a ghostly fish behind the wheel of her car.

Ted felt calm and clammy. He hadn't anticipated the rush of actually spotting her.

She left her car engine running and got out of the vehicle. "Ted? What are you doing? You're going to get hit by a car. Why are you in the middle of the street?"

Dressed in a dark suit, she looked serious and addressed him in her firmest tone. What was he doing? For a moment, he stood perfectly still, too entranced to do anything.

"Get out of the road," she said.

Her worried tone snapped him out of his reverie. "No. I'm trying to get your attention."

"Mission accomplished. Wait..." She crossed her arms over her chest. "Is this from a movie? Does a man get hit by a car on a busy street? Is that it? Is this some sort of symbolism?"

The only film that fit that setup involved an amphibian puppet trying to sell a musical about his life story to Broadway producers. "No, of course not. And I'm fine. I've been here for a few minutes, and I haven't seen another vehicle go by. Read the poster."

"How did you know where I was?"

"I listened. You said you love eating at the food truck and would miss it. I figured you'd take this opportunity before Abby closed up shop for the year." He shook the posters in his arms. He'd poured his heart out into a confession of everything that held him back. "Can you read the poster from there?"

"And Abby was helping you? Did you call her?"

He nodded.

"Oh, thank goodness." Stephanie dropped her arms to her sides. "I was getting really worried about her."

"When I called you, and it went to voicemail, I remembered what you said about the food truck."

"My special treat. Abby didn't disappoint. Her new hushpuppies are amazing."

He didn't want to rush her, but he was worried they'd gotten off track. He glanced down, trying to reach the play button without dropping the cards. He should have practiced this part. He didn't think it would be hard. It was so easy in the movie. "One sec. I'm sorry." He lifted his gaze.

"You look nice. Did you dress up for me?"

He had. His dark slacks hung in the very back of his closet. The white shirt still had its price tag in it when he grabbed it off the hanger. "Will you read the poster?"

"I think I have to come closer. Your handwriting is hard to read." She wrinkled her brow, folding her arms over her chest and strolling forward. "I'm sorry. I still can't tell what it says. Am I supposed to understand the reference?"

The classic pop song filled downtown. Finding the old school stereo had been the real hitch in his sister's plan. Meg scoured her inventory at the antique store but had nothing. Joe came through via text on his lesson planning break. His love of history wasn't strictly professional. In his spare time, he fiddled with video game systems and, in a cardboard box full of parts he was working on with his class, he had a plastic, two-cassette boombox. Ted swung by the school to grab it.

Educating Stephanie on movies and TV shows promised a lifetime's worth of fun date nights. *I need to ask first.*

"Yes, it is a reference but never mind." He stopped the music, hating to end the song at the first build up to the chorus, and set the boombox and cards on the ground.

He dusted his hands on his pants. Why not segue to a reference she would understand? "How about I ask you what kind of sandwich and drink pairing you'd like for your dreams tonight? Perhaps Pastrami and Buttermilk?"

"Like the movie?" She widened her gaze. "That one I get. But seems a little personal."

Her mouth twitched like she suppressed a smile. He was glad to have a shared joke. "Good. I'm glad you understand."

She kept her mouth in a solid, straight line. She was emotionless.

He'd done that. He'd ruined the sunshine that bubbled up from inside her. With his rainy personality, he blocked her light behind his clouds. "Nothing makes sense without you. The whole town needs you." *So do I.*

She wrinkled her forehead. "Anyone can run an event or teach a class. What I do isn't special."

"You know that's not true. No one can advocate for the kids or the town like you. No one cares as much as you. And that's why I can't let you leave."

"I'm not. If your whole speech is about convincing me to stay. It's fine. Don't worry about it. I'll keep going." She smiled. "Same as I always do."

The happy expression didn't reach her eyes. Up close, she looked almost sad. Was she so practiced in smiling for her students she could wear the expression without meaning it?

"I told you I couldn't be the man I was."

"You said he was a stranger," she said.

"Yes. The man I was is so far in the past. I couldn't pretend to be him if I tried. With you, I'm someone different. You're transforming me. I've been shut down for so long. I don't know how to act or what to do."

"I'm sorry," she muttered.

He stepped forward. "But I want to try. Because I need to break down the barriers between us." He stretched a hand out, stroking her shoulder and dropping his arm away. "I'm ready to give us a chance."

"I need more than words," she murmured.

"I know." *I was counting on it.* He didn't smile. He wouldn't. Because then he'd give away just how much he already knew her. How deeply he already loved her. And he wanted to say the words to her so she could see and hear and believe him. He put two fingers in his mouth and whistled, loudly. "I'm not hiding."

She widened her gaze, her cheeks turning bright pink.

He stepped to her side and waved toward the Golden Crown.

Meg, Ryan, Hank, and Jen stood a few yards away. They waved as they emerged from the restaurant to gawk from the hitching post out front. He'd invited them. They helped him search for the items of his plan and encouraged him to follow his heart. Had he overstepped? Was this too much?

He swiveled, spinning on his heel, and several locals exiting the general store on the other side of the street. He bit the end of his tongue. He couldn't go back now. Boxed in by the community on all sides. "I wanted you to see I have no fears about everyone knowing how I feel about you. But. . . I didn't want you to feel put on the spot. In my head, this felt much more like a grand gesture and not much like peer pressure."

She met his gaze and smiled. "I can appreciate the spirit behind the grand gesture. For future reference, I'm more of a private, no public displays sort of person."

"Future reference?" He held the words to his giddy heart.

She tipped her head back and raised both eyebrows. "I like hand holding in front of everyone. But maybe not what Hank's sign is suggesting?"

"Hank made a sign?" His voice cracked. His stomach filled with lead and dropped to his ankles. Dread covered him like a sticky syrup and he slowly turned his head.

Hank's poster board was no-nonsense and direct, like the man himself. The white sheet read *KISS,* the black lettering clear with its thick outlines.

Ted provided Joe a day off from Hank's meddling. Now Ted was glad he hadn't been more of a distraction. *Good luck, Joe.* "I thought I grabbed all the posterboards. I'm sorry."

"Welp. Guess I'd better respect my elders."

Ted shook his head. He saw the playful gleam in her sparkling eyes and her half-smile. But he never wanted her to ever feel coerced. "Listen, Stephanie. I'm sorry it took me so long to realize what was only feet away from me this whole time. But I'm awake now. I've snapped out of my coma, and I'm ready to live. And I want to, with you. You were right when you said I used excuses to push you away. I did. And I'll probably screw up again. I never stopped caring about you or wanting the best for you. I just didn't think I could possibly fit that bill."

"But?" She teased the word and nibbled her bottom lip.

"I love you. If you'll take a chance on an old fool like me, you won't regret it."

"You won't turn out to be one of those millennials with no savings because you're addicted to avocado toast?" She teased.

He chuckled. "It's fine. Give me your best generational slaps. I've heard them all. It's the curse of my age."

She stepped forward, draping her arms around his neck. "I love you, too."

He lowered his mouth to hers. He put every ounce of hope and every single promise he had into the kiss, tightening his grip on her waist to let her know he'd never let go. The chorus of "oohs" that could have been a canned audience response from a sitcom were enough to assure him this town would never let him forget what he'd done here today.

And wasn't he lucky.

EPILOGUE

Stephanie loved being with Ted. She didn't need much. She didn't need fancy dinners, romantic movies, or sparkly jewelry. Time together in any capacity, from working side by side to reading their books, was her love language. Every second was special.

"You're really sure you don't mind?" Ted asked.

In the shotgun seat, Stephanie squeezed his hand. "Of course not. Have I ever minded when dinner and a movie becomes a ranch event?"

He shook his head. "No, you haven't. You've been a really good sport."

She liked the way the smile reached the corners of his eyes. She liked so many things about him, more than she had ever guessed at during her years of unrequited pining. From deep conversations to silly moments and every comfortable silence in between, she connected with him more every day.

He parked in the semi-circle drive. With five vehicles already in position, he angled at the very back of the line. "One day we'll do something fun." He released her hand and turned off the engine. "I promise."

"You make our time together fun. Even when we have a bunch of spectators for our date."

"Well, not so many anymore." The words were almost under his breath as he opened his door and exited the vehicle.

In the month since they had started dating, after the failed romantic moment in the middle of the street—that ended up being witnessed by no less than fifteen people. Who knew so many people were free in the middle of the day? Bystanders and interruptions had become part of being together.

For the first few weeks, date nights at the cabin became family affairs with the tight quarters. Stephanie hadn't minded too much although it was awkward to have one of her students witnessing her casual moments. Long walks around the property had become their go-to for time together.

Instead of waiting for the new year, Maddy and Jen had moved out of the cabin at the beginning of October. An apartment building in a great location had a sudden vacancy.

Jen jumped on the chance. While Stephanie knew Ted was glad to have his space to himself again, she could also see the sadness in the last week since he'd been on his own again.

Before she finished grabbing her purse and unbuckling, he had her door open.

"Thanks."

"Are you really sure you don't mind?" he asked. "We don't have to stay for supper. We could make it a quick visit."

Stephanie shook her head. "I have to see Maddie and Colby's Halloween costume. I've heard all about how hard your sister has been working on it at school."

"It's something." He chuckled. "I haven't seen the whole look pulled together. I've only been called in to help wrangle Colby for measurements. Have you ever held a dog still so it could be measured for a hat?"

She widened her eyes.

"And the weird thing is, the dog didn't really mind. I've never known a dog that likes costumes," he said. "Colby might be more person than dog though."

"Or she just likes attention. She gets a lot of it," Stephanie said. "Before we go in there, how are Ryan and Meg's wedding plans going? I don't want to say anything and step on anyone's toes."

They had reached the front of the ranch house.

Instead of continuing up the front steps, he pulled her to the back, taking the long way around the covered porch from the backyard and making their way to the door. They weren't visible from the front window yet.

He darted his gaze around the porch. "Would you believe me if I told you I think Ryan might be a groomzilla?"

Stephanie chuckled. "If he needs any help. . ."

"You're sweet to offer. Take my advice. Stay out of this one. You'll have your hands full with Frontier Days and starting your master's degree. You don't want to get involved."

She wanted to argue. Herd wasn't known for its options. She assumed she'd plan the event easily because each item only had one choice. Cake? General Store. Catering? Abby Whit's food truck. Photography? The Old West studio. "I'm sure I could handle it."

He shook his head. "You can handle logistics no problem. But dealing with a finicky groom? The situation is already tense."

"Oh really?" She wrinkled her brow. "Tensions between the couple? That's a shame."

"More like a groom and his grandfather. And the grandfather's insistence about the wedding planner."

The front door opened with a crash.

Startled, Stephanie leaned around Ted and spotted Hank.

"Come on inside. It's not getting any warmer out here, and the food is getting colder by the second inside," Hank said. His voice was deep and scratchy, almost a snarl.

Hank's words were harsher than normal. While he embraced the appearance of a gruff cowboy, he had never behaved as such. The old man was a sweetheart.

She held tight to Ted's hand as he steered her towards the door and inside. Once she crossed the threshold, she stepped back.

Hank shut the front door.

She stilled Ted with their interlaced hands and shot him a look before turning to their host. "Mr. Kincaid? Are you feeling alright? We don't have to stay long if you'd rather have the house to yourself."

"Oh, I'm sorry." Hank scrubbed a hand over his face. "Just trying to talk sense into my grandson again."

She nodded.

The pair disagreed often about big decisions. Between a wedding and a full-scale construction project, they had plenty of opportunity for strife. The town had rallied to help the Kincaids clear the debris and start the new build. In record time, plans had been drawn, submitted, and approved. With the foundation poured, the crew worked on putting up the walls and roof in a race against the weather.

"If I can be of any assistance, I'm glad to help. I could get Joe started on the timetable for planning a wedding."

"Don't you worry about it, darling." Hank forced a smile. "Joe and Abby will figure it out. Ryan is the one leading the charge and driving everyone to distraction." He patted her hand. "I'm glad you could come. Supper is on the table. You know the way."

Together, they continued down the slate tile hall to the large kitchen at the back of the home. A swinging door that had been installed to provide privacy during tourist season was propped wide open, letting light and sound spill out. The room was warm, inviting, and smelled of chicken pot pie. Her stomach growled. Ted led her to the table, and they sat on the bench opposite Joe, Meg, and Ryan.

"How is your book coming, Joe?" Stephanie asked as she unfolded a paper napkin over her lap.

Joe blew out a sigh. "Slow. I had hoped to make more progress by now." He shrugged. "I'll get it done. Maybe not in time for the centennial, but I'd rather do my best work than rush."

Hank took his seat at the head of the table.

"Don't eat yet," Ryan announced. "We have our special guests coming down the stairs."

Meg turned toward the door. "I am so excited to see what they are wearing. Do you have any ideas, Ted?"

"None," Ted smiled. "My sister and Maddie have been determined to keep this a secret. I was only called in for back-up but not given enough clearance for the classified intel."

Jen appeared in the room from the open doorway. "Is everyone ready?"

Nods and murmurs of agreement erupted around the large plank table.

"Okay." Jen pulled out her phone and it tapped the screen.

Familiar music filtered into the room. But Stephanie wasn't sure where she had heard it before. She couldn't quite place the melody.

At her side, Ted folded his arms and shielded his mouth with a hand. He shook slightly.

Then the opening line was sung as Maddy and Colby entered the room.

"Sisters, sisters. . ." The music played, and Ted and Jen sang.

A dog and a girl dressed in matching powder blue tuille dresses and sequined headdresses entered and spun in a circle. Maddy held an ostrich feather fan. Colby sat and wagged her tail.

"Oh, she looks like an angel," Meg exclaimed.

Stephanie glanced away from the charming tableau.

Ryan rested a hand on Meg's shoulder, his eyes crinkling and softening as he gazed at his fiancée.

Stephanie bit her lip to still her tongue from a cheeky response or a chuckle. Maddy was precious, but Meg meant the dog.

"See how well she can do? She has to be the maid of honor and ring bearer," Meg stage whispered.

"Ring bearer, maybe. You cannot have a dog as a maid of honor," Ryan replied.

The dog and girl danced and wagged to the end of the song. The audience dutifully applauded their efforts.

"You look marvelous," Stephanie said. "Do you need help getting changed for dinner?"

"Thank you." Maddy beamed. "Mommy has to help me, Miss Patricks."

"I'll help, too," Meg said and scurried away from the table. Walking away, Meg and Jen leaned close together, leading the dog and girl away.

Stephanie smiled. All three women had become friends. A few years ago, Stephanie had only considered Kelly and Lauren part of her inner circle. Over the past six months, however, she'd expanded her friend group by two and was glad. Jen had quickly become part of the community.

Stephanie turned toward Hank at the head of the table. "Mr. Kincaid? Have you ever thought about you know who and," she lowered her voice and leaned close, "Jen?"

Hank stroked his chin. "I had. She is a nice woman. But. . . no. I'm only more convinced than ever. There is somebody for everybody, and Joe would get bored with anyone else. He needs conflict." Hank patted her hand on the table. "You leave them to me. I know what I'm doing. I have someone else in mind for Jen."

Hank had brought enough strife to Joe with the event planning. Would the phrase if you want something done give it to a busy person prove true? Stephanie wasn't so sure. She couldn't argue with the mischievous twinkle in his eye. She was only grateful she'd escaped his notice but found love anyway.

Ted reached for her hand under the table and squeezed.

This was the good life. She'd savor every moment.

UNMASKING A
Cowgirl

BOOK THREE
MATCH MADE IN MONTANA

Rachelle Paige Campbell

CHAPTER 1

Some days, Abby Whit forgot she was hiding behind an alias. After two years and change of living in Herd, Montana, she fully embraced her cover story as a food truck chef, passing through town. To anyone who asked, she was working for herself after stints being the sous chef for chefs from Kansas City to Las Vegas. Her family didn't put down roots. Those were the kernels of truth. But she'd arrived with a plan.

Determine the public's perception of her family and assess the feasibility of taking back her land.

On the frosty March morning, she parked her food truck in the gravel lot behind the bright red barn on the Kincaid ranch. Against a snowy backdrop and overcast sky, the new construction building popped amidst the open land that had been owned by one family for over a century. Credited with saving the local economy by modernizing their ranch into a cowboy spa, Hank and grandson Ryan Kincaid were undisputed winners in the town's founding families' feud. Her family, the Whittiers, were the first losers. The good citizens of Herd considered her ancestors the villains in the town's history. If she had given her full name on arrival, she'd have been kicked out of the state.

Hating the Kincaids on principle, given her history, would have been expected. Prejudice hadn't suited her. They had never questioned her sudden appearance and purpose in the tight knit community. They'd supported and encouraged her. Their kindness was the reason she continued to debate finally making her legal claim to the small patch of land near the church where she parked her food truck. The deadline approached.

The hum of the idling truck wasn't loud enough to silence her whirring thoughts. Helping out others in the community had been equally about establishing good karma for herself and treating others with the kindness she valued. No one had been better to her than the Kincaids. She didn't think she'd done nearly enough to redeem herself in their eyes once they learned the truth.

Joe would be sure to highlight her villainy.

She shuddered. Joe Staunch, middle school teacher and ranch tour guide, was her very vocal critic. She was careful to never cause anyone offense and yet she'd somehow made an enemy of him.

He either ignored her or complained about her—often within her earshot. Some people rubbed each other wrong. She accepted that fact. The trouble was that she liked him. Her heart wouldn't be reasoned into submission.

She cut the engine and exited the truck, leaving the vehicle unlocked.

An icy breeze whipped past her, burning her ears, and carrying the scent of a nearby fire. She crunched the gravel under her feet as she made her way to the barn.

While she agonized over the decision, she only had two choices. Either she claimed her inheritance, or she gave up on it forever. Security lingered so near she could almost smell the roasting meat in proper ovens and feel the stability of the solid walls and roof from her own restaurant on her land. She couldn't stall much longer. But she didn't want the town to feel she'd betrayed them. She hadn't told bald-faced lies. Neither had she shared the complete truth.

The side door stood slightly ajar. Muffled, deep voices carried out.

She slipped inside and rubbed her hands together. "Hello?" she called, her teeth chattering, from nerves and the low temperature.

"We're here," Hank Kincaid replied.

She blew on her icy figures and approached the men standing in the center of the room.

"Sorry, the new furnace arrives by the end of the week," Ryan Kincaid said. He stood next to several toolboxes and a stack of drywall.

"No bother," she said, waving off any concern like she didn't notice the unfinished walls with wires poking out and gaps visible in the boards. A little spray foam insulation and a working system would solve the heating problem. "I hope the first week in June is warm enough and we won't have to be concerned with turning on the heat. I don't want to add *fix furnace* to either Hank's ninetieth birthday extravaganza or the wedding budget." She plastered on a smile to stop her teeth from chattering.

"Bad luck to replace the furnace twice in one year." Hank Kincaid shook his head. "Makes me worried what the third calamity will be."

"Doesn't the fire count as the first strike of poor luck?" Ted Stirling frowned. "Rebuilding this barn from the ground up is at the top of my list of bad things."

She darted her gaze between the three cowboys.

As the oldest, white-haired, and permanently tan, Hank Kincaid often touted tired cliches and old wives' tales as guiding life principles. "No, that was last year's number two after my trip to the hospital."

Hank's grandson and heir, Ryan, rolled his eyes. Standing well over six feet and with a perpetual scowl, he was the town's stalwart visionary. Practical and forward thinking, he had revitalized his family's legacy and the entire community through a clear and unexpected plan. He didn't waste time looking for signs of divine intervention.

The third, Ted Stirling, was the thoughtful ranch hand turned trusted confidant. Often found stroking his jaw in consideration, the slim man with thin streaks of silver threading his dark hair didn't jump to conclusions. He'd been hired to work cattle and, over the past decade, switched direction to managing people.

Abby had overheard the stories enough from Joe. She almost imagined a first-hand recollection despite only living in town for two years. For the past decade plus, the three men guided the town to an unprecedented economic recovery thanks to their varying character qualities, forming a strong pyramid. If one side wobbled, the other two assumed the weight of the struggles and balanced the load.

What would they do when her revelation rocked them all?

"Was there a number three last year?" she asked.

Hank tapped a finger against the deep cleft in his chin. "I don't think there was unless you count Colby's trip to the vet after she ate that pan of brownies."

Colby, a rescue mutt, was arguably more human than dog. She hadn't been shaken by her life-or-death accident over Thanksgiving weekend. Meg, her owner, and Ryan's fiancé, however had been an emotional wreck.

"No more of this talk." Ryan held up his hands. "Don't even put the energy out into the universe. We have too much going on in the next few months for anyone to go looking for a curse or believing in superstition."

Hank nodded and turned, flashing crossed fingers behind his back.

Abby glanced at Hank's crossed fingers and snorted. She rubbed a hand over her face. "Sorry. Must be allergies."

"Why did you need us to stop by today?" Joe Staunch asked, his voice carrying from the sliding glass doors in the center of the back wall overlooking the deck behind the building. "Couldn't this be a phone call or email?" he asked as he approached.

Abby gaped. She was well-versed in his curt words but had never heard him so short with his friends and bosses. In the summer, Joe served as a tour guide for groups interested in historical excursions on the ranch.

"Yes, keep us on task. Thanks, Joe," Ryan said, glaring. "I wanted you both to get a sense of the space. Abby, we have added a small prep station but besides the sink, dishwasher, and single oven, it's not a fully functioning kitchen."

She nodded, pleased for the prep area. "Can I park the truck close to that space?"

"Yes, we have a service door leading to a spot for you with hook-ups," Ted said. "The plan for Hank's ninetieth birthday and the wedding has expanded."

She widened her gaze and met Joe's. As reluctant partners, she hoped for a second of commiseration to thaw his icy demeanor.

He shook his head and glanced away. He wore his disapproval and doubt like a pair of well-worn jeans. Whether he liked it or not, they were tied to each other.

They were stuck together in planning the event. For the better part of ten months, she had been working on her contribution, catering, and communicating mostly by email to Joe. She trusted him to carry his weight, not that he shared much of his progress.

"Meg and I have decided since we are only getting married once, we need to do it right," Ryan said. "No more simple ceremony. We want a full weekend of events."

"Oh." Abby tipped her head to the side unsure she followed what that meant. Ryan's fiancé, Meg, wasn't the sort to make a big fuss. A full weekend could include multiple events on each day. She'd have to carefully plan the menus if she was expected to cater everything. She wouldn't want to repeat any meals.

"The birthday celebration remains on Friday night. Saturday will be the rehearsal dinner. Sunday will be the wedding," Ryan said.

Abby nodded. Including one more event, the rehearsal dinner, wouldn't zap her creative spirit. Her worst-case scenario had been avoided but didn't alleviate all of her concerns. She would be doing a lot of cooking in a short amount of time. She couldn't turn down the opportunity. To stay in town, she needed to expand her business. She'd started a catering side-hustle on the ranch to pad her bottom line.

With more events, she needed more space and capacity. Her truck didn't have the refrigerator space to store enough food for three-days of events. She'd have to use what space she could find at the Kincaid's house and ask her friend James Rabbitt at The Golden Crown saloon, the only full-service restaurant in town. She knew he'd agree for the special, one-time-only weekend. If she wanted to be the go-to caterer for the ranch's new wedding and events business, she needed a better plan.

I have one. But it'll make everyone hate me.

"Let me see what I can do." She smiled until her cheek twitched. She hated the chicken and egg predicament she'd landed herself in but neither could she turn her back on the easiest solution. Claim her inheritance and build. Of course, if she was black-listed in town for being a Whittier, kitchen space wouldn't matter. "Do you have any ideas about the food for the rehearsal dinner and wedding? I can cook whatever you like. Ian is almost finished with my new traveling smoker. Depending on the wedding start time, I could be out here all-day roasting meat."

Hank licked his lips. "Sounds good to me. Now I regret asking you to cook all those fancy little things for my birthday."

She chuckled. "I can switch. I haven't put in the order yet. You let me know what you want. Canapes and small plates or a sit-down dinner. Or buffet. I can do barbeque or Tex Mex or steak."

"Could you send me a few sample menus for both options?" Ryan asked. "I'm in charge of the food."

She pulled her phone out of her back pocket. The lock screen flashed with a reminder. *Meeting with lawyer.* She'd hoped for some sense of moral clarity before facing the attorney in the next town over, but wasn't likely to discover it here while the Kincaids were being so considerate and kind. She unlocked the screen and typed in the note. "All set, I'll send you a mock-up in the next day or so. How many guests are you thinking?"

"We've set aside enough rooms for a hundred guests to stay on property," Ted said. "Give or take. Would you mind including Stephanie in the email exchange? She's taken up the wedding planning. She can coordinate with you and Joe."

"Of course." Abby smiled. The simple project was twisting and turning into a complicated knot with each additional person. Maybe that was a good thing. She could work closely with Stephanie, a kindergarten teacher and one of Joe's colleagues, at the local public K-12 school. Stephanie knew how to handle Joe and the bubbly woman remained nonplussed by anyone's moods. "I'd better head into town and discuss the changes with James."

"If you say so," Joe muttered.

Abby spun and faced her partner slash nemesis. "What does that mean?"

"Nothing. If you think you can't handle a big event, you need to get help. Sounds like you already know your limits. At least in this instance." Joe folded his arms over his chest and stared her down.

Her cheeks flamed and red-hot anger bubbled up inside her.

She'd been careful to be overly nice to him. He was an interesting person, rattling off more facts about the town than anyone else alive, including walking encyclopedia Hank Kincaid. If anyone could uncover her secret, it was him. While pursuing her own research about her family, she'd often bumped into him at the library. Despite the need for self-preservation, she was curious about his work and asked questions.

History wasn't immune to bias. Joe's outspoken search for truth heartened her. Whatever happened with her position in town, perhaps he would save her family's reputation.

But she'd never won his friendship or even a bare level of grudging respect. Trying to make a success of her business on her own, she was plenty used to naysayers. She prided herself on her thick skin. His comments were typical of his conversation with her. But the cumulative effect meant each word cut her a little deeper. Death by a thousand papercuts.

"I know what I'm doing. I'm very good at making things happen. In case you hadn't noticed?" she asked.

Joe dropped his arms to his sides and turned his gaze away.

His response wasn't a victory, as far as she was concerned. He'd needled her into a verbal spat in front of people she respected and counted on. With any luck, she hadn't disgraced herself too much. Yet. She faced the trio of cowboys once more, blocking Joe from her line of sight as best she could. "If you don't need anything else from me?"

"Thanks for coming out on such short notice," Hank said.

"Yes, we really do appreciate you and all your help with the ranch." Ryan's smile crinkled the corners of his eyes. "We're here for you, too."

"If you need any assistance with loading or unloading your truck, you can always call," Ted added.

She glanced between the three and saw pity in their pinched expressions. They felt bad for her because of Joe's poor treatment. She prayed her one-sided crush wasn't public knowledge. As long as these men didn't pity her ill-fated attraction, she could walk away with her head held high.

She rubbed a hand over her tickling nose. She'd pretend she hadn't noticed their solemn expressions. "Thank you for..." Tears stung her eyes for a different reason. Guilt and shame for her secret. "Thanks for everything. I'll start menu planning immediately." Spinning on her heel, she crossed through the barn, her snow boots leaving a slushy trail behind her on the thick pine boards. As she slid the door open a crack and slipped through the opening, she heard Hank berate Joe.

"What is wrong with you, boy?" The old cowboy's gravelly voice carried through the opening as she carefully shut the door.

Stuffing her hands in her pockets, she dropped her chin into the collar of her coat. With each step, she crunched gravel and snow under her boots. Maybe she just imagined what she wanted Hank to say. She spent enough time lost in her thoughts, preparing herself for the worst. Before long, she'd have to face facts and she wasn't sure she was creative enough to prepare mentally for the town's reaction to her real identity.

If I don't take the land, nothing will change.

Without the land, she couldn't move forward in a meaningful way, and she'd have to leave. Life didn't stand still. Whether she liked it or not, everything was changed by the mere passage of time.

She wished her goal wasn't so tightly wrapped around her secret. But if Joe hadn't figured it out by now, she was in the clear. Probably.

Joe studied the thick pine boards under his boots, searching for the grain in the wavy patterns like he'd uncover the secret of life. He'd do anything to stop from tracking her as she blessedly left the barn, taking the faint scent of butter with her. A cold gust of air swept through the barn. After last night's snow, they were due for a reprieve from precipitation. Not that anyone in Herd or the surrounding area would complain about snow or rain. Last summer's drought had caused major issues for the prairie including a wildfire that consumed the historic barn on the Kincaid ranch.

"Hey, did you hear me?" Hank said.

Joe glanced over his shoulder.

Ryan took a step back and held up both palms.

"What is *wrong* with you, boy?" Hank asked again.

Joe poked his chest with his index finger.

Hank nodded.

Joe flinched. He'd assumed Hank mean Ryan. Joe wasn't addressed as *boy*. Hank saved the moniker for his grandson. Joe gulped. He must have really messed up.

"Well?" Hank glared.

If Joe knew the answer, he'd solve a lot of his own problems. He wasn't sure exactly what it was about Abby Whit that grated on his nerves only that her presence—no matter how pretty she was—set his teeth on edge.

He was being unfair and unkind. He prided himself on being the opposite, treating others with a magnanimity he wished in return. But he couldn't stop his displeasure with her and in turn only grew angrier at himself. It was a vicious hamster wheel he wanted to leap out of but hadn't figured out how.

"I'm sorry. I'm just..." Joe ran a hand through his hair. He'd had big plans for how to spend his spring break. Giving up time to argue with his nemesis wasn't part of his schedule. He let his frustration with himself and his lack of progress on his passion project, a history tome on the town, spill over. "I was wrong."

"Hmm." Hank grunted. "I'll leave it to you to apologize."

Joe nodded. He knew better than to try to explain himself anymore. Hank had eased up on matchmaking Joe and Abby over the winter. With the wedding and upcoming birthday celebration, his attention was directed elsewhere. Joe was glad for the break. And one morning of a walk-through wasn't going to throw off his schedule for the rest of the week. He had interviews lined up and appointments scheduled at the county records office. "Is Stephanie really on board with the wedding planning?" He turned to Ted. "What about her other commitments?"

Ted shrugged.

Joe read the resignation in his friend's shaking shoulders. Stephanie was always busy. If she didn't have three jobs at once, she claimed boredom. This summer, however, she had plans to continue her education with the goal of becoming a school administrator. She'd also be teaching a yoga class on the ranch and running the town's summer festival. Joe supported his friend's ambition whole-heartedly but wondered if she was taking on too much. "Does she have time?"

"Does she ever?" Ted asked. "I've stopped asking her if she needs help and jump in. She won't give up her responsibilities."

"Someone has to be in charge. Meg really wanted to get married in a field." Ryan sighed. "I want to give her the day of her dreams, and she's giving me nothing to work with."

Joe met Ted's wide-eye gaze. Meg was the sort of person who knew her own mind and wasn't shy about letting it be known. If she said she wanted to stand in a field and recite her vows, she wanted to do exactly that. Joe appreciated her frank, up-front personality. He never had to guess around her. *Unlike other people.*

On the surface, Abby was everything sweet and smiling. Eager to please, she pitched in at every town event and joined almost every club. He hardly went a day without running into her at some group. He'd spotted her planting annuals in the reused oak barrels up and down Main Street the week before Memorial Day in the past. He'd nearly been impaled by her knitting needles as she barreled out of the saloon. And, of course and most unfortunately, she asked him incessant questions when he was researching on the second floor of the library. She had no reason to be there, quizzing him, unless she was trying to aggravate him.

"Okay, groomzilla. Calm down. We'll make sure your big day fills every one of your childhood dreams," Joe said.

Ryan raised an eyebrow and widened his stance. The twitching muscle in his cheek flashed a warning.

"If Steph is on board, are you sure you'll still need me? She can probably take over my side of the planning, don't you think?" Joe asked. He tried to keep his words modulated but couldn't completely eliminate the hopeful tone of up speak.

"No. You know what I like," Hank said. "You're practically an expert on everything Kincaid ranch."

Practically but not officially. Joe smiled. The old cowboy knew how to cut straight to the heart of the matter. Earning undeniable credentials, elevating himself from the anecdote guy to indisputable historian was his ultimate goal. After five years, he wasn't any closer to achieving his dream. Of course, the past two and a half had added the distraction of the sudden appearance of Abby Whit and figuring her out was his go-to distraction.

"Meg wants to make a go of weddings and events. She has already worked with Stephanie on pulling a lot of the tasks together. She's developing master lists for the future," Ted said.

"You must unify and execute our visions of the event. You'll know what to do," Hank said.

"Besides you won't be totally on your own. Stephanie will function as a wedding day coordinator," Ryan added. "Her focus is on the ceremony. You can't believe how much needs to get squeezed into such a short amount of time."

The field sounded better and better to Joe. But Ryan was nothing if not a meticulous visionary. He'd have some exacting image of what he wanted. Stephanie might be the only person up to the task. "Is my timetable for the birthday celebration still adequate? Parade, cook-out, fireworks?"

Hank nodded.

"Will we need to hire more staff for clean-up?" Ryan turned to Ted.

Ted shook his head. "All taken care of. If you can support the coordination with the town council, I'd be in your debt."

Joe drew back his shoulders. If he'd earned anything on his own merits, it was the respect of the council. "Of course. We should be set. As long as the new herd doesn't cause too much calamity in town, you shouldn't have too much to worry about."

Ryan scrubbed a hand along his jaw. "We'll find out in a few weeks."

Initially settled at the end of the nineteenth century on a false claim of gold in the creek, Herd was named for the overwhelming number of bison in the area. The eradication of the animals within a few years of the founding was one of many stains on the past. At one time, three ranches surrounded the town. Only the Kincaid family remained, absorbing all the land in the process. Ryan sought to reintroduce the bison. Many remained skeptical about the impact.

"How's the research going?" Ted asked.

"Slow." Joe exhaled a heavy breath. He found himself so easily distracted by the personal stories that he'd lost his main thread of the book several times in the process. He'd refocused around an unshakeable through line, the Kincaids. Betrayals littered the past, but the family found strength from ingenuity. Ryan was only the latest in a long line of smart, risk-taking businessmen.

Joe felt the direction of the book, an undeniable American story, would resonate with readers across a broad spectrum of ages and backgrounds. If he could only finish. "I'm heading to the library, unless you need anything else from me?"

Ryan shook his head.

"I'll walk you out." Ted strode forward, clapping a hand on his shoulder.

The decisive grip was unshakeable. Joe wouldn't fight. Of the three, he'd least expect a lecture from Ted. Maybe he was that far gone that only his friend's warning would suffice. "Sure, thanks." He waved to the Kincaids and followed Ted out of the barn via a side-door.

Joe stepped onto the deck and raised a hand to shield his gaze against the bright glare. The door shut behind him with a dull thud.

Pristine snow covered the wooden boards and sparkled in the faint sunlight of the overcast day. Beyond the railing, the prairie rose and fell in gentle undulations. With the snowfall, drifts created drama and mystery. In the summer, wildflowers grew amidst the tall grasses, brightening the otherwise monochromatic view.

Joe hated to wreck the pretty winter picture with his booted steps. But if he was going to be yelled at, he didn't want an audience. He lifted one foot and then the other into the eight inches of snowfall, trudging across the deck.

"I keep forgetting to add *shovel the deck* to my chores." Ted chuckled.

"I can't even imagine your list." Joe raised his hands to his mouth and blew on his icy fingers. "Did you want to talk?"

"Are you okay?" Ted tipped his head to the side.

No. "Same as always." Joe forced a grin. He hoped the twist of his lips was more welcoming than the grimace he felt. "Maybe a little more pressure this year with the events and the end of school coming. Why do you ask?" While considerate, his friend wasn't the type to poke around another person's private business. Until recently, stoic Ted had been allergic to feelings. But then everything changed. The life he'd seemingly left behind crashed into him.

Joe was happy for Ted. The cowboy of a few words might argue otherwise, but no man truly wanted to live alone. With the arrival of his sister and niece, along with opening his heart up to love again after a decade plus as a grieving widower, Ted couldn't seem to escape the influence of one woman without being under that of another. And he never scowled anymore.

Ted flushed.

Shaking his head, Joe stuffed his fists into his coat pocket. He wasn't against love. But he was actively anti-manipulation. Why Hank decided to pair him with the most suspicious woman in town, Joe would never understand. "I'm okay. Feeling a bit impatient to hurry up and prove myself. If I'm being honest."

"All in good time. You don't have anything to prove. You're valued."

Not to me. Joe was tired of feeling so out of sync with himself. Abby was the only person who seemed interested in hearing his history tidbits and facts. She'd quickly become part of the fabric of the community and wasn't leaving. He'd have to deal with her for the rest of his life.

"If you want off the project, I can probably talk to Steph about it."

Joe shook his head. "No, don't do that. I didn't realize how high-maintenance Ryan was going to be about the wedding. She's going to have her hands full with his demands."

"Okay. If anything changes, let me know. I've got your back. Good luck with your work this week."

"Thanks, Ted. See you later." Joe strode across the deck and jogged around the side of the building to his car parked nearby. Shielded from the worst of the drifts by the barn, the gravel lot was exposed. Joe unlocked his car and hopped inside, turning over the engine.

His love of history was rooted in learning about personal connections to important moments. What seemed small to someone at the time ultimately became a barometer of a broader sentiment.

And if he didn't hear someone else's tale, he often filled in the details on his own. Storytelling was embedded deep in Joe's soul. He'd never met a dog without developing a backstory for the creature or witnessed an event without stringing together motivation for what unfolded.

He backed his car out of the parking lot and coasted onto the two-lane road heading to town. He needed distraction from Abby Whit. Her unexpected arrival bugged him over two years later. With each passing day, the chance of uncovering her secrets grew more unlikely. He couldn't shake the burning questions that simmered at every encounter.

Who was she, and why was she here?

CHAPTER 2

On the raised wooden sidewalk outside the rough-hewn stones of The Golden Crown saloon's façade, Abby crunched the remaining layer of snow and ice under her boots. The pathways around town were neatly shoveled. Road salt was avoided to protect the integrity of the wooden boards that comprised a big part of the Old West charm.

She snorted. The town was founded on a murky tale. A hopeful prospector claimed to discover gold in the creek now located on the Kincaid ranch. In truth, he had only found a gold tooth. The mistake wasn't caught until long after three families from the East Coast were well into their ranching operations, dividing the land between them in a decades long campaign of backstabbing and betrayal.

With the toe of her boot, she pressed against a patch of ice, cracking the thin sheet. Completely clearing the wooden sidewalks was almost impossible without the help of portable outdoor heaters. Near the saloon's front door, where warmth had escaped, the snow had melted and reformed as ice.

If she went inside, she wouldn't have to bother with the chill or the slick patch. She drew back her shoulders and filled her lungs with a deep breath. Asking for favors never got any easier for her. She did her best to offer her help and support whenever and wherever she could. She especially was proud of herself for those moments she anticipated someone's need and offered before being asked.

How many good deeds must she accomplish to wash herself clean from her deceit?

A lie by omission was still dishonesty even if it wasn't malicious. And strolling into the building that ultimately pushed her family out of town never got easier. Long ago, on one drunken night, her family's fate was sealed. Hoss Whittier had kicked over a kerosene lamp and set this entire side of Main Street ablaze. And then, after the buildings had been rebuilt, he did it again.

Shipping stone this far out on the prairie bankrupted the wealthiest family in town. Hoss's father sold the ranch to the Hawkes and Kincaids, splitting the land that had been the barrier between them down the center. The Hawkes wasted no time and built a pretty clapboard house on their newly acquired property, inching closer to the Kincaids. A few outbuildings remained, but the Whittier home was razed. If the Hawkes and Kincaids were determined to eradicate the Whittiers from the land, they had been successful. Only a spot of land, two acres, near the church at the far end of Main Street remained under Whittier control.

She'd often wondered why. If the townsfolk were so determined to push them out, why had her ancestors held onto anything? Since her arrival, however, she was grateful. Because Herd was the sort of place a person longed to call home.

For good measure, she rubbed the sole of her boots against the historic iron boot scraper. She pushed inside the swinging door and blinked, her vision adjusting to the interior. With the snow almost blinding under the gray sky, she needed a second to recollect herself under the replica kerosene lanterns hung throughout the open dining room.

"Abby?" A deep voice called.

She turned toward the bar, a polished walnut relic that ran the length of the western wall. "Hey." She waved and approached.

Behind the smooth counter, James Rabbitt, owner and proprietor, wiped glasses with a cloth. Dressed in shirt sleeves held in place with garters and a striped waistcoat, he complimented his historical dress with a neatly trimmed, waxed moustache. He was known for his friendly demeanor as much as his facial hair. He never kept one look for too long. Switching from mutton chops to an Imperial from one week to the next.

"Are you here for knitting club?" He tipped his head toward the tote on her arm.

She glanced down at the bag, almost forgetting the other purpose of her visit. She held onto the strap. "Yep. I'm still not ready to get off the loom, but my scarf is coming along."

He chuckled.

"Actually, I'm glad to bump into you." Her voice cracked, and she frowned. The words were stilted, awkward, and rehearsed. The last point was perhaps the one she feared the most.

When the truth came out, because even if she didn't claim the land someone was bound to uncover her real identity eventually, she didn't want to be accused of acting her way through the past several years of her life. She'd been honest and real about everything except her name and purpose.

She cringed. How much worse would the truth sound out loud?

"Do you need to pick up a few more shifts?" James asked.

She shook her head. James and his wife Heather, had been big supporters. As the only restaurant in town, they had welcomed a little friendly competition and sent business her way during the busiest time of the year. In the winter months, when she could not operate her food truck, they employed her in their kitchen. Without their help, she wouldn't have lasted more than the first summer in Herd. Once she opened her restaurant, she wouldn't need to burden them so much. She could be their friend and equal. "I came from the ranch. Ryan's wedding sounds bigger than I initially assumed."

James shook his head, lifting the corner of his mouth in a grin. "I told you. He never does anything small."

"Isn't the wedding day supposed to be all about the bride? I thought for sure Meg would win out with her intimate ceremony."

"I subscribe to the happy wife, happy life mantra. Heather told me where to be and when. But I think Meg doesn't want to fight. Besides, it's a good chance to launch their new business. Can't overlook that."

Abby nibbled the inside of her cheek. No one could ignore a single opportunity. While Ryan redeveloped his land, he could not have revitalized the town on his own. Every business had to step up and take charge of their future. Weddings and events at the ranch promised Abby a good deal of business growth. She couldn't lose the opportunity, or she'd never get the chance again.

"Are you here to ask for more refrigerator space?" James threw the cloth over his shoulder and crossed his arms over his chest. "Do you need another oven?"

Yes, and yes. She couldn't throw herself on his mercy without showing she was determined to help her career on her part as well. "Ian should have the new smoker ready well before June. I won't need all of your ovens. But yes, I definitely need more refrigerator space. I'll tap into everything I can at the ranch but the new barn doesn't have a fully functioning kitchen, just a prep space."

"We'll come together and help. It's a big weekend for the town. But if the weddings do take off at the ranch, you'll need to find another solution."

"Thank you, and yes, I know." She nodded. Her budget wouldn't stretch far enough to purchase property in town. She barely had enough to build on the land she already owned.

"Looks like they're here." He pointed behind her.

She spun and spotted Heather and Kelly Strong, one of the local kindergarten teachers.

The pair waved and strode toward their usual table next to one of the thick structural wooden beams with a light positioned directly above the circular oak, table.

Turning back, she met his gaze. "I'd better not be late. Thanks again, James."

He smiled.

She crossed the room to the table. Since coming to town, she started a wide variety of hobbies in an effort to get to know her neighbors and figure out if she wanted to settle here. She decided long before she arrived that she wouldn't claim the land and immediately sell for top dollar. The Whittiers already had a poor reputation. She didn't want to solidify them as a scheming, inconsiderate, money-grabbing family. They had left town because they lost the faith of the community. She wouldn't twist the knife and make the wound irreparable. Claiming the land and using it was less likely to cause backlash.

"Good morning." Abby pulled out a chair and sat, setting her tote bag on the table. "Meeting up during the day to knit is always such a treat."

"Spring break never feels like much of either," Kelly said, her eyes sparkling with humor. "Until I get together with you ladies."

"You'll make me blush," Heather said.

No nonsense Heather wasn't the sort to be embarrassed by anything. Abby laughed. She wished for some of that self-esteem. Rifling through her bag, she retrieved her circular, plastic loom.

While the others worked with knitting needles, she stuck to the knitting hook. She'd made good progress, considering how many times she'd started the scarf. With ten inches of teal hanging off the loom, she traced the accidental rectangle she'd created near the bottom edge. On her second day, she'd hurried to get started and e-wrapped the wrong way, making the yarn double the thickness and almost breaking her hook as she attempted to loop the yarn over the loom.

Once she realized what she'd done, she could have undone the knitting and started for the tenth time. Instead, she wanted something different. She would leave this error in plain view as a reminder of what she screwed up.

Inevitably, during every project, she lost track of what she was supposed to be doing and made mistakes from her impatience to plow ahead instead of understanding what she needed to do. Overcomplicating her life and preparing for the worst was just what she did.

She wanted to change. Coming to Herd had been about more than restoring her family's good name. It had been about putting down roots and fighting to belong somewhere. The longer she stayed in town, the more she wanted to have a permanent position.

Her military parents were both children of military parents, and so on stretching far back into the past. They loved to pick up and start something new. She'd thought she loved it too. Until she'd started researching the family history and learning more about the motivation of what became her nomadic family. She was tired of running away. After culinary school, she'd had one-to three-year long stints with major chefs at restaurants around the world.

After a few rows, she stopped knitting and examined her progress. She'd lost track of whether to purl or knit. *Focus on the moment.* This hobby forced her to do that or end up with a bumpy, messy piece. She reviewed the sheet of paper tracking her progress, marked off what she'd knitted, and then studied her companions.

Kelly hummed as she knitted with her needles.

Heather kept her chin down, focusing on her work with a narrow-eyed gaze.

Abby couldn't ever just live in the moment. Her companions were good examples to her of what she could find if she stayed present.

Heather frowned. "Are you stuck?"

"No, just trying to gather my thoughts and set them aside." Abby smiled.

"How's the big event coming?" Kelly asked.

"I think it's getting even bigger," Abby said.

"I'm glad to hear it. It's sort of like our town's royal wedding. The two founding families finally coming together?" Kelly beamed. "I can't wait. I feel like I need to order a new dress and a hat for the occasion."

Heather snorted. "We're not in London. Don't expect to see them drive through town, waving to adoring fans lining the streets. Or to spot commemorative plates and tea towels with their faces in the shop windows."

"That's not a bad idea." Abby crossed her arms over her chest, content to ignore her knitting for a moment as she pondered. "When the British royals have a wedding, it is a huge boost to tourism. I'm not saying we start screen printing every mug we can find with the wedding date. But maybe we do need to play up the town's involvement more. Why not have them drive through town? With a western twist, riding around on horseback?"

"Better call, Stephanie," Kelly said.

"She's already on board but yes, I better run some ideas past her." Abby studied the table, unseeing. Because maybe if the third founding family, the disgraced, shame-faced Whittiers, worked extra hard to celebrate the other two, past sins could be more easily forgiven. This was another shot at redemption. And she couldn't blow it.

Joe paused the recording playback on his phone. Slipping the wireless headphones off his ears and onto his neck, he let the white-noise of the busy coffee shop drown out his inner demons. He didn't often treat himself to sitting around and working in public. Usually, after an interview, he completed his transcriptions in the comfort and silence of his home.

When he left the interview in Miles City, however, he decided on a change of venue. What was the point of a week off if he didn't get out of town? An hour away wasn't exactly the prototypical, tropical spring break destination, but he was glad for the scenery change all the same. Raising his drink, he blew into the lid and sipped the mocha, savoring the rich sweetness on his tongue.

Today's interview hadn't been of any extraordinary significance. He'd met with a family that had moved out of Herd in the sixties. The surviving members didn't have first-hand memories but shared passed-down recollections.

Joe often pondered when the real depth of the project would become clear. Too many of his interviews slipped into myth-making with unreliable narrators. The only consistent thread remained the villainous Whittier family.

With each retelling, he became more conflicted. Hoss Whittier had set fire to downtown twice. Reportedly, he'd been drunk both times. The town had demanded reparations and exile. His father had sold almost everything he owned to rebuild the saloon and post office in stone. Hoss had left.

The family had retained the small plot of land near the cemetery. After Hoss's father died, the family had disappeared forever to become part of the legend of the town's founding. If a person only lived as long as those who remembered them, Hoss was immortal. Joe wanted the rest of the story. He wouldn't mind a pro-Hoss bias if that meant answers.

The door opened and a blast of cold air rushed into the space.

With a shudder, he set his coffee on the table, drew his coat tighter, and crossed his arms over his chest. Leaning forward, he scanned the notes he'd typed so far. The crowded coffee shop meant he increased the volume on his headphones than he should. Scanning the laptop screen, he frowned. He'd included too many question marks in his transcription to continue the endeavor in his current locale. He wasn't saving himself any time or energy. But he doubted heading home would be the relief he needed.

Today's interview was probably a bust. After the reprimand at the barn this morning, he should just write off the whole day while he still could, go home, and do better tomorrow. He wouldn't let anyone down by retreating. *Except myself.* With a heavy sigh, he scrubbed his hands over his face, wiping away the crust in the corner of his eyes. He knew what he was to his friends and neighbors. A joke. He hated that. He wanted to be taken seriously with official credentials.

She takes you seriously. He bristled. Abby Whit's endorsement was hardly his end goal. He needed the rest of the town's support.

"Fancy seeing you here," a feminine voice said.

He drew up his shoulders and then his chin, preparing for an unwanted visitor. And then relaxed when his gaze met his companion. "Hi, Steph. Care to sit down?" He shut his laptop and cleared the small bistro table, putting his computer securely in the messenger bag on the third chair.

"Thanks. I didn't think it would be so crowded in here today. Especially not in the afternoon." She twisted her neck from one side to the other. "Although, I really should have." She chuckled.

The perky blonde sat in the free chair.

He scanned the packed coffee house. Every bistro table was claimed, including his in the front window next to the doorway. He selected the worst seat in the house out of necessity. Eyeing the overstuffed chairs near the fireplace, he fought the longing to move nearer the blaze. "Not many places to go around here during Spring Break."

"Unless you like snow-shoeing." She scrunched her nose. "I definitely do not."

He chuckled. "Were your ears burning this morning? I was at the ranch and learned all about your wedding day duties."

"Oh, yeah."

Her voice was oddly flat. As the town's go-to coordinator extraordinaire, Stephanie handled many major events. If this ceremony gave her pause, how far in over his head was he? "Is everything okay?"

"I'm sure it will be fine." She smoothed a strand of hair behind her ear. "Meg called me in a panic, and I agreed to help."

Meg panicked? His stomach felt heavy. "Did she explain why?"

"Ryan has a very clear vision. She wants him to be happy so she'll go along with whatever he wants. But she needs help."

And maybe an intermediary. Meg was smart and—after nearly a lifetime—she knew Ryan better than anyone else save his grandfather. If she decided to put distance between herself and Ryan's plan, she must have a good reason. Joe wouldn't be the fool to insert himself into the groomzilla's path. But he couldn't exactly turn his back on a friend either. "I'm done planning Hank's celebration. I have a few details to go over with the council." Namely, how big, how bold, and how bright the fireworks at the end of the night could be. Hank insisted on a sky as light as the day. Joe wasn't sure anyone would agree, including the FAA. "I can help you and so can Ted."

Stephanie blushed. "He already told me the same."

Of course, her boyfriend had. Although the relationship hadn't passed the year mark, Ted and Stephanie were a team. They complimented each other. Ryan and Meg's coupling was the sort of inevitable pairing that was easy to take for granted. But witnessing Ted and Stephanie stirred up something in Joe he hadn't felt before.

Jealousy. He'd admit he wanted someone who had his back and who valued him. He didn't have the time for love but with everyone settling down, he had less time with his friends without their significant others around. He wanted someone to care about and focus on and help him through the mess he'd created.

But instead, he spent his time worrying over the person who drove him to distraction by her mere presence. What was Abby's secret? Was she genuinely as easy-going and charming as she wanted everyone to believe? Beautiful and giving and kind? She seemed too good to be true, but she'd been consistent in all three since coming to town. At what point would her pleasant façade slip, and she revealed her real self? No one was always giving to others without asking for something in return. "Can you manage a wedding? Do you have the time?"

"I'm working on the timetable at the moment but am sure—once I hand that over to Ryan—he'll have some other more elaborate to-do list to tack on. I'm stalling as long as I can." Stephanie raised her mug and sipped. "You are right. I will be busy enough this summer. I don't need to seek out more ways to occupy my time. But I won't give him the opportunity."

Joe chuckled. Stephanie was a master at managing people. The skill set served her well in both her volunteer work and her full-time job as a kindergarten teacher. She needed Ryan to be distracted.

"When does your program start?" he asked, remembering her plans to earn accreditation to move into school administration.

"Mid-May. I'll be swamped with the end of our school year and Frontier Days in addition to the Kincaid events. I'm dreading May. But by mid-June, everything will be in the rearview, and I can focus on learning. Studying will be a relief." She smirked.

With the big events happening at the start of the summer season, Ryan wouldn't have more to focus on until the *I dos* were over. Maybe Joe could help with another distraction. If Ryan didn't have time to obsess over every tiny detail, he'd be happier. *The unclaimed land...*

Ryan had already put him off about seeking to officially lay claim to the several acre property near the church at the end of Main Street. He'd said it was a waste of time. The prime real estate would revert to the town soon as long as no one came forward with a familial claim. The Kincaids told Joe it was an expensive headache to get lawyers involved in taking ownership of the property.

Joe worried it was a ticking bomb, and no one knew the countdown to detonation. He wasn't suggesting the Kincaids add to their impressive acreage total. He hoped the land would become some sort of civic spot like a small park. An area for skateboarders or dogs would be welcome. Any use, as long as the land didn't revert to a Whittier, would be a positive for the community. With the family's history in town, a descendant would just as likely set the ground ablaze as build some sort of terrible eyesore structure. "You've given me an idea."

"A good one, I hope."

"We'll see. Sorry to run off."

She blushed. "Actually, I'm meeting Ted's sister and niece here. I'm glad I bumped into you, or I never would have found a table."

Honest to her core. That was what made Stephanie so easy to approach and befriend. Abby could learn from the younger woman. "Have a nice day." He drained the rest of his mocha, grabbed his messenger bag, and headed toward the exit.

As the county seat, Miles City boasted a more complete collection of historic materials. Both the county records and the library offered information far more thorough to what Joe had access to at home.

Herd didn't have a library until Susie Kincaid and Betty Hawke established one a few decades ago. They had donated their own historical records, dusty boxes of ledgers and journals from their ranches. But the Whittiers were excluded. What could he find in materials from a town established almost twenty years earlier?

Since he was already in town, a visit to the library wouldn't be out of the ordinary or remarked upon. Small town living meant never truly shaking off the eyeballs of his friends and neighbors, not even in the nearest city. He didn't mind. As long as he was in control of the narrative.

CHAPTER 3

Abby tucked her chin into her coat collar as she made her way down the busy street. She hated feeling like she'd answered a summons. The lawyer was working for her and not vice versa. Still, Harrison Wolff was the best around and had taken her on pro bono. She couldn't afford to offend him, or she'd bungle her future.

The drive to Miles City had been blessedly as boring as ever. She hated driving in the winter. Between pot holes, black ice, and snow blindness, she often had car trouble. Or, rather, truck trouble. Two years ago, she had invested almost everything into her food truck. Driving the huge vehicle around was great for advertising but poor for keeping a low profile.

The investment had been sound. She'd earned back her costs and then some, saving a tidy nest egg for her restaurant. A costly auto repair would eat a huge chunk of her money and set her back. Following her complicated morning, she readied for the worst.

As she turned into town, however, her luck turned around. She pulled into a large, parallel spot for two vehicles a block away from the office. She exited the cab and crossed to the pavement, avoiding the slush near the curb. Maybe she could make quick work of her summoning.

She wasn't sure she knew what she'd say to the lawyer. The more logically she approached the situation, however, she couldn't miss the chance. Strolling slowly on the sidewalk, the hairs raised on the back of her neck, and she turned her head from side to side. She had the off sensation of being watched. Glancing up and down the busy street, a few pedestrians passed on either side and cars zoomed past. But no one paid attention to her. She was being ridiculous and giving in to her guilt.

The sooner she settled this business the better. She knew what she had to do, and there was no point in backing down from it now. With her focus on her feet, she didn't look up in time to see the familiar face. Not before a hand reached out and grabbed her elbow. She turned and shot her knee straight up into the offender. "Joe?" She covered her mouth with both hands.

Joe hunched forward, groaning.

She felt bad. Joe didn't like her. Kneeing him in the groin wasn't likely to earn her his friendship. She'd tried so many times for something warmer than his cool disdain. Now she'd caused him physical pain, proving he was right to keep distance.

And yet, she was proud of her natural instinct for self-preservation. She wouldn't apologize for defending herself. He couldn't just grab a woman on the street. He had no right to touch another person without permission. "What are you doing here?"

"Trying to save you from getting splashed by that truck." Straightening, he pointed to the street.

She dragged her gaze to follow his direction and spotted the pick-up barreling down the road. "Oh, I didn't notice." Stepping toward the storefronts, she tugged her knit hat low over her burning ears.

"Clearly." He dragged in a breath and frowned. "What are you doing here?"

She could ask him to answer her since she asked first, but she wouldn't. She wasn't rude even if the man always suspicious of her never gave her cause for being polite in return. Neither would she give herself away. She found her resolve in the face of his harsh niceties. "A little of this, and a little of that. What about you?"

"I had an interview." He bit the words tersely. "I'm stopping by the library."

"Of course. How's your book coming?" She knew asking would irritate him. But needling him wasn't her motivation. She was genuinely curious about his project. During her research into her family tree, she often bumped into him at the library in town and always asked about his work. He was a passionate historian and his fervor pulled her in, piquing her curiosity. She supposed that made her a moth flying straight into a bug zapper.

"It's fine. I'd rather wondered if maybe you had an interview in Miles City."

She widened her eyes. "Me? For what?" She wasn't working on a book. Why would she be at an interview?

He shrugged. "A job. You're talented. You should be a head chef in a big city."

None of his compliments sounded positive. He had a way of delivering *hello* like an accusation. He would've been great during the inquisition of centuries gone by. "I've done the urban center guidebook rated top marked restaurant thing before. I wanted something else. Besides, I've got more business than ever with the events at the ranch, what would they do without me?" She forced a chuckle.

She meant the words light heartedly, but deep down she was worried. She needed the town a whole lot more than anyone needed her. If she showed weakness to the one person always looking for it, however, she'd be kicked to the curb. "Why aren't you a professor of history somewhere? You definitely love research. You could easily be on a university campus. Wouldn't your talent be better served with more history to uncover than in middle school in Herd?"

"It would."

She rolled her eyes. He didn't have a shred of self-deprecation. Why would she expect anything less of the man with the biggest ego around for hundreds of miles.

"I work hard to inspire the kids. We live in a place where it doesn't seem like there are a lot of opportunities for academics. These kids need me."

He wasn't wrong about any of it. And she wouldn't question him further. She was just annoyed that he was constantly finding flaws in her very similar argument. She wanted one meeting where she wasn't knocked off balance. He showed her his annoyance with her presence at every turn. And she stood there smiling like a fool every time.

He lifted his arms, glanced at his sleeve, and dropped the limb. "Look at the time I have to go."

She nodded like he hadn't just pretended to look at a nonexistent watch as an excuse to be rid of her. But at least he was leaving before he could see where she was headed. "Of course I'll see you back in our town."

He tensed, tilted his head, and strode past her.

She counted to five before continuing on her way. She wouldn't turn around to see if he followed her progress. The skin-crawling sensation of being watched was gone. She didn't need visual confirmation he disappeared. Neither could she shake off the grin that hadn't reached his eyes.

She continued to her destination, entering through a communal lobby, and pulling open the door to the lawyer's office. She checked in with the receptionist and sat in one of the tapestry-covered side chairs in the waiting room. Tucking her ankles under the chair, she focused on her breathing, drawing upon her short-lived tenure in the meditation class led by Stephanie.

Harrison Wolff hadn't become the best without playing a few mind games with everyone who bumped into him along his path, including his clients.

She glanced up at the slogan displayed prominently near a muted TV. "Need justice? Trust a Wolff," she murmured.

When researching who could help her, she only had two options. A lawyer with a wide range of expertise in property and estate law. Or an ambulance chaser. While she didn't love Harrison's slogan, it was better than his competitor's catchphrase: *Want justice? Give them the Brass (knuckles)*.

After one morning of watching TV, she had decided to go with the former. Over the past six months, however, she learned more about Harrison. Her association with him made her almost as uneasy as their business together.

He had moved to Miles City from Herd and graduated high school in same class as Ryan Kincaid. She'd learned he fancied himself a rival. From him. She'd never heard either Kincaid mention Harrison's name.

But Harrison always circled back to Herd's first family, slinging mud with petty comments. Nothing she could call out. He was too savvy for that. His pro bono help also advised her to bite her tongue. She couldn't afford his legal fees on her own. One internet search informed her of the exorbitant cost of the over-inflated ego.

"Ah, Abby Whittier. Good to see you," a deep voice boomed.

She drew her shoulders to her ears, shrinking like a turtle in a shell as she turned.

With arms outstretched, Harrison approached in his tailored, navy-blue, three-piece suit. "Come on back. Let's get the paperwork settled."

Abby stood, tucking her icy hands into the pockets of her puffy coat. In her salt-stained boots, knit hat and scarf, jeans, and t-shirt, she felt shabby next to the lawyer. She followed dutifully behind him.

He opened his office door and waved her ahead.

On the double-sided walnut desk, paperwork was fanned across with flags marking spots for her signature. "Wow. This is it?" she asked, slightly breathless at the somewhat underwhelming moment. Changing her future and the shape of town as her neighbors and friends knew it should have some sort of trumpet blast heralding the occasion, not a few scratches of a pen on a sheet of paper in an unremarkable office building an hour away.

"Yes, this is it." Harrison boomed. He strode around the desk, pulled out his chair, and sat. Rifling through the top drawer, he reached for a pen and handed it over. "Just a few signatures and you get to take back your land from the Kincaids."

She didn't like the gleeful gleam in Harrison's eye. With a frown, she accepted the pen and pulled out the chair opposite him. She stared, unseeing, at the papers. "I'm not taking anything away from the Kincaids. I'm reclaiming land from the town that is undeveloped. This shouldn't impact anyone."

He scoffed. "The Kincaids are the town. It's one and the same."

She didn't correct Harrison. She hated the comment. She loved Herd and didn't want to ruin anything.

Instead, she grabbed the documents and read, dragging her index finger along the left margin, and tracking every line. She reached the middle of the first page when Harrison interrupted her.

"Oh, now you don't trust me?" He chuckled, low and deep.

His amusement scalded her skin like she grabbed a tray out of the oven without a mitt. She'd always been a slow reader, needing time to digest and absorb every word. She wanted to argue that no matter her opinion of him, she would read every line before signing.

But she met his gaze and froze. Her good girl instincts activated and insisted she quiet down and not agitate anyone by advocating for herself. She uncapped the pen and flipped ahead to the last page, writing her loopy, full signature.

In this instance, she knew that her goals aligned with the lawyer. She wanted a chance to reclaim her good name and redeem her family history. No one in town knew what had happened after Hoss was kicked out of town and exiled from his family. How he devoted his life to God, becoming a pastor in Minnesota, raising a family, and earning the respect of every community he preached in. He worked hard for redemption. In her small corner of the world, she wanted to broaden the narrow understanding of history. "You'll keep my claim anonymous?"

"At the start. But the truth will come out sooner than you might want."

She nodded, swallowing the lump in her throat. *It always does.*

At the library, Joe struggled with focusing on the text in front of him. Research grounded him. Usually. Joe couldn't quite shake off the dull ache after Abby's self-defense demonstration. It wasn't just the physical discomfort from her surprisingly strong reflexes. For that pain, he was mad at himself.

Joe deserved to be kneed. He should never have grabbed her. He wasn't even sure why he had. What did he care if someone he didn't like was splashed by a sloppy, slushy puddle? But he had.

While he'd been minding his own business striding to the library, he suddenly sensed a shift. The air changed around him, and he caught the faint hint of her intoxicating, no nonsense bar soap and butter scent. He paused on the sidewalk and studied his surroundings. Then he spotted her.

He didn't want to. He would love to not notice her or how she had kind eyes that studied him with too much clarity. But he couldn't seem to block her from his consciousness, no matter how hard he tried. And she hadn't said thank you for his concern.

Why was she all the way over in Miles City? His love of story took the form of filling in the blanks, often where none existed. He knew it was a bad habit. But he couldn't stop himself from inferring an entire back story based off of one clue. The problem with her, however, was that he had never rationalized her presence with a history. She came to town, fully formed, in the middle of the action.

His questions had been delivered from a place of frustrated honesty. She could go anywhere. He wished she would. *Then I won't have someone to project all my imposter syndrome feelings onto.*

While he had been observing her, he felt the deep rumble before he saw the truck. In slow motion, he reached for her and pulled her back. In the end, the truck driver spotted the pothole at the last moment and swerved. For his troubles, he'd been kneed hard. And she hadn't really apologized. No good deed went unpunished.

His valiant efforts had once again been in vain as far as she was concerned. He'd been so annoyed with himself that he forgot why he was studying her so intently. Since childhood, the public library welcomed him like an oasis. He'd always been warmed from body to soul by stepping inside, no matter the location. The hushed tones, the smell of musty books, and the ambient light of research table lamps and overhead fixtures, was a warm welcome. As a kid, he stopped in for books every week. He struggled to read, wanting to be a good reader but taking his time to make sense of each sentence. He wasn't content to memorize and throw a fact away. He wanted knowledge and operated at a slower pace because he wanted to retain every single word.

He began to read faster in college, because he had to. And he found the more he read the better he read. But he still wanted to be as smart as everybody thought he was. Many days he felt like a fraud.

And somehow, with her thoughtful questions, she saw through him. *What if my best isn't good enough?* His greatest fear laughed at him, taunting him every time he extolled to his students the ethos their best was more than he needed. He longed to believe it; a twisted version of fake it till you make it.

Exposing her secret before she could learn his, grew in importance with every passing day. She almost tripped him up today with her smile and questions. He was put off by the sense she wasn't upfront.

Why did he care? He wanted to stop thinking about her with a fervent desperation. He couldn't shake the unnerving sense she hid a huge secret. But what? And why did she seem almost surprised by his logical train of thought that she was interviewing for a full-time job?

Her truck was mostly closed during the winter. She helped the Rabbitts in their kitchen. What else did she do?

He couldn't waste more time caring. He had too much to do on his limited time off school. After spring break, he was on a collision course with the end of the school year. Projects and testing would dominate his days. He pulled out his headphones and queued the recording on his phone. He'd make another attempt to transcribe the day's interview, once again a third hand recount of the epic fallout between the Whittiers and the Kincaids.

Taking a deep breath, he inhaled the scent of paper and dust unique and universal to every library he'd ever entered. He slowed his racing pulse and hit play. His fingers worked almost independently of his mind, quickly dashing across the keyboard. Words appeared as if by magic, from his ears to his eyes.

After fifteen minutes, however, he stopped typing. He paused the recording and rubbed his weary eyes. He'd lost track of the interview and begun to channel his inner dialogue onto the page.

Why didn't the Whittiers sell the parcel in town? Why didn't the entire family leave? Where are their descendants?

Leaning back in his chair, Joe folded his arms over his chest. He couldn't shake the nagging inner voice that had grown from a whisper to a shout. Some big piece of the puzzle was missing and left the town vulnerable.

What happened after Hoss left? His research had turned up nothing. Struggling against his demons, he'd probably lost the battle. But what if he hadn't? Where was his family? Would they come back to Herd and demand payback?

Ryan had advised Joe not to get involved and not to worry about the unclaimed land. But Joe hated a loose end. What happened if a Whittier came back and snatched up the plot and built some awful high-rise or something equally obscene. Then the landscape of the quaint town was changed forever and once again a Whittier was to blame.

Ryan was too busy building his empire and planning his wedding. Joe didn't blame him for not wanting to take on one more task. But what was stopping Joe from taking up the mantle?

On his laptop, he pulled up the website for Tom Brass. The flashy lawsuit lawyer wasn't his first choice, but he was the only option. The more reputable attorney-at-law, Harrison Wolff, considered himself Ryan's high school rival, and Harrison never shook off his second-place attitude. On several occasions, he had returned to town, strutting like a peacock with a snide remark and seeking to somehow dethrone the man that single-handedly brought about an economic recovery. He hadn't been received well at the high school reunion, and he had left just as quickly as he had arrived.

Joe dialed the number and held the phone to his ear. The line rang and rang. Was this a mistake? Probably.

"Tom Brass speaking," a gruff voice answered.

"Hello, Mr. Brass, I had a question about property," Joe murmured. "Can you handle ugh…" Joe scrambled to make sense of his thoughts. How could he say this over the phone without sounding like a fool and a complete waste of time? "Do you handle real estate closings and such?"

"I can when I need to. But mostly that's Harrison Wolff's territory."

"What if there's a potential for a lawsuit?" Joe asked.

"Are you talking about bringing about a lawsuit or preparing to be sued?"

That was a good question, and Joe had no idea. The spur of the moment call was a mistake and each passing second made the error more glaring. For the sake of the other patrons and his own self-preservation, he should hang up.

"Because Harrison Wolff is still the man to talk to about property. Of course, if this has to do with his big case moving forward."

That piqued Joe's interest. "What big case?" He already sounded like an idiot. He wasn't sure he should push his luck that much further. But he had nothing to lose.

"Some unclaimed land."

"In Herd?"

Tom grunted. "Listen I can't talk about a colleague's business over the phone. Should we make an appointment? This could be pretty interesting. Haven't gone head-to-head with Harrison in a while. I'd enjoy it."

Joe shuddered. He wouldn't. "I'll give you a call back if I move forward. Thank you for your time." He ended the call and flipped the phone screen-down on the library table. The loud clatter echoed in the cavernous space.

Had he opened a major can of worms? Was his curiosity about to spell his doom? Was his imagination getting out of hand? Or was something bigger at play?

What were the odds the lawyer mentioned another, distant plot of land in the state of Montana? It was a big state. Tom hadn't disputed or confirmed the location.

What would a legal battle against Harrison Wolff look like? Probably protracted and expensive. No matter if Joe started the suit, he knew the Kincaids wouldn't leave him on his own—no matter how foolhardy the decision to pursue.

If they did nothing, what happened to downtown? He'd urged Ryan to purchase the land on behalf of the town, to be proactive. Ryan hadn't seen the need, preferring to wait until the end of the claim.

How would the return of a Whittier—a family that would have no warm feelings for the community—change the town? He couldn't shake the uneasy feeling his powers of deduction had been too late and definitely too little.

CHAPTER 4

If Abby had learned anything during her time in Montana, she had reached a new appreciation for the beauty of nature. Strolling down Main, she admired the brilliance of the wide-open sky on a sunny day. The blue overhead was almost cobalt, a rich shade that somehow warmed her despite the cold air. The colorful facades of the false front buildings on one side of the street shone.

Would she be able to help the town with its efforts of being a year-round destination? Without mountains, Herd couldn't lure snowboarders. A few intrepid souls had attempted to snowshoe and cross-country ski around the Kincaid ranch once but needed rescue by Ted after mistaking part of the creek for solid ground.

She wasn't sure one restaurant would be enough, but it would be a start. And her contribution to town would make her proud. As long as everyone supported her, including Joe.

Replaying yesterday's encounter, she was sure he had inserted a dig somewhere into their conversation. With the rest of her day devoted to tying herself up into knots about the decision to file her claim, she chose to reflect on the positive of the encounter. He pulled her back from a very soggy fate.

If he didn't care about her, even a little bit, he wouldn't have touched her. Maybe she was making inroads with him after all this time. Which would be great.

Because she needed as many friends as she could find.

After signing all the documents, she insisted on a promise Harrison would keep her name anonymous as the proceedings started. She couldn't hide forever, although she'd done a pretty good job of concealing her identity for the past couple years. She wanted to broach the subject on her own terms, first with the Kincaids and then with her other friends in town. She'd been supported and wanted to continue to keep everyone's goodwill.

At the General Store, she blinked, doing a double take at the crowded room.

The occupancy wasn't quite *standing room only please take a number*, but she stood in line behind another customer at the coffee counter. For the typically sparsely occupied store, any amount of time in a queue was remarkable. The weather hadn't warmed up enough to lure tourists to town. Every head she spotted she recognized, if not by name at least in passing.

She scanned the seating area along the back of the building, past the bakery case and souvenirs for sale. The four booths and six bistro tables were all claimed. The General Store was the nearest thing to a coffee shop and bakery. Their biggest selling food item was their homemade fudge. In summer months, Will Buck, owner, used a marble topped table to work the Wolff 's chocolate into a delectable treat in view of tourists. The rich smell was often enough to drive traffic into the building.

Besides a few muffins and coffee, and the occasional special-order cake, Will didn't sell a meal. So why was the room full? Spring break alone couldn't account for the buzz in the room.

The customer in front of her paid and left the line.

Abby stepped up to the counter.

"Good morning, Abby. Can I make you a Chai latte?" Will greeted with his typical broad grin.

"Hi, yes, please." The coffee shop owner knew her order by heart. Familiarity was one of the perks of small-town living and warmed her from the inside out. She opened her purse and pulled out her wallet. "What's up with the crowd? You giving coffee away this morning?"

He chuckled as he rang up her purchase. "Hardly. We've got other big news in town. It's unverified so maybe I shouldn't say anything."

The hairs on her neck raised. "Is it gossip?"

"I don't think so." He handed over her change. He moved to the gleaming espresso machine and started preparing her drink, heating the milk. "If it is, it's not much to go on," he said, loudly. "And you should know. It affects you most of all."

Her stomach dropped. Oh no. Harrison filed but hadn't kept her name concealed for the time being? "What do you mean?" she asked, her voice cracking.

He finished her drink, secured a lid on top, and slid the paper cup into a cardboard sleeve. "The unclaimed land by the church has an owner. Some Whittier descendant is back and stirring up trouble. You'll be kicked off the spot, I'm sorry to say."

"I will?" She accepted the hot beverage with shaky hands. Raising the cup to her mouth, she blew into the steaming spout. At least she had reason to look concerned with the drink in her grip.

"I haven't heard any details. But the Whittiers were always combative. Get yourself ready for a fight."

"Do you know the family?" She frowned. "I thought they'd been kicked out like a hundred years ago."

He shook his head. "They were. Let's just say they left a lasting impression."

She shuddered. She knew what she'd been up against. Changing an entire community's perception of the past was a tall order. But she'd always had hope. The neighbors she'd gotten to know—Will included—had been so kind and welcoming. Surely, they wouldn't hold onto prejudices that should have died several generations earlier? "Thanks for the heads up."

He nodded.

With one last glance at the full seating area, she decided her next step. She needed to check with Ian on the progress of her new smoker. The town's blacksmith had been a professional welder for years. He had lucked into a job tapping into his hobby of old-fashioned metalwork. She had a destination and a purpose. So why did every step feel like she beat a hasty retreat?

Following the scent of burning metal, she blew into her drink and strode down the covered, raised, wooden walkway. Under the awning that protected this side of the street from the elements, she felt exposed. If she glanced to her left, she'd spot the stone edifices marking her ancestor's ultimate fall from grace. The elegance mocked her.

She couldn't stop her plan now. She had no choice but to move forward. She'd meet with an architect in a few weeks to discuss how to build on her property. At the end of the street, she jogged through the intersection toward the blacksmith shop.

The clanging of metal on metal punctuated the air as a wave of warm air filtered out from the open doorway. The dirty smell of burning fuel mixed with the earthy aroma of hot iron.

She entered and knocked on the door, banging loudly.

Ian pounded the red-hot iron and dropped it in a bucket of water. Steam rose. He slipped his protective mask up and waved. "Hey, Abby. Come on in."

She stomped her feet on the mat outside, stepping over the threshold. With a few seconds in the toasty room, she relaxed.

The building had been built as a replica of the original. Ian hadn't changed dirt floor with anything permanent. He'd been talking about laying a brick floor. If she helped, could she still count on him as a friend?

She couldn't do little chores or pay for upgrades for everyone in town, or she'd be broke in a day. Bribery wasn't an effective way for building meaningful relationships. "What are you working on?"

"Well, maybe nothing. I came up with a couple of brands for the bison."

She widened her eyes. "Does Ryan want to mark them?"

Ian shrugged. "I don't know. He's still thinking about how to best keep track of managing the herd. I'll admit, I'm a bit skeptical."

"You are?"

"Sure. The Kincaids have plenty of land for the animals to roam. But that doesn't mean the bison will stick to the ranch."

Abby crossed her arms over her chest. "The Kincaid ranch is partially fenced. Ted does a good job of maintaining the barriers."

"How well can you explain the rules to wild beasts?" Ian snorted. "If an animal that big and strong decides to break down a split rail fence, the wooden posts have no chance against it. I don't want to find myself in a stand-off trying to get in or out of my store."

Had he shared his doubts with others in town? She never questioned any of the decisions Ryan and Hank made. Of course, what they enacted wasn't restricted to their kingdom alone. Consequences could be felt far beyond the borders of their ranch. She was living proof. While she hadn't stepped foot in Herd until adulthood, she'd been shaped by her ancestor's exile. Since Hoss had been kicked out, the Whittiers never stayed in one place for too long. "It's not just a split rail fence," she said. "Ted installed a tall square wire fence along the closest section to town. And besides, I don't think they'll be a disruption. What would buffalo want with town? It's full of people."

"And food."

"I thought bison eat grass?"

Ian shrugged.

If Ian was set on his opinion, she couldn't dissuade him. Still, she had to try. "Won't the noise be a discouragement? Loud voices? Trucks?"

He shook his head. "Let's hope so. The best-case scenario is once they get settled to our community quickly."

She nodded. Maybe she should work the angle of the new animal arrivals and redirect everyone's attention and energy off her claim. But that felt disloyal and she added shame to her list of the day's woes.

"Did you hear about the land? Can't believe a Whittier is coming back to claim the last scraps." He whistled.

"Scraps?" Heat crept up her neck and burned her cheeks. She'd been proud of her location in town. While the sidewalk didn't extend to include the spot, she had high hopes of being able to encourage the development with time. In the summer, she often had a line around the cemetery. But her property was the leftovers? The assessment stung.

"Sure, hope this won't hurt your business. That would be a shame. But really, what would you expect?"

"Well, I don't know what to think." Her voice cracked. She dried her clammy palms on her jeans one at a time and sipped her tea. She needed another angle with this ally. He prided himself on being a free-thinker. Why conform? "I'm surprised you have that opinion. You're a transplant too. Have you been totally indoctrinated in the town's old beliefs?"

"Good point, maybe I have been guilty of falling into line too much. I'd better do something reckless soon, or I'll get a good reputation," he said. "The smoker is ready to go. Just let me know where to drop it off."

"Until I get an eviction, I'm keeping my truck where it is." She lifted her chin.

He smiled and nodded. "Sounds good."

It sounded fake. She was pretending to be brave against some unknown foe. When, in reality, she was up against herself. Her own worst enemy? Yep, that fit.

Joe held the legal pad full of questions and concerns he'd heard around town about the bison. The herd wasn't due for another month, but he liked to stay ahead of a problem, especially when he had the time to do so. With the week off from both of his jobs, he leaned into his other projects. He'd met with frustration about his progress for his history of the area.

He wanted a new angle. Every interview only reinforced long held beliefs. The oral history had turned more into a recounting of local legend than illuminating town tales. After his frustrating day at the Miles City library, finding nothing of importance for his project in the census records, and leaving with an unshakeable sense of doom about the call with personal injury attorney Tom Brass, he was almost glad to think out worst case scenarios and anticipate questions about wildlife.

He jogged across the gravel drive and climbed the front steps of the ranch house. Every time he approached the house, he marveled at the strength and beauty in the old construction The solid stone foundation held the timber frame of the two-story home. A low hanging roof covered the wraparound porch.

The house rose from the land rather than fighting for attention.

Lifting a fist, he knocked on the door.

"Come in," Hank's deep voice called.

Frowning, Joe twisted the knob and stepped inside. The Kincaids spent most of their time too busy to monitor the comings and goings at the ranch house. Had they waited for him with bad news? His stomach clenched. "Hello?"

"We're all over here in the war room," Hank called.

War room? Joe shut the door and wiped his boots on the bristle mat inside before slipping off the slush covered footwear. In his socks, he slid over the slate tiles, passing the staircase and heading into the front room.

With a large couch facing the fireplace and a pair of wingback chairs in the window overlooking the front yard, the room hadn't been transformed into the make-shift lobby for the summer season yet. At the moment, it was still a comfortable family living space.

Ryan leaned against the fireplace, glowering.

Ted stood perfectly ramrod straight on the other side.

Hank turned around on the couch, Colby the black and white mutt at his side. "Come on, Joe. We need all hands-on deck."

Joe gulped. Was he on trial? He'd only meant to give an update on the rumblings he heard around the saloon and school. He hadn't intended to alarm anyone. "You didn't have to go to so much trouble for me. I didn't make photo copies. I thought we'd keep this causal."

"Huh?" Ryan asked.

Ted shook his head.

"Hard to keep it casual when the whole fate of the town is at stake but come in and sit down," Hank said, smoothly, ever the statesman.

Joe approached the group, standing near one corner of the couch.

"If you want to tell me you told me so, you're out of luck," Ryan said.

"About what?" Joe asked, meeting Ted and Hank's serious expressions.

"You haven't heard?" Hank asked. "A claimant has come forward for the Whittier land in town near the church. You told us to get it handled. You were right."

"We'd almost run out the clock, too," Ryan said.

A shiver tickled Joe's spine as a pair of thoughts emerged simultaneously. He'd guessed the cryptic warning from Tom Brass was about the land. Was this the secret Abby hid? He had no reason to jump to the second conclusion except his own ever-present feeling something was off about her.

He'd bumped into her downtown. She could have been on her way to Harrison Wolff's office. He hadn't spared her a glance after he'd righted her. He wanted her out of sight out of mind. If only that actually worked, he'd be better off. "Harrison Wolff is involved?"

Ted nodded.

Joe really didn't like Harrison, always flashing his fancy cars and nice clothes, displaying his perceived superiority to those he left behind. To Joe, the man's attempts were sad. No one seemed to care about the high school popularity besides the attorney. Everyone else had grown up.

"That's about all we know at the moment. The heir is keeping their anonymity for the time being. Can't imagine what will happen once they are officially announced," Ryan said.

"Do you think it's someone in town? Someone we know?" Joe asked.

"Why else would the person insist on not being named? Why would we care about someone we don't know?" Ryan added.

Joe considered that. With the last name Whittier, everyone in town would have their opinion pre-determined. "I doubt that. If it's someone in town, why wait all this time?"

By that logic, I can rule out Abby. She'd been in town for years. He breathed a little easier. While he couldn't shake an uneasiness about her, he didn't want her to be so duplicitous. He wanted her secret to be inconsequential like she was a secret millionaire living in town to bestow money onto unsuspecting good Samaritans. Not that he'd ever had any such hint. He didn't want her secret to bring her downfall.

"What do you need from me? How can I help?" Joe asked. He'd keep the news about reaching out to Tom Brass to himself. Luckily, he hadn't divulged any identifying information besides his phone number.

"We don't have time. I'm frustrated. I was warned. You were right to do that but I still don't think it would have been worth the cost. Guess we'll have to wait and see," Ryan said. He hunched forward, looking defeated.

Joe had never seen him less than absolutely certain. In good times and bad, Ryan held himself with a stoicism and seriousness fitting for his role as the head of a major business.

"I worry about Abby," Hank said.

"Abby? Why?" Joe tipped his head to the side.

"She'll be kicked off the land she parks her truck on. We'll have to see if we can give her more space out here to help make up for her lost revenue," Hank replied.

A pang of guilt burned him. Joe looked away. If he hadn't dissuaded Ryan from an idea to build a restaurant for Abby, he wouldn't be complicit in pushing her out of town. He knew she wasn't telling him—or the community—everything. But he had a heart. He didn't want her ruined and destitute to prove a point.

"I wonder if I can convince the new owner to put in a pickle ball court," Hank said, stroking his chin.

"Pickle ball?" Joe asked.

"It's the hot new sport everywhere but here. I had my eye on campaigning to the city council to develop a court," Hank said.

Ryan snorted and rolled his eyes.

"Maybe I'd be better off discussing it with the new owner. Since some members of the community are set against getting with the times," Hank added.

Colby whined and laid her head in Hank's lap.

"She hates it when I'm unhappy," Hank said, petting the dog's belly in long strokes. "I am worried about Abby, pickle ball or no."

"The events might help her out," Ted said. "We'll have plenty of catering jobs if the bookings sell well."

"Speaking of," Ryan said. "I have to head to a meeting with a vendor for the wedding. Are those the notes about the complaints in town?"

Oh, right. The reason for his visit. His succinct plan felt silly in light of the news. He'd spent hours thinking of problems only to be dumbfounded by a real issue. Joe held up the legal pad. "Yep, more concerns than anything. We can't anticipate the problems, can we?"

Hank snorted.

"Thanks, Joe." Ryan stepped forward and grabbed the legal pad.

Ted nodded and followed his boss.

As the pair left the room, Joe considered the new information. Would the descendant provide the direction he needed for the book? If he could meet the person, he had plenty of questions. Perhaps he'd finally get the answers—and a direction—he needed.

"What's wrong?" Hank asked.

"Just feeling a little off-balance," Joe said. "Guess I'm not sure how to take any of that news."

"Agreed. All I know is, I won't join the mob that is forming in town. Whoever it is, I won't make them an enemy before learning the motive and goal. The whole thing could be overblown with fearmongering," Hank said.

Joe wanted to agree. Too many odd occurrences aligned recently to tie everything together as the result of coincidence alone. "Do you really think we know the person?"

"I'm not the one who solves the mystery's around here."

"I was a kid detective," Joe said. Had Hank been paying attention every time he claimed his former hobby?

Hank huffed. "Coulda used you when Ryan and Meg were young. Can't tell you how many pies were stolen, and no one was ever brought to justice. The only time those two ever worked together was to steal my dessert."

"And you're sure you want to move forward with their wedding?"

Hank grinned. "Oh, yes. They can't walk off with a multi-tier wedding cake. I'll have the photographer guard it until they cut it at least."

Joe lifted the corner of his mouth in the closest approximation of a smile he could manage.

"Let's get coffee in the kitchen. You have time for my interview today, right?" Hank asked.

"Yes, sir. I blocked off the whole morning."

Hank pushed off the couch. Colby nimbly jumped to the ground at his side. "Good girl, Colby." Hank smiled at the dog. The pair ambled around the couch.

Joe followed. Was the obvious answer, right? Or was he doubling down on his prejudice against her? Was Abby tied into the whole mess and in a bigger way than losing her spot in town?

If she was the descendant, she'd definitely want to tell her side of the story. But why hadn't she made her claim years ago? He couldn't ignore that he'd bumped into her in Miles City. He never paid attention to Harrison Wolff's business address and for all he knew, she had been in the neighboring city for an innocent reason.

He'd focus on what he could control. His interviews and his work with the town council regarding the bison. He'd deal with people later. Or better, never.

CHAPTER 5

Abby frowned at her rudimentary sketch. Her artistic skills and penmanship remained subpar even when she applied her best effort. At least she could afford to hire an architect because no one would be able to make sense of her work.

Sitting on the hard oak chair on the library's second floor, she shifted but found no comfort. Worry caused her physical pain she couldn't escape no matter her position. After meeting with Ian, she was left more uncertain than ever. Her instinct was to head home and hide out. Her truck was closed today. No one expected her anywhere. She could spend the rest of the day under the covers in her bed, cozy and snug and pretending her life wasn't on the verge of implosion.

While she wasn't particularly passive aggressive, she avoided conflict with every ounce of her soul. Throughout her life, she'd been insulted and snubbed, but she never rose fought back. Maybe that's why she'd done so well being partnered with Joe for so long.

She sniggered and glanced about the empty space. Instead of retreat, she sought sanctuary. Only after she'd climbed the spiral staircase to the second floor had she realized she headed to the ultimate site of her undoing. If she was spotted in the genealogy section, would someone put the pieces together? If she wasn't in town, would anyone notice and question why she was avoiding her neighbors?

Understanding her current state of paranoia didn't alleviate the fears. Her claim was progressing as she'd been told. No one suspected her. She'd spent too long daydreaming—with the help of the library's collection of interior design magazines—about her new building.

She was going forward. She was putting down roots with a property she could live and work on. Some of her friends would still believe in her and understand her motivation. She just needed a plan to deliver the news with care.

Heavy footfalls echoed off the metal risers.

She turned toward the staircase and spotted Joe.

Warmth spread through her from head to toe. Maybe this was a sign. She had the overwhelming urge to tell him everything. Since he already judged her, he'd be the easiest person to confess to. She couldn't go any lower in his opinion.

Joe turned and spotted her, waving a hand. "Oh, hi. I didn't realize anyone else was here."

"Yep, just me, don't worry," she said. *No one that matters to you.*

"Did you hear the news?" he asked.

She stiffened and glanced over her shoulder. The second floor was empty. He was pursuing a conversation with her. His tone was warm and genuine. She held a hand against her churning stomach. A total change in character didn't happen overnight. Unless he'd had a dire news-inspired epiphany.

With his shoulders back and his chin lifted, he strutted toward her. The smoothness of his gait shouldn't be possible with heavy outerwear. As winter lingered, she moved slower, trudging through her days in worn snow boots and puffy coats. *Stop staring. He asked a question.* "I'm sorry. News? What's going on?"

He dropped his messenger bag at the table next to hers and leaned against the top. "Apparently, some Whittier is coming back to town. You'll have to find a new place for your truck."

She stared. If she didn't know any better, she'd assume a certain level of friendliness in the warning. For once, he delivered a sentence to her that didn't drip with condescension or suspicion. How did she respond?

"I already spoke to the Kincaids," he continued.

Her jaw dropped. She was stunned into silence. He brought up her welfare to the Kincaids? He spoke on her behalf? She couldn't feel her face. The muscles in her jaw and tongue were frozen liked she'd been injected with anesthetic.

"I was up there about something else." He shrugged. "They mentioned letting you park on the ranch more often. Right now, their offer wouldn't be very helpful. Over the summer, you'd have a steady stream of business."

"That's really nice of them," she murmured. And so typical. Ryan and Hank were kind. If she was lucky, the animosity between their ancestors hadn't carried over to the present.

Joe had no longstanding roots in town, but he carried the torch against the Whittiers like so many others. He was practically the leader of the movement, stoking and recording beefs for posterity. Joe's project would ensure no one ever forgot the Whittiers were the bad guys. Once Joe knew the truth, she feared he'd regret his moment of kindness.

"I heard some talk." She wouldn't compound her sins by pretending to have learned the information today.

Joe crossed his arms over his chest and stared.

She broke away first. She had to act normal. But how when he was behaving so unusually? His steady gaze unsettled her. He looked like he wanted to speak. She longed to get out of his way. "Why were you up at the ranch? A meeting about the celebrations?"

"No, just reviewing a few concerns about the bison."

"Oh, right." She almost sighed. "You'll have your hands full. I don't think everyone is on board with the latest plan. I've heard concerns about the town being overrun by the animals. I know it's highly unlikely to happen. I tried to defend the plan."

"While I appreciate your help, I can promise you I have everything well in hand." He tipped his head to the side. "Why are you changing the subject? Don't you want to get your future settled? Aren't you more worried about what will happen to you?"

"Am I changing the subject?" she asked, her voice squeaking. She cleared her throat. "I guess I don't want to anticipate problems. I'll deal with it when it comes. The thing that comes out of worrying is stress."

"Is that your usual M.O.?"

Why do you care? She shrugged. "More my family's motto."

"Where did you grow up?"

With a shaky hand, she tucked a strand of hair behind her ear. She forced a laugh. "Are you actually interested? I thought I was far off your radar for your project."

"Everyone has a story."

Unfortunately, she had quite a history to tell. Not regarding her immediate family. Growing up as a military brat, with her family in the armed services as far back as anyone could remember, she learned not to let herself get overwhelmed about tomorrow. Because the future inevitably meant change.

She both lived for and loathed the chaos of uprooting her life. As an adult, she finally got to make the decisions for herself. While her siblings continued in the family tradition, she had been happy to travel around from kitchen to kitchen. Until she actually went looking into the past and found Herd.

At the moment, she had nothing else to offer that would placate Joe. She wasn't sure what was standard for her anymore. She hadn't been actively deceptive over the past two and a half years. She'd pursued her standard, putting off something bad for another day, techniques, becoming an expert in delay tactics.

"Sorry, I shouldn't interrogate you." He scrubbed a hand over his face. "Old habit I guess."

"Why?"

"Excuse me?"

She gulped. She knew enough of his opinion that she didn't want actual confirmation. But some nihilistic side pushed her. If she was going down, she might as well burst into flames and leave only a pile of ash where she once stood. "Why is it your habit to treat me with open disdain?"

"I wouldn't say disdain." He flinched, breaking away from her gaze to study the floor.

At least he had the decency to show a little embarrassment. *Once he learns the truth, he'll only feel vindication.* She should stop talking while she was ahead. She gained nothing from their stand-off. "I would," she said, forcing the issue. "I've been nice. Other people like me."

He lifted a shoulder. "Do you want the truth?"

No. She swallowed the sharp metallic taste in her throat, pushing down her fears, and nodded.

"I have this sense that you're holding something back. Maybe it's just my love of story-telling. You pop up with considerable skills in the middle of nowhere. I try to fill in the blanks. For projecting onto you, I apologize. We're almost done with the party planning and then you don't have to deal with me ever again."

I don't want that. She pursed her lips and dropped her gaze to the table. She skimmed over the pile of incriminating papers strewn across. She'd had enough fight and now was flight time. She gathered her papers, clutching them to her chest and swinging her purse onto her arm. She'd never taken her coat off, the second floor boasted a legendary draft year-round. "I'll get out of your way."

She turned nearly bumped into him. He had taken a step forward and stood too close. The papers slipped from her grip.

Her cheeks burning from his nearness, she bent and grabbed the scraps of paper. "What's this?" He reached down, grabbing a sheet off the floor. "A map?"

She widened her eyes. Why couldn't he have found her poor building layout or list of punny business names? No one would expect anything nefarious from *Home Skillet*. Why did she have the worst luck? *Because I'm a Whittier*.

He met her gaze. "It's you?!"

Joe rubbed his eyes, blinked, and then squinted. Was seeing believing? Or did he believe so he saw? In this instance, he hated being right.

Abby hadn't changed in the past few seconds. Her appearance remained the same. Her hair was still a mop of brownish reddish curls. Her green eyes flashed with a startling clarity, demanding his attention. She remained completely herself, the woman he didn't care for because of an indefinable something. The one person he couldn't stop thinking about and noticing. He felt like she should have morphed into an entirely different person. Or at least pasted on a cartoon villainesque moustache.

He wanted her to change from the person the town loved to a grotesque monster.

Because how could the woman who—he grudgingly admitted—earned the town's friendship have betrayed everyone so thoroughly? Couldn't she whip off the curls like a wig and take out the color contacts and be some other person hiding underneath? Hiding in plain sight—and lying by omission—was so much worse. "I was right?! This whole time. It was you?"

"Shh." She furrowed her brow, snatched the paper out of his hands, and scanned their surroundings.

The spiral staircase terminated in the center of the room. With shelves on the perimeter, the second floor was one large open space. There was no place to hide here.

She wanted discretion? She'd hardly earned the right to set the terms of her confrontation. But yelling and screaming wasn't his style. Luckily for her.

He pinched the bridge of his nose. Under the flare of anger, he poked at something deeper. He had spent the morning defending her and the better part of two years ignoring every sign telling him the truth. "I've felt bad about something and now you've made me sure I shouldn't."

She frowned.

They were going to build you a restaurant. You wouldn't have had to backstab anyone in the process. Try as he might, he still couldn't quite feel okay about standing in her way and stopping the Kincaids' proposed business partnership with her. Scrubbing a hand over his face, he studied the ground. He didn't want this to be her big secret. He'd grown used to her as a scapegoat but this felt too low. "I hate that you are the heir," he murmured.

A single, deep belly chortle responded.

Frowning, he looked at her. He meant what he said. It might be the most real thing he'd ever uttered in her presence. Her reaction rankled him. "I don't want you to the be villain."

"Why?" She shook her head. "You don't like me. You've never made that a secret. And I know all about secrets."

"I... I..." He had no argument. She was right.

She rolled her eyes. "It's bad manners to call you out. I'm sure you'll chalk that defect up to my questionable heritage."

She stuffed her papers into the tote bag on her arm.

Did he imagine the catch in her shallow breaths? He was wrong to treat her the way he had. But he hated that she could be throwing away everything she had worked for and the community's goodwill. She'd built something for herself out of nothing. Would she stay? Leave?

She strode forward, eyes downcast.

He reached out and touched her elbow with a light press of his fingers against her sleeve. He only felt the down of her puffy coat. It was enough.

She stopped in her tracks and glanced up at him.

He watched her thick lashes flutter. Up close, he studied her. The shiver wracking her body couldn't be hidden. Anger? Or something else? Standing inches apart was madness. "I'm sorry." The words rumbled out of him, low and soft. "It's not that I don't like you. I just felt like you weren't being honest."

"You were right." She lifted her chin and met his gaze. "I wasn't entirely truthful about who I am or why I came here."

"Now that I know the truth, I have a question. What comes next? We're almost done with the wedding and birthday planning. You won't need to worry about whether I like you or not."

Her chin trembled.

What wasn't she saying? He shouldn't push her but why hold back now? "You don't care about my opinion."

"I do. Actually. You're setting yourself to be the go-to expert on all things Herd. You want to tell your version of the town's history." She stepped away, breaking contact. "Not the truth."

"What are you talking about? You know how much work I've put into my project." He didn't want to argue. He was supposed to be taking the high road, but he couldn't. He'd defend his integrity to the end. "I've conducted years of interviews. I'm presenting the most unbiased picture I can."

She snorted. "The town remains very patriarchal. The men in charge aren't bad or wrong, but their view points are limited by their experiences."

She poured salt into the open wound of his imposter syndrome. He was not simply retelling the story of how the Kincaids won. He resented her opinion. How many in town shared her assessment? No, he wouldn't let her flawed judgement hold him back.

Joe knew history wasn't black and white. And in their community, facts were almost secondary to legend and myth. It suited the founding families to be seen as pursuing something greater through hard work, the American manifest destiny dream. But the reality was greed and backstabbing.

Establishing Herd in the early days was more a story of survival amidst constantly shifting allies. In the end, the cleverest among them won. The Kincaid family took a ranch overrun by bison and sold them off at a steep price for every head.

Ryan and Hank understood their luck and attempted to do better by truly putting community ahead of themselves. Joe wasn't sure what they would think of the book once their family's history was printed. He didn't want to hurt anyone, including Abby.

"Isn't everyone's life colored by the stories they've been told and those they tell themselves?" he asked. Hank and Ryan had been her biggest supporters, more than she knew. "The Kincaids will defend you to the end of time. I think the bigger concern is the man you've chosen to partner with."

She scrunched up her face.

"Don't be oblivious. You're being used."

"How do you figure?" she asked.

Joe swallowed the sigh building in his throat and kept his eyes steady. Expressing his annoyance wouldn't help the tense situation. Could he explain her troubles without being accused of using a condescending tone? For the sake of the town, he could. "Harrison Wolff has always been out for his best interests and to take down Ryan Kincaid."

"So? Why tell me that?" she asked.

Joe gasped. He didn't bother to shield her from that reaction. Standing on the top floor of the library, anyone could stumble onto the scene. He almost wished someone would and save him.

"How does an old grudge involve me?" she asked.

Her directness unnerved him. "You're being used."

"Maybe." She shrugged. "Even a broken clock is right twice a day."

"Meaning?"

"I'm not a fool." She readjusted the bag on her shoulder and took another few steps toward the exit.

Had he detected the tremor in her voice? She was firmly on the defense. This would be the easiest of the battles she'd face in the days to come.

"I know Harrison is a viper," she said. "For the moment, my professional interests align with my lawyer's. That's it."

Joe nodded like he understood. But he didn't. The history of Herd reflected much of the greater area. The town had been founded and shaped based on vengeance. If it was best served cold, hers was perfection. Her reveal was glacial.

"How are you going to tell the others?" he asked. He almost hated himself for the question. Her cold demeanor told him to stay away. But he couldn't. He'd been proved right at the expense of everyone he cared about. The victory was worse than hollow.

"What do you propose? What would satisfy you? Shall I pin a crimson *L* to my shirt for liar or tattoo Whittier across my forehead?"

"Will Harrison keep your identity secret? Do you trust him?"

"He's already moving forward on my behalf. What other choice do I have?"

She would experience a fierce backlash. The community was warm and welcoming of newcomers. But they'd feel stupid once the truth came out. In hindsight, they'd wonder if she was laughing at their easy acceptance of Abby Whit without questioning her. Her name wasn't even a major attempt at concealing the truth. Every good lie held at least a kernel of honesty.

Her worry and hesitation were obvious. She must have felt justified in her actions, probably even compelled. If he hadn't stopped at the restaurant, would he or anyone have ever learned the truth? And why throw a jab at him and his project? Striking first?

"Good bye, Joe." She walked away.

He didn't stop her. Her steps echoed in the quiet second floor and her descent on the staircase rang out like a clang of the church bell.

They'd had a common goal but would her ambition drive them apart? He was disappointed. With the mystery solved and the evidence presented, he just kept not believing the truth. He'd let her, or her lawyer, break the news. He wasn't going to intercede. Unless she asked for help.

CHAPTER 6

Over the next couple of weeks, Abby kept telling herself she wasn't a coward. She hated how she had behaved with Joe. He had always provoked her but his faux concern had really pushed her over the edge from civility to hostility.

Why pretend to care about her? After the run-in at the library, she'd been left shaken and scared. He had confirmed her worst fears. That everyone would hate her.

And she'd proved him right.

She wasn't sure which angered her more.

As talk settled down about the big bad Whittier in their midst, the town returned to normal. By the weekend, she hadn't heard any mention of the land she parked her food truck on. Harrison hadn't publicly named her. Neither had Joe shared her secret. The days passed without any change, leaving her in a sort of anxious lull.

As frustrated as she was with Joe, she was also grateful. He'd never liked her but hadn't sought her ruin. At least, she knew that now. She had a lot of respect for him and what he was trying to do with his book. In many ways, she was jealous. He belonged to the community in a way she might never attain. Her name would always create a distance. She was glad to know he held a sliver of the same emotion for her in return.

Her reprieve was temporary, of course. As soon as she was named, she would have nowhere to hide. In big sky country, she would be conspicuous as a skyscraper. And so she steered her food truck to her destination, doing what she should have a long time ago. Telling the truth to Hank and Ryan and letting everything else fall where it may.

The vehicle made her every movement conspicuous. For someone who'd spent so much time hiding, the truck was an unexpected choice. She'd be glad to be done with secrets. She parked her truck and scanned the surroundings for Hank or Ryan as she approached the stone and timber house. The snow had started to melt, patches of dead grass poking up through the pristine white. In other spots, mud marred the sparkly snow surface. Snow was pretty for a day and then a slushy pain for weeks.

She loved all four seasons and couldn't imagine living in a place where the change of the weather didn't provide an opportunity for a fresh start. By the start of April, she was wiped from dealing with the cold and ready for spring. The next two months, coinciding with the lead up to Hank's birthday and Ryan and Meg's wedding, promised no break, unless they fired her for her deception.

She climbed up the front steps and wiped her boots best she could on the doormat outside. The covered front porch that wrapped around the house was a welcoming spot, even on a chilly Monday morning. Fisting her mittened hand, she knocked on the door with muffled thuds.

"It's open," Hank's deep voice boomed.

She smiled and twisted the doorknob, letting herself inside. The house was rarely locked.

The Kincaids' happily welcomed visitors dropping in at all hours of the day. In a few months, the building would serve as the lobby for the resort as well. Maybe after the wedding and once Ryan started a family, they'd want more privacy from the business and their personal lives. But she doubted it.

The family was as wrapped up in their legacy as they were in their individual identities. She had only recently come to appreciate the heavy weight of that responsibility. They were the good guys in the town story thanks to a lot of hard work and sacrifice. And—if anything—the town's opinion was perhaps the heaviest weight of all. A two-ton anvil wrapped around their necks.

Shutting the door, she leaned a hand against the solid oak panel for balance as she slipped off her boots. The wood was warm against her icy palm. A nice welcome she wasn't sure she deserved. "Hello? Hank?"

"I'm in here. We all are," Hank called.

We all are? A terrifying thought. Was she about to be put on trial in front of the original tribunal? Ryan's fiancé, Meg, was the last Hawke in town. Once she married Ryan, she'd consolidate the two families into one for the rest of time. *If I have a kid that marries their kid, then the town would really belong to the Kincaids.* She shook off the thought.

Spending so much time with Joe had scrambled her heart and her brain. He disliked her and didn't pretend otherwise when confronted. She couldn't seem to stop the butterflies fluttering in her stomach with every encounter.

She tiptoed across the slate tiles toward the front room. The surface was uneven from natural flaws and over a hundred years of wear. The Kincaids lived with a permanence in direct contrast to her nomadic upbringing. They weren't leaving. None of them.

In the front room, Hank and Meg sat on the leather couch. Colby the mutt lounged on her back in between them, receiving belly rubs and chin scratches from both humans. Ryan sat on the fireplace hearth, holding a steaming mug of coffee. In the corner, Ted stood perfectly straight and silent. Usually, Abby found the stoic cowboy's presence comforting. He was steady and stalwart like an old Roman statue. Today, she was intimidated.

"Good morning," Ryan said and stood. "Can I get you a cup of coffee?"

Abby shook her head, darting her gaze wildly from person to person. "No, I don't deserve it."

"What?" Hank twisted in his seat, craning his neck until it cracked. "Girl, you don't have to earn your morning cup of ambition. It earns you."

"Are you okay?" Meg asked. "You're pale."

Ryan approached and guided her toward one of the wingback armchairs. "She's right. Sit. Catch your breath. Ted? Can you get her a water?"

Ted nodded and strode out of the room.

Abby sank into the chair's green velvet upholstery like a bag of stones dropped on the ground. Her stomach churned. Her vision clouded. Her head spun. If she didn't blurt out her news, she might be sick. She shut her eyes, scrunching her face to block out her view. "It's me."

"What's you?" Meg asked.

"Come again, girl?" Hank asked at the same moment.

Abby breathed through her nose and opened her eyes. She had to do what her family couldn't. She had to face the other families and ask for forgiveness. After Hoss had been kicked out of town, his father had left without a word. Never acknowledging the epic mistakes that had cost the town families their livelihoods and eventually came for their own. She met the frowning stares of Ryan, Meg, and Hank.

"I'm the Whittier," Abby said.

"Oh, thank goodness," Hank said and exhaled a shaky breath. "That's it? Don't scare me like that. I don't want to spend another birthday in the hospital."

"Whit? Should have seen it," Meg said, shaking her head. She flashed a smile.

"Why didn't you say anything before?" Ryan asked.

"Well..." Abby stared at the glass in her hands. She still felt nauseous, but the bile had retreated enough for her confession. They hadn't demanded she leave their land and never return. "I don't..." She sighed. She couldn't lie. Lifting her chin, she stared at them through her watery gaze. "I was scared. I know how much everyone hates my family. I wanted to see if I could claim the land or if I'd be kicked out of town the moment I set foot in city limits."

"It's been over two years, Abby." Ryan retreated to his spot on the fireplace hearth, pinching the bridge of his nose.

"I know. I shouldn't have let it go on so long. To be frank, I wasn't even sure about claiming the land at all. I might have let it lapse but then with the ranch hosting events. I need a proper kitchen to cater and it just seemed like..." Abby shook her head. Her words came out too fast and sounded accusatory. She alone would accept responsibility for her actions. "I'm sorry. I didn't think I'd love Herd as much as I do. I didn't think I'd want to stay. But the longer I'm here, the more it breaks my heart to think about leaving. I can't afford to buy land and build. But I can afford to build on land I own." Her vision blurred. She sniffed, scrunching her burning nose. "I can't apologize enough. Now that the truth is out, it's okay if you hate me."

"We don't hate you," Hank said. "I worry about what everyone in town is gonna say about your secret. We still support you. We still choose to partner with you."

Abby offered an approximation of a smile. She couldn't move her face much more or she'd loosen the tears in her eyes. She wanted to believe Hank, but he wasn't the ultimate decision maker anymore.

Ted strode into the room, his boots announcing his progress. "Who don't we hate?" he asked, twisting his neck from one direction to the other.

"Abby's the heiress we've been scared of," Meg chimed in.

"Oh." Ted strode toward her with the glass of water.

Abby gratefully accepted the token of kindness and hospitality. She took a sip, cleared the awful metallic taste out of her mouth, and swallowed.

"Everyone in this room has dealt with judgment of our neighbors at one time or another," Hank said.

"We support you," Ryan said. "You're going to need to earn back trust and goodwill. It won't be easy."

Abby nodded. Coming clean to the Kincaids was a good place to start.

"I do have a change I'd like to run past you about the wedding and birthday weekend," Ryan said.

Am I officially fired? Abby clenched her jaw, keeping the cords inside.

"We want to simplify," Meg said. "Or, at least, try to. We are moving the wedding to Friday night. Hank's birthday. No rehearsal dinner. No second event. Just one big night to remember."

"Are you all in agreement?" Abby asked.

Hank flashed a thumbs up. "I'm giving up my parade to make room in the schedule. It's the least I can do."

Ryan nodded. "Not that the change of plans will make the headcount any easier. It's still going to be an educated guess. We want to include everyone in town and any guest at the ranch who wants to join."

"Can you handle it?" Hank asked, his voice soft.

"I'll find a way. I won't let you down," Abby said. If anyone heard the tremor in her voice, they didn't react.

Instead, Ryan turned toward her and smiled. "Don't worry about the other thing. We'll do our best to help smooth over the backlash in town. Herd has a long memory. You have supporters and friends. The community will come around."

Abby nodded. She knew that well enough. She'd have a lot of apologies. As long as she stayed a step ahead of Harrison, she'd be okay. She wouldn't worry about Joe. She'd finally given him a reason to hate her, and she'd stay away.

In the teacher's lounge, Joe blew across the top of his coffee. He didn't need the drink and probably should give up caffeine in general. He hadn't enjoyed much sleep for the second half of his vacation or the few weeks back at school, but he didn't think his diet factored in.

He couldn't stop replaying the moment in the library. Finally, he had been validated. In an instant, he had understood how ridiculous his entire campaign against her had been. He had only sought acknowledgement of being right. The win was hollow at best and petty at worst. Why had he cared so much? Did he really let his ego drive him?

He sipped his coffee, not tasting the brew but only absorbing the heat. On the seat, he shifted forward but found no comfort in the soft padding.

How would the community respond? His worries shifted gear from protecting history to shielding her. He wouldn't mind eavesdropping to get a sense of what was being said in town. Since the initial announcement of the claim, he hadn't heard any a whisper. Talk about the mysterious Whittier had died down. She wasn't safe from discovery. She needed to tell the Kincaids before they found out from Harrison Wolff.

With his connection with the Kincaids, he assumed many would consider his stance against the claim a given and not even broach the subject. His known association made presenting himself as an unbiased source impossible. He would get an opportunity to take the pulse of the community tonight at the last town council meeting before the arrival of the bison herd. The gathering was meant to be a question-and-answer session for the town to present their concerns. He should have spent his free period this morning running through potential rebuttals to possible town concerns. But he couldn't stop thinking about her.

The door between the office and the lounge opened.

He straightened and turned his head. At sight of the newcomer, he slouched in his chair again. "Hi, Stephanie."

"Worried I was the principal?" She chuckled, clutching a stack of photocopies in her arms.

"A little bit," he admitted. "Mostly just worried I was needed."

"Post break blues?" She set the papers on the round table and crossed to the staff fridge, grabbing a bottle of iced coffee. She returned and pulled out the chair, uncapping her drink. "Cheer up. One standardized test is behind us. Only one to go. We're almost ready for the end of the year alphabet countdown, too."

"Something like that." He traced the edge of the particle board table. The white laminate top yellowed over the years and flaked away in sections, exposing the sharp shards underneath. "Just trying to get back in the swing with everything else on my plate."

She widened her eyes. "You and me both. Nervous about tonight? I've heard some rumblings in town."

"Really?" He leaned forward, searching her face for any hint. "About the bison or the mysterious landowner?"

"Both although I think talk has died down about the Whittier descendant. It has to, right? Hard to stay mad at a faceless, nameless entity."

Not as hard as you'd think. In his interviews, he was increasingly disappointed that the townsfolk accepted legend over fact. Abby had a war ahead of her. And he couldn't stop himself from wanting to help. She wouldn't accept his assistance. Not unless she had no one else to turn to. He feared exactly that situation becoming her reality. He didn't want to be the last person left on earth who had her back. He wanted her to choose him.

What? He took another sip of his coffee, cutting through the lump in his throat. Did he like her? He'd spent most of the past year trying to fight Hank's matchmaking. But could the old man have been right the whole time? Was he supposed to be with Abby? Did they have anything in common?

She was an outsider. He fought to earn his place. She struggled against prejudice based on her name. Maybe they did make sense on paper. "Can I ask you a hypothetical question?"

"Of course," Stephanie replied.

"If the Whittier descendant is someone we know, would that change things for you?"

"Is it someone we know?" she asked, crossing her arms over her chest.

"Hypothetical, remember?"

She rolled her eyes. "I guess it depends on the situation. Has the person always known they are a Whittier? Was this a recent DNA discovery? Context is important."

"You wouldn't rush to judgement?"

"You can tell me if it's you," she murmured.

"No. It's not me. And we're speaking hypothetically, remember?" He almost wished it was him. If he could shield Abby from what might happen, he would. Jealousy impacted his behavior from the start. Every day, he struggled against feeling like a fraud. He wanted to be an expert, an undisputed leading figure. She quietly—and competently—showed her talents to any who approached her business. She didn't have to tout her qualifications. The proof was in the pulled pork.

Now her future was at risk. He hated that he couldn't figure out how to help her. She deserved to stay in the community she loved. But how?

"Joe? Hey, are you feeling okay?" Stephanie snapped her fingers and waved her hand.

He shook his head. "Sorry, did I miss something? What were you saying?"

She sighed. "Yes, your eyes glazed over, and you missed quite a bit. But that's okay. I was just saying I might need more back-up on the wedding than I thought."

"Why?" He tipped his head to the side.

"Ryan has very specific wants for his big day. I'm going to need the groomsmen to help run interference."

"I'm sure we can manage him."

She narrowed her gaze. "Well, I'm not."

Joe laughed. The ranch owner had become quite the groomzilla, ruining his reputation for having a cool head with his exacting demands and wedding day expectations.

"Do you want to practice your speech for tonight? Try a mock meeting?" she asked. "I can offer some hard, ridiculous questions."

"Such as?" He was intrigued.

"What if a bison poops in my yard? Should I call Ted to come clean it up?"

"I'd love to see that happen." Joe smirked. Stephanie's light-hearted conversation lifted him out of his mood and refocused him on what he could control. "Yes, call Ted."

"A bison is standing in the middle of the road. Do I drive around it? Honk?"

"Back-up and detour." Joe was on a roll. "Give me another."

"Can't. I have to get back to my classroom before they finish gym class."

He smiled and nodded, appreciating the difficulty of both their jobs. She had to deal with boo boos and hurt feelings. He navigated around a class half in puberty and the other still in childhood.

Finishing his coffee, he stood and rinsed his empty cup before loading in the dishwasher. The bison might prove a worthwhile distraction for everyone in town. Give the community something else to talk about while she navigated her way through the truth. With any luck, she'd start her explanations before she lost her chance and her nerve.

Because he'd pity her if the truth came out via Harrison Wolff.

While winners recorded history, some villains didn't understand their place in the story. Aligning herself with the town's biggest antagonist since her ancestors would spell her doom for certain.

He liked having her around. Especially as she provided a new insight into what so many took for granted. Especially on the eve of the town's biggest event ever, Herd's very own royal wedding as two legacy families officially became one.

CHAPTER 7

Behind the open windows in the food truck, Abby welcomed the spring breeze snaking past the row of customers and inside her vehicle. Parked on the lot where Main Street intersected with Church Street, she operated steps away from the heart of town. She liked to think Mother Nature provided her with the light wind to cool down her truck's interior from the ovens and cooktops and waft the aromas of her buttered cornbread and roasted meats downtown, luring customers her way.

With her typical steady crowd at lunch, Abby wasn't worried anyone had heard the news yet. She was annoyed with herself for putting it off for so long. The morning conversation at the ranch had quickly steered into the normal business of wedding and birthday celebration talk. Abby was grateful. While navigating Ryan's demands with Meg's more laidback approach gave Abby a headache, she was glad to resume their normal friendship.

At least one hard discussion had gone well. But she still had a whole list of people to apologize to in advance. She'd rather rip off the bandage entirely instead of letting it dangle, but she couldn't rewind time. Her elevated stress levels were her own fault. She'd gone this long without her secret being revealed, another couple hours wouldn't hurt. As soon as she closed for the afternoon, she'd head to the blacksmith shop and then the saloon. Her arrival at the latter would coincide with the start of knitting club. She could have the talk twice more and be done with her apology tour. She didn't owe everyone an explanation, only a few important people.

She served the last customer in the queue, leaned out to scan the lot for any more guests, and pulled down the retractable metal curtain. Locking up the truck, she left it in its spot and exited on foot. Herd's tiny downtown was perfect for strolling, but she needed a vehicle to otherwise get around the sprawling community. She loved walking as much as she could, and today's stroll was calming. The bright blue sky held only a few puffy clouds and shone on the colored facades of the wooden false-fronts on one side of Main Street. Across the road, the stone exteriors of The Golden Crown Saloon, Post Office, and grocery co-op gleamed like they'd been polished.

"Hey, Abby. Are you sure it's okay to leave your truck there?" Will Buck asked.

She smiled and waved at the man standing inside his shop's open doorway. "It's fine. Thanks," she called.

Better not to respond with anything she couldn't take back. Turning her back to her land, she strode with determination. She kept her chin down, tucking it into her coat collar. The brisk breeze whipped past her ears, scalding her, and propelling her forward. She didn't need to lift her gaze to follow her path. She relied on her nose.

Past the last traffic stop, she breathed deep the smell of the forge. In another life, she imagined becoming a blacksmith. She was always cold and would welcome the heat, even in summertime. With her spate of mishaps, however, she'd probably have set her building on fire before getting the hang of handling the irons.

There is a precedent for accidental pyromania in my family tree. She shook off the unhelpful thought. Hoss had had his own demons. She, of all people, wouldn't judge him. He'd more than made up for his shortcomings after his exile. Not that anyone would ever care to listen to his redemption story.

The door stood a few inches ajar.

She knocked on the door twice but received no answer. With her fingertips, she gently pushed the entry open, scanning the interior.

Ian sat on a stool, studying something in his hands. A cell phone? His visor was pushed back, but he still wore his leather apron.

He hadn't heard her knock? He was too engrossed to respond to her heavy, booted footsteps? The distraction didn't line up with the friend she knew. He hated technology and railed against the use of smartphones to any who would listen. For a millennial, he was as staunchly opposed to digital advances as most were in favor. He'd shared his hatred of selfies and social media often and loudly. Why turn to his cell phone now?

"Hello? Ian?"

He lifted his head and stared at her.

She fought a shudder. He looked at her unseeing. Like she was a stranger. Not the best greeting for starting her confession. She stepped deeper into the room, rubbing her icy hands together.

To the side, she spotted the smoker, a gleaming cylinder on a wheeled stand. She approached and lifted the lid, smiling as she glimpsed inside. Staggered racks accommodated maximum production with every use. The smoker would greatly increase her output, enabling her to cater the large wedding. "This looks great. Thanks so much. I should have driven over."

"I'll drop it off later."

His words were flat. She faced him. With several yards between them, she wasn't encouraged to approach any closer. His brow knit together in a solid line and his mouth was almost comically downturned. He looked like he might spit.

Just say it. Her inner voice shouted over the bad vibes rolling off him in waves. "Hey, I wanted to talk about s—"

"I don't have time." He stood and stuffed his phone into his back pocket. Crossing to the mounted hooks above his work bench, he pulled on his thick gloves and lowered his welding mask.

Like a knight shutting out the world as he prepared for battle. Without another word, he turned toward the forge. He stoked the burning embers with a poker, giving his work his full attention. The coals flickered and then flamed, the fire roaring to life.

What had she done? He was never so cold. She'd have to figure out an apology when he dropped off the smoker. To get his attention now could have dangerous consequences. With a nod to his back, she left the shop.

Raising her coat collar, she gripped the lapels with one hand and stuffed the other into her pocket. She headed toward the saloon. School had let out an hour earlier. Kelly Strong would be at the usual table. With any luck, although she wasn't sure how much she'd used up this morning, she could catch the Rabbitts as well.

This time, she focused on her destination and not her feet. With her chin raised, she met the gazes of a few pedestrians. But her smiles weren't returned. She gritted her molars.

At the saloon, she pushed through the front door and froze.

The buzz of conversation immediately cut to silence.

This time she knew what the problem was. Her. Squinting, she surveyed the room.

In the back corner, a few diners ate at two tables.

In the center, the knitting club focused furiously on their work.

She turned toward the bar.

James focused on polishing pint glasses with a scowling determination.

She approached him first. He'd been her staunchest ally. Surely, if she could explain, he'd have her back. She owed him the first and biggest apology. She rested her hands on the smooth bar top. "Hi, James. Do you have a minute to talk?"

"Who am I talking to?" He stared at her, his gaze icier than the wind. "Abby Whit? Or Abby Whittier?"

The blood drained out of Abby's limbs. Any practiced comeback died on her tongue. In the moment, she was colder than a January morning. Because she saw so clearly what she had done. She'd lied to the town. More than that, she hadn't been honest with people who had cared about her and helped her. People—like James and Heather—who treated her better than family. She had proved herself unworthy.

"How did you know?" she murmured. Fear at discovery didn't quiet her voice. Shock subdued her.

"Harrison Wolff officially listed you and your alias on the documents filed at the county clerk's office. You know how fast word spreads, especially about something so inflammatory."

"I... I'm sorry," she murmured.

"I don't understand why you didn't say anything. Aren't we friends? Haven't we supported you?"

She nodded, scrunching her nose from one side to the other. She sniffed and blinked. Tears threatened to spill, but she wouldn't give in to the luxury of expelling the hot emotions stoked up inside her. She did this. She had no one to blame.

"I would have been happy for you to have the land. We all would. But it's clear you don't think much of any of us." He shook his head and grabbed another spotless glass.

Dismissed. She stood in the spot wanting to argue and defend herself. Wanting to trot out the explanation that she really owed the Kincaids the truth first and she'd only just told them a few hours ago. They didn't hate her.

What could she say? She turned and walked out the front door. She'd had over two years to come clean. While she had at first assumed she'd be judged for her ancestors' actions, and she might, she had neglected how many of the people in town would not be swayed by generational prejudice. She could have had a chance to make her case if she'd been honest from the start.

But she'd prepared for the worst and never let herself imagine the best. Fear had controlled her actions from the start and held her back from telling the truth. Responding instead of acting, she'd never given anyone a chance. She understood now.

The whole mess was her fault but she couldn't just give up. She'd have to find a way forward. And it didn't involve hiding or running off. She'd leave Main Street now and avoid making a scene. But she had a bone deep certainty. She was the Whittier who belonged in town, and she wasn't going anywhere.

As a rule, Joe didn't live with regrets. He dealt openly and honestly with everyone, not wasting time on holding a grudge or concealing his feelings. As emotions arose, he acknowledged and handled them. Like an adult.

But then she'd called him out for his behavior, and now he couldn't stop rehashing what he should have done differently. After school, Joe headed home to change and eat before driving to the ranch. Since Ryan had called the town council meeting to discuss the bison, he made it clear he'd host the event. He had plenty of space for parking and a full set-up to livestream the meeting for those at home. At a table in the back of the room, Meg and Hank fiddled with a laptop and camera. Putting that pair in charge of technology was a questionable choice probably made to keep them busy.

Joe began setting up the metal folding chairs in neat rows. He worked to one side of the room as Ted mirrored him on the other. Monotonous work typically calmed his worrying mind, his anxiety settling as he accomplished a task. Tonight, however, he couldn't stop wondering if he'd have the chance to do better for Abby.

"All done?" Ryan called from near the French doors centered on the back deck. A cool breeze snaked into the room as the doors shut.

Joe finished the last chair in the front row and headed towards Ryan. "Yep. You think you'll really get this big of a crowd?"

Ryan nodded. "I do. Although the bison probably aren't the big draw of the night." He shook his head.

Ted crossed to the room. "Did you hear?" he stared at Joe.

"Me?" Joe drew back his chin, twisting his neck to take in both men's expressions of concern. "Hear what? What's going on? What's happening?"

"Turns out the Whittier in town is Abby," Ryan said. "She came here this morning and told us so herself."

Joe nodded.

"You knew?" Ryan asked, leaning close.

Joe's throat closed. Should he have confessed to the Kincaids as soon as he found out? She would have expected that. With his often-childish behavior around her, tattling wasn't out of the realm of possibility. But he had kept his mouth shut. "It wasn't my secret to tell."

"That's true enough," Ted said.

"How long have you known?" Ryan crossed his arms over his broad chest.

"A couple weeks ago." Joe shifted his weight from foot to foot. "Since spring break. I confronted her. To be honest, I probably knew for longer. I didn't want to see it."

"Why?" Ted asked. "You are her number one critic. Seems like this would have proved you right."

No one could cut through to the heart of the matter in less words and fluff than Ted. Joe wasn't sure he liked the categorization as a hater. It bothered him. A rational explanation for his feelings would make him look better. But he'd behaved with prejudice based on nothing. And now he was ashamed. She'd been correct in her estimation of him, too. She'd humbled him about the bias he fostered on his project. "I don't know."

Ryan snorted. "Come up with a better answer if Hank asks you, or he'll think you're softening on her."

Maybe he's right. Joe turned around to glance at Meg and Hank. The older man made no move like he'd heard his name. Why would Abby's identity be a subject of gossip tonight? Joe spun back and stared hard at Ryan. "Did you tell the town her secret?"

"Never. Harrison Wolff filed the paperwork today," Ryan said, shaking his head.

Joe clenched his jaw, swallowing the swear forming on his tongue. Had the lawyer promised Abby discretion? Had Harrison used her in his war on Ryan?

Worse, had Joe's unfriendliness made him complicit in her destruction?

"I like Abby," Ryan said. "She did right by us, she came and told us the truth. I wish she hadn't been so scared and waited for so long."

Joe nodded, memories niggling the back of his mind. How many times had she questioned him about the Whittiers? He remembered a couple conversations about the continued animosity towards the family. Had he been part of the problem? He'd railed against the family with a venom as if he'd lived the history first-hand. Had she cared so much about what he thought she let his opinion override good sense? Why did he get a slight thrill to imagine his words mattered to her?

The doors at the front of the barn opened.

A low buzz of conversation suddenly filled the room.

"Guess we finished in the nick of time," Ryan said. "Excuse me."

Joe stepped to the side, letting his boss pass. He hung back and observed the scene as neighbors and friends filtered into the room. The neat rows were dismantled as chairs slid forward, back, and sideways. Each scrape against the pine boards did the same to his heart. He could do his best and still have his hard work disregarded by the public. Until she walked into the room, he hadn't realized he'd been holding his breath.

Abby slunk in, her back rounded and her chin down. She didn't want to be here. But she came anyways. If that didn't tell everyone what they needed to know about her and her dedication to town, he wasn't sure what else they wanted. She found a chair in the back on the end of a row, near the table with Hank and Meg. Hank spoke with his typical animation. Meg smiled. And Abby looked slightly less uncomfortable. Joe's heart ached for her. He wished she had believed more in herself to come out with the truth long ago. The town might have bad memories of her ancestors, but they adored her.

"Are you ready?"

With a start, Joe whipped his gaze to Ted, holding the microphone stand.

Ted strode to the front of the chairs. Centered by the sliding glass doors, he set the stand into position.

Joe approached and flashed a thumb's up to Ted's retreating figure. "Yes, thank you." He nodded. "Good evening, everyone and thank you for coming out." The microphone crackled and his voice boomed. He backed up a few inches. Maybe he didn't need to be so close to be effective. "I appreciate you taking the time for this special meeting. And if you're watching from home. That's some kind of miracle given tonight's IT team." He gestured to Meg and Hank.

"Hey now," Hank called.

The crowd chuckled.

Joe hated public speaking and yet he seemed to constantly put into that path. As a teacher, as a tour guide, and as the face of the bison project, he couldn't escape the spotlight even if he wanted. Was it foolhardiness that propelled him or the surge of adrenaline after he accomplished something that terrified him?

"I want to start the evening by addressing the biggest concerns. The bison will be introduced on ranch land miles from town. The animals are wild and can't necessarily be monitored and controlled. But we are not anticipating a disruption to downtown. The occasional animal might wander past a store, but there is nothing of interest on Main Street."

"Speak for yourself," a deep voice called.

The crowd sniggered and murmured.

He scanned the good spirited group, darting his eyes through the friendly faces. He spotted Will Buck and an older lady next to him. The Rabbitts sat in the front row.

Abby met and held his gaze.

He offered her an encouraging smile. He hated seeing her shrink. With her talents, she wasn't meant to hide.

Should he tame the bucking bronco in the room and broach her identity with the crowd? "I also wanted to take this opportunity to talk about the other big news. We now know the land at the end of Church belongs to our own Abby Whit. I'm sure I'm not alone in expressing surprise but also my relief at the revelation."

Frowns marred the faces in the rows. A pretty picture of prairie pride cracked.

"Yeah, what a relief," a sharp voice called.

Derisive snorts of laughter accompanied the jest.

"I am relieved, and you should be as well. We don't have to fear development of some awful skyrise or whatever other fear we've stoked."

"She lied to us," another male voice shouted.

A chair scrapped back.

Ian, the town's blacksmith, stood. "She's pretended to be someone else this entire time. How do you know she won't sell the land to a developer? How can you be so sure she won't take advantage of us?"

"Because I know her." Joe met and held Abby's gaze in the back of the room. He wanted her to hear him and to feel the truth of his words. "She has shown us who she is. She was scared of her last name. Can't say I blame her considering the immediate backlash against her."

"Why go about everything in such an underhanded and sneaky way?" Ian asked, forging ahead. "Her family screwed up and was ruined. Isn't she proving why we can't trust the Whittiers?"

The angry question didn't encourage the same general murmurs of support and agreement as the earlier comments. Joe was glad the room wasn't becoming an angry mob. Abby had lied about her identity, but she hadn't committed a crime. The town's people needed time to process the information and make their own, individual determinations about what to do next. He hoped others would forgive her.

"Everyone deserves a second chance," a female voice called.

Joe wasn't sure if the words had come from Stephanie or Kelly Strong, another kinder-garten teacher at the school. He was glad for some assistance outside of the Kincaid ranch network.

"I don't trust Harrison Wolff," Will Buck said, standing and crossing his arms. "I'll give Abby the benefit of the doubt. But he is cunning and crafty."

Joe would concede part of the town's issue was Abby using an outside, big city firm to lay her claim. Harrison's history hadn't endeared him to long-time Herd residents. Joe wasn't prepared for her to be burned at the stake for seeking legal counsel. He held up a hand. "I understand. We considered her one of our own, and she wasn't truthful. Many of us feel used. I won't fault her for seeking a lawyer's guidance and neither would any of you, after you've had time to process and cool down."

"She should have come to us. She didn't give us a chance," James Rabbitt said.

Joe paused and nodded. More than anyone, James and Heather had supported Abby. "Fear makes us do rash, fool-hardy things. She wants to settle and stay. Her actions have always been kind and neighborly. Let's move forward. I know Abby will be able to fill in some of the gaps in our town's history. I look forward to providing a fuller picture of Herd in my book. We accept legend and lore as truth. History isn't infallible. I will give her the opportunity to explain her side. I hope you'll give her a chance to do the same."

Ryan strode down the center aisle between the rows of chairs, his eyes flashing a warning. He stood at Joe's side and clapped a hand around his shoulders, leaning close to the microphone. "Thanks, Joe. Let's open it straight up to questions about the bison."

Joe stepped away from the stand, relinquishing the microphone to his boss. Was he being saved or condemned for aligning himself with Abby? He surveyed the crowd again and spotted her leaving the room. At least he'd tried. Had it been too little too late? He wanted to run after her and apologize, get her interview on record, and move on from this whole business. He felt bad about his part in the sad affair.

He wasn't a big public gesture sort of guy. But he'd tried. He hoped she appreciated the effort. The only way to know for certain would be to follow her and ask.

But he couldn't, because he had a job to do. The rest of the questions returned to the bison and the more pressing concerns about property and insurance and care. He couldn't stop thinking about her and prayed she'd endured the worst and could rebuild from here.

CHAPTER 8

As a rule, Abby avoided camping. While she didn't consider herself a particularly high maintenance person, her skincare regime relied on grocery store brands and she treated herself to two haircuts a year, she required a few basics. A mattress—not air filled—central heating and cooling, and indoor plumbing.

In the cab of her food truck, she shivered in her three layers of pants. If she wasn't so against roughing it, she might have been better prepared for her long night ahead. A sleeping bag would have been useful. She leaned her aching shoulders against the worn-down captain's seat in the front of her truck. The padding on the second-hand vehicle never bothered her much.

She wasn't in the habit of taking her truck for joyrides or road trips. Her life savings was tied up in the expenses that encompassed her livelihood. What cash she had earmarked for her restaurant would dwindle quickly if she had to purchase a place to live. She doubted another landlord or apartment complex would allow her to park her truck overnight. Then, at the minimum, she'd have to buy a car and leave the truck on her lot. Would she be vandalized as quickly as she was villainized? Dollar signs flashed through her mind with an old-fashioned cash register chime accompanying each image.

When she had purchased the vehicle, she had been thinking of a bright and shiny future. Now, she faced the harsh realities of her actions. A long night in the cab of her locked truck.

The wind whistled.

She folded her arms on the windowsill. The cold glass was inescapable. With a groan, she folded her arms over her chest. She shut her eyes and leaned her head back against the rest. The cracked leather scratched her skin. She had to hold perfectly still to avoid smelling the stale odor of degrading foam and to stop from scratching her tender skin.

Every muscle in her body ached, including her jaw from prolonged clenching. She couldn't sob if she wanted. She was utterly drained of any excess energy. The day had been an emotional rollercoaster of her own making and all she wanted now was sleep. What a joke that, in the immediate aftermath of the town meeting, she had felt heartened. Joe, of all people, had defended her. He'd used the community gathering to support her, risking his solid reputation. He, the one person in town who hated her, had spoken up for her.

Of course, she couldn't help but argue that he had no choice. The Kincaids hadn't publicly defamed her. Joe would bolster her to show his solidarity with them.

If he was only saying what he felt he had to, he wouldn't have been so eloquent. She could analyze his actions all she wanted, and she'd never reach a clear conclusion. No one was all good or all bad.

She'd been overwhelmed by his speech and had fled. She'd heard enough whispers and hisses on the streets and in the new barn to know her heart couldn't take any more public displays of either scorn or support. She'd made it into her vehicle as the call came.

After learning of the situation, her landlady had declared the contract, signed as Whit, null and void. The eviction was delivered with such succinct respect, Abby was almost glad. At least, in one instance, the situation was all business. Abby had boxed up all of her belongings and stuffed the truck to capacity and left her home.

She had spent a considerable amount of time scrubbing the furnished one-bedroom apartment and leaving a note that simply said *Thank you. I'm sorry.*

Her conscience wouldn't let her do anything less than leave the basement suite as she found it. She might have been exposed as a liar, but she had determined to prove she only deceived about the packaging and not the person. She wouldn't seek her security deposit. She hadn't thought of the ramifications of signing only part of her name. She would accept the consequences and move on.

Unfortunately, with her funds tied up, she didn't have an excess of cash to splash on an indefinite hotel stay. With her entire life now contained within her truck, she was vulnerable. She couldn't leave her worldly goods unattended. She was completely exposed now. Was this the bottom? She hoped so.

The wind picked up from a melodious howl to a sharp screech. She'd spent enough time on the plot of land beside the cemetery to know all the sounds. She'd endured plenty of blustery days. At night, however, the location became ominous. She recalled Stephanie's suggestion to host haunted events. *Please let the ghosts stay away tonight.*

Tomorrow, she'd have a plan. One night in her truck wasn't the worst thing in the world. She could do this and perhaps earn herself a hotel stay in the morning.

An insistent knock on the truck's metal door startled her.

Opening her eyes, she turned and squinted, peering through the glass to the ground and the small figure standing there. She trusted her strength. She'd easily overwhelm the mystery guest.

In the dark, she couldn't quite make out who her visitor was, other than a woman. Who was here? Why? Throw rotten vegetables at Abby and her truck?

The figure stepped back into the beam of lights from a small SUV and waved.

Meg.

Abby pressed her lips together, unsure how to proceed. Did she invite the other woman in, offering whatever meager hospitality she could? Was it better to be yelled at on your own turf?

Abby wrenched open the door and slowly lowered herself out of the truck to the ground. She couldn't hop or jump with her usual ease. Muscles in her lower back strained and tensed. With several pairs of pants on, her movements were restricted. Slowly, she shut the door, gripping her keys tight in her fingers, and crossed her arms over her chest against the chill in the night air. "Hi."

"Are you sleeping in there?" Meg asked with no preamble.

Abby's cheeks and ears burned. At least the dark hid her visceral response. She lifted a shoulder in a half shrug. Did her nonchalance land? Was it even visible?

"What happened?" Meg's features were hard to make out in the dark. Her tone sounded sincere. Meg had always been friendly. If Abby had to speak to anyone right now, she was glad it was Meg.

"Nothing I didn't deserve," Abby said.

"I doubt that. Were you kicked out of your place?"

Meg's succinct and spot-on assertions would put Joe to shame. Abby never wondered what Meg was thinking. With a second of conversational lull, Meg would fill in the blanks.

"Is that allowed?" Meg asked. "Why would she throw you out into the cold?"

"I signed Whit instead of Whittier on the contract. It's a legal issue. Don't be too hard or quick to pass judgement." *Hopefully my ex-landlady won't file a lawsuit.*

Abby would be glad to end her association with Harrison Wolff as soon as possible. She'd rather not become further embroiled with the lawyer and his sneaky tactics. He served her best interests, she couldn't argue that, but his methods seemed aligned to some other motivation.

"And you have no place to go." Meg sighed. "I'm sorry. Truly."

"Thanks."

"Where are your things?"

Abby appreciated the direct, no-nonsense line of conversation. She couldn't let any of the emotions threatening to bubble up inside her boil over, or she'd lose all her nerve. "In the back. I don't have much."

"That's good."

"Why are you here, Meg?" Abby asked, hating the crack in her voice but unable to don anymore disguises. The blackness of night was the only veil she had left. In the morning, when the whole town would learn of her situation, she would be laid bare for everyone's examination and gossip.

Rumors spread quick through town thanks to a few long-winded folks. A flicker of strong opinion flamed into an engulfing blaze of gossip after a few retellings. Most of the time, notoriety burned itself it. But she had an inkling she'd forever be a topic of conversation. For the rest of her life, she'd be another one of those Whittiers. It didn't require much imagination to summon the shaking heads and wagging tongues that would follow her every move.

She couldn't leave now. She would have to find a way forward. If anything, her refusal to remove her truck would solidify her place in the landscape.

"I was worried about you, after the meeting," Meg said. "I couldn't stop putting myself in your shoes, and I wanted to make sure you were okay. I guess I had good reason."

Abby's heart ached. She was glad to know she could count on the other woman as a friend. But she'd hoped Joe might have suggested Meg look out for Abby. "It's late you should get home."

"Late? No, it's not late."

Abby pulled out her phone and glanced at the screen. Nine ten? Really? She'd hoped it would be almost midnight. Instead, she'd only suffered through forty minutes. The night would be longer than she'd anticipated. Abby snorted. Oh, Meg's instincts were spot-on.

"What will you do?"

"Tonight?" Abby asked, sliding the phone into her outermost back pocket. "Get some rest."

"And in the future."

"I'm building a restaurant on the plot, and I'll have a two-bedroom apartment upstairs. It'll be nice." *And mine.* No one could kick her from her property. Tomorrow, she'd go to a big box store and buy supplies. A tent. A sleeping bag. She'd stay on her land.

Abby wouldn't give up on her dream. She'd called Harrison Wolff earlier. Unsure what to do next, she wanted a trusted opinion. He hadn't offered her advice; however, he'd cared only about how Ryan and Hank responded to the news. He hadn't given her a chance to ask a single question about her next steps. "If we speak any more, I'll have to charge you," he had said before abruptly ending the call.

"What about right now?" Meg asked. "Where will you go?"

Abby turned toward her truck. She shuddered, involuntarily and wished she could feel her limbs well enough to kick herself or wiggle a toe. How quickly did hypothermia set in?

She didn't know if her gas budget would extend enough to running the truck all night to stay warm. Maybe she could turn it on every hour for a little while. If she was already losing feeling in her extremities, however, she probably needed to keep the engine on until the truck ran out of fuel. And then she'd be back to sitting in her cold truck, risking her health.

"Come to my house," Meg said.

Abby faced her friend and shook her head. "I can't. You don't want to roll in the muck with me."

"I won't abandon you," Meg said and stepped forward grabbing Abby's icy hand and squeezing. "I've had my share of feeling unwanted and unwelcome in a place I love with my whole heart. I know first-hand how hard it can be. And you won't have an easier time for not sleeping."

Abby pulled her fingers out of the other woman's warm grasp. Meg had a point.

With every secret exposed, Abby could start to rebuild her standing in town with every interaction from this moment on. The entire town would dissect her comments, appearance, and behavior. Wouldn't she be better served by a night in a real bed? "Okay but only for tonight."

"No, you can stay until your apartment is ready, or you find another place to rent."

"That's too much. My building won't be ready for at least a year, and I doubt anyone in town would rent to me." Long before news of her identity spread, she had had a difficult time securing a place to rent that allowed her to park her truck outside.

"No, my offer stands. But we can work out particulars later. Do you want to follow me in your truck?"

Abby shook her head. If she was going to spend the night, she'd leave her truck in its place. She'd risk leaving everything she had out in public rather than move the loud vehicle to Meg's house where it would definitely not be hidden. She didn't want Meg to be dragged down to her. She'd leave it be and pretend everything was normal.

Could she fake it till she made it?

"Let me grab a suitcase and lock up. I'll ride with you if that's okay?" Abby asked.

"Sure. You can come back into town with me in the morning when I open the store."

As long as Abby wore a hat and dark sunglasses. She walked back to the truck, checking the locks on the exterior of the truck before entering the cab and throwing a few things in the bag. She was blessed and lucky for the kindness of Meg and wouldn't let anything harm her friend. Joe might have had mixed feelings and reasons for why he stood up for her, but she could count on at least two people's genuine support.

On Saturdays during the school year, Joe treated himself to a lazy, late start. In an area with deep roots of caring for the land, the citizens of Herd kept sunrise to sunset hours. Traditions engrained for generations couldn't be so easily forgotten. Waking up at eight was considered sleeping in.

With his self-imposed book deadline looming, however, Joe found himself pounding the slats of the downtown raised wooden sidewalk by seven fifteen. He slid a few thank you notes into the mail slot outside the post office. Gratitude wasn't a mere act of polite behavior. He carried a grateful heart with him into every day. While many in town might consider his project as superfluous or a demonstration of vanity, he understood the value in listening. The interviewees shared personal narratives, giving the town history a layer of intimacy and connection. The biggest worry was entirely out of his control. What had happened to all the stories that hadn't been collected? Were some chapters already lost to time?

He'd admit his ego played a large part in motivating him to finish the work. But his efforts weren't only to prove himself worthy. One day, everyone would understand the importance of his actions. *Is this how Abby feels about her choices? Justified?*

He released his grip on the mail slot's handle, the opening clanging shut. Her decisions weren't his business. Or anyone else's for that matter. In the heat of the moment last night, he had made her his concern during the meeting. And then spent the rest of the night berating himself. Should he have intervened? Was he wrong to do so? Had he said enough in her defense? He wasn't sure. He'd felt right in his convictions at the time. But he knew his words weren't the last on the subject. Could she, would she, stick around for long enough to prove herself?

Shaking his head, he scanned the street.

The street was nearly deserted. A few vehicles were parallel parked in front of businesses. The saloon opened for breakfast as did the General Store kitty-corner from the post office. The road was free of traffic.

He jogged across Main.

A car door slammed shut.

He spun toward the sound and spotted Abby and Meg at the end of the block. They were a curious combo. Had they decided to eliminate him and Ryan from event planning? He couldn't deny that would simplify matters. But he felt an odd pang and rubbed the ache under his breast bone.

Meg entered her store, but Abby remained on the sidewalk. She twisted her neck side to side and stalked down the street with determination. The hunch in her neck looked uncomfortable as she stared at her feet.

The door to the General Store opened, and a rush of warm air invited him in as two women exited. He stepped forward to hold open the door. The women smiled and nodded their thanks. He returned the gesture and then froze.

Abby strode past, her steps clicking in determination.

The women spotted her. In a second, their pleased expressions were wiped clean, marred with deep wrinkled frowns. And then, as if he was trapped in a bygone era, the women turned and gave Abby their backs.

She continued past.

He prayed she didn't notice.

The whole episode was over in a second.

The women departed in the opposite direction.

Abby was no doubt on her way to the food truck.

He remained in place holding open a door and gaping. His mouth could catch flies. He was too shocked by what he had witnessed.

A snubbing? He had heard enough about them from his deceased grandmother. He had never expected to observe one in action. At least the women hadn't said a word in the process. It was a small thing to be glad about, that they didn't compound their behavior with blatant pettiness, but still he was grateful.

He shut his mouth and stepped inside. He rubbed his palms together and approached the coffee station in the corner of the store.

Will Buck poured refills in several mugs at the bistro tables.

Joe waited at the counter, scrubbing his hands over his face to erase his expression. He was ashamed of his lack of reaction in the moment outside. While he was stunned by the women's behavior, he hadn't done anything to stop it or help Abby. Maybe she hadn't noticed him? He added that wish to his growing list.

"Hi, Joe. What can I get you?" Will asked.

"A coffee and a moment of your time, if you have either to spare," Joe replied.

Will darted his eyes to the side and leaned forward. "Is this about you know who?"

Joe frowned at the fervent whisper. When he had been the only person in town wary of Abby, he would have welcomed commiseration. No one wanted to discuss his concerns and worries back then. In the end, he'd been correct in his assessment and hated the end result.

He'd been so adamant against a plan Ryan Kincaid floated last fall, to partner with Abby on opening a restaurant on the ranch. And now Joe wished he could go back in time and sign the contracts himself. With a partner, she would have had what she wanted and had protection. No one would have ever needed to learn the truth.

At least she didn't know, and it had never been more than an idea. He'd always feel guilty. He'd inserted himself into her life to block and complicate her path. Could he help her somehow? He hated to be the cause of anyone's misery but especially hers. Since learning the truth, he found himself longing for her company. She was a remarkable person.

"Actually, it's about cake," Joe said at last, breaking the awkward silence. "I'd love a coffee, too."

Will grabbed a mug and filled it to the brim. "Cakes I can discuss."

"Great." Joe reached for the coffee, letting the warm ceramic sink into his chilled fingers before taking the first sip. "I guess I need to know lead time on the orders for the ranch's big weekend. If you can make enough, all of that."

"I'd like to have the order at least two weeks out if not more. I'll accommodate, no matter what the numbers."

Joe had expected such an answer. He didn't need loyalty. He wanted truth. "We won't have a true count for either Hank's birthday or the reception. Ryan wants to invite everyone. The ranch will have around fifty guests that weekend alone. Maybe two hundred people for each event? Maybe three hundred?"

Will nodded. "For both events, my plan is to make a multi-tier display cake that can be cut for photographs. But I'll have sheet cake in the back to slice and serve. Same cake and frosting flavors but much more efficient."

"Do you need help?" Joe wasn't sure why he asked. He survived off microwave meals and takeout. Who could be of assistance? Abby?

Will shook his head. "With enough lead time, I'll be set. Cake can be frozen. My grandma is very excited to help. In fact, I'm glad you stopped by. She wanted to know if you'd be interested in interviewing her for your project. She's a few years younger than Hank so she wasn't sure if you wanted to talk. She figured you probably had enough stories from her generation to fill four volumes with your connection to Hank."

Joe chuckled, glad for the lighthearted moment. "She isn't too far off the mark. I'd love to interview her. Every perspective matters."

"Great. When can I tell her to be ready?"

The door opened, sending a gust of chilly air into the store.

Joe glanced over his shoulder as a couple strolled inside, making their way to the counter. His time was running short. "I need a few more weeks? I have to put my interviews on hold for the moment as I sort through the latest round of event planning and work with the bison introduction. But soon. I'll let you know." Maybe Joe would have more answers by then, especially as concerned Abby. He drained the rest of his coffee and left cash under the mug. "Thanks."

He turned before Will could tell him it was on the house. Joe didn't want anyone to feel awkward or obligated. As he strode through the store, however, he caught the snippet of a conversation.

"I can't believe it. I've never seen her drink. Have you?" A sharp, female voice asked.

He spotted Miriam, the town librarian, chatting with Wendy, the school secretary near a display at the front of the store and slowed his steps.

"I haven't noticed anything about her, if I'm being honest," Wendy said.

Joe stared at a display of postcards, feigning fascination while straining for every word. At least he could continue to count on Wendy's kindness.

"They say it can run in families. I suppose the Rabbitts will pay extra attention now," Miriam said the words with an edge of warning like a serrated knife blade.

"I don't want to speculate," Wendy said.

From the corner of his gaze, Joe openly stared now. He caught Wendy's eye. Miriam opened her mouth to speak. Wendy shook her head and rested a hand on her friend's arm. She tipped her head to the side. Miriam followed the direction and widened her gaze, her nostrils flaring.

Joe cleared his throat, breaking himself out of his daze, and strode out of the store. Only a few weeks ago, he would have been guilty of the same train of thought. He'd have looked for the Whittier claimant amongst the patrons who stayed too late and were cut off at the saloon. Now, he felt ashamed for his generalization and offensive prejudice.

He'd shown his public support for her, but he hadn't done enough to help her. Regardless of what came next, Abby had accomplished one thing. She had opened Joe's eyes to his own blind spots and challenged him to examine himself. He had never been more ashamed.

CHAPTER 9

Abby had never thought much about being the town outcast. In a theoretical concept, she'd tried to put herself in her ancestor's shoes. When she had first made the decision to scope out the town and learn if it was worth her while to claim the land, she had experienced such friendliness, even as townsfolk repeated folkloric gossip and hatred, she couldn't truly understand what it would mean.

Having never been shunned, she only had a hazy sense of loneliness for the prospect. Her new reality was a throwback to a bygone era. After the first time a neighbor turned their back to her and blatantly ignored her *hello*, she nearly laughed out loud at the ridiculous behavior. She'd only stopped herself because making light would not have improved her town standing.

As the days passed, she had become the center of a community-wide, targeted, snubbing, and she found less reason for amusement.

When her former part time employees wouldn't pick up the phone, she let the frustration roll off her back. The unexpected check from her former landlady was a nice touch, though. She was grateful to have her security deposit returned and to not be spending money on salary when she had no customers. Every cent added up while she began work on her future. She found, over the course of the next several weeks, she didn't mind solitude. Meetings with architects had filled her days better than sitting around waiting for no one to show up at her food truck. At least during the summer, tourists wouldn't know she was persona non grata. Their constant influx meant turnover on a weekly basis, and would keep her afloat.

Truly, she couldn't complain for her situation, but she was frustrated that no one would take her phone calls regarding the wedding and birthday celebrations. She hadn't shared the tidbit with her roommate. Every morning, Meg cheerfully marked another day off the calendar with a bright red X. She remained upbeat and unphased by the countdown to her wedding as she flipped to the month of May. Nor did she complain about carpooling into town most days.

Abby had driven the truck to the Hawke ranch only when she could be sure no one was aware of her movements. She had unloaded her belongings in the spare bedroom overlooking the back of the house and felt quickly at home. The sunny room was filled with antiques lovingly cared for and passed down. Meg had delighted in sharing the story of every item in her home. While Abby had felt awkward using family heirlooms, she had been chastised. Meg had insisted on using what she had to honor the memories of her loved ones and keep their spirits alive in the home.

Abby had never stayed in a home long enough to ever consider herself or her family tied to the space. Seeing the Hawke home through Meg's eyes, however, Abby understood the desire to cherish and hold on to the past. Every moment held a reminder of love. What a gift.

She could not wait to put down some roots of her own. In the meantime, she had taken every precaution to lock up her vehicle securely in town. When she had returned to her lot, she was mostly ignored. She hadn't experienced any physical violence or threat of retaliation, but she wasn't sure when she'd be welcomed again.

The Kincaids had remained resolved that she was their go-to caterer.

She'd have to figure out how to get more refrigerator and counter space to be able to fulfill her contract. The Rabbitts hadn't participated in any sort of active hostility. But neither had they assisted her, even when she attempted to order lunch one day at the saloon.

Perhaps they really hadn't heard her, since they had been passing each other on the way to and from the kitchen. But she hadn't wanted to cause more of a scene by raising her voice and trying again. She would give them time and space. She was more worried about someone else.

Since Joe's declaration of friendship and public show of support, he hadn't sought her company. It should be a relief to have at least one person no longer actively hating her. She missed him even if she felt judged in his presence. When she got the email about meeting up to review and finalize the menus for both events, she'd been thrilled. The hurried text that came an hour ago, however, put her on edge. Meg wanted to meet with Abby and Joe at her store. Would they mind stopping by?

Abby agreed even if she hated to drag them through the mud of guilt by her association.

From the safety of the alley on the side street adjacent to Main Street, near Finders Keepers Antiques, she watched and waited. Meg had asked her to meet to discuss the catering menu. As roommates, Abby could have easily produced a few samples in the kitchen without anyone knowing. Instead, Meg wanted a formal meeting and suggested Joe join them.

Abby would be grateful to speak with him and clarify the situation. But she didn't want to hurt anyone else's credibility in town. She'd taken great pains to conceal her residence at Meg's house by riding into town early and asking to leave late. She refused to be a liability to Meg because of her kindness.

With her ponytail threaded through a ball cap and a pair of oversized sunglasses shielding half her face, she felt more like an undercover starlet than a small-town restauranteur. Still, she waited. She wouldn't drag down anyone else.

Joe strolled down the street.

She could race inside the antique store before drawing any attention. She attempted just that. Stepping onto the curb, she took a step forward and slammed her foot into a slushy puddle. Dirty water sloshed over her ankle boot. So much for incognito. With each squelching step, she continued to the antique store. At least her ankle wasn't twisted. As she opened the front door, a bell rang overhead.

"Welcome to Finders Keepers," Meg called.

Abby shut the door and breathed in lemon furniture polish scented the air. She turned slowly and found only Joe and Meg.

The pair stared in confusion.

Abby pulled off her sunglasses, tucking the eyewear into her coat pocket. She released a shaky exhale. "Hi." Walking to the glass case and cash register, she focused only on her path forward and didn't let her gaze drift to either side.

"Thanks for coming," Meg said. "Both of you."

She said the words with significance that was lost on Abby. Frowning, she glanced at Joe for a clue.

He shrugged. "Of course. How can we help?"

"I know you have everything well in hand for the birthday celebration. I am also aware that my groom might be..." Meg scrunched her nose. "Over enthusiastic about the wedding."

"He has a lot of opinions," Joe said.

Meg laughed. "I am grateful that you two are acting as the coordinators. But I want to stress, if any of the requests are too much to handle. I'm not expecting miracles. Let me know, what is out of the realm of possibility and I'll break the news to him," Meg said.

Abby frowned. The wedding and birthday celebration were straight-forward. With the events happening simultaneously, she had a lot less work to handle. Meg's statement was ominous. Abby's stomach dropped. "Is this because of me?"

Meg had a pinched expression, her face wrinkled in concentration. "Not exactly."

Joe smiled but it didn't reach his eyes.

"If you want me off the projects, I understand. You don't have to feel bad. I get it." Abby dropped her shoulders. She felt boneless like she'd melt into a puddle of goo on the floor.

"No, I want you on the project. I love your food. So does everyone in town." Meg reached a hand out, grabbing one of Abby's limp arms. She squeezed. "Give them time, they'll come around."

"I haven't changed. Doesn't it count for anything that I was liked before?" Abby asked, fighting back the burn behind her eyes and in her nose.

Meg squeezed her hand again. "It does to me."

"If Meg didn't support you, she wouldn't have asked you to room with her," Joe said smoothly.

Abby gasped. "How do you know? Who told you?" She darted a glance at Meg but quickly sobered. Small town living. Of course he'd know. Everyone would. Secrets didn't last long. And—on the off chance they did—grudges developed.

She swallowed a snigger and studied the glass case under her fingers. Pretty, old things rested on velvet. Watches, cigarette cases, brooches, and snuff boxes. The sort of little items cherished and passed down from one generation to the next.

Her family didn't have any antiques. Growing up surrounded by other families constantly on the move, she never noticed. In Herd, where roots rand deep, she saw history everywhere.

"I was going to let the claim lapse," Abby said slowly. "Until I needed to expand for catering, I had a call scheduled to tell Harrison to drop it."

"Why don't you tell the town?" Joe asked. "If you explain, you'll be vindicated."

Abby met his desperate, wild-eyed gaze. Did he want her to be the hero? She shook her head. "Because ultimately I assumed control of the land." Could've, would've, should've were excuses. She stood by her decision. "And I have been lying. How many people only gave me business out of pity? How many people worried I was about to be evicted at any moment?" Abby asked.

"You're wrong about the pity, but I'll concede you have a point about the other thing. The town cared about you, and you hurt people that trusted you. You have to own it but also stick it out. Give them another chance," he said.

Abby shrugged, dropping her gaze to the glass case full of tiny pretty things on a velvet lined shelf. She couldn't look at him or she would break. His Freudian slip neatly explained her situation. Past tense, not present. "The moment the news came out, no one would give me the time of day."

"How are your plans?" Joe asked.

Abby lifted her head. She wouldn't wallow when she had so much to do. "I'm okay. Plans are moving forward for my new building. I'll start construction in June. I'm grateful for the ranch. Ryan is letting me park onsite for the summer. With any luck, tourist season and events catering will keep my income in a positive direction. I might never recover in town."

"You will," Joe said. "Of course you will."

His confident words, delivered without a second's hesitation, warmed her from inside out. She smiled at him. A little of his faith could go a long way.

"I also wanted to stress," Meg said. "You need to lead the tasting. Ryan would never interrupt you while you're speaking. He thinks he has an idea what he wants for the food. He has no clue. Don't let him talk you into doing something you know is wrong."

Abby smiled. She had been mostly shielded from Ryan's demands but knew tomorrow would be her big debut. "Got it."

The bell jingled overhead.

Abby froze. If she could shrink and hide, she would. In her pocket, she fumbled for the sunglasses.

"Welcome to Finders Keepers," Meg called, leaning around Abby and Joe to address the newcomer. "Please let me know if you need any help."

"I'd better go," Abby murmured, pulling out her sunglasses with shaky hands.

Joe reached for her wrist, lightly stilling her with his warm touch.

Abby fought a shudder. His kindness might break her even worse than his pity.

"Let's go to the saloon and chat," he said.

She shook her head. "I don't think that's a good idea."

"I do. I insist. My treat." He turned and offered his elbow.

Abby widened her eyes.

"Go on. Don't hide," Meg said.

Joe moved closer.

"Okay," Abby said on a sigh. She looped her hand through Joe's arm, fumbling with her sunglasses.

"Put those away. Let them see we're friends," he said.

She stared, mouth agape. Was he serious? Why would he want to be friends with her now? She had nothing to offer and he had everything to lose by association. Slowly, she shut her mouth and tucked the sunglasses back in her pocket. She let him led the way out of the store and across the street.

For the first time in a long time, she had the oddest sense of safety. How ironic that it was on the arm of the man who hated her. It felt a lot like coming home.

Until Joe walked out of Finders Keepers with Abby on his arm, he hadn't thought much about next steps. His defense of her at the town meeting almost a month earlier hadn't been enough. He should have done more. With the return to school and the frantic rush to the end of the year while also working on his new programs for the summer season on the ranch and compiling his notes for his book, he hadn't had another moment to think about what else to do. Meg's call had snapped him out of his daze.

He hadn't realized how low Abby felt until she showed up at the antique store. With her reddish-brown hair hidden under a hat, she looked diminished and anonymous. His heart broke for her. Without her in his life, his days had been a monotonous drone. He'd missed her.

"Whoa," she breathed. "Is that a bison?"

He turned and followed her finger pointing down the street towards the blacksmith shop.

A dark shadow with a big hump meandered into view. The fence was supposed to discourage the bison for their safety and the town's.

Shielding his gaze with his free hand, Joe squinted. The shape became clearer, a massive furry figure almost improbably supported by slender legs. "Yep, that's one of the bison."

Joe couldn't judge his distance away or the size of the creature. It looked like it was nowhere near the businesses. Which was good. He'd assured the town that the animals wanted nothing to do with them and vice versa.

But he wasn't a hundred percent certain that was true.

The conservation group had included some animals that had exposure to humans as both domesticated animals in private zoos and a couple from a circus. The hope was that with wide-open spaces the animals would return to their natural habitats and leave the humans alone. Of course, many of the bison had never lived in herds. Could the animals learn instinctual behavior? *Could humans?*

"Looks like he's well past the blacksmith shop." *Thankfully.*

"I know they've been in the area for a few weeks," she said. "I hadn't seen one before. It's sort of startling."

He understood. While Herd might look like an Old West town, it was as sanitized and commoditized as the rest of the country. The bison would reinstate the wild moniker to their West. "I've been out at the ranch a few times, but I haven't seen one wander close to town. The fence deters them."

"How many bison are there?"

"About two dozen, give or take. The adults are mostly females with their young. A few males were included."

"Hoping for some babies next spring?" She winked.

He liked her playful tone and the cheeky gesture. "I don't think that's the plan. Teds in charge of caring for the bison. He'll know more. I'll give him a call to let him know we have a wanderer in the midst."

She chuckled. "Maybe that one is being helpful and eating up the dead grass. Would be nice to have a little bit of natural wild fire control."

"They're not goats."

She glared, her green eyes glittering like emeralds. "Just looking for the positive."

He liked her slightly annoyed and feisty. Playing the victim didn't suit her. And she had a point. He spent too much time focused on the worst outcomes. He had a tendency to predict his own demise. Instead of the positives of a self-fulfilling prophecy, he carefully plotted his own doom. He needed to look at his life from a different perspective. She was good at reminding him about that. "I'd be a lot happier if I followed your lead."

"Glad to hear it." She lifted the corner of her mouth in a tilted grin.

He stared at her lips. She twisted her mouth to create the most fascinating shapes to express every emotion. Anger, frustration, and amusement were the three he'd witnessed the most. What else could she do?

She darted her tongue along her lower lip.

He flexed his hand at his side, fighting the itch to reach for her, pull her close, and do something inopportune like trace her mouth with his tongue.

The wind blew past and knocked her cap off her head. Without waiting, he raced after it and grabbed the hat in a couple yards. He returned with the prize, and she accepted, stuffing the cap back on her head with short, jerky motions.

"You know you'll get an earful from Ian about the animals too close to his shop," she said.

Joe sagged his shoulders. With that statement, the moment of romantic potential was officially over. But she wasn't wrong.

He narrowed his gaze for one last look at the bison, but couldn't discern if it was the troublesome male that had been treated more like a pet than a wild beast. Lover Boy had shading around his eyes that made it look like the top of a heart. Once he got to town and spotted people, pushing him back onto the prairie would be a challenge. Joe couldn't see anything from his position, but he'd shoot Ted a text, just to be sure.

Continuing across the street, he held the door open of The Golden Crown and waved her through first. As he crossed the threshold, he spotted James behind the bar. The other man lifted his chin in the tiniest nod of greeting possible. Joe smiled. He wouldn't hide now that he saw his part in her path forward. He strode toward a table almost in the center of the restaurant. If people were going to notice and talk about them, Joe would rather be seen in the open. He couldn't control other people's opinions or craft a narrative that suited his needs, but he wouldn't be accused of skulking in the corner.

He pulled out a chair for her, but she'd already grabbed the seat across the table. He frowned and scrubbed a hand over his features, not wanting the scowl to linger. Of course, she wouldn't expect him to be courteous and chivalrous. He had a lot of poor behavior to atone for.

James approached with two glasses of water. "Good afternoon." The delivery was as flat as the beverages.

Joe smiled broadly. "Good afternoon. Thank you. I know it's a little early, but could we order the spinach and artichoke dip?"

James nodded and turned his back, striding away.

Abby leaned closer. "Are you sure? That can take a while."

Her voice was barely above a whisper. "I am." He rose his voice to a normal level and said, "Are you ready for tomorrow's tasting?"

She nodded. "I think so. I've never catered a wedding before. But I have experience in accommodating a wide range of palates and dietary restrictions. My menu is both a crowd pleaser and scalable. I can add or subtract without too much fuss. I'll be able to carry it out no matter what."

He reached for his water and sipped. He hated her preparing for a worst-case contingency of no help from the town. From here on out, he had to make a bigger show of his support. A sudden thought popped into his brain. "Actually, since we're here, I was hoping I could convince you to help with my project."

"Me?"

He nodded. "Yes. You can finally shed light on what happened to your family after Hoss was kicked out of town. But I'm also asking for your assistance with some of my upcoming interviews."

"Are you sure?" Color drained from her face. "You might get the door slammed in your face."

He shook his head. "No way. Give them a chance."

"Let's see how tomorrow's tasting goes first." She lifted the corner of her mouth.

He extended his hand across the table. "Shake on it?"

She clasped his hand and shook once.

Her grip was surprisingly strong and firm. Good. He didn't like her at a disadvantage. He preferred her as a worthy foe. *Not anymore.* "Can you tell me more about your family? Do you know what happened?" He brushed the pad of his thumb over her knuckles. For someone who worked with their hands, her skin was surprisingly soft and unscarred.

She pulled her hand back. "If I tell you, you won't believe me." Her playful tone lifted the mood.

He straightened. "Try me."

She drew in a deep breath, sitting taller. "Hoss got sober. When he was kicked out of town, he was exiled from his family as well. His father never forgave him. At his lowest, he found forgiveness through religion."

Joe's jaw slackened. "Seriously?"

She nodded. "Hoss attended seminary and became a minister. He rebuilt his life and created his own family. But he never stayed in one place for long. That became my family's sort of creed. Military as far back as all the stories I've been told."

"Wow." She was right. He didn't believe it. "That is quite a story."

"I have documentation and old journals and such, if you want them." She reached for her water.

"I'd love to see everything." But he was struck by her family never putting down roots. He was glad they had survived and thrived. But to live as nomads broke his heart.

His family had been one impacted by Hoss's fire-starting accidents. It was a many times ancestor but the story sparked his interest in history. Personal anecdotes connected the present with the past in a way nothing else could. While every person was the hero of their own story, they didn't get to be the center of someone else's.

Herd had long cast the Whittiers as villains, and never let them be anything else. But that was wrong. Granting people the grace and space to change was what community should be about. And he hoped he could help her do that. Maybe they'd both win for telling a richer story and setting the record straight.

"How are your plans for your restaurant going?" Joe asked, leaning forward. "How is Harrison?"

"I haven't really dealt with him much lately. I get the sense he did his job and is happy to be done with me."

She smiled but the expression didn't quite meet her eyes. Joe had opinions about Harrison but was slowly learning the value in discretion and respecting others' assessments.

James returned to the table with small plates and napkins.

Abby stiffened.

"James, I hope we can still count on your support for the Kincaid events," Joe said.

"Of course. I gave you my word. I won't let you down." James replied, his voice with a hint of modulation and emotion.

"I'm sorry if you felt that I did," Abby added. "Truly."

James folded his arms over his chest and shifted his weight from foot to foot. "I can appreciate you were in a tough spot. We didn't have any preconceived ideas about you."

"But you've lived here long enough to know how many people do," Joe said. "Come on. Casual prejudice against the Whittiers is like the town's citizenship test."

"I suppose that's true." James rubbed the back of his neck. "I guess now I should be grateful you never let me put you on payroll. Otherwise, I might have fraud issues. Let me go check on your food."

"Thanks," she murmured.

Joe reached across the table and rested his hand on hers. Her fingers were ice cold. He wanted to warm her up in both his palms. He burned where his skin touched hers. Instead, he dragged his hand away. He could be her friend. That was it.

CHAPTER 10

A beep echoed through the food truck interior.

With the metal curtain still closed, the chime rang with fervor, every surface reverberating and vibrating. Abby needed the sharp, piercing alert. She moved as slow as molasses. Up since the early hours of the morning, she'd been checking on the meat she started smoking the night before for the day's menu tasting. She'd decided to add another couple pounds in case the wafting aroma of the smoker filtered down the street and lured a few customers her way, despite their best intentions at a continued snubbing.

She shut off the timer and pulled a batch of skillet cornbread from the oven. The sweet scent filled the truck with a heavenly aroma. If she wasn't exhausted, she'd be tempted to cut a slice.

Instead, she crossed to the coffee maker and poured herself the first cup of the day in the biggest container she had on hand. She gulped the hot liquid and started to feel more in control of her day. Rituals were important. She didn't empower coffee to super-charge her in an instant, but the hot drink queued her brain to get started.

She checked on the trays warming in the lower oven and then the pre-portioned cold sides in the fridge. She was as ready as she could be. Perhaps even more so than she would have been before yesterday's meeting. Meg and Joe had restored a bit of her self-confidence. Neither had shied away from being seen with her in public. For a second on the street, after leaving the shop and before heading into the saloon, Abby had shed her troubles as easily as slipping off her boots. She had shared a moment of wonder with Joe as she had marveled at the bison in the distance. She hadn't felt so conspicuous. And she had felt like Joe saw her and not some unwanted burden.

It had been nice.

At The Golden Crown, James had slowly thawed during their exchanges. She was glad he had said what he did. While painful to acknowledge, she hadn't considered how her actions impacted others. Her occasional work at the saloon had been seasonal and sporadic. She'd been paid in cash and dealt with handling her own taxes, thus avoiding giving him her tax information. But she hated to think she'd left James vulnerable to an investigation by the IRS or anyone else because of her lie. Would some irate townsperson flag her to the federal authorities?

As they had finished the appetizer, the dinner crowd and Joe's poker group had filtered into the saloon. Joe made it clear she didn't have to run off. He was just being kind. She knew that but couldn't shake the hope that she held against her heart that maybe he could become a friend.

She raised the metal curtain and grabbed her sandwich board. Carefully maneuvering the folding sign out of the truck, she propped it open next to the back wheel. With a stick of chalk from her back pocket, she listed the day's specials.

"Mustard coleslaw with pulled pork on pretzel roll?" Hank Kincaid's deep voice boomed. "Count me in."

She smiled to herself as she stood, slipping the chalk into her back pocket, and dusting together her hands.

Hank, Ryan, Joe, Ted, and Meg approached from the parking lot.

Abby waved and swallowed the sigh building in her chest. She knew they were all coming. No sense in getting intimidated by the show of force now. "Good, that's one of the menu items for the tasting. I made extra in case I get some business today."

"You will," Hank said, nodding. Dressed in his hat and boots, the older man was every inch a cowboy. With his wrinkled, visage tanned from years in the sun, he could be intimidating. If he wanted to turn a weathered look on the town and frighten some locals into supporting her business, she wouldn't stop him.

"I've set up the picnic table with clipboards and menu sheets. I'll serve each item, and you can make notes. We'll discuss after you've had a chance to sample everything," she said.

"Very organized. I appreciate that," Ryan said.

Meg winked.

"Let me step inside to get the first course," Abby said, turning back toward her truck.

"Go and help her, Joe," Hank said, his gruff tone brooking no opposition.

"Of course," Joe replied and reached the truck first, holding open the door.

With a smile, she climbed the steps.

He shut the door behind him with a gentle thud. "Good work on the printed menu. You've already impressed Ryan with that touch."

Abby glanced over her shoulder at Joe. "I took Meg's idea seriously about setting the tone."

Joe chuckled. "He cares about details. As do you." Joe pointed to the full spread she'd prepared.

She'd probably overdone it. Would the leftover food spoil in her fridge after tasting? Was she wasting money and time? She'd need a lot of customers to get rid of it all. For the Kincaids, however, she'd spend whatever it took with a grateful heart. Their support meant everything.

"I don't take the opportunity for granted. I never do. And especially not now." She leaned against the counter. "Do you think I overdid the tasting menu?"

"Not at all. Go big or go home, right?"

They both knew she had no real home if she didn't cement her position in town. She had courage and wasn't giving up the fight. The sentiment had a casual delivery but cut through her like a knife.

He cleared his throat. "Bad cliché. My apologies." He rubbed his hands together. "I'm here to help. I worked in food service during college. I have some limited experience."

"Oh, that's great." In years past, she hired line cooks for the busy summer season. She hadn't even thought about placing an ad in recent days.

"Don't get too excited. My skills are mostly related to dishwashing."

She smiled. "I'll never turn down a good dishwasher."

He stroked his chin. "Will you pay in food?"

She nodded.

He licked his lips. "Then I'm all yours."

Her stomach tightened. He meant nothing with his accidental double entendre. "I wanted to thank you." Her voice cracked and heat crept up her checks. "You didn't need to stick your neck out for me like you did at the saloon. But I am grateful."

He shrugged. "I'm glad I could help."

She was too. Turning toward the oven, she grabbed a mitt and pulled out the first sheet pan. She set the warm tray on the stove and grabbed the coleslaw out of the fridge. Opening a drawer, she pulled out a pair of disposable gloves and a spoon. She handed both to him. "I'm going to transfer the sliders to another plate, and you can top with the coleslaw."

He accepted the utensils and gloves. "Aye aye, captain."

She pulled on another pair of gloves.

For a few minutes, they worked in silence. Surprisingly, it was companionable. With her secret now revealed, she was more of an open book than ever before. She'd shared her deepest hope with him. Establishing some place as home even when the location of her choosing seemed to be star-crossed. "Dare I ask why Stephanie isn't with the group?"

"She said she'll be along. She had to do something first. Don't worry. She's on your side."

"I hate that there are sides," Abby murmured.

He scooped the last slider with coleslaw. "Don't think about it like that. My poor choice of words is no indication of the general sentiment."

Of course he was right. Still, she couldn't shake her worry. She topped each small sandwich with the other half of the pretzel roll she'd made from scratch. "Okay, I'm all set."

"Hey, before we go out there, thanks for helping me with my interviews tomorrow."

He held her gaze and looked at her intently, not even a flicker of his lashes to break his stare. She didn't feel pity from him only reverence like she was a valued equal. She wasn't sure she was worthy of the high level of consideration, but she appreciated it all the same. She wanted a way to thank him for his display of friendship that would be organic and jotting down notes while he interviewed someone seemed the best option. "My pleasure."

He nodded and strode to the door, descending first and holding the door open for her.

She made her way carefully to the picnic table.

The bride and groom sat on one side, facing the cowboys in their midst. In the center, Abby had stacked plates, forks, knives, and napkins.

Hank tucked a bandana in his shirt and licked his lips. "I'm ready."

Heat crept up Abby's cheeks. She was glad someone was still enthusiastic about her food. "This is the special from the sign, pulled pork sliders. It's bigger than a one-bite appetizer, and you'll need a fork. So, this wouldn't be a good option for passed appetizers." She set the platter down in front. "Please serve yourselves."

The group each reached for a slider and started chewing.

Ryan lifted his head and flashed a thumbs up. He stuffed the rest of his sandwich in his mouth. Then he grabbed another off the platter.

Hank and Ted did the same.

Meg chewed slowly. She set half the sandwich on her plate and dabbed her lips with a napkin. "I think these would be great whenever we serve them. No one would mind using a fork to get every single bite."

Abby smiled. Good. Because she had brisket to serve next. "Let me run and grab some waters for you."

"I'll help," Joe said, following her. Inside the truck, he opened the oven door and peered inside. "Can I grab one? I'm not sure Ryan is planning on leaving any leftovers."

She chuckled. "Go for it. Not like I'll have to worry about serving too many customers today." Opening the refrigerator, she pulled out the coleslaw again along with several bottled waters.

"I wouldn't be so sure." His singsong tone was followed by his finger pointing to the front of the truck.

She stared at him for a long moment. He had to be teasing.

He tipped his head to the window.

Abby turned and sucked in a breath.

Stephanie appeared with Kelly Strong. Both women smiled and waved.

"Oh, wow, hi," Abby said. "Good afternoon, ladies. How many I help you?"

"Two of the specials, please," Kelly said with a grin.

"Absolutely. Coming up." Abby turned toward Joe. "Do you think you could help me run these waters out to the table? And I'll get the next course ready?"

Joe nodded and grabbed an apron off a hook on the door. He wrapped it around his waist. "Sure thing, boss. Just tell me what you need."

A lot of forgiveness and a little grace. She curled her toes in her shoes. Maybe she'd come out okay after all. His friendship was better than she could have imagined. But she'd stop her daydreaming there.

Joe had worked in food service during college. But he hadn't shared the truth of the situation with her. He wasn't embarrassed. He valued hard work.

At a fast casual restaurant, he'd been able to work around his schedule during the school year. Long hours on his feet and dealing with angry customers persuaded him to stay the course and finish his education. But he'd been grateful for the paycheck and learned a lot about diffusing an argument that came in handy for teaching.

He never stopped to consider the industry as a career path. At her side, however, he viewed the whole endeavor through another set of eyes. Inside the food truck, he marveled at her cool-head in the chaos of the lunch rush. She had seemingly bottomless energy and enthusiasm. For each order, she devoted time and care to crafting the meal.

Without missing a beat, she prepared every dish with precision. The portions were exact. The presentation was impeccable. To the soundtrack of constant motion—the clanging of utensils as served, water rushing from the faucet, and customers conveying their orders and conversing together—he was hit by an awful realization. She was an artist. He was jealous.

In a rush, he understood his earlier apprehension at the beginning of their acquaintance beyond her keeping a secret. She had attained a level of skill in her field far exceeding what he could imagine. No matter how many hours he devoted to study, he would never be as accomplished. He toiled.

By comparison, his achievements were feeble. His project was like a last grasp for respect. No wonder he'd held a subconscious grudge. Now that he saw the truth, he couldn't hide. He didn't want to. She might outclass him by miles. He wouldn't be intimidated to stay away. He wanted to help and—in doing so—earn the gratitude she had heaped on him. For too long, he'd allowed envy to influence his distrust. He was ashamed.

He hadn't noticed her focus and determination before. Because he'd been so busy looking for her faults? He could kick himself. After helping serve the rest of the tasting menu to the Kincaids, he carried their kudos back inside the truck and helped her.

He smiled at the line forming in front of the truck. While he didn't spot the Rabbitts, not surprising given they'd be handling their own business, he smiled at many familiar faces, including Miriam the town librarian.

He was glad. If he had paid even tiny bit of the debt he owed her by publicly friending her yesterday, after his proclamation at the ranch a month earlier, he did something right.

She kept her cool between serving customers and the wedding tasting. After the last customer in line was served, he faced her. "Finished."

Grinning ear to ear, she glanced over her shoulder and sighed. "Oh, thank goodness."

"And just the perfect amount of food, too." He scanned the empty trays, platters, and containers.

"Somehow it worked out. I'm glad I woke up so early."

He smiled. "I'm sure the delicious smell of the smoker wafting through town played a big part."

She untied the apron on her waist. "I owe the line to Stephanie. Thank you for helping. I couldn't have managed alone."

"I'm not done yet." He crossed to the sink and turned on the water.

"You really don't have to do this."

"I wasn't joking. You can bring me the dishes and dry." He tossed a dish towel at her.

She caught it, threw the cloth over her shoulder, and grabbed the trays.

He wouldn't have anticipated the quiet companionship he found in completing a chore with her. But every day seemed to surprise him.

He rinsed the last container, turned off the faucet, and slipped off his apron, drying his hands. He couldn't help but wonder if he'd hindered her in the long run. If he hadn't been so negative against her for so long, would she have found the courage to come out with the truth sooner? He didn't deserve her praise.

"Oh, my."

He spun back. Something in her tone was equal parts wonder and worry. He wouldn't worry about how he knew the sound. "What is it?" he murmured.

"Well. Oh goodness. It's one of the bison. And it's huge. Should I be worried?"

He stood at her side and stared out through the open ordering window. "The last orders were to-go, right?"

She nodded. "Do we have anyone at the picnic tables?"

"We shouldn't. What do we do?"

He scrambled his brain for the crash course Ted set him on recently. "We stay put. He'll move on."

"If I was a real cowgirl, I'd know what to do."

"What's this?" he asked.

"Nothing just..." She grabbed a dishcloth and rubbed the counter.

He studied her from the corner of his gaze. The stainless steel was already spotless. But the motion seemed to soothe her. He liked observing her and noticing the little things he'd missed. She never asked for someone to take care of something for her but jumped in and did hard work, figuring out if she needed help along the way.

Her open-ended statement was another opportunity to assist. "Have you been getting flack for your heritage? For not being Western born and raised?"

"Not that exactly. Herd isn't opposed to outsiders, thankfully."

He nodded.

"I hear things. Not necessarily meant as jibes but still not quite polite."

About alcohol? Of course, the biggest worry about a Whittier's return was the most unfair, that the drunkard descendant would stumble around and set fire to the town again. The community as a whole seemed to expect any descendant of Hoss would seek retribution or total destruction. Accepting the truth, someone they'd known and liked who wanted to put down some roots, didn't line up with what had been ingrained for so many years. "Are you suggesting that you should be able to go out and round up the bison purely because you're a Whittier?"

"When you say it like that it sounds really dumb." She sighed. "But shouldn't I be more of a cowgirl? Shouldn't I at least know how to ride a horse?"

"Do you want to learn?" *I'd be happy to teach you.* To his surprise, he rather liked the idea of instructing her in how to embrace her roots. He wasn't the best equestrian but knew enough for leading his tours.

"Actually, I'd hate it." She scrunched her nose. "I tried once, and I freaked out."

"Why?"

"In the saddle, I was too high off the ground. I'm scared of heights."

He had no response. Could a fear be aggravated by such a small impetus? He wanted to argue she'd be fine. With his help, he'd quickly get her comfortable and riding like a professional. But that wasn't fair. It was okay for people to know their limits. It was up to others to respect that.

"Should I close the curtain?" she asked, pointing out the window. "Is he being led here by the smell?"

"He shouldn't be attracted to meat. Bison eat grass."

She turned towards him and put both hands on her hips, glowering. "Wait, was I right?"

He frowned. Facing off against a wild animal, and she jumped onto a chance to win an argument? "What do you mean?"

"When I said maybe the bison could help with wild fire control by eating grass?"

He scrubbed his face with both hands, hiding the smirk.

"You said they aren't goats."

He dropped his hands. "You're right. I'm sorry. The truth is, I have no clue." He leaned closer and narrowed his gaze.

The bison's distinctive coloring around his eyes was just visible from the hundred yards of distance. A light, irregular ring in the fur looked like a heart.

"I know that bison. That's definitely Lover Boy. He has no practical skills." Joe sighed. "He was a pet. I think he heard people and got lonely. I'll let Ted know he's out here."

"Is he friendly?"

"Very much so." Joe pulled his phone out of his pocket and pulled up his texts. "At least, for a bison. He's a wild animal. Don't approach him. Keep your distance."

She rested her hand on his phone screen.

He glanced up.

"Maybe don't tell Ted. I wouldn't mind the company for a little bit. It's lonely at my truck right now," she said, softly.

He vowed to be nicer then and there. No matter how everything played out in town. If she earned her redemption or not, if he was able to help her or not, whatever the costs, he would be her friend. Because he couldn't stand to think she was lonely and he'd been the cause. She was kind and sweet and talented. She deserved the world and way better than what he'd given.

But he had another chance, and he wasn't going to spoil it. He slipped the phone back into his pocket. "I'll let him know in a bit. Do you suppose your affection for a bison is your ranching ancestry coming out?"

She giggled. "Not in the slightest. I can't twirl a lasso."

"I don't think—technically speaking—lassoes are twirled."

She pursed her lips.

Joe laughed. The expression highlighted her perfectly kissable mouth. No, he tamped that down. Spending time with her had nothing to do with attraction, and everything to do with righting his past behavior. Her fun personality made the situation a bonus. He saw no harm in prolonging their encounter for another hour. "How else may I help?"

"You've done more than enough."

Not nearly. He had a lot of apologizing to do. Manual labor was one way to repay his debt. Maybe he had a better reason to spend time with her again under the guise of friendship. "Will you join me at my interview tomorrow?"

"Do you think I'd be welcomed?"

"I do." Because he wanted her company. He suspected the more time he spent with her the more he'd want to see her. He might be making a big mistake. If Hank Kincaid caught a whiff of their changed status, he'd push his matchmaking again hard.

"I'd be delighted."

And—to Joe's surprise—so would he.

CHAPTER 11

Abby smoothed her hair behind her ears and shifted on the passenger seat in Joe's SUV. She should have worn a ponytail or a bun. With the weather warm enough she could leave her knit hat at home and the humidity still low enough not to inflame her naturally wavy mane, she couldn't resist leaving her hair down. But now she worried for another reason.

She stood out. Everyone knew the auburn hair was the mark of a Whittier, enemy to town. Some might have forgotten about the family's coloring but once her identity was known they'd all be sure to notice. One good day wasn't going to be enough to suddenly atone for her sins. She wasn't a fool.

Joe parked the car in the driveway and cut the engine. "Ready?"

She smiled, not feeling the emotion but desperate to fake it. She patted the purse in her lap. "All set. I've got a notebook and pens. I vow to sit quietly and take diligent notes."

"Well..." He wrinkled his brow. "I didn't invite you to be silent. If you have a question, you are free to ask as long as you don't interrupt. And I've learned over the past few years, you need to pause for longer than you would in a normal conversation. Once the interviewee starts reliving their memories, they need time to process. A comment or question asked too quickly can throw the interview off track."

She nibbled her bottom lip. She was famous for fast-talking and jumping into conversations. Essentially, she'd have to bite her tongue to give anyone enough time.

"Can you do that?"

She flashed a thumbs-up. "I'll do my best. I should be an expert in waiting for others to speak first after the last few weeks."

He nodded. An air of solemnity heavy in the vehicle.

"Besides," she said, rushing ahead before silence ensued. "I used to be obsessed with a kid detective TV show on public broadcasting. Patience solved those cases."

"*Ghost Writer?*" he asked.

"Word."

They both chuckled at her invoking the show's catch phrase.

"I cut my teeth on those episodes," he said. "I sent in a self-addressed stamped envelope to my local public TV station for the sticker for my notebook and everything."

She smiled. She'd done the same, anointing one wide-ruled single subject as her official casebook. It was nice to learn how much more they had in common than she'd ever suspected.

Their mutual respect for the other's abilities warmed her, too. She'd do her best to be an active, but unobtrusive, participant. "Who are we meeting?"

He grabbed his phone from the cupholder and scrolled through the lock screen to his calendar. "Will Buck's grandmother."

"Will Buck? Like owner of the General Store?" She drew in a sharp breath.

"Yes. He didn't grow up in Herd, but apparently his grandmother did. She moved away when she got married and then Will wandered back." Joe lifted a shoulder. "Doesn't seem so odd, all things considered."

"I suppose not." She rolled her eyes at his playful tease. But the smile that followed was genuine. Still, she couldn't fully shake her trepidation. It clawed at her with an icy burn.

"Will is at the store. And, according to Ted, Will is taking Jennifer out on a date after work. He shouldn't be here today. If it makes you feel better."

"Thank you. I'm not trying to avoid anyone. I just don't want to make your project awkward for you." And in a small town, everyone seemed to know everyone else's business. Will was dating Ted's sister so those in either orbit would know his plans.

"I'm grateful. But you are fine," he murmured. For a moment, he held her gaze and smiled.

The crinkles at the corners of his eyes reflected his sincerity. Her stomach flipped. She craved his gaze only to squirm under his focus.

"He'll come around. He's not a bad sort. And trust me, the rest of town will forgive you, too. We better head inside."

She unbuckled her seatbelt and exited the car. Rounding the bumper, she followed him up the front path to the door of a snug colonial revival home.

Joe rang the doorbell.

She glanced over her shoulder, taking in the neighborhood. Built in the seventies and eighties, the homes in the subdivision were the most recent, major construction project in city limits. An apartment complex with a strip mall had popped up off the highway a little further out of town. But with no great demand for housing, no one had broken ground any closer to Herd despite plenty of available land. Her restaurant's construction would have been the subject of scrutiny regardless of ownership.

The front door opened.

"Hello? Mr. Staunch?" A petite, silver haired lady dressed in a sweater set, pearls, and pressed chinos answered the door.

Abby felt shabby in her jeans. She should have dressed in nicer clothes.

"Yes, good morning, Mrs. Buck. Thank you for taking time to meet with me," Joe said smoothly.

"Are you Abby Whittier?" Mrs. Buck asked.

Abby drew her shoulders up tight, hoping the sneer or whatever else she'd come to expect of the townsfolk would bounce off her. When she met the pleasant expression of the older lady, she relaxed. "I am." Answering to her real name felt almost as foreign as those first few months using the alias.

"Don't suppose you've brought any food?" Mrs. Buck licked her lips. "I love your brisket. Willie brings it home for me when you have your specials in the summer."

Willie? The nickname soothed a little of the sting from the grandson's continued anger. "Oh, that's so sweet of you to say. I'm sorry. I didn't know," Abby's voice cracked.

"It's okay. Next time." Mrs. Buck winked and held open the door. "Please come inside. I'm very pleased to have both of you here."

Joe waved Abby through first.

She passed the threshold into in a short entryway leading to a living room on the right and stairs to the left. She followed Mrs. Buck into the living room and settled on the sofa. Beyond the next open doorway, sunlight spilled in from a sliding glass door, illuminating a large eat-in kitchen with a southern exposure backyard.

Joe settled down next to her, rifling through his messenger bag.

Mrs. Buck sat in an arm chair, facing the sofa.

Abby pulled out her notepad, silenced her phone, and studied her surroundings. The fully furnished rooms had bare walls. No knickknacks or commemoratives took up space on a table, shelf, or cabinet. The khaki color carpet blended into the beige wall color and cream tiles in the connecting kitchen. Joe told her the home belonged to Will and that his grandmother moved in. She didn't see any personality to the space.

Perhaps Mrs. Buck had a suite of rooms decorated to her taste, with warmer colors and specific details. Will's home was bland. Because he spent so much time at work? Abby wouldn't have to worry about making that mistake, when the time came. She'd be living just above her business and decorating as she chose.

"Mrs. Buck, do you have any questions for us before we start talking?" Joe asked.

"I am curious, if I change my mind and want to redact some of what I've said, how I'd be able to do that?"

Abby's eyebrows stretched into her eyebrows at the woman's question. How many scandals had Mrs. Buck witnessed? Abby came to the right interview.

"Is there anything in particular you are worried about?" Joe asked. "To be honest, no one has brought this up. I haven't been trying to uncover gossip or old stories, if that's your concern. My interest is purely in trying to understand how the town has changed. You're not being interrogated."

"I know you're friendly with the Kincaid family. And... I just don't want to say anything that might upset any of them," Mrs. Buck said.

Abby shut her gaping mouth. She was brimming with follow-up points but silently counted to ten. As neither Mrs. Buck nor Joe said anything, Abby inserted herself into the conversation. "Mrs. Buck, I can assure you the family are very reasonable. They've been forgiving and welcoming of me. You won't need to fear retribution."

Mrs. Buck smiled. "Well, it's nothing damaging. I've known Hank a long time. I doubt he'd remember me. I had an opportunity to see him over Easter, but I caught the flu. Not that he would have known I was absent."

"How did you meet Hank?" Joe asked. He hadn't turned on his phone's voice recorder and made no move to uncap the pen in his hand.

"My maiden name was Everson. I'm the kid sister of Hank's high school girlfriend, Ava," Mrs. Buck said.

"He dated someone before Susie?" Joe asked.

Mrs. Buck nodded, interlacing her fingers, and lowering her chin.

Wide-eyed, Joe met Abby's gaze. *What?* He mouthed.

"And you are concerned Ryan might be hurt by stories about his grandfather's first love?" Abby added.

"Exactly. I don't want to upset him," Mrs. Buck said, pressing a hand to her heart. "I lost my sister about a decade ago. Hank and Susie came to the funeral. They were very kind. I went to Susie's service. I kept telling myself I should reach out to him for a chat. It would be good to catch up. I didn't want to force myself on him."

She looked wistful and girlish. Abby smiled. "You should call him. You can never have too many friends, right?"

From the corner of her gaze, she scanned Joe's grin. She relaxed. She feared her instantaneous response betrayed the code she'd agreed to follow.

Joe reached inside his pocket for his phone. "Do you mind if I record our interview? I can type up my notes and send them to you. Anything you want to strike from the conversation, you can."

"Yes, please," Mrs. Buck said.

Joe turned on the dictation app and set the phone on the coffee table. "Mrs. Buck, wherever and whenever you want to begin."

"Hello, I am Lana Everson Buck."

The older lady continued, but her words became almost white noise to Abby. Instead of participating, she found herself content to observe. Joe was a thoughtful, patient, and considerate interviewer. Treating Mrs. Buck with respect, he earned the same in return tenfold. His reputation in town was well-deserved. She knew he wanted to be an expert, a trusted historian. He didn't need credentials or accolades. He already was an important member of their small society.

The more she learned about Joe, the more she valued and liked him. Maybe being scorned by the town had provided the unexpected chance to become allies. But she was almost glad for it.

His friendship had come to mean so much. She had the urge to reach for his hand and squeeze. But she wouldn't risk asking for too much. Instead, she'd just sit in the comfort and warmth of his companionship. She wouldn't ask for more. Even if she wasn't sure what she felt as far as Joe was concerned.

Joe drove the SUV down Main Street as the sun started to dip on the horizon. The sky was washed with pink and orange and blue. It looked sugar-sweet just like his day.

They'd ended up spending the entire afternoon with Lana Buck. She brought out old yearbooks, scrapbooks, and more memorabilia from the high school and town than he'd ever seen. She had buttons and bumper stickers from Herd's celebration of the American bi-centennial and even more saved from Herd's big party in the 1990s. He'd been too young to think about keeping anything, and his mom wasn't the nostalgic sort.

The talk was illuminating and charming. And not just for the bygone tales Mrs. Buck told. Whenever he was at a loss for words or the next question, Abby jumped in.

She was never flippant or off the cuff. She thought quickly though, faster than he did. Her statements were insightful and encouraging. She enhanced the interview. He almost wished he could re-interview everyone with her at his side. What would he learn now with his new double act?

He drove slowly through town. The lights had turned on, spilling onto the street, and raised sidewalk. He hoped someone would see them. He didn't want to hide their association anymore.

He drove past the General Store. Will should be heading home soon. Lana was making his favorite meal, chicken pot pie. Joe envied him having someone there who cared. Joe had been as eager as anyone else to leave home for college and hadn't ever truly returned to living with his family. He hadn't missed it. Until the past few months or maybe even the past year, when his friends started to couple off and had less time. Then he'd envied those who had someone else—whether romantic or not—in their lives.

"Do you think she'll call Hank?" Abby asked.

Her voice was soft and sweet, almost wistful. Joe smiled. "I'm going to make sure I give Hank her number, too. They should spend time together and catch up."

She turned in the seat and arched an eyebrow.

From the corner of his eye, he spotted the incredulous look. "What?" He continued to Church Street and turned into the parking lot. "What's that look for?" He pulled to a stop.

"No look." She shook her head.

He rolled his eyes. She wore every single expression like a costume. Happy, sad, mad, and confused were broadcast with her expressive eyes. And yet, somehow, she'd concealed her identity, hiding in plain sight.

"Oh, okay, fine." She exhaled a heavy sigh, turning towards him and loosening the seat belt. "I can't help but wonder if you're turning the tables and setting him up now."

He grinned. "Turnabout is fair play. They both still have a little spark."

She tapped a finger to her chin. "I hadn't thought about it like that. Maybe we should be careful. Those two are both feisty. Together, they could start a fire."

He laughed, the chuckle flowing out of him with ease. Being with her had shifted so abruptly from pain to pleasure. Joe wouldn't mind a little heat as long as he wasn't engulfed in the flame. Since Hank backed off of setting him up with Abby, Joe finally came to understand what would have inspired the old cowboy to make the match in the first place. Unlike the match Hank had engineered for his friend and boss, Ryan, Joe hadn't known Abby forever. Sure, he'd gone a year and a half without seeking her out. But was Hank's push really what prompted him to change his opinions about her?

He wasn't so sure.

"I think it would be nice for Hank to have a companion. But Ryan might get jealous," Abby said.

"He doesn't have the time. Between his wedding and his business and his new wife, he should be able to let his grandfather do what suits him. Hank should enjoy himself too. He raised two kids almost thirty years apart. He should relax now while he can."

She shuddered.

"You okay?" He turned the key in the ignition, warming up the engine and restarting the heater.

"Sure, I'm not cold so much as... I guess it all just hit me. Everything Hank's lived through. So much pain and loss. He's so steady and so positive. A lesser person would have keeled over from any number of his hardships. But he's still here. That's..." She sniffed and swiped at her eyes. "Inspirational."

Joe fumbled in the glove compartment for his stash of tissues and handed her one.

"Thanks." She accepted the square and blew her nose.

"Herd will come around and accept you. You haven't done anything unforgivable. Your reasons are understandable. The town holds its prejudices. You've made them all wake up and realize what they're taking for granted."

"If you say so," she mumbled.

"I do. In fact..." He shouldn't do it. He'd barely had a chance to update it over the past few weeks since learning of her claim. But he wanted her to see she had a friend. "I want you to read what I have in my manuscript so far."

She widened her eyes. "Are you sure?"

"I am. I have some hard facts about your family in there. I need to edit and compile all my recent notes. But I want you to see what my goal for the project is. If you have time?"

She nodded. "Of course I do."

He reached behind her seat, unzipping the front flap of the messenger bag. He grabbed the stack of two-hundred recycled paper sheets bound with a thick binder clip and pulled them out. In his hands, he scanned the neat, white stack. This latest version hadn't had his red pen and sticky note treatment yet. "You can mark it if you want. This is not the final edit by a long way. But I'd appreciate your thoughts."

She accepted the pages and held them to her chest.

Her actions were tender. She cared and understood the enormity of his vulnerability in handing over his work for her critical inspection.

"Will you have another interview with Hank? Now that you've met with Lana?" she asked.

"That's a good thought. I have follow-up questions about his high school days." Joe stroked his chin. "If I do speak with him, will you come?"

"Depends when it is. I'll do my best. I'm meeting with Harrison Wolff and an architecture firm this week. At least, Harrison is supposed to be there. I rather think he might have changed his plans."

"How do you like working with him? Has he been treating you well?"

She lifted a shoulder in a shrug. "I know you don't like him."

Joe scrubbed a hand over his face. He wouldn't pretend he hadn't publicly railed against the aggressive lawyer. But that didn't mean he wasn't concerned that she get the full benefit out of the association since she'd already pursued it. "Don't put any stock in my opinion. I don't matter."

"Well, the price for working with Harrison is right."

"It is?" Joe had been turned off by the lawyer's website stating his fee as *market price*.

She shrugged. "Hard to beat free. That's why I think I won't see much more of him. I can't afford his time."

Harrison waved his fee? Joe had misjudged the lawyer. Not that she gave a glowing review. But perhaps the disgruntled Kincaid rival had another, better side. "I'm wondering if I should get a legal opinion about my project before going too much further."

"Like to determine if you can be sued? What are you writing?"

He chuckled. "I like to be prepared for the worst-case scenario. I appreciate advice."

"Oh, then he's definitely got that." She smiled. "He's good at what he does, but he can be determined. Clients and other parties don't know what's best. As far as he's concerned, his opinion is the only one that matters." Abby rolled her eyes. "Are you sure you need him?"

No, Joe wasn't. The problem was his need for validation outweighed every other consideration. He wanted someone—anyone—to approve of what he was doing and encourage him to keep going. "I don't know what I need."

"You're a smart guy. Can't you do it on your own?"

"Self-publish?"

She nodded. "That's one path, sure. Or reach out to publishers on your own."

"Maybe." Perfectionism held him in its sharp talons. If he made the wrong move, would he doom his career and his future? He had spent a lot of time imagining worst-case scenarios. "I want to be sure I'm not putting myself in a bad spot. Legally speaking." Libel was a handy excuse for the real source of his professional procrastination.

"Don't you need to build a presence in your field? Get a reputation as an expert? Or do you publish first?" she asked.

"Again, a good question."

"I believe in you. Whatever you choose."

He held her gaze and for a second, something changed. The air electrified, full of a charge that might zap them at any moment. It was a heavy moment like the lead-up to the final seconds of a game. He almost had the urge to kiss her. He stared at her lips, berry pink and full, slightly parted. He might have leaned forward.

A low moan, deep and rumbling, carried in the air.

"What is that?" he asked, turning toward the windshield.

"Oh, it's just Lover Boy. He likes to hang out by the truck. You're right he loves people."

Joe frowned. He wasn't sure the pairing was for the best. What if the huge beast decided to knock against the food truck? What if the creature ran at her vehicle when she left?

The door opened and shut.

He turned toward the sound and frowned. She'd hopped out of the car?

He rolled down the passenger window. "Hey, are you okay?"

"I'll be fine. Good night and thanks for this." She held up the pages. With a wave, she unlocked her food truck and strode inside.

Lover Boy stood near the picnic tables, keeping watch.

Was Abby running away from one or the both of the men outside? He wasn't sure. But it wouldn't last. If something was going to happen between him and Abby, it would have a long time ago. Before Hank's meddling and during, they had never rubbed well together. Her needing a supporter changed the tenor of the relationship but that wasn't sustainable. She was a confident, capable woman. And if she'd been interested, she would have kissed him moments ago.

He backed the SUV out of spot and drove home. He knew Ted's advice so he wouldn't bother with the call. Ted would tell Joe just to leave the animal, and he'd learn. Animal instinct would kick in. Lover Boy would go back where he belonged without any unnecessary human intervention. Maybe—in that respect—the bison was smarter than him.

CHAPTER 12

"Of all the wedding tasks," Joe said. "I would never have imagined Ryan delegating this one."

Abby smiled. Seated at a folding table set up to one side of the General Store, she surveyed the eight-foot surface. Slices of cake with buttercream frosting set on small plates filled the tabletop.

"Right? I would have thought tasting the cake was his top priority," she agreed.

Ryan had been an eager participant in her food tasting, firmly stating his selections. She wouldn't have thought he'd pass off the cake sampling. But she wasn't going to question her good luck.

At four o'clock in the afternoon on a Friday, the General Store drew a steady stream of traffic. When she'd received the text from Joe about meeting up, she expected to find a space carved out in the back so Will could hide her away from the public. Instead, he'd welcomed them both warmly and invited them to sit as he started to bring out the cake samples. Perhaps his grandmother convinced him. Or he decided on his own to give her another chance.

The third option, however, was Joe had a hand in this change of heart. It seemed the most likely and the one she hoped had caused the change. Joe was finally, and truly, her friend. Every meeting, she learned something new about him and enjoyed a fun, sparkling conversation.

Abby scooted forward on her chair and reached for a plate. "I'm not going to complain about being asked to do this job."

Joe chuckled and grabbed another. "But," Joe said, dragging the word. "In his defense, it isn't surprising he doesn't have time. He's too busy trying to source potted wildflowers. I don't think he took Meg's request to get married in the field of wildflowers seriously until this week. He wants to fill the barn with enough that she won't mind the locale."

It was a sweet sentiment, even if it took the groom a while to appreciate the bride's sincerity. "I'm certain Meg will love his efforts. He isn't quite the over-the-top, grand gesture guy like Ted. But it'll be perfect."

"Until last fall, I would have pegged Ryan as the public display guy. But Ted, standing in the middle of Main Street and reenacting multiple romcom cliches, proved me wrong."

"Yeah." Her single word reply was delivered more breathless than she intended. Her cheeks burned.

"Do you like public displays?" Joe asked, studying her.

She shrugged. "I've never had one. I guess I don't know." She stuck her fork into a slice and stuffed the cake bite into her mouth. Glad for an excuse to stop talking. She'd never been in a serious enough relationship to warrant such an idea. But in her gut, she knew. She'd love it.

As she chewed, a bright burst of lemon cake hit her tongue first followed by the raspberry curd that cut through the tart bite. She chewed and swallowed, setting her fork to the plate. "Well, that's the winner for me." She slid the plate to Joe.

He frowned, hovering his fork over the cake, reading the plate. "Ryan said no citrus."

Will had used paper plates and written the cake and frosting flavor on the rim in permanent marker.

She slid the plate back over. "Then I claim this whole slice."

"We don't need to act like pirates, laying siege."

"Do you want some?" she said between bites, sliding the plate between them.

"I'm just giving you a hard time." He shook his head. "I'll give the chocolate cake with chocolate fudge filling a taste." He slipped his plastic fork into the cake and it stuck. "Well, maybe not. This is thick. The fork isn't budging."

"Are you sure you don't want a bite of mine? Lemon cake is my absolute favorite. I can attest to the superiority of both the crumb structure and smooth filling." She forked another bite and stuffed it in her mouth.

"I'll trust you since you sound like an expert. Good to know your favorite."

She smiled as she finished chewing. His sincerity warmed her. "What's your favorite?"

"Pie."

She giggled, but the laugh turned into a snort. She covered her mouth and nose with both hands, her cheeks burning.

He grinned broadly.

"Did someone say pie?" Will asked, wiping his hands on his apron.

Joe turned away.

She felt sort of sad to lose his attention. She liked being under his focus. He had a depth of caring she hadn't even guessed at. For two years, she thought she knew him, and she'd been flat wrong. The only saving grace was that she could say the exact thing about him regarding herself. At least they got a second chance.

"Ryan wants cake for the wedding," Joe said.

Will pulled a chair over and sat down opposite. "Understood. He is very traditional."

Abby snorted again. "Sorry, allergies."

A cheeky grin tugged at the corner of Joe's mouth again. "Sure, of course."

"I was wondering if we could have a little more freedom for Hank's celebration?" Will asked. "I know it's the same event. But after the cake cutting, couldn't we do something different for Hank? He won't mind as long as we sing happy birthday."

It was a good idea. While she had spoken with him enough to have heard he didn't mind, she still wanted to make Hank feel special and not like an afterthought. The whole weekend had been all about him, celebrating in grand style after a health scare landed him in the hospital on his birthday last year. Ryan had slowly usurped Hank's event.

Abby cleared her throat. "Sure, what do you have in mind?"

"I wanted to have a dessert bar. I'll have a cake for Hank to blow out his candles. But I wanted to display a variety of sweets," Will said.

"Like fudge?" Joe asked. "Was that real fudge in the chocolate cake?"

Will nodded. "Yes, it was. Our signature dessert."

No wonder Joe couldn't move his fork through the slice. The fudge had the reputation as the go-to pulling solution for kids eager for a visit from the tooth fairy.

"The General Store's fudge has many fans. I love to make pies and bar desserts. If the events do take off at the ranch, I'm hoping to expand my bakery business," Will said. "I guess I figure might as well take this moment to really showcase what I can do, besides standard cakes."

"Good idea," Joe said.

Abby nodded. "I agree. Hank would love whatever you came up with and especially if it's something you're passionate about."

Hank was the town's encourager-in-chief. He hadn't always been. Stories told about him thirty plus years ago showed a man very stringent and stuck in his ways. But at some point, he'd become flexible and open to new ideas. At the time when most people would have doubled down on their old patterns, he became someone new. Hank showed an example of how Abby hoped she'd be in the future too.

"I will." Will smiled. The bell over the front door jingled. "If you'll excuse me?" He walked away to help the customer.

Abby turned to Joe. "Okay, which flavor is next?"

"Right... here's the thing. I know which cake Ryan wants."

"You do?" She gazed at the table full of sweets, darting her tongue over her bottom lip. Will had baked twenty cakes and whipped up different flavor frostings and curds for a full sampling. Had his work been in vain? Could she eat a few more slices before fessing up?

"I do," Joe said. "Ryan wants chocolate cake with white frosting. Meg agreed to it."

"Well... Now I feel bad. Are we wasting Will's time?" She drummed her fingers against the table.

Joe reached for her hand and squeezed. "I couldn't think of another legitimate reason to meet so I agreed to go ahead with it."

His touch sent a shiver along her arm. She licked her lips again. This time, the action had nothing to do with sweets. She stared at his mouth, his full lips curving into a mischievous expression. She'd thought he might kiss her the other day and felt the same charge between them again. "Do you need an excuse to see me?"

"No. But I worried you'd be too busy otherwise."

Good answer. She should hide her smirk. He knew her, and she was glad. "I had a chance to read your manuscript."

He drew back his hand and scrubbed his face. His actions were slow and deliberate. "Oh? What did you think?"

"It's good. Really good. I think you should talk to someone. If Harrison Wolff can help, let him." She managed to keep her voice even.

With time to think, she had accepted the lawyer's curt behavior in the immediate aftermath of her exposure was to be expected. He had been right. She couldn't afford his fee. She would have appreciated his help, but he had never pretended to be her friend. "He has all sorts of contacts in a variety of industries. Or you could strike out on your own. I'd help if I can."

"I don't know that Harrison would want to work with me. I'm close with Ryan."

She wanted to assure him she'd put in a good word with Harrison. But she wasn't sure he'd be at the meeting in an hour. Instead, she reached a hand into Joe's and squeezed. "I know he would. People can change, right?"

He squeezed her hand in return and then lifted her fingers and kissed her knuckles. "You are too kind."

The light touch sizzled her skin, like he'd branded her. A strange and searing feel but not unwelcome. She grinned. She hadn't imagined anything good coming out of her public outing as the big bad Whittier. But then everything worked out better than she could have imagined. "We better get to work eating all these cake slices, so Will won't feel put out."

He winked. "Your wish is my command."

A little thrill zipped along her. Reluctantly, she dropped his hand and reached for another plate.

She hadn't given him any notes.

Joe sat behind his keyboard and stared at the blinking cursor on the computer screen.

The wall clock flashed seven pm, but it might as well have been midnight. The hours had dragged as he mentally berated himself.

Without anything to change or delete, he had no other reason to stall in his writing. He still had to finish adding in Lana Buck's stories as well as figuring out how to restructure the early chapters to include the history of the Whittiers that Abby had shared.

But she hadn't told him the manuscript was garbage, and he should throw it all away. She hadn't offered any critique whatsoever. He'd prepared himself that she might hate his words. Instead, she had praised him. And now he found himself almost immobilized.

Because if it wasn't awful, if the work might be okay, then he should finish and present his study to the world. Maybe that was the whole point she'd tried to get him to. He needed to take a chance with no guarantee of success or the greater reception.

He smiled. She was a leap *whether or not she looked* sort of person. He wanted to be that brave. He hadn't realized how he envied that quality until the past few weeks. She wasn't sure her best was good enough, but she still tried.

While he found the thought terrifying, he witnessed her give each day her all despite the unknown. How much of his perfectionism was imposter syndrome? And how much born of cowardice?

He reached for his water and took a long sip. After cake tasting, he'd grabbed dinner at her food truck, pleased to join the line. The town had again embraced her.

She had rushed to unlock the truck and start cooking.

He had waited patiently at the back of the queue. He bounced on the balls of his feet. The plates of cake provided an overwhelming rush of sugar to his bloodstream. He'd crash hard soon. But he wouldn't regret it. He could have called in the order but then he wouldn't have had the chance to learn her favorite flavor or hold her hand in public.

When his turn had finally arrived, he stepped up to the window and heard the now familiar low moan of the town's lonely bison.

A breeze swept through.

Joe bundled deeper into his jacket and placed his order.

"Would you look at that?" she had asked in wonder.

He turned and spotted the bison.

The wind had blown a hat onto Lover Boy's head. Now a permanent fixture at the food truck, he had looked almost jaunty with the accessory covering one horn.

"You said he was a pet. But I wonder if he wasn't in the circus or in the movies," She had asked with a tone full of such wonder as she.

"I don't know of any celebrity bison."

"He has presence. If any animal deserved their turn in the spotlight, it's Lover Boy."

The statement encapsulated her sweetness. He envied and longed to share her optimistic view of the world. "You're really something special. Did you know that?"

She blushed and handed Joe his order.

He almost kissed her then. Their location, however, had kept him in check. He wouldn't have the whole town as an audience for their firsts, so he held himself back. He had walked around to a picnic table and eaten his dinner, pleased to see a wide variety of faces both familiar and foreign.

School only had a few more weeks until summer break. While she'd told him of counting on tourists to keep her business running, she must be at least a little relieved the town wouldn't abandon her totally, despite their initial reception. When her restaurant opened, she'd have year-round business.

He set the glass to one side and scanned the document again. He still needed to make changes. He hadn't formally interviewed Abby yet and hadn't added her story into the manuscript. The history he presented on the page remained the one-sided version everyone had grown up with. It was time for the town to get comfortable with being uncomfortable.

He grabbed a pen and a legal pad. Writing longhand wasn't the most efficient choice. Often, he had trouble reading his penmanship when he typed his work into his saved document. But he liked the freedom of expression, the connection between his brain and his heart that only the pen conveyed.

What if the ending we've accepted didn't capture the entire picture? What if Hoss's exile ultimately started the man on a path to redemption? Would this explain why his father remained in town for several years following the departure, hoping for a day he could welcome his son back into the fold?

Hoss Whittier left Herd and took a surprising path, finding faith alongside his sobriety. He raised a family. But he never felt a connection to another place, relocating often. His legacy lingered through his own family until one brave descendant returned to challenge the town's myth-making of the early days.

He wasn't sure he quite captured the spirit and gravity of what had occurred in the past and the impact being felt in the present. Would he ever? If he didn't establish some sort of external deadline, he'd never finish the work.

His cell phone rang.

Frowning, he grabbed the device off his desk and swiped his thumb to accept the call from the unknown number. "Hello?"

"Joe? It's Harrison Wolff, calling."

Joe's mouth dropped.

"Listen, I heard you might have a book, and I might have a contact."

In his icy grip, Joe lost his hold on the phone. The device slipped and clattered to the floor. He dropped to his knees and reached for the device. "Sorry. Can you back up?"

"I had a call from Abby this evening, and she shared that you might be in touch. We've never worked together, but as you can imagine I don't like to beat around the bush. If you're serious about your work, you should send me what you have, and I'll put you in touch with my contacts."

For a fee? Joe didn't know much about the publishing industry but Harrison's proposal sounded all sorts of backwards and out of order. Was he going to act as an agent? Approaching Joe felt sort of aggressive? Was this his first moment to test his new found resolve to try?

He'd want a lawyer to review any contracts on his behalf but hadn't anticipated the attorney would seek the sale. What percentage would Harrison expect as both legal counsel and pseudo manager? Fifty percent? An even more outrageous rate?

Trusting someone else for guidance was meant to ease the pressure. But Joe had leaned on someone he expected to stab him in the back. He had set himself up for this moment. A self-fulfilling prophecy. He dragged in a shaky breath.

"Listen, I know this is unexpected. Both that I would call you and that I would want to work with you," Harrison said.

Joe was glad the lawyer couldn't see his smirking face.

"But," Harrison continued. "I'm expanding my practice and looking into pursuing IP in any capacity."

"IP?"

"Intellectual Property."

"Isn't that more like patents? I'm writing a book."

"You need to think broader. Your writing could launch into a variety of media."

Joe doubted the commercial appeal of his work. Harrison wasn't known for his flattery, and he didn't waste his time on any venture without some personal or professional gain. If anything, Harrison surprised Joe by meeting with Abby. Joe had the impression the lawyer had washed his hands of her association since she hadn't managed any vengeance against the Kincaids.

"And I wouldn't mind seeing the Kincaids taken down a few pegs." Harrison chuckled. The lawyer had read his mind.

"I'm kidding," Harrison said. "It's a joke."

In Joe's experience, the people who had to point out their mean comments were meant to be funny had very little sense of humor.

"I grew up in Herd, too. I mean no offense to the Kincaid family, but I am glad your work will highlight the entire community's history and not focus solely on the last legacy ranchers. People like you and me count, too."

"You're absolutely right about the scope of my project," Joe said, calming down. While he didn't entirely trust the lawyer's motives, he vowed to keep his wits through the process. "If we move forward, what's the next step?"

"You send me a copy, and I reach out to my contacts. A few editors and a couple agents. We get a feel for the interest."

Literary agents? Or film industry professionals? Would that be realistic? A big screen adaptation hadn't been part of his plan. That didn't mean the path was meritless. Joe was getting ahead of himself. He swallowed. "I'm not finished."

"You don't need to be. This is more of a proposal than anything else. Let me see if it's even worth your time to complete the work."

Joe furrowed his brow. If his life's work wasn't deemed valuable, he walked away. From a logical standpoint, he understood. But the black and white nature of the prospect skewered him through the heart.

Was Joe really going to consider involving himself with someone who'd make that sort of comment? Harrison never understood Joe and that hadn't changed. Joe pinched the bridge of his nose. What would the Kincaids think about this?

Hank would encourage him to do what he needed. Ryan wouldn't like it but he'd never begrudge anyone a career opportunity. "Okay, what exactly do you need from me?" Joe asked.

"Write up a couple paragraphs, like the back of the book. Then I need two to three pages of synopsis. Send me those along with the manuscript you have so far. By Monday."

Joe almost chortled. Oh sure, no problem. The number of pages was overwhelming. How to sum up all of his interviews and research into an enticing couple of paragraphs and a synopsis? He'd devote his weekend to the work. At least he had a deadline now. On his own, the project would never be completed. "Okay. Fine. By Monday."

"Great."

Are you sure you want to work with me? Joe held back the insecure question. He knew the lawyer never did anything he didn't want to do. Joe's lack of confidence wouldn't endear him to the person he turned to for help. But his imposter syndrome lurked just behind his smile. "I'd better get to work."

"Please do. We'll be in touch," Harrison said and ended the call.

For a few seconds, Joe sat in silence. He'd probably been oversold. Abby's enthusiasm for his work had been relentless. He wanted to trust her opinion about the value of his project.

He pushed off the floor and strode the length of the room. Harrison made the entire process seem simple. Joe wanted to trust the path wasn't as complicated as he'd been making it in his head. Regardless, he had his work cut out for him if he was going to update the manuscript with what he'd learned from her and Lana. And only so many hours in the weekend.

CHAPTER 13

Abby opened the front door of the Hawke house, bracing for impact.

Colby loved to greet everyone at the threshold. The mutt didn't particularly care if a person had only stepped outside for a moment to check the mail. If a human walked inside, the human must submit to a thorough sniffing as Colby happily wagged her tail.

But today, Abby walked in without an elaborate welcome.

She frowned and peered over her shoulder through the still open doorway. She'd driven herself home, not wanting to hold up Meg. Since everyone knew where Abby now lived, she saw no purpose to the subterfuge besides reinforcing the town's opinion of her behavior as sneaky.

Meg's car was in the driveway.

Where was Colby? The pair were always together. Or almost always.

A lump caught in Abby's throat and her limbs were heavy. She hadn't grown up with dogs. In the short time since moving in to the pretty white ranch house, however, she'd become accustomed to the pup and glad for the freely given kisses.

"Meg?" Abby called, shutting the door, and slipping off her shoes. She padded through the empty first floor, from the front door through the living room to the dining room.

"Colby? Are you here?" The dog loved to sleep. Perhaps she'd curled up on her dog bed in the kitchen.

The kitchen was empty too.

She returned to the front hall. "Meg? Are you home?" Abby tried again and climbed the steps.

On the second floor, she heard movement. Tiptoeing down the hall, she kept her back against the wall. Her pulse pounded. She wasn't going to walk into a crime scene. She attempted to reason but couldn't fight the bile rising in her throat.

At the front bedroom, she eased the not quite shut door open with her fingertips, holding her breath.

Inside, Meg danced around her bedroom.

Abby entered and sighed.

Meg shrieked.

Abby jumped.

"Abby?" Meg removed a tiny earpiece. "Gosh, you startled me."

"You startled me," Abby said, bracing her waist with both her hands and dragging in deep breaths. "Where is Colby? What are you doing?"

"I'm packing." Meg held out her hands.

Abby assessed the stacks of fresh, never folded cardboard boxes near the window. Several large wardrobe style boxes sat open near the closet. "Packing? Already?"

Meg patted her bed. "Colby is spending the evening with Hank. She gets worked up whenever I pack, even for a weekend. She'll be happy once we are there. But the process overwhelms her."

Abby crossed the room to sit on the soft mattress, her hands gliding over the worn quilt. She knew Meg planned on moving into the Kincaid ranch house. During the summer, the ranch house operated as the lobby for guests, not offering privacy for newlyweds. But moving one person versus two was preferred.

In the past few weeks of cohabitating, however, Abby had blocked the knowledge from her mind. She liked living in the gracious, warm, welcoming home. More than that, she enjoyed Meg's company. She hadn't started to look for another place yet. She wasn't sure anyone in town would rent to her again. Moving to the apartment complex outside town would give her more of a social life. Stephanie and many of the other young, single people lived in the modern building stocked with amenities. But the drive would be burdensome. Abby wasn't sure any complex would have the parking necessary for her vehicle.

Meg grabbed a flat box and began to assemble. "Are you okay? Everything go alright today?"

"Yes, it did. Sorry." Abby shook her head. "Didn't mean to give you the wrong impression. I just...forgot about the move. I really shouldn't. I was cake tasting for you today. I know you're getting married."

Meg chuckled. "Were you pleased with the options? Were the cakes good?"

"Will had a lot of choices. I wouldn't have been able to narrow it down." Abby could still taste a hint of lemon. She licked her lips. "I'm surprised you didn't want to join us at least to enjoy free dessert."

"I agreed to whatever Ryan wanted so I didn't want to change my mind with options. Ryan is the picky one in the relationship," Meg said, her right eye twitching. "I can't believe he didn't join you. I'm slammed setting up the framework for future weddings. I want to use our big day as a test run for clients so I spend my time looking at the big picture, getting samples, reviewing contracts. I can't get lost in the details. I'm glad you and Joe are taking care of the minutiae." Meg finished taping the bottom of the box and crossed to her dresser, grabbing sweaters by the armful. She dropped her pile into the box and repeated the motion. "I'm glad we are starting our events business with our own. I'd rather not use a paying customer as a test run."

"How do you think it is going?" Abby shifted on the bed. She hadn't had a chance to pick Meg's brain about the new business. The success of the ranch impacted Abby for better or worse. While they might not be true partners, they each felt the consequences of the others' choices.

"Slow but steady. I'll know a lot more after the event. Thank goodness we won't have another wedding until next year." Meg sealed the full box and set it on the ground, pushing it to the wall. She assembled another box.

"I can help you build some boxes." Abby held out her hand.

"Thanks." Meg carried a stack to her along with the tape.

Abby began to fold the first box and secure it with the clear tape. She slid the completed box onto the ground and started on the next.

"I can't believe I'm leaving," Meg said, sighing.

Abby glanced up.

Meg didn't stop moving.

Abby reasoned she couldn't. The countdown calendar in the kitchen now flashed with a warning. "What will you do with this house?"

"In the long term? I'm not sure. My mom owns the house. I don't think she has any intention of selling. But houses need to be lived in. They need care and maintenance. I don't want this place sitting empty."

Abby nodded and moved on to the next box in the stack. After growing up in Chicago, Meg had relocated to Herd. The house was her mother's childhood home. Meg craved the small town her mother had escaped. Would her children do the same? Or would they love the land like her husband-to-be's family?

"Would you want to stay?" Meg asked.

Abby met her gaze. "Does that mean you'll let me pay you rent?"

Meg bristled.

"I can't keep squatting on your property." Abby hated being treated like a victim.

Meg scrunched her nose. "I hate that word."

Abby shrugged. She didn't have a better word choice to define what she was doing.

"Until your restaurant opens, you'll need a place. Construction might last a year. I'd be happy for you to stay here. I hate to think about it empty."

"I won't stay unless I pay you something."

"Fine."

"To be honest, I wonder if it's too much for me." Abby shivered remembering the chill that snaked up her spine when she thought an intruder was in the house. Without the dog to greet her, she hadn't entered with the same sense of homecoming she had begun to take for granted.

"Why not ask Stephanie? Her lease is up soon."

"That's a great idea. She's swamped with studying. I bet she hasn't even looked into what she'll do next. I'm sure Ted would like having her close."

Abby agreed. Stephanie's long-time crush turned boyfriend was the lead cowboy on the Kincaid ranch next-door. "I'll give her a call."

Meg stuffed another box to bursting and taped it shut. "What about you? Any changes to report?"

Abby's cheeks burned. Hank Kincaid, Meg's soon to be grandfather in law, had made no secret about his matchmaking. He'd had Abby and Joe in his sights for over a year. But it was moot. No matter that Abby liked Joe. Until recently kept himself slightly removed. He was a historian and, by default, an observer. He wasn't the type to get in and live. He'd study and analyze.

Sure, over the past six weeks or so, he'd changed and become a friend. But he'd always have a separation, like he looked at her through a pane of glass. She didn't always mind his gaze. What would it feel like to be in his arms?

A low, deep moan sounded from outside.

Abby hopped off the bed and joined Meg at the window.

Outside, Lover Boy nudged the side of her truck and grunted. The bison must have traveled at top speed to follow her. They were a surprisingly fast animal. Abby hadn't noticed a lumbering animal running behind her. But she was more than a little distracted lately.

Abby chuckled. "That's all the romance in my life I can handle."

"Is that okay?"

"Ted thinks so. But I better start leaving the truck on the ranch to keep him safe," Abby replied.

Lover Boy didn't quite fit. Despite his best efforts, he remained misguided. She was exactly the same. What a pair they made.

At the kitchen table in the snug cabin, Joe stared at the cards in his hands. Unseeing. He blamed his location for his lack of focus.

Ted lived across the lake from the spa barn, guest cabins, and the bunk house for employees on the Kincaid ranch. With the arrival of the seasonal employees, the ranch was coming alive once again. In a few more weeks, the summer would kick off with the resort's Memorial Day weekend opening. And then the big celebration.

Final details for the celebration as well as his summer tour guide job demanded much of his time. Coming to the ranch was no longer the peaceful break in an out of the way location. The ranch was—once again—the center of the local universe.

And Abby's.

She could distract herself with her restaurant all she wanted, but she couldn't hide what was so clear. She didn't have enough customers to keep going in the off-season. She'd need the support of everyone in town, and she wasn't quite there yet.

It hadn't occurred to him before how much the Rabbitts had kept her afloat at the saloon in the colder months. Should he intervene on her behalf with the couple? Would the return of the summer guests be enough to sustain her? She planned to build on her lot but how feasible was the endeavor. He didn't know her financials and worried about how quickly expenses could add up. Because he didn't want her to leave.

"Well?" Ryan asked, arching a brow.

Poker night wasn't the time for his mind to wander. He knew better.

Or at least he used to.

He used to be sure of so many things. The longer his project continued, and the more twists and turns he uncovered along his path to prove himself, however, the more doubt crept in. He should welcome the emotion like an old friend and pull out a chair at the table. They were already a man down. They could use another player. "I fold."

"Call," Ted said.

Ryan laid out his cards and crossed his arms over his chest, leaning back and raising his chin.

Joe examined the hand. A royal flush. At least the other man earned his smugness.

Ted tossed his cards to the table.

Ryan collected his winnings, neatly stacking the chips into a tidy pile. "I feel as lucky as Hank. Not sure if either of you has noticed his chipper moods lately. He practically started singing today."

"What's he up to tonight? Why isn't he joining us?" Joe asked. Hank loved to challenge the younger men to any sort of competition. With each passing year, however, he preferred sitting down events to level the playing field. He rarely missed a card game.

"Trying to get Colby comfortable in the house," Ryan said.

"She isn't?" Ted asked, gathering the cards, and shuffling the deck.

"Not according to Hank. He made her a steak dinner and bought her several dog beds. I think he's concerned she'll sleep in my room after the wedding," Ryan answered.

Joe wasn't sure what to say in response. Before Colby came into Hank's life, the older man treated animals like animals. Colby softened him. Now he bribed a dog for affection. Love was remarkably powerful at changing hearts and minds.

I should know. Mentally, he kicked himself. The tenderness he felt was the appropriate amount for friends to share for one another. He wasn't a lovesick fool. "Is Meg officially moving in?"

"She is." Ryan grinned. "I wouldn't mind a little separation from work and home over at her place. But I know better than to ever suggest Hank move."

Will Abby be back on the streets? Joe hadn't known about her momentary homelessness until long after the fact when Meg let it slip. She'd stepped up. Thank goodness for her kindness. But learning about Abby's plight—no matter how short—filled him with a despair and hopelessness he could never have guessed. She mattered to him, and he hated that he hadn't realized her precarious situation. He should have been the one to help.

"Stephanie and Abby are going to rent the house together," Ted said. "Steph called with the news a little while ago, all excited. She's stressed about continuing her education and keeping up with all her other tasks. I'm glad she won't be on her own anymore."

"Oh, that's nice," Joe said. "A good solution for everyone."

"To get back to Hank," Ryan added, clearing his throat. "He's acting strange. I'm telling you. Do either of you know why? Does he have a new scheme afoot? Are you two taking his advice about something?"

Could the secret source of Hank's happiness be Lana? Had the older woman kept her word and called him? Joe kept his mouth shut. He wouldn't seek to poke the bear and Ryan was no less wild and grizzly than the massive beasts.

Ted stroked his chin. "Maybe he's happy because Joe is finally being nice to Abby."

"That's the extent of it. No romance. I don't have time." Joe sighed. "I can barely sleep. I'm focused on the wedding slash birthday and school and my tours and the book. That's it. That's more than enough."

"What about your amateur detective agency?" Ted asked. "No more cases to solve?"

Joe shook his head and reached for his cola. Investigations were his forte. But he also came to appreciate that he'd let bias and prejudice keep him from the truth. Or had that been his heart?

"Ted, you ever notice how someone swears off love and then falls head over heels?" Ryan asked.

"No, not me," Joe's refusal was adamant and immediate. "I don't hate her, and that is enough." His mouth filled with an awful sour taste and his stomach churned. He hated denying his feelings to his friends. But he couldn't have more focus on what was happening. Or he worried nothing would change. Pressure made diamonds, but it also cracked glass. Could what he shared with Abby become more than friendship if given space and time?

"If you say so..." Ryan said from the corner of his mouth.

"Are we going to play?" Joe asked.

Ted dealt and the sounds of cards sliding against the wooden table and ice cubes clinking in glasses restored the balance to the room. Joe couldn't find his equilibrium so easily. He hadn't been helpful when she'd needed him. Could he step up in another way?

He grabbed his cards and studied them, shielding the view of his hand from the others. A queen and a king weren't any guarantees of success. In this as in all things, he must make his own way. "I did want to ask about the bison that keeps wandering into town."

"Have we had complaints?" Ryan frowned.

"Not that I'm aware. Why won't he fit in with the herd? Is there a reason?" Joe asked.

Ted shrugged. "Some animals are loners. Can't force everyone into a mold. No matter how it might make your life easier."

The words reverberated within Joe's soul like the clanging of a bell. Joe wanted to make sense of his world by framing it within the larger scope of his moment in history. He wanted to know what would happen next so he could take away the uncertainty of having to make his own choices. He grappled for anything to hold onto.

"I could call the conservation group. Let them know we're having trouble," Ted continued. "But he isn't a nuisance. I worry that the solution suggested will be final."

Ryan dragged a finger across his throat.

"No, don't do that," Joe said quickly. "The town hasn't really opened for the season yet. Maybe we can find a solution."

"Is he attracted to Abby or the truck?"

"I'm...not sure."

Ted stroked his chin. "Huh. Maybe it doesn't matter. As soon as she moves the truck out here, the herd will take him in. Problem solved," Ted said.

If only Joe's issues could be so easily resolved. He'd have to give himself the permission to succeed and finish first. "She's moving here?"

Ted nodded. "Yep. Figured we'd give her some space away from the construction on her lot. Once the crew begins, she'll have a tough time keeping dust and dirt out of her truck. Her customers won't appreciate the noise, either." He stroked his chin. "Actually, she could settle here now."

No. The word was an immediate, knee-jerk response.

Ryan nodded. "Makes more sense than what she's doing at the moment. She lives at Meg's. Would be easier on everyone if she didn't have to run back and forth all day. Might give the bison a chance to get used to the ranch and move on."

I'd miss her. How would Joe stop by and see her without notice? The plan was sensible. But not for him. "Don't you think you should let her make her own decisions?" Joe asked.

Ryan leveled a steady stare. "Of course. I'm not a dictator. Why are you so bothered?"

"Hey, cool down both of you," Ted said. "Abby can make up her own mind. She's an adult and a business person. Ryan will give her a choice."

Joe stroked his chin. "Under pressure, she won't have a choice. To keep everyone happy, she'll agree."

"Fair enough. You ask and give her the option," Ryan said. "She has no problem saying no to you." He chuckled.

"Great," Ted added. "Now pick up your cards and let's play."

Within a few seconds, the tension evaporated in the room as bets were made and laughter shared. Joe wasn't sure if he'd defended Abby or passed some sort of fidelity test with Ryan. Or both. But at least he had another reason to seek her out. That was a good win from a tense round.

CHAPTER 14

Abby frowned at the spray-painted lines on the ground and slowly meandered around the outline. Somehow, ten thousand square feet better resembled the chalk shapes on police dramas. She shuddered. She sure hoped not. What was the crime? The murder of her dreams?

At least the weather was mild for mid-May. She turned her face up to the sun and let the warmth sink into her for a moment. The land near the cemetery was peaceful and quiet.

The air was sweetly scented by lilacs planted near the entrance. Typically, her food truck's cooking overpowered the location. Taking a break from her smoker and ovens, the natural aroma of her plot sank into her, reminding her of the first day she'd come here. When she'd felt like she'd known the landscape by heart because she'd found home.

By the end of the month, she'd witness the ground breaking as long as she approved the architectural plans. After a few changes to allow more privacy in her proposed two-bedroom apartment upstairs, she couldn't think she'd change a thing. Of course, she'd been surprised a lot lately.

She turned toward the picnic tables and approached the builder.

Corey came highly recommended from the over-booked architecture firm. She liked his no-nonsense demeanor. Maybe she should have gotten a second recommendation, but she trusted him. Besides, she wasn't sure who she could have asked for their opinion. Harrison stopped returning her calls. At the ranch, the Kincaids trusted Ted and a work crew of tradesmen to help patch up and fix things. What she wanted was a little more specialized than a barn raising.

Corey spread out the blueprints across the top of one of the picnic tables, weighing down the sheets with rocks and condiment jars.

"Thanks for mapping it out. I still can't exactly visualize it. But that's on me, not you," she said with an apologetic smile. While she'd hired the man, she couldn't shake the trained good girl instincts to make amends for any hint of a slight.

417

He chuckled. "I should thank you for feeding me first. You've definitely given me the encouragement to get your kitchen up and running."

Making a wrap from leftovers taking up her limited fridge space helped her more than him, but she'd accept his thanks for her hospitality.

She crossed her arms and studied the plans spread on the table. The proposed build lurked at the top end of her budget. She was paying a premium for speed as much as anything else. The sooner she was officially up and running, the better. Business was slow and the only major events slated for the summer were the opening week birthday celebration and wedding double act.

She hoped she wouldn't have to content herself with utilizing the food truck and the limited kitchen space in the rebuilt barn. She needed to make time to meet with the Rabbitts and discuss their collaboration. Would the meeting be civil? Had enough time passed to move beyond hurt feelings and deal with each other in a strictly professional capacity? At least, after her building was complete, she wouldn't need their help so desperately.

"If I want to expand?" She tapped her finger on the blueprint.

The proposed two-story building would be in the Western style with a high-false front stretching a half level above. The curve to the roofline would differentiate it enough from the appearance of the rest of Main Street to be unique without off-putting. Her goal was to compliment the town and not stand out.

But she didn't want any comments about *if you can't beat them—or burn them—join them*. She wanted tourists to view her business as a natural extension of the rest of the town. Without the raised sidewalk, she'd already be separated. She didn't want any more distance.

"You'll have plenty of space." He pointed to the back of the building. "You could always add a patio. The kitchen is set to the eastern wall. If you wanted to expand the building, you could add another wing and create an L-shaped footprint with a semi-courtyard in the back."

She liked the idea. She could string lights between the two halves outside. It would be like magic during the summer. She could almost feel the warm breeze and smell the sweet grass. Anything was possible with enough cash.

A low groan shook the ground.

She smiled at Lover Boy, standing a few yards away. Of course, she'd need to establish some sort of bison defense system. She wasn't concerned about the tourists' safety. Lover Boy needed protection.

"Whoa, stay back." Corey grabbed a rock and shook his arm.

"Stop, no." She jumped in between the builder and the bison. If she didn't physically block the animal from the man, she worried what either's next move would be. "He's a sweet animal. He's harmless."

"He's a bison. No such thing as harmless."

"I know and don't approach him. But he'll wander away. He doesn't get close," she said.

"If you say so..." Corey eyed the bison and—without looking away from the animal—pulled the blueprints off the table and rolled them up.

The tension dissipated. Her breathing slowed to normal. She really did need to take precautions.

Corey stuffed the blueprints into a cardboard cylinder. "I will get these submitted. I don't anticipate any issues."

"Neither do I." She smiled at the sincerity in the statement. The restaurant would succeed. She'd prove her sincerity in putting down roots.

"If the Kincaids can keep their wildlife under control, then we won't have any problems."

She frowned. "I'll speak with their lead ranch hand about Lover Boy. Let me assure you, the animal is fine. He is passive."

"He is, until he isn't. You don't want to use up your liability insurance before you've even opened your doors." Corey capped the cylinder and extended a hand. "Have a good day, Miss Whittier. I'll be in touch."

She accepted the brief hand shake and dropped her arm to the side.

He strode away toward his car in the parking lot.

She gazed at the horizon, studying Lover Boy. Why did everyone want to see him as the villain? He was a misguided animal struggling with a life many couldn't comprehend. Joe had called the animal a pet. Had he been discarded by his owner for growing to full size? Was his crime reaching his potential? She worried that was becoming her fate. Building on her ancestor's land meant establishing herself and not budging. She refused to be shoved aside, and she'd fight for Lover Boy, too.

Pulling back her shoulders, she strode toward Main Street. With her chin held high and—she hoped—a pleasant expression on her face, she walked with purpose, her steps clacking against the raised sidewalk. If anyone noticed her, they'd glimpse a woman standing tall. She wasn't shrinking anymore. She pushed into The Golden Crown, nearly deserted at ten forty-five.

"Good morning, we aren't..." Heather said behind the bar, pausing with a rag on the walnut top. "Oh, hi, Abby."

Abby wouldn't let herself be deterred by the flat delivery. She owed too much to the Kincaids to disappoint them. *Joe would approve.* The rightness of the stray thought sent a shiver down her spine as she approached the counter. "Hi, Heather. I was hoping for a minute to speak about the wedding?"

"We promised our help. We're always true to our word." Heather focused on polishing the wood.

Abby refused to flinch or otherwise react from the verbal slap. "I hope I have shown the same. I want us to move forward with mutual respect for each other."

Heather didn't reply. But she lifted her gaze and scanned Abby's face.

What did she find? Her former friend? Abby hoped so. She hadn't really apologized. Time might diminish the immediate pain of her betrayal, but she hadn't spoken honestly and from her heart. She owed the Rabbitts better.

"I am sorry. Truly," Abby said. "I lied to you and James. You have always been so good to me as a friend and occasional employee. And for all your trust I rewarded you with deception."

Heather nodded; the firm set of her mouth wobbling. "I suppose you were scared."

"I was. But I should have had faith in you and James. You both have been kind and respectful. I can't apologize enough for my behavior."

Heather picked up the rag and rubbed the bar top again.

From her winter-time stints at the restaurant, Abby knew the gesture wasn't a brush-off but a sign of consideration. Heather needed time to process. She valued giving thoughtful responses.

"If you can send me your menu, I can see what we can prep here," Heather said.

Abby released a heavy, stuttering sigh. "Thank you. I'll be running the smoker almost non-stop starting in the days leading up to the wedding. I'll be driving my truck out to the ranch to get set-up."

"Is it a buffet? Or plated?"

"Plated."

Heather whistled. "That'll take some planning and organization."

Abby chuckled, the laughter both a release and a nervous response.

"Would it make sense to use the truck's kitchen for the appetizers?" Heather asked. "We could plate dinner more efficiently in the barn's galley if so."

Abby nodded. "That's a great idea. I will send you everything I have. Thanks."

Heather extended her hand.

Abby shook and offered a shy smile. The gesture wasn't a complete thaw. But it was the start she needed.

Joe took a sip of his iced tea. Seated at the large farmhouse table in the Kincaid's kitchen, he shifted on the hard bench seat. Only one person could claim the comfortable high back and padded chair at the head of the table. And Hank Kincaid wasn't likely to stop holding court from the throne-like position.

At the moment, Hank steepled his fingers together, pressing the hands under his chin.

With sunlight streaming into the warm room, Joe was almost tempted to remove his sweater. But he didn't want to do anything to disturb the old cowboy. Instead, he sat patiently waiting for Hank to jog his memory.

Joe sent the paperwork as requested by Harrison Wolff on Sunday night and spent the rest of the week grading papers and playing catch up on the hundred other tasks he'd let slip. The end of the school year might be a slippery slide for students. But teachers had no let-up on the work.

What free time he did have, he devoted to finishing the project. If nothing else came from the outside interest, he'd at least use the push as the motivation to complete what he had by the end of June. He had plenty of things he wanted to do, changes to implement and edits to tackle. He couldn't keep letting the roadblocks he created impede his path. Done was better than perfect Or so he hoped.

"Ava Everson. Oh, she was something," Hank said, his deep voice gravelly. "She was beautiful, sure. We had a town full of pretty girls. No, Ava was almost like a cat. I always had the sense she was playing a game. Letting everyone chase her until she caught them."

Joe widened his eyes. "And you dated her before Susie?"

Hank rubbed his chin. "I did. The ratio back then was about three girls to every guy. But Ava had everyone chasing after her. As the quarterback and captain of the football team, I was her prize."

"Football? Ryan says you're against tackle sports."

"I sure am now." Hank shook his head. "We didn't know too much. I'd never risk Ryan's health. But back when I was a kid, we all played. Ava was a cheerleader." Hank's eyes sparkled.

"So…" Joe darted his gaze through the room and strained for any noise above that of the dog snoring on the bed in the patch of sun in the center of the slate tile floor. He didn't want to have the conversation around Ryan. "What happened?"

"We never had…" Hank dragged out the moment. "Zing."

"Zing?" Joe asked.

"A spark. You know? An undeniable chemistry together," Hank continued.

Joe understood. The air sizzled between him and Abby.

"Ava was bold and brash," Hank said. "She captivated me. But when we finally dated, it sort of fell flat. Maybe two big personalities are too many."

Joe nodded. Hank was more than enough to fill up a room all on his own.

"We were better friends. In fact, we were still dating each other when we met our spouses," Hank said.

"Really?" Joe asked.

"We went on a double date. I sat across from Susie and next to Ava. Wouldn't you know, I couldn't keep my eyes off Susie. She was so sweet and so different. She only said maybe two sentences. But one was the funniest thing I'd ever heard. And the other was so insightful." Hank stared past Joe, resting a hand over his heart. "She was always the smartest and most thoughtful person in any room. But never showy. She wasn't a braggart. She saw the world with clarity and joy."

Often, when speaking of the love of his life, the cowboy seemed to enter a different plane. What would it feel like to so cherish and adore another person that—long after they'd gone—a memory could still bewitch? Joe envied him.

"I did call Lana. Thank you for the number," Hank said.

"Oh, good. I'm glad," Joe said. He wasn't sure if Lana approved. She had asked for Hank's phone number. Perhaps she had wanted to take the lead in their friendship?

Footsteps echoed off the tiles.

"You're glad about what?" Ryan asked.

Joe turned and smiled at Ryan and Meg entering the kitchen. With an under the breath woof, Colby scrambled to her feet and padded over to Meg. Meg knelt on the ground, scratching the dog under the chin. Colby's tail swished like a propeller.

"Glad that I have a date to the wedding," Hank said, lifting his chin and crossing his arms over his chest.

"Excuse me?" Ryan gasped. "What did you do? What did Joe put you up to?"

"Oh, Hank, really?" Meg beamed. "How lovely!"

Ryan twisted his neck from the table to his fiancé and back again. "What? What? What?"

Hank grinned. "Thank you. I wasn't looking for anything special. But I got a phone number out of the blue and figured only a fool would miss a chance with a fine woman. Something Ted and I talked about recently really resonated."

"Ted?!" Ryan almost squeaked. "What did he say?"

"That I shouldn't give up on living," Hank said.

The group fell quiet.

After Hank's health scare and the old barn's fire, none of those present took a single day for granted. As the silence stretched, however, the lack of noise became oppressive.

"She's a real nice lady," Joe interjected. He'd witnessed enough moments where Hank pushed his grandson to exasperation to revel in this one. The wedding had Ryan truly on edge.

"What?" Ryan glared at him. "You know who he is talking about? What did you do? Give her the number?"

Joe almost turned away. How else could he hide his guilt from his friend?

Hank dropped his hands to the table. "Don't get yourself all worked up. It's Lana Buck. She'd probably be at the wedding anyways as Will's date. I'm claiming her for myself."

"And how do you know her? Since when have you been dating?" Ryan glowered.

Hank rolled his eyes. "I'm not dating. Although, maybe I will be. She's an old friend. She was the kid sister to the first girl I ever dated."

Ryan flared his nostrils.

"Long before your grandma gave me the time of day," Hank added.

"Well... well... good for her," Ryan sputtered. "Grandma had a lot of sense."

"How lovely to reconnect with someone," Meg exclaimed. "I can't wait to meet her." She pushed off the ground and approached the table. "How about you, Joe? Any date for the wedding?"

"He's working." Ryan frowned, wrinkling his brow even more.

The lines could be etched in stone. Unfortunately for Ryan, he was in a room surrounded by those who knew him too well to be fooled by one of his bad moods. "I might. I have to ask her first."

"Maybe you should," Ryan said. "I've decided on a change of plans. You and Ted are no longer groomsmen."

The back door opened and Ted strode in, his boots loud against the tiles. "Morning. What did I miss?"

Joe gritted his molars and shook his head, trying and failing to grab Ted's attention.

"I no longer require your services, or Joe's, as groomsmen at the wedding. You won't be standing up at the front with me. You'll both be sitting in the first row," Ryan bit out.

Fired? Joe wasn't sure if he should be offended or relieved. With any luck, losing his official position meant he wouldn't have to perform the dance for Meg. Neither would Ted. Joe didn't dare ask for confirmation or dart his gaze at Ted. Was he expected to sit between Hank and his date? Whatever Ryan wanted; he'd get.

Joe flashed a thumbs up.

"If you're sure, boss," Ted said.

"I am." Ryan lifted his chin. "Meg didn't have a second attendant, only her mom. I think this will line up better. I'll ask you both to please be ushers and help seat everyone. But I only want Hank standing up for me."

"Do you mean it, boy?" Hank asked, his voice thick with emotion.

"Oh, Ryan." Meg sniffed. "How sweet. My mom and your grandpa as our attendants. I love it."

Hank leaned forward and covered his grandson's hand with his big palm. "I'd be honored."

Joe watched the tableau and couldn't help but analyze the touching scene. Ryan was quick-witted and had no doubt come up with the alternative on the spot as a way to keep his grandsire away from a love interest. If Joe could be finished with the dance lessons, however, he wasn't going to be cynical about the change of plans. He could hardly wait to commiserate with Ted out of earshot.

Joe drank the rest of his iced tea and slid off the bench. "Thanks for meeting today, Hank. I think that'll be it. I'm all wrapped up on the interviews for my project."

"Congratulations," Meg said.

"Really?" Ryan asked, dropping his jaw.

Joe would feel put out by the expression if he hadn't shared the opinion that he'd never finish. "Thanks, Meg. And yes, Ryan. I wasn't sure I'd ever be done." *But then Abby stepped in.* He was glad she'd made him set a deadline. "I've already be in contact about reaching out to publishers with the help of Harrison Wolff."

"Are you sure you can trust him with your work?" Ryan asked.

"I'm keeping my options open. But I can't ignore an opportunity if he really has the network he claims," Joe said. He grabbed his messenger bag off the bench seat and slung the strap over his shoulder.

"You'll be great," Meg replied. "You're smart. You won't be a pawn. Besides, Harrison is a professional. He's done right by Abby. I guess we need to give him the chance to do right by the rest of us. He wouldn't want a whole, growing community mad at him."

Joe nodded.

Ryan dropped his shoulders. "What she said. Sorry. I'm on edge. I just want everything perfect. No mistakes."

Meg wrapped her arms around Ryan's waist and leaned her head against his back. "It's one day. Don't stress about perfection. That's boring. It'll be wonderful no matter what happens. We're starting our lives together."

As she cooed, Ryan relaxed.

Joe watched, transfixed by the transformation. Could he have a love as deep and unending as Hank's for Susie and as life-affirming as Ryan and Meg's? Joe wouldn't find out standing around the kitchen and letting life happen without him. "Good afternoon. Thanks."

The group waved.

Joe saw himself out of the kitchen via the hallway and the front door. Now he needed to push himself. He owed Abby a proper date. He didn't care who knew or what they thought. For so long, Hank pushed them together and Joe resisted. If he hadn't been determined to avoid the meddling man's snare, would he have reached the point of almost being happy earlier? He wouldn't get mad worrying about would've, could've, and should've. Instead, he'd be glad for second and third and fourth chances.

As long as he had breath in his body, he had an opportunity to go after what would make him happy. Joy was a choice. He'd been setting up so many stumbling blocks to prevent him from truly enjoying his life. He was done with nonsense.

CHAPTER 15

Abby draped the cloth napkin over her lap and crossed her ankles under the chair. She scanned the interior of the upscale restaurant again. For the past hour, she'd marveled at the building, absorbing every detail to see what she could apply to her business. Her restaurant would be far more casual, but she appreciated the high-end without feeling snobbish ambiance created through a mix of custom and box store furnishings. After she spent the rest of her week touring a tile store, picking options for flooring, backsplashes, and the bathrooms, she more easily spotted what she would have previously overlooked.

In fact, she'd perhaps spent too long detouring from the table to the washroom. She was at the bistro on a date. Or, at least she hoped it counted as a romantic dinner. From under her lashes, she glanced at her companion. "Sorry, if I was gone too long."

"Everything alright?" Joe asked.

"Yes, fine. I was being a little nosy. The kitchens are on the way, and I was curious about their set-up."

He chuckled. "I understand. Professional curiosity. I get that way at any place with even a hint of history."

"Really?" She leaned forward, closer. Despite over two years of acquaintance, she was only beginning to know him. She rather hoped he'd always be a little bit of a mystery.

"Oh, yes. Museums, homes, public buildings, heck even a field. If it has a hint of historical significance, I'm there."

Every new fact drew her in with another chance for an inside joke. They had developed a sort of easy, friendly intimacy she couldn't have imagined. While they had never been true enemies, their frenemy status had created a barrier. She was only too glad to dismantle it one conversation at a time. "Don't go to the East Coast then, or you'll never leave. George Washington has supposedly slept and stepped foot in so many locations, you'd be utterly absorbed. Even parking lots have historic markers."

"I already have a favorite, significant parking lot. Very close to home." He winked. "And plenty of reasons to stay here."

Her cheeks burned, and she reached for her water.

"I take it the construction is off to a good start?"

"It is. I was picking out floors and finishes this week. I guess I almost feel like this dinner is a celebration."

"Mission accomplished. I have so many questions about your restaurant, but I don't want to overwhelm you."

She shrugged. "I'm sure I can handle a few. But I can probably guess. Yes, we will be open for breakfast, lunch, and dinner. Yes, I will continue to serve a mix of barbecue and Tex-Mex style flavors. Other than that, I'm still figuring out details."

"Fair enough. You are so incredibly talented and creative. I admire you a lot. To be honest, I'm a little jealous of your talent."

A moment of silence fell between them. She liked the pauses in their conversations equally as much as the chatter. Time to absorb and reflect on what the other had said somehow strengthened the trust she put in him.

She darted her gaze through the bistro. Taking in the white linen topped tables and customers in dressy clothes. Her business wouldn't be nearly so upscale. But dressing up and putting in an effort about her appearance felt nice to do for a change.

She exhaled a sigh. "This is really nice. You didn't need to take me out."

"Of course, I did." He smiled and raised his wine glass. "And you deserve it."

She clinked her glass against his before sipping.

"What don't I know about you?" he asked.

She flinched, carefully setting her wine glass on the table. Had anyone ever asked a more loaded question? "I think we've covered it all."

"Sorry, that came out all wrong. I meant like...first date small talk." His cheeks turned bright red.

She liked him off-balance and unsure. It was a refreshing change from the man who always had an answer. *First date?* She liked the categorization, too. With candles on the table and chandeliers overhead, the dim lighting set a romantic mood. The occasional titter of laughter rose above the low din of private conversations lured her to lean close and speak softly.

He reached for his water and gulped.

"I supposed this could be a chance to talk about hobbies?" she asked, offering him a reprieve from the hot seat. "I don't really have any. I was knitting for a while at the saloon. I liked spending time with the group. I haven't really continued on my own. How about you?"

"Same," he agreed. "Not about the knitting. I have a poker group. We don't play for money, and I'm terrible at cards. I like the companionship, and I'm glad it doesn't revolve around sports. I am clueless about professional, collegiate, or high school teams."

She'd tried softball in third grade and only lasted half the season in outer outfield, a position created for her. "I suppose we could join forces and start a P.I. firm, now that we're aware of each other's lifelong passion for solving cases."

He chuckled, shaking his head. "I'm happy to put my sleuthing days behind me. Learning your secret was the biggest mystery I ever cracked. And that was all intuition."

She smiled but didn't feel the expression. "I guess the truth wasn't very exciting. I came here to assess the situation and the value of the land. I didn't want to put down roots when I came. Now I can't leave."

"And aren't we lucky?" He held her gaze with an intensity that sent a shiver down her spine.

She wanted to belong to Herd and maybe to him, too.

426

The server approached, topping off their glasses of wine and setting a lava cake in the center with two spoons.

Abby smiled at the man as he retreated before turning her attention back to her surprising date. Nothing about the evening had been typical. Then again, she wasn't sure she'd ever expected to join him on a date at the steakhouse midway between Miles City and Herd.

When he had called and invited her out, she'd been speechless. Sure, she hoped he'd ask her to dinner but thinking wasn't doing and it had been little more than a silent wish. She hadn't prepared for the call but stammering her way through her acceptance.

She'd managed a little better through the meal, returning to the table after she slipped the server her credit card during her washroom and kitchen detour. "How did you know I liked lava cake?"

"A good guess, and they didn't have anything lemon."

She slid the spoon through the ice cream and warm cake, scooping a little of each in equal parts. The gooey sauce poured onto the plate. "This is a promising sign. If my spoon stuck like Will's fudge cake, we'd be in trouble."

"Don't remind me."

Raising her spoon, she savored the first bite. Sweet and rich, the dark chocolate was neither too bitter nor too sugary. The dessert provided the perfect finish to the meal. She swallowed and dabbed at her mouth with her napkin. She'd have to take notes for her menu.

"Good?" he asked

She slid the plate closer to him past the imaginary dividing line. "Dangerously so. Maybe even addictive."

He scooped up an oversized bite and moaned as he chewed.

She laughed. When had she ever enjoyed a first date? She knew Joe. Their conversation had flowed so easily all night, she almost forgot this was any sort of start.

"You're right," he said, his voice muffled through the napkin covering his mouth.

"I usually am."

"You are." He nodded. "Did I tell you Hank is bringing Lana to the wedding as his date? They spoke over the phone, and he asked her out."

"Oh, that's so lovely." She was glad for Hank. If nothing else, he'd appreciate companionship with a peer. He was so spry and witty; it was easy to forget his real age. Everyone needed somebody. Maybe she had found her someone? "And fast."

"Hank doesn't waste time. Ryan was a little annoyed. But he'll come around. Speaking of Kincaid business," Joe said. "Ryan says you can move the truck to the ranch anytime."

"I hate to ask my customers to drive out of their way. But I can't operate on a construction site. The noise is impossible to escape and dust seems to slip in through every crevice. It's not very appetizing."

"It's only a temporary change. Your food is worth the road trip." He winked.

"And I'll update all of my social media feeds. Maybe I can ask Ryan to add me to the ranch's website too."

"Might help with Lover Boy, too."

"Oh, that's one of the big selling points for sure. That would be a big help." She breathed a little easier.

If the bison needed a little encouragement to explore the wide-open prairie, she'd be glad to assist. But she'd miss the chance for a run-in with Joe under the guise of needing advice. In a few weeks, he'd be at the ranch every day leading his tours. Could she go that long between their run-ins?

"Madam? Sir?" The server asked, stopping by again. He moved silently. "Can I get you anything else this evening?"

"Just the check," Joe said.

The server met her gaze and smiled. "Have a good night." He backed away from the table.

"You paid?"

"My treat." Now she had the chance to wink. "I guess you'll have to take me out again."

He reached for her hand across the table and squeezed. "I guess I will."

Inside her heels, she curled her toes. This was the start of something special. She was excited to see what happened next. "After the wedding?"

"Sure, I'll offer a raincheck."

"I can't believe how fast time is going."

"It's only another week and then we get our lives back. Won't that be nice?" he asked.

Then she wouldn't have any excuse to hold her back or any reason to hide. She wasn't quite sure what to make of that. Was she ready to fully step into the next phase of her life? If she focused on her restaurant, she was ready. With Joe, she was in no rush. She enjoyed the toe-curling excitement of every encounter.

"Abby? Joe?" A familiar voice called, booming in the space, and drawing all the attention.

She turned toward the sound and almost deflated. Such a lovely evening, full of firsts on a road to forever, should only have one possible ending. The man striding toward them promised nothing like a happy resolution.

Joe might have growled. He wasn't the sort to lean into his animalistic urges. He was enjoying his night and didn't appreciate the interruption from Harrison Wolff.

When Joe had selected the restaurant, he had accepted the possibility the flashy lawyer might be here. Arguably the nicest place for a few hundred miles, Joe wanted to pull out all the stops to show Abby what he thought about her. He'd told her plenty of times. But he wasn't sure she really heard him. Until tonight.

Their conversation had been relaxed. Despite being on a first date, he had none of the usual apprehension. It had been a long time since he'd taken a woman out to dinner. Perhaps the most surprising of all was how natural the night felt.

"Harrison, hello," Joe said, instilling the two words with polite curtness. He didn't want to engage in a conversation.

Harrison faced him, turning his back on Abby.

The move felt unnecessary and cutting. Joe frowned. What was that about? Would Harrison throw Joe away as soon as their project together was completed? Abby hadn't brought about any sort of revenge for Harrison against the Kincaids. It was an unfair assessment, but Joe couldn't shake his conviction.

"Glad I saw you. I might have a lead on your work," Harrison said.

"Wow, already?" Abby asked.

Joe heard the disbelieving upspeak in her tone. He shared the same sense of wonder and smiled across the table at her. "You move quick." He addressed Harrison but focused on his date.

She covered her mouth with a hand but couldn't hide the shake in her shoulders.

Harrison glanced down his nose. The effect was almost a sneer. Like he'd noticed a pest. Joe wanted to be wrong.

"What do you need from me? Sample chapters? Should I refine the pitch?" Joe asked.

"I'll take another look at what you sent. I might make a few notes, and I'll share those with you later in the week," Harrison said.

"How lucky you have so many connections?" Abby asked.

Harrison bristled.

Joe didn't like the man's continued snubbing of his date. Of course, after the past month, Abby must be used to being ignored. Her comment had been delivered kindly if somewhat questioning, and she deserved an acknowledgment of her presence. The other man had interrupted their date after all. "Yes, how lucky," Joe said. "Thanks to Abby for putting us together. I wouldn't have approached you without her encouragement."

She blushed slightly.

"I'll be in touch. Have a good evening." Harrison tipped his head to Joe and strode away without another glance.

Joe didn't like that the lawyer had no manners for Abby. Was she no longer of any value and thus below his notice? Maybe. That's how Ryan had always described the man. Joe wasn't sure getting into business with Harrison was a good idea. He hadn't signed anything yet. He wasn't tied into a legal tangle. He still had options. "Shall we leave?"

She nodded.

He pushed back his chair, left his napkin on the table, and quickly came around to pull out her seat.

She stood inches away. "Thanks."

The murmured word hung in the air between them. He stepped to the side.

With a soft smile, she passed, brushing his shoulder, and continuing through the restaurant to the host stand. He handed over the coat check token and a tip. The maître d bowed and made quick work of grabbing the coats. The maître d returned. Extending Joe's coat, the man retained hers, holding it out for her to slip into.

Joe didn't comment, but he was a little disappointed. He wanted to take every opportunity to be chivalrous. He pulled on his wool overcoat.

Abby thanked the maître d and buttoned up her coat.

Joe reached the door to the vestibule, holding it open for her and then quickly crossing ahead and grabbing the front door.

A chilly breeze blew in like a wave crashing against the shore. She stumbled back. He reached for her elbow, steadying her.

She chuckled. "I don't know why I'm always surprised by the cold weather."

"Because it's May, and you're longing for warmth." He tucked her arm tight against his body and steered her toward the parking lot, careful to navigate around the slushy puddles. "On the bright side, we're almost done with the current cold snap. And at least it's a clear night."

She snuggled closer to his arm. "I suppose so. I do love stargazing in Montana. No other sky comes close to matching the visibility."

Big sky country. The catchphrase was apropos. And he'd prepared for just this moment, on the off chance it came. With his free hand, he pointed overhead. "Do you see the cluster over there?"

She nodded.

"That's Andromeda, and if you follow up the chain you reach Pegasus."

"Really? Are you sure?"

"Of course. I didn't spend an hour of my day on the internet for nothing."

She laughed, her whole body shaking. "I know nothing about stargazing. I look up and see a bunch of spots. I have always wanted to see the Northern Lights."

"You should. Glacier is a good spot."

"Did I miss it this year?"

He opened her car door and held it as she hopped inside. "Not necessarily, we could go in the late fall." He shut the door hoping she'd take the hint.

He filled his lungs and slowed to his normal gait as he rounded the vehicle. He felt like he stood on the edge of something, and he'd never been much for patiently waiting. He opened his door and slid inside, turning the key into the ignition. "I think I need to let the engine warm up."

She snuggled into her jacket with a shaky thumbs up.

"Oh, I'm sorry." He hit the heated seat dial to max and turned toward her, holding out his hands.

She put her icy fingers in his warm palms.

He encased her hands, rubbing quickly to jumpstart her circulation. "Nights like tonight make me wish I had splurged for a remote start car or heated steering wheel."

"Not on my account." Her teeth chattered. "I'm always cold."

"I would like to do better for you," he said, unsure whether he should be honest about his upset at what had just happened. Keeping secrets had erected a stone wall between them at the start. He didn't want to risk what could develop with any more omissions or little white lies. Every tiny untruth was a pebble in another barrier. He had to share his feelings. "I don't like what just happened back there."

She stiffened.

"Not you. You're perf..." He cleared his throat. "I meant Harrison." Joe ran a hand through his hair, tugging the ends. "That behavior doesn't sit well with me. How he treated you was abhorrent. I should have called him out."

"For acting like himself?" She lifted the corner of her mouth in a sort of wry-sad smile. "I'd be tempted to use our newly established, fictional P.I. firm to get to the bottom of Harrison's problem. If it wasn't so lame and obvious as a high school grudge."

Four years younger than Ryan and Harrison, Joe never witnessed the rivalry first hand. "At the risk of sounding smug," Joe said. "I am always shocked some people can't stop living in the past." Because if he hadn't shaken off his misconceptions, he wouldn't be here now with her. He'd be just as bitter as the lawyer.

"Regardless, Harrison wasn't outright rude. You couldn't have called him on snubbing me without risking your project. I'm glad you're pushing yourself and seeing this through. Good things will come to you. But..."

"But what?"

She drew in a shaky breath, the inhale almost as loud as the winter wind.

He gritted his molars. He hated preparing for the worst but couldn't stop his instinct for self-preservation.

"I've done a little research on the internet."

He relaxed. "Ah, yes. Search engines tend to rule our lives, don't they?"

"I was curious about the steps to become a non-fiction author. And I really don't think you need Harrison. I'm not saying that because of what happened in the restaurant." Her words tumbled out in a rush.

"I wouldn't accuse you of that."

"Most non-fiction authors get book deals after they've established themselves as an expert in their field. You could do that. Easily. You start by building a platform. Get yourself credentials by sharing your knowledge."

He stopped rubbing her hands and held her fingers in his. "How?"

"First, you need to set up a website and social media. You could share selected excerpts of your interviews or interesting facts you've learned. For official documentation, you could link to the Kincaid Ranch's website, ask to be listed as the resident historian. Then start getting out there. Interviews, podcasts, lectures. You have what it takes to be a big success. You don't need Harrison."

"My social media feed is pretty lame. I don't think anyone wants to follow me."

"Luckily for you, you have an expert on your side." She winked. "I've learned how to utilize hashtags and posts to advertise for the food truck without a marketing budget. You've got this. Trust me. You're the real deal."

"I feel the same about you." He stopped rubbing her hands and held her fingers in his. "I'm glad you're moving forward, and that you're staying put."

She leaned forward. "I'm glad you are, too."

With only the center console between them, the setting was intimate and comfortable. The distance shortened from inches to centimeters to a breath. Her warm exhale tickled his nose. She was as near as a person could get.

But he didn't want to take any chances. Now that he found someone who really mattered, he wouldn't ever act like he knew best. He wouldn't ever do anything without her consent. "Can I ask you a question?" he murmured.

She nodded.

"Would you want me to kiss you?"

She darted her tongue along her lower lip. "Hmm. Why do I feel like I should be circling something on a note passed during class?"

He chuckled. His approach wasn't smooth at all. "I suppose I spend too much time around middle schoolers. I have no game."

"I think you're smooth enough." She squeezed his hand. "And yes. I'd like you to kiss me. I'd like that a lot."

He pressed his lips against hers, still clasping her hands in his. She sighed and deepened the kiss, opening her mouth slightly. He cheered inside. It was like coming home at last, and he couldn't understand how he'd ever been lost in the first place.

CHAPTER 16

For most of her life, Abby felt time was not on her side. In the past, she had come to ideas too soon and lacked the self-confidence to execute a plan only to learn of another's success with a similar concept later. Or, and perhaps worse, she had arrived at a conclusion too late and missed the benefits of the idea by years, months, or days.

With Joe, however, she couldn't help but smile.

She had, for once, met someone at the right moment.

Maybe two years of barely concealed animosity had—in hindsight—served a purpose. Neither of them had been ready for anything serious. She had been lost in discovering who she was, if the sum of her experiences was enough to subtract the infamy of her family's past, and so had he, in his own way.

He had been on a journey to establish himself as an authority. While she understood the thrill of power, she had lived a life almost in the shadow of such figures. She trusted he wanted to use his position for good.

Of course, the start of any relationship was easy and lovely. And she was probably jumping way ahead by even declaring an attachment after one evening and a perfectly swoon worthy kiss. Inside her newly purchased cowgirl boots, she curled her toes.

He had been so sweet and earnest. Not pushy. Not demanding. When she had pulled back, she hadn't been greeted with a frown or mark of frustration. He had kissed her hands and driven her home.

Dating him wouldn't be casual, but he had already showed he could be patient. She was glad for his calm demeanor. The timing worked in her favor because of her packed schedule.

Their date had occurred the week before Memorial Day weekend. She was simply too swamped with business and preparation to stew over their encounter. Between final tasks for the combination birthday wedding and serving the first wave of tourists at the ranch, she didn't have time to think let alone overanalyze about their shared meal. All she could do was savor the memory of his lips on hers and smile whenever she saw him. He returned the expression with a quirk of his lips that sent a tingle down to her toes.

On Wednesday, she had an especially overscheduled day. Meg's mom arrived that evening, and Abby had to make it home to help clean and prepare a welcome meal at the Hawke house. She had agreed to close her truck tomorrow to enjoy a bridal shower spa day with Meg, her mom, and Stephanie. Without any wedding attendants, Meg had avoided any sort of bachelorette shenanigans at the hands of her friends.

Stephanie had balked at Meg's insistence she didn't want to do any more celebrating besides the wedding. Abby had joined forces with Stephanie. Meg was happy to share her wedding with her grandfather-in-law's birthday. But she deserved a little spoiling. And especially with all of her kindness, Abby wanted to pamper her friend.

She rang up her last order and handed the change to the customer. She fought the urge to sigh. She was grateful for her welcome on the ranch. She hadn't had a chance to stop by the restaurant site all week but had placed a sandwich board with news about her temporary location. Hopefully very temporary.

At her station, she made quick work of frying the hushpuppies, loading the last of the pulled pork on the pretzel buns, and topping with a heaping spoonful of mustard coleslaw. "Order up," she called at the window.

The husband and wife approached, an older couple who talked Abby's ear off about returning for the wedding of the century. Or, at least the wife had. Marcia and Clayton Ford were a pair who swore they couldn't miss the wedding when they were the first to see the spark between the pair. Abby rather doubted the truth but wouldn't argue with a customer.

Marcia and Clayton accepted the baskets with thanks and retreated to the picnic tables.

She lowered the window and began to clean. While her truck would be closed, she wouldn't be taking a day off cooking. She'd need the extra time to start smoking the brisket for the wedding. The Rabbitts had volunteered their ovens as well, and Abby intended to take them up on their offer to roast chickens. Cooking for an undetermined number of people was daunting and nearly impossible. She was grateful for the help of the Rabbitts and Will Buck. Without their assistance, she would be totally lost.

Herd rallied when it mattered. And she hoped she'd shown her heart hadn't changed just because her name had. She scrubbed a sticky corner off the griddle. Focusing on her work was all she could control. She'd learned that lesson well over the past few months.

Her feet ached in the tight boots. She'd let Meg talk her into embracing her cowgirl roots with the purchase. Abby would have been better off finding an already worn-in pair at Finders Keepers, the antique store. But Meg didn't have many leather goods in stock at the moment.

Abby had bought the boots online and decided to break them in today. In a few minutes, she could head home and slip off her footwear in favor of soft loafers. If she wanted to connect with her past, she'd be better off sticking with the riding lessons Joe had promised. And she wouldn't mind another excuse to spend a day together.

A low moan almost shook her off her sore feet.

With a jerk, she glanced at the clock hanging on the back wall. Couldn't fault the timing. She hopped out of the truck and made her way around.

Lover Boy had returned. His custom on the ranch had been to stop by for a visit in the late afternoon. While he seemed to like people, he was smart enough to be wary of crowds. He preferred when only a handful of humans gathered near his truck.

Abby was glad someone loved the vehicle as much as she did. She worried about the bison. In the weeks she'd been relocated, she hadn't seen him close to any other of the free-roaming herd. Being on one's own was great, she'd attest. But she hadn't realized how much she had been missing out on until she'd made a friend in Meg. She was grateful to continue on with Stephanie as a roommate. She wasn't ready to go back to being alone.

"Wow, look at that," the woman said, her voice breathless and wary.

"He's okay as long as you don't approach him. Or feed him," Abby rushed to add.

She put herself between the guests and the bison.

Lover Boy stopped in front of the truck, as was his custom. He faced the grill.

Could he see himself reflected in the chrome? Was he in love with his reflection? Abby shook off the ridiculous thought. Not everyone was motivated by romance.

"Can we take a photo?" the woman asked.

"If you stay where you are, yes. You may. He won't react to the noise or a flash," Abby said.

"Was he someone's pet?" the husband asked.

The question was delivered in a tone of wonder. The very idea was awesome in the clearest definition of the word. That a giant creature capable of destruction could have been domesticated was almost too fantastic to be believed. And it was the absolute truth. "I think so. But we don't go near him."

"Oh, of course not," the man replied.

Abby pulled her cell phone out of her back pocket. She needed to call Ted. With the tourists returning, the situation regarding Lover Boy took on more urgency. While the beast's presence on ranch land wouldn't shock anyone, the animal's safety could be compromised by his seeming docility.

Her grip on the cell slipped and she opened her inbox instead of pulling up her contacts list. An email from Harrison Wolff appeared at the top of her messages. What could he want?

He'd made his dismissal of her quite clear with every interaction. She was sure the Kincaids embrace and encouragement had frustrated the lawyer with a grudge. She opened the message. Within seconds, her skin chilled and her palms went clammy and cold.

"Great angle. How backstabbing built the West."

She raked her gaze over the pitch. No one was spared. The Kincaids were greedy and ruthless, grabbing land like a mad board game. The Hawkes acted as double agents, befriending one side and then the other, never staying loyal with their support. And the Whittiers were fools, easily manipulated by the more clever families and townsfolk. How could Joe write such an attack piece? And why? What did this history serve but to disgrace the entire community?

"Are you feeling okay?" the woman asked.

At the hint of concern, Abby raised her watery gaze. She swiped at her lower lashes and glanced at the husband and wife. "I am perfectly well. But I unfortunately need to ask you both to grab your food and walk slowly to safety. I need to head to the barn to get the lead cowboy. He'll handle the situation." *And I'll handle mine.* "Follow me, please."

And without turning to be sure she was followed, Abby pulled back her shoulders and strode forward. Hyping up the founders' feuds. Replaying the past so many wanted to forget. Why? She wanted answers.

If Joe thought his troubles had been solved by Ryan's abrupt wedding changes, namely firing the groomsmen, Joe couldn't have been more wrong. He wouldn't explore being a medium, palm reader, or any other sort of psychic channeling energy and auras. He didn't know people as well as learning their family's history had led him to believe.

Standing in the barn with only two days until the wedding, Joe held as still as a statue. If he didn't move, perhaps he'd escape detection.

Ryan certainly stalked around like an ancient predator. From one corner to the next, he jerked his gaze so hard his neck cracked. He grabbed a ladder leaning against one wall.

Ted ran after him, holding onto one end of the sixteen-foot steps to keep it from swinging around and crashing into the tables that had already been set up.

Ryan stopped in the center of the room and, with Ted's help, set up the ladder. He climbed and glared at the ceiling.

Ted held the ladder in position.

It shouldn't be possible to fix an inanimate object with an evil eye. But Ryan found a way. Joe shuddered. At least he wasn't the one standing closest to the groom. Falling off a ladder a few days before a wedding was probably a bad omen even for a witness. The closer to the incident the worse off the luck.

"How did this happen?" Ryan asked.

The question was rhetorical and more moan than query.

"We didn't think we'd need a chandelier, boss," Ted said slowly.

Joe tried to meet the cowboy's eye.

Ted avoided him.

Probably the smart move. Any show of commiseration between the pair would only rile Ryan more. He was practically a peacock the way his non-existent feathers stood at attention.

"Well, now we do," Ryan sputtered, climbing down the ladder.

Joe pressed his tongue against the roof of his mouth. He knew better than to counter that the bride to be wanted to get married in a field. She didn't need a chandelier.

"The deck is set. We have the poles in position on the railing and the lights strung up in between. You'll have plenty of light. It'll be magical," Ted said evenly.

Joe widened his eyes. Ted wasn't one to speak with such whimsy. But Ryan was too overwrought to notice.

"What if it rains? What if we can't have the ceremony out there?" Ryan spun in a circle.

"The wildflowers are still in pots. We can move them in as needed," Joe interjected.

Ryan's concession to his bride had been to create a field of flowers on the deck. Meg had expressed her disappointment that they wouldn't be married outside with quiet resignation. In Ryan's defense, he had been correct that the field wouldn't have been much more than grass at the moment. But that was the only argument Meg had brought up. Ryan had won of course but his victory looked hollow from the outside.

"And the paint? Is it too white in here? Will it be blinding? Should we put up darker paneling? Re-paint?" Ryan asked.

Joe widened his gaze.

This time, Ted did meet his eyes.

After a fire last fall, rebuilding the barn had been a herculean task. The town had united to get the structure built before the snow came. The activity had been a callback to the long-ago days of barn-raising. Hurdles, including local bureaucracy and state laws, hadn't existed when the structure had first been built. The community had rallied to overcome those, too.

The fact that the building had paint on the exterior—let alone paneling inside—at all was a miracle. But Ryan wanted perfection. His clear-eyed focus had transformed his ranch and helped rebuild the local economy. Getting in his way was never a good idea.

"The forecast is bright and sunny all week. You could still get married outside like Meg wanted," Joe said. "You won't even need to take everyone. Just the pastor, Meg's Mom, Hank, and the dog. By the time you get back here for the reception, you won't even notice the paint. The sun will start to dip and the color won't be so strong."

Ted rolled his eyes.

It had been a low blow. But Joe felt the need to remind everyone the scale of the event on a day that was supposedly the bride's had ballooned. Abby didn't even know how many people she'd be feeding. She'd shared her attempts at meal planning over a few stolen moments and phone calls.

He hated that he couldn't sweep her off her feet. Following the best first date of his life, he wanted to repeat the experience. He wanted to spend every second in her company. He'd dated women in the past but Abby was different. Their connection was more special. And more fragile.

With a rough start behind them, he wanted to solidify his place in her good graces. He wanted to wash her dishes, take out her trash, hold open her door, and help in any way he could.

"I know," Ryan said, hanging his head. "This is a little more public than either of us understood. But we'll do it for Hank."

Joe wasn't sure that was quite right either. Hank's birthday celebration had morphed into a joint event. Once he had made his intentions to bring a date clear, he had been forced into the bridal party. Nothing about the event lined up with Hank's wishes. But Joe wasn't going to say anything else.

Ted clapped a hand on Ryan's shoulder. "We'll help. Everything will go smooth."

"Even without a rehearsal?" Ryan asked.

"What do you need a rehearsal for? You don't have any kids involved, and you only have two attendants," Joe said.

"And the dog," Ryan replied.

Colby was better behaved than many adults. "You'll be fine. It's better without a rehearsal. How would you feed them all? Abby wouldn't have time to smoke enough meat for that dinner too."

"Yeah, Abby. How is that going?" Ted asked.

Joe gaped, darting his gaze between his friends. "Excuse me?"

"I understand you've taken her on a date," Ted said.

"Did you tell him?" Joe asked Ryan.

Ryan shrugged. "Didn't have to. Meg, Stephanie, and Abby are friends. They chat."

"Maybe they shouldn't," Joe murmured.

Ted howled with laughter. "Hey, I didn't say anything in front of Hank. I didn't put you on the spot."

"Thank you. Although I'm sure he'd appreciate hearing he was right," Joe said.

"Oh, please save me from that," Ryan added. "Don't give him another ego boost. At least let me get on my honeymoon before you start building him up."

Joe smiled. Hank had been right. Abby and Joe were a good fit. While he was frustrated the busyness of the past few weeks had meant no quick follow-up date, he had been glad too. They had known each other for so long, they weren't going to be casual. They were destined to go from enemies to friends to committed relationship pretty fast.

And they'd avoid some of the inevitable sanding down of each other's rough edges. Perhaps the past two years had been the worst of the conflict they'd ever have. Now they could go forward and just be happy.

He found a wonderful woman and his big project was nearly complete. After years of doubt, he'd finished his book. He had found the self-confidence to tell the story. He had silenced his imposter syndrome, in large part thanks to her. The pair weren't mutually exclusive. Life didn't get much better. If he had to deal with a little taunting and a little decorating, he could take it.

The barn door slid open with a whoosh.

"Speak of the devil," Ted muttered with a grin.

Joe spun and spotted her. He waved and froze. Her face was pinched and drawn. Her posture was tight.

"Excuse me," Joe said and crossed the room. He held his arm out as he approached, and lightly grazed her upper back. "What's wrong?"

"We need to talk."

Under his palm, he noticed the tremors. "Of course, come on, let's head outside."

She nodded and spun, stalking back to the still open door.

By the time he got outside, he couldn't find her. He shut the door and strode around the barn to the deck on the side.

She paced the boards, her body radiating with energy.

"What's wrong?"

She approached and thrust a phone into his hands. "This."

He squinted and read the screen.

Harrison Wolff's email didn't make sense. The pitch he presented didn't represent any of the material they'd discussed. "What is this? Why do you have it?"

She snorted and crossed her arms. "Good questions. I don't know. I have no answers."

He didn't like her defensive stance or the snark in her tone. He turned back to the email. Harrison hyped up the founding feuds against every family. Why would she assume Joe wanted this angle? She'd read his manuscript. She knew what he had to say about the town.

"That isn't what I read. I can't believe you would re-write the whole thing to be a hit piece."

"But you do," he countered. "You do believe it or you wouldn't have come storming into the barn."

"Just tell me you didn't do this." She dropped her hands to her hips. "Tell me you haven't been twisting everything."

No, I shouldn't need to. In every draft, he had worked hard to create balance. Sure, at the beginning without another side it was a classic western good guy versus bad guy scenario. But he'd changed his opinion and so had the work. He struggled to establish the nuance of the situation. The end result still wasn't perfect but allowed for more interpretation. He had faith a good editor would help him hone the tone.

"No response?"

"What do you want here? What are you really looking for? Do you want me to rewrite the history of what happened?"

"I expected fair treatment and an understanding that winners write history, but that isn't the whole story."

Her words were measured and logical. Her delivery, however, pricked deep like a burr to tender skin. Was she picking a fight?

"Come on, give me answers," she said. "Tell me you didn't write the book with my family as the scapegoats."

You should know I didn't. He hadn't given her any indication of duplicity or subterfuge. But she had.

The long simmering frustration bubbled up from the depths inside him. If anyone had the right to feel betrayed, it was him. He'd been magnanimous and kind. Did his treatment not matter? Weren't his actions stronger than a few words?

"Why? Why are you confronting me?" he asked. "Are you here seeking your own validation? Are you looking for me to build you up and tell you you're good enough for this town?"

She scoffed.

"I'm serious. I don't appreciate your accusations, and I'm going to walk away. But I need you to know. You don't need to be good enough for me, for Hank, for the town, for anyone but yourself."

"My self-confidence isn't on trial here."

"Isn't it? Bye, Abby." He walked away while he could. He had phone calls to make regarding his intellectual property, he needed to reframe his understanding of the situation because maybe the last jibe wasn't only meant for her. Maybe he needed to be enough for himself as well. He might never be the expert he needed to be to prove himself worthy. What came next?

CHAPTER 17

Abby didn't consider herself a spa person. Sitting around, sipping flavored water, and listening to new age music in a robe while waiting for a stranger to rub her body held no appeal. But, until Thursday, she'd never had the chance for the experience. And she had to admit, don't knock it until she'd tried it, might be her new mantra.

In the private waiting room, Abby reclined next to Meg and opposite Meg's mom, Carole, and Stephanie.

The water was chilled, the room warm, and the air lightly scented with eucalyptus and lavender. Abby hadn't enjoyed a massage or pedicure yet and was already a me-time convert.

"This is so nice," Meg's mom, Carole, said for the hundredth time.

Meg sighed.

"It really is," Abby agreed, hoping to distill some of the nervous energy rolling off Meg. With each hour closer to the wedding, the more Meg tensed.

After Abby's confrontation with Joe, she had waited at her truck until she had calmed down enough to close up her business and put out her closed signs in a safe perimeter. She didn't want Lover Boy spooked by any curious tourists while she was gone. She had called Ted for a ride to the Hawke ranch, and he had promptly picked her up and driven her back.

They had not spoken.

She had been grateful for his silence. She wasn't sure if he had overheard any of the conversation between herself and Joe. She wasn't sure if she cared. She needed space to process what had been said.

Joe's shock at the email had seemed genuine. His parting words, however, had been a jab. If she had been congratulating herself on timing hours earlier, she had been mistaken by her afternoon.

She had reached the house only a few minutes before Meg's mom. The house had been full of energy, both good and bad. Meg's mom fussed and fretted. Each mention of the wedding had visibly aggravated the bride to be.

Meg had drawn her shoulders together and flinched. She had grown quiet and reflective. The stress of the wedding had finally caught up and infiltrated her calm.

Abby hadn't had the heart to run upstairs and shut herself off, to focus on her hurt. She had to be there for a friend who had gone above and beyond for her. Maybe she was simply delaying the inevitable. Maybe she was once again guilty of living a lie. But she couldn't let Meg down.

"When you're on the ranch," Meg said, "do you ever feel like you've set foot onto the set of *Hey Dude*?"

Abby chuckled. She hadn't thought about that TV show in years. "Too much grass here. Wasn't that filmed in Arizona."

"You're right. But I wonder if we shouldn't embrace the nostalgia a little bit more," Meg continued.

"What is *Hey Dude*?" Stephanie asked.

Stephanie's lack of pop culture knowledge wasn't only due to being eight years younger than Meg and three years younger than Abby. Stephanie didn't watch TV or many movies. Moving into the ranch house and further away from the hustle and bustle happening close to her current apartment building wouldn't be an inconvenience. If anything, relocating to the middle of nowhere made perfect sense for someone oblivious to trends.

"Thank you for inviting us to join you," Stephanie said. "I haven't used the spa before."

"Neither have I," Abby added and leaned forward, catching Stephanie's eye.

Stephanie gave a barely perceptible head tilt.

"Have you had a chance to sort out your something old, something new?" Abby asked, slowly, deliberately enunciating each word. She didn't want to push the morning into another stressful meltdown.

Carole leaned forward.

"The dress counts as new. I'll probably have my nails painted blue. And I have plenty of options for old and borrowed at the store," Meg replied. "Mom, did you remember to bring the six pence penny?"

Carole flashed a thumbs up.

Perhaps the mother had caught on to some of the off-vibes from her daughter, finally, and wasn't jumping into any more conversations.

"Abby and I brought you a few things," Stephanie said and reached behind her chair for a tote bag she'd insisted on bringing with her. "Something new, something blue, something old, and a special something borrowed." She handed the bag to Meg.

Meg accepted the cloth bag, scrunching her nose. "You didn't have to go to so much trouble for me."

"Of course we did," Abby said. "And this is all Stephanie."

"Abby helped," Steph replied. "You'll see. Open it."

Meg reached inside and pulled out a lacy, bright blue skirt slip. She threw back her head and laughed. "Good thing the skirt has plenty of layers. Otherwise, you'd be able to see my something blue from space."

Abby dropped her shoulders a fraction of an inch and grinned. The merriment dispelled the ever-present threat of a meltdown. The bride could crumple at any moment. "That's from me. I had to dye it. Many times." She was glad she'd had the foresight to get an old pot from the donation store or she'd have ruined her cookware.

"Thank you." Meg smiled, tears in the corner of her eyes.

"Keep going," Carole urged.

Meg opened the bag again and pulled out a pressed handkerchief, embroidered with her new initials. "Oh, wow," she breathed and met Stephanie's gaze.

"I can't take credit. Kelly is a master with a needle," Stephanie said.

"One more," Carole murmured.

Taking a deep breath, such a large gulp she nearly sucked all the oxygen out of the tiny room, Meg looked in the bag one final time. Her nose twitched, and she sniffed. "I don't want to cry."

"What is it?" Abby asked, sitting on the edge of her chair.

Meg retrieved a faded, blue velvet box and opened it, displaying a strand of pearls.

"Wow," Abby gasped. She had done her part but hadn't asked about the other items.

"These belonged to Susie Kincaid," Meg said slowly.

The significance of the moment created an air of solemnity and awe.

"And these," Carole began, producing a box from the pocket of her robe, "are from your grandma. She wanted you to have these on your wedding day. Your borrowed and old." She handed her daughter a box.

Meg opened the last box, revealing pearl and diamond studs. Tears streamed down her eyes.

Carole embraced her daughter, kissing the side of Meg's face. "They are watching. I know it."

Abby sniffed and dabbed at her own eyes.

"How?" Meg asked, her voice muffled against her mom's shoulder. She pulled away from the hug and wiped her tears with her hand.

"Stephanie wanted you to be fully prepared for your big day," Abby explained. "It was all her brainchild. She approached Hank about the pearls."

"He was very happy to lend them," Steph said. "Abby had to jot down your mom's number so I could call and fill her in on the plan."

"I can't believe you all went to such trouble for me," Meg said.

"It's your big day, sweetie. You have to make every moment count," Carole said. "Trying to start a business around weddings can take some of the excitement away." Carole patted her daughter's hand. "We won't let you miss a moment."

A knock sounded on the closed door.

"Please come in," Meg greeted, her voice still lower than normal but slightly above the whisper their surroundings invited.

"Miss Hawke and Ms. Hawke?" Two women dressed in the pale blue kimono uniforms greeted them. "Are you ready for your massages?"

"Yes, please," Meg said on a heavy sigh. She shut the boxes and put everything back in the bag, clutching it to her chest. "Thank you all. Truly." She stood and crossed to the door with her mom. "We'll meet up with you two for lunch before our nail appointments."

Abby wanted to say it was too much. That Meg didn't need to go to so much trouble or expense on their behalf. But the slightly frantic look in Meg's eyes, the twitch of her pinched smile, told Abby to hold her tongue. Meg was trying to hold on to every ounce of control she could. Abby wasn't going to disagree. She nodded.

Stephanie flashed a thumbs up.

"See you two in a bit," Carole said before exiting behind her daughter.

The door shut softly behind them.

Abby turned to Stephanie.

The other woman widened her eyes.

Abby released the nervous laughter she'd been holding in for eighteen hours.

"Wow," Stephanie murmured.

"Seriously," Abby agreed. The tension could be sliced with a cake knife. Weddings brought up all sorts of emotions, dealing with heightened feelings. "Hopefully Meg will relax with the massage or as soon as the wedding is over. I know I'll be glad for a break. Luckily, James agreed to keep an eye on the smoker so I could sneak out here."

"That was smart." Stephanie nodded. "I'm glad you're here and I know Meg is, too. She is under a lot of pressure. I wouldn't want to get married with the whole town watching."

Abby shrugged. "I can't see their big day going any other way. I anticipated a much more elaborate and involved weekend. Their plans seem tame."

"True, but I'd need a head count at least." Stephanie chuckled.

"Are you thinking about weddings?" Abby asked.

Stephanie blushed.

"Sorry, I shouldn't tease." Abby didn't want anyone poking around her love life and knew better than to do the same to others. Especially when, despite his accusation that she needed to be enough for herself, she couldn't stop missing him.

His words didn't even make much sense. Of course she was enough for herself. She believed in herself. She invested in a future with everything she had. How much more did she have to show to prove she wouldn't ruin the town?

On further reflection, she hated her immediate antagonistic response. Of course, Joe wouldn't be involved in bashing everyone in town. The proposal from Harrison left no one in a good light. She had reacted irrationally, ready to strike before she was hit. She should know better than to trust anything from Harrison. He used and discarded people. She was proof. But how could she apologize when Joe cut her so deep with his words. Better to push it aside and get through the wedding the best she could. They could go back to being strangers as soon as the event was over.

"How are you?" Abby asked her friend instead. "How is everything going?"

"Good, but busy," Stephanie replied. "Although, I don't know how to function without being overbooked."

"I'm glad you're moving into the house with me. I didn't realize how much I liked having company." *Until I lost it.* Abby wasn't letting Joe ruin her day.

"It'll be nice to have someone to talk to," Stephanie agreed. "How has business been treating you? Welcomed back into town?"

"Summer season isn't a good indicator of local popularity." Abby shrugged. "I have had a nice, steady business." She didn't want to unload on Stephanie. With her own packed schedule, Stephanie didn't have time to work through all of Abby's problems. But they would be roommates soon. They would need to understand the other. "It's okay. I'm on better terms with everyone in town. Thanks to Joe."

"No, I don't think so. You've done the work on your own."

"Joe helped pave the way."

"Maybe. But you stand on your own merits. You aren't the sum of the people before you or town opinion."

Abby hoped so.

Joe was grateful Ted had suggested heading over together. Instead of cards at the saloon, as Joe had anticipated, the groom had requested a campout. Joe wasn't a huge fan of sleeping under the stars. No matter how much padding he brought, he could never seem to get comfortable sleeping on the ground. But he wouldn't mind a night away from town and his mistakes. He piled his gear into the four-wheeled gator and headed out.

You don't need to be good enough for anyone but yourself. His harsh accusation echoed in his mind.

He'd been talking more to himself than her. His whole endeavor with the town history had been an exercise in establishing his identity and his role. He wanted to be an expert to solve his own inferiority complex. None of that had anything to do with her and yet he'd looped her into the situation. He'd been hurt that she'd jumped to the conclusion he was in cahoots with Harrison Wolff. Joe should have avoided the weasel. He should have known better. Even if he hadn't only believed the stories told him by Ryan and Hank, after witnessing Harrison's abhorrent behavior of Abby, Joe should have steered clear. Instead, he'd entertained the idea of working together and he'd ended up with what he deserved.

But he shouldn't have said what he said to Abby. And now he didn't know what to do next. Ted drove further and further away from the ranch. Into the unknown. The green hills against the blue sky were an endless sea of possibilities. The gator climbed a hill and finally the campsite came into view.

Two figures sat on collapsible chairs.

With an hour until sunset, they didn't have too much time to spare for setting up their tents.

A large fire burned, the orange flames licking the sky. Surrounded by huge stones, the blaze was well contained.

After losing the barn, Joe was surprised Ted had approved the evening's plan. Helping put out the fire and cleaning through the mess that followed, both physically and emotionally, had strained Ted. Witnessing it had been a lot for Joe. But his friend came out the other side all the better.

Joe stopped the vehicle several yards away, hopped out and grabbed his tent and sleeping bag.

Ted did the same.

"What are we in for?" Joe asked under his breath.

"You'll be pleasantly surprised," Ted said and strode to the other men.

Joe followed, leaving his tent and bag in the pile of gear, and taking an empty seat. "Hey, are you two fighting yet? Or have you decided to take a night off?" He asked Hank and Ryan.

"Ha. What would we fight about tonight? Hank's getting his way, and I'm not against it for once. He was right about Meg. And I'm happy to say he told me so." Ryan reclined in his chair, hands behind his head and legs spread wide. "Glad you could make it."

Joe didn't detect any warbles or intonations. From the corner of his eye, he studied the groom. Ryan was the picture of contentment. No tension, no sighs, no frowns. How strange. Joe couldn't remember a time he didn't witness a big reaction out of the legacy rancher.

"Were you taking a nap?" Joe asked.

Hank guffawed.

Ryan rolled his eyes. "No, just taking stock of the landscape before it changes."

"What is this spot?" Joe asked, turning to Hank. "I've never been here before."

"The old barrier between Kincaid and Whittier land. It's the last vestige of the ranching past. The cowboys used to have to set up a vigil out here, keeping an eye on the Whittiers. After the Whittiers left, the cowboys maintained the spot. Hauled out the stones and built the firepits, kept the ground level and worked on drainage." Hank poked a toe in the dirt. "I used to take Meg and Ryan camping out here."

"That's a generous assessment," Ryan said, lifting the corner of his mouth. "Meg never lasted a whole night out here."

"True." Hank grinned. "I'd have to leave Ryan out here and haul her back to the house. Good thing he wasn't afraid of the dark."

"Of course I was. I'd stick close to the fire until you came back. I probably ruined my vision staring into the flames. But won't have to worry about that anymore. We're thinking of developing this spot into a med spa," Ryan said.

"You'd need a new building," Joe said.

"We would," Ryan said. "We'd need a lot we haven't required before." He held up his fingers one by one. "An architecture firm. A land survey. Collaboration with medical professionals. All sorts of certifications. Running utilities all the way out here won't be easy or cheap."

To Joe, the process sounded complicated and unnecessary. Constant change overwhelmed him. He'd thought Herd escaped the rat race. But by staying the same, the resort risked becoming tired and obsolete. "What would a med spa offer?"

"Cryotherapy. Vitamin IVs. Infrared sauna. Blood analysis. Naturopath stuff," Ted replied.

It sounded sterile and clinical. Not exactly fitting with the rough and tumble West image they sold guests. Joe flinched after every word. "Huh. Really?"

Ryan shrugged. "It's the next level in high-end spa services. We'd build out here though. Wouldn't want people on cleanses smelling the barbecue. It would need to be self-contained."

Joe didn't disagree. He scanned the horizon again. The spot was secluded. Establishing utilities would be its own headache and hassle. "How would you staff?"

"My sister has friends that have left traditional nursing to pursue alternative medicine. She'd be a big help," Ted said. "Early days and all that."

"First events and now a new spa," Joe said. "Never any rest for the boss, is there?"

Ryan smiled. "I wouldn't want it any other way."

"Glad to hear it," Hank said. "Does that mean you are building pickle ball courts, too?"

Ryan groaned.

Ted shook his head.

"Pickle ball?" Joe asked. The gym teachers taught the kids how to play the popular sport at school, but Joe hadn't realized how far the pastime had spread.

"Don't," Ryan bit out.

"Lana and I play together," Hank said with a grin. "We've joined a league. It's one of our favorite activities."

"And, your doctors cleared this activity?" Joe asked. He waded into dangerous, fast-moving waters. After Hank's health scare last summer, however, he wasn't allowed to do a lot of things. Like eat candy. Not that a disapproving doctor stopped him.

"No," Ryan said at the same moment Hank replied, "of course."

"Whatever keeps me moving, keeps me going," Hank added. "And you should be supportive. The alternative is I could be spending all of my time at her place, or parked in front of the ranch, necking."

Ryan shuddered.

Ted stood and threw another log on the fire. "Everyone good with hot dogs and s'mores?"

Joe was glad for the break from the sudden discussion of Hank's love life.

"Not quite the bachelor party I expected," Hank replied.

He wasn't kidding. While the typical bar hopping slash strip club bash wasn't an option in Herd—or appealing to any of the group—Joe imagined he'd find Ryan pacing and pulling out his hair. Joe anticipated heavy lifting with calming last-minute nerves. Ryan was sedate. Joe scanned for empty beer bottles or cans, anything to indicate the cause, and spotted nothing.

"Everyone ready for tomorrow?" Joe asked. He hated to poke the seemingly calm bear but was taken off-guard by Ryan's complete nonchalance.

"Absolutely," Ryan said.

"No rehearsal needed?" Joe asked.

Ted glared at him.

"Nope. Not as long as Hank is on his best behavior," Ryan answered.

Hank grinned. "I've got Lana to keep me in check."

Ryan rolled his eyes but didn't otherwise rise to the bait.

"And the honeymoon is all set?" Joe asked.

"They'll be in a yurt for two weeks, giving me and Colby plenty of space," Hank said. "I'm looking forward to some me-time."

"We'll go on a trip in January. I want a week of sun and sand with Meg. When the weather is unbearable here, and there isn't too much for us to be doing, we'll be gone," Ryan answered.

On the ranch, there was never an off-season. Joe would have to follow up later with Ted to see if he needed help watching the herd or Hank.

Ted stood again and moved to the cooler, grabbing a package of hot dogs, and tearing it open. "Why don't the rest of you work on your tents? I'll start dinner."

Joe nodded and walked to the pile of gear, grabbed his tent, and headed to a clear spot. Ryan picked a spot beside him.

"Ryan, I have to say I'm shocked and impressed with your demeanor tonight," Joe said, glad for Ted's back so he couldn't experience another withering look. He unzipped the bag and pulled out the poles and fabric.

"I'm not stressed at all. I wanted everything perfect. I've done all that I can. Now I can sit back and just enjoy the moment. I'm marrying the love of my life. I couldn't be more ready," Ryan replied.

Joe wanted a simple life. Make a choice, be confident in the decision, and let everything play out. He had made a mistake, lashing out at her with words meant for himself and in doing so had cut her deep. He saw her pain. He knew the consequence his action had earned. She'd give him space. They'd be worse off than before. He'd be lucky if she ever spoke to him again.

Joe finished laying out the tent and started slipping the poles into position. He'd bought an easy to assemble pop-up tent from a big box store. The first time he watched Ted and Ryan put up the tent with a pole, stakes, and sheet of canvas, he had decided to opt out of future camping. Today, he made an exception.

"I can almost guarantee you that Meg is spinning her wheels now," Ryan said. "I plan and work out all the details in advance, looking for the issues before they arise. Meg is calm because she knows I'm taking care of everything. But now she has plenty to do that I am in no way involved with. Now she has to worry about details. Have you heard from Abby?"

"No." *I'm not likely to.*

"They were having a spa day today. Wasn't sure if you heard any updates about Meg?"

Joe shook his head and pulled the rain cover on to the tent. He moved to stake the bright orange shelter.

"Anything you want to talk about?" Ryan asked. "I know we've been focused on me and my life. I'm not completely oblivious to the rest of the world."

"I rather hoped Lana and Hank were enough of a distraction."

Ryan groaned. "As long as she doesn't move into the house, she can date Hank. I won't get in the way. What's going on with you and Abby?"

"A fight. A big one."

"Don't waste time stewing. Tell her you're sorry."

Joe drew back his chin. "How are you sure I'm the one at fault?"

Ryan didn't reply, too focused on the canvas for the tent.

Joe needed to apologize but in a big way. A gesture so undeniable she'd understand the depth of his feelings. He glanced back at the group as he finished assembling the tent, before staking the construction into his spot. An idea sprang into his mind fully formed. This group of men that had rallied for each other could be counted on. "Do you mind if I ask for a favor at the reception?"

"Make it a good one," Ryan grinned. "And I'm in."

"I need a grand gesture. I have to show her how I feel," Joe said. "Whatever I do, it has to be at the reception. I don't want anyone to question my loyalty."

"Then we'd better loop in Ted. Although, to be honest, I'm a little afraid of what he'll come up with." Ryan chuckled.

Joe was too. But Abby deserved a big declaration of love. No matter how much ridicule he'd earn from the public display.

CHAPTER 18

For the better part of three years, Abby had bemoaned her place in the town history. Her family's loss over a century ago had started a chain of events no one could have known. From Hoss to her siblings, no Whittier had ever found a permanent home. Their curse was inherited. She wondered how different their lives could have been with generational wealth. While owning land in the past was no guarantee of the future, property did set some people ahead of others and gave a head start on reaching their greatest potential. Some people built their lives off each victory until almost guaranteed a positive outcome in the future. Not everyone had that chance, but she wouldn't bemoan the hand of fate today.

In Herd, three wealthy families from the East Coast had been lured west by a false gold claim. Three families had plotted and backstabbed one another. In the end, only one had been left standing.

From the deck off the barn's kitchen, she watched a perfect punctuation mark to one of the town's enduring chapters and the start of a new legacy. Instead of crowing over past victory, however, the winning family had held out a hand to lift the other two up. The Hawkes and the Kincaids would now be forever linked through marriage. And the Whittiers would have their chance at a return through Abby. She couldn't help but cheer for it all. Today's wedding was a healing of old wounds.

"You may now kiss the bride," the pastor said.

With a stunning sunset backdrop, standing amidst pots filled with colorful wildflowers on the barn's deck, Ryan wrapped his bride in his arms and kissed her, dipping her slightly.

To either side of the happy couple, Meg's mom, and Ryan's grandpa grinned. Seated in a chair, Hank held Colby's leash and petted the dog on the head. The black and white mutt woofed. The crowd seated inside the barn, watching through the pushed open accordion French doors, swooned, clapped, and cheered.

Abby swiped at her lash line and got to work, striding into the prep kitchen. "Ready to start?" she asked James and Heather Rabbitt at the counter.

Near the oven, he raised an oven mitt clad hand in salute. "Sounds good."

"I'll send the wait staff out to bring in the appetizers," Heather said.

"Great. I'll head to my truck and then I'll come in here to help with the entrees." With a smile, she exited and made her way to the foot truck. For the next hour, Abby operated without thinking. Moving by rote helped her finish trays and pass them off to the servers in a never-ending line.

Occasionally, laughter poured out from the celebration inside the barn, carried on the wind along with a contagious joy Abby wanted to soak in. She wanted the happiness to wash away every last ounce of longing and hurt. But she couldn't so easily turn off her emotions. Luckily the crushing chaos of catering kept her busy.

When the appetizers were finished, she lowered the curtain over the window, and locked up the truck.

Fortunately, Lover Boy had stayed away.

She scanned the horizon but couldn't see much of the prairie past the cars filling every available spot. Perhaps he couldn't spot his love, the food truck, in the crush. Or maybe he had found company among the herd and was safely away from the noise.

As long as he wasn't hurt somewhere...

She pushed the thought from her mind, dusting her hands on her pants, and strode around the side of the deck again.

She appreciated the care that had gone into the barn's construction, to allow for her to enter and exit more easily. Today, however, she was a little sad to miss a chance to see the crowd. A glance at her watch disavowed her of any idea to sneak into the reception. She didn't have time.

Entering the kitchen, Abby checked on the brisket, pulled pork, chicken, and began to position the sides for the assembly line. While a buffet was the typical style of service at the barn, Ryan had requested a sit-down dinner for the reception. The barn could comfortably—and safely—seat two-hundred.

"Ready?" Heather asked.

With a nod, Abby took her spot at the end of the row and using an assembly line began plating. In wordless unison, the four moved through. Abby felt like she engaged in a dance or meditation. More than that, she felt like she belonged. She'd offered to hire more staff to help with plating but the Rabbitts and Will had balked.

Once again, she was part of town. She'd take the baby steps to regain her foothold. She wasn't going to make a misstep again. She wished Joe was at her side. One perfect kiss was all they'd be to each other. She had to accept it and move on graciously.

Heather handed the final plate to Abby.

Abby dished a helping of all three meats and passed the plate to the server. Turning to the group, she exhaled a heavy sigh and rolled her neck. "Anyone hungry?"

The trio laughed and grabbed plates, serving themselves.

Abby dished herself a heaping pulled pork sandwich and savored the bite. She ached from the marathon cooking and serving. She had left the boots at home. All the work of the spa staff to alleviate her aches and pains was in vain. But it had been worth it to make her friend's day special. The kitchen crew still had to plate and serve dessert. They'd earned at least a few minutes break.

"How is your restaurant?" Heather asked, standing next to Abby as she leaned against the wall.

"We're making progress. The plans are approved, and the footings poured. Thank you for asking," Abby said, touched. She had never thought her business would be competition to the saloon. If so, she wouldn't have pursued it. But in the time since she'd been painted as a villain, she wasn't sure what anyone's perception of her future brick and mortar business were. Construction noise would keep her in some people's complaints. But she couldn't do anything about that and was almost confident only Miriam would bring it up.

"About a year do you think?" James asked.

"Hopefully," Abby replied with a tentative smile.

"Good," Will added. "We need more businesses downtown to help us all to keep visitors in the off-season. Will you open for breakfast, lunch, and dinner?"

"That's my plan, unless that's difficult for you," Abby said.

"Not at all. We will welcome it. The saloon traditionally never served breakfast," James said. "We added it on in the last couple of years to keep pace with the demand. To be honest, I'd be glad to give it up if you took it over."

Abby took a huge bite of her food. She was heartened by the sentiments but still a little hesitant. *You have to be enough for yourself.* She hated him for saying the words. The more she had time to consider what he'd said, however, the more she had to give him some amount of credit.

Without taking away anything from those around her, she could be enough. *But what about pursuing a romance with him?* She wasn't seeking external validation from his approval. She missed him.

"How is your blanket coming?" Heather asked.

Blanket? Abby furrowed her brow and then remembered. Her life had changed since she'd been wordlessly kicked out of the knitting club. It was almost hard to recall what she had been doing. But not the reason why. She'd been looking for friendship. When she'd been at her lowest, however, she'd found connection from other—some surprising—people. "Not very well," she said, blushing. "I might end up with more of a shawl. The loom is hard to manipulate. I've made very little progress."

"Whenever you want to come back to knitting club, you'll be very welcome. Kelly mentioned she could help you work off the loom. If you're interested on progressing to knitting needles, you'd have our full support."

Kelly and Heather had discussed her. Abby wasn't sure she wanted to leave the safety of the plastic figure eight pegs for the freedom of traditional knitting. If she put her work down, she knew exactly where to resume. Working with needles was a few levels ahead of her skills. "Oh, that's nice. Kelly did a beautiful job embroidering the handkerchief for Meg."

"She is quite talented," Heather said. "I hope you will come back. Even if you don't want to test your skills, you are still very welcome. A little positive peer pressure might be a good push to finish your project."

Abby took another bite and flashed a thumbs up. Anything to save herself from a response. Or she might say something embarrassing about her gratitude.

"Is Abby in here?" Stephanie asked, appearing in the doorway.

With a walkie talkie and a clipboard, Stephanie wasn't quite a guest either. The town's go-to events queen couldn't sit still long enough to simply enjoy the day.

Abby stepped forward, swallowing her bite, and raising a hand. "I'm here. What's wrong?"

"You'll see." Stephanie grinned. "Come with me. You're needed."

Abby had never heard a more ominous phrase. Was something wrong with the food? Were the bride and groom unhappy? Was Hank? She fought off a shudder. "I'll be back to help with dessert."

The other three nodded and flashed thumbs up before dishing themselves seconds.

At least she knew the three toughest food critics in town didn't take issue with her food. But what could she have done wrong? Stephanie dragged her through the crowd to the edge of the dance floor next to the bride. With a leashed Colby at her side, Meg looked serene. Appearances could be deceiving. Abby's stomach clenched. "Meg, is something wrong?" Abby whispered. "Where are the tables?"

"No, everything has been wonderful. The food was perfect. We pushed everything back for dancing before dessert. Look." Meg pointed to Ryan, Joe, and Ted in the center of the dance floor with their heads down and their hands clasped in front of them.

"What are they doing?" Abby asked.

An orchestral song cut through the noise of muted conversations. Abby twisted her neck from one side to the other. Guests had cell phones angled at the trio.

"Baby, baby, baby, baby, baby, baby," K-Ci and Jo Jo sang. The piano music began for *All My Life*. Abby hadn't heard the song in years, but the hit of nostalgia from her youth overwhelmed her. Her skin prickled with goose bumps from a sense of anticipation for what might follow and a hint of worry she'd be involved somehow. She did not love the spotlight.

In the center, Ryan turned on his heel and strode toward his bride. Joe and Ted raised their chins and copied the pivot turn sequence. Ryan led Meg to a chair they'd blocked from the crowd's view.

Meg darted her gaze around at the three men dancing around her, holding tight to Colby's leash.

The dog wagged her tail against the ground, the thump thump thump a loud addition to the bass line.

When Abby's gaze met Joe's, she was hit by a wave of amusement and second-hand embarrassment for his nineties dance moves.

"What is this song?" Stephanie asked loudly, leaning close to Abby. "What are they doing?"

Abby grinned. If she used the term cabbage patch, she wasn't sure Stephane would be enlightened. She probably wouldn't even ask if the dance had to do with the stuffed dolls of the eighties and nineties. She'd miss that connection, too.

"Is this the electric slide?" Stephanie followed up with earnestness.

Abby shook, her whole-body shuddering from holding in laughter. Stephanie's lack of pop culture awareness didn't faze her. But she spotted the annoyed expression on Joe from the loud comment.

Ted shrugged.

Hank ambled onto the dance floor to grab Colby's leash and led the dog away from the crowd. The guests clapped for the pair. Ryan reached for his bride's hand to help her up and twirled her into his arms, slow dancing to collective oohs and aahs.

Joe and Ted strode forward.

Joe held out his hand to Abby.

She hesitated, pressing her lips together.

"Please?" he asked. "This is all for you. To show you and everyone else what I'm feeling and where my loyalties lie."

She widened her gaze. "For me? Based on the choreography and music, I figured this was another Ted special."

"He helped. But it's for you," he called back. "I couldn't find the *Ghost Writer* theme song."

His voice carried over the music, loud enough for everyone to hear. But he didn't hesitate. He was making a show of his feelings in front of the whole town. She offered him her hand.

As the song finished, he led her through the crowd on the dancefloor to the doors leading to the deck. "Harrison's pitch was heavily edited and had nothing of the actual text in it."

"I know," she sighed, dropping his hand to cross her arms over her chest. "Or, at least I guessed after I calmed down and had time to think."

"Thank you. But I want to be honest. He did capture the spirit of one of my earlier drafts. At least, as far as your ancestors were concerned. I am sorry for that."

She shrugged. "You didn't have all the facts. I can't blame you for the correlations you made."

"No, but as an aspiring historian I should be more aware of bias and should fight against it harder. History shouldn't be so one-sided but it is. We can at least change that with the real project. I won't be working with Harrison."

"It's fine. We're fine. You don't need to miss a chance because of me." Her voice warbled. She wanted to keep the emotion out of her responses but she struggled.

He shook his head. "No. I will pursue another partner on the project. I was flattered by Harrison. I don't want to be a pawn, and I'd hate for him to make money off my hard work. I'll query literary agents. Or better yet, I'll take you up on your advice about building a platform. There are a lot of paths to success."

"If you're sure..."

Joe reached for her hand and raised it to his lips, kissing her knuckles. "I am. I shouldn't have agreed to work with him anyway. He fed my ego and gave me an easy path. I know better. Getting published might take longer on my own, but I'll do it. I don't need him." Joe cleared his throat. "And no, we aren't okay. I don't want to go back to being acquaintances. I said some hurtful words to you that I didn't mean. I wanted to be taken seriously and the only person who did that I pushed away."

"But you weren't wrong. I do need to be enough to myself. I need to stand on my own." She turned up the corner of her mouth. "I think I am."

"Can I be part of your future?" he murmured. "Did my grand gesture sufficiently demonstrate my feelings for you?"

Tears stung the back of her eyes. Emotion caught in her throat. He held her gaze with a steady intensity, conveying so much more than the words he spoke. She saw flashes of what they could have together and how much better they both would be as partners. She'd come to Herd to claim her family's land and find out if a second chance was possible. Ultimately, she'd discovered herself. Along the way, she'd found him, too. She wouldn't give up this chance. "Do you want to be?"

He stepped closer, narrowing the space between them from feet to inches. "I would." He tipped up her chin, a soft smile playing across his lips in the second before he pressed his mouth against hers.

He wrapped her in his arms like she fit. She wasn't letting go, ever. They'd have plenty of disagreements in the future. They'd probably always have some sort of fire burning that needed to be stoked or put out in equal measure. And wouldn't life be better for it.

A low, deep moan shook the deck.

She pulled away and drew back her chin. "Was that... you?"

He gaped. "What?"

The sound came again.

"Oh no, Lover Boy is back," she murmured. She broke free of his arms and raced around the side of the barn. No one else was outside. Yet. But in seconds, guests would start filtering out onto the deck to enjoy the evening breeze. Some might leave. If the animal got spooked by the crowd and vehicles, he might charge and endanger someone. Then he'd risk himself.

She raced to the food truck, twisting the back door, and diving inside in a swift motion. Her shoulder ached. She'd probably pulled something but she didn't stop. She had to get up to the driver's seat and steer away from the crowd.

The truck shuddered. Lover Boy must have bumped into it. Utensils clattered and pots clanged as drawers and doors opened and spilled their contents onto the ground. She kept going, squeezing through the door into the cab and climbing behind the wheel.

The bison moaned and nudged the truck with his shoulder. The vehicle shuddered and rocked side to side. While guests had been directed to park their cars some yards away from the truck, the truck falling over could crush a few sedans in the best-case scenario and start another fire in the worst case.

She patted her pockets and pulled her keys out, slipping them into the ignition. The engine wouldn't start. "Come on, come on," she pleaded as she twisted the keys again and again to no avail.

"Where is Abby?" Ted shouted.

"ABBY," Joe yelled.

She was in trouble. Joe sounded worried. Lover Boy knocked the vehicle again with more force than he'd ever attempted. She'd made a bad choice and had to hope she would have the chance to never repeat this mistake again.

"What are you doing?" Joe yelled from the passenger side, his voice cracking.

"I wanted to move the vehicle. I don't want him to get hurt," she shouted through her open window. "But the battery is dead."

Now she was going to be hurt. Or worse.

"What do we do?" Joe shouted behind him.

Ted must be behind the truck. He couldn't see the bison. Both men were at risk and it was her fault. "Lure him away," Ted shouted.

Lover Boy kept up his assault, moving to some sway of his own beat.

"How?" Joe sounded frantic.

If he was nervous for her, she was scared. She darted her gaze through the cab. She needed anything that could distract the bison. Her emergency kit with road flares was in the back next to a fire extinguisher. Could she throw something out the window for him to chase? Did bison fetch like dogs?

A higher pitched moan carried through the window. Abby turned and stared at the prairie. A pair of bison stood nearby, the closest any of the other herd had ever come. The larger of the two grunted and snorted.

Lover Boy stopped rocking the truck. Slowly, he turned and grunted at his comrades.

The smaller bison grunted.

Lover Boy walked away.

Without a backward glance, he followed the pair, and, after several minutes, the trio disappeared into the dark night.

Joe rushed to the cab and wrenched open the door. "Are you okay?"

"I am. How bad is the truck?" she asked, letting him help her to the ground.

The side of the truck had dents, and the back tire was flat. "Not as bad as it could have been."

"Do you think he's found love? He's moved on for good?"

Joe pulled her into his arms. "I think everyone has earned a happily ever after."

"Your heart is racing," she said.

"A bison rammed your vehicle. Of course, my heart is racing." He held her tight, resting her head against his pounding chest. "Are you okay? Really?"

She nodded, her hair brushing his chin. She was glad for his strength. Her limbs felt boneless and without him holding her up, she'd have melted into a puddle on the ground. But this wasn't a moment for recrimination. They'd finally reached understanding and she wasn't about to ruin it with apologies and excuses. She pulled back and lifted her chin. "Kiss me and find out."

EPILOGUE

ONE YEAR LATER...

In front of her bathroom mirror, Abby smoothed her hair back into a bun.

She loved her bathroom mirror with the polished chrome frame that she had selected and purchased for installation in this very spot. It was a small detail. For many, it was an afterthought. By that point in the construction timeline, she shouldn't have cared what she selected, but to Abby, everything mattered and deserved her full attention.

A lump caught in her throat. Or maybe it was her heart leaping out of her chest. Her blessings were abundant. The living situation was only the most obvious—and biggest payout—of her struggles to claim her legacy. She had never owned anything new before. Her truck was second-hand. The two-bedroom, two-bathroom apartment was not only brand-new but designed specifically for her over her restaurant on her land. Hers, hers, hers.

A knock shook the door.

"Come in," Abby called.

Stephanie appeared through the crack, slowly widening it. "Hey, are you almost ready? We have to head downstairs soon. Everyone will be here in the next ten minutes."

"Yes, I'm glad it's only the soft launch for friends. I made it easy on myself."

"Easy?" Stephanie bulged her eyes. "You've been cooking non-stop for the past three days. What about *that* is easy?"

Abby chuckled. All things were relative. And in Herd, the tight-knit community was like a giant extended family, stepping in when needed without much notice. After the building was ready, she had gratefully accepted the keys. Ted and Joe moved their boxes over from the Hawke farmhouse. Stephanie's friends, Kelly, and Lauren, painted the apartment. And thanks to the Kincaids recommendations, the restaurant booked reservations two weeks in advance.

After nearly a year as roommates, Abby couldn't imagine being alone. She might have to figure it out soon. According to Joe, Ted was getting very close to a proposal. Although, knowing Stephanie, Abby was almost sure Stephanie would be the one to ask the big question.

No sooner than they had moved out and Meg's mom Carole had settled back in her childhood home. The sudden relocation had been shocking and the biggest news in town. Abby had been grateful to finally be shoved out of the gossip circle.

The speculation reached a near fever pitch until the announcement of Ryan and Meg's impending bundle of joy. Of course they had shared the news on Hank's ninetieth birthday. He had gladly shared his day once again. With Lana as his date, he was glad to avoid some of the limelight.

With one last glance in the mirror, at a happy face Abby almost didn't recognize, she smiled at her friend. "Let's go."

Abby led the way through the apartment and down the spiral stairs reaching the main floor of the restaurant. She opened the employees only door that would—as soon as the business officially opened—be locked to all except those with keys and crossed down the back hall to the main open dining room. With dark paneling, oversized crown molding, historic photographs, and a few tasteful touches of antlers, she had decorated with a Western Cowboy chic look she hoped wouldn't date the restaurant too soon.

The clattering of metallic utensils and low conversation from the open kitchen spilled into the main room. The sounds of cooking filled her with gratitude. Staff had been easy to find. Cooks were eager to work. High school aged kids applied for busser jobs. She'd hired college undergraduates home for the summer for front-of-house staff. With more employment opportunities, the community thrived. Her family's historic misdeeds officially erased from current local memory.

At the front, Abby spotted the small crowd gathering outside the plate glass windows. "Come on inside," she greeted, pushing open the door and held it with her back as they poured in.

"Wow," Meg said as she passed. "If I'm not careful, I'll lose our events to you."

"No, I'll leave the big productions to you," Abby replied, hiding her shudder. Meg's idea to expand the ranch's offering to include weddings kept a steady stream of tourists in town through the fall. Occasionally, a big event popped up on the calendar in mid-winter too. After assisting with the Kincaid wedding and birthday celebration, however, Abby didn't want the stress of being actively involved in day-of logistics. "I'm happy to cater but that's it."

Abby had moved her food truck there in a semi-permanent spot to help with catering events. That was the official reasoning and it made sense. In truth, she'd been worried about Lover Boy. Since he nearly flipped her truck, however, he hadn't ever gotten close again. Every so often she'd spot him with another pair. He'd found his place too. He belonged.

"Actually," Joe said slowly, pausing to kiss Abby's check. "You've already lost one. I'm hosting my book launch here."

Abby let go of the door and waved her guests to the large table in the middle of the room. "Just the one."

"Maybe a few more," Stephanie added. "Not weddings. I promise. The restaurant will be part of Frontier Days this year. Joe is a featured lecturer, and Abby is hosting his talks here."

"What a great idea," Meg said.

"Don't forget anniversary dinners," Hank said with a cheeky grin. He hadn't brought Lana as his date tonight. But the pair were quite the couple around town. "It's a nice, romantic spot."

"Please stop," Ryan muttered.

Abby shut the door and scanned the room, warmth filling her from heart to hands at the scene. Under the brass sconces and hanging fixtures, the dark stained paneling held depth in the grains. Dotted with historical prints of the town, sourced by Joe, the décor was a mix of past and present, inviting and familiar and new all at once.

Cheerful chatter from friends who had become family added to the atmosphere. Herd was worth fighting for. She was so happy she'd stayed in the battle and—ultimately—won the war.

"Are you okay?" Joe murmured, reaching for her hand.

She hadn't moved from the doorway. She didn't want to disturb the picture-perfect scene by inserting herself into it. She squeezed his fingers. "I'm great. Never better." Her voice cracked, and she cleared her throat. "Did you see the sky tonight? I thought I saw something green and wavy."

"The Northern Lights? This early?" His face crumpled.

"I assume so. Pretty cool, huh?"

He scowled.

"What's wrong?" she asked.

"I planned a trip at Glacier for the fall. I already booked it."

Her heart swelled. "For us?"

He nodded and, his mouth down turned. "I figured it would be a nice way to celebrate the end of my lecture circuit and thank you for all of your help with building my platform and getting my book published."

"I'm pretty sure your agent gets the credit for that."

"Without your hard work getting my social media visible and reaching out to libraries to get me notice, I never would have had the confidence to approach a literary agency. You get all the credit."

She stepped close and wrapped her arms around his waist. "In that case, yes, I'll take you up on your offer. It's a date." She leaned into him, kissing him until she was breathless. She'd come to Herd unsure of what she wanted for her life. Along the way, she'd been unmasked as a cowgirl. Now she was more than ready to ride off into the sunset and live her happily ever after.

CHECK OUT THESE OTHER GREAT TITLES FROM ROWAN PROSE PUBLISHING!

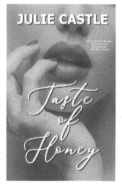

Rachelle Paige Campbell writes contemporary romance novels filled with heart and hope. She believes love and laughter can change lives, and every story needs a happily-ever-after. Check out her blog for updates on current projects, and sign-up for her newsletter to learn about upcoming releases and announcements: rachellepaigecampbell.com